THE QUEEN OF STORM AND SHADOW

JENNA RHODES

THE ELVEN WAYS:
THE FOUR FORGES (Book One)
THE DARK FERRYMAN (Book Two)
KING OF ASSASSINS (Book Three)
THE QUEEN OF STORM AND SHADOW (Book Four)

THE QUEEN OF STORM AND SHADOW

The Elven Ways: Book Four

Jenna Rhodes

DAW BOOKS, INC.

DONALD A. WOLLHEIM, FOUNDER

375 Hudson Street, New York, NY 10014

ELIZABETH R. WOLLHEIM
SHEILA E. GILBERT
PUBLISHERS

www.dawbooks.com

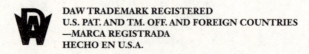

In memory of Charles P. Ervin, gone far too soon. He was my daughter's husband, my granddaughter's father, and our son and brother. He loved sports, music, books and movies, had an impish sense of humor and a great empathy for his fellows. To say he is greatly missed cannot express the loss.

Dedicated to:
James, for coming home and promising to visit more often.
Stuart, for joining our family and bringing his
own wonderful family with him.

Acknowledgements to my incredible friend, editor, and publisher Sheila Gilbert, in partnership with the estimable Betsy Wollheim, and a grateful thanks to all the rest of the awesome DAW staff. Couldn't do any of this without you. Another round of thanks to all my readers for their interest and support.
And to the cats, because . . . well . . . cats.

Prologue

Kerith

"HE ASKS ME to tell the truth, and yet all Vaelinars are liars. That's how they raise their fortunes, and that's how they inevitably collapse, taking all of us down with them. He cannot put himself out there, so he asks me, Kerith-born, to do it for him."

Lily placed her hand over her husband's. He could feel the calluses from the looms on her long and slender fingers, as well as the strength within them. She squeezed lightly, so as not to crush the letter he held. "Would you count our Rivergrace among them?"

"We raised her differently. She's one of ours, Dweller down to the bone, with the good sense any of us have. She just looks Vaelinar." His mouth skewed a bit to one side, bringing the wrinkles that aged him to prominence. He brushed the palm of his hand over his salt-and-pepper hair and took a deep breath.

"And what about Lord Bistane? He's as good a man as we can find, he and Verdayne, both Bistel's sons, and the late lord—rest his soul—raised them in his footsteps. They are all good men."

"I won't haggle that with you, most especially when you're right. But, woman, you know it as well as I do, with the rest, untruth leaps more easily to their lips than truth. They are more untrustworthy with it than a trader with your gold." He waved his pipe about. "The lot, even Lariel, rest her soul, wrap their tongues about lies any time it favors them to do so. And we live and die on truth, Lily. We don't use magic to build our homes and protect our families. We do hard, honest work."

"You can walk down the street to the pub and be hard-pressed to prove that."

"Bah. What do you want of me?"

"He asked you to tell the truth."

"Bistane asks the impossible of me, and he should know better. A Vaelinar doesn't know veracity. He can't carry it in his heart or his blood or his senses. And his asking will get us all killed because they do not like it when their dark underbelly gets exposed to the light." Tolby Farbranch smashed the letter in one hand, knuckles turning white. He did not care for being enmeshed in Vaelinar politics; for all that he had friends and allies within the high elven, those trusts and entanglements would cost him his family. Since the day that sorcery had blasted its way into his world and deposited the lot, they'd done nothing but cause trouble. True, they'd brought wonders with them, magics and knowledge, but so interwoven with tribulations that he questioned their worth. The Dwellers were practical folk, their neighbor Kernans wanted to profit and explore, and the Galdarkans had been left to their own devices, nomads who ranged the continent after the Mageborn who'd made them self-destructed in magic-wrought wars. Vaelinars, though, that lot wanted to rule the world almost as badly as the Mageborn had. "What truth? His? If I'd done what Lord Bistane wanted, stayed with Lariel so that she could have her heir near, we'd all be dead, slaughtered in Larandaril. This letter tells me that. Do you think the assassin started with just one room in mind? No. He undoubtedly watched and observed the manor for days before he went in, looking for the children and us first before he went after the Warrior Queen, but we weren't there for him to find. I left in spite of his protests, but I was right, curse it, I was right! I've lost one daughter to their damned schemes and now Bistane warns me I might lose Nutmeg unless the truth comes out. Tressandre ild Fallyn is openly moving on the throne again because she can, because Lara sleeps in an endless night. It's been out, Gods curse their truth. They've taken Nutmeg before to get at the throne. They'll do it again." The farmhouse trembled with the thunder in his voice. Dust motes skittered and danced with the force of his gesture.

Lily slid her hand over his fist. "Don't you think he knows that? But the ild Fallyn hide in corners and shadows, and we can take that away from them."

"Bah. You and he—you think they'll scuttle away from the brightness. They're like any other pest. They'll hide until the shadows return. They live on hatred and bitterness, and they'll not relent until every cursed one of them is gone." The tenseness in his shoulders did relax a bit as his wife leaned her head on him. "They are Vaelinar," he reminded her. "They are born to power and live to treble their birthright. Only this isn't their world. It's ours, but they cannot live quietly in exile."

Lily half-smiled. "If it were you, Tolby, you'd never go quietly."

"Never! Not until I had my family and world back." He caught himself and cleared his throat. His voice lowered. "Too right you are. I would not go quietly." She turned his fist over and opened his fingers for him.

"Then you might start by telling the truth as we know it."

He opened the crumpled paper between both hands, smoothing it down. "My way."

Her smile blossomed wider. "I do believe that's what Bistane had in mind."

"Devious Vaelinar."

"Aye, and he's one of the best, the ones who shared better ways to farm and create and educate our minds. They've shaped the way we live today. They didn't know how they came here or why for hundreds and hundreds of years. They thought they were lost and now they know they were exiled. High elven or not, I pity them for that. History is one of the greatest teachers, and theirs was torn from them. No wonder they've stumbled so here while trying to find their way." Lily raised her head, kissed his cheek, and crossed the room. She paused at the threshold. "But they've always met their match on Kerith, and always will. We Dwellers thrive on stubbornness." Still smiling, she left him alone in the room to do as he would, knowing he'd think on her words.

Tolby chuckled then, and kicked out a chair to sit down and read the letter again. He swept his desktop clean with one arm to make way, sending papers ruffling to one side and rattling the inkpot.

He would start, he thought, by reminding his audience that his daughter Rivergrace and her man Sevryn disappeared from the battlefields of Larandaril in hopes of stopping the master of death Quendius as he strode from one world to another with an army of Undead slaves at his heels. She stepped onto a bridge of light and magic, heading to another world which had swallowed her up and not given her back. He would remind them of his loss, because they'd all had losses, and would understand. He'd give them the truth as native born on Kerith knew it, and hoped that would sate Bistane's intentions. And then, then, he would offer them hope, if he could only think of how he could do that.

Chapter One

Trevalka

I STAND HERE ON A BRIDGE on a world where I was never born, remembering my name is Rivergrace, and holding onto myself as hard as I can. This bridge does not span across water; it arches between worlds. At my heels follows my warrior and the love of my life, Sevryn Dardanon, because I whispered to him "Follow" and he did. We are come from a battlefield in the sacred valley of Larandaril, on a world called Kerith, where our friends are fighting and dying, but this bridge, this rift, from one world to the next will destroy all who survive the war. I have no choice but to pass. I led him through betrayal and sacrifice, through skill and slaughter, through the just and the unjust, through victors and losers to this point where all bets are placed and all destinies weighed. As I prepare to look these Gods in the eyes, and see the ancestors of the Vaelinar—haughty, proud, magical beyond belief, and entitled parents of those exiled who do battle behind me, I realize that I can't do what I set out to do crossing these worlds. I am lost. Sevryn won my heart and my life long ago and now, I fear, he must win my soul. But first he must tear it from the being who weighs me now.

When the Cold Lady of Death claims you, it's said she lets your regrets parade through you so that you can face and embrace each one and put it to rest. Dwellers talk little of their Cold Lady, but they respect her. There were a few who held some disdain—the Cold Lady comes often for those born of Kerith, and rarely for the elven Vaelinar. I don't know the face of Vaelinar death, though their blood runs in my veins. I am Dweller raised and loved after they rescued me, and they are my family, save for this true love of mine. The sight before me frost-burns my eyes as well as my soul as Death holds me tightly.

I can feel my heartbeat slow until it barely registers, each thump a painful spasm in my chest, the sound of it spun out into threads. Each thread lingers only to be caught up in Death's icy hand to be examined, spider silk floating on the air anchored by a tremulous touch. I can feel the slightest breath on my strands, each one as if plucked by fingers of steel, stretched to their utmost limit and then released like a shot that vibrated inside my being, threatening to shake me apart. The moment stretched to unbearable limits until I thought I might die again. Then the Lady examines the web of souls I have anchored about me, my feeble attempt to protect what life and mortality they have left. She strokes their strings as she has mine, and I feel each quaking thrill shock throughout me.

The Cold Lady looks at me one way and the other, head tilted, eyes blacker than a moonless night in examination. "What are you?"

"I am Dweller." My voice rasps in my throat. I cling to my memories as a Dweller, spinning out laughter and love, sunlight and harvest. "And I am Vaelinar." Pearls of moments lanced by magic and love and hatred and betrayal stab through me.

The Cold Lady drops her hands from the weavings of my life and says, "I will visit you again. Remember." She strips away my sense of self, leaving my soul unbalanced and spinning like a toy she has been tinkering with.

She steps aside, the wake of her movement thrusting me across the bridge toward another impasse, this one beyond her domain of Kerith. My heart starts to beat in rhythm again, but I have no way of knowing how long it will last this time. My steps freeze between worlds.

Chapter Two

SEVRYN SET HIS SIGHT on the back of Rivergrace's shoulders, crossing what felt like a simple plank bridge, albeit shaky, under his feet. The sound of war behind him shushed to a muted roar as the smell of a salt marsh, replete with bird dung and other strong aromas, filled his nostrils. A heavy mist billowed into the air about them until he could see nothing beyond her slender form, and even less to either side of himself. The smell of the salt marsh bled from him, only to be replaced by the sharp and acrid smell of burning Raymy carcasses, far less pleasant. It coated the back of his throat with an unpleasant oiliness that went far beyond his sense of smell. A hacking cough rose as if offended, and he stopped to clear his throat. By the time he could wipe his streaming eyes and swallow again, the smell had whisked away. A fragrance neither awful nor wonderful drifted across him as he hurried to catch up with Grace, but he needn't have bothered, for she had stopped still on the bridge, mist roiling about her.

He stared at her, imprinting in his mind the many changes since he had last been with her. Always slender, she looked even thinner, but underneath that there was a hardness of frame. Her garb looked both rough and ancient, her boots borrowed and ill-fitting, her lustrous chestnut hair tied back with a scrap of fabric she might have torn from the sleeve of her colorless dress.

His jaw tightened. He did not want to think of what she might have endured at the hands of Quendius and her deranged father. He'd suffered under that yoke once himself, nightmares of slavery at the weaponmaster's forge he'd buried in his past. They had left the stink of Cerat, the soul-drinking demon, all over Rivergrace and in the cage of tenuous threads that covered her like a spiderweb of black-and-gold gossamers. If he reached now to touch her, he would feel a faint thrill of answer from those threads, lives which Quendius claimed for his own Undead but which she still held in thrall to her. The demon caused that; his power through hers that tethered the souls and anchored them to her own, but did she feed it—or did it feed her?

He had never seen sorcery which could create those Undead who had followed Quendius across the battlefield of Larandaril but had no doubt it existed—he had seen Quendius bid the dying to follow, and they had. He hadn't seen the leashes woven until Rivergrace touched him and opened his eyes, and then made a similar lead from her heart to his. That magic had nothing to do with the Undead, and glimmered now between them, filled with light and life, not like the strands caging her. He wanted to slice through the bondage and watch it slip away from her, yet knew that no knife he could wield would sever that cage. Sevryn only knew that it imperiled her—if not now, then soon. She needed him more than she knew. And still, she did not move on the path she'd asked him to follow, frozen as if a part of her had died there.

Did Quendius and his Undead block their way? The assassin guild of the Kobrir had trained him well, but he wasn't prepared to face an unknown horde. Not yet. He had to study what drove them, what they were vulnerable to, and what mortal traits if any they retained. He couldn't let Rivergrace throw herself into an attack now. He could not sense them and he told himself that if the hulking weaponmaster waited in the mists ahead, he'd know it. He'd know it by the clenching of his gut and the dryness of his throat, by the prickling of the hair on the back of his neck and by the narrowing of his eyes as if they sensed a target to focus upon. He'd know it beyond a shadow of a doubt, even with heavy fog between him and the Vaelinar he hated most in life. Soot-skinned and silver-eyed, coarse and mean, the man had been unstoppable, but Sevryn knew that their time drew near. For once and all, they would meet again. For Rivergrace's sake, if not for the whole world left behind them.

He took a step back to draw her in retreat with him and felt the edge of the bridge crumble behind him. He stepped forward sharply at that, and then he slid a foot to the side. The brink fell off very close at hand. Where they stood/walked was so confined that the skin at the back of his neck crawled with every instinct he had. No quarter to run and damned little to fight in. "Grace?"

She said nothing he could hear but only a breathy word or two he couldn't decipher. Neither did she move or look as if she'd heard him. They couldn't stay in place, wherever they were, for the chances of attack were far too great. His nerves screamed with that warning.

He stood close enough to be spooning with her, his body outlining her slender one. He put his lips to the back of her ear. "Rivergrace."

A quiver ran through her body. "Sevryn," she answered softly.

"We need to move. We cannot stand like this."

"They're blocking the bridge."

He squinted into the shroud of fog in front of her, seeing nothing, not even with Kobrir-sharpened perception. "Who is?"

"Can't you see them?"

"No. Are they armed?"

"They are sitting . . . well, some of them are sitting . . . at a curved table . . . and the whole scene reminds me of one of Lara's conferences. But that's not what bothers me." She paused for a long moment. "Each of them is Vaelinar, men and women, and each has a cage of souls like mine, only theirs are woven from many hundreds more strands than mine, and much finer. It's like the difference between crude homespun and the finest, softest cloth you can imagine. And it's far more translucent and lightweight, so much so that they seem almost unaware of it. And I've no idea who they are or what they want. They've deliberately blocked my path, but they have yet to acknowledge us." She made a little noise of disgust. "Ild Fallyn arrogance."

"Move forward, then. I've my daggers in hand. We cannot stay here; the bridge is giving out behind us."

"Oh!" She stirred then, sliding one foot forward cautiously, following with the other. He could feel a tension in her body as though she faced an unseen obstacle or barrier that would deny her.

"Let me go first."

She paused and turned sideways, barely moving, as if she felt the verge of the bridge even more strongly than he had. He slid past and immediately felt an oppression, a weight on him, telling him that it would deaden his limbs and press his breath out of his body if he moved onward. Sevryn chose not to believe it. He couldn't see the cloud-sitting table with its occupants, but he had no doubt they were watching him as he strode forward, one deliberate step at a time, Rivergrace's hands on his hips as he pulled her along with him. Slow progress, but they were making it.

Grace gasped softly behind him.

"What is it?"

"I cannot hold . . . everything . . . unraveling. Pulling me apart."

He glanced over his shoulder. She'd paled, but looked fit. As fit as she could, both of them splattered with the crimson-and-copper blood splatter from the fighting on the other side. "You're fine."

"It's from the inside." Her hands tightened their hold on him, fingers curling in desperation. She freed one hand to pluck at the air. "They are trying to Unmake me. All that weaves me together . . . My River Goddess—"

"She is part of you and you her." He could feel the desperation in her grasp. "Don't let them. You are truly woven. Every part of you is hard won, and I love you. Fight to hold on. You have to." He could feel her shudder, and as she did, the firmament under his boots also trembled. The fog wisped about him, thinning, giving him flashes of form and color ahead of them but nothing he could recognize. But if she said she saw Vaelinars, he held little doubt she did. That they could be both so powerful and cold sent fear deep into his own core.

He moved forward a bit, thinking they might get past. She shuffled in his wake, with a muffled groan. "A little more," he encouraged. "Can you see how far we need to go to get through?"

"I can't see beyond them, but . . . I can smell. Can't you? Salt spray in the air."

The smell of the salt marsh had come back. Did they traverse the world they were breaching in such a wide arc that even a slight movement meant massive gain below? Or were they merely stuck in a cesspool of smell and air and dead ground? He tried to pinpoint whatever views he could gain through the murk and saw very little, but something moved ahead of them. Several somethings. He saw enough to account for targets, and the palms of his hands itched. What forces backed them up? They had just left a war. What kind of war would he start if he attacked the unknown beings blocking their way on the bridge?

She had her hand on his back, between his shoulder blades. Sevryn narrowed his eyes, trying to pinpoint what he almost saw, and then he had a thought.

"Grace. You're the lady of the Silverwing, its River Goddess. Disperse the mists. Let them know what it is they face."

He heard her suck her breath in slowly. She murmured, "I can't summon much power."

"All you need is enough."

Her fingers curled his shirt into a knot, holding onto him tightly.

Then she shoved him aside as the mists fled, and he could see what she had described, a curved table with figures about it, some sitting, a few standing, and a few pacing. Vaelinar, in all their regal bearings.

Her voice rang out and he hummed, sending his Talent of Voice just below it, underscoring her words.

"Let us pass. You have no right to hold us and you are unable to Un-make me. My God comes from a different land, and we are offended by the war and venom you are spilling into us. I have come to set matters aright."

Seven faces turned to them, attentions fixed. He could feel the tension in Rivergrace's body increase.

Seven Vaelinar Gods stood before them.

"Let us pass!" Rivergrace demanded a second time, her voice ringing across the span.

Sevryn could feel that maddening itch in his palms crawl out and over his wrists; he ached in containing the urge, the need, to react, gripping his weapons tightly.

She took a step forward. She raised her right hand, palm up, and rain-drops from the now thin air fell to fill it. Deliberately, she raised her left hand palm up, and a flame danced there. "I am of Kerith and of Vaelinar, and I claim both rights."

"Give us a name," the Vaelinar standing at the table's edge called out. He stood as tall as any they'd ever met, his shoulders wide, and even his neck thick with muscle. His leathers were scarred and patched, battle-worn, and he wore a baldric lashed about his barrel torso, filled with weap-onry. Thick black hair curled about his skull, and echoed down each arm. His eyes blazed brown and gold at them, with flecks of obsidian in their hard gaze.

"Nar," whispered Sevryn. "The God of War. He has to be." He stayed on one knee beside her, attention rapt on the cadre but mentally counting up the weapons he had left on his body and their placement. Not enough to dispatch seven, not unless he closed with one or two.

Two stood hip to hip, the woman with silvery-soot skin and long, curl-ing white hair, her eyes of softest gold and the man bonding with her, of coppery skin, his short and straight hair a blend of that same copper and streaks of ebony, his own eyes banded black and gray. He thought they might be the Gods of Light and Dark, but his involvement with Vaelinar religion was sparse. The one who commanded his attention most was the being both male and female, body alight with flame from the glowing coals of its bare feet to the streaks of blue-white that comprised its hands, and the trailing river of molten red running in a constant stream from its brow to its waist. None of the others stood near this being, Dhuriel of Fire, and he imagined they feared immolation as much as he did. Spikes of heat speared at him even across a distance.

The others he would sort out in his memory, when this moment passed—if it did. Dhuriel struck fear in him that none of the others had, but the fiery being also seemed the least interested. Perhaps it had devolved into the more primal aspect of its constitution, and the petty grievances of the flesh disinterested it.

As if confirming his appraisal, Dhuriel made a diffident noise and strode away from the table, disappearing into the abyss beyond it, leaving the other six behind. His going left the background streaked with oranges, reds, and pinks like a glorious—or ominous—sunset.

Rivergrace spoke for his ears alone. "Vae, Nar, Daran, Lina, Rakkan, Dhuriel, and Banha."

"And you know them how?"

"Rufus taught me. I believe he learned from Quendius and the others at the forges."

That thought stopped him for a long moment: the idea that a Bolger of Kerith would know the Gods of the Vaelinar or that he would have learned them from the irreverent Quendius, for Bolgers were the most primitive of hominids. But they were deeply spiritual, on a level that Sevryn respected. Perhaps he'd held his knowledge of the slaver's Gods like a shield about him, for whatever protection might be given.

"Give us a name," repeated one of the women, stepping forward, a woman whose long, golden hair was streaked with a faint echo of red, her flowing gown of greens and golds embroidered with vines stretching ever upward to the suns she wore on each shoulder, epaulets of gold-and-silver light. Her skin glowed like the finest of porcelains, translucent and radiant as she looked upon them.

Rivergrace hesitated but a moment longer. She had a name, one given to her at birth and forgotten during her life, though being stored by a River Goddess. She never used it, and thought it didn't delineate her or her memories and experiences but would satisfy those waiting. She whispered her reasoning to Sevryn before proclaiming, "Vahlinora."

Sevryn put his shoulders back, wary even after her explanation. Names held power, especially to such as these.

The word dropped among the Vaelinar Gods like a pebble into a pond, sending rings of resonating power outward as it did. He was not as certain as Grace seemed to be that this name could not bind her. "Aderro," he murmured. *Beloved.*

"What business have you here, amongst us?"

"Did you stop the others before us?"

The Gods drew back a step and bunched together. They might deny having seen Quendius and his Undead, but their body language would call them liars, and loudly. Sevryn immediately noted who each among them trusted, and who each did not. The God of War stood alone, confident and ready. His Kobrir-honed senses crawled up and down his body, warning Sevryn not so much of the man all too ready to pick up his sword and rush him but of the unknown wielder of that fine looking bow off to the side of the tableau. That weapon had range, and where they stood now, they were more than vulnerable to it. He let his muscles relax into a balanced stance as he tried to decide who among those facing him suited the bow best. He put his hand to the small of Rivergrace's back.

"What business have you with us?"

"I am following those who passed before. If you stopped them, we are free to turn aside. If you did not, I've no choice but to follow."

"The leader carries a strange power."

"A power," she said softly to Sevryn, "they both fear and covet. They let him pass while they decide what should, or could, be done."

He read their expressions as she did. "I agree. They wonder if they can use him to their advantage."

"Vaelinars do not change from world to world, it seems."

Her upheld hands trembled barely perceptibly, but he caught it and wondered if those who blocked them did, as well. Rivergrace took a deep, shuddering breath. She had given much before they even entered this passage, and she wasn't limitless. He ducked his face down, lest they catch his words. "Push them while they hesitate. Quendius has come and gone, and we can't afford to be stopped."

"As Gods, you've failed in your guardianship. I will pass!"

And she did. Taking a running step forward, with a deep, guttural shout of defiance, she threw what she held at them, a breaking wave of pounding water to one side and a bolt of blazing fire to the other. The Vaelinars

scattered, retreating in a disorderly mob, their flesh tearing apart the un-
earthly clouds that framed them. Their power flared, untargeted, and yet
its strength buffeted the two of them and nearly drove Sevryn to his knees.
Rivergrace staggered back a step, bumping Sevryn. He could feel her
trembling.

One alone stood. She, or mainly she, although she held some of the
aspect that Dhuriel held of being both sexes and neither, raised a hand at
Rivergrace. Mud-brown hair tumbled down to her shoulders, cloaking her
lush figure wrapped in sun-warmed colors as she turned and stepped
calmly away. The stone and earth churned in surrender beneath her feet at
each step. He could feel the answering thrum in the bridge below him, and
realized that she—whoever she was—frightened him almost as much as
Dhuriel.

She paused, twisted about, and beckoned to them to cross. "Do you
harm Trevalka, you will never leave, River Goddess and warrior. I, Banha,
promise this." And then she sank with each subsequent step, deeper into
the earth until she disappeared.

The bridge began to break apart beneath them. Sevryn bounded to his
feet, grabbed Grace by the forearm and hauled her after him before the
others could gather their wits and stop them. He didn't get them far before
the structure collapsed and they fell, endlessly.

Chapter Three

HE COULD FEEL RIVERGRACE tumbling above him, hear her startled gasps and chokes as she struggled for air, and he reached for her blindly. Mist roiled around them and he caught, in flashes, sights of booted feet, a dress or apron hem, a hand with fingers wildly outstretched, her pale face, auburn hair flying about it, her eyes wide in fright. He caught a pinch of cloth and reeled it in like a starving fisherman desperate to keep the fish on the line. He hugged her close, her heart beating wildly against his chest as he enclosed her, and then with a WHUMP! they landed. Water sprayed up about them, the awful salt and marsh water he'd smelled earlier, but thanked now as its icy cushion frothed about them. He rose to the surface, bringing Rivergrace with him in his arms as they both spat and choked and fought to get their feet under them. He plowed to the muddy shore, dragging her in his wake and they stumbled out, reeds and nettles bending every which way as they clambered onto land that was only a little more dry.

Rivergrace coughed harshly before wiping her mouth on the back of her hand. "If this is the old country everyone wanted so badly to come home to, I'm not impressed."

Sevryn found a laugh as he reached out, slapping what looked to be leeches off her clothing and then off his. The sluglike creatures wriggled away in the mud and back to the water, looking as offended as Grace did.

"What were those?"

"Nothing pleasant, I imagine. Leeches, perhaps."

"They're freshwater."

"This is not home."

Rivergrace bent over, wringing her hair out. "I know," she answered, her voice muffled. She combed her fingers through knotting curls and gave up with a muttered curse, standing back up to braid her hair, fingers flying, into some semblance of order. "We need drinking water."

He looked at her. "And you need decent clothes and walking shoes."

Rivergrace spread her hands out over what looked like an herbalist apron made of boiled leather and the rough cloth of an ancient blouse and skirt under it. Leather shoes curled about her feet. "The skeleton which owned them did not object to my borrowing them." She met his glance. "Mist cannot carry clothes."

"Mist?"

"The river took you away in one form, and me in another. It called to me, like the dew or the rain, and I . . ." She spread her hands beseechingly.

"Water like that has no soul, no memory. I could have lost you!"

She nodded, eyes downcast. "I know. It was an escape I'll think long and hard about before I ever seek it again on purpose, yet it calls to me. Water will always call to me." Her gaze came up then, and rested on his face. "What about you? I cast you upon the Andredia in full flood and prayed the river could take you far, far downstream ahead of Lariel's anger." On the banks of that river, Lariel with Bistane and her troop had cornered them, the Warrior Queen's anger and fear that he had betrayed her ruling Lara's heavy-handed actions.

He shifted. "Don't ever do that to me again. I can fight for you, Grace, but not if you put me aside."

"I heard the anger in her voice. She would have killed you. And I was afraid you'd hesitate, unwilling to answer her fury, hoping you could turn it aside. She wouldn't have let you. She would have cut us both down."

"Neither I nor Bistane would have let that happen."

"I couldn't risk it."

"So you risked yourself and put me aside."

She looked aside. "I couldn't just stand there. I sought help of any kind, and the Andredia answered me. I didn't go with you because it wanted more from me than I wanted to give it."

"More?"

She lifted and dropped a shoulder. "It does nothing without sacrifice."

"What did it ask of you?"

"It wanted to know love. So I gave you away, with the vow you'd be safe. I prayed you'd come back to me, knowing the river might take you down into its arms forever." She looked up at him, worry and sorrow glistening in her eyes. "I did all I knew to do, hoping it would be enough. The Andredia is more than a river, more than wild water and the earth that holds its pathway, and its will is strong. In the end, I fled it as much as I fled Lariel."

He shifted his weight uneasily. "It carried me well, as sturdy as a ferry under my feet. And, when I finally came ashore, there was an old Bolger waiting for me by a campfire on the shore."

"Rufus?" Her face lit up.

"None other. He said the clan shaman had told him to go there to fish and wait. He was a little cranky at having caught me rather than something to eat."

His words brought a happy blush to her face, pleasing him, and he reached out to gather her up. "We need to dry out and find a safe place for a camp. And then we need to plan."

"Quendius could be a month's travel or more away from us."

"He could be half a world away."

"I can find him when we need to," Rivergrace told him quietly and spread her arms, webbed with threads, to remind him.

"Then we need to be ready, when the time comes that I go hunting."

"We will be." A violent shiver cut off the rest of her words. She hugged herself tightly. "The wind is cutting me to shreds."

"You need that fire." He took her by the hand, pulling her away from the salt marsh shore and across the boglike lands toward small hillocks where a fringe of brush and shrub began, promising forest beyond. She trailed after him, his hand more than guiding her as he could feel her frail strength ebbing away. Finally, he stopped and took her into his arms, finding her slender weight even lighter than he'd imagined, and headed for whatever shelter he could reach.

She rested her temple on his shoulder, her hands lightly laced about his neck, her hair smelling of salt as it dried in the sun. He could feel her breathing steady and deepen as he strode through the landscape, the reeds and tangling grass of the marsh giving way to the sturdier growth on the slopes. A fringe of a tree canopy peeked up over the horizon, an omen he welcomed, and he headed for it when her arms suddenly tightened about him.

"Hear that?"

He stopped in his tracks and then shook his head. "Nothing out of the ordinary."

"Yes. Listen, you must hear it. I think it's Vaelinar, a soft weeping, not too far away."

She paused, and he could tell she was holding her breath so he could better hear. His Talent itched along the curve of his throat from the sweep of his chest up to the line of his jaw, a Talent of Voice, of sound, of projection and influence and power, but under it was the opposite of that, the need to listen, to hear, to understand. A shadow of his ability, as it were, enabled him, and he made out a wisp of noise. He turned in its direction.

Rivergrace nodded. "Yes," she spoke in his ear. "I think it comes from that way, as well."

"Spoken words. Broken. In pain." He began moving in the direction he faced. "This may be trouble we don't need."

"Out here, alone, how can we refuse to help?"

Sevryn reflected that her heart might one day get him killed again. He drew close enough that both of them could hear the soft voice, crying, words edged in pain and fear. They cut through whatever reluctance he'd felt. He stooped to set Grace lightly on her feet. She nodded as he did so, his hands sweeping his Kobrir garments for a dagger and a throwing star. She didn't protest when he put her slightly behind him and at his elbow. The voice came from behind a rise, a dune of sand and ground with bent, sweeping grasses covering it, the sea breeze rising sharply over it and as they drew near its crest, they could see that an army had passed here. They both stopped and turned about to carefully survey their footing.

"Quendius," he said.

"Do you think?"

"I can smell corruption and death on the air, faint but sure. Can't you?"

She gave a quick shake of her head. "I've been immersed in it for weeks. I can't discern it anymore."

Sevryn answered her by grabbing her shoulder and drawing her to him for a fierce kiss. She stepped back with a blush and an answering curve of her mouth. He cut the air with the blade in his hand. "I'm going down there."

"I'm going, too." She slipped a short sword out of her apron. Nicked, but of good metal, it had seen wear and war and looked ready for more in her small hand.

They moved to crest the dune and their gazes fell on the scene below. The wind swept up into their faces, and now the coppery scent of fresh

blood came to them clearly, as well as the small sounds of someone struggling, and low moans of agony.

Sevryn identified the livery of the fallen soldier as that of Larandaril,
which meant that she had been taken up from the battlefield, reaped as
Quendius passed, and then left behind on the march here. Rivergrace
stumbled downward, going to her knees beside the badly wounded woman,
taking her head and shoulders onto her lap.

"We're here. You're not alone."

Clouding green eyes focused. Bloody bubbles danced on the finely
molded lips which opened. "Rivergrace."

"Dylane, isn't it?"

"Yessss." The soldier struggled, her hands pressed to her torso, crimson
seeping through her fingers, staining her uniform and pooling onto the
sandy loam beneath her. "I . . . I wouldn't let him . . . turn me."

Rivergrace's fingers trembled as she brushed Dylane's copper-streaked
brunette hair from her face and forehead. Pain etched the other's face
sharply. "He is making Undead as he marches?"

"Not me. I would . . . rather . . . die. So they left me behind." Her fingers closed about Rivergrace's wrist. "The queen?"

"Alive. Bistane and his men arrived, with Abayan Diort close behind.
The tide has turned, and now we hunt Quendius." Sevryn secured his
weapons and went to one knee beside the two women. He raised his Voice
ever so slightly. "Your pain is fading. You can feel the warmth and peace of
the sun. You won't be afraid or hurting."

The heavy lines on Dylane's face began to ease. "So far from home . . ."

"Not that far," Grace told her, holding her a bit closer, heedless of the
spreading blood. "You'll be back before you know it. Larandaril calls you."

The barest corner of Dylane's mouth curved. "Good. That is the home
I know."

"You honor us all." Sevryn took her other free hand. The flesh felt chill
to his touch but Dylane did not shiver, warmed by the suggestion of his
words.

She took a breath that rattled through her broken body and ended in a
choke, and then she sighed, another bubbling sound, and did not breathe
again. Rivergrace held her tightly for a long moment.

"Lara would be proud."

Grace traced the fine wisps of hair about the woman's face. "Yes. It took
a lot to ask for death instead of what Quendius offered."

He waited until she lowered the body to the ground and stood.

"We can't bury her."

"I know." He stood as well, and searched about the trampled ground. "She brought her kit bag with her." He pulled the leather bag out of the brush. "This we'll take."

She looked at him.

"It'll have supplies. Maybe even a change of clothes. Quendius won't search for that if he or any of his passes this way again, although he will expect to see remains."

"All right, then." Rivergrace added softly, "Thank you for what you did for her."

He didn't answer because it hadn't been enough, and they were both painfully aware of that. He looked, instead, across the small trail of destruction left behind Quendius and his Undead. "We do not go that way," he answered pointedly.

"Not yet, anyway." Grace inhaled deeply, bent over Dylane's remains, and tugged her soldier's boots off her slender feet, tucking the leather objects under her arm. "Tirn'da, ambrel Dylane," she murmured before spinning around and heading back the way they'd come, sand churning from her feet.

"We salute you, soul of Dylane," Sevryn repeated and followed after. He would carry her again in a little bit, but for the moment, he let her walk off her sorrow.

Rivergrace tucked her feet under her and watched Sevryn bank a small fire carefully. "Are you sure . . ." She let her question trail off as she watched the thin, blue plume of smoke rise among the trees and dissipate in the tall canopies.

"They're not looking back. Not yet. And, as you can see, I'm mostly using this to warm the stones I've got lining the pit. They should keep us warm during the night."

She put a toe out to the flat rocks he'd gathered and could already feel a slight heat emanating. Her feet, battered and sore from weeks in old, ill-fitting shoes were now encased in the top quality soldier's boots. She'd scrubbed sand over the bloodstains to little avail, but she knew the practicality of having taken them. She pulled her foot back.

Sevryn sat, a pleased expression crossing his face over the fire he'd built. "Let's see what we have here." He swiftly unwound the leather cords holding the kit bag closed. His hand dipped inside and pulled out a rolled bundle. "Pants. Excellent. And a shirt and jerkin." He tossed a second tightly rolled bundle at Rivergrace. "Some medicinal herbs. A few spice bags. No food."

"Good thing you've got a . . . whatever that is . . . rolled up in leaves and baking for us."

Sevryn took a pondering glance at the meal he'd set to baking. "It should be edible. Smelled like good flesh and blood."

"It squealed when you killed it."

"So would most of us." He took his stirring stick and shoved the bundle closer to the heating rocks and kindling that had begun to glow red among the ashen gray tones. "At least it wasn't slime dog."

Rivergrace couldn't contain her shudder. He chuckled. "I wouldn't be eating that either." He nodded at the bundles. "Not changing?"

"I feel crusty. If we find freshwater, I want to bathe first."

"All right, then." He rolled up the clothes and repacked them. "Close your eyes. I'll wake you when the . . . whatever it is . . . is cooked."

She rolled onto her side with a sigh and was lost to sleep in three breaths. Sevryn tilted his head slightly to watch her sleep, telling himself that she had not closed that core, that selfless part of her he found so endearing. That she had changed, as he had, was undeniable. He hoped that she would find that part of himself he hid away to preserve himself for her as endearing. He poked the cooking bundle again. It would be a while, at this slow heat, to cook itself tender. He put the stick aside carefully and lay down next to Rivergrace, drawing her carefully into his arms. The web of anchored souls encasing her buzzed a bit angrily at him, stinging him faintly much like the hornets' nest their tiny voices imitated. But he did not let her go, only hugged her that much closer to him before he dared close his own eyes.

Chapter
Four

BECAUSE IT WAS FORESTED, they'd found enough water to drink but not enough for bathing as Rivergrace wished in the morning. He made a bucket out of the leather bag and filled it for her three times from the tiny freshet which bubbled up between tree roots, as she sat in a sun-dappled spot and peeled off her old clothing, bathing a bit at a time. He helped her, and before she was finished, they turned into each other's arms and spent the last of the bright sunlight learning each other's bodies again, not because that much time had passed but because they had both experienced so much since the last time they'd made love. He spanned his hands about her waist, bent his head and kissed each rib he could feel and see so clearly now. She found and stroked each new scar taken in Kobrir training, her fingers smoothing out the scar tissue and ridges until they nearly faded completely away, although she could not take them entirely as healing was not her strongest Talent. He curled about her and kissed the new muscles on her shapely legs, pausing delicately on the inside of her thighs before moving deliberately upward until she sighed in soft pleasure. When she cried for more, he entered her, the two of them thrusting against each other in movements growing ever stronger and faster until they both shouted in triumph and collapsed to hold each other closer. Many, many things had changed but not . . . this. Nor the love that accompanied it.

She swept his hair behind his ear and tucked it there, running her fingertip over his point as she did. Her own were softer, gentler echoes of her Vaelinar heritage, but it wasn't a gender issue. Familial, perhaps. He smiled into her face.

Rivergrace frowned a little in return.

"What?"

"Your scars."

"And yours."

"Yes. But you seem to worry only about the flesh, bone, and muscle of them. You accept them, you even embrace them."

"But."

She gave a little irritated shake of her head. "They are more than skin-deep."

"Aderro." He pulled her into his shoulder, muffling her words and his against her skin. "Don't you think I know that? I can feel each and every bond you've woven, and the anchor driven into your soul, and the worry and care that pulls on you."

"You can?"

"I know that Narskap has taught you a way of dealing with his demon Cerat." He ran the palm of his hand over her shoulder, feeling her bare skin shiver under his touch.

She swallowed. He could feel her throat grow tight against him, and the muscles constricted harshly. She pulled away from him. "How can you love a person who does such a thing?"

"I don't love just any person, I love you."

"I'm not the person I was."

"And you think I am?"

She put her hand over his. "I know the Kobrir honed you, but you were already a finely made and tempered blade. They could not have changed your soul if they tried."

He felt his eyes narrow a bit in sorrow. "You might be surprised."

"No. No, I would not because I am not. But I'm not talking about you." She took her hand back and curled it upon her chest. "Me. I am the one carrying Cerat again, only this time he's not bound in a sword I can hold sheathed across my back. He's buried in here. Deeply buried."

He knew the soul-drinker almost as well as she did. "I know what he feels like when he's burrowed inside of you, and you're not carrying that rage, that burning agony. You've got him caged. You use him. For these, I imagine, so they won't ever have to face the brunt of becoming his totally." He ran a fingernail across the threads he could see glimmering over her forearm. He imagined them like fine strings on a lute, murmuring at his touch. He also wondered if she felt the tiny sparks when he stroked them as he did.

"How can you think of touching me?"

"I have spent many days thinking of little else."

She squeezed her eyes shut for a moment before flinging them open again and glaring at him. "Sevryn."

"Do you intend on calling them to follow at your heels? Have them kill for you? Conquer Trevalka or Kernan for you? Rape and pillage for you?"

"How can you think such things?"

"Because you think that I might be thinking them. I know if you have them anchored, it's to give them one last chance, one last hope at escaping what Quendius and Cerat have planned for them. Your father could not have brought you into his schemes if you did not think so and he had not told you as much."

"You believe that?"

"With every breath I have."

The fist at her chest relaxed, fingers uncurling slowly. "Long ago," she told him softly, "You won my heart. Now, I fear, you will have to win my soul."

"You never had to ask." He wanted to smile at her, reassure her, but knew she wanted to take him absolutely at his word.

"Now," and she glanced up at the sky. "We're losing the sun altogether, and I could use some warm clothes."

He passed her the bundles and helped her adjust the items which, although made for a slender female figure, still hung on her in a place or two, and cuffs had to be tucked deep into the high-topped boots. When she stood, she looked a little like a woman-child who had decided to step into her mother's too-big clothing for a day. He reminded himself that River-grace was still young, even among the Vaelinars—young and too thin. Another one of those squealing rodents for dinner would not help terribly, but it would keep a bit of food in their bellies. He stretched and stood, readying to go hunt.

"What will you do when I'm gone?"

"Study the wildlife. See if I can figure out what vegetables we can eat and what we can't."

He raised an eyebrow.

She pointed overhead. "They're not silverwings, but I still seem to attract fisher birds."

As his sight followed her pointing hand, he could see a restless wing move, and the flash of other feathers on green branches overhead, and a nervous coo or two as the birds settled and shifted among themselves. "Interesting."

"I thought so. Just don't bring one of them down."

"I'm not that hungry. Yet." He stamped down into his boots as she put up her hand, called to a creature, and it answered her.

It did not seem put off by her cage of souls, either, as it put its beak to her knuckle and made bird noises to her.

When he returned, he found her with a bird perched on her shoulder and another on her head, plucking a hair or two away at a time, evidently intent on using her tresses to further its nest building, and a variety of pulled roots and berries piled at her feet. She glanced up with a laugh, one of the first lighthearted looks he'd seen on her face in a very long time. He approached quietly and sat next to her, sending only one of the birds surrounding her off on the wing, disturbed.

"Perhaps we've misunderstood your true calling."

Grace's smile spread brighter for a few seconds. "It's not me, it's the River Goddess."

"Who is as much you as anyone."

"True. She had an affinity for the fishers, I know, and they for me. Nutmeg and I used to chase them up and down the riverbanks and leave bits of cloth from Lily's weavings for them, and they'd leave bits of herbs and berries and an occasional bright object like a lost button for us." She soothed the back of her finger down one breast and listened to the bird murmur in soft pleasure. "Anyway, these seem to be edible." She fanned her other hand over the pile.

"On whose authority?"

"Well, they eat them," Grace amended. "We can try a bit. If they're disgusting, spit them out, so that if they're pernicious, we should survive."

Sevryn did not answer for a moment, thinking of the herbs the Kobrir had introduced to him that were quite deadly even by a bare pinch of quantity. But having been through their tutelage, he thought he could discern what he needed to about these food items. He crossed his legs to watch the flock of six or seven birds preen and jockey among themselves to get closer to her. The one plucking her hair flew off, to be replaced by another content to sit on the second shoulder. She reached up to repair her braid, scattering both birds off her with the movement, their blue-and-green wings flashing brilliantly in the sun as she did. They landed a bit away and watched her, slightly aggrieved, with bright, dark eyes circled by feathered rings of sable.

"Time is not on our side," he remarked, finally.

"But it might be. We know that the queen still lives and that time here is not what time is at home."

"We still can't afford to tarry. While we pass time here, time gallops at home, if my perception is correct. You risk losing Nutmeg and the rest of your family to the ages."

Her hands paused in gathering up the bounty the birds had brought to her. "I wouldn't mind that, I guess, if I knew they lived to a ripe old, deserved age. But it's not likely."

"No, it isn't."

"What do we need?"

"A water source. Steady food. A shelter out of the elements, and a home base to strike from that is not encumbered by distance and circumstance. Mounts. Allies."

"I'm used to being on a march. I'll count myself well-rested by tomorrow. You?"

"Yes, and ready."

She reached out to rest her hand over his knee. "You set off to dispatch Tressandre and Alton."

"A destination I didn't reach for quite a long time." He swept a hand over himself. "This intervened."

"The Kobrir captured you?"

"Eventually, yes, but I blame that on Bregan. He led me into an ambush."

"Bregan?" She sat back, a little astonished at his mention of the Master Trader. "Bregan has been more than eccentric these past few years. However did he get past your defenses?"

"You can blame that on my old mentor Gilgarran. The trader seemed to have an inkling of plots behind the plots and distracted me enough that I decided to follow his lead." He cradled his fingers back over her hand. "He didn't do it by himself. The old Gods of Kerith have begun to awaken, and they decided to bedevil him."

Rivergrace raised an eyebrow. He nodded. "Almost beyond belief, but I decided to believe him. He offered a way through the old Mageborn tunnels that would save me days and days of travel, and I was in a hurry." He paused as if to gather words. "Grace, he hears them. He does. It has driven him crazy, but it's also awakened powers in him that none of us have. Kerith is beginning to rise, I think. Whatever we do here will have a terrible impact there."

"What kind of powers?"

"He can manipulate travel through those tunnels. And, it seems, time."

She shook her head in disbelief and he tightened his hand over hers, as if to restrain her reaction. "He took me back centuries. Unintentionally, but he did it, through those tunnels. I witnessed the choosing of the Warrior Queen."

"Lariel?"

"Yes. Coming into her own, and with the help of powers that most Vaelinar consider forbidden."

She frowned. "But Lara had labeled you traitor before that . . . before you witnessed that day."

"Because she let me into her thoughts, and I read the possibilities long before I actually witnessed them."

"We do not mind read."

"We are not supposed to. Neither are we supposed to possess."

Rivergrace took in a breath that hissed a little through her curved lips. "No wonder she fears you. And me."

"She uses her power with great restraint."

"And yet." She looked away for a long moment. "That she uses them at all means her life is forfeit, doesn't it?"

"Yes."

"And Sinok protected her from that."

"He was the old Warrior King and her grandfather, and he had no doubt about his successor. Gilgarran, too. I think, from what I've seen of his journals, that he had a fairly good idea of what her Talents were, and deflected the criticisms of her detractors who felt she had little enough Talent to earn and keep her title."

"The family of ild Fallyn among the foremost opposition."

"In a way, I can understand that, but once the title had been contested for, and won, they should have retreated. They should have become the ally that would have strengthened all of us, rather than divide us, but they have never had that mindset."

"They coveted what they felt should have been theirs."

"And they will not stop. That's why you decided you had to remove them, for all our safety."

"They've earned it." He paused. "Alton died an ugly death. Tressandre will never let that go, not until she is gone herself."

"You killed him?"

"I had a part in it. The other—" He paused. "You didn't see it?"

"No." She waited a long moment before he continued.

"Lara wore armor, light mail, that Tranta had made and interwoven with shards from the Jewel of Tomarq."

"The destroyed Way?"

He nodded. "Tranta refused to believe the Way was gone, that her protective powers no longer existed. He had an affinity for the Jewel and couldn't, wouldn't, let it go. The gems still fired for him."

"A fiery blast for enemies."

"Yes." He rubbed his thumb along the silhouette of her hand. "Lara wore a pectoral, bracers, and girdle of chain mail set with the gems. Alton got to her before I could stop the blow or parry him back. The . . . protection . . . reacted to his attack. He sliced her, but the gems—it was like watching a bonfire explode into a thousand sparks and flames. I cut him again, more out of mercy than anything." He cleared his throat. The man had been screaming, he remembered. He'd had to attack Tressandre as well, the woman driving in to administer the killing blow Alton had failed to deliver. He knew he'd hurt her, how badly he could not guess. "I left a Kobrir dagger in Lariel, and Lariel in Bistane's hands."

"You struck her?"

"I had to. The blade was coated with a potion that would simulate death by slowing the body down into a deep sleep. It was the only way she'd survive, and the Kobrir can revive her when her body heals. She will heal, slowly. I believe."

"Her body is torn in a race between healing and dying?"

He nodded. "And healing should prevail." He knotted a fist. "It has to. We need Lara."

Rivergrace crossed her boots at the ankle. "I wonder about the babies."

"Whose?"

"Nutmeg. And Tressandre."

He made a noise of disdain. "Tress will have a great deal of trouble proving she carries Jeredon's heir. If Nutmeg is fortunate, her child will be clearly stamped as Jeredon's, Dweller blood mingled or not. Plus, she should have months before Tressandre gives birth. She is bold to claim her child is Jeredon's, the very nature of maternity is against her."

"But the ild Fallyn have a loyal following, plus they're not afraid to strong-arm the weak-minded." She gave a little sigh. "It won't be easy. It's never easy." She went silent.

"Was it ever?"

The corner of her mouth tilted upward. "When I was young, and Nutmeg was the only sister I knew, and our brothers the only menace—besides bad weather and tree rot in the orchards. Yes, there were easy times, long before I thought of myself as Vaelinar."

"I'm sorry we had to ruin it for you."

"Oh, you didn't ruin my world. You Vaelinar expanded it, and I grew up. Lily always told me the world would be a different place as I grew into it."

Lily Farbranch had been, to his mind, as much a weaver of fate as of fabrics. She'd woven good values for her children to grow into. And, Rivergrace's foster father, Tolby was as shrewd and stout a man as he could ever hope to have on his side, notwithstanding his stature as a Dweller.

Rivergrace uncrossed her ankles and stood up smoothly. "You're right. Time isn't on our side. I don't want to cross that bridge again and find them gone. To find that the life they lived could have been better if only I'd been there."

"First, we have to stop a queen and kill a master of death."

She put her finger up. "First, we have to make dinner. Then, we make plans."

Chapter Five

"I T'S OUR FIRST VILLAGE."

"Hardly big enough to be called one, but yes."

"And you think we should approach it."

Sevryn put aside the throwing dagger he'd been sharpening with a promising rock and answered, "Yes, I think we should consider it. I've been observing it—"

"I know that."

He continued smoothly, "Observing it and it's underpopulated, if anything. They're fishermen, primarily, but in the mornings, there is a regular exodus of the young and able-bodied. For what or why, I can't determine from our perch up here, but it appears to be voluntary, if necessary. No matter. With the men out to sea and the others gone, it leaves us a handful of people to make contact with. Easily manageable."

"The lame and the feeble."

"No. There are bakers and wisewomen aplenty down there." He looked over the sea cliff toward the scattering of huts. "Most importantly, Quendius has not come through."

"That," Rivergrace conceded, "is a winning argument. So we go in tomorrow to test the waters?"

"I think so. The weather is changing; I'm thinking we're not at the end of winter here but at the beginning of it, even though the leaves are still green. It's getting damp and chilly enough that autumn may be closing in."

"You're thinking of better shelter."

"And you should be, too." He found a sheath for his weapon. "We also need to get an idea of communication and what they do or don't know about the current state of affairs."

"They look isolated."

"Perhaps all the better for us if they offer shelter."

Her chin jutted out with a touch of stubbornness he recognized. "What are your thoughts?" he added.

"I don't want to be hunkered down all winter. I think we need to move, and move now. Trevilara may not know of us, or Quendius where we are, but the Vaelinar Gods know and they will not tolerate us."

"You feel this."

"I feel it deeply." Rivergrace brushed a stray bit of hair from her forehead. "They're watching. Evaluating. And when they decide what to do, they will *strike*. I don't know what we hope we can do against a God."

He settled back against a thumb of rock that jutted up from the sea cliff. Lichen flaked from its surface as he did so. "We've been moving well these past two weeks, but we don't know where we're going, and we've no way to orient ourselves. Those fisher folk down there know exactly how isolated they are."

She relented. "All right. But I'm going with you."

"I intended for that."

"Oh." And she leaned the side of her face against his shoulder.

"I expect a great deal of talk between women."

She laughed. "Ah. Now I see." Rivergrace punched his arm lightly. "I should have realized."

"Yes, you should." He rolled flat to the ground, taking her with him, and said to her neck as he buried his face in it. "You really should have thought of that."

Crouched by the scruffy ring of brush that had possibly been coaxed into a hedge to fence off a more vulnerable side of the village, Rivergrace held her breath lightly and watched the line of people begin to leave. She poked Sevryn. "They're carrying jugs. Sevryn, they're going for water."

"But they have a well and a freshwater source running into the salt bay."

"They trust neither of them, and I'd say with good reason. Illness or poison, and most likely illness."

"You think they would have abandoned this bay."

"Fishing might be good, in spite of that. Illness fades." She stood carefully, stretching her knees and lower back as she did.

Sevryn pinched a corner of her tunic. "Wait until everyone is gone. If it is illness, like the plague, it could be what infected the Raymy. We saw that at Calcort. It's deadly."

"They believe it's in their water."

"And they may very well be right."

"We need allies. If it is the water, I might be able to restore it. That would mean a great deal to them. As it is now, they can't grow even small vegetable patches or crops. Rain must be dear here, too." She brushed her hand against his hold. "I need to see what it is." She marched out of the brush and toward the villagers.

Her words were ignored by most of them, but one or two dropped out of line and hung back. The youngest, a girl of silvery skin and dark, dark hair and eyes that flashed gold sparks among the rings of deep brown, eyed her in suspicion. When she spoke, Grace realized why she was mostly ignored: their Vaelinar barely resembled the language she'd been taught. She answered slowly in an effort to be as clear as possible. "Why do you gather water?"

The girl cut the air in disdain. "It kills. Who are you to ask?"

That stopped everyone in their tracks to turn and look. The walkers drifted back, slowly, their arms full of clay pots or leather pouches, their faces etched with resignation.

"The running water or the well?"

"Both. What does it matter?"

Rivergrace looked among the scattered huts for the well and found it, well placed, and marked by a tall pole with several skulls hanging from it. Mortal skulls. Her eyelids fluttered in surprise at that. Sevryn stepped in place behind her. "How did you think they would mark danger?"

"I just—it seems—I don't know."

"The last skull is recent enough that it hasn't even weathered yet. Some brave soul must have decided that the water surely must be clean by now."

Rivergrace lifted a hand. "May I examine your water?"

Scoffs at her strangely accented words and someone, a boy with voice breaking on the threshold of manhood said, "Go ahead, but we won't be burying you."

She skirted the growing crowd to cross the pathways leading to the well. Weeds, twisted and contorted, sprang up from ground not often trod, but even those growths did not prosper. Their stems went limp and brown and curled in upon themselves. Bad water. And as she grew closer and closer, she could feel it.

Water had no scent, she'd been told. She disagreed with that, knowing that animals could find water, so it must be her nose that was deficient. But this well carried, if not a scent, a miasma of things most foul. Of ill-will. And a power, a dark and suffocating power. She stumbled as she drew near and Sevryn caught her by the elbow to steady her.

"What is it?"

"The well deserves its reputation. Can you feel it?"

"I feel a certain repulsion, that's about it. Not enough to force me away if I were thirsty enough."

"It's all I can do to keep from bolting," she told him, her words low so they did not carry to the curious villagers shadowing their steps.

She leaned over the lip, an effort that took a great deal of nerve, and looked into the still waters below. Dark water greeted her. Like a quiet, waiting eye of evil far below, it looked back at her and made the skin on her body prickle in answer. She thought she had met this evil before, although not in such a quantity, such a concentrated entity. She couldn't remember where or when, but that didn't matter now. Now, all that mattered was how she might deal with it. Like oil, it lay upon and infused the sweet water seeping up from the ground below, swirled into its depths. She would have to immerse her hands in it.

She reached for a dangling bucket, but Sevryn took it from her hands and ran the pulley himself, bringing it up full, its sides damp and running. She put her hand out and dipped it into the chill water.

Like ice, it burned and numbed her senses before going cold. If ice was what it wanted to imitate, she could deal with that. She called on her Fire and burned the cold away. She took the bucket from Sevryn's hands and put it aside, on the ground.

"This water is clean."

Murmurs grew loud. Arguments broke out, words hurled at her like spears or arrows of denial. She turned to look at the villagers. "One bucket will do you no good. I intend to cleanse the well." She turned back to Sevryn. "Lower me down."

"It can overwhelm you."

"It will try, but I don't believe it can. It is only a well, and there is something down there—a token, a talisman, a plant, a pouch—something dropped to its depths to spread its poison, something that has to be removed, like a growth. In this form, it's effective and long-lasting but it can't concentrate itself. I'm not likely to meet a greater infusion, no matter how deep I can go, if you understand."

"If you're up to your neck in poison . . ."

"Well, you won't lower me that far, will you?" She bent to remove her boots and roll her trouser legs up. "Foot-deep, that's all I need."

He looked at the simple pulley system. "The rope is old." He called over his shoulder, "I need more rope!"

The boy who'd denied her a burial pelted away from the crowd in answer. He came back with a length of rope coiled over his shoulder. The cord smelled of salt and sparkled with fish scales in the sun as he handed it to Sevryn, but it looked pliable and stout enough. He secured it about Rivergrace in a harness saying, "You're going to smell like the catch of the day when I reel you back in."

"As long as I don't smell like death warmed over, right?" She held on to him for a moment longer than necessary as she perched on the stone rim of the well before she kicked over lightly and her weight hit him.

"Stop!"

He couldn't stop, she'd already gone over, but he braced himself at the imperious voice that rang out behind him. With a knee braced to the side of the well, and its none-too-steady side, he noted, as gravel and sand loosened and the rock seemed to shift a bit, he looked to identify the voice.

He thought for a moment the reedy but strong tone had come from a woman, but he looked instead at a man, a thin whip of a man, with a swoop of a nose and a knotted frown that was too many years fixed into his face to relax now. Lank gray hair swung about his shoulders as he halted inside the ring of villagers, just outside of Sevryn's reach—that is, what reach he'd have had, if he let Rivergrace and the ropes go.

"Do not lower that woman of darkness into the well."

Sevryn felt his jaw tic. "She is no bringer of evil, and she intends to clear your well, or do you wish otherwise?" At the other end of the rope, he could feel Grace swing and then thud to a stop, perhaps gaining a toehold or handhold on the inside. The burden didn't lessen, but the rope steadied.

"If wishes cleaned our water, it would have been sweetened long ago." The man tilted his head, sizing him up. The quick, sharp eyes fastened on him, moved away, and then refocused like a bird of prey sizing up the immediate field of vision. He pointed at the fresh skull. "That one took a week to die. The others less than a day. Whatever poisons our water weakens. Is that why the two of you are here? To restore the poison? We are far from Trevilara's shadow, out of the queen's notice. We don't need strangers here!"

Sevryn let himself shrug, lowering Grace surreptitiously a bit more as he did. He got an answering tug as he did. "There is no doubt that you lie far from anyone's notice. Is that why you've gotten no help here? No new well dug? Why is your river cursed as well?"

The protester's lip curled. "We're cursed because we are independent. We're out from under the thumb of any who would rule us." His gaze slid away for a moment. "Of course, in our misery, who would want to rule us and claim the responsibility? But we are free and proud of it!"

Grace's voice echoed hollowly from the well. "Then be free with sweet water. We're here to help."

"Do you think me simple? Them?" And the reedy man beckoned his hand over the villagers crowding him.

"We think you're without clean water, and you send the better part of your people every morning to collect it. Why not dig a new well?"

"Because the water does not stay clean. No matter what we do."

Grace said faintly, "Sevryn, I think it's because this well seeps back into their ground water. Let me down a bit more . . ."

The reedy man threw himself at Sevryn, a strangled cry deep in his throat and the rope spun out of his hold, and he could hear Rivergrace cry out before a tremendous splash drowned out any further cries she made.

"Aderro!" Sevryn called before the man hit him, and his resolve not to kill bit deep as he wrestled with the fanatic. It happened as he feared, they sensed that one man could not bring him down, but in force they all might be able to, and he dodged water jugs, fists, and feet before he had his attacker under his boot and the others at bay.

"Rivergrace?"

Faintly. "I need a moment. Bring me up in a moment." Her voice sounded strong but even farther away than it should, as if she'd gone dreaming in the poisoned waters.

He shoved the unconscious body from under his foot and went back to tending the rope. He pointed at the crowd, now on their knees or stomachs, most of them, laid out before him. "Stay out of my way, or you'll have more than bruised heads and ribs to worry about."

A woman pushed forward and sat cross-legged. "We will wait," she said firmly, and crossed her arms. She had black hair so dark it held purple highlights, but her eyes were of the clearest, brightest blue, and he knew what she promised would be followed by the others.

This one was the leader.

He turned his attention to the well, knowing not only she watched him but her fellow villagers. What was Grace doing?

Chapter Six

HER STOMACH PLUNGED as her body fell without warning, the rope harness going slack, sinking her into the chilled waters. The shock numbed her, sending coherent thoughts out of her mind, filling her mouth with incoherent cries and sputters. And then the water claimed her, sliding slickly over her skin wherever it could touch: her hands, her arms, moving up her throat to her mouth, seeking to own her entirely. She spat it out and that act revived her. She couldn't drown, she couldn't give in to the poison, she couldn't let it saturate her being, and she couldn't let it shove away her intentions. Grace kicked gently, forcing her head to bob above the surface, and tread water.

Muted noises from above came to a halt. Sevryn must have been attacked, or the rope wouldn't have gone slack. If she got pulled up now, she didn't know who would meet her at the well's rim. He might have recovered, or he might have been overcome. Those thoughts worried at her even as the water tried to worm its way into her body and soul. It slithered along her skin like a thing alive and determined to dive down her throat. It crawled up her face to her eyes and lids, as if it thought it could peer inside her, and she blinked fiercely in response, knowing that poison in the eyes could be trebly fatal. She shook her head lightly, fighting it, but keeping her movements subtle because that kept her afloat. Thrashing would only bring her down below the surface that much faster.

Her toes felt like icy pebbles only vaguely attached to her feet. She wiggled them slightly as she pedaled through the water, glad she'd taken her boots off before being lowered into the well. Her hands felt only slightly warmer as she waved them, back and forth, forth and back through the surface. The water pulled at her, trying to drag her down. She ignored it, thinking of summers spent swimming with Nutmeg and their brothers in sun-warmed, lazy pools. She thought of hanging onto the side prying her fingers into handholds in the well itself, but she didn't trust what might be growing down here, slippery mosses that might be adding to the water's corruption. So she stayed afloat where she'd dropped and concentrated instead on warding off the element that fought to consume her.

Like a foggy mist, it curled around her, trying to creep into her nostrils, her ears, her eyes which she could not shut tight enough. And it gained a voice, a soft, deep, sinuous voice that cajoled and coaxed, asking for surrender, for submittal, for everything. She thought she remembered that voice, oily and ingratiating, holding just enough truth that she had to listen to it to be able to tell the difference. As its watery hold wrapped its silken arms tighter around her, she remembered then what had eluded her. She'd not felt the dark water before but heard it . . . and fought it . . . deep in the ridges that bordered Larandaril, pooled in the tunnels and caverns that bubbled throughout seemingly solid rock.

It had coaxed her then. Showed her bits and pieces of life as it had been and as it might be. Frightening scenarios that she could change if only it could merge with her. Share powers. Mold destinies.

Being chased by Lara for treason she neither committed nor fully understood, and having sent Sevryn off safely, the dark water had come to Rivergrace at a time when she had never felt more alone or uncertain. She would sink even lower when captured by Narskap and Quendius after, but then, at that moment, she had found it within her to deny the dark water.

It bit at her now with cold sharpness, washing over her relentlessly, trying to pull her down. Rivergrace took a slow breath to gather her thoughts and tried to search through the well water, looking for the heart of the darkness, the seed from which all this venom bloomed. She fought her body's desire to go liquid itself and be free of this contamination, instead going down and out, searching. She kept her head above water as long as she could, but when her search jerked her down and under, she went with it, praying she could hold her breath long enough, knowing that her flesh might flee into mist rather than death if she failed. She opened her eyes, squeezing them shut tightly after every blink, willing the poison out of them, shaping whatever touched her into sweet water, potable, living, clean. The seductive voice, the liar, went silent. She went searching for its center, determined to ferret it out, and stayed down until her lungs ached and her throat felt like bursting and she let herself rise to the surface, thrashing a bit. The oily coating over the water thinned under her touch as her fingers fanned and she let herself feel a bit of triumph. It was backing away from her, ever so surely.

Releasing the triumph took effort. She had to let it go, because she knew that the moment could be deceptive. The battle hadn't been won, it had barely been enjoined. To act as if it had would be to court disaster.

She shook her head. Above her, she could hear the ring of words, Sevryn's voice distinctive, though not what he said. Smiling, she took three great deep breaths and dove again. This time she kept her eyes wide open, blinking only when silt scratched at her face or the water rose with a particular bad splash of corruption. She banished the waves a hand touch at a time, her fingers tingling as her Goddess rose in answer.

Two more surfaces, quick and clean, and one last gulp of breath, she marked the sides of the well this time to determine where she'd searched and where she lacked. Then she found it, her foot kicking over a large, flat brick or stone at the well's farthest depth. A bright green wink of light, a flash, a moment of panic and nausea, a stab of ill-intent and she had it, something clinging to the other side of the weight. She pried it off, losing half a nail in the attempt and brought it with her as she went up for air.

Slimy. Loathsome. It shimmered in the palm of her hand, scarcely more than a pinch of—whatever it was. Rivergrace stared at it and then, after a long moment, smiled crookedly. She wove a black-and-gold thread out of the air, out of her soul, and bound the curse to herself, a curse embedded in a speck of someone else's soul.

Once caged, the water went clean in a touch. With a fan of her hands through it, the last of the corruption thinned into nothing and she threw her head back with a shout. She could taste the clear, snow melt water surging in from the depths as it should, icing up, a fountain of renewal.

"Sevryn! Pull me out!"

The sun dried her, but slowly, clouds heavily dappling the sky until it finally settled into a leaden gray, overcast until nightfall. They accepted a bowl of fish chowder which they shared between them, knowing that the hospitality of the village couldn't go far and not wanting to strain it. The wiry man stayed in a corner of the cottage, watching them sourly, his arms crossed over his chest and one shoulder put to the wall. The woman Sevryn had made allies with, more or less, had given Rivergrace a blanket and a shawl and also watched them with few words, as they met the others and shared their portion.

"That unnerved me," Rivergrace told him later, as they crossed the meadow.

"The judging?"

"Yes, if that's what it was."

"More or less. I used a bit of Talent on them to accept us and not betray us, but I won't gamble on that holding."

"How would they betray us?"

"From words passed while you were cleansing the well, I gather the queen and her forces travel from village to village, rooting out traitors. Whole cities have been known to vanish."

She halted. "What?"

He nodded. "She puts to fire the plague-ridden, the treasonous. Sometimes a city is more one than the other, but since gone is gone, with no one left to argue the point, who knows?"

"How can she keep her people?"

"I don't know. She does, but I've no idea of how she engenders loyalty. Fear can rule a people but not for long. As a weed grows stubbornly out of the most well-tilled and kept field, so will truth."

"And you learned that from . . ."

"Tolby Farbranch, actually." Sevryn grinned at her.

"Figures. We Dwellers have always had a handle on things."

"Mmmhmm. So where are we heading now?"

Rivergrace pointed in front of them as she began walking again. "The river. Not its origin but upriver a bit."

Sevryn's silvery-gray eyes narrowed as he looked ahead of them. "Poisoned, too?"

"So they say. They had to trek inland to another freshet to fill their buckets." Rivergrace lifted her left wrist thoughtfully.

Sevryn could not see it, but she'd told him about the new bit of soul she'd woven to herself. He didn't like the idea she'd done it. "What's guiding you?"

She tilted her head as she forged ahead through bracken and scraggly, salt-swept grasses. "Not my water sense. This bit would pull if I let it. It nudges at me as it seeks a bigger part of itself."

"Could that have come from Daravan?"

"No. Nothing at all like his sorcery. Or even Vaelinar Talents. I wish there were someone with us who could identify the source, but I don't need someone to tell me it's corrupt."

"Evil."

"Yes. It's a predator without mercy. Its sole aim is to cause destruction."

"And you're carrying it around with you."

She threw a look at him over her shoulder, framed by auburn hair caught in the late afternoon wind as it gained strength over the meadows. "I couldn't destroy it. Fire, ordinary fire, won't."

"I would say ice, then, but we know it prevails over water."

"You understand."

He didn't want to, but he did. She carried on her a touch of soul, a desperately evil soul that she could not destroy. He could not bear to think of a time when it might get free and destroy them both.

She started to speak then, and he thrust his hand up to cut her off. "I know what to do if that happens."

She made a little strangled noise as if to say something more, and then shook her head as if tossing away anything else she might wish to say. She did, however, stop in her tracks and point upriver. They could not see the river itself, but the growth along its banks was visible, greenery striving to survive despite the poisons in the water. It could be heard, too, sounding along the rocks in its bed and along the banks, a faint burbling melody. "We're close."

"Keeping your boots on this time?"

"Unless I have to go wading." She began to hurry.

And he, as he had promised himself long ago, followed.

Chapter Seven

THE RIVER SANG TO HER. Its voice, like that of the well, held a not-quite-familiar lilt, but whether she heard it that way because of its stain or because it was not of her world, she couldn't tell. She let its call fill her, searching for that wrong, discordant, harsh sound that pulled at her roughly, insistently, as if the tether she'd made encircled her throat rather than her wrist. She stumbled over rough ground and felt Sevryn catch her elbow to steady her, but she didn't hear his voice at her ear. All she could hear was the river song, flooding into her, like a torrent of rain after a dry spell. It called to that which she held embedded deep inside her, the River Goddess, bereft of its own and that gave her pause. Just in time, for Rivergrace found herself on the edge, the meadow trampled into a muddy bank.

Sevryn's fingers tightened on her elbow. "You're not listening."

"I couldn't. The river was singing to me."

He gave a slight sigh. "Look about you."

She did, and saw then what troubled him, and stepped back sharply. Boot prints stamped into the muddy, footprints, and a multitude of them. "Quendius crossed here."

"I didn't know what drove you."

"I'm sorry. It was the water." She looked upstream, where the river grew both narrower and deeper, its blue-gray waters racing toward them. "It's not far upstream." She could see the oily stain spreading down toward them. She put her hand over his, feeling the slight chill in his fingers. "Are we safe here?"

"This looks to be at least a day old, if not two." Sevryn slid his hand free and knelt down. "The mud has dried. The grass, too, where it was broken. I can't see that they drank here."

"The Undead don't drink. Not water, anyway. They don't eat much either, although they do have to . . . blood . . . prey now and then. They have an unquenchable thirst for blood."

"He must have them on a tight leash because I don't see any carcasses in their wake."

"No. Not yet." A shudder thrilled through her.

"We're safe for a day or two, if we follow after. It would be best to return to the village and stay the night, I think."

She thought of the wisewoman. "Zytropa?"

"The one with the brilliant blue eyes. She could be related to Bistel and Bistane, with eyes like that."

"I wonder if his hair will go snow-white like Bistel's did."

"It could hardly help it, courting Lara and keeping Tressandre in line diplomatically."

She let Sevryn reach out again, to guide her over the trampled bank to virgin ground upstream, talking to him with half her attention and listening for the seductive voice of the oily stain as she walked. "Would it be wise to return?"

"I believe so, for a day or two. They are grateful if wary. I didn't see any bird keepers, so any communication would likely be by sea and take a while longer. They like their isolation from what I gather."

"Independent."

"Exactly. They are beholden only to the sea for whatever bounty it gives them, and it exacts its toll from them."

"How does the land feel to you? The sea?"

Sevryn tilted his head for a moment's thought. "If I had to characterize it, I would say old. It feels old and worn."

"But not comfortable."

"Not at all. Why do you ask?"

"Because it struck me that way, too. While the lands of the First Home are raw, new, primal, this world feels different to me. As if it has been beaten down by circumstance and weather—and man. Strange to think of a place like that."

"You've not seen most of the ruins of the Mageborn, or you wouldn't say that."

"And you have?"

"Gilgarran was a most thorough teacher and mentor. Also, he held a curiosity that some said was unhealthy about the pools of sorcery left behind in the badlands."

"The contaminants."

"Yes. Still viable even after centuries, but in a most unpredictable and often virulent way. I almost lost a foot accidentally stepping in an unseen pool."

"Almost."

"I did," he said sorrowfully, "lose a very well-made and practically new boot."

Her head whipped about. "Speaking of contamination."

"Here?"

She winced. "It shouts at me. But . . ." and she dropped to her knees. "I don't think it's placed deep in the creek. In fact, it feels like it's just tucked in about . . ." She had her arm in, fishing around the bank and finding a water-carved overhang. "Just about here." She pulled her fist out, fingers curled over a pulsating bit of yellow-green that radiated the venom it produced. It squirmed and pulsed against her hold, flaring out between her fingers so much that she narrowed her eyes to a slit to look at it.

"You're not going to bind that to you."

"Cage it tightly is more like it, and yes. I don't have a choice right now until I find a safe way to destroy it." Eyes still near shut, she quickly wove a bit of her soul into a tight thread that she wrapped about it like a spider would cocoon a prey and hooked it onto her as she did her other anchored threads. She could feel the two minuscule bits of evil rotate toward each other and buzz in mild irritation when her thread kept them from merging.

"You're frowning."

"I can't let them merge."

"The first bit to the second? I should think not." He leaned over to brush stems and damp dirt from her knees. "Can you identify the soul?"

"Not yet, and there's a strong part of me that never wants to know whose soul it is."

"A wise reaction, but an unlikely outcome." His hands ringed her calf for a moment. "Is it mortal?"

"The soul?"

"Yes. Or could it be a demon, like Cerat?"

She chewed on the corner of her lip thoughtfully. "My anchors are souls. But at the other end . . . Narskap and Quendius use Cerat. They offer a dying man a pinch of Cerat in exchange for their true soul, and their Undead are the ones who accepted."

"But you . . ."

"A pinch of myself. Life. And their life."

He stood. "Why?"

"A chance to keep them from the abyss. There is an abyss out there, I saw it, if only briefly. It wasn't for me, but it waits for a number of us, don't you think? And even though death doesn't frighten me, being there alone does. So when their death approaches, I can save them from that brink, I think."

"You don't know what will happen if you retrieve those anchors you set."

"No. I don't. Narskap had a vision and was instructing me step by step, and we . . . we didn't get a chance to talk about his final purpose."

His lips thinned. "He talked you into using your own soul. How could he have asked this of you? His only daughter."

"He had none of his own to give."

"Grace, you gave bits of yourself away. I don't know if, we don't know, how the soul heals. If it's infinite or like a biscuit with only so many crumbs to be had from it. He made you deal with Cerat, and we both know what that demon is capable of, and if Cerat realizes that you're at the other end of those strings—"

"He won't." She added, "I don't even know if the demon thinks or can rationalize as we do, or if it just exists."

Sevryn fell silent and she could not follow his thoughts, but saw the lines deepen at the corners of his eyes and downward along his mouth. "But you don't understand what it is you're dealing with here," and he gestured at the new threads she'd added.

"I know." She ruffled his hair with her fingers. "What if it's not a demon? What if it's Trevilara?"

"Then we'll know the songs they sang of her for centuries are wrong."

"One of the few things remembered from the exile, and it's wrong." She echoed the irony.

He offered her his arm as he straightened. "If we're lucky, if we succeed here, they'll never have to know." He put his face to the wind for a moment. "We should make it back to a sturdy roof or two before the evening drizzle hits us."

"Rain is coming?"

His eyebrow lifted. "What? You can't feel it?"

"At this point, everything feels damp." She leaned slightly against him as they began the long walk back.

"You need to take that up with your inner Goddess," he told her, his breath tickling the top of her head.

"I will."

It rained for an evening, and then came two fair days when no one stayed inside and the well water was tested with great caution. Then celebration was followed by work, and even Rivergrace spent a good part of a day helping to mend nets. When she took a break, she did so at the meadow's edge where a girl with tousled hair and blue eyes that spoke with vibrant laughter sat down next to her and busily picked a lap of wild flowers to braid into a chain.

Rivergrace had found some herbs which, as described by three or four of the village women, were good for basic healing arts and sat preparing them to take with her. She was more tired than the cleansing should have left her, and the hard work hadn't helped, so she rested when Sevryn couldn't see her and worry about her. The two of them worked in comfortable silence for a short span until the girl spoke.

"Mama says you're high Vaelinar."

"Oh?" Grace tried to smile, felt the expression slipping away too quickly in her exhaustion. "And you are not?" Did she mean royalty and common?

"No. Our powers are small, compared to yours. Even our whole village couldn't have cleaned our well and the waters that feed into it. We tried once or twice. Our elder died trying."

"That's . . . that's awful."

"It's life." Her small hands paused in the twisting of her flower stems before her nimble fingers quickly righted the braiding and then finished with a triumphant twist before shoving the flower crown at Rivergrace. "It's for you. A thank you."

"Oh! And, thank you." Rivergrace took the crown, doubled it and put it on as a bracelet rather than the crown.

"Mama says we should thank those we can while we can. Not to wait."

"She's very wise."

Her companion's dimpled chin bobbed in agreement. Her gaze, which had been fixed on her flowers, looked up now. Pretty Vaelinar eyes, of that blazing blue with tiny sparks of green. She ought to have the power that accompanied her bloodline, Grace thought.

"I'm Hobina."

"Rivergrace."

"I know." The girl paused for a long moment. "When are you becoming a God?"

She couldn't have heard right. The language she heard here was so different from what she learned at home, a blurred version, she often had trouble following. "A . . . what?"

"A God. That's what Queen Trevilara is going to be." She wrinkled her nose. "I think she will be a black, awful Goddess, but my mama says she wants power."

"Does everyone become Gods?"

"Oh, no. Only the special ones, even among the high ones." She peered up at Rivergrace from under her bangs, the late afternoon light catching the sparks in her eyes. She put up her little finger. "Most of us only have this much Talent. The High have this," and she put up her whole hand, fingers wiggling. "Queen Trevilara and you probably have this much." And she put up both her hands, fingers extended widely. "But I won't tell anyone."

"And why not?"

She pushed her hair from her face and stared right into Grace. "Because she'll come and kill you if she hears about you. The others said so."

Rivergrace felt the corner of her mouth draw upward. "She may try," Grace told her young admirer. "But she won't be able to do it."

"Good," the girl said firmly. "That's good."

She bent closer to Hobina. "And do the others talk about how one becomes a God?"

"They rise on the power we give them. But most of them take it, Mama says."

"And your mother would be . . . Zytropa."

"Yes! How did you know?"

"You look much like her."

Hobina dropped her gaze to her lap as she prepared another chain of wild flowers. "Not yet," she allowed. "But maybe someday. Mama says those who would be Gods put their hooks into us and never let go. They ride on our backs."

"Ride on your backs?"

Hobina nodded firmly. "We let them chain us and give our powers to them."

Rivergrace sat back on one hip, remembering the cage of threads like and yet unlike hers, tightly woven and too numerous to count spun about the Vaelinar Gods. Mortals, who made themselves immortal? Gods who were not Gods but whose powers were stolen? If so, then they would have much more trouble confronting Trevilara than they'd hoped, for every so-called Vaelinar God would be allied against them, in self-defense. They could sap the strength of an entire people to feed themselves.

On the other hand, Sevryn might be a bit happier knowing all they faced were mortals, or those who had been, once. Gods were not killable. Mere mortals were, even though pretending to Godhood. That might cheer him considerably.

But thinking that did not warm the cold spot of fear which had begun to form inside her chest.

Whatever steps they took from here on would have to be carefully planned and well-guarded. And they had to keep Quendius from crossing paths with Trevilara, at all costs.

Hobina put her grass-stained fingers on Rivergrace's knee. "You look very pale. Are you all right? You're not poisoned, are you?"

"No." Rivergrace found a small smile. "I will be fine."

A long shadow fell across them as Sevryn approached. Hobina's eyes narrowed with worry, and she got up to skitter away after a stammered good-bye. Sevryn watched her coltish figure run from them.

"You're too like the authority, I think," Rivergrace told him as he frowned and squatted down next to her.

"Do you think?"

"I do. You've the discipline and self-reserve. I don't know what Trevilara has done to this village; no one will talk to me yet, but I am beginning to form an idea."

"Then let me drop some more information on you." He paused to pluck an herbal stem from the ground and sniff it. He dropped it in Rivergrace's lap. "I think that might help stem bleeding," he mentioned. "I've run across something like that the Kobrir use."

"Perfect. I'll test it, of course, but I could use that in my simples kit. What did you find?"

"This was more than a plain fishing village. What we see here," and his hand swept across the landscape, "is a quarter of what used to lie here. I found massive outbuildings that were burned down, and the stubs of dry dock cradles down at the harbor."

"Boat builders?"

"So it seems, and once very good ones. Their past is a memory from their grandparents' time and they don't willingly reveal it. Trevilara brought a punishment of fire down on their heads for it." He sat back on his heels.

"For building?"

"For crafting vessels that enabled cities to escape her hold."

"Ahhh." Rivergrace twisted a bundle together and dropped it in a pocket, the scent of fresh greenery, bruised by her fingers, filling the air. "The women are saying little of her, but Hobina," and she nodded after her departed companion, "talks of a two-caste system. The higher tier holds the magic, and the power, and the longevity, from what I can glean. There is a deep-seated fear and respect, but I'm not sure if we can count on a rebellion."

"We haven't time to build one, anyway." He picked up a handful of pickings and spread them across his palm to examine them. "What are these good for?"

"Headache, toothache, I'm told."

"Eaten?"

Rivergrace grinned at him. "I've seen few topical cures for those." She laughed as he tossed the gleanings at her.

His own white teeth flashed. "That would be a sight, wouldn't it? A green paste spread across the brow or cheeks for pain."

She gathered the cuttings back up again, her fingers nimbly catching them up and twisting them into a bundle, long-stemmed buds with showy white-and-blue pods. "More like they would crush to a bluish goo, but since they're dried and put in a tisane, I'm not likely to know." She pocketed her flowers.

"What do we do?"

"We gather whatever they want to give us for payment and move on—and move quickly. They fear another fire-hazing that will destroy what the last one did not, and I don't think we're safe here for more than another day or two. Their gratitude will be greatly strained by then. Our main advantage now is that they're not in communication with any local government seat, let alone Trevilara's throne, so they've no one spying on them and they're not spying back. But—" And he paused. "That's not to say they wouldn't give us up willingly, especially if they stood to regain some of their old favor. There's plenty of lumber here to go back into the old business. They long for the security that will give them."

"Then we won't stay."

"Tomorrow?"

She got to her feet and brushed the last few stems and leaves off her skirt. "Early, I think."

"Yes, and I think we will leave in one direction and double back, in case anyone thinks to mark our trail."

"Meaning you're not sure about spies."

"In this world," and he stood to join her, his lips brushing her ear, "I'm not certain of anything except you."

Chapter Eight

"**I** FEEL LIKE I CAN SEE forever from here," Rivergrace murmured. She laced her fingers together about her knees as she sat and felt the early morning wind tease her hair about her shoulders.

Her attention darted to Sevryn and then back to the harbors in the shore below their cliffside perch. "I don't wonder. Look at them, like a many-fingered hand of the sea stabbing into the land, demanding to be noticed."

"I am thinking of Tranta."

"We would, with the sea in his blood and his hair the color of a warm tide pool. He never quite seems of the earth, does he? Those harbors—they're naturals, all of them, and it's no wonder we saw a fleet of fishing boats take to the tide at dawn." He dropped down to sit next to her. He brushed the aura that surrounded her lightly, and the touch against the barely seen yet tangible cage of gold-and-black threads sent a buzzing tingle over him. He leaned slightly away to avoid that touch again. "And, yes, Tranta would have loved seeing this. I think he would have talked me into stealing a sailboat with him and going out for a season, if he didn't think he'd have to convince you first."

"I think if he'd gotten out on a wild sea, he'd never come back. The desire is too strong in him."

"The Jewel of Tomarq was his anchor. When Quendius shattered her, he almost went to pieces as well, but he made smaller, just as potent, sentinels out of her shards. He made light armor for Lara, pieces of the Jewel inlaid in it, and that's what destroyed Alton when he tried to kill her. I saw their flare immolate him. I felt their heat." Sevryn shook his head in memory. "Tranta is determined not to let his Jewel go. She is a Way that was broken and yet still exists."

"What do you suppose he's doing now?"

Sevryn pulled at some of the tall sea-reeds that grew at the cliff's edge and examined them, as if deciding whether to eat them or weave. "It's hard to tell," he answered, as his fingers decided to braid the flat-leaved stems. "Time passes differently here, we know that much. Daravan's sorcery which sent us blasting to Kerith happened but a century or two ago here—and more than a thousand years ago on Kerith. We have to be mindful of that. As for Tranta, he could be married with children or still fastening his gems into watch-posts, hoping to extend the Jewel's Way. Time could snap into place with us here. We've no way of telling."

"It's like when I escaped the mines and forge of Quendius, cast out on the raft in the flood, and the Goddess caught me up. She wove us together to save me. Time passed and I never knew it."

"Possibly. Yet time passes everywhere."

"Nutmeg's child is born."

"Now that, I would bet upon. She could hardly have grown much more pregnant."

Grace slapped at his wrist and he laughed. "And we're wasting time!"

"We're not. Today, we're resting and evaluating our new situation. Caution is not only wise, it's necessary." Sevryn sniffed his fingers to see if the reeds had any discernible sap or odor. He couldn't tell. He nodded, finished his reed diadem off with a twist, and settled it on her head, her glossy auburn locks shining in the sunlight. He knelt beside the fire and spit, where their meal dripped fat into the ashes and sizzled as if it might be done. He pulled the carcass toward him, dividing the small roast in two, and they both ate hungrily without words.

Grace set her bones aside to lick her fingers, her mouth pursed as if she had words she needed to say and couldn't. She examined her wristlet and let her hand drop into her lap. "I feel empty."

Sevryn abruptly lowered the quarter leg of meat he held, its fire-crisped skin hanging loose from now tender flesh, and then offered it to her. "I've had enough."

She pulled a face at him. "That's not what I meant. I've had my half, now you eat yours."

Frowning, he brought the haunch up again. "What do you mean?" His neat, white teeth ripped into it, with a bit of juice escaping the corner of his mouth. She watched it glisten on his chin.

She spread one hand into the air, palm up. "I wish I had a better way to say it. Just . . . empty. As if I can't be filled, no matter how deep I breathe, or how much I drink or eat. As if I'm searching for something that I have to consume but can't, because I don't know what it is or where to find it, and everything else is nothing. Sometimes I feel almost frantic. And it weakens me."

"I find little wonder in that. You've cleansed three settlements in a handful of days, it has to be wearing."

"It has to be done."

"Yes, but not all at once! The water had been fouled with plague for decades at the last village," he told her, and cut his bone through the air. "They could have waited another few days while you got your strength back."

"If I can get it back."

He bristled. "I will shove you back into Kerith if I have to, while I stay to deal with Quendius. It's those souls draining you. It has to be."

"Possibly." She twitched her fingers in the grass near her thigh, rolling the stems between her fingertips. "We're resting today," she added mildly.

He tore meat off the bone with a savage bite, not answering.

"I don't know what it is. If I did, I'd tell you . . . and I think I'd know if Cerat was chewing at me the way you're chewing at that."

He swallowed. Then again. "Perhaps."

"It could be the Goddess. We're not home."

"No, we're not." He looked up, to the eastern quarter of the sky where a very small silver crescent rode the darkening blue. A songbird in a faraway branch faintly trilled. "We don't have three moons. Although that one is hardly big enough to qualify." He dropped the rest of his portion to a leaf platter. "It could be that, which means it's vital that we move against Quendius soon. Our time here could be even more measured than we figure, if it's wearing on you adversely."

"I didn't want to tell you."

He reached out and caught up her hand, squeezing it lightly, and the aroma of the grasses between her fingers spread on the air. "You didn't have to. I can tell. I was wondering when you might say something or if I would have to pull it out of you. You look pale. You act as though you feel transparent."

He held up their hands. Hers, pale against his tanned ones, her fingers long and tapered, his callused and scarred but showing strength. His skin warm against hers.

"Lily would make me eat my greens."

"And Nutmeg would bring you fresh apples."

The corner of her mouth pulled. "Yes!"

"And it would help."

She pulled their knotted hands to her forehead, pressing them close. "Yes, it would. So what will help me here?"

"Getting done what we came to do, I imagine, and finding our way home."

He freed his hand gently so that he could finish eating.

"If the bridge can be rebuilt."

"Daravan did." He pulled a crispy bit of skin free and eyed it between his fingers. "A number of times, as far as I can determine."

"What do you mean?"

"He entered Kerith at least half a dozen times, by what Gilgarran and I have noted. Not that either of us were eyewitnesses, but there were anomalies. Gilgarran noted the appearance of the Kobrir assassins and surmised they had been an imported race, such as we were. We know Daravan came to the Ashenbrook and the Ravela, and then to the Andredia in Larandaril. That's twice. Not the same bridge, or he'd have had the same landing point, do you see? He picked his geography."

She grew still, thinking. Then, "He did, didn't he?"

"Oh, yes. He came close to piercing Calcort but could not hold it. I'm not sure if the spell needs to be docked or anchored to complete, it's not a Talent I can even imagine, but it seemed he couldn't manage it there. The Raymy came spilling through but not him."

She shivered at the memory.

Sevryn finished off the meat on his bone and sucked at the marrow. "He didn't want to come through there; he knew he wanted to be in the heart of Lara's kingdom. Because of the Andredia, it was the last place any of us would think an invasion and attack could succeed."

"And it didn't."

"But it almost did."

Rivergrace busied her hands by pushing them through her abundant tresses and pulling them back, and weaving them into a knot at the back of her slim neck. With one hand securing the knot, she plucked up a sturdy, thin twig and inserted it to complete the style. "But it didn't," she said, laughing.

Sevryn threw another twig at her. Then another and another, until she got to her feet and ran to hide behind a tree. She stuck a hand out and waved. "I surrender."

"For today anyway."

Grace nodded. "You'll be scouting?"

"Just a bit after sundown." He stuck a thumb at their next destination. "That's a town, Grace, nothing like what we've dealt with already. With outlying farms and roads and businesses as well as that good-sized port. We risk a great deal going in there."

"Perhaps we should do it in early sunrise. Contact no one, if we can help it, but the water-gatherers and launderers will be up and about, readying for their day." She peered at him from around the tree. "I should be able to know where I have to go."

"They won't have a well and bucket system. That's a fairly sophisticated town down there, as well established or more than Calcort. There will be sewers and the like. Ponds and cisterns. Aqueducts and culverts. Piped water will be calling you from every direction and most of it buried under their roads and buildings."

"Like a web."

"Exactly, and you searching for a spider which is most likely nowhere near the center of it. I'll have a bit of trouble protecting you."

"I have faith in you."

He smiled but it didn't warm his silvery-gray eyes. "As I have in you. Not tonight. Don't press me to let you go tonight. I want to have a better idea of the town's layout. We don't know what we'll find there—it's prosperous, the port is open from what I can see—we're not likely to find allies there. More like a people toiling under the obstacles they must, and others spying to make sure it's done. It's possible the town hasn't been tainted."

"We have yet to find a place where the name Trevilara is not a curse."

He held a hand out and pulled her to her feet. "We've been at very independent, outlying communities, the sort that have always rubbed against rulers and rules. The first time we find a civilization that is loyal, unless we're very cautious, could be our last."

"All right, then. You go be cautious and I will nap."

He tapped his index finger on her chin. "Exactly what I hoped you'd say."

*   *   *

Although, deep inside the city, he found he worried about leaving her behind, that the heavy forested hills to the south of the town were not secluded enough. She could defend herself, he'd no doubt of that, unless she slept so deeply she could not hear an approach . . . He heard steps nearby, a presence he hadn't noticed for worrying about Rivergrace and chided himself as he moved away quickly. He ducked behind an eaved building and slid into the muddy shadows of what had to be a tavern, smelling of roasting fat, and beer and urine, with the pungency of stables nearby. His nostrils stung. Really pungent stables. Someone ought to be after their stable lads for their lack of work ethic and basic care of horses.

He rolled on his shoulder blade around the building's corner, out of the deeper shadows, and almost into an illumination from a streetlamp which had just been lit. He saw the lamplighter trundle his ladder up over his shoulder and with a broken, whistling tune, make his way down the street to the next lantern pole.

Again, thinking too much of Rivergrace and too little of his own caution. And what would she do when he didn't come back with the dawn?

Come after him, of course, no matter what sort of trouble he might have run up against. And he knew she would, too. The corner of his mouth pulled into a half-smile. With that in mind, he found a drain pipe and shinnied up it until he could gain the rooftop and from that advantage, watched the streets below as he moved through the night.

He froze in place at the sound of voices. He sussed out words and accents, and finally drew on his Voice to understand more clearly, warming his Talent and listening as finely as it allowed him to. A breath or two and then the surliness came through as he lay down on his belly in the dark.

". . . marks not the border, y'see, and she cares naught if anyone dies out there!"

"Shut yer mouth. She has ears and eyes everywhere."

"Only if there's money in't. If it's just flesh and blood, Trevilara won't be caring. And there's an army out there, I tell you. A dread army of shadow and steel that bleeds whatever it crosses and throws the carcasses to the side and doesn't care at all for gold or gems."

"Only the dead don't care about money."

"Exactly, I tells you. Something unnatural is out t'ere and it cares not a whit for money or prayer or the queen, flames and all."

"Yer wrong. She marks it, she has to. That sort of army could do for her."

"Nothing does for her. She cannot die, our queen, no matter who might wish it."

"So whut are you sayin', then?"

"Don't take your caravans that way, no matter what bounty she offers, or it'll be you and yours drained dry and thrown aside like a sack of dried bones to the road. That's all. I told you the warning and what you do with it is your own cursed business."

"Bah. Th' queen has offered a fair bounty to travel for goods that way. I'd be a fool to turn it down."

"And I jus' told you why you're a fool if you go."

"A dread army." A scoffing sound. "She has never let an army stand against her. The last one she blasted off th' face of Trevalka for even thinking of going against her, and who has ever heard of those Houses since? Eh? Brave warlords and knights and fighters all, blown off the face of the earth."

"In your father's time. If it happened. I say she opened a pit and buried all the bodies, every rag of the traitors, down to the last dog and wagon wheel." Boots scraped the alleyway. "Yer goin' despite whut I say, right?"

"I have t' go. I have contracts to fill and bills t' pay. I can't run from armies I never heared of before, now can I? And I trust th' queen. She wouldn't send anyone inta harm's way, not for goods she needs. 'Tis a pretty bonus she's payin' when I bring the caravan home."

"Think on it, lad. Why the bonus? 'Cause damned few are comin' home!" Another shuffle of boot soles in the wet and grime. "Bah. I tol' ya. It's all I can do. Light on ya, and hope you make it back."

The voices dropped beyond his hearing. Sevryn pulled back tightly. It sounded like Quendius and his men had taken a stand on a crossroads, living off the fat of the land there and waiting to see what authorities they might draw after them. Rivergrace hadn't told him that the Undead fed so voraciously, but then she might not have known. Quendius would not keep them under wraps the way Narskap had, mostly to protect his daughter, a worry Quendius did not feel. Now, with that constraint gone, the appetite of the Undead seemed to have grown in leaps and bounds, making Quendius the master of a very unruly pack.

And it might well be a calculated move. Quendius would have a formidable reputation when the time came for him to meet Trevilara, a background of bloodthirsty and relentless action. The weaponmaster might even hope that Trevilara had built up a reluctant respect for him and would treat with him as an equal.

Sevryn breathed in, long and slow, and went to his hands and knees to make his way across the rooftop. His path took him crisscross over the town, but he never heard a conversation that piqued his attention quite so much as the first one. No word of bad water, only talk of plague, and those few who mentioned it did so in hushed, frightened words that told him the plague was feared, under strict control measures and no longer in daily outbreaks. He culled the information he needed as he drew close to the center of town, near the town guard headquarters, from the gossip on the air as well as the grousing of tradesmen. Among the most important tidbits he heard was the location of the stables in the opposite quarter of the town. Rivergrace would walk no farther, he decided, not with Quendius nearby, and changed his rooftop route to go in pursuit.

He did not see the rotted corner of the next roof he crossed, not until too late, when it collapsed with a thunderous noise, dropping him to the streets where he lay and tried to catch his breath. In the next blink of an eye, he found himself surrounded by city guard, their spear points down and glinting sharply in the pale light of city lanterns.

He meant to leave her sleeping, but she couldn't. The smell of the fire ebbing down to little more than glowing ash filled her senses, along with a restless wind that did not blow steadily into the trees but fitfully, so that each new gust rattling branches came as a little bit of a startlement. The noise of predators moving far off, twigs snapping now and then, a faint yelp of a prey caught—those came to her as well. Nothing could be as noisy, though, as the sounds of her own body: the rush of her pulse in her ears, the knocking of her heart, the whoosh of her breathing, the occasional gurgle of her stomach, the pounding of her thoughts. She hated that he had gone without her though she knew he could move faster and quieter without her. Always dangerous, his stint with the Kobrir had given a razor-sharp edge to his abilities. They had meant to. His captivity had not been accidental but fortuitous, he'd told her. He had been sharpened so that he could face off against Daravan and deliver the man to the Kobrir for justice. His prey had no intention of going willingly, so Sevryn failed in that regard, though Daravan could hurt and manipulate them no longer. He counted that as a victory for the Kobrir, though far from their intentions and he might have to settle with them when—or if—they ever returned to Kerith.

Rivergrace shifted to try to find a more comfortable position. If they returned. She had not thought that far ahead nor did she now. Her father had had a plan in mind when he insisted she anchor the souls of the Undead, but he'd never told her the extent of his thoughts. His voice echoed in her half-dreams. "Remember this," he'd told her. "Cerat is never diminished no matter how many times he is divided." And then, "He lives to corrupt. Innocence is the most perfect bait to catch him. He is most powerful whole . . . You'll understand if you remember."

She remembered, but she was no closer to understanding what he meant or what he'd hoped the two of them could accomplish, the legacy that he'd passed to her. Narskap was not always in his right mind, seldom actually, but in his moments of lucidity, he could do great things. That was why Quendius held his leash and kept him close as his Hound. He had known another way, she thought. Had planned that he would have time to impart his scheme to her, and failed.

What had he meant?

She was the innocence of his statement: that was the only fragment of his words that she understood and she knew that he had been mistaken then and now. She would work with that element when the other parts of his statement fell into play. She knew one thing with surety. He'd been speaking of dealing with Quendius. She'd have to worry at it like a dog over a bone until she knew how to do what she must. Quendius would be stopped.

She turned onto her back. The night, not as dark as it could be, lay sprinkled with stars, unfamiliar stars, not like the ones she and Nutmeg used to picture from tall orchard trees they climbed up and perched in on lazy summer nights. Her faraway sister used to tell her that there was no problem that couldn't be solved by climbing a high enough tree to get a new view on it. She wondered how Nutmeg was, after her loss of Jeredon, and how the baby was, and if they were doing all right. She wondered if Nutmeg thought she'd died when she went through the Gate at Larandaril and given up on her, telling her baby about the lost aunt, like the lost father. How Tolby and Lily fared, and her brothers—Garner, Hosmer, and young Keldan—thrived, if they did. Garner had a free-roving spirit and likely had taken to caravan guarding, like his father, with more than a little gambling on the side. He might never come home again, to Lily's sorrow, but she let her son go. He was, after all, more than man grown and how could she scold away the traits that helped her to fall in love with her husband, his father? Hosmer was grown, too, now a captain in the city guard, as solid as an emeraldbark tree. Keldan, now, like the hot-blooded horses of the Vaelinar he so admired, could set a wild eye on you as if he would bolt away at the first suspicious word, but his craft and kindness with animals couldn't be disputed. Rivergrace wondered if he'd become a healer and trainer of them. All three were bound to be doting uncles for Nutmeg's child. If Garner stayed true to his wandering soul, he'd still send gifts back, trifles he'd found along the way that he thought might be loved or useful.

Rivergrace fell asleep, listening to her mind's memory of Lily sitting at a loom and singing softly to herself, working on a soft yarn garment that would undoubtedly be a baby's blanket.

She awoke to the smell of blood and death.

Chapter
Nine

GRACE MOVED SIDEWAYS, blending into the wind-twisted trees that ringed the campfire. It had sunken into banked coals, little she could do about that, but she could disappear from sight. The stiff-needled branches of the nearest tree bent around her form reluctantly, its sap scented sharp and clear. With the toe of her boot, she dragged her kit bag under cover with her and bent to grab the strap and hoist it over her shoulder. Her other hand dropped to the hilt of her blade. The smell of blood grew stronger. The blood scent came to her fresh, as though just spilled and still wet and crimson, but underneath she thought she detected a familiar dry and musty rot.

She shut her lips tight. She slipped her fingers into her bag carefully, searching for the sharpest bit of steel she could find. The curved blade bit her, slicing across her index finger lightly. She grasped the handle and drew it out, breathing as lightly as she dared, not wanting to alert the other. If it were hunting, if it were crazed by the blood it had spilled, she had no hope or reason to save its unlife and her tether would take care of its soul. Beyond that, the balance lay between life or death, and she would choose life.

Grace put her forehead against the tree trunk whose branches sheltered her and tried to look through the looming darkness. A barely lit night, the moon not bright enough to illuminate much, if at all, but the unmistakable odors reaching her told her the being moved steadily closer.

It couldn't be hunting her. Like a gaze hound, the Undead looked for movement as well as the heat of the blood within its prey, and she stood still, still as silence and shadows. The shroud of threads she wore shifted about her, and she could feel a ping of awareness down one of the lines.

The back of her neck went chill. His awareness of her or her awareness of him? And did she even have a soul anchor on this particular Undead, for Quendius had been reaping the dying on the field of Larandaril with every step he took across the battlefield heading to the gate between the worlds. She had flung her own soul out, capturing as many as she could, but she could not possibly have caught everyone. Not all of them. So did this tingle she felt come from the approaching Undead or from within herself?

The light breeze stirred the branches around her; one brushed over the top of her head and across her brow, like the light and feathery touch of an inquisitive hand. She looked upward and then shoved her blade into her boot, put her hand up to a sturdy branch and began to hoist herself up. The tree gave way quietly, surrendering to her climb, as silent and sure as she could accomplish it, her thoughts filled with remembered climbs with Nutmeg, in the same quiet, so that their brothers could not discover them. The fitful night wind covered the occasional creak of limb or crackle of bark as she made her way higher and higher until she could travel no farther safely and settled down in the fork of her tree. She ran her hand down the shaft of her boot, ensuring that the curved blade remained nestled securely, and then looked over the canopy of trees to see what she could.

She would not have seen him at all if the faint light of the moon had not caught and reflected in his eyes.

He didn't dare take them out, though he had no doubt he could do so. If it had been a pack of street thieves in a back alley, he would have. But these were town guards and their numbers would certainly be missed and the motives behind any attack would be keenly probed throughout the city. He rolled to his knees and froze, open hands in the air. Even though he'd made the decision not to provoke or fight, he noted his targets and how he would most efficiently attack: to his left, grab the end of the spear and throw the holder across the semicircle into the two standing to Sevryn's farmost right. That would bring three down for a moment, in which time he could pull two men together and take one out by a kick to the face and the second by hamstringing as he went down and turned in the kick. Then he would take out one of the spear-carriers by a blow or kick to the temple, roll, get back on his feet, and face the remaining three. His actions would depend on theirs: spears, swords, knives, or fists. He hadn't been particularly lethal yet and would go for the knees, preventing them from running after him efficiently when he took his leave. He would have a spear in his own hands and could use it to both block and sweep anyone else off their feet, as well as deliver some ringing blows to the side of the head.

But he stayed still. His lungs inflated a little with his thoughts, preparing for the attacks, and his balance shifted, ever so subtly, but he kept his eyes level on the town guardsmen.

"What're you doing up there?"

"Watching and listening. My girl walks down thatta alley. Thought she might be meetin' a fella." The accented Vaelinar felt strange coming from his throat and mouth and, to his ears, he didn't quite have the pitch of it, but they did not seem to notice.

The big guy in the middle, with a scar across his upper lip that looked like he'd taken a losing slice in a knife fight, dipped his spear point in the air. "Make a habit of crawlin' on rooftops, do you?"

"Only when I don't want t'be seen. My bit catches me spying on her, it'll be a cold day for me, eh."

"No more'n you deserve. A woman needs respect."

"Indeed." He sketched a slight bow. "By the Queen, no less, a woman does."

The guards traded looks. Had he gambled on Trevilara insisting on a woman's equality correctly? It would be no less than he expected, but backwater towns could hold backward perceptions. Someone grunted.

The big guy waved his spear. "Inta the drunk wagon with you. I think t'would do you good to sleep the night off."

Sevryn heaved a sigh. He bowed his shoulders. "If you will."

The spears all moved closer to him, herding. "Git along."

They prodded him into a quick walk, along the gutters of the alley and into the main street where lanterns flickered feebly against the curtains of night. The march took him to a foul-smelling enclosed wagon hunkered down by the side of the road, four droop-headed horses waiting in the traces, and a guard sleeping on the high seat to the fore of the wagon. Sevryn did not want to enter the wagon but went anyway, with a spear end thumped into his ribs to encourage him, and sat down, breathing through his mouth against the stench of urine and alcohol vomit at his feet. His throat burned with the effort. Two huddled-up figures exchanged nods with him and a third lay curled up on the filthy floor, snoring fitfully. He braced himself with his elbows on his knees and fixed his fellow passengers not as comrades but as points of diversion and possible shields when he broke out.

The wagon gate slammed as he settled. "That's enough for a stop at t'jail."

A heavy fist thumped the side of the wagon, vibrating through its thin boards, and another voice called out, "Halt there. Not the jail." A new voice. Somewhat cultured, by the accent of it. Perhaps an officer had joined the guardsmen.

"Not the jail? Why't not?"

"The good queen is in town, standing at the Lord Mayor's hall. She wants a look at our miscreants, see who's up to mischief and who isn't. For all I know, she might need a subject for one of her experiments and such."

"She's been sending spies out to take a look at that army gathered at th' crossroads." A flat declaration.

"Of course she has! Think anyone stays a queen supreme as long as she has without a lick of sense? She's got eyes fixed on that group, studying, gathering. I heard"—and the voice dropped low enough that Sevryn had to lean forward on his elbows to take the whisper in—"that the army is most unusual. Only one man has gotten back to tell of it, and his mind so addled only she can pick the truth out of it."

"What sort of truth?"

"I heard that the army is unnatural, riddled with curses as well as magic, and the soldiers are blood drinkers."

A collective gasp from the listeners. "No! No such thing exists."

"It does now, if the survivor has it right. But who knows? The queen herself may have to travel out to meet this menace. Our trade routes have been blocked for days now, and she is furious over the lack of goods and revenue. She says her people suffer."

Someone muttered something even lower than Sevryn could catch, and a scuffle followed the muttering and then a hard thump of a fist to flesh. Another thud of a body hitting the street.

"Throw him in th' wagon until his head clears." Big man, clearly.

The cultured voice added smoothly, "Fitting. We'll have no dissent among the guard, for pity's sake. She's been our queen for three generations and shows not a day of it, but her mind has wisdom we cannot even begin to comprehend."

The tailgate dropped long enough to roll a limp form in. The body came to a halt at Sevryn's boot toes and he stared down, trying to decide if the man could be an advantage or not. The gate slammed shut again, and this time the horses took off with a jolt and whinnies of protest against a whip snapping against their rumps. The wagon lurched forward unsteadily before settling down into a pattern of bumps and sways. The men around him pitched back and forth, except for the loose-limbed unconscious guard on the floor and the sleeping drunk in the back, who Sevryn had come to suspect, was neither as drunk or asleep as his fellow prisoners thought. Now there was a dangerous man, and one Sevryn hoped to keep a lid on until he made his own move. He slid a boot over, quietly and slowly, until he could toe an outflung hand. A slight tension ran through the supposedly sleeping man. Then, he aimed his Voice, low and steely at him, filled with compulsion. "Don't."

The tension increased as did the snoring. Sevryn drew his foot away, fairly secure that the man had been warned and taken it accordingly.

Under them, the wagon wheels went from relatively smooth road to graded but much less hard dirt roads. After a space of time traveling along this corridor, the wagon turned again and ran over paved roads, although the paving seemed erratic and somewhat in need of repair. The Lord Mayor, it would seem, spent the funds of his high office on projects other than roadwork. Perhaps on an excellent wine cellar and larder? If he was entertaining the queen, that would undoubtedly be indicative. He let idle thoughts wander in and out while he kept a rough calculation on how far they traveled and knew that, when he did make a run for it, he would need a mount. Might as well get that second one for Rivergrace he'd been contemplating earlier that night.

Wagon wheels rolled onto a much smoother, harder, and consistent roadway, the horses' hooves ringing out. Wherever it was they were, they had almost arrived. Sevryn sat up and cleared his throat, preparing to grab whatever shadows he could with his Voice and disappear into them, when the vehicle jolted to a sudden stop.

Light flared about the thin wooden sides of the wagon, light and heat. Torches? A lot of them, if the driveway were lit that crudely but lanterns could put out neither that much illumination or temperature. Had to be a veritable fiery lane of torches. Was the queen afraid of the dark and its many shadows? Did she presume that assassins hid around each and every corner to cut down her despotic self? Or was this a fetish of the Lord Mayor, to burn into the darkness a miniature sun holding forth on his grounds? Either way, it would make it difficult for Sevryn to slip away.

Very difficult.

He sat up, gathering his legs and balance under him, ready despite the circumstances. As figures came to the wagon gate to lower it, he moved to the far corner, as two of his fellow prisoners got to their feet in anticipation.

Beyond them, he could see the trailing edge of flame—orange-, red-, and blue-tipped waves—eating away at the night. In the midst of the bonfire stood a woman. She might have had copper skin or it might have been the reflection from the wall of fire that surrounded and protected her, but she had hair as black as ink cascading over her slender neck and shoulders to cup the bottom of her firm behind. Her gown, of ivory with gold filigree and needlework, hugged her figure close, revealing high mounded breasts, nipping in at a slender waist, and then falling smoothly to the floor, only hinting at the shapely legs it covered. He could not tell if the hem was clear of the flames or if its edges burned as well. He thought he might be able to smell it if the cloth had caught fire, but he couldn't. He had no doubt, however, that he looked upon Trevilara.

"How many subjects have we?" she asked crisply.

"Four or five, Your Highness."

"I see four." She retreated a step, the fire's path following her. She raised her voice, which was lush and seductive even when reciting the business of the evening. "Gentlemen, let me congratulate you on the job you are about to perform for me." She lifted a slender arm, her long fingers grasping a vial. It gleamed in the light she cast, its fluid ruby red like a fine wine, but not like blood. It held a shimmery glisten to it that spoke of artistry, not nature, in its depths, like liquefied gems. He instinctively drew back, his nostrils flaring as if it contained all the unsavory odors of the prison wagon and more. Of evil.

"As you know, I have been on a long quest to rid my country of the plague and this elixir is the latest culmination of my hope to find the proper antidote. You shall have the privilege of testing it for me. With your help, and your names will be sung in the Halls of my palace, I shall prove its worth."

Or not, thought Sevryn. And first, one had to be contaminated.

Trevilara put out a finely shaped ankle to kick her hem aside, so that she could pivot. When she did, her fiery wall shifting to remain with her, her movement exposed a barred cage to view, a cage filled with two Raymy, their reptilian spines up and their wattles puffed out, and their skin bursting with the nasty pustules of their disease. They hissed as she took two steps toward their pen. Its bars rattled with their agitation.

She made a motion with her hands. Her fiery enclosure opened and took the Raymy within its confines as well, and she laid her palm on the top. The Raymy hissing grew loud and shrill until she kicked a bar, and they scuttled back into a corner and cowered. They knew her, knew what she could do to them, Sevryn thought. And it wasn't a pleasant knowledge.

As the last two men climbed reluctantly over the tailgate, Sevryn took advantage of the long shadow they cast and hit the ground as well, behind them, and then quickly peeled off to the side of the wagon where it cast its own silhouette and absorbed his.

A brace of guards rode up, one of them nearly brushing him as it passed where he stood. The horse jerked his head and flicked his ears, indicating his presence, but his rider only had eyes for the queen, it seemed, and halted to stare at her. His partner swung down, pushed his reins into the other's hands and went to gather up the prisoners who stumbled about as if in awe, pushing them in a bunch toward the fiery queen.

He did not blame them for their sudden silence and numbness. She stood in power and beauty, spectacle and sorcery, and he was afraid to look away himself. He decided on two things. One, he could not let Quendius ally with this person. And two, to do that, he must escape her presence that night, at all costs. Then, thirdly, his most important realization sank in. She must never meet Rivergrace.

A low and powerful voice spoke at his back. "Your Grace. You mustn't overlook this sacrifice. The shadows seem to have an affinity for him."

A knifepoint, aimed at his kidney, poked him in the back hard enough to break skin, urging Sevryn to step forward.

From her vantage point, Grace could see the shambling half-man below her as he pushed through the twisted grasses and low-hanging branches. Wetness slicked his clothing black. Yet, if the sun had been up, she was almost certain what she saw was blood, dampening and sticking his shirt and ripped trousers to his body. She could smell it, coppery sharp and pungent. Mortal blood? She'd no way of knowing. What she did know was that the Undead, while in her father's grip and being herded for Quendius, had little actual need for food or drink although they liked to blood small vermin now and then. Bigger game stayed mostly on the plates of the living although Quendius would sometimes throw raw, bloody portions to his followers as a treat. She'd never seen any of the Undead bathe in blood although she'd sensed the potential.

Cerat had risen in this one. Taken over. It seemed alone, which meant that even the stranglehold Quendius had on his army had not kept this one in line. And it hunted.

She knew that because the thing had stretched up, standing tall as it must have done once in its mortality, and laid its hands on the trunk of her tree, and made a noise of satisfaction.

It had found her.

She held her breath but all that did was make its panting all the louder. It backed up a step or two, to cast its gaze up at her and said, "Want."

It took a moment to get the word out, rolling the sound about in its throat as if it had forgotten how to speak as a mortal speaks rather than verbalize, and when it did force the word out, the sound of it shivered over her, chill and piercing.

With little thought but a lot of purpose, she took hold of her knife and let herself fall from the treetop straight down upon the thing. She hit hard, and it buckled under her weight. They hit the ground together, the Undead squalling in anger and surprise. On its back, she grabbed for greasy strands of hair and yanked its head back with one hand, and cut through its throat with the other. The curved scythe went through its flesh like a hot knife through soft cheese, decapitating him. The body continued to buck under her convulsively and stilled only when she jumped off it and threw the head aside.

Her heart pounded so hard in her chest she thought it might burst through. She wanted to drop the scythe knife, but her fingers white-knuckled about the grip and she had to pry each one away. The blade fell to the ground with a dull thud, the only noise she could hear in the night-cloaked forest. She quickly bent and picked up the knife, scrubbing it dry on the grasses. The thing at her feet bled very little, as if its desiccated flesh absorbed all that it had devoured earlier and still found it inadequate. She prodded it. It felt . . . light. Not absurdly light, but insubstantial. She could drag him, she thought, to the fire pit. She could burn the evidence. Not that she wanted to, but she didn't want to leave this undead and rotting thing here, so close to camp, where it might attract other predators, hunters that did not mind eating spoiled carrion.

Her netting of threads itched. She put a hand up, as if she could bat away a spiderweb even though she knew she could not. Her hand snapped on a single thread, a thread that felt cold in her hands, its color gone to gray, its life pulse shuttered. She tugged it. The headless body twitched again.

Rivergrace secured her knife and bent to do the unsavory, and it was not until she stood by the burning corpse that she realized Sevryn had not yet returned. She could not leave a fire raging on the cliffside; she dared not draw attention. She pulled on her anchored string to the dead man-thing's soul and fed it to Cerat. The demon swelled in the body in victory, and its own fire burst open, eating through the remains far quicker than even a brisk stack of logs could. She watched sadly, knowing that she could not have saved this one, no matter what she had done, but a part of her hated that she'd let the demon claim him, after all. What would Sevryn think of her?

Rivergrace hugged her arms about her torso. If Sevryn did not return by dawn, she would have to go down into the city herself. If one of the rogues from Quendius' army could make its way up here, the possibility that the man himself might be in league with the powers down there had grown much greater. She couldn't leave Sevryn to an unknown fate. Her hand, unconsciously, settled back on the grip of her scythe knife.

Sevryn felt the shadows shred away from him reluctantly as his assailant marched him forward. His Voice halted in his throat. Much as he wanted to use it, if he were ever to be among Trevalka's more powerful and elite Vaelinar, this would not be the time. It would not be prudent to reveal his nature before these two. He could feel Trevilara's gaze slide over him, casual at first, and then a narrowed, close examination, as if she could see through his very skin. His eyes would not reveal him, but his ears most definitely showed that he had Vaelinar blood, if not strong, somewhere in his lineage. She would underestimate him because he did not have the multihued eyes of a strongly Talented Vaelinar.

Or so he hoped.

Their gazes locked just as the knife point in his kidney relaxed, ever so slightly, and he came to a stop in front of the queen, the heat from her barrier washing the front of him to stop at his throat. He could feel her weighing what she examined, shadows of thoughts chasing each other like silvery clouds in eyes of jewel green. Forming judgments and thinking of tests. He'd never seen eyes of her color, cold and warm at the same time.

Her smooth face showed no sign of any decisions she had made, but her eyes gleamed with a vivid alertness. Let her think anything but eliminating him out of hand. He watched her puzzle over him as if he were made of pieces she could glide back and forth over a table while she put him together—and undid him.

This was what a good ruler did, although she had been far from a good ruler. Perhaps he meant strong ruler, he thought to himself, letting himself flinch under her assessment as a lesser man would. If she had any inkling of what she faced, of his birthright, of his training on Kerith under both the Vaelinar and the Kobrir, she'd drop him on the spot, no questions asked.

He had to live long enough to determine what weaknesses and strengths Trevilara might hold, and then escape to Rivergrace.

"Come here," she said.

Her soft tones wound about him, seductive and dark, sweet and savory, but he did not hear Talent in them. Merely the self-assured and sultry confidence of a woman who knew just what she had to work with, and how a man would respond to her. He thought of Tressandre ild Fallyn and that same tone and assurance. It hadn't worked on him for her, and it wouldn't work on him for Trevilara, but why not let her think it did?

He pushed a foot forward as if spellbound, but did so cautiously so that the kidney stabber would not spring back into action and careful of the wall of flames the queen kept so vigilantly ignited around her. He did not expect her to quell the barrier and she did not, although she opened a tiny pathway through and as he stepped into it, the Raymy began to hiss and wail at him, a warbling of belligerence and misery. Sevryn had to believe she had a bit more in mind for him than simple contamination but even if that resulted, he also had to believe Rivergrace could take care of him, as long as he got back to her.

Flames licked up the side of him as he passed through, close but not close enough to ignite his clothes though the heat brought beads of sweat to his forehead that ran like raindrops down his face as he slowly moved toward his goal. Closer, he could see lines of age about the corners of her mouth, in her gracefully arched neck, and in her hand which she held out to him in a half-beckoning gesture. Air sucked up from the ground in oven temperatures, passing over him and whirling upward, drawing faint wisps of smoke with it. Whatever she burned, it left little behind—no debris or ash and only the faintest trace of smoke. He felt on the edge of suffocating. Did she burn the air itself?

Whatever Trevilara did, it effectively kept everyone back, and those other prisoners cowed and on their knees as they awaited being called to her as well. It would not eat a well-placed bolt or arrow, but the updraft might well carry the instrument so far off target as to make a hit near impossible. Anything else would be defeated. She protected herself well. Perhaps she told her advisers and those close to her that it was to keep the plague burned away, but he had little doubt she used it against assassins as well. Poisoning? All she needed were food tasters kept close. This woman would be near impossible to kill. He wondered what she did for lovers. The corners of her eyes crinkled faintly as she observed him. Yes, she took lovers, the expression on her face clearly wondering if she might do that with him. She tilted her head and gave a ghost of a smile.

"Who are you?"

His throat closed for a second, parched dry, and his nose stung with the heat, before he managed, "Dardanon." He wouldn't, couldn't give her his first name. Names had power and power in this or any other world could be spun into great, life-losing, consequences. He felt his heart pinch tightly as she caught onto that part of his name he did give her and tested it for its truth. It passed. And still the flames swept near him, close enough to embrace, and Sevryn felt himself drying inside out, as though he'd been staked out in the sere Kobrir desert and left to die. He realized then that the fire consumed him. Not her, but himself and anyone else who might step within its perimeter. He put a hand out, certain that if he touched her, he would find protection, but Trevilara pulled her hand back, ever so slightly, and he could move no closer.

"Do you know what beasts these are?"

Sevryn froze. Did the population here know of the Raymy or had she bred them only to send into Kerith? And even if the population were familiar, what would they be called? He had no clue. He licked chapped lips. "They are death, my queen."

She shook the vial she still held. "Perhaps. Perhaps not. Are you brave, Dardanon?"

"Middling."

That brought a throaty laugh out. "Indeed? Not too brave, but honest. I might find a use for you, better than this." She extended her hand then, catching him by the cuff of his sleeve and drawing him to her side, and as she did, a coolness swept him. So this second layer was how she protected herself and so like his own Rivergrace, the gift of water and fire in one person. Only she seemed far more in command of her gifts than his love was of hers.

They must never meet.

He let Trevilara have a crooked smile. "However I can serve."

"Pick one, then. I have a mind to fill the rest of my evening more pleasantly."

"Pick . . ." She wanted him to choose a subject for her experiment. He wanted to do no such thing but now, next to Queen Trevilara, he seemed to be the center of attention. He jerked a thumb toward one of the faces he could see through the flames.

"Good." She nodded at her guardsmen and opened the breach in her barrier wide to let all three men through. The subject in question would not get to his feet and began sobbing into his palms as they dragged him forward on his knees. Trevilara tucked her vial inside her bodice and bent over the cage, a steely silver blade in her hand. Both Raymy were dead before Sevryn could blink, the knife going in the eyes of the one and the ear of the other.

Her guardsmen opened the cage door and pushed the sobbing man inside, where he tried to roll into a ball in the one clear corner.

Trevilara shook her head. "It's not done that way." She jerked her hand and the other three were pitched inside quickly, the cage filled body to body. She motioned for her men to set it on its rounded side and begin to trundle it like a wheel. The dead mixed with the living with bloody, mucus-covered efficiency as they rolled the cage out of their sight, the men wailing and begging for her mercy.

"Tomorrow," Trevilara promised with a great deal of satisfaction, "they ought to be contaminated enough to try the elixir and see what, if any, effects it has." She swept her appraising gaze over Sevryn again. "In the meantime, I have another test for you, I think. One of great stamina."

"My Queen," protested a man outside the flame's shadows, one he could barely see but who was undoubtedly the kidney sticker.

"I know what I'm doing," Trevilara answered him loftily. "I suggest you go about your business. Pay the town guards and return their wagon. Set guards up for the night. Retire to your rooms."

She pulled Sevryn's arm up over her own and swept away down the lane toward an enormous manor house that emerged from the night. "The Lord Mayor is indisposed, I'm told, so we have the run of the second floor tonight. You won't mind, I'm sure."

Actually, that would make things a great deal more convenient for him. As they passed the first soaring threshold, she quenched her flames and the night suddenly became a good deal darker as she drew him inside.

"Tell me how you did that bit with the shadows?"

"Oh, lady, that was nothing. A trifle. The only bit of anything I inherited besides the point of my ears. It does help me earn a living, however."

"You're a thief." Pleased, Trevilara chuckled. A wing of her dark, silky hair fell over their arms and he could smell the scent of her shampoo and oils, with a strong underlying smell of burning. "I might let you steal a bit of something from me tonight."

"You're too gracious."

She took the curving staircase. "I am bored. I am never gracious, and you would do well to remember that." She took the stairs quickly, familiarly, and he practically had to run to stay in step with her. No one followed them. Another stair or two and he would see how many men awaited ahead of them.

She moved onto the landing, out onto granite flooring. Soot marks stained its polished beauty. Banks of windows looked upon them like a multitude of mirrors. He sent a quick glance about them. Alone, save for himself. Trevilara turned on him with a sudden look of triumph in her expression. "And now," she said, "we shall see what you are truly made of," and dropped her hold on him. Flames roared into being, and he caught within them. She meant to test him, and he had no intention of giving her the satisfaction.

Red-hot, he opened his Voice and shouted, "Arise!"

His Talent hit the barrier and fueled it in answer. The fire answered with a roar. Its flames soared up, to the vaulted ceiling of the corridor, driving Trevilara back and he turned on heel and dove headfirst out of the nearest window, an inferno licking at his heels.

"And that's how you got away from her?"

"After her, the few guardsmen below were relatively easy to deal with. And I was able to steal not one but two horses." He nodded at the two horses cropping contentedly on grasses while the dawn clouds began to shred on the horizon.

"Clever, using her own fire against her."

"Oh, not against her, she's too well shielded. But she hadn't a chance of seeing me or what I was up to until she gained control, and all I needed was a moment or two." He paused. "She's dangerous, Grace. Without a conscience and powerful."

"We'll have to keep that in mind."

Rivergrace tucked her heels close to her bottom as she sat next to him. He passed a quick kiss over her cheekbone. "And that's what I was up to. Mind telling me what we're burning at the old campsite? It stinks to cold hell."

"A body, although it should be done far quicker than regular flesh and blood." She pointed at the second fire, a clearing away.

His eyebrow rose.

She shrugged. "Time for me to explain," and so she did. He watched the desiccated body burn, sparks crackling and spitting skyward.

"Desert dry. It took nothing to set it alight."

"I don't want to think about it."

She became quiet. She reached for him and tugged his shirt off without protest, then took his leggings and put both in a pannikin of water and began to scrub the sticky blood and soot off them, moving more by touch and smell in the darkness than by sight. When she finished, she hung them over nearby branches where they dripped to the ground. Then she cleaned her own clothes and shivering, lay down next to Sevryn, holding up a blanket for them both.

"We have to make plans for Quendius," he said to her ear, his breath tickling the fine, loose hairs about her face.

"We are doing nothing until our clothes are dry."

It seemed they had the beginnings of a plan.

Chapter Ten

Kerith

TWO YEARS GONE. Bistane slowed his horse as it moved down the inner slopes leading to Larandaril's innermost valleys, and he rubbed a hand to the back of his neck. He didn't know if he could actually smell the smoke and blood hanging in the air as he rode down, but he couldn't be sure—the battle which had been fought here stayed that crystal clear in his memories, as did its consequences. Two years since Lariel fell in his arms in a drug/poison-induced coma for which he had no antidote but had been promised there would be one. Time he had spent watching the Warrior Queen whom he loved look more than dead but far less than in peaceful slumber. Did she fight the betraying ild Fallyn in her unconscious state? Rail at Sevryn for saving her life even as he put the poison that still consumed her into her system? And yet, for all the days he spent taking care of her and her kingdom, and his own, he could hardly believe the count of days into years.

If Sevryn Dardanon were about, Bistane would gladly throttle him because he had trusted the man and then Sevryn had disappeared beyond any knowable reach. Rivergrace had gone after Quendius through the portal to the old world and taken Sevryn in hot pursuit with her. Had the young half-blood who had been Lara's faithful Hand before being accused of betrayal even survived the transit between worlds? Bistane had found no clue. No word sent back by any means of the welfare of Sevryn and his ladylove, Rivergrace. It was not a journey Bistane would have recommended, not following upon the heels of an Undead army and its head Reaper, but Sevryn had always had a destiny that Bistane could not quite fathom. Perhaps crossing the Bridge had been part of it. He would look again, today, for signs of life beyond the portal but hadn't much hope. The rip into the fabric of their world remained open, if only barely so. No one had managed to close it. And, by the grace of whatever Gods had awakened on Kerith, neither had anyone been able to force it wide open. He prayed that he would find it unchanged this day.

His horse sidled down off the last gentle slope and broke into a canter, without urging, over flatter ground. He settled more easily into the saddle as the site of the battlefield came into view.

His mount pranced aside from the great, black gashes across the meadows where pyres had burned for days, grass still not growing back, not even the slimmest yellow-green stalk. Perhaps there was something inimical in Raymy blood that poisoned the soil. The inside of his nostrils stung, as if he, too, could scent whatever the horse winded that upset it. It would get worse the closer he rode. The wind shifted, imperceptible particles floating across his line of sight that ought to be pollens or small insects wafting above the flowers and grasses but looked almost like ash.

He brushed the back of his hand over his nose to abolish the stinging and, taking the horse in hand, guided him wider around the expanse than he'd intended. It mattered little. He would cross the tent city which had sprung up on the edge of the meadow whether he wished to or not. Squatters determined to worship the anomaly which might or might not lead them back to a world that the traitor Daravan declared had been their original home. They'd no proof of it, but it was clear that the gap had opened to and from a somewhere, and why not home? Why not a paradise that malcontents everywhere invariably hungered for? He had issued orders for the Returnists to decamp and return to their own lands; he had been studiously disobeyed with every order, no matter how forcibly presented. Lara would strike him down for letting squatters flourish in her realm, especially Returnists who quoted Tressandre ild Fallyn from dawn till dusk. He held a certain authority but not one that went unchallenged. He could keep the city from growing but not enough to sweep them altogether out of the valley.

Bistane slowed his mount as he caught sight of the first of the tents. They were not allowed to build frameworks or anything that might add any permanence to their chosen homes and finally had accepted that edict after he'd brought in a company of men to tear down those that had been built. Under notice that he would burn them out if they violated that restriction again, the Returnists had reluctantly complied. His tashya complained at being restrained as well, although this by bridle rather than a writ and tossed its head while working at the bit. It wanted to run, where the ground was both firm and yielding, without critters that could dig holes for unwary hooves to be caught in, with the spring tide upon them. He wanted to indulge his hot-blooded horse but held him down to a walk. Hooves struck the now muddied ground with emphasis, the horse letting it be known he did not wish to be muted.

He halted the horse beyond the boundaries and dismounted, looping the reins easily over his left forearm, leaving his right free to draw arms if need be. Bistane knew they would provoke him, they always did, these Returnists. He just was never quite sure if it was intentional or accidental.

Someone had been bold enough to hoist a flag. He narrowed his eyes at that. Several children playing outside one of the longhouses put aside their grass necklaces and mud pies, got to their feet, and fled. That was . . . new. And disturbing. It meant that someone felt guilty and had cautioned the children. Now he had to discover what had transpired to cause the guilt. He shrugged off his riding gloves and slapped them against his thigh before securing them in his belt. Behind him, he could hear the distant thud of his backup troop, just a handful of Lara's men, in case he needed them. The worry that he might nibbled at the back of his thoughts as he approached the residences.

The worry gave way to irritation which began to grow into anger. Instead of knocking on the door barring his way, he kicked it, the door shaking as a result of his action.

It flew open.

"Everyone out," Bistane ordered. "I want everyone where I can see them clearly." He stepped back, resting his wrist on his cross-body sheath, and watched the longhouse empty. From the bodies emerging, he could tell he'd interrupted a town hall meeting of some sort, one that had perhaps begun with the hoisting of that flag. He said, to no one in particular, "Get everyone else here, as well."

A slim, dark-haired boy balanced on his toes, ready to take off on a run, but was halted by a head shake from a meaty man, his body clothed in trader's garb, his thick hand cutting through the air for emphasis. Bistane stared at him. The man stood still a handful of seconds before fidgeting and stepping back. Bistane then looked to the youth. "He does not countermand my order. Go fetch what other adult residents you can."

The trader reset his stance as Bistane faced him. "A name," he said.

"Trader Gantermitt."

"What guild hall?"

The thick-bodied man put his foremost chin out. "I am from the east."

"I am educated. What hall?"

"Norist."

"Southeast, near the bay of Qiram."

A look of surprise flashed over Gantermitt's face. "Yes. That would be . . . correct."

"You've come a long way to sit on your haunches."

Gantermitt drew his stocky body straight. "I would like to see my home."

Bistane turned on his heel a little and pointed a thumb to his right. "Qiram and your hall would be that way."

Someone tittered in the growing group behind the trader and Gantermitt's face knotted. "Lost Trevilara has beckoned for many of us for hundreds of years."

"You forget to whom you speak."

The trader put up his chin again, somewhat reducing the wattle of his abundant neckline, as well as increasing his belligerence as he stated, "I know exactly who faces me. Warlord Bistane Vantane, of the Northern Aryns, self-appointed regent of Larandaril."

"You have forgotten that I am the son of Bistel Vantane who was the oldest living survivor of the sorcery which brought us to this world, and that we were both on the banks of the Ashenbrook when Daravan revealed that we were not lost on Kerith, but sent here to exile and death. You have forgotten that we temper our skills at war with our magics of the aryn trees and our fields, and that we came bidden to Larandaril because of our alliance with Queen Lariel, and you are here unwelcome."

The hand of men at Bistane's beck and call dismounted and joined him silently during his proclamation and the murmuring that had begun at his speaking hushed, leaving one man's voice to stand out as he said, "To say nothing of his bastard half-brother."

The corner of Bistane's eye ticked a bit as he raised his voice. "I do indeed have a half-brother, but he's no bastard as my father duly married his Dweller lover and has bequeathed them lands and holdings in accordance with Kernan law, as well as with Vaelinar love and decency. Verdayne has been acknowledged and accepted since his birth, and my brother would show far less tolerance for you than I have. He believes in earning an inheritance, you see, not whining for one."

Bistane rocked back in his stance. "The flag comes down. These are Lariel's lands and will be respected as such. Those of you following other alliances are being told to quit this encampment and return immediately to your Houses. As for the rest of you, I will repeat what has been suggested a number of times to you: get out. You are squatters here and not welcome."

"Try to force us out and meet with the wrath of other Vaelinar lords," someone muttered from the rear of the assembly.

Bistane's head whipped about to find the speaker and failed as the entire crowd shifted, perhaps to protect the speaker, perhaps out of mutiny, perhaps out of fear of his reaction. The shadows moved in ribbons of ild Fallyn black and silver, in defiance. They were there and they taunted him. His teeth clicked shut on the words he wanted to shout.

A wiry woman, her violet-colored shawl wrapped closely about bone-thin shoulders, called out, "Then let Queen Lariel herself come and tell us. Let her deny us the right to go home to Trevilara. Does she yet live?"

That would be the question. Bistane could not answer, for he hadn't been to the manor himself yet, but he'd had no word otherwise. Expected none. To his flank, Lieutenant Firan said briskly, "She lives and thrives and when she does come to take you to task, you'll rue the day."

But no one moved, except the freckled girl dispatched to take down the flag as ordered, and he could feel their stares on his back as Bistane and the others mounted, reined about, and rode out.

The back of his neck tensed and he put a hand up to rub it. To his flank, Firan rode up to pace him.

"We were informed when you passed the border," the man told him. He looked well enough, a scar down his left cheekbone that puckered into his throat had healed well as, no doubt, had other scars hidden beneath his uniform. The deformity jarred otherwise handsome features and the hair on that side of his head had gone white, mingling slowly into warm brown tones. He had hazel eyes, of relatively few hues for a Vaelinar, telling Bistane that whatever Talents the man held, they would be light in power. It didn't matter to his loyalty and soldiering ability. He'd been there for Larandaril years ago and would be there in the future.

"I'd like to see that border closed," Bistane answered.

"So would we all, like in the old days, but only the queen has that ability."

"Any change?"

"None that we have noticed. She does seem more restless when you are gone."

"She moves?"

"We find her position shifts from time to time. Nothing significant, mind you. It may be a tilt of the head or a hip so that one leg may turn over another. The healers move her to keep sores from developing, as you know, but they have noticed differences they did not initiate. Healer Sarota keeps a diary."

He hadn't been aware of that. The tension running up the back of his neck cramped down into his shoulders uneasily, but why? He changed his balance in the saddle and shoved his feet deeper into his stirrups, yet nothing seemed to help.

"How is recruiting?"

Firan shrugged. "Difficult. Not like it used to be in the old days. Weather and economies always drove Vaelinar back here to the First Home provinces, but now we lack a general and a Warrior Queen to train them, and put them to use. To offer estates outside Larandaril when their terms were up. The only one effectively recruiting now seems to be the ild Fallyn." Firan paused to spit his contempt to the ground, just missing the flashing hooves of their horses. "And we've always suspected their recruiting consists more of abduction."

"Difficult to prove, but I agree with you. Who guards the manor?"

"A triad at the doors. It's been quiet."

He shot a look over his shoulder at the six who accompanied him. He did not like the numbers and his immediate response as his gut tightened was to shake the reins, and lean over his horse's neck, asking for speed.

His pulse quickened as the knots in his shoulder and neck tightened, and Bistane felt a fear that he wished he did not hold. The manor house was not far away, but neither was it as close as he needed it to be. He wanted desperately to be wrong, but knew that in all likelihood, he would be far too correct.

The ild Fallyn depended on quiet.

Chapter
Eleven

THE STABLE YARD WAS EMPTY of personnel, but not of horses, which stuck their heads out stall doors and whickered, hooves thudding against wood impatiently. Impatient for being let out to pasture or watered and fed by stable boys who had not appeared. Bistane dismounted before his mount came to a halt, dropping rein and running across the eerily silent courtyard. Firan followed after, calling, "What is it, Lord Bistane?"

He did not have an answer, for he didn't know what it was, and came to a halt facing the back side of the huge manor, tilting his head back to look up three stories, seeing that the men at the doors as they approached still stood guard. How they could not be aware of the near abandoned stable yard, he didn't know. There was distance, yes. And the horses were of little concern to them, neighs and whickers only background noises to the life of this part of the estate. Nothing alarming about a hungry horse, unless you knew that no one had been left alive to tend to them. Bistane twisted about.

"Count the dead."

"The dead?" Firan stumbled to a halt next to him.

"In the stables." Bistane pointed at the most visible stall where the mare knocked her hoof persistently against the door and tossed a head with the whites of her eyes showing and her nostrils flared in distress. "They smell blood."

Firan paled, swore, and swung about, drawing his sword with one hand and dispersing the other riders with wild gestures. Bistane hesitated to breach the manor. The enemy might still be hunkered down in the stables, trapped now, knowing their opportunity had been missed.

Or had it?

He could smell dinner cooking, its aroma wafting from the kitchen door. Spring onions and orange root vegetables and braising meat . . . nothing interrupted the meal preparations in the kitchen. Then why the assault in the stables?

Was he wrong?

Firan had disappeared inside the cavernous barn. He came out, shoulders sagging, one arm dripping blood. "No one," he called. "Alive."

He turned and pelted for the back door, yelling "Stand aside!" even as the bewildered guard stumbled forward a few steps in Firan's direction. "What do you mean, no one alive?"

Bistane shouldered past him. "After the queen! Firan, surround the buildings with whatever men you can. And archers! Find me archers!"

As he flung himself in through the kitchen doorway, in the corner of his eye, he saw a window shutter high up, slam in the wind. Lara's rooms.

Alarm already raised, all he could do was pelt upstairs as fast as he could, taking the stairs in great leaps, the wood sounding underneath as he conquered them. Lara's men followed after, shouting in confusion between themselves, and he leaving them behind in his wake. No one stood at her door. There had been for months on end and even when he'd left to take care of his own estate for a span of months, but not today.

Not this moment, when all depended on it. He kicked the door open, uncaring of the wood that splintered or the tremendous crash as it sprang open, or the man who spun about in triumph, his blade flinging blood on the walls as he moved to face Bistane.

Lara's blood.

He could see her bed, her bier, clearly beyond the assassin's crouch and saw the blood cascading to the floor, to pool there, wetly crimson, hotly warm, and inevitably fatal.

Or so the assassin must think.

Bistane heard the threshold behind him fill with bodies. Mutters of anger. Sounds of boots filing to the left and right of him, but he locked his sight on the assassin's face. Clothes, indistinct. Weapon, a common, curved dagger though its edge looked wickedly sharp. No House garb or livery. No badges or jewelry. Hair freshly shorn so Bistane could not tell how it had been worn before.

No telltale eyes of unmistaken House heritage, or complexion, or hair color. The only thing Bistane knew was that this was no Kobrir, and he had come to assassinate Lariel Anderieon regardless.

"Put your weapon down."

"No surrender."

"You are a fool if you think you can kill her."

"I already have."

Bistane shook his head slowly.

The other smiled thinly. "Too late."

"Not yet. You might think so, if you did not know what I know."

"I slit her throat."

Bistane's gaze slid behind the boaster, to the floor. "She does not bleed." He tempted the other to follow his look.

The assassin's attention wavered. He wanted to look, Bistane could tell that every nerve in his body told him to risk a glance, but he did not dare. Not with a room full of men waiting to close on him, and deadly Bistane far closer than he should be.

"Bled out already."

"No. She breathes."

"Her throat grins at the ceiling."

"Listen. She wheezes. You've injured her grievously, indeed, but she lives and she does not bleed."

Bistane could see her. His heart tore for the agony he saw on her face, in one hand that bunched up helplessly even in her sleep to go to her throat and stop the bleeding. The sounds she began to make, of pain and the effort to breathe, could bring tears to the eyes of those who cared.

As he did. He blinked back whatever reaction he had.

She lived. She hurt terribly. She managed to thrash one leg out and at the sound of her movement, the assassin jumped back, heedless of leaving his flank open, with only one thing on his mind.

To finish the job.

Bistane knew he would move before the assassin himself had decided. He sprang at the killer, striking deep in the flank, splintering ribs aside, puncturing lungs, shoving deep into the torso and then lodging deep in the heart. Spitted, the assassin flailed his knife about, cutting uselessly at the air, blood gushing from his mouth, crying wordlessly in his dying throes. He went to his knees, his eyes locked in horror at his victim who lived despite the viciously cut throat gaping open at him.

"How . . ."

How, indeed. Bistane let the weight on his sword slip to the floor, after giving another thrust and twist to the body impaled on it, hearing the death rattle gurgle out. He stepped over the body to Lara's side. Her eyelids fluttered. She must hurt. She must know she'd been struck, yet again. She must somehow *feel*. There wasn't a sleep deep enough to cocoon her, to protect her from this.

Bistane put his hand over the wound which had already begun to clot. "Get a healer in here! Sarota should be about. She lives but needs tending. We need to prevent whatever scarring we can, internally and out." And he looked to the dagger in her thigh, Sevyrn's dagger, coated with the Kobrir poison king's rest that would not let her live, but neither would it let her die.

Not just yet.

And today, for the first time in many, many months, Bistane found himself glad of it. The poison that slowed her body, that entrapped her, was the only thing that kept her alive in this moment.

Firan joined him. He toed the assassin's body. "Who sent him? He wears no identity."

"He is ild Fallyn."

"So I would guess, if I had to, but we can't guess at this."

Bistane turned his head slowly and pinned him with a hard look. "This isn't a guess."

"My lord, I don't want to contradict you, but—"

"But nothing." Bistane pointed his hand, fingertips coated with Lara's warm blood, at the window. "He broke in from outside, and he didn't scale the walls to do so. None of the guards at any of the other doors were taken down, and the exit he planned to use was the same one he took coming in. The only damage he did was in the stable, where he must have been discovered when he came in and took refuge there, to observe the manor for the best opportunity."

"Then how . . ."

"The signature Talent of the ild Fallyn. He levitated." Bistane straightened as the healer came running in, pale of face, her apprentice behind her with a bowl of fragrant water and a bag of clean cloths.

"Levitated," Firan repeated. "We won't be able to prove it. We can't confront Lady Tressandre with this."

"No, we can't." Bistane showed his teeth briefly. A soft moan of pain escaped the sleeping Lariel and he winced. "But I won't be forgetting it, either."

A guardsman called from the hallway, "My lord, one of the men has found the mount the assassin used. He is holding it for your inspection."

He didn't want to leave Lariel, but knew he could be better used elsewhere. As he started out the door, the healer caught him with a gentle hand on his elbow.

"She won't die," Sarota told him. "And she's no longer bleeding out, but she has lost a lot of blood. There may be a cost for this, Lord Bistane, one that she cannot pay."

"Meaning?"

"I don't know if we'll have our queen back when she awakens. Severe blood loss does affect the mind. I cannot tell you if the Kobrir poison will protect her from that, one way or the other. This has been unprecedented, and there's no way of knowing until the day she wakes."

He removed her hand carefully. "You won't be blamed."

"I know. I am just trying to prepare you."

Bistane nodded. "Consider us all prepared and take care of her as well as you're able."

"Always, my lord. As Lara has always done for us."

He felt a coldness arc through him as he left the rooms. When the queen awoke, if she awoke, what would they both face?

The Kobrir would find him acquiescing no longer. He'd waited long enough for them to come and heal Lara. They had a duty to fulfill, a promise, and he would hold them to it if he had to wage a vendetta on them wherever he could find them. They would do well to remember that he was a Warlord, and he would not hesitate to remind them. He had men who could dig them out of their holes to carry a message to those who held rank among them. The Warrior Queen must not be left to sleep any longer. Her time was now!

And he had a duty to tell what had happened, a duty to protect her legacy which the ild Fallyn would assassinate as surely as they tried to murder her person. A slow smile crept into one corner of his mouth. He knew one man who could spread the truth (and a tale or two) better and faster than any other.

He called for a scribe to bring ink and fresh paper, and a rider to make preparations for a hard journey to Calcort.

Chapter
Twelve

"NEWS! News from the high court of Larandaril! Reports and intelligences from our own Tolby Farbranch! Today! Now at th'
Bucking Bird!" A runner streaked down the dirt runs of Calcort, a Kernan
street boy by the looks of him with his tousled brown hair, flyers in his
upheld hand, bare feet pounding the thoroughfare. His cries stopped
strollers on the walkways and carts on the main road. As people looked
after him, he tossed papers into his wake where passersby caught them up,
intrigued by his cries: "Pints and cider half price! Storytelling by Tolby
Farbranch at the Bucking Bird pub!"

The curious and the customers headed to the pub in question, joining
a thirsty throng already packing it full. They shoved past one another: tall,
golden-skinned Galdarkans and even taller Vaelinars, Kernan traders and
scholars, and the barely chest-high Dwellers who grumbled until they
were let to the front where they could see their own cider maker and vintner hoisting himself up to sit on a tabletop.

With sharp elbows and hobnail shoes, patrons shoved and stomped
their way inside, making room where there was little enough to be had.
Their sleeves and skirt hems held the fragrant odors of whatever work
they'd been at: potion making, tanning, smelting, cooking, stabling, print-
ing, weaving, matchstick making, and whatever other jobs took place
throughout the busy quarters of the city. Kernan and Dweller, with a
golden-skinned Galdarkan or three, grabbed whatever mugs they had tied
to their belts or could wheedle away from the pub owner and settled back
with their libations, intently watching the Dweller who sat on the countertop end, legs crossed, tamping down his pipe. He had a few years on

him, sun-seamed into his face and hands, his hair gone salt-and-pepper, but his physique stayed Dweller-strong and steady, and not a man in that pub thought he could best Tolby Farbranch in a fight, fair or otherwise. It was rumored he'd been a famed caravan guard in his younger days.

They muttered among themselves: "Is she dead?"

"Na, I heard she still but sleeps!"

"Who cares about a pointy-eared queen, I want to know if they've found and hung that king of assassins yet!"

A Kernan pulled at his vest adorned with gold buttons even as he muttered, "I've got provisions contracts. I want to know what's going on with the Vaelinar roads and Ways. They're unstable lately, they are, and dangerous, but what roads have I got to use?"

To all of which someone at the back growled, "He'll know, he'll know! And if you quit yer bellyaching for a minit, he'll be telling us!"

Tolby took his time getting his pipe out of his jacket pocket, and then a pouch of toback, packing and tamping it down carefully before lighting it with a certain amount of deliberation as the Bucking Bird filled to its capacity and spilled out onto the streets. Its doors and windows flung open wide so that all within and nearby could see and hear, somewhat. He drew on his pipe, teeth clamping down on the stem, and then exhaled deeply. He looked across the pub to a far wall where a brace of Vaelinar stood, apparently at ease, but their strong, slender-fingered hands never strayed far from their weapons' belts. They'd come from their watch at his farmhouse to the far end of the quarter, where he and his family had taken a vineyard and made it thrive and ran a grand cider mill in addition to the winery. The Vaelinar stood at the queen's orders to guard his daughter Nutmeg and her daughter, the heir to Larandaril, for all that she was scarcely two years old. He wasn't much concerned about the feelings his words might ruffle; he couldn't be.

His listeners hadn't seen much of Tolby's brood in the last three seasons, for Nutmeg had taken up residence at the queen's domain, and he'd just brought her home not too many weeks ago with her daughter, nanny, and the nanny's own half-breed toddler. That meant gossip and news to them, for which they hungered as a feral predator wanted fresh meat. Nutmeg's child held a claim to the Warrior Queen's throne, being the only child of her brother Jeredon Eladar, though not legitimate, and Bistane had wanted Merri raised close to Lariel and her kingdom. The Warlord held reign over two birthrights, his to the north and Lariel's, while he waited for the queen to awaken. Tolby had developed a dislike for the Returnists who squatted at the edge of the battlefield ruins, and close to the rip, and often gave honor to the ild Fallyn and not the House of Anderieon where they perched like birds of carrion. Bistane had done what he could without starting a civil war, but Tolby didn't have to let that sit with him, and he hadn't. Now he had fresh news that clenched his fists and riled his innards and put a chill to the back of his neck. He smoked to calm himself, thinking on Lily's words and his daughter and grandchildren.

Blue circles of toback smoke drifted in the tavern air for a moment. He sucked in his cheeks and his throat before saying, thoughtfully, "This is the Tale of the Queen who could not die and the River Goddess who vanished."

"A tale? Not news? The papers promised intelligences. Reports!"

He looked askance at the speaker buried deep in the crowd and nodded. "Oh, 'tis news, surely, for we've all lived the facts of it, have we not? So it's a report, and still it's a tale because I haven't had ears in all the shadows and nooks and corners of this thing, and neither have any of the lot of you."

He took a deep breath. "And I heard someone asking if she had died, and this is the tale of it, for assassins have struck yet again."

A gasp stilled the room. Tolby paused a moment to look at the two toddlers sitting under a nearby table and his booted feet, the one a sturdy Dweller lass with a heart-shaped face and smile, the other a solemn-expressioned boy of Vaelinar elven looks, crossed with just a touch of Dweller. "That is, if you are all wanting to hear it."

Merri pushed her mass of curls from her forehead with one hand, peering up at him. A ribbon meant to hold her lustrous amber hair back looked as if it had unwound and perched as if by accident on her head. "Listenin', Grampy!" She pursed her mouth into a pensive line and tilted her head.

Evar, the lad, crossed his arms over his chest and scowled. His lips thinned. Tolby raised a salt-and-pepper eyebrow, and the two stared each other down for a moment.

"Are ye listening, Evarton?"

The boy held his elder in a stare, not to be backed down. A pile of sticks and twigs rested in front of him, lined up as though he'd been playing soldiers.

"Let the lad be. Give us the tale!" someone shouted from the back of the pub, and thumped his mug on the tabletop.

"Aye, then. Well, that I'll do."

Tolby let his words begin to encircle them, as if it were a cloud of pipe smoke in itself, well spoken with authority and deep timbres of honesty within. "First, but it will not be the last of what I have to say, an assassin has struck at Queen Lariel. The cowards who sent him could not wait for her to die in her sleep, or the Gods grant wisely, yet awaken. He came in through a high, unguarded window and his blades found their target. Yet . . ."

And Tolby looked across the room, sweeping it with his tense gaze, stilling his audience. "She lives. She survived this vile deed, as Lord Bistane discovered the assassin at his work and killed him for it. Her body heals from this last treachery. My daughter and heir I had already brought home, here, to be safe. As for why, well, it's all in the story, isn't it? Mind you, though, that the assassin struck the house from without, no aid of ladder or rope . . . and that only the blood of the ild Fallyn carry the Talent of levitation. This is not an indictment, though," and he leaned back to listen as his words were repeated and traded throughout the tavern. The Vaelinars guarding the far wall watched him steadily, as a hound watches for prey to bolt.

He drew on his pipe. "Why? It's not an easy tale. Most of us have lived through it, and yet know not the whole truth of it, for it concerns the Vaelinar and the mysteries they keep close. The Queen who cannot die is our own of Larandaril, survivor of not one but two great battles with the Raymy and the traitors Daravan and Quendius—" Tolby paused here to lower his pipe and look down upon the children. "Know who they are?"

"'Course," said Evar while Merri just nodded before sagging onto Evar's shoulder as if he were nothing more than a pillow for her body grown suddenly sleepy.

A sharp-nosed Dweller woman leaning at the far end of the bar man's counter sssted through her disapproving lips. "That Daravan, playing at being th' gentleman for centuries while he waded through our histories, stirring up our fates like a cook with a spoon in her soup kettle."

"Indeed," agreed Tolby. He settled back as the pub owner caught his eye. "More to be said, but it's dry. Everyone served?"

"We've a crowd sittin' outside, Tolby. Give us a chance." Moments of shuffling and calls for ale or a cider, amid the throwing open of various items so those outside could have a possibility of hearing followed. When all had settled, Tolby looked about and then squared himself.

"For as much as we all here know, this is still a long tale. I will be telling it from my beginning in it, and there are those of you who know the start of it as well, so give me forbearance. Calcort is a crossroads of many, and there are those from the Eastern lands amongst us that do not know what we've been through. It might start six, seven years ago, when that drought began to bother all of us with fields or groves, but it stretches a mite farther back than that, when my daughter Nutmeg pulled the girl who would become our daughter Rivergrace off a flimsy raft on the spring-flooding Silverwing."

"Mummy," murmured little Merri drowsily and shoved even more snugly into Evar's body. He put an arm about her, his free hand fiddling with his sticks, arranging and rearranging them.

Tolby smiled down at his grandchild. "Aye, your mum and your aunt, tied forever together by a moment of fate and the Silverwing."

"It may not seem odd t' any of you listening that our hearts went out to this orphaned lass and took her in. But it might in that she was clearly Vaelinar, near half-starved, and she had scars from shackles and cuffs on her little arms and legs. That took us aback, it did—who would have the power and mind—the balls, forgive me, ladies, to enslave a Vaelinar so ruthlessly? Doubtless, there were others who tried the escape and did not survive as the child barely did. Who would come after them? Who would hunt this child and those tryin' to help her?

"We kept her anyway, knowing that the Vaelinars who invaded us centuries ago keep magics and secrets, but the child who came into our lives needed us. Lily, my wife—many of you know her for her great skills as a tailor and weaver—had just lost a wee one of her own, and glad to have another join our family. We were happy and prosperous for a good many years. Though I don't mind saying that I kept a sharp weather eye out for any who might come looking for an escaped Vaelinar slave."

Tolby stopped and reached for a mug of cider, his own crush and one of the best not only to his satisfaction but to the tastes of many, waiting at his elbow. A murmur stirred through the throng of listeners, many muttering about the elven Vaelinar, and others declaring the valor and goodness of Queen Lariel. He set his mug down and the room quieted.

"The drought that hit eventually bought Ravers down on the farms and groves along the Silverwing. We dared not stay after several attacks, Worse, they seemed t' know of Rivergrace. She drew them like nectar draws bees, and we never knew the why of it, just the danger. While the Warrior Queen

Lariel and her brother Jeredon played at politics with their ambitious rivals at Fort ild Fallyn, wheels of deception began t' turn faster and faster. Rivergrace found a suitor, Sevryn Dardanon who was no less than the Hand of Queen Lariel herself, and Nutmeg fell for the dashing Jeredon, her brother. The famed river Andredia turned corrupt, and began to foul the fertile valley of Larandaril. It took a quest to clean the sacred river, to thwart the plan of the rogue weaponmaster Quendius and his Hound Narskap. The two of them summoned demons, they did, and trapped them in weapons. It was one of their forges that spilled foulness into the font of the Andredia."

Tolby counted on his hand: the sword named Cerat, caging no less than the demon Cerat Souldrinker itself, the war hammer Rakka which cracked stone and split earth when struck and was carried by Abayan Diort, and later the arrows which tore not only life's blood from those struck down but the soul as well. He leaned back. "And those were the evil that stained that river's precious, life-giving waters."

"Led by Queen Lariel, this small group fought their way to the heart, the very font, of the Andredia and the sword met its end and the river was cleansed. Lara gave part of her hand to renew her family's blood pact with the river and the Gods of Kerith, but hers was not the only sacrifice. Jeredon, of the queen's own, was struck down on the way and became paralyzed. Rivergrace and Sevryn died."

He paused as a gasp swept the room.

"Aye, a shock that because all of you know that Rivergrace and Sevryn live yet today. A River Goddess held two souls in her hands and saw a love that death would not stop. She brought them back so that they could finish that love, a second chance that the lot of us is never likely to see again. It was meant to be, though, for when Quendius made his pact with the Raymy to bring them for war on us all, it was only by the grace of the Gods' mercy that we all live today. So do not doubt that we have Gods or that they watch us from afar." Tolby grinned about the stem of his pipe, breaking from his solemn tone. "Thanks be that they are afar, or many of us would be in trouble, eh? 'Tis hard to live a saintly life!"

Laughter swept the room, amid the noise of mugs being clunked together in approval. Tolby nodded as he resettled on the countertop.

"The great war came where the Ashenbrook crosses the stony Ravela, two grand rivers embracing the armies of the Vaelinar and the Galdarkan Abayan Diort. Diort had the war hammer Rakka and used it to bring the broken empire of the East back together. He marched mercilessly toward us, the First Home lands of the west, and seemed unstoppable. The armies faced each other. Had Diort come to conquer the west coast as he had conquered the Eastern lands? No one could be sure. But when the Raymy led by Quendius came pouring out of the mountain tunnels, the two armies merged to fight a bigger and more vicious one."

"Curse those foul froggy beasts!" called someone from outside the pub, leaning in on his elbows through the windows.

Tolby pointed to him in agreement. "The Raymy cannot be called mortal in any way. Their blood is cold, their skin the warty and ofttimes scaled pelt of a reptile, their hearts misplaced, and their tempers vicious. We know now that the Ravers are their insect scouts, dread fighters on their own, but if they fall in battle, they are nothing less than fodder for the Raymy who drive them."

"We faced this foe, knowing that victory was not likely, not trapped between the rivers, and no knowing when or if reinforcements might come. Fall came, the leaves dry and sere, the ground cracked from a hard spring and summer, and no rain in sight. We dug in, flanked by the two rivers, and fought.

"'Twas our own stout hearts that saved us, that and Vaelinar magic. Daravan woke his Ferryman brother and the two worked a magic that swept up the Raymy army and took it elsewhere, else when. We knew his magic would falter sooner or later, but any time he gave us at all, we would take to arm ourselves the better.

"The accounting of that war was terrible. Warlord Bistel died on the banks of Ashenbrook, along with many soldiers, men and women. So did Jeredon Eladar, leaving our own Nutmeg with child and alone. Many, many more fell and are mourned with all our hearts to this day, some two years and more later."

Tolby drew vigorously on his pipe, sending up a fragrant cloud of smoke.

"Talent rides within the Vaelinars. It shows in their eyes of many colors, but it does not always bloom early. It bloomed that day for Rivergrace on the banks of the rivers. She found the way to make the skies rain, and the long drought finally lifted as the blood from the war washed away."

"Blessed rain," murmured the tavern wench weaving her path through the crowd, a pitcher in each hand.

"Amen," echoed the crowd.

Tolby waited for quiet. "As our rivers and lakes filled that following spring, the Raymy began to return. In spits and spurts, like big omens, falling from the clouds overhead. The ild Fallyn began to plot the death of Jeredon's unborn child, the only heir to Larandaril, Queen Lara's chosen successor. Abayan Diort's army withdrew, but stayed on our borders, his intentions still murky. The Galdarkans were guardian servants of the old Mageborn peoples who warred each other into nothingness and chaos, and we did not know if Diort held the same chaotic mind.

"We lived in uncertainty. Then the inevitable began, and it became clear that Daravan's magics failed and could no longer hold the Raymy at bay. They carried plague and war wherever they touched.

"What we did not know was that Daravan had not gathered up the Raymy to save us. It was his retreat. The armies belonged to him, given to Quendius to ravage our lands at will. He saw their defeat at Ashenbrook and Ravela that day and used all the power he could command to turn that defeat around, to retreat with his army still intact, and took it, sweeping them up with his magic and that of the Ferryman who could transport across water and time. We thought we'd won. The bitter notion came soon enough to us that we had only bought a little time. With the Raymy gone, we started eyeing each other again in suspicion.

"Queen Lariel saw her own assassination and named the killer as her own faithful Sevryn who took Rivergrace and fled her retribution. Sevryn, son of Daravan whose own traitorous conspiracies began to reveal themselves. Sevryn, named as the king of assassins."

Tolby lowered his pipe and tapped it against the edge of the counter. He sighed. "My Rivergrace loved him, and because she did, I gave him the benefit of doubt. Though his father was a traitor, that man had also turned his back on his own son, and Sevryn did not even know of his paternal bond until those dire times. And Daravan had kept his traitorous nature hidden. Sevryn worried more than I did that he might follow unknown footsteps. I did not believe my daughter could treasure an unworthy man."

He pointed his pipe at the ceiling. "Wonders dread and terrible were learned that winter and spring. We had rain again, a near miracle. And death had come to many of our families, a tremendous sorrow. But we did not know a dead man would rise from the battlefields, a bloodless man, a man who neither lived nor died, and a man who could hold the demon Cerat at bay and use him to create the Undead. That being was Narskap, still enslaved, bound forever to Quendius. Rivergrace was torn away from

Sevryn and used by Quendius to force Narskap to build an army of Undead, while the weaponmaster waited for Daravan with the Raymy and his own dire soldiers to return."

He looked out at the crowd, his brow knotted, his eyes fierce. "They plotted nothing less than the death of all of us. When Daravan came back, only a few would stand to face him. Ever devious, he struck at the heart of Larandaril when all expected the armies would return to where they had been swept up at Ashenbrook and Ravela. Queen Lariel was caught alone in her kingdom, with only a smattering of her troops. Rivergrace and her Sevryn against Quendius and the battalion of Undead he commanded. Young Bistane, Bistel's son and heir, kept the bulk of his troops for some reason and came riding like a whirlwind in fury to Larandaril. And the Guardian King Abayan Diort, taking fresh troops to Ashenbrook turned instead to the sacred valley on a whim. The battle fell in the heart of Larandaril where only a few companies under the queen stood against the Raymy. The ild Fallyn came as well, but their soldiers came to make sure Queen Lariel fell and would not rise again there.

"Their battle shook the earth to its core. Th' very fabric of our lives tore open. Daravan had sorcery as well as Talent, and it was he who tore the universes apart, linking the old world of the Vaelinar to fight this new world of ours where they had taken refuge."

Hisses went around the room. "Aye," agreed Tolby. "Our Vaelinar, chancy and devious as they can be—well, they've blessed us as well as chafed us. We learned it that day. The old world had cursed itself, filled itself with plague and hatred and wanted to spill into ours. We stopped it. We won that day. Bistane and Diort brought their troops thundering into Larandaril, the valley that had been pledged never to know war or drought or famine or pestilence. The Raymy were fought to the last one. Quendius saw Daravan cut down and he took his Undead Army through the hole in the universes in flight. Rivergrace and Sevryn went after, to heal the grievous wounds between two worlds, and stop Quendius.

"They did not save Lara who was cut down and lies today in a sleep like death, yet she does not die. Bistane stays at her side. Her wounds heal, but she does not awaken. The ild Fallyn lost their son, Alton, but their daughter Tressandre remains as ambitious as always. Some circles say it was her blade, or her brother's, which cut Queen Lariel down. No one has proved— or disproved—it yet. It was said she, too, carried a child sired by Jeredon Eladar who would claim the Anderieon throne, but rumor came to us that

she lost that child after the fight in Larandaril. Does she plot bitter revenge? Likely."

Tolby clamped his lips tightly about his pipe stem for a long moment.
"The Raymy plague is still about, but never unleashed upon us as it might
have been. For that we may be thankful. We drive it out with fire wherever
it erupts, and so far, we've not lost many lives of Kerith to it.

"And my daughter Nutmeg has given birth to the rightful heir of the
Anderieon Warrior Queen." His gaze fell upon the two sleepy children
under the nearby table, and he smiled.

"Rivergrace, Goddess of fire and river waters, has not returned to us.
Nor has her love Sevryn, king of the assassins. It's been two years and a bit
more. The rip between our world and theirs remains, often very slight but
sometimes great, and the world shakes whenever it opens. It is an eye that
watches us as closely as we watch it."

Tolby rocked back on his perch and drained the last of his mug of cider,
thumping it down empty beside him. "Yet that is only part of the story, for
any tale involving the Vaelinars mean wheels spinning within wheels and
the knowledge that much is still hidden."

He cleared his throat, preparing to tell them what Bistane had asked
him to share. Outside, where some of the listeners had been crouched on
the roadway or leaning in the windows, bodies began to straighten and
shuffle off, leaving their mugs in a congenial pile by the thrown-open
doors. Dust spouts followed their footsteps, swirled about by a beginning
afternoon wind. The breeze grew stiffer and gained a voice, a howl.

Then someone screamed.

"THERE ARE GODS HERE!" Bregan spun around in the barren wasteland, flinging his arms out as if he could catch one to embrace.

Abayan Diort, known to his people as the Guardian King, sat in his leather chair as the briefest of travel canopies fluttered in the breeze overhead. Despite his kingly presence, the man he watched dance seemed oblivious of him. His gold-hued skin, a marking of the Galdarkan people, glowed in the morning light, and the woman who knelt next to him smiled softly as she basked in the warmth of his presence. She put her hand on the arm of his chair. "There are Gods everywhere," she called back to Bregan. A tangle of hair escaped her scarf, exposing her curved and exquisitely pointed ear, her own marking of her Vaelinar blood. "Especially to Bregan."

His eyebrow went up at the naming of the half-mad Kernan in Diort's guardianship. Self-proclaimed, for no one heard the Gods as loudly or as often as Bregan did, the madman styled himself a Mageborn in a land which had not seen Mageborn for over a millennium—nor did they wish to. Mageborn held magic like the Vaelinars did, but unlike the Vaelinars, they quarreled themselves to death with it and left reservoirs of corrupt, unpredictable magic behind them that still soiled Kerith to this day. If Mageborn had indeed returned to the face of the earth, one could question: why? To what purpose? What good would it serve? And no one would have a good answer. Certainly not Bregan, once a handsome young Master Trader with all the wealth and education that conferred, whose current level of mind skill ranged between deliriously incoherent to raving maniac. Galdarkans had been bred centuries ago to rein in the Mageborn, to serve as their bodyguards and protectors and, in some cases, even their conscience. Diort could not deny he had found a deep, instinctive maternal response within him to Bregan's plight. One which he often wished he could ignore.

"So you and I know." He pointed his chin toward the still spinning Kernan. "I am not so sure what our madman perceives." He watched as the personage who had once been the prince of the most powerful Trading Guild on Kernan began to topple, dizzied, from his activity. He wore a brace of elven make on one leg, his right, weakened by a magical attack from the being known as the Ferryman, but Diort had his doubts about the kind of magic. He'd seen similar injuries among the fortunate few to have survived a lightning strike. The striations on the skin, the muscle weakness, the nerve damage. It was not for him to say, of course. He hadn't been there decades ago when the young scion had taken umbrage with the Ferryman about the trade caravan's passage across a treacherous river and taken a sword to him. Diort would not have done such a rash act. The Ferryman had been a Way, a knot put into the natural fabric of their world by the Vaelinar, a knot which should never have existed but did because they'd taken up a few of the threads which made the natural world and *changed* them.

Those knots existed throughout this coast where Vaelinar Houses were more populous and powerful, and their unnatural magics remained potent for the most part, although every now and then a knot simply frayed apart and the threads sprang back into place. When that happened, energies would be released, and a backlash occur, but nothing disastrous. Nothing at all like the lands blasted by their own past wars of the Mageborn. Nothing at all like the cataclysmic pools of corrupt power sunk into the Kernan soil, cesspools of disaster waiting to flare at the slightest touch.

The man he watched eddy to the side and sink slowly to the ground was Mageborn, or so the Gods told him. The only one after centuries of extinction by the will of vengeance of angry Gods. Kernan Gods were distant. They had once talked to their people and now they were mostly silent, either discouraged or complacent with the civilizations they had stirred into being. Galdarkans had been born to be guardians of the willful Mageborn, to protect the magic wielders from each other and themselves. They had ultimately failed at their task as the wars erupted. Diort wondered vaguely if he would fail at this new, resurrected task.

"Bregan. How do you fare?"

Bregan lay on his back now, spread-eagled. "Marvelously dizzy."

Diort had no answer to that. He looked down at the woman flanking his chair. "Ceyla."

She smiled wider. "He is childlike, is he not?"

"Indeed. I'd like to know why he ran away and I've spent the last two weeks tracking him this far."

Ceyla spread her hands, palms up, and eyed the faintly pink skin. "It didn't take him two weeks to get this far."

"No. With or without the Mageborn tunnels, he is still on foot."

"I surmise," she told him softly, "that a God carried him this far."

His attention snapped to her. "Why would you think that?"

"He's not journey-worn. Not tired or hungry or thirsty. He doesn't show any of the strains of having been running for days, even though he escaped from your care."

"And does he show how he escaped?"

"Not that. If he felt compelled enough, he would have escaped however he could. Perhaps he hung underneath one of your supply carts as it went through the gate."

Diort made a scornful noise. "When he was young, perhaps, but he's not in that kind of condition now."

"Yet he's here, brace and all, and he's even euphoric."

"So that means to you one of the Gods carried him this far, but you cannot prove it."

"Of course I can't." She shook her head, dislodging her scarf further and finally reached up to remove it, loosening the glorious bounty of her hair over her shoulders and down her back. "Nor do I think he could give an account of it."

Diort sighed. "I do not wish to be in charge of a madman."

"It's what your people were created to do."

"Not I. I didn't conquer the earth-shaker Rakka so that I could be a nursemaid. I brought broken cities together. I was born to heal what the Mageborn tore apart!" He clenched his fists.

Ceyla's face smoothed into a curious, neutral expression. "Following him will lead you to your destiny."

He looked sharply at her, noting the expression and the position of her hands. He said not a word until she shivered and suddenly dropped her hands to her knees.

"Would you repeat that?"

She shrugged a shoulder. "I said I doubt Bregan could tell you himself how he got here."

He paused for a long time, gaze searching her face before looking away and getting to his feet. "I suppose we need to ask him where he intends to go from here." He bent to give his hand to her. "Or should I wait until you divine his road?"

Ceyla slipped her slender hand into his great one, standing easily. "I may be your oracle, Abayan Diort, but those words don't fall easily from me."

He brushed a bit of dirt from her hip. "Perhaps, like Bregan, they do, but you cannot give an accounting of it."

"Bitterness doesn't ride you well."

"My people were born to it evidently, but that doesn't mean we like to embrace it. At least I didn't have to bring an army after this fool."

"This time," Ceyla murmured softly behind him, as she dropped into place to follow him.

His voice drifted back to her. "You are more accurate than my last oracle, but she was not tempted to talk behind my back."

Ceyla shut her mouth firmly, but couldn't help smiling as she followed the man, whom she considered great, to the man all knew was a fool.

Bregan sat up as they neared and looked as if he had, for the first time since they'd made camp that morning, just noticed them. His childlike expression brightened. "Oh, good! You've brought horses." He ran toward them, his brace working as smoothly as if a living limb in itself and he swung up on horseback, snapping the bridle loose from the horse line and setting his heels into the animal's flank. It bolted with a shrill whinny, and the madman galloped out of their encampment.

Diort sprang forward with a curse and commands, and the camp came apart in a flurry of men, tents, and equipment, in pursuit. Like a hill of ants broken apart and swarming up in furious activity, his army flew apart to form up again. Another army might have taken a day to pack and prepare to follow, but his came from nomad stock, and he watched in pride as they were ready in less than a candlemark, outfitted and eager, awaiting him.

Ceyla sat on her mare, toying with the tasseled mane, waiting for Diort. Their eyes met, and she smiled at him. "I await."

"As always, since the day fate gifted you to me." His gaze lifted from her face, and his answering smile warped into a scowl. "What in cold hell—"

The horse Bregan had stolen ran scampering back to them, its eyes white with wild fright and its tack entangled and dirtied as if it had been caught in a massive dust storm, tail and mane knotted and thrust about with brambles and even stones.

Ceyla began to shake. She put a hand out as soldiers spread out to catch the frightened horse and bring it to a halt, its flanks heaving and lathered. It put its nose to the ground and made terrible noises. She swayed at the sight of the poor beast and let out a cry herself.

The dream struck her down as cleanly as if she'd been cleaved in two by a sword. Ceyla felt herself go limp and then drop at the feet of her liege, his shout ringing in her ears just before everything went dark.

Her mind did not stay dark, as the dream welled up inside her, until she thought she might explode from it. The sights, sounds, and smells of her prophecy swelled until her head could hardly hold it all and she reached out with both hands, grasping, crying, "I can't remember all this!" in terror. The scene ripped in front of her and swirled away into gray mists, leaving her ears ringing from it all, and her lungs gasping for air. She awoke panting, her fingers clawing in front of her.

Abayan Diort took her hands in his to still her fighting. His large hands enveloped her in strong but gentle warmth, and Ceyla felt his strength wash through her, a comforting feeling as he helped her sit.

"I have known for some time that dreaming is not easy for you, but this looked like a deadly struggle. Yet, I knew I should not awaken you."

Her heart had been beating like that of a racing horse but now began to quiet in her chest. She took three deep breaths before saying, "So much. So much I don't know if I can tell you all."

"Try, if you wish. If you wish not, that is your will. Your dreams aren't mine to command," Diort told her. His bulk stayed between her and the sun, shading her in gold, like the hues of his skin, not yet deepened to bronze as it did in the summer, but golden enough. Thick skull ridges shaded his eyes deep in his face, and the tattoos of office and manhood offset distinct cheekbones, his face both barbaric and handsome at the same time. To a Vaelinar, she thought as she freed her hands from his. To one of Kerith, he looked perfectly acceptable. Galdarkans were nomads of the great eastern part of the continent, although this man had united most of the tribes and forgotten cities. They were not in the east, though. He lingered in the First Home lands, on the western coast, and Ceyla knew he wondered if he should take a bride from this region or if it would be seen as a grab for even greater power. She knew her lord had power enough and that he found himself lonely. A Guardian King did not marry for his feelings; however, he married for his people. Would taking one of the Vaelinar cement or help his kingdom?

She had no answer for him, not yet, not in this dream.

He smoothed an unruly lock of hair away from the corner of her eye with his thumb. "I have the scribe here, waiting."

She blinked and twisted about to see Mallen kneeling nearby, his instruments at the ready. The old scribe winked at her and raised his pen in readiness. Diort rubbed her shoulder. "If you are ready."

"I dreamed of Bregan."

With Bregan gone running, disaster could surely follow. "We were following, but you were struck down."

"But now I know what he is up to, and he must be stopped!"

"Colobrian!"

Soldiers answered, with the aforementioned Colobrian in front. They dropped to their knees. "Abayan Diort."

"You may encamp here. It's fruitless for all of us to be in the chase. I will follow, as I am the madman's guardian." Diort's gaze rested on Ceyla a moment. "Any idea in which direction from here?"

She looked into Diort's eyes. "We need to get to Calcort."

"We will then." He waved at Colobrian and the others. "Dissect the trail between the border and Calcort, just a few scouts. Send word if you cross him, though that seems dubious. The oracle sends us to Calcort."

His men jumped to their feet in obedience.

"Listen, Mallen, and listen well."

Ceyla shook her head. "We haven't time."

"We have as much time as it takes. Your first fear, when you woke, was that you would not remember. Every waking moment takes us that much farther in the direction of your fears. The scribe awaits."

Ceyla raised a trembling hand and the elderly scribe leaned forward and pushed a water vessel from his blue-veined and ink-stained hand into hers. "I await," he told her gently.

She spoke then, telling of visions in the past and mostly in the future of the things she had dreamed. She drank only when her voice faded to such a reedy whisper she did not think anyone could hear her, swallowed, and then spoke more.

The wind deposited him on a scruffy bit of herb garden in the corner of
the town. He only knew it was an herb garden because of the familiar, and
slightly delicious, aromas that enveloped him when he stood up and dusted
himself off. The wind slapped him in the chest, and Bregan instantly de-
duced that he had been an ingrate and dropped to his knees to lift his voice
in a prayer of thanks. The God spun away then in a whirlwind, the omis-
sion mitigated somewhat, and Bregan got up a bit clumsily and righted
himself. He scratched at his head, dislodging another fragrant bit of herb,
and peered out of the garden.

It took a moment for him to realize where the whirlwind had borne
him, and why. He stood in Calcort, slightly juxtapositioned from the infamous Farbranch Vineyard and Cider House, as he read on a sign which
showed only the slightest amount of weathering. The Farbranches, it
seemed, had not lived there all that long.

As they should not be living there at all.

Bregan bent to secure the straps on his Vaelinar-made brace that caged
his right leg, giving it both strength and flexibility. The metallic cage
showed little wear. If he'd had a sword made of the same stuff, he'd rarely
have to hone it for sharpness or notches and wear. He did not. The straps,
of the best coachmen's leather, had to be replaced from time to time, but
the gadget had done well for him. He ought to take it off and not be the
hypocrite he was. But if he took it off, he could neither stand nor walk
easily, let alone run or hold a swordsman's stance, and he did all of those
things rather well. Cursed if you do and cursed if you do not, he told himself, and let himself out of the herb garden.

He hadn't known exactly where he was going when he'd bolted from
Diort's gentle care, only that a destination lay ahead of him and he had to
get to it. He still would not have made it, stumbling through the wilderness, if the God of Wind had not picked him up and delivered him. Now
that he'd seen the Farbranch name, his duty struck him in the middle of
his throbbing forehead.

Tolby Farbranch must die. To that end, he began gathering his power
as he walked into the street. Will. Intent. Target. His fingertips tingled as
the magic he called to him began answering. He did not, however, turn to
the farmhouse and its outbuildings. The target pulled him, as if having
caught him up by his earlobe, down the street where he could see a crowd

gathered at the pub he knew as the Bucking Bird. In his lesser days, he'd both drunk and gambled there, freely and stupidly. The side of his face felt on fire until he turned directly into both the sun and the face of the small, Calcortian tavern. He could hear the murmured asides of the crowd.

"Hear that? Tolby says the queen lived."

"Did she? I missed that bit!"

"What troubles would we have at all if not for the bloody Vaelinar?"

"Naw, don't you believe it. Galdarkans, Bolgers . . . we got trouble aplenty with or without 'em."

The crowd shouldered one another aside to have a go at the broad windows lining the building, shutters thrown open for listening and viewing. Goblets and cups flashed in hands as frequently as did grumbles.

Then someone stepped back from the window. "That's it. Beats all, doesn't it? Took a knife to the throat and she still lives. Th' black and silver tried to do her in!"

" 'Taint natural."

"That be the truth of it. 'Taint natural." Talkers and listeners began to drop their empty cups for the tavern servers to retrieve.

A Kernan backed into Bregan who'd moved ever closer to the crowd and the doors. He turned around. "Sorry, master. Feet and hard cider don't always mix well, aye?" He pulled at his hat brim in sincere apology.

Bregan's foot stung despite his boot and he lifted a finger—not a hand, mind you—and pointed at his fellow Kernan. A bolt shot out, yellow-gold, thin and fiery, striking the offender in the chest and dropping him to his chin in the dirt road. A woman screamed as she saw him felled.

"Get out of my way," Bregan ordered. "All of you. Now. This retribution comes from the Gods of Kerith, upon the head of Tolby Farbranch for the lies he serves up in the name of other Gods!"

He raised both his palms and his hands disappeared in a fiery halo of light. The crowd scattered before him, and he inhaled deeply in pride as they recognized his worth. He felt as if he could shut off the light of day, if he wished.

If it be the will of the Gods.

They hadn't asked him to, yet, nor did he think he had developed the power, but he would attempt it. His chest swelled at the thought. No more trading for mere gold and gems for him. He traded in *power*. It filled him.

"Tolby Farbranch!" he called. "Come meet your punishment!"

*   *   *

Ceyla watched as both Diort and his lead tracker leaned out of their saddles to survey the ground ahead of them. Her head still hurt from her dreams of the day before—or perhaps it was from hitting the ground when her body had abruptly folded—but she gained little satisfaction from knowing part of what she'd glimpsed she'd interpreted correctly. Bregan had indeed slipped his caretaker and gone running into the wilderness, with little or no preparation such as a horse or waterskins. Driven, the caretaker had communicated.

Driven mad, she had no doubt. She'd seen Bregan when Diort first came upon him as a Mageborn, and she knew the delusional ravings which ravaged the poor man. She'd seen him taken on a quest against the Far-branch heir which was why they now halted on the trail while her thighs burned like fire from the rough riding to get this far in a hurry.

Diort finally swung off his mount. He wore Galdarkan desert garb, and his voluminous pants hid the muscular lines of his long legs. He went to one knee by the sign, and craned his head to look back at his tracker. "I've seen nothing like this. What do you, if anything, make of it?"

"I cannot say, sire, except that it appears he disappeared into thin air." The tracker pulled a face of both apology and puzzlement before wrapping his scarf about his face.

"Impossible."

Ceyla let out a sigh. "Ponder it all the two of you want, but I've already told you what happened."

Diort very slowly and deliberately turned to look at her. "Do repeat it then."

"The Gods picked him up and carried him to Calcort from here."

The early, barely morning sun glanced off Diort's frowning face. "We are half a day's ride from there. At a run."

"Then we have a chance at making it in time before he kills Tolby and the children."

"Which you foresaw."

"You heard my words." Ceyla's hand twitched irritably on her reins, and her horse tossed its head from side to side in answer. "I said he would attempt it and the subsequent results. Whether he succeeds or not depends on whether you succeed or not, forewarned as you are."

"I have to ask myself what is the will of the Gods. If Bregan was transported there . . ." Diort straightened and stepped back to his horse.

"Perhaps it might occur to you to ask if the Gods of the Mageborn are the Gods of Kerith."

Abayan closed his mouth. He blinked once or twice in thought before tweaking the stirrup to his feet and stepping up. "I had not thought of the enigma in quite that fashion."

He arranged his reins across his palm. "Perhaps if I do, it would solve a number of questions. If I am to comply with your vision, Oracle, then I should get to Calcort as soon as possible." Without waiting for an answer, he kicked his horse's flanks, setting him into a run. Ceyla's horse threw its head up to answer the challenge, leaping after. Behind her, the tracker let out a smoldering curse and sprang to get aboard.

Tolby reached the children first before the scream's ringing tones even finished. He gathered them up in his arms, Evar protesting until Tolby put his tobacco-scented lips to his forehead, saying, "Peace, my boy. Quiet. We've trouble."

Merri stopped in mid-yawn, her chubby little hand curled over her mouth. "Twouble?"

"Indeed." He kissed her little fist. "Now be quiet for Grampa."

He watched the room empty, or attempt to empty, through the doors and if not the doors, by the wide open windows. His brace of Vaelinar guards dropped back to flank him.

The taller of the guards, a copper-skinned, hard-muscled woman identified the voice for him. "That's Master Trader Bregan."

"And babbling about Gods."

Tolby hugged his grandchildren closer. To the public, the two were presented as the heir, precious Merri with her Dweller looks, her ears only slightly pointed, her eyes of subdued hues for Vaelinar blood, and her nanny's son Evarton looking more like Jeredon every day to the point where they would soon not be able to carry off the lie about the twins. Neither were expendable, both equally precious to him and their mother, and Lariel who had never been conscious to meet them. If Bregan had come, deranged of mind and intention, to take those twins away from him, he would have to have all the Gods of this kingdom and a dozen more to get through Tolby Farbranch.

"Tolby Farbranch! Don't let yourself be branded a coward by the Mageborn!"

He had to admit, Bregan's voice had a bit of a ring to it. He handed one toddler to one guard and the other to the second. Firmly, he pointed to the backroom. "Back door that way."

His tone brooked no disagreement. The two Vaelinar guards went to the back.

Tolby headed to the door.

Nutmeg straightened and rubbed the small of her back, and then rolled her shoulders to ease the strain of working over the loom in front of her. Handmade from the finest woods, the loom occupied a very large part of her workroom as did various children's toys: blocks, a rocking chair made Dweller child size and a second chair, bigger and more elegant for a Vaelinar child, and various dolls and animals stuffed with colorful patchwork skins. But the room stood absolutely silent when she stopped the loom. Nutmeg pushed her stool away and bent down just to make sure no one curled up on the floor under her work, because Merri often liked to find a corner below and watch the colorful threads at play as the shuttle moved back and forth. Evarton, of course, would have been at the bucket of blocks and toy soldiers while his quieter sister watched the loom. But neither of the children was in the room, and Nutmeg had forgotten when they'd left. Corrie had probably swept in and taken them while she worked out the intricacies of the pattern she wished. Probably. Should have. Undoubtedly, most capably had.

Irritated at herself for not knowing where the toddlers were, Nutmeg tugged at the hairband holding back her curly, unruly mop and walked into the main farmhouse, refastening the wrap about her rebellious crop. She ought to take the shears to it. Summer was coming and with it the hot, lazy days that ripened the fruit in the vineyard and left the back of her neck and even her scalp damp with perspiration. Nights she would tie her hair up so that she could feel a bit of a breeze through open windows and under the small ceiling fan her father had installed in her room. She called gently, "Corrie?" not wanting to wake anyone if the children had gone down for a nap. It was about the time of day that claimed Merri for a short one, although they'd grown so much now she couldn't predict naptimes.

Corrie came out of the kitchen, drying her fingers on the apron wrapped about her ample waist. "Taking a break, Mistress Nutmeg?"

"And looking for the little ones."

The Kernan nanny frowned a bit. "Tolby didn't tell you? He was supposed to! He took them with him down to the Bird for a bit of cider and a walk. He's giving one of his tales down there."

Nutmeg sighed. "He's a gossip, through and through. Is Lily with them?"

"No, your mother's gone to the shop. The guards followed, though. Do you want me to go fetch them?" She fussed with her apron. "I should not have let them go!"

"I'll go down and see what is in the wind." Nutmeg brushed herself off, bits of fluff and floss drifting about her skirts as she did. Corrie dropped a very slight curtsy before returning to the kitchen.

She wasn't the first nanny they'd had—the first had been a wet nurse who'd moved on when the babies' teeth came in—but Corrie had left her own family for theirs, and made herself indispensable. Her two . . . the heir and the unspoken of second . . . were a handful. She did not like representing Merri as the only heir to Larandaril and Evarton couldn't be hidden much longer, she feared, because of his resemblance to his father Jeredon. Merri held some of the same resemblance, but her Dwellerness tended to overwhelm first impressions and Nutmeg did her best to ensure that casual acquaintances did not get close. Already the Vaelinar guards had begun to mumble among themselves. She would have to request Bistane change these two out, if their secret were to be kept. Merri posed as little threat to the ambitions of the ild Fallyn dynasty as possible. She looked Dweller, despite her delicate ears and her shining eyes with their multiple colors. Nutmeg knew that Tressandre had descriptions and perhaps even quick-study portraits of the child, and that Tressandre hopefully felt that she could depose the child easily as not being Jeredon's or Vaelinar enough to follow as Lariel's heir. Not that Nutmeg could know a mind as devious as that Vaelinar's, ever, but it seemed the likeliest reason that Merri's life had not been taken yet. That and vigilance. Tolby had taken them from Larandaril and, it seemed, just in time after the news came in about the latest attempt on Lara's life.

Evar, now. Evar would be a real worry in the next few years, especially as he grew. People would say that he did not resemble Corrie at all, who stood in as Evar's mother, and that he did look like Jeredon; even as that brave man's face faded from their memories, there were portraits enough of him at Larandaril that would remind them. They'd been lucky in their deception so far: Corrie's substitution for the first nanny had gone nearly unnoticed, the two Kernan women being quite alike in ample stature and graying brunette hair and even brusque manner of speech for both had come from the same region, to the southeast. No, it wasn't the nanny Nutmeg had to fear. It was her son himself as he daily and undeniably grew into his birthright.

Nutmeg fanned her face as she stepped onto the road and cast her attention to the south, to where the Bucking Bird stood, nearly out of eye and earshot—praise good red apples—for she hated the sounds of drunks and screaming . . .

Screaming! She could see a sudden flurry of action that carried into the road, patrons spilling here, there, and everywhere, and her heart jumped in her chest. She whirled quickly and ran to the cider barn. Nutmeg hung on the barn door, panting. "Dayne! Dayne! They're attacking the Bucking Bird."

Verdayne Vantane swung about from the rough-hewn worktable where he had been patiently drying ancient manuscript leaves. His hands shot out to grab both his aryn staff and his sword sheath. "Who? The children?"

"Dayne Vantane, this is serious! I cannot tell from all the yelling and screaming down the road, but Dad is there and the children are there. They toddled after Tolby, and Corrie is frantic. I'm frantic!"

He had already crossed the barn and passed her in the doorway, but took a step back. Sword buckled on, he had fingers free to squeeze her shoulder. "I'll bring them back," he told her before breaking into a run straight at the heart of the trouble.

Nutmeg inhaled and followed after.

"Blasphemers!" screamed Bregan, his thinning hair standing on end as if it had a life of its own as he yelled. The two Vaelinar guards, having taken the children out the back way and told them to run home, came forward now, shoving the crowd aside to reach a clear spot in the street opposite him.

"Master Trader," called she of the copper skin. "Rest easy. There are none here who wish to argue with you about the Gods."

"You! You are the worse of the worst!" He pointed, and a veritable bolt of gold flame lashed from him, spearing into the woman who dropped in the midst of a scream. She hit the ground shaking, her tremors becoming weaker until she lay absolutely still. Bregan put his shoulders back, lifting his chin, adding, "Give me Tolby Farbranch!"

"That will not be happening," Dayne answered at his flank and set himself, left-handed with the aryn staff across his chest, and his right hand on his left hip to draw his sword. "Master Bregan, the Gods are warring in you today, and that's not a good sign. Before you do any harm"—and his gaze fell upon the fallen guard who moaned softly from her sprawl on the ground—"I suggest you consider having a draft of good, cold cider and rest yourself."

"Is that what you think I am? A drunken fool? I know you, Verdayne Vantane, son of Bistel Vantane and a daughter of Kerith, and my mind is just fine, thank you."

"Actually," said Dayne mildly, "From here, it looks like it might be on fire."

Bregan turned on him, quicker than the eye could follow, blasting him with a flick of his hand. The aryn staff caught it and lit up with the glow, the wood illuminating in a warm rose-gold from the inside out, delineating its grain and occasional whorls of the tree from which it came. The blow of the blast knocked Dayne on his ass in the dirt, but the staff held. More than held, it reflected a portion of its power back at Bregan, striking him in the shoulder and knocking him back a step or two, his shirt smoking from the heat. Dayne hurriedly got to one knee, getting up to follow the advantage, but Bregan recovered faster, spinning about and firing again, knocking him to his side, and dodging before Dayne could knock some of the force back at him again.

"Enough!" shouted Tolby, shouldering through those onlookers gathered at the road's edge, too entranced by the spectacle to run off, though they should have. "You know who I am, Master Bregan."

Nutmeg pelted up, her hair tousled, dust flying from her shoes, to pull the children from the doorway, where they crowded at Tolby's heels, having squirreled away from their guard. She swung them up defiantly, but Tolby stepped in front of her smoothly. "He's out of his mind, lass."

Evar kicked his heels against Nutmeg's skirts. "Down," he insisted.

She wrapped her arms tighter and put her lips to his forehead, murmuring something that only the two children could hear. They quieted.

Bregan had no choice but to face the man he'd cried out for. Tolby locked gazes with him, stepping out away from the crowd, one hand beckoning to Nutmeg to get away. She moved reluctantly to the side of the pub, letting its thick stone walls buffer her. Meanwhile, Dayne got to his feet, spat dirt out of his mouth as he settled his sword back into his sheath, and twirled his staff about in his hands. The aryn wood seemed unaffected except for faintly glowing wisps that wafted off it as it cooled. He moved closer without catching notice.

Tolby grinned. "Attack me if you would, pup. I remember you when you were a guild apprentice trotting at your father's heels, scarcely taller than his belt buckle. I remember when I gave you some of your first lessons with a sword."

Those words halted Bregan who pulled his jaw in as if he'd been slapped and ran a hand through his wild hair, both of them crackling with sparks as he did. His desert scarf ran out from his neckline like a banner, as if an errant breeze had found him and him alone, or perhaps the energies from his magic set him into motion.

His lips worked, forming no words, and his hands raised again, little blue discharges of energy flitting from one tip to another.

"Come at me, then," Tolby said. He set his feet firmly. "We Dwellers have been the salt of Kerith's earth for longer than you Kernans have claimed to own it." Bregan stood a good two heads taller than he did, but he barely raised his chin to look the maddened trader in the eyes. "Come on."

Bregan leaped.

The crowd screamed as Dayne swung his aryn staff into Bregan and swept the stick up into a solid thwack under the chin that stopped the other in his tracks as sparks and lightning rattled up and down his frame with the smell of summer lightning and the heat of the full sun. Bregan's teeth had clamped shut with the hit and he screamed through them, a whistling screech of pain and anger. Dayne ground one end of the staff into the dirt and swung about it, bringing it up behind Bregan's knees and sweeping his feet from under him. Tolby followed with a swift kick to the downed trader's abdomen, sending him gasping for air from lungs that would not cooperate. Dayne pinioned Bregan against the ground with the staff, the aryn wood absorbing the Mageborn fury and sending Bregan into a stunned silence, his hands pinned to his chest under the staff.

Merri's little voice spoke up. "Grampy wins!"

"Yes, my babe. Grampy and our Dayne," Nutmeg answered, with not a little bit of pride, as she lowered her two to the road and stood with their hands in hers.

Evar pointed toward the city gates. Horse hooves pounding along the road scattered the crowd, but the citizens of Calcort did not look up to see their guard, as they thought. Instead, the Guardian King Abayan Diort rode in, a handful of soldiers and a woman in his wake. His horse slid to a stop near the combatants, and he swung off in a swirl of desert silks and haste.

He looked down at the confined Bregan who looked up and then put his head back limply, settling into a kind of collapse. One last spark drifted off him, a blue star whirling into the air and then extinguishing with a pffft.

Diort swung his gaze to his oracle. "It seems we were not needed, after all."

"Oh," said Ceyla. "I didn't mean that you had to be here to save Tolby and the children, or even Dayne. No, no. You had to be here to save Bregan."

"I WOULD NEVER," Dayne said firmly, "have put Bregan down. He is a madman and pitiable, and now even dangerous, but he's not an animal."

Ceyla tapped the aryn staff which now rested against the trestle table where they all sat. All, save for Bregan who lay trussed up and sleeping in a cool side room away from the kitchen. "The staff absorbs energy as it is meant to. You wouldn't have done it a-purpose, but Bregan has no control over what rules him now, and the aryn staff would have drained him of everything, down to the last breath of his life as long as he fought."

"Really."

"So I feel. Didn't you feel it?"

"Something like that."

"You Vantane have surely suspected the aryn wood properties for the hundreds of years you've used it here as barriers against the ruins, the pools of chaos left behind."

Dayne ran his hand down the staff. "I admit nothing. I wonder if it stores the energy or merely discharges it."

Tolby lifted his eating knife and pointed. "A topic to be examined later. Trials and demonstrations are in order."

"The calamities of the Mageborn Wars could have been much easier withstood if we'd known," said Diort mournfully.

"We didn't have it then, my king. It's not a wood that springs from the seed of Kerith." Ceyla moved to refill his glass with cool cider and reseated herself. "He still sleeps."

"Good. Less trouble later."

"What sent him our way?"

Diort shrugged. "Master Tolby, this one here has it that a God carried him here. I've no proof of it, but he traveled in a manner physically impossible, so . . ."

"A God carried him?"

"A whirlwind," Ceyla said confidently as she put her hand out for the breadbasket. "I saw it."

Nutmeg dusted her hands off, standing at the table's end, now bereft of the two children whose voices could be heard fading away into another room with their nanny. "You saw what he did not." She pulled a stool out and found a place near her father.

"In here." Ceyla tapped her forehead. "I don't often see, but when I do, I try to understand what I've dreamed."

"You're the one." Tolby leveled his attention on her. "The ild Fallyn who got away."

Tanned almost as golden as the Galdarkans, she blushed anyway, her cheeks coloring hotly. "I am that one. You may ask, rightly, who my dreams support and I answer: Abayan Diort. I risked my life escaping the fort and finding him, so that I could send him to meet destiny on the fields of Larandaril."

"So that's how you got there in time." A smile quirked the corner of Tolby's mouth as he spread his fresh bread with soft cheese and put a bit of grape jelly on it.

"You tell the tale."

"As it was told me, but now I hear it from the source! Truth is as precious as gold." He popped the hunk of bread in to chew enthusiastically, beaming at Diort.

"Are all the Mageborn destined to be mad?"

Everyone at the table paused to stare at Nutmeg. She lifted an eyebrow. "It has to be asked, doesn't it? Look at our past. Look at our present."

"Bregan needs training, and his mind may be too broken. I was born for this, but I haven't had training either," Diort told her wryly. "You may well be right. I have been sending riders out to my lands and other Eastern holdings but we've not uncovered other Mageborn. He could be the only one, or—" He halted.

"Or?"

"His might be an inherited magic. From my knowledge of Bregan as the son of a wealthy trader, and one in his own right, he might have a scattering of bastards from one end of these lands to the other. It could be a long search."

"The only magic the elder has is his ability to pinch wealth until it squeals."

Diort laughed at Tolby's mutter. "I've heard that, too! More important than my search is my care of him now. I do what I can. My presence usually calms him, but he's been most agitated this last handful of days. And, as long as we are sharing truths, I've never seen him with power that could be considered dangerous."

"He could have killed my father. He meant to. And one of my guards lies stricken, although our herbalist says she should recover with but minor weakness. It was as though lightning had struck her. I hope she doesn't have the infirmities of such a strike."

Diort shook his head slowly. "I have never seen that ability from him before." He put a hand up as Nutmeg sputtered. "Not saying he didn't do it. Only that he couldn't before."

A look traded across the table. "The Gods filled him."

"Possibly. What quarrel have you, Tolby Farbranch, with the Gods?"

"Only one I can bring to mind." Tolby set his eating knife down with a thump. "I am aligned closely with the Vaelinars. I sheltered and adopted one, and Nutmeg's child is fathered by one."

"Not all trouble on Kerith comes from the Vaelinars!"

All heads turned to the angry outburst from the corner of the room where the lone guard left standing stood, his jaw jutted out in protest.

"The lad has a point," Tolby remarked. "But not necessarily a valid one. Trouble follows the Vaelinars closer than their shadows do. Even Queen Lara would not gainsay that."

The guard folded his arms across his chest and leaned back against the wall until Nutmeg said to him gently, "Merri is in the other room," and he stalked off to oversee his charge.

Ceyla lowered her hand from her face. "Not that you're wrong," she told Tolby. "I think that you're probably right in this instance. The Gods slept, thinking the world safe after the purge of the Mageborn, and here we come, stirring things up again. We meddle with their people and the very threads of the world itself. If we don't anger them, what would?"

"Your people have been here hundreds of years. Why now?"

"Who knows what time is to a God?" She finished by picking up a piece of hard cheese and nibbling on it delicately.

"So a God set Bregan against me."

"Possibly. One carried him here. It's possible Bregan could have summoned him, but why would he/'"

"Why, indeed." Diort drained his cup dry and licked his lips. "You were speaking at the pub?"

"Aye, news mostly. There was an attack at Larandaril—"

"Old news," the Galdarkan interrupted.

"Not this one. An assassin got into Lara's apartments and slit her throat while she slept."

Diort knocked the cup over. "What?"

"She lives. By mercy, but she lives and heals. Bistane sent word that he encountered the villain and took him down. No proof, but the manner of attack says he was ild Fallyn."

"Not Kobrir."

"No. And they've been relatively quiet since Daravan's fall at the great battle of the Andredia. Perhaps they toil as the rest of us do until someone pulls their strings to force them to kill. At any rate, Lariel lives but yet sleeps." Tolby fingered the hilt of his utensil. "People have been curious since I brought my family back, so I thought to get them a bit of gossip along with their tidings."

"Why did you bring them back?"

They looked at one another.

"I am," said Tolby, "a Dweller through and through, for all my dealings with the rest of us who live on Kerith. We have good roots, when allowed, and I deemed that my daughter Nutmeg needed her father and her mother more than she needed a sleeping queen. So I brought her and hers home."

"Being at Larandaril is pointless, anyway, without Rivergrace," Nutmeg added quietly. She stood with the empty breadbasket and disappeared into the kitchen, where a cupboard could be heard as it opened and closed and a pan or two clattered.

"No word of the two?"

"None. The Returnists are squatting determinedly by the Eye between worlds, but it neither opens or closes. Sometimes . . ." Tolby paused and reached for his drink, taking a hearty gulp before continuing. "Sometimes things get pushed through."

"What sort of things?"

"Bloody bones. A bit of fur. Once, a cloak, ripped to shreds and muddied unrecognizable. Nothing of any consequence or good."

Ceyla shivered. "Bones?"

"Aye."

"No wonder you brought everyone here."

He gave a fierce grin. "One of the reasons."

Ceyla's fingers curled, and Diort looked down at her hand, a thoughtful expression crossing his face. She looked up at him and then shook her head, ever so slightly.

Dayne and Tolby did not miss the exchange nor did they remark on it.

Nutmeg came out with more fresh bread, neatly sliced, and a cup of butter taken from the cold cellar. "That will have to hold us over until I set dinner to fixing, although we have stew in the pot, simmering, and I've added to it, for company."

Diort stood. "My thanks for the hospitality, but I think I should return Bregan as soon as possible. I'll need to engage a wagon." He waved a hand, and his handful of soldiers who had been sitting quietly to the side jumped to their feet and passed through the kitchen to the outside door, each of them snatching up a nubby piece of bread as they went, Nutmeg laughing as they did.

Ceyla put up her scarf and followed, but he lingered a moment beside Dayne.

"A staff or two might be useful," he said finally, as if he'd thought carefully before choosing his words.

"There are trees on your border."

"We treat them as sacred. We don't cut them or use them for any lumber."

"Use the lumber. You have my permission as a son of Vantane."

He inclined his head. "Thank you. I'll send word if we have any interesting experiments to report." He touched his chest in a farewell salute.

Tolby followed him out the door and they paused together in the cooling evening air. "A word or two on his motives would be helpful here."

"You will know as soon as I do. Or if Ceyla dreams it." Diort smiled and took Tolby's forearm in a shake. "May the queen awaken soon."

"May we all find peace." Tolby released him and watched him stride off to where his men and Ceyla waited a-horseback. Lariel's guards dragged Bregan out to the courtyard and stood him up where he blinked in the sun while they untied his trussing and held him steady until he stopped swaying.

A slow smile eased across the man's face who now looked for all the world like a beggar. He twirled in the dusty courtyard.

"Enough," snapped Diort, as he bent to hoist the man up in the saddle behind him. "The Gods are done with both of us for the while."

Bregan laughed as he threw his arms about his Guardian King, and they rode out of the farmyard.

"What do you think Bregan really had on his mind?"

Dayne shook his head at Nutmeg. "I might doubt there was even a clear thought in his muddled mind."

"A shell which an angry God held sway over for a time?"

"As likely a reason as any." His chin lifted, part of his attention attracted by the sounds of the twins squabbling in the back room, and his eyebrows lowered a bit. He called out, "Evar. Don't tease Merri."

The argument subsided a bit.

"It might be a hatred for the Vaelinars."

"He attacked your father."

"Who was holding discourse on Vaelinar news at the time." Nutmeg ironed out an imaginary wrinkle in her apron with her fingers. "He was nearly destroyed by the embodiment of the Ferryman when he attacked that Way, his mind cleaved in half, like a stroke victim. It's a wonder he lives at all."

"Or that he hears Gods." Dayne looked back to her. "That could be the simple explanation."

"But his Mageborn blood?"

"Oh, that was bound to happen to someone, sooner or later. As long as life walks here on Kerith, there is a chance a Mageborn might turn up. Gods' work or not, I can't imagine wiping out a bloodline or a people in their entirety. Can you?"

Nutmeg tugged on a stray curl brushing the edge of her ear. Her rounded Dweller ear looked as though it had begun to develop a definite upward swoop and tip like that of a Vaelinar. Dayne's roaming attention now fixed on that for a long moment before he realized she had realized he stared, and he looked away.

"I can't, nor do I believe the Gods meddle. We build our own fates, I think, splinter by splinter, until we've built a tree of life. It might be a vast, wide-branched tree, or a scraggly bit of shrubbery, but there it is."

"All up to us."

"And those around us. I mean, I didn't start a war, but there I was in the middle of it."

"So some branches might intermingle a bit."

"If you want to call it that. Tangled, the way I see it."

He sat down, near but not too near her. "Some things seem inevitable, though."

"Aye, well, apples will rot no matter how cool the cellar." She crossed her ankles and eyed them, still slim and well-turned despite the two children.

His throat ached with words he wanted to say and couldn't. He finally shot to his feet and got halfway out of the room before calling back over his shoulder, "I'd better finish up in the barn." And he was gone.

Nutmeg looked after him. It occurred to her that while apples might rot, even more constant was the sun rising every day no matter how cloaked by clouds and ill-weather, its light hidden but welcome.

BISTANE HALTED in the narrow manor hallway as a page approached, his senses and mind still filled with the intense spring of the outdoors. He rubbed his hand down his thigh, brushing his leathers, no longer white as he used to wear but now a color somewhere between lustrous brown and burnished cherry. The warming spring day crept slowly indoors despite the shutters and hangings, and later, he knew he would wish he had worn one of his light shirts instead of armor over his torso. The chain mail hanging from his shoulders down to his hips would gain weight as the day went on, but it might well save his life again as it had saved him and Lara just a few weeks ago. He rolled first one shoulder and then the other to settle it better about him, watching the page coming down the hall. Pages. Seneschals. Head of the Grange, all trouble which Lara handled with far more alacrity than he did. Tolby had been attacked by that raving Mageborn Bregan had morphed into, proving that even the country life held no safety. Lara lived, but would she become aware again? Be able to even think again? Thoughts pounded his head from the inside out and his shoulders ached from being bowed over Lariel's coffin-like bed for days.

The assassin's wound healed. Her color returned somewhat, though she'd been pale since the battlefield attack, shut in her rooms. She almost looked, once again, as if she were simply a prisoner of sleep, locked inside a dream too inviting to leave. A dream of quietude.

The hallways and rooms also held the quiet of a tomb, without Nutmeg and the children. Nothing like the head-knocking common sense of a Dweller to dispel a mood.

He never thought he would so thoroughly regret Tolby Farbranch's clan leaving (and taking Bistane's brother Verdayne with them), but he did. Wholeheartedly. Now he had no one he could trust to watch over his queen while he took a break. He'd not had one word to his two frantic missives to the Kobrir, urging them to provide the promised antidote for the king's rest. He was a warlord, but his duty held him here. He could no longer return to see how his fields and groves fared, to walk among the beloved aryns, to lance at words with the librarian Azel d'Stanthe at the nearby Library, to drill his new recruits and otherwise tend to the family business. His pledge kept him at Larandaril to ensure her safety. He'd have to keep his trust in his own seneschal, Pieter.

If he had Verdayne with him, he could leave Dayne on guard. But, even as Bistane had, his brother had made his own decision and chosen to keep watch over Nutmeg Farbranch and two bouncing children, and probably for many of the same reasons Bistane had made his. Duty. Loyalty. Love. Dayne did not think that Nutmeg would ever look at him as he looked at her, but he hoped so, he'd told his brother. One day. Bistane consoled him, gave him hope, but did not tell him the truth as he saw it. Nutmeg had never had to make the choice with him. Verdayne had gone into her life, become her protector and her strong right arm, and she had never had to ask herself what she might feel for him if he were not always there.

Dayne fretted to Bistane in his own brotherly fashion that Nutmeg might worry about the gap between them. He was, after all, half-Vaelinar, his father the great Warlord Bistel Vantane and his mother a long-lived and prosperous Dweller woman, and he himself more inclined toward the Vaelinar portion of his bloodline. He would live long, too, although nothing approaching Bistel's time whose lifeline had exceeded most of his peers and reckoned over a thousand years. Had that made Dayne's life far too formidable? Did Nutmeg worry that she would grow old long before he did? She carried no sign of her years, but she was Dweller, and a Dweller seldom stood taller than a Vaelinar's elbow at the most, and lived perhaps a tenth of the elven lifespan, forgetting war and plague.

Not to put Dayne's worries aside as if unworthy, but Bistane knew that women mated to Vaelinars often inherited a portion of their longevity. Dayne's own mother had lived nearly twice as long and Dayne himself approached two hundred years and was just now into his young, hot blooded prime. Nutmeg had loved a prince of the Vaelinar and carried his child. That alone increased her years, and if she became Dayne's, that would go even further. Not a reason to marry but certainly not a reason to not marry.

Bistane knew that the council he'd given his brother hadn't gone far. Verdayne held too much fear deep inside of him for that, and neither could he blame his brother for it. Being half-Dweller among the arrogant Vaelinars was its own peculiar, cold hell.

As for himself, he loved a woman who was married to her kingdom. If she ever did reach out for a partnership, it would no doubt be for one steeped in political and strategic advantage. That was what one did, after all.

If she ever awakened.

And when she woke, would she look at him and realize why he stood watch at her bedside, moment by aching moment?

Footsteps tattooed his thoughts.

Bistane inhaled and lifted his gaze to the page who finally stopped in front of him, boot heels tapping together quietly but firmly.

"Sir. There is a personage at the back kitchen door, asking for you."

Bistane's eyebrow arched. "Kitchen door."

"Yes, lord. Not a formal visitor, he said, but necessary." The page's young face had creased in upset. He swallowed hard. "I couldn't send him away, lord, and the staff is near paralyzed in fear. It's a Kobrir, sir."

The words punched him in the gut. He would ask if the page were certain, but Kobrir couldn't be missed. Their dark garb and face veils left little to the imagination even to those who had never seen one but certainly had heard the stories. He looked over his shoulder at Lariel's closed door. "I want two guards at the door, and one inside."

The page nodded and ran. When the additional guards were in place, and only then, Bistane went down the servants' stairs to the kitchen to see what awaited him.

The Kobrir sat cross-legged near the back door, the kitchen staff occupying the quarter of the kitchen farthest away, darting looks over their shoulders when they dared. The assassin looked totally unaware of them, as though they did not exist. Bistane knew that if any one of the five had made a move, they'd have a dagger buried in their neck. Without word, without thought, and without regret. And then the other four would be dropped just as quickly and quietly.

The last Kobrir with whom Bistane had been face-to-face had been Sevryn Dardanon, just after he'd plunged his knife into Lariel's thigh. Most of his last words had been to Bistane: "She's not dead. She's not dying. My blade is poisoned. It mimics death. Don't leave her side till she wakes. It may be days. It may be weeks. She will heal if you tend it. Don't take the blade out. Do you hear me? Do you understand? Don't take the blade out until she heals. The poison on the blade is the only thing keeping her alive as she heals."

Kobrir poison. He'd sent to them for the antidote when her body had almost finished its sluggish healing, with her deep in its coma. They had sent back they could not help. Every season he sent to them. Her healing had been nearly complete when the assassin breached her apartments and nearly killed her again. Bistane had insisted the Kobrir dagger remain in her body, and she survived again. Her scars pink but sealed, he had sought help one last time.

Now, finally, this spring season they had sent one of their own. The surprise held him silent for a few heartbeats as he looked at the assassin sitting in the queen's kitchen.

The Kobrir looked up at him.

"Do you have it?"

"May I see the queen? If allowed?"

"You're an assassin. How do I know you're not here to finish the latest attempt?"

The Kobrir tilted his head. "Latest?"

"Someone tried to slit her throat."

"Is the Kobrir dagger still in her body? Does she yet heal?"

"Yes."

"Then your assassin was not Kobrir, for one of us would have succeeded. And we would have removed the dagger which prolonged her life."

"That gives me little faith to let you near her now."

"You had enough faith to plead for an antidote."

"Sevryn told me you had one. I've yet to see it."

The Kobrir unfolded agilely getting to his feet. "I have some news on that request."

Bistane suddenly felt a heat from the staring kitchen staff. He dipped his shoulder and turned about sharply. "Follow me, then."

The Kobrir moved after him, relatively silent on boot soles that seemed to be felted rather than leather, up the stairs, avoiding the boards that breathed or groaned with every step, a shadow in Bistane's wake.

The hair on the back of his neck prickled, reminding him he was being followed by an enemy. Bistane did not turn about until they reached the third-floor landing. Then he looked to the Kobrir. "Another letter refusing aid would have been sufficient."

"We told you we could not help. Not that we would not."

Bistane cut the air with his hand. "Playing at words as if they held a knife edge."

"But still true. Our master herbalist, the Kobrir who taught Sevryn much of his knowledge, including that of the poison called the king's rest, died in our camps while the battle to save Larandaril raged here. He took with him the knowledge of the antidote. We couldn't help you, even if we had wished."

"That explanation would have been appreciated." Bistane felt his jaws tighten.

The Kobrir gave a fleeting smile. "But then you might have let the queen slip away, thinking your efforts and hopes futile. We couldn't let that happen. By thinking us stubborn, heartless perhaps, you kept her in her sleep, hoping we might change our minds."

"And you're here now."

"Yes. We've been testing what we know, and we believe we now have the antidote our master intended. He always told us that maidens nodded and bowed before a king. We thought it a fanciful philosophy. Then one of our young potion makers remembered the flower you call the maiden's nod. I believe the meadows of Larandaril are full of them, this time of year."

Bistane blinked slowly. He inclined his head.

"We have been brewing and testing, and we believe this is satisfactory." The Kobrir opened the pouch at his belt and took out a corked, brown glass vial. He held it up but moved his hand swiftly when Bistane attempted to take it.

"Enough games!"

"She must be healed, or nearly so if she has grievous wounds, or she'll die on you yet."

Bistane tried to relax his clenched hands. "She is, as near as our healer can promise me. That last attack was swift and brutal, but only to her throat. The wounds she took in battle had been far worse. She would have bled out in a dozen heartbeats if Sevryn hadn't acted. Now . . . she's not perfect. She's very pale. We can tell she's had a lot of blood loss, particularly with this last. But it's closed. We don't believe there is any internal bleeding. Now it hurts her to linger. I have to let her live, or let her go."

The Kobrir inclined his head. "The king's rest cannot be in her system indefinitely or it will act as a true poison. Shall we see if this works?"

Stiffly, reluctantly, Bistane led the assassin into Lara's rooms.

It smelled like . . . he couldn't put a finger on the word he wanted. Like a sickroom, an odor of illness and near death, hiding under the scent of herbs and flowers, of spring wafting into the apartments through a barred window. Bistane flicked a glance at that window, out of habit. That was the window the ild Fallyn bastard had come through. Then it had merely been shuttered, and the flick of a knife had swung it open. That had been remedied. The floors were freshly sanded and oiled where the body had lain, blood pooling underneath it. He'd had Lariel's bed moved, too, after her mattress and linens were taken out and burned, her own blood staining them heavily, but he'd moved her so that she could catch the breeze a little easier. Her maids had thanked him, for that now made it easier for them to make the bed and move her. The healers who came up kept the bed sores away and dictated periods of exercise, twice a day, moving her still body about as though Lara were nothing more than a puppet. Sometimes the incision where the dagger was buried to its hilt in her thigh would leak a few drops of blood. Most often it would not.

She seemed closer to dying than ever before. Despite their care. Despite his worry.

The Kobrir looked to him. "You must be certain before we do this. Do you need to call a council to certify your decision?"

"Why?"

The Kobrir shifted weight. "We tested our poison and antidotes a number of times. We found a danger of not removing the dagger in time, or removing it too soon."

"Too soon?"

"That's a deep wound. She could bleed out from it, if the king's rest doesn't clot the bleeding properly before it is excised from her system."

"So we remove the dagger and wait to apply the antidote."

"Not precisely. If we wait to apply the antidote, the king's rest will turn deadly."

Bistane cut his hand through the air impatiently. "If it hasn't killed her by now . . ."

"No." The Kobrir's dark eyes watched him intently. "That's a hollow-bladed knife. Pulling it out releases a reservoir of poison within, flooding the wound. A fresh application, if you will."

"Cold hell." Bistane took a step toward Lariel. "You people are diabolical."

"So we were created to be. It distresses us almost as much as it does you."

"This might kill her."

"It could very well."

"Then why come to me now? Why not wait until you're certain?"

The Kobrir shook his head slowly. "We had a success. When we did, we knew we had to come to you as quickly as possible." His slender fingers tightened about the vial. "No one has ever awakened from a king's rest as long as Lariel Anderieon has slept. She slips with every day that passes now."

Bistane took another step, then two, until he reached the side of her bed. He brushed a finger alongside her cheek. She always felt cold to him, now. Who would he ask for an opinion and permission? Sevryn and River-grace were gone, lost two years now beyond that unholy break between worlds, swallowed and lost for good. Tranta's body had come in on the tides below the cliffs of his shattered gem. Bistel, long since passed. The ild Fallyns wanted her dead and didn't care how it happened. The Guardian King Diort had no say in the matter, though . . . and Bistane hesitated a moment . . . his oracle might prove useful. Still, if rumor was correct, Ceyla herself was an ild Fallyn, for all her loyalty to the Galdarkan, and Bistane couldn't feel any trust in himself for the girl. "I don't need a council. We'll take the antidote." He looked back at the Kobrir. "Do I need a healer in here?"

"It wouldn't help. It's the timing."

"Timing?"

"I put the vial to her lips. She swallows if she can—"

"She drinks. Not much, but we keep her hydrated." The sacred Andredia River kept its vow with her and its waters kept her alive, he thought privately, as much as healers and the king's rest did.

"Good." The Kobrir joined him at Lara's bedside. "Then this is what we do. I give her the vial, pour it down her throat at a measured pace. It has to be administered drop by drop, for all intents and purposes. You withdraw the dagger when I mark the vial as half gone."

He thought he understood what the other intended. He'd worked with wounds in the field. A good many times, the blade, if left behind in the soldier, blocked bleeding even as it slashed deep. Removing the blade before adequate bandaging could be provided could be as dangerous as the original wound, unless a vital organ had been hit, in which case internal bleeding doomed the soldier anyway. "The antidote will burn most of the poison from her system and begin to attack the bleeding of this last wound, even as I create it?"

"Yes. Then you will need to put pressure tightly, a dressing on the cut, while I force the second half of the vial into her at once."

"And then?"

"We wait. We see if the bleeding slows appreciably. If it does, we've won. The queen should awaken. If not, we still have some hope that pressure on the wound will work. That she will not bleed out almost as soon as she gathers consciousness."

"Some hope is better than none." Bistane grabbed up the utility table which contained scissors and dressings, as well as thin gauze bandages which were placed to keep the dagger steady whenever Lara had to be exercised or otherwise moved. He put it near at hand.

"Ready?"

"As we will ever be." He smoothed her arched eyebrows with his hand, found it shaking, and stopped. "Forgive me, Lara, if this doesn't work. But I don't think you'd want to linger until the poison has wasted every bit of you to nothing. Nutmeg's child, Jeredon's, thrives if we can't save you, but I think this is your best chance. You're a fighter. Meet me halfway on this, and we'll win through. We'll take this chance." He took the scissors and cut away the wrap about her thigh, exposing the carved handle of the dagger buried in her flesh.

Carefully, the Kobrir arranged the tiny pillow under Lara's head. Her healers had cut her hair to shoulder length, its platinum-and-honey-blonde strands curling down her neck. A few hairs fell loose as he pillowed her head, another sign that the poison had begun to work its more deadly traits on her body. "When I say begin . . ."

"Pull the dagger swiftly."

"As you can, and pressure on the wound."

"I have it," Bistane told the Kobrir. He steadied his hand. "Does the poison work on contact?"

"It can. I suggest you wrap and secure the blade as soon as you can."

"Ready."

"We begin." The Kobrir uncorked his vial, put his hand behind Lariel's neck, arching it slightly, bringing her mouth slightly open, and began to tip the potion over her lips. As he did, he started to speak.

Bistane barely caught the sound and sense of it before he realized the Kobrir chanted. Slow-paced and deliberate, it no doubt helped him calculate the dosage. The chant buzzed at his ears a bit. Did this Kobrir have the Vaelinar Talent of Voice? If he did, what he said might be as important as what he poured. The fact that he thought the Kobrirs might have Vaelinar blood in them, he tucked away to be considered later. That he might well bring before a council.

He could see a ripple down her throat as she swallowed. Once. Twice. A third time. The pallor of her skin took on a faint blush. Bistane thought he could feel a delicate heat in the leg near his hand. The antidote burning out the poison? Or the poison rising to fight its cure? Either way, a battle waged inside Lariel's pale body, bringing heat and color to her skin.

The chant rose a little louder. Bistane could feel his pulse slow to match its cadence.

"Begin."

He put his hand to the dagger to pull it quickly, cleanly—and could not. The blade burned into his hand, searing his palm and curled fingers. Bistane spat out a curse but did not let go. It refused to budge under his grip.

The chanting stopped. "What is it?"

"It burns. It won't come free."

"It has to come free. Don't let go of it!"

The heat seared through him. He could feel unshed tears of pain pool in his eyes, but he kept his grip. He could feel the blade in his mind as if it held a consciousness. It held on stubbornly, relentlessly, to its victim. *Sevryn wielded you. Now I free you from your destiny. Surrender to me.*

"Get that dagger out of her or we'll lose her."

Agony seared to his bones, through flesh, nerve and muscle. Bistane could feel sweat dripping from his forehead and leaned into it. He would lose his hand before he failed Lara. It began to slide from her thigh, crimson welling up in its path as it relinquished its hold. Its last act of defense was to jump and twist in the air, biting at him, but he had the wrappings up and ready for it. Captured, he threw it to the floor and stomped a boot over it. He grabbed the fresh, clean gauze and covered her wound as the Kobrir quickly poured the last of his vial down her throat.

His bandage soaked. He tossed it to one side and grabbed a second handful, swapping one for the other. It soaked the gauze as well, but more slowly.

Lara's eyelids fluttered rapidly.

The Kobrir stepped back, his voice dropped into his chant once more. The blush that had colored her face now lit her throat, the hollow of her bosom began to glow. She moved her free leg and shifted as if to move the one he held tightly. Her hand swept across his. He heard her take a deep breath.

Awakening or in a death throe?

His palm grew damp. He applied more clean gauze. The incision still welled with blood, but it did not fountain as it had. Nor did his hand show burn marks, though he still felt the pain of the dagger throughout, from the palm to the back of his hands. He thought he could even feel heat through the tough leather sole of his boot. He would have to take the dagger to the forge and have it disposed of properly, because it seemed to have a life of its own. He wondered just what sort of man Sevryn had become, to carry and use such a weapon. The thigh tensed under his hold, as if she tested her body now.

Lara raised her head. She choked out an inaudible word and swallowed tightly. Then she put one slender arm behind her and levered herself upright in her bed. Her arm trembled and her body swayed with the effort. She ran her tongue over her dry lips and tried again.

"How long? How long has it been?"

Chapter
Sixteen

L ARIEL SAT UP, shaking in every limb, her legs hanging over the edge
of her bed, the sheets rumpled under her, bracing herself with her
arms. Bistane bent over to help, but she stayed him. "Don't."

"You're weak."

"I'm . . . awake. Finally." Her multihued blue eyes focused and then
narrowed. "With a Kobrir in my rooms."

The cult member bowed from the waist. "Your Grace."

"You brought the antidote."

He must have smiled, for the corners of his eyes crinkled slightly,
though his mask hid most of his expression. "I did."

"Thank the Gods." Her efforts to hold her head high failed, and her
chin dropped down. Bistane placed a goblet of water into her nearest hand.
She grasped it and then brought it to her lips, water spilling out of the
quaking vessel, sprinkling her in dampness, but she got most of it down.
Took a very deep breath. Her hoarseness had nearly faded when she began
to speak again. "What of my brother's child? Nutmeg? That damned ild
Fallyn? The Raymy?"

"The Raymy are dead and burned. Nutmeg is well and you have an
heir. They were staying here at the manor, but—" Bistane paused. "You
remember some of this?"

"It was like falling asleep. I remember being sliced by Alton ild Fallyn
and then Tressandre. Sevryn caught me falling from the horse. Drove a
dagger into my leg, but that didn't hurt. And he told you what it meant
when you caught me up. I couldn't keep from slipping, I could hear the
trumpets and fighting about me, but no more could I wake than I could

have run. I was so weary. A kind of darkness took me. There were times when I could hear voices speaking. I understood them for a few moments and then lost it. I knew I'd been moved. That the war was behind me, but whether we'd won or not, I couldn't tell. I thought I heard children playing by my bedside once or twice. I knew when the healers came, sometimes. They moved me about. I knew when you were about, often." Lara realized water dappled her chin and shoulders, and tried to shake it off a bit and rearrange her robe about her.

"The children," and Bistane smiled in remembrance. "Little Merri, and Evarton, the son of a wet nurse Nutmeg hired. They had an attacker as well, early on, and the wet nurse died. Nutmeg kept both children and has a nanny, an auntie, to help her raise them. Nutmeg would sit in the corner and do some stitchwork and let the toddlers play here. She said you knew they were here, for you'd laugh in your sleep from time to time. Evarton took his first steps holding onto your bed linens as he staggered from your side to Nutmeg's knee. He prefers to be called Evar. Merri has a Dweller temperament, but she has Vaelinar eyes and Jeredon's pointed chin. There's no doubt, Lara. She is an Anderieon."

"Is she here?"

"Not presently. Sometimes I think the boy—who is also of mixed blood—resembles your brother as well. You can see a bit of the Dweller in him, particularly in his stubbornness, but he has the eyes, the ears, and the hair color. I can understand why Nutmeg fosters him as well."

She sagged suddenly. Both men moved to brace her against the backboard of her bed, with pillows behind her so that she could remain sitting up, and she gave them a trembling, fleeting look of gratitude. "Does she have Talent?"

"She has the eyes, Lara, so she must have the Talent. And she's a bit fey, but what the main ability will be, we can't say yet although I've had some inklings. She's grown fast and matured, so much so that people say she is like an old soul. She is not taking her time as most Vaelinars do."

"Born to the pace of Kerith?"

"Healers have examined her. They deem that she'll have most of our longevity. She is just growing fast, perhaps due to Nutmeg's blood. And Nutmeg is a good mother. Excellent. Both children thrive under her, and I think Evar is good for Merri. He is more Vaelinar, so she is already learning to deal with our inborn ways. She copes well. I think, although as I said we cannot be sure, that she might be a natural-born healer." He paused.

"Both children show a remarkable maturity within. You can see it in their eyes."

"And you find that disturbing?"

He tilted his head slightly before answering. "I always thought children should be children. There's no doubt, however, that Nutmeg does well by them."

"I never thought Meg would be other than an excellent mother." Lara straightened herself out as she began to list to her right. She plumped up a pillow with a fist. "Tressandre's child?"

"No sight of it. Rumor has it she miscarried after the battle. We can't get confirmation of it, but there's been no word in the last two years. She's rebuilding. She lost Alton, half her army, but she's like a snake coiling, readying to strike again. Her breeding program," and he cleared his throat on that as if ridding himself of an unpleasantry, "is filling in her troops."

Lara touched her throat thoughtfully. "I don't doubt she readies. She has always done so. What of Sevryn and Rivergrace?"

"Gone."

"Gone? Dead? Or where?"

"After Quendius, through the eye, the tear, the thing that Daravan wrought to take the Raymy from here and then bring them back."

"To Trevilara? To our beginnings?"

"So we believe."

She stifled a yawn, her eyes far livelier than the rest of her expression. "So they follow the death master. That begs the questions: What would Quendius want with Trevilara? And what would Sevryn and Grace want of him?"

"In that time he fled from you, he was taken in by the Kobrir. He trained as an assassin. I think he went after Quendius with the hope of bringing him down. The death master, true to his name, had a small army of Undead with him."

"My Gods. And he slipped through our hands?"

Bistane sat down on the edge of the bed. "We were a little preoccupied at the time."

"You called them Undead. Are you certain of this?"

"We captured one of them which had fallen on a dead body to eat. They need blood and meat, as fresh as they can get it, to slow the corruption of their own flesh. They are cold. They think, but little beyond survival. The one we held had been a mercenary and fighting was braided into his being, his muscles, his memories. He lived on the brink of dying and knew it, and fought for the next breath, the next heartbeat. He had a trace of the demon Cerat buried inside him. We think that's what kept him as an Undead. They seem bound spiritually to Quendius and, as such, are slaves to whatever he wishes."

Lariel looked away from Bistane and the very quiet Kobrir, her gaze seeking her window which, though barred, let the sun and spring inward. "Always Quendius, somewhere in the shadows, always lurking. Gilgarran had been hunting him diligently, but he's the only one who seemed to worry about Quendius. Even when the weaponmaker fouled the Andredia and broke the pact my family had with the sacred river, even when he drove the first armies of the Raymy out of the mountains to Ashenbrook, we discounted his place in the scheme of things. What does he want, I wonder? Do you think he goes to meet the queen on the other side?"

"We can't know." Bistane fisted his hand and then uncurled his fingers slowly. "You ask questions to which none of us can divine an answer."

"She could cut him down or could ally with him on the other side."

"She could. Or Sevryn and Rivergrace could seek to put an end to it all."

The Kobrir stirred a bit to say quietly, "He seeks power."

"But to what end? What would he do with it when he has it? Who will he seek to rule? Who will he crush?"

The Kobrir shrugged. "He is a spirit. Always there yet one we are unable to grasp. He and Daravan pulled at our strings for many a decade, but we still exist, as do they." He put a hand out to Bistane. "I have done what I was sent to do. May you and your queen unknot the future." And he was at the threshold before Bistane could blink.

"Wait!"

Framed in black, much like the shadow he'd condemned Quendius to be, the man turned.

"Name your reward."

The Kobrir stilled. Thought ran through him like floodwater through a spillway. Bistane could see it plainly. Then the Kobrir shook his head. "We give death freely. It's enough, for once, to give life."

Lariel had lifted her chin and now kept it high. "We don't know you as a people. Perhaps we shouldn't. But I rather like thinking my life has a certain value, and I would like to thank you for saving it. Name a reward, not just for yourself, but for your clan."

He shuffled his foot. That odd felt sole of his shoe made little noise, as befitted a person who lived and died by stealth. "We have a . . . bit of land to ourselves."

Lara nodded.

"It is a difficult place to live, but it suits us."

"And . . ."

"It would help us, as a people, to be able to have a grove or two. At the far south end of Larandaril, away from the sacred river, there are sloping hills and small pockets of runoff to keep it green. . . ."

"Done," Lara told him. "That section will be yours as long as I reign. Plant what you will. I'll set it down in writing and post the edict at Hawthorne and Calcort and anywhere else you might deem necessary, and put posts at the boundaries. Three hundred acres, with the water rights to the two artisan wells there and watershed, and mineral rights below. Does that answer your question?"

The Kobrir's jaw had dropped while she spoke, and he fell to one knee. He put his hands to his head and held them there a moment while Lara waited for his answer. He choked out, "Thank you, my queen. Thank you."

"I ask only that you not draw blood on this land or train your skills. It is farmland."

"Understood." He looked down and seemed to realize he'd fallen to his knee, and rose swiftly. Disappearing through the doorway, his words trailed after him. "Let it be done."

Bistane waited a few heartbeats to be certain the hallway had cleared. "Well. That's a bit of diplomacy."

She reached for his hand and held it a moment. "It won't stop them from accepting contracts, probably. It's what they do."

"They could train for caravan guards. There's demand enough for their skills there. We've been having a run of banditry."

"Indeed." She pulled him slightly toward her. "What else has happened?"

Bistane scratched at an eyebrow. "Abayan Diort is raising a Mageborn."

"What?" Her voice rose sharply enough to make her cough, and he hurriedly fetched another goblet of water for her.

He watched her drink, her face animated and her slender throat swallowing, remembering that her hand on his had felt warm, unlike the chill of months past. She lived, and he realized with a knot in his own throat, how wondrous that was to him.

"We have a fledgling Mageborn among us, and Diort has found him and is now his guardian," he repeated slowly.

"Some Kernan waif?"

"Not exactly."

She held the goblet and, for a split-second, looked as if she might toss it at him, in the way the old Lariel would have. He grinned at the realization and held his palm up in surrender. "It's Bregan Oxfort."

"Bregan?" She paused. "Why am I not surprised anymore? The man has always been a bit peculiar since his run-in with the Ferryman Way. He nearly killed himself and I've always thought it possible the forces he tangled with fried his nerves. He ran that scam with the pottery shrines for the Gods to speak and listen, if you recall."

"No longer a scam," Bistane told her quietly.

"My . . . Gods." She blinked off whatever thoughts now seemed to race through her eyes.

"Indeed."

She put a hand to her throat. "It hurts to speak. I should probably rest a while. Then you'll have to get the staff together, and Farlen—wherever he is—and I should make an appearance."

"You should." He left her side and crossed the room to her dresser and picked up a mirror. He gave it to her, positioning it so that she could see the thin scar across her jugular.

Her hand shook and the mirror fell from it, dropping to the bed linens. "The other scars I expect from the attack I remember, but this? What happened?"

"An assassination attempt while you slept. We got the fool."

"Anyone we know?"

He shook his head. "No, but we know his House well. Ild Fallyn. No one else could have accessed these windows. That's why I had them barred."

"I was going to ask." She ran her fingers over her skin, tracing the small line of the scar. "It's still tender. When?"

"Two moons ago. It would have been worse, was planned to be worse, but Tolby Farbranch had moved his family out of the manor, and so they were not here to meet the blade as well. The Returnists squatting just west of here unnerved him. Said he was safer among his own folk than Vaelinars."

"Who can blame him?" She picked the mirror up again to examine, her face, not so much in vanity, but to look at her condition Bistane realized as he watched her. She tugged on the ends of her much shortened hair, her lips tight, but she made no comment.

She finally looked back to him. "We'll have to deal with the ild Fallyn once and for all. I've put it off far too long, and now their roots have stretched far and wide." A shadow fell over her face. "She has been making alliances while I've slept. I don't want a civil war. We have to be very careful what we do."

He nodded. "When you've strength."

"What else have they been up to?"

"Not the ild Fallyn, but the Galdarkans. Diort has an oracle—"

"Does he now?"

"A good one. She steered his troops here, to meet the Raymy threat and come to our aid. She'd seen it, knew he had to be here or Larandaril would fall. Or so she says."

"I hear mistrust."

"You do." Bistane crossed his arms. "Diort's girl is the result of the ild Fallyn back-breeding program. She says the program has had little real success, but it exists. They are herding people, Lara, like animals."

"And she's a seer."

"She claims to be. Diort seems to be convinced."

"That is a very rare Talent in any of our backgrounds. Their program could be more successful than she knows." Lara fingered the golden frame of her mirror. She closed her eyes for such a long while Bistane feared that he'd lost her to sleep again.

"Lara?"

Her eyes opened. "I'm here. Just thinking the Gods of Kerith are awake, and wondering what they think of us, meddling with the threads They used to weave their world. What are the Gods of Kerith, as it comes down to it? Will they move to meet us? Deal with us? Stir the pot so vigorously we destroy ourselves?" Her stomach let out a tiny growl and she dropped her hand to it with a laugh. "More practically—go get me something to eat! I think I may be starving."

"As I am commanded. Something light, though. You've been existing on dreams and the waters of the Andredia."

"With apologies to the sacred river, it no longer seems to be enough. Save me once again and get me something to eat!"

Laughing, Bistane hurried to do her bidding.

Chapter
Seventeen

LARA COULD NOT BEAR the vein in her throat that began to pulse as she stepped out onto the balcony to view her valley. It sent a painful throb down the curve of her throat down to the too sharp edge of her collarbone where it collected to the point of agony. Larandaril was not her kingdom: it was her heart and her trust. The wind off its green hills and vales comprised her breath. Her Vaelinar heritage was her blood, cold perhaps as some claimed. The Kobrir had been rewarded and left, and she could hear Bistane clearing the room, giving her space, giving her time. She'd drunk her fill of cool, clear water and allowed herself to be spoon-fed bread dipped in broth, but now she wanted to stand and exist on her own. It was time. It was past time. Nearly two years, they'd told her.

She put her hands on the stone railing, and curled her fingers tightly. Dark black scourges marked the land like scars, gashes of war carved deeply into the firmament, emitting faint puffs of gray, greasy looking smoke. As the smoke drifted upward, it did not thin but coalesced with other wisps of smoke into webs that caught upon the canopy of the trees and hung there. She wondered for a moment if the dark blight upon the branches had any relationship to the black mold that had been affecting the Books of All Truth at the Ferstanthe Library, eating them away and if the librarian had found a cure with the help of Tolby Farbranch while she slept. She marked that thought as another question she must ask. Answers, so many answers she had to have. Questions she had to remember to ask. Life that had passed her by while she slept without dreams, without knowing, without hope.

The Andredia River sliced through the valley, its waters so bright blue that their reflection hurt her gaze upon them, but even that brilliant river faltered where it traveled through the scars. The pastures nearby seemed nearly empty, the breeding herds thinned, few mares with foals trotting at their sides. She could see the magnificent dapple-gray stallion Aymaran, Sevryn's favorite, pacing the railing of the stallion paddocks. He hadn't gone to the killing fields of the battle. She could see his influence in several of the foals, their coats a dark, flinty gray that would, as his was doing, whiten as they aged. But his bloodline could not save the hot-blooded tashyas. She would have to appeal to the other Houses and holdings for both studs and brood mares.

And she could not bring them to graze on corrupted fields or drink from tainted waters. The Andredia cried out to be cleansed, for her to fulfill her blood vows, and to keep the valley as she had pledged. She could not see beyond to the actual battlefield itself. Bistane would have to take her there, if he would. She anticipated an argument. He would say she was too weakened, and he would be right. But she could not wait a moment longer. Her pulse drummed in her neck and hummed and beat hotly at her collarbone. She had work to do.

A step scuffed faintly behind her. She asked, without turning her head, "Bistane?"

"Never far from you."

"I heard you. In my dreams. Or my waking. Sometimes I seemed to see things, even though I could not move or react to them."

"You would open and close your eyes, sometimes," he answered. "We couldn't leave your eyes open . . . the healers were afraid they'd dry. So we would close them, and you'd stay for days—weeks—with them closed, and then I would come one morning and you'd be looking out. I knew you weren't dead. Sevryn told me that the toxin would be all that could keep you alive, at first, to heal. But I could never be sure that you'd really live again, either."

"You sang to me."

"I talked. Sang, once in a while. Sat, and worked."

"Sevryn." Lara opened her hands from the balcony rail, and stepped away, turning slightly. "Rivergrace took him through the Gate."

"Yes."

"Have either of them returned?"

"Not yet."

"Are they expected to?"

"We don't know. The Gate has stayed open like an eye that's barely slit, since the battle. There are those who would force it, but that is a matter better discussed when we have the others here and you're rested."

"My being awake doesn't solve everything at once?"

His mouth twitched. "It seems as though it should, but it does not."

She traced a fingertip over the half-moon scar along her throat. Unlike her other scars, this one hurt and her touch quickened nerves to tell her so. "What was it Sevryn gave me? It wasn't the death blow I feared, but it felled me all the same." Her hand drifted to her thigh and rubbed along the robe as if she could see the small scar left by the knife he'd plunged into her.

"His dagger was coated with a potion called king's rest by the Kobrir. It plunged you into a coma, so that you might heal instead of die, but then you were trapped within. The dagger couldn't be removed until the antidote was verified by the Kobrir, but it seems they'd lost their master . . . poisoner . . . leaving no one quite sure of the potion. With a sacrifice or two, they eventually recreated it."

"I understand the time span for that. But this." She tapped her neckline. "But this is still sore."

"An assassin broke into your chambers. If you hadn't been within that healing coma, that slice would have killed you, but your heart refused to bleed out."

Her eyes narrowed. "How did he get in?"

"Jumped to the window and in. Or, I should say, levitated."

"Ild Fallyn."

"One of their Talent line, yes. Dead now."

"You sound as if you regret that."

"He did not live long enough to tell me what I wanted to know."

"Mmmm. So I healed yet again under the influence of this poison, the king's rest."

"Yes. I sent another appeal to the Kobrir. I told them that none of them could walk safely upon Kerith until the poison was cured."

"And so they found they had the antidote."

"Eventually, yes."

"Do you think they stalled on purpose?"

"They gained no advantage by it. Actually, they had not planned the poison for you at all."

"Oh?"

"No. It was intended for Daravan. The more particulars of that, I could not tell you. Sevryn had precious little time to tell me anything, and the Kobrir were even less inclined to give me information, even when they sent one to administer the cure."

"Daravan was the target?" She turned to face him fully, one hip braced against the balcony, unable to admit her legs felt unsteady. She could not be weak. She could not afford to show it.

"Yes. He brought the Raymy army back on us en masse with purpose, to bring Kerith and all its peoples to their knees. We thought his control weakening, by the small troops that kept dropping here and there, but it was him practicing his control until he could hit you in force here in Larandaril."

"Do we know why?"

"Other than he wanted to rule? No." Bistane spread his hands out, palms up. "Sometimes there is no more reason than that."

"Not with Daravan. Never a single rationale. You may be certain of that." She paused. Her throat, her mouth, felt terribly dry. "For years I've wondered if he plotted Gilgarran's death at the hands of Quendius. What Gilgarran might have spared us from, if he had lived. He taught Sevryn much as his protégé, but not enough. Not nearly enough." Her voice faded. She turned her chin to cough lightly, but that turned into a terrible hack that set her shoulders to shaking and racked her entire body.

Bistane darted back inside her rooms and returned with a tall glass in his hand. "Come in. Sit. And we will talk some more."

Chagrined, she accepted the drink and emptied half the glass before she felt she could even thank him. "I feel," she added, "like a spring shoot, just out of the ground where it can be annihilated by the slightest drop of rain or tug of wind or even a too bright ray of sun."

He put his hand about her waist. "Then come in and be protected for a while."

Lara let him guide her to one of her padded chairs. He sat in the carved wooden one at her secretary desk, after having pulled it around to draw close to her. She finished her drink, water sweetened with a bit of honeyed mead, and waited as he refilled it. The drink both cooled and warmed her.

"First, I wanted to talk about Sevryn."

"He was no traitor to you."

"No. No, he wasn't. I feared it. I had . . . seen it. And that brings me to talk to you not only about Sevryn, but myself. Things very few have ever known." She sat back in the chair, heard the material rustle like silk at her touch, felt it cushion bones that had too little flesh left over them. She'd gotten horribly thin, she realized, and looked down at her arm. Pale, almost translucent skin showed the tracery of her veins beneath the surface clearly; old scars tracked spidery-white etchings over it. Translucent and fragile looking, like the pages of a very old book, holding ancient knowledge. She pulled her sleeves down over her arms, suddenly feeling chilled.

"You don't have to tell me anything," Bistane said softly. "It's unnecessary."

"Not to me. I have been an unknown quantity most of my life, to those important to me, and who trust me in spite of that which has never been revealed." Lara took a deep breath. She folded her hands in her lap. When had her fingers become so slender, so frail looking? And the stump for her missing finger looked almost as if it had melted away, rather than been sliced expertly. "Sinok kept many secrets and for a very long time, I was convinced it was to protect this throne. But it wasn't. It was done to protect him and what he felt was his legacy. Sinok was not only my grandfather but my father. When Jeredon grew older, he took stock of his grandson and found him lacking in the Talents he needed to rule. Jeredon's father met a fatal accident. Jeredon was disinherited. My mother remarried again, an even more unwanted match, and he also died but not before he could give the impression he'd impregnated her." Lara looked away from Bistane's face and earnest expression. "Sinok had raped her. She gave birth to me and raised me in the truth, in shame and silence that Sinok demanded from both of us. Eventually, I lost her as well, and he trained me to succeed him. I had inherited his Talents, or I would have been shunted away, too, I believe."

"I think Gilgarran suspected and was quietly gathering evidence. I know that Sinok tried to have him assassinated at least once. But Gilgarran also supported me. Whatever sin there was in the matter fell on Sinok's shoulders, not mine. So. That is where I came from. What I can do has been whispered about since I could walk. I could become as a vantane and ride the winds, gathering information no one else had. I could think faster than my opponents could react. I could always stay several sword strokes ahead in my battles. How I did it, no one knew. Now Sevryn, wherever he is, knows. And so will you."

She stretched out a hand, found it trembling, but placed it on Bistane's leather clad knee, anyway.

"You have foresight. Extremely rare, and valued." He sounded triumphant in having guessed it.

Lariel shook her head. "No. It may seem like it, but that's not what I do." She leaned forward, her voice quieting. "I am a Possessor, Bistane. I possess another's soul and observe. For those moments, I know all that soul knows and what it will do, based on its knowledge. And I am able to go into the future and possess in order that I might know what happens then." She looked away from him. She could see from his expression that he was trying to understand and accept what she was telling him. But she didn't think he ever would, or could, truly understand. "I saw myself struck down in the Raymy attack, and it looked as if Sevryn was doing it. I realize now that the soldier I possessed saw it from an angle which hid the truth, that it was Alton ild Fallyn and Tressandre who struck at me, but when I came back to myself, all I knew was that Sevryn had been there, blade in hand."

"And you woke up screaming assassin."

"I did." She took her hand from his knee, her flesh warmed by the touch, her body still shaking faintly. "I didn't want to die there, Bistane."

"No one would."

She tried to lift her chin, to look him in the eyes. "I can't die. It's important I don't, and not for my sake. There will come a moment when the existence of all that is Kerith will depend on me, and I have to be alive to see that moment. I've seen it, and it wasn't easy, and it's nothing I want—but I love these lands. I don't want to fail them."

Bistane's posture had changed, just by the barest amount, one shoulder higher and tensed, as if his body fought to lean back and he fought against the reflex. He met her gaze steadily, his eyes so like his father's, intense blue on blue, clear and piercing. "I cannot promise you that you will meet this moment in history, but I can promise my loyalty and silence." He paused as if he wished to add one more thing.

"But?"

Bistane tilted his head. "No, nothing more. Not yet." He did sit back in his chair then, with a sigh that might have come from relief or weariness. "So do all your observations come true?"

"Yes. It's not something I've ever done lightly, but only at great need. I wonder if I have ever tampered with the threads of fate or knotted what should be our true history, but I don't have any evidence of it. Except that last battle when I thought I saw myself die. It wasn't quite the same as what I'd envisioned, but when I fell, I found myself thinking. Not now. Not yet.

I have something I must do for the others. And I haven't loved yet. I can't die because I'm not done living."

"No different than any of us."

"No. No, I suppose not."

"Your Talent gives you an immense power."

"Perhaps. I have only been allowed to learn a very little. It's rather like looking through an arrow loop, nothing more than that narrow slit in stone that my archers use. But perhaps that's the way it's meant to be, or I might be meddling in things I should not."

"You've never tried."

"It seemed wiser not to. I've saved myself, but I've never been able to—quite—save anyone else." She looked away from him then, suddenly unable to meet his gaze.

"You must have seen things you couldn't bear to see."

"I didn't go looking. What I searched for, Bistane, were answers to an immediate crisis, a knot that I had no way of cutting through without knowing what might happen if I took a certain action. And it's not easy for those I possessed." Her chin dropped, and her left hand joined her right in its trembling. "There are those who did not withstand being possessed. In the early years, Sinok had them killed so they could not talk. In later years, I—I—"

"Don't say it. You did what you had to."

"It was never done lightly."

Bistane thrust himself to his feet. "I doubt it could have been. When did you know? Were you taught?"

"I learned what we all did when we were young, that owning another was an abomination. That people who could steal your soul needed to be put to death."

"Lara, that wasn't quite—"

"What I did? But it was." She put a hand up to the cuff of his sleeve to keep him from withdrawing from her totally. "I took them from themselves so I could witness what they were meant to experience, and when I was done, I couldn't always leave them untouched. Particularly when I was young. I learned the hard way how to disengage without destroying the mind I touched. Those were some very difficult lessons. Very difficult."

His hand covered hers briefly before he finished stepping away. "You were raised in secrecy and shame."

"For me, yes. Sinok took no shame in any of it. He enjoyed possessing those who were weaker. He enjoyed making them put a knife to their throat and use it."

Bistane's mouth tightened, white lines about his lips. She knew he was remembering the death rate during her grandfather's reign. "I'm surprised," he noted finally, "that the Andredia kept her pact with him."

"The River Goddess is among the few elementals awake on Kerith, and I have no reference on how she dealt with him, only how she deals with me. The only reasoning I could find was that it was Vaelinars who came to grief under him, not those of Kerith."

"We only hurt ourselves, hmmm?" He took another step across the room. "That would make some sense of it. Thank you for telling me."

Lara stood up. "I'm not asking your forgiveness."

His eyebrow arched. "No?"

"No. I've told you because I wanted you to know what—what you're dealing with, when you deal with me."

"Did Jeredon know?"

"Yes! Yes, he did. He anchored me on my . . . voyages, I suppose you'd call them. He'd guard my body. He would keep me safe till my mind could return. He didn't have most of our abilities, but he could kick out a trespasser, if it came to that, and once or twice it did. He was my safety, my home, my rock."

Bistane asked quietly, "Was he your lover, too?"

"Does incest run in the family, do you mean?" Lara gave a laugh that sounded bitter to her ears. "No. I loved him dearly, as my half-brother and protector, and I shall never stop missing him, but he wasn't my lover. He had one love in his life and we all know her as Nutmeg Farbranch, as unfortunate as that was." She sighed, and sank back into her chair, suddenly feeling as if not a bone in her body could hold her together. She added simply, "I'm tired, Bistane."

"Then you've got to rest. We'll see to the Andredia and Larandaril tomorrow, as soon as you wake in the morning."

"You'll be here?"

"Nowhere else." He smiled at her, and she thought to herself that it looked genuine.

Then a thought kicked at the back of her mind. With a Vaelinar, who could tell?

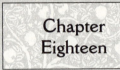

Chapter
Eighteen

NOT ALL SPRING MORNINGS, even those when one feels newly awakened and reborn, are sunny. This one dawned gray and misty, dew cloaking the ground heavily and clouds covering the sun with heavy veils that it might or might not burn through as the day wound on. She swung aboard the tashya being held for her, a young gelding, splashy in color and a little nervous for her tastes, but the fight had devastated her herds and he'd been in training this last year while she slept. He pawed the ground as she settled into the saddle, gathered her reins, and nodded at the stable lad, not a lad actually but a grizzled veteran she knew well, his left shoulder bunched up in a crippling injury from that same battle. Garlen let the gelding go and gave her a half-salute.

"Good to see you up and about, my queen."

What was it she should say? Then she remembered what Bistane had told her. "Good to be seen," she answered, but the veteran rewarded her feeble response with a hard squeeze to her booted foot.

Bistane, swinging up on his large chestnut, flashed her a grin. "You look ready."

She did not feel ready. She'd bargained for this, so many walks, so many meals, so many naps (after all that sleep, why must she nap?) and now that she had the outing, she felt uncertain. The horse seemed bigger than she remembered. The ground farther away and hard-looking, even carpeted in lush spring growth. The air nipped sharper. The wind held a keener note to its howl off the hills. Larandaril seemed on edge and sinister.

Her missing finger let out a lingering pulse of pain inside her glove. She rubbed it absently. Would the River Andredia call for an accounting when she came to its banks where the Vaelinars, the Kernans, the Dwellers, the Galdarkans, and the Raymy had fought? So much blood had already been shed there, but did it call for more, from those it blamed for the massacre?

Did it want her blood?

"Lara."

Her attention shot to Bistane. "What?"

"You're thinking."

"I might be. It's better than dreaming, is it not?"

"That would depend on what it is you're thinking and dreaming, my queen."

"Bistane, you're many things, but a mincer of words you're not." She lifted her hand and her splashy horse broke into a slow lope, rocking gently under her. Bistane put a heel to his and matched her speed quickly. Behind them, a handful rode in a rearguard, and the misty gray morning sped by them. She could feel her leg muscles quiver as she kept her seat. Her heels refused to stay in position, and the horse's ears flicked forward and back on the confusing signals her body sent him. She, who had been riding since before her earliest memories, now had trouble.

"You're fighting yourself and Dhuran," Bistane told her. He rode his horse close enough to her that their legs brushed, and his mount peeled back his lips to show Dhuran his teeth as the smaller, younger horse dared to crowd him. "Take a breath. Quit trying. Relax and let it come naturally. Your muscles are weak, but you don't need to tell them what to do. You know how to ride."

She forced down a tight breath and let her hands drop. Dhuran took the opportunity to veer a half-length away from Bistane's mount, and snorted as he did.

"Little snot."

Bistane laughed. "He intends to dominate someday, when he's full grown. One of the reasons we had to geld him. He was nigh untrainable otherwise."

"I think he's forgotten that he was cut."

"Possibly."

She looked at the fiery chestnut splotched coat of his, realizing that his name, based on the Vaelinar God of Fire, seemed most apt. "He's one of the last get of Banner High, is he not?"

"Yes."

Lara bit back her response to that. The old stallion had been one of her favorites, just another part of her heritage lost to the Raymy attack.

"We should probably buy from the ild Fallyn to rebuild the breeding herd."

Bistane's face pulled. "I didn't want to resort to that."

"We don't want to inbreed."

"I was hoping for other options. I brought down a herd of my own younger mares, in foal to Falcon's Lance and they've all dropped successfully and are carrying again."

"Yet we're pressing immature stock into training."

"He doesn't seem the worse for it."

Dhuran shook his head, bit and bridle rattling, his luxurious mane tossing about as he did.

"True that," Lara admitted. "He's got a good gait."

"Neat hooves on that one. Nice legs. You might want to keep him around."

"I might." Lara inhaled and exhaled gustily, realizing that as she had relaxed, both her body and the horse had stopped being quite so uncomfortable. She picked up a hank of Dhuran's mane between her fingers as she held the reins. The last time she could remember crossing this terrain, she and her troops had been riding double-time as they realized that the enemy came to make a stand in Larandaril, rather than returning to Ashenbrook and Ravela Rivers as anticipated, and they were all that stood between the Raymy and total annihilation.

Dhuran let out a nicker as her sudden tension sparked through him. He bent his head against the bridle, trying to lengthen his stride. She gently brought him back, all the while sweeping her lands with a keen gaze, looking at the overplay of the threads of its well-being that she could see with her Talents. She put one hand out to Bistane, signaling her desire to halt, and reined in her mount. She could see the hurt rising in Larandaril, like a haze over the fields and trees and while she could, she would put to rights those little things she saw, that she knew inevitably added up to a much bigger whole. With her guard at her back and Bistane at her side, Lara took a deep breath and stretched out her feelings, her commitment, her love for her lands and the threads which bound it together. Tiny frays here and there she smoothed and strengthened. Gaps she darned as she would a hole in a sock, nipping her power in and out, over and across. She did not alter what she touched, for her skills did not lay in the making of ways, nor was she creating new works out of old. She was dusting away cobwebs and dust specks that ought not have landed in the pattern of her kingdom, mending rents here and there, filing down rough and jagged edges where they appeared. The wards gaped open as though wounded, but she hadn't the strength to repair them, not yet. Those repairs would take a melding of her will as well as the Andredia's.

When she was finished, Lara closed her eyes, finding them suddenly dry and at the same time, ready to shed tears, and held them closed for a ragged breath or two. When she opened them, the gray morning had turned to a fitfully overcast and sunny day, shadows moving over them. Dhuran stood like a statue, only his ears moving.

Bistane unhooked his water canteen and passed it over.

She looked at him before realizing her mouth felt dry as sand and took it from his hands and first wet her mouth, and then swallowed two or three times in sudden thirst.

"You've been mending for about two candlemarks," he told her.

"That long?"

He nodded. "I had the guard dismount and rest their horses, but Dhuran would not give you up, so we stayed."

She passed the canteen back and then dropped the palm of her hand to the horse's neck, where she rubbed him in praise. Bistane took a good pull before capping it and relacing it on his saddle.

Lara ran fingers through her hair. "No sight of the squatters."

"They are there. Around the second bend, you should see the ramshackle buildings and tents they've raised. I run them out every season, but they filter back."

"To keep a watch on the portal."

"Yes. And the kingdom."

A thin-lipped smile rode her face. "They won't be expecting me in person."

"Those who know you will. But they do not."

"All right, then." Lara touched a heel to her horse's flank, setting him back into brisk motion.

There were banners up, around the bend, but not permanent flagpoles. Lariel held up at the sight of the tents and lean-tos, at the jagged edge their forays had torn into the forest shading the banks of the Andredia. Most of all, her eyes narrowed at the flags. These were traveling banners, and they bore Tressandre ild Fallyn's proud insignia, a jade T against the Fortress flag of black and silver. Lara felt her lips curl at the sight and her jaw tighten.

"How dare she," Bistane muttered, an echo of her own thoughts.

"Because she thinks she can, and should. I will give her that much; she thinks as many rulers do, in what she perceives as owed her."

"Do we truly think like that?"

She glanced to Bistane. "Not you or I, I believe, but many a tyrant over a small patch of ground wishes that patch to be bigger—and more malleable."

"Hmmm. An imperceptible scratch that begs to be itched."

"Precisely. Let's go stop her from satisfaction in my lands." Lara lifted her reins.

Black-and-silver–garbed men jumped to their feet outside a lavish, silken pavilion as they rode up, but their voices froze in their throats as they tried to call out both a greeting and a warning to their mistress. One managed to gulp down his astonishment and fall to one knee, even as the canopies around him stirred in great agitation and the inhabitants of the pavilion poured out into the open air.

Tressandre ild Fallyn exited last, her hair of dark honey colors flowing down the back of her shoulders, her ebony pants tucked neatly into the tops of her calf-hugging boots, her silver-and-black–daggered blouse hugging her curves. "Well, and a blessed day," she said smoothly. "Do I see our Warrior Queen not only awake but astride as well?" She tilted her head in curiosity, eyes wide but examining the scene closely, as if she expected that an imposter might ride in Lara's place.

"Awake, astride, and aware," Lara answered, bringing Dhuran to a pawing halt. "The battle is over. My lands are closed."

"Closed?" Tressandre turned on one heel, twisting her body about smoothly, hands in the air. "But we've good people here, guarding the portal for you."

"She's guards enough and these . . . people . . . have been warned about their trespass." Bistane dismounted and drew his sword in one movement, though he held his weapon across his chest.

"Trespass?" Tressandre repeated, with a slight pout of her full lips. "And we so quick to respond to the need for aid along the Andredia."

"Your brother died at my feet, his final act one of treason and attempted murder." Lara felt the attention snap to her, all except for Tressandre who turned to face her with liquid poise.

Although the ild Fallyn's face had to look up to her, she did so in such a way that Lara felt their gazes met on an equal level. Disdain fell across Tressandre's expression openly.

"My brother was blasted while trying to protect you from a Kobrir assassin's blade, an attack of extreme cowardice and surprise from a battlefield."

Lara felt the corner of her mouth curl up. "That assassin put his life in between mine and your brother, and foiled a slice from you as well, if I remember correctly. I may have fallen there, but I remember what I saw—and felt—as I went down. I did not die there, Tressandre ild Fallyn, nor did my memory. Alton died because my armor, studded with shards of the Jewel of Tomarq which has always stood against treachery and betrayal, flared out and caught him as he tried to remove my head from my shoulders. He failed, as did you. Do not think that because you and I are both Vaelinar that I have any love or consideration for you at all. Get off my lands. Stay off until and unless some twisted knot of diplomacy and circumstance forces me to treat with you."

Tressandre smiled briefly. "Royal courtesies are so uncommon and, obviously, difficult to deliver." She beckoned to her guardsmen to begin to pack up. "I may go, but my . . . our people . . . might stay."

"Not with my permission."

"How can you deny them, Lara? They came to view Trevilara through this hole between the worlds. They pray for a sight back on the world that birthed all of us. To return, if the hole ever widens and the bridge returns. We are exiles here, Lariel Anderieon. How can you deny them passage back, indeed, how can you not promise them safe passage, if the bridge appears again? Why would you send such hopeful hearts away?"

There were murmurs at her back, and they grew louder as Tressandre fell silent. Lara looked at them. Traders, farmers, a smith from the looks of him, a carpenter, at least one herbalist in the bunch as well as their sullen-faced partners and children. A few dozen, but she knew they had branches throughout the villages and cities of the First Home lands and what she did now would carry.

"Elect two families amongst you to stay and watch. I will allow NO more to stay on my lands that are not from Larandaril. That is my word. My men will see to it that it is carried out, and my good ally and friend Bistane Vantane is here to assist me as he has stood by me and the needs of my lands for all these seasons. Do not mistake his even nature for one that can be duped or misled into unwarranted mercy."

Bistane nodded to her. "My Lady."

Tressandre stepped forward and offered her hand. "Fairly done," she said, but ice gleamed in her eyes. She stripped her glove off, forcing Lara to do the same, bared skin to bared skin, as was customary.

Tressandre's power leaped through her hand to Lara, charging blunt into her, a brutal assault on Lara and she sat back in her saddle a bit to brace herself and, biting into her lower lip hard enough to draw blood, she brought her own strength up to meet Tressandre. All fell into quiet around them, their eyes locked, and Lara fighting the tremor of her grasp. She could not fail in this, or the ild Fallyn would run roughshod over her weakness. She shoved back and gained no ground on the forces pounding through their bodies, but neither did she lose any more. It was like, she thought at the back of her mind, two great bruising men at arm-wrestling, but this contest struggled in silence and unseen.

Except she could see it. Could see Tressandre's fair skin pale a touch. The lines at the corners of her eyes deepened as she summoned up more of her will. Lara felt the back of her throat go coppery in taste. Her jaw tightened and a tic hit the corner of her right eye, a rhythmic spasm that was ever so slight and very annoying.

She could not give way. Lara reached out to the power of her lands, of the River Andredia, and felt her country answer her. Faintly. Sluggishly as if it had separated from her in her sleep and just now realized she'd awakened and so had their bond. She found a depth in her that the Andredia lent her, new strength, clean with new hope. She reached out to the wards which held the boundaries of her kingdom and touched them, fleetingly, retasking them and they answered. With a magical jolt, they told these invaders they were not welcome and that they would never be welcomed until Lariel herself let them pass. A feeling like fire ants would begin to swarm up their skin and grow ever more fervent until they left. The wards would harry and hound them to their deaths or Lara's guards found them first.

Tressandre's eyes flashed, and she let go of Lara's hand. She traded one last, appraising gaze with her.

"Choose your representatives wisely," she advised the Returnists at her heels. "I won't be here often to give guidance and support as I have in the past." She moved past Lara, her hair fairly crackling with energy as she did.

Lara turned Dhuran about sharply. She did not know if she could stay in her saddle. "I will meet you at the manor," she told Bistane, and set her mount toward home.

He caught up with her not far from the manor, for she had lost all ability to ride except for the effort just to stay aboard, and Dhuran had taken the bit in his teeth and headed to the stable yard, good lad, looking for dinner.

"Seven stayed back," he told her, "but otherwise, consider them routed."

"Good." She forced the word out through clamped teeth, set to keep from chattering like some snowbound idiot who did not know how to come in out of the cold. And cold? Why was it so blasted cold on this, a spring morning? Even one with hints of an evening rain?

Dhuran turned into the stable yard with a snort and a toss of his head. She steeled herself and found no steel at all within her. She might as well be as boneless as an egg.

She fell more than dismounted from her horse and took a staggering step before collapsing. Her body cramped into a tight knot, making her pant and gasp with the pain of it. She threw her arms over her head in defense and lay there, crumpled, her limbs turning back on themselves in agonizing knots.

Bistane hit the ground beside her. "What is it?"

"Cramps. Knots, everywhere." She could hardly talk. Even her lungs squeezed tightly.

"You're depleted." He swept her up, with a mutter that might have been "Fool woman." Or not.

Lara pressed her throbbing temple against his chest and tried not to feel the agony of her body. She felt the jolt in his body as he kicked the door open to the kitchen, shouting for juice as he made his way to the back stairs and took them, two at a time to her rooms. A figure darted in front of them to throw open her apartment and hastily pull the coverlet straight on the bed just before Bistane put her down on it. She stayed rolled on her side, intense spasms driving all thought but pain out of her head.

"Help me get her boots off. And the shin guards, too." Bistane's strong hands tugged and drew on her feet and ankles until her boots gave way and she sank back with a sob. "Is that juice?"

"For the breakfasts, aye, but what has happened?"

"I'll take that, and nothing you need know about."

A babble of voices, one of which she recognized as Gundrid, her chief cook, and Bistane thrust a glass into her hand and up to her lips. "Drink."

She could barely hold the vessel. More juice splashed onto her chin than through her lips, and he stepped close to hold it steady.

"What's wrong with her? What is it?"

"She just overextended herself. Now get out and let me get this down her."

"Going, Lord Bistane, going. Call if you need anything else."

She could feel the sweet wetness going down her throat now, uncurling her lungs, her arms, but her legs stayed furiously cramped up as she let out a deep moan of hurt.

He simply said, "I'm here" and tilted the last of the drink down her before moving to her legs. "Take deep breaths and listen to me." He poured another round from the jug and fed her sips. "Too much, too soon—but you know that. I should let you rest, but I can't. You burned out everything you had, even your Talent, and your body is going into shock. But you'll recover. This time. You can't show anyone else your weakness. It will get back to the ild Fallyn, it always does. So you'll drink for me and bear the pain."

Lara gave a feeble nod. Her mind began to work properly again. She isolated and then shoved her pain down into her legs and prayed for survival. Her limbs twitched. His fingers found the knots in her muscles and bore into them, hurting keenly at first before forcing them to submit and loosen.

"Why do you care?"

His hands paused. Then began working away at her again. "The correct thing to say would be that you are my Warrior Queen."

"But that's not why."

"No. Because . . . That was admirable," Bistane told her, as he straightened her out and flexed his strong hands about her legs, patiently massaging away the cramps.

It took her a moment to find her words. "How can you say that? I nearly got myself killed."

"But she didn't know that. Only you and I know that."

"She does know she nearly had me."

"She's nearly had you a dozen times in your life. But Tressandre only knows that she's never been able to kill you, and that you have never tried to kill her, only defend. That's got to hurt, in her small world." He stopped talking for a moment, concentrating on one stubborn knot in her left leg, fingers working until her foot smoothed out and toes relaxed. "Take your victories where you can."

"Now you remind me of your father."

He kept working at sore spots in her lower limbs, making her kick feebly in protest every now and then as he hit a particularly troublesome area. "Would he have been wrong? Am I wrong?"

Lara let out a soft, hissing sigh. "No. Neither of you."

"Nice to be acknowledged."

"Then why do you sound peeved?"

Bistane drew his hands away from her and stood up. "Because you knew you weren't ready. Because no advice I would have given you would even have been considered. Because you nearly got yourself killed."

She stretched one slender leg out, achingly free of cramps and knew it would be sore the rest of the day, but whole and flexible. "I thought we covered that already."

"Not entirely." Bistane pulled up a stool and sat by the edge of the bed, his leathers creaking slightly as he did so. "You need to pick your battles wisely."

"I have done, mostly."

"What was it that drove this one?"

She sat up and leaned over her other leg, rubbing where he had stopped. She wasn't nearly as good at it as he was, but this way she didn't have to look him in the eyes. "I'm not quite sure what you mean."

"I think you have a good idea. I'm asking, Lara, if it was your decision to go after Tressandre or if the Andredia asked it of you."

"The river."

"The river with which your family has a blood pact. The elemental of that river."

"You ask me things of which I cannot speak." Lara spoke quietly as she worked on the arch of her right foot, her toes splayed uncomfortably. The pain of the cramping hurt far less than his words.

"I'm not asking you to reveal the words of your sacred pact, damn it, Lariel. I am trying to understand what drove you to attack a formidable enemy when you had neither the ability nor the justification to do so."

"I thought you had my back."

"Always. I just have never had your trust or your love." Bistane stopped abruptly, as did her hands working her foot and ankle.

Lara found she could not quite breathe or swallow for a few moments. Then she looked up uncertainly. This time it was he who could not look at her. The silence stretched out until she had to break it. "I trust you."

"Let me amend that to—you've never trusted me as you did my father."

"He was an experienced warlord."

"True. And I rode at his side for most of those centuries, and now I have become the warlord. Most people do not bother to separate us in their considerations."

Her foot cramped harder, and they both reached at the same time as she curled in response to it, his warm hands over her cool ones. He brushed her fingers aside gently.

"You're right, of course." She watched his hands as he worked at her sore points. "It's not that I don't trust you."

"Is it not?"

"No. It's that I've lost Gilgarran. Osten. Jeredon. Bistel. Tranta. Sevryn and Rivergrace are gone, and might be lost, no one knows for certain. All allies that I could, and did, lean on. I'm afraid to lean on anyone else, lest they be taken, too. It's that simple. I can't afford to lose any more trusted friends."

He cracked her foot gently and dropped it to the cushion before sliding up to work on her calf. "Loss and gain are part of life."

"Don't wax philosophic at me. Half those I named died far before their time, and you miss them as much as I do."

"I miss them, yes, but that's not kept me from reaching out for others. My brother Verdayne and I are closer than ever. We have long lives and we avoid death as we can, but it comes to all of us, and none of us like it." He tapped her ankle. "How do you feel?"

"Bruised but no longer in spasms. Thank you." She sat up and swung her legs over the side of the bed. She took a deep breath. "I take your criticism that I acted rashly. My pact dictates that I owe the Andredia reparations, but never would the sacred river ask for more death. That was my choice. My wish. My desire. I hate Tressandre." She sucked in a breath. "But I wasn't ready and defeated myself as much as Tressandre did."

"Then train for it. You've been abed for years, Lara, and only up for a week. You're in no shape to be the Warrior Queen you were."

She nodded. "I realize that. I will begin training again."

"To what end?"

"To being better. To being prepared because Tressandre will try again, and she won't stop until I stop her."

"No," he agreed mildly, "She won't stop. She is queen of a stony fortress built on rock and ice. Larandaril has always looked like a promised paradise to her, one that comes with power and respect. It's no wonder she covets it."

"No wonder at all, but she doesn't deserve it. She never has and never will." Lara stood gingerly, one hand up to stay whatever aid Bistane might give. "About that other thing."

A shadow swept his face, disappearing. "Mmm. That other thing."

"I love you, too."

He watched her face. "But . . ."

"I was always told that whenever I married, it would not be for love, but for the ties of alliance and compromise."

"Of course."

"Time hasn't changed that."

He got to his feet as well, pushing the stool out of the way with a shove of his boot. "It won't, when viewed that way."

"Am I wrong?"

"I don't know. Yet."

"When I am, will you tell me?" She reached out and put her hand on his forearm.

"I intend to speak up loud and clear."

"Good." She turned her back to him. "When you go out, tell the staff I don't want to be disturbed." She made a face which he could not see but heard in her voice. "I fear I have to take a nap."

"And when you wake, we'll have to consider the import of this. One of the Returnists gave it to me." He pulled bloody rags out, the garb of a Kobrir assassin, like those she'd last seen Sevryn Dardanon wearing.

"Where did they come from?"

"Once in a while, very rare occasions, something material comes through the portal. We have an ally amongst the camp of Returnists, and she took up this find and held it for me—for you—when next one of us would come check on them."

She stirred her hand through the rags. "They have to be Sevryn's."

"But he is not wearing them."

The blood had dried, stiff and rusty brown, but unmistakable to anyone who had ever been around war and battle and injuries. "Not now."

"Perhaps there was a Kobrir among those who followed Quendius across."

She shook her head slowly. "No. I don't think so."

"Nor do I, but I am not fond of any other explanation."

She managed a deep breath. "If anyone can cheat death, it's Sevryn. Was there anything else? Sign of Rivergrace?"

He shook his head. Lara curled the rags to her chest. "I do have to sleep," she told him. "But now I'm afraid I might dream."

He wrapped his arm about her shoulders. "Don't be. The best dreams lie ahead of us. I'll do whatever I can to make certain of that."

Chapter Nineteen

TRESSANDRE ILD FALLYN brought her horse to a halt, taking in the small croft and its garden, and a somewhat bedraggled looking field beyond it. Her mouth thinned. Chased out of Larandaril by a woman barely off her deathbed who could hardly think. Yet Lara managed to hold her at bay. Her, the pride of ild Fallyn. A bitter taste ran down the back of her throat. If there had been no witnesses, she would have slipped her knife from its wrist sheath and put it deep into Lariel's gut and twisted and twisted . . . Just as she should have been the one two moons ago to slit her throat while she was still locked in sleep. A multiple failure, that had been. Neither Lara nor her heir had been successfully terminated. She knew now that the assassin had no chance at the child, the filthy Dweller kind had been taken away but not out of harm. Calcort would be far easier to penetrate than the manor at Larandaril. She would reach in and squeeze the heart of the heir into death throes soon enough. If only she could have dispatched Lara.

But she could not and had not and now she was barred from Larandaril, its legendary wards once again activated. The wards were not of Vaelinar Talent and magic, although it took a Vaelinar to activate them. No, they were part of a blood-and-flesh pledge made to the River Goddess of the River Andredia, a pledge that Tressandre had long considered how to corrupt and break. So far, her research and efforts had proved fruitless. The border wards, invisible but pervasive, walled in Larandaril successfully. She could get past it, but she would have to consider her options carefully, because when she entered the kingdom again, she wanted no alarm or warning. She would take Lara down.

In the meantime, she faced this insignificant and scrubby collection of abodes. This was Kerith as it had been before her people had arrived and elevated the civilizations they found. Before their priceless contributions had been ladled out, like a life-giving soup. Tressandre wrinkled her nose at the backwater settlement. A hedge ran its borders rather than a fence and it did not look as though it had been terribly successful in keeping out pests, with frequent, gaping holes in its evergreen branches. The cottage fared little better, listing a bit to one side as if its builder had not known how to build on the square. A loose shingle or two flapped in the spring breeze. Even among the poorest on her stronghold estates, she'd seen nothing like this. The cottage would never have survived the harsh coastline of her territory or its windy winters. This was free man's land, and what good did it do them? They barely existed at all. She set her heels down in her stirrups and waited for her man to emerge. If this were not the place she had been informed it was, there would be cold hell to pay. She would brook no more failures. Her fingers tightened on the reins.

"What is taking so long? Either we have the right place, or we do not." No one dared answer her.

The wind circled about to tug on her hair, tangling the dark honey-colored strands that had escaped her riding scarf. It felt like it had tiny feet embedded in its touch, scribble-scrabbling across her skin wherever it could touch her. Annoying. Chiding.

Tressandre stood in her saddle a moment to stretch her legs. It had been a long ride, and it had better not have been without results. The curve of her full mouth thinned more, along with her temper.

"If he's not out in three breaths, we ride off without him."

"Lady Tressandre, he'll be outnumbered. Even with nothing but knives and hoes, the villagers could bring him down. We can't leave him behind."

Her chin went out. "Then he does not deserve to be called ild Fallyn, and his end would be a just one."

"But we can't just leave him here—"

She turned in her saddle to look upon the man, Kreshalt, who paled as soon as she did. He clamped his lips shut.

"The first bit of wisdom you've shown," Tressandre remarked. She settled once again.

A handful of similar cottages were scattered about this small settlement, and she'd no doubt there were noses pressed to the shutters, eyes fixed upon them. Unlike Kreshalt, however, she did not fear their numbers.

All the better to crush them, as they would fumble in each other's way, uncertain and untested in battle.

Tressandre took a deep breath. If Alton were here, she would have no need to worry about the quality of the intelligence she was acting upon now, nor the ultimate result, or who would be warming her bed enthusiastically tonight. No worries at all. But her brother was dead and gone these two years, and her chest tightened at the memory of him. Half-blasted to a crisp and shriveled as if lightning-struck, the other half near sliced away from him by a blade. Fallen and dead far before his time, no matter that he was attempting to assassinate the Warrior Queen in the middle of battle. No matter that Alton had not been able to achieve the moment for which they had planned nearly their entire lives. No matter that that which others called betrayal they, the ild Fallyn, knew was only fulfillment of their destiny. The moment spent, blackened, dying and dead at her feet.

She would kill Lara with her bare hands for that memory.

The ragged wooden door to the croft banged open. A man, woman, and half-grown boy stumbled out, followed by Nikton, the man she'd sent in. His black-and-silver garments shone in the meager sun like the richly woven clothes they were, in brilliant contrast to the drab homespun wear of the other three. The man of the family went to his knees. "Mercy, Lady ild Fallyn. We have done nothing."

She could barely discern a recognizable face behind all the grime. Tress shifted her gaze to her man. "Are these the ones?"

"Husband, sister, and son," he answered. "I am certain."

"They are under your guardianship, then. You know where to take them. No need to let them gather any goods. The poorest of what we will give them will be the richest of anything they've had."

"Yes, Lady."

She pivoted her horse about and let her hand fall, hard, upon the horse's shoulder, and let it take to its heels. She'd enough of stinking poverty for the day. There were things she had had to do and steps that still lay ahead of her to exact the vengeance she had in mind. Her horse threw up its head and nickered a challenge to the wind rushing at both of them, and she leaned lower in her saddle to urge it faster.

Chapter Twenty

"EVARTON, that honeycomb is better on the inside than out. You're making Merri all sticky." Nutmeg dropped her mending in her lap for a moment, eyes narrowed, daring the two children to turn and look at her stern reprimand although neither did. In fact, Evar scooted over on his bottom so as to present a broader view of his back. Merri raised a chubby arm in the air and then let her hand fall on her twin's auburn curls, golden honey dripping from between her fingers. Nutmeg closed her eyes for a moment, envisioning a sooner-than-later bath time.

She put her mending aside and got to her feet. Her slim dress fell in graceful folds to her ankles as she made it to the children's sides in three quick strides, grabbed each by an ear, and called for their Auntie Corrie. Evarton tried to squirm away from her fingers pinching his ear. "Don't need Auntie Corrie."

"Possibly, but you do need a bath. Rotten apples, but you've got honey from head to toe."

He danced about, giving her a crooked grin and a look. "I smell sweet!"

"Me, too!"

Nutmeg bent over to give each a kiss and smacked her lips. "And taste good, too!" She straightened. "Corrie?"

No answer. Gryton, one of the Vaelinar guards on duty, poked his head in from the threshold. "The auntie is not about the household."

"Oh. That's a long walk she's taking." Never mind that it was afternoon, with sunlight blazing its way into the farmhouse windows, illuminating her two mischief-makers and making their honey coating sparkle here and there. Merri giggled and waved her free hand at the erstwhile guard who saluted back before retreating to his guard position.

"That's it for the mending for a bit, then," and she leaned down and picked up Merri.

Evar's brow knotted. "My turn for carry!"

"Your turn was yesterday, aye? So today is Merri's turn."

He folded his arms over his chest and his lower lip stuck out. He countered. "Auntie carry both us."

"Well, Auntie is a good bit taller than I am, is she not? I've got shorter arms as well as legs."

"Mum's better."

Nutmeg smiled down at Evar. "That's a sweet thing to hear! But you're still getting a bath. Keep up with me now."

Evarton threw a beguiling look up at her. "Outside?" he suggested.

"In the trough?" Nutmeg hugged Merri a bit closer, shifting her weight. "I suppose it is warm enough. Outside it is!" And she marched them out the backdoor to the horse trough, sitting in the sunlight next to the sweet water well that Rivergrace had restored their first years in Calcort. On the way out the door, Nutmeg reached out to snag a bar of soap and a rough towel from the kitchen shelves. She dumped Merri into the trough, clothes and all, as Evar grabbed the wooden side and swung himself in as if he were mounting a horse. She dared not help him, but the effort was touch and go until he got past the tipping point and literally fell in. After the splash, he emerged with a triumphant grin on his face.

Bath or not, she had both children laughing and squirming as she washed. Evar, as was his habit, loved the water and the splash more than the soap, but Merri took the bar from Nutmeg and scrubbed herself, little face scrunched in concentration as she did. Then Nutmeg ran a dipper of clean water over their heads. The clothes came off midway to be draped over the next hitching post, and when they were all done, the children helped her tilt the trough to let the dirty water run off. She lifted both out and set them on the ground. "Now, don't be getting yourselves all dirty again!"

Two shiny faces grinned up at her. Evarton huffed and puffed as he pumped the trough full of clean, fresh water. The water ran through their toes and Merri stomped until she had a mud puddle squishing up through her toes.

"Oh, no, you don't!" Nutmeg told her and grabbed her up, holding those little feet under the pump as Evar gave it a few pulls "for Merri."

"A'right, then, that's done it. Clean clothes and blocks for you two."

He marched beside her, wiping his bare feet on the reeds covering the back steps, his mouth pursed in attempts to whistle, a skill he'd not yet learned but kept trying, inspired by Verdayne's melodic skills. His wheets and whoots trailed behind Nutmeg as she led the children in and quickly redressed them. She sat back on her heels before using the same rough towel to quickly wipe down their play area where tiny drops of honey glistened on the floorboards. It seemed her whole day was filled with the care of these two, something she could never have imagined before. Before, she filled her days working at her mother's tailoring shop and early mornings and evenings at her father's vineyards and presses. Not to mention the adventures and mishaps that often followed Rivergrace and their friends.

Friends like Jeredon. Nutmeg sat back and watched her two children play. She wouldn't be able to hide Evarton much longer as their auntie's son. Every moment that passed, he grew more and more into the likeness of his father. His bloodline showed not only in his physical features, the high elven blood obviously, but in his coloring so like Jeredon and then the most telling—his attitude. He walked like the man he'd never seen, he laughed like him, he looked on life as Jeredon had with a zest for the dangerous as well as the humorous. He charmed everyone around him, especially his sister. He would never be as tall as Jeredon, but Evar walked in his shoes, no doubt. And he could brood as his father did—deep, dark moods that no one, not even the sister he adored, could dispel. She also saw his stubbornness (that would be her), his dogged determination to accomplish what he wanted (Tolby), and his love of colorful things (Lily).

She saw a multitude of wonderful things in Merri, too, but it wasn't Merri who worried her. Who put those few silvery strands in her own hair that would no doubt turn to all silver in its own good time without Evar to hurry it!

Would she still have loved Jeredon if he hadn't been who he was? She couldn't imagine how he might have been as a father. He had had little patience with himself when he had been injured and she had spent a season nursing him. If she hadn't, perhaps he would still have been too crippled to fight at Ashenbrook and Ravela, where he met his life's end. If . . . if . . . if.

She felt as petulant now as Evarton could get.

She watched as Merri attempted to soothe him over some imagined slight. Perhaps she had taken more than her share of the building blocks, for her peace offering was to slide a few over toward him, especially two of the bright red ones that she favored. He slapped them back. Merri's face crumpled up for a moment as if she might cry. Instead, she shrugged and took them back, adding them to a pile in her skirted lap. Nutmeg bit the inside of her cheek trying not to laugh at the two of them. But that was the way to treat the pouter. Shrug off his emotion in indifference after trying to give him what he wanted. She wondered where her small but capable daughter had learned that. Surely not from—

"Nutmeg?"

"Hmmm?" Out of the corner of her eye, she caught Dayne looking into the room.

"Brista said you were looking for Corrie?" The second of their two Vaelinar guards.

"If anyone around here wants their socks darned and their buttons replaced, I am." Nutmeg nudged her basket of mending.

"She's walking home now." Dayne stepped in and grinned at the two who were now head to head, playing and chattering to each other in childish nonsense although Evar still carefully had his back to his mother. "Want me to spell you?"

"No, I'll wait. She shouldn't be long." The stout Kernan woman worked from sunrise to sunset to help with the twins, and she lived in a comfortable, newly built corner room of the farmhouse, constructed after the place had been half-burned down by an attack from the ild Fallyn, seasons ago. Nutmeg had been carrying then, big as a house, and yet she and Dayne had nearly eluded capture even as pregnant as she was. That, they hadn't escaped until days after, but they had. Otherwise, who knew where the children would be today, or if Tressandre would even have let them live. The ild Fallyn did not treat for ransom. It was power or death, to them.

Dayne put his back to the wall, settling comfortably. He stayed silent, as if unwilling to disturb her thoughts and did they show, tumbling around in her stubborn head? She could often see Merri working things out, but she also had this way of sticking her tongue slightly out of the corner of her mouth as she did. Little pink tongue and apple red cheeks.

"Do you think it's writ in the blood?"

"It has to be, doesn't it? That and how we raise them," Dayne said easily.

"We won't be able to hide him much longer."

"Hopefully, we won't have to. I have had some news that a Kobrir has come to Larandaril."

"The one that tried the last assassination?"

"No, no. My brother says that one was one of Tressandre's and he doesn't say such things lightly or without proof. No. He's been looking to the Kobrir for a cure. Perhaps one is on its way."

"Or they're giving up entirely."

"Now I don't know who in your family tree is such a gloomy pessimist, but I wouldn't have said it was you!"

The two of them suddenly became aware that the room had gone very silent, and they turned their faces to see both children, quiet and still, listening.

Dayne chuckled. "I think, Mistress Nutmeg, that discussions are best held at naptime."

"In matters of state, I think I must agree with you." She stood and straightened her skirts, and bent to pick up her basket. "Watch them for a few while I see if Corrie is in sight?"

"Most certainly."

But Dayne did not stay with his back to the wall as he had been. Instead, he crossed the room and got down on his knees, to examine whatever it was they had been building, and the children started talking again, to each other and to him. Meg smiled as she went out the doorway, he and the children passing blocks back and forth.

Evarton drew back and let his sister work on whatever it was she was concentrating on making, her little mouth drawn into a bow of total attention. He leaned against Dayne's elbow quietly for a moment or two. Then he announced, "Wanna dog."

"What? A dog? Ah, lad, but no. No, no. Your mom's got enough trouble to take care of, without bringing a pup into it. Maybe when you get a bit older, I'll find us a hunting dog or maybe a good pest runner."

Evar's lip trembled. "Wanna dog now."

Dayne put his hands about the boy's shoulders. "Not today, lad. But I'm not saying no forever, you understand? In a while."

Evarton sighed and leaned forward, intent once more on gathering up his fair share, and then some, of the building materials. Dayne sat back on his heels, watching. If there was one fault Nutmeg had, it was that she hated to say no to either of them, which made the occasional denial hard for them to take. Merri would often find some other amusement to make herself laugh, but Evar could be quiet and dark about it for days. Verdayne didn't know what his father had been like, so he couldn't agree with Meg if it had been writ in his blood or not, but it worried him. Life would be stuffed with nos along the way, and it was best to know when to be stubborn about it and when to accept it.

When Corrie returned, she smelled of the sun and citrus. Evar immediately knew that she'd eaten a sweet fruit without bringing them one back, too, as their mom or Dayne would have done, but he didn't belong to Auntie, not really, even though he had to say he did. She often didn't share. She came in with a cheery "Allo" to Dayne and lowered her bulk on the wooden rocking chair, which creaked ominously as she did. Dayne eyed it and made a mental note to check the joints on it the following day, whenever it was unoccupied. She waved him off. "I'll take charge from here."

"Did you have a pleasant outing?"

"Bracing. Fair bracing it was. Passed a brawl out by the tavern." She shook her head. "Some men simply cannot hold their drink. But I'm back in one piece, so all's well."

"Get a letter, did you?" Dayne smiled as though his face might break.

"I did and enjoyed every word of it. Now go on wi' you. This is my job here," and she looked fondly on the two playing somewhat quietly in the corner near their beds.

Dayne nodded and stepped out before she could commandeer him for some task or other, as she was wont to do. Without looking at their auntie, Evar said to Merri, "Sleepy."

"Nuh-uh!"

He put his slender hand over her full lips. "Ssssh. Sleepy," and he looked at their auntie this time.

"Oh," Merri mumbled from behind his hand. Then she thrust it away from her face and shook her red block at him.

He pinched her knee lightly but not enough to hurt and they went back to building towers as high as they could get them, which, with their dexterity was not very. After a few moments and a nudge to the ribs from her brother as a reminder, Merri began to hum a little song. She could carry a tune, surprisingly, and her pleasant little choice mimicked the one both Lily and Nutmeg sang while at their looms. It paced the movements of weaving nicely, with a repetitive cadence that soothed as she sang it. Before long, Auntie Corrie let out a snorting snore and then settled in to a steady, rhythmic noise of her own.

"Sleepy," noted Evar in satisfaction. He took up one of the red blocks, wrapping his hand and fingers about it, the block nearly too big for him to hold. He stared at it for long minutes, until a frown mark deepened in his forehead, like a wrinkle come to stay. He gave a little grunt. When he opened his hand, he smiled at a shiny red apple which he handed to his sister.

She took it and promptly crunched her pearly little teeth into it. It sounded like a crisp apple being eaten, but she made a face and spat it onto the floor. "Yuck." She dropped the apple on his lap.

Evar picked it up, eyeing it closely. He finally sniffed it. Then he took a tiny nibble from it himself. "Ugh. Taste like dirt."

"Dirt better," Merri told him, and went back to constructing her tower. She tapped the apple. "Empty. No life." And she sat it on the top of her structure where it wobbled a bit and then steadied and she grinned.

Evar went on his belly to pull something out from under his bed. It scraped along the floorboards with a horrible noise that almost disturbed their auntie's snoring. He positioned it proudly, a stone statue of a war dog half the size of Merri. He patted it on its head. "My dog."

Merri nodded. She pointed at her blocks. "Mine."

Evar laughed at her, a soft indulgent chuckle. He drew his stone dog closer and wrapped both hands about it. He murmured, "Wanna dog." He looked at it, into it, and drew his forehead together tightly. For long, long moments he did not move, his breathing quieted, his heart pounding so loudly that Merri tilted her head to hear it.

The stone began to change under his fingers. It went from stone gray to clay red, then the dappled chestnut sheen of a living coat. The pelt spread, slowly at first and then rapidly, covering the entire sculpture. Then nails, black-and-ivory ones, sprang from the feet. A black nose. White whiskers. Eyes grew out of the stone and opened to look at him. The dog . . . for dog it appeared . . . the Vaelinaran war dog, took a shuddering breath and opened its jaws. White fangs showed from lips curling back.

Evarton sprang to his feet and backed off as the beast snarled. He grabbed Merri by the elbow and shoved her behind him. The thing lived. It breathed. Its tail went down as it clambered to its four legs. It swung its head back and forth, opening its jaws wider. A tongue flopped out, but it was not a wet red tongue. It had withered and blackened. Its breath stank as it panted anxiously. The dappled coat rose in hackles along its neck and shoulders.

Evarton could hardly stay on his feet, the effort to transform it had drained him so badly, but he staggered back in shock. This was not a dog anyone would want. He didn't know what he could do. It began to growl deeply, its tail down at its haunches, its eyes flat and dark as it slunk forward.

Evarton gulped, but it was Merri who let out a piercing scream.

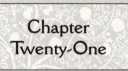

Chapter
Twenty-One

CORRIE CHARGED TO HER FEET, and the war dog swung its massive head in her direction.

Before Merri could gasp for breath and start another yell, she grabbed up her immense shopping bag dropped by the side of the rocking chair and swung it at the beast as it pivoted to leap at her. "Run, fast as you can!" She looked about and reached for the chair itself to fling.

Gryton lunged through the threshold and barreled past the auntie, his short sword down and aimed at the creature's chest. Evar stumbled to one side, carrying Merri with him as the guard and dog clashed. The beast shied away, a shrewd intelligence in its coal-black eyes, snapped its head about, and grabbed the spear shaft behind its point to shake it violently. Gryton, off balance, went to one knee to keep hold of the weapon. He gave out a shrill whistle to signal Brista, the other guard on duty, to come to his aid even as the dog spat out the spear shaft and launched a twisting charge into the curve of Gryton's neck before he could get back on his feet. He plunged into the guard's shoulder, twisting him around on his knee, and doubled back with a slavering growl to sink his fangs deep into his prey.

Crimson spurted. Gryton yelped, as did the dog, as his free hand swept up with a wicked short knife buried in his fingers, scraping across the dog's skull. Blood, thick and dark, welled up from the cut as though the beast did not wish to bleed. The dog gave no sign of pain. Did it even know it had been knifed? He managed to shake his attacker loose, but his neck wound gaped open, blood flowing freely. Gryton grappled with the animal as it plunged again and again at his neck, blood slicking both of them and splattering the floor. The dog's toenails scrabbled against the floorboards for traction as it dug in, jaws snapping and slashing at Gryton's hands, the guard frantically trying to protect himself, his lifeblood spurting out with every heartbeat. Corrie found the courage in her to haul up the rocking chair and approach the fighting two, all the while crying, "Get back, get back!" The dog grabbed hold of the chair's runner, his jaws splintering the wood before spitting it out and gathering his legs under him for balance. The beast returned to Gryton, determined to keep his prey down and helpless.

Brista entered and skidded to a halt, her green-gold eyes sweeping the room and taking in the situation. She grabbed Auntie Corrie by the shoulder and threw her outside the room, clearing it, but she could not reach the children, for they huddled on the far side of the attack, with only a wall and open window at their back. When the dog finished with Gryton, it would turn on them or Brista, and she made a determined noise, already in the process of attracting the beast away from the children.

With the blunt end of her spear, Brista tried to engage the snapping dog, to fill its jaws with wood, to turn it from Gryton who sank lower and lower to the floor in weakness, his movements growing more feeble by the heartbeat. The dog paused in its attack long enough to swing its sight to her.

"Evarton. Get your stool. Climb out the window. Help your sister, too."

The dog left off worrying at Gryton and dropped into a crouch, preparing for a leap in her direction.

"He'll follow." Evarton reached out a shaky hand and began to drag his little stool toward them and the window. Blocks scattered every which way as he did, and the dog's ears flicked, hearing.

"Outside?" Merri added, as if the guard might not be right.

"Outside," Brista said firmly. "Get outside and climb the fire ladder."

The ladder affixed to the side of the house had been installed after the last fire when the ild Fallyn attacked, its purpose to aid bucket carriers in getting to the vulnerable roof. She knew the children climbed it sometimes, when they thought their mischief wasn't being noted. She and Gryton had noted, but not stopped, their explorations. Climbing a ladder seemed a good survival skill, and what would be the harm in learning it? Maybe a sprained wrist or scraped knee if they fell?

"Now," Brista ordered and could say no more as the war dog launched itself at her. It hit her spear point, heavy as a barrel full of mud bricks and her spear did as little damage as it could, the point snapping off in the dog's chest and then falling out, to the ground. She had a second in which to feel astonishment before having to swap ends of her spear yet again, this time aiming the blunt end at open jaws snapping at her. She tried to gouge an eye, but the wood merely slipped off the dog's thick skull and in the end, she let the spear be pulled from her hands as the dog caught it in its jaws and worried at it.

She pulled her sword and moved to her right, drawing the dog away from Gryton's now inert form. His body spread out limply, blood slowly pooling under him, bleeding out. She could not save him, and he was not her ward. Her duty rested with the children. Brista's glance flickered to the movements at the window. Merri had gained the sill, stretching out her hand to Evar.

"Move!" she cried to the little heir. "Leave him if you have to!" Lara's heir ranked most important, but the son of a wet nurse could hardly matter. She had no more time for words as the war dog came after her in earnest, its dark eyes gleaming with malice. She backed up toward the doorway, determined to keep it at bay yet keep it occupied. Behind her she could hear sounds, Nutmeg hurrying in and shaking Corrie to get a coherent word out of the hysterical auntie and behind them, Verdayne. His calm words put them both in the background and out of range.

Verdayne could be counted on for backup. Brista smiled grimly. She slashed out at the dog's forepaws before it could charge her again, jaws agape, and it danced back, its growls filling the room. The dog seemed impervious when she did land a hit, blood barely welling up from the slice, the contact only making him growl louder and snap at her quicker. She sized up her opponent, with the looks of a war dog but perhaps less than half the size of one, and certainly none of the training. At the same time, it was built like a brick guardhouse. She would exhaust herself trying to hit at it, hoping to make a dent in it. It couldn't be hacked apart, built of squat and heavy muscles, and yet fast enough to dodge her strokes again and again. She parried against his attacks, but she had to brace herself again and again and found the dog hit like a barrel of stone. She could not hold it back much longer and had no idea of what it would take to drop it. No ordinary beast this, not any war dog like she'd ever seen on the battlefield, or even a mongrel trotting down a country lane or street. Witchery? Perhaps. With a grunt, she parried against another lunge.

She spared a glance at the children, only to catch Evarton standing atop the stool to watch the fight. "Get out!" Brista ordered. "Now."

He gave her a look before turning to obey.

At her back, Verdayne Vantane said, "I have a crossbow. Soon as the lad is through the window, I dare shoot."

"Single or double bolt?"

"Double."

"That might bring him down. I fear Gryton is dead."

"You look to be right." Dayne spoke evenly behind her, his voice an echo of both his brother Bistane and the older, mourned, and gone Bistel. It always took her aback to see him barely head and shoulders above Dweller height, but that was mixed blood, always surprising.

The dog went for her ankle and caught her around the boot shaft, teeth sinking into and through the leather, piercing skin sharply and not letting go. She sliced off an ear and the beast seemed not even to notice it.

Dayne's dry observation. "You've anchored him. See if you can broadside him my way."

Lip caught between her teeth, Brista tried to swing her weight and bring the determined dog about, jaws clamped to chew her foot off. Pain thrust through her, but she did not scream, afraid to distract Evar and Merri; both would come back to the window to see what was happening.

The dog rolled his underbelly toward her. She took it, ramming her sword in all the way to the hilt. If the dog felt it, if it hit any vital organs, if it slowed the beast in his mauling at all, there came no sign. His teeth ground down harder on her ankle, and she thought he'd hit bone as agony lanced her.

"Lean back." Quiet, but urgent from Verdayne.

"Aye." She sliced off the other ear, doing no real damage that the creature took note of, but a slow, curling curtain of blood began to make its way into the dog's eyes and it blinked rapidly, growls muffled by her agonized flesh filling its jaws. Brista pulled the dog about another half a hand and then leaned back sharply.

"Now." Bolts whistled past her so near she could smell the oil on them from the windlass of the crossbow. He hit his target dead center and hard enough that the animal let go of her with a surprised yelp and fell to its flank, pawing at the floorboards, and turning its snapping jaws to the feathers sticking from its side.

Painfully, Brista got to her feet and raised her sword again. She cleaved a shot to its neck, cutting deeply, but not beheading the dog—which ought to have happened. Dayne cranked his bow for a second shot, saying, "Get out of my way."

She did. He advanced into the room and shot again, one of the bolts piercing so far through the dog's upper leg that it sank solidly into the floor, and the other headed to where a heart or lung ought to have been. He kept coming, pulling his long, thin dagger from a wrist sheath and sinking it into the nearest eye savagely. Yelps grew faint. The thrashing slowed.

Finally, the dog stopped moving.

"What, from the cold pit of hell, was that?" Brista collapsed to the floor, her hands wrapped about her ankle, trying to slow the bleeding.

"I've no idea. It was in here with the children when you came in?"

"Yes, hanging onto Gryton's throat. The auntie got out, but the children were cornered."

"I saw them go out the window." He looked up, frowning, and there the two stood, faces pale, watching him, little hands braced on the window frame.

Nutmeg ducked in. She bent to help Brista to her feet. "Let's get that tended to." She paused at the doorway.

"I'll get them," he told her, seeing her look the children over carefully. Meg nodded before hurrying the much taller guard out, her arm over her shoulders.

Merri stepped onto the stool, Evar behind her.

"I don't want you to see this."

They looked at Dayne and shook their heads. "Too late," Evarton said.

"How did the dog get in? Who brought him in?"

Evarton's eyes grew moist. "I made him."

"What do you mean?"

Merri's ungraceful tumble behind him, nearly knocking both of them off the stool and onto the ground, took Dayne's attention. He reached out and steadied them, and set them both down on the wooden perch.

"What do you mean, you made him?"

Evar brushed his sleeve against his nose. "Wanna puppy. I made him."

Merri shook her curly head. "No good. No insides. Told you!" and she elbowed her brother. "Like apple."

Evar sniffled. "Was dog."

"Was not. No insides."

Evarton gave her a little nudge, but she held her ground, mouth stiff.

Dayne looked to the carcass of the dog. It bled very little from any of its wounds. It had already stiffened into a rock-hard pose. He reached his hand out and poked it. What warmth it might have had, as the living did, had already fled. Disbelief rippled through him, leaving behind an icy track. Made him? He saw traces now and then, of things Evarton could and did alter. Nutmeg's ears. Her height, though barely perceptibly, although that had been a gradual thing over the seasons. Her eyes, too. Certain toys Evar liked but wanted a little different, like a coat of paint. Dayne was never sure if anyone noticed but himself and perhaps their mother. He had never heard of a Talent that created life out of . . . nothing. No being could. He looked Evarton over. Never in old Sinok's bloodline had there been a hint of this ability. Not Lara and certainly not Jeredon, although . . . he had heard stories that Jeredon could sense and recognize new life. He knew when favorite hounds or horses had conceived. Dayne shook his thoughts to clear them. He could not make the leap from recognizing the conception of life to forcing such a conception.

Evar stared at him, face pale and wide-eyed. Little Merri trembled behind him.

Whatever Dayne thought, the dog had to have come from somewhere. "What did you make it from?"

"My stone dog."

He looked into Evar's eyes. "My stone dog, you mean."

Evar's face flushed. He looked down at his knees. "Yeah."

He had had a stone dog, a parody of a war dog, sent to him by his brother, as a jest. It was to "hold down" his place in Bistane's heart and estates. The statue had disappeared. He flicked a glance at the beast lying pinned to the floor. Yes, it was about the same height and bulky weight as his stone-cast mascot. Evar had brought that to life?

But not a proper life nor even an Undead. Merri knew. It was her piercing scream that had sent him to the weapons' rack and brought him running to her. It was empty, unfinished, a construct without true life. Without soul. How had she known?

How had Evar done what he did?

Dayne took a deep breath. He did not know what to do with the knowledge he'd just been given, only that it put these two in even greater jeopardy. He put his hand out. "I won't tell that you took my stone dog if you promise not to tell that you tried to make it live." He waited. Two heads nodded. "All right, then. Let me get the two of you safe. Perhaps a trip to Lily's shop."

"Cake shop there. Grandma's friend," Merri informed him.

"Oh, is there?" He smiled down on her. Of course he knew it well. He and Nutmeg often had their hands full marching the two past it.

She squeezed his hand with her little warm one. "Yes, right there."

"Then if you and Evarton are good, we might go visit the cake shop."

"Mum?"

"I imagine she's the one who will walk you down." Dayne looked at them sternly. "You cannot go by yourself!"

"Oh, no. Never." And Merri squeezed his hand reassuringly as they walked by the bodies, seemingly not even noticing.

Evar's head, however, swiveled and he did not take his eyes off the two until Dayne led him through the playroom door. He whispered as he walked out of range.

Sadly. "Not alive."

Corrie watched the small family pass her by, without a word for her frayed nerves or thumping heart and head. She scratched at her right brow as the door closed, shutting them away from her. She hoisted her bag onto her lap. It seemed filled with inconsequential things: a boy's shirt, home-spun but with intricate embroidery on the collar and cuffs; a man's ring, crude but stamped with a seal not unlike one a noble might use; a woman's handkerchief, also embroidered, fancier than the boy's shirt but possibly done by the same hand.

Her son. Her husband. Her sister.

She knotted her fingers into the shirt. She never should have left the farm, but she needed to, they hadn't been doing well, and Tolby had bought spices from them for cider mulling and had made a generous offer. It had been generous, too, just as it had been generous for Tolby and Lily to take in the orphaned child of their wet nurse and raise it alongside their own granddaughter as if he were one of their own, and he a half-breed. It should be said in Merri's defense, Corrie thought, that the sweet little girl was a half-breed, too, although her Dweller nature far outweighed that of her Vaelinar blood. Still, as Corrie's father had said before her and her husband said now, blood will tell. It always did. It reared its ugly head in animals, proving traits both good and bad, and it showed in mortals, too. Still, the offer had been generous. Enough for them to think about buying new equipment, new seed, perhaps even hiring a man to work alongside her husband as they increased their holdings, and she herself had a grander home in the meantime. Tolby had offered her a five-year contract and paid for the first year in full, and that nearly gone now, but the money would be steady. He was a man of his word. She would be given a few weeks off, to go home, to love her own loved ones instead of making do with the children here.

Corrie sighed. She didn't know how the ild Fallyn had found her family. In the long year, she hadn't talked. Not once. She had done her duty as an auntie and done it well. Someone back at the village must have gossiped, and that spread to the wind, and the wind eventually came to rest on the rugged cliffs where the ild Fallyn stronghold perched and now she was left with this. This! She knotted her hands tighter into her son's shirt.

Tressandre ild Fallyn had taken her family hostage. Terms would be known later, as soon as she acknowledged the contact. Corrie could disavow her family. Ignore the demands being made upon her, but to do so would be to sentence her family to torture and then death. Lady ild Fallyn had said so.

That meant Corrie had no choice but to spy, didn't it? If she wanted her own family safe and free someday? To watch and report on the children. And such a report she would be writing as soon as she had the spare time to find paper, ink, and a messenger bird. Merri and Evarton had made a stone dog come to life. Nutmeg and Dayne were very careful not to mention it in front of her, nor even ask any questions about the incident, but Corrie had fallen asleep, hadn't she, her drooping gaze fastened on that self-same stone dog sitting in the shadows under the lad's bed.

Now missing. Or smashed to gravel, however it had been dispatched. It had come to a vicious half-life, growling and leaping at the same children who'd given it life.

No one acted as if they knew Corrie had seen a thing, but she had. A fistful of things that could not be explained away easily, and no one had asked her about the incident or inquired of her health.

It seemed to her that she had been paid well, but not well enough for this. The little girl had witch powers in her, the like of which hadn't been seen since the days of the Mageborn wizards. It hadn't come from her Vaelinar blood, for no one spoke of any such abilities among the High elven. No. Buried deep in her Kerith heritage lay a Dweller witch of incredible power, and it had leaped generations, as it was wont to do, and landed in little Merri. Corrie shuddered. She would have to watch the child like a hawk, and then decide what grains of knowledge to pass along to the Vaelinar mistress.

Gods help her, but she was walking a narrow line between the cold pits of hell and the sunbeams of the saved.

Corrie put her head down and sobbed, quietly, into the shirt crumpled in her hands.

Chapter
Twenty-Two

Trevalka

"WINTER IS ON OUR HEELS."

"It feels even closer." Rivergrace could not help but hug herself, the banked fire at her toes doing little to warm anything upward of her ankles. Her jaw ached from the chill and her nose had gone numb the moment she slipped out from under their meager blanket.

Sevryn dropped that poor ragged thing over her shoulders even as she thought of it. "I think I've found our haven."

Holed up deep in what she called wilderness, Grace couldn't think of anyone he'd been watching except for a small band of trappers. She said as much.

"They're the ones. Relatively isolated."

"And suspicious."

"To our advantage."

She peered up at him. "They'd be just as wary of us as they would anyone else."

"Not . . . exactly."

"The waters in these mountains are clean. I can't make friends by cleansing them."

"I don't think they are."

She dropped a corner of the blanket. "What?"

He squatted down close to her, his heat joining with hers, and for a moment she felt almost comfortable. "They're trappers, yes, but they also have a relationship with the trees. I've been watching them set up for the winter. We're north here, quite a bit north of the capital, and winter hits early here, so they're preparing for it. I'm not sure what they're doing, but it looks like they're bleeding the trees."

"What?"

He shrugged. "Your father is the farmer, the orchardist. I surrender to your expert opinion."

"I . . . I don't have one. Tree's blood, I've never heard of anything like that."

"I'll take you down to the outer edge of their range, but the thing is, they have tasted the sap and don't care for it. I think it's been tainted, by deep water, from their reaction. It's not extreme enough to do more than sicken them a bit, but it's in the trees. In anything that grows."

"Sap," Rivergrace repeated. She turned the thought over in her head. "It's nothing I'm familiar with, but if their ground water is corrupted, that I can handle. It would present in the sap, although what they're doing—I can't begin to guess. The river we've been at, I haven't detected much. It has to have gone deep, into the soil and rock. We know rivers run below, and the tainted source must have gone that way. We would have to search for where the water went underground. That may take a few days."

"Then we can start today and be prepared to produce a miracle for them to accept us."

She stood and began to fold her blanket. "A curse to drive them away and a miracle to bring them back. What have we walked into?"

He put his arm about her waist to draw her close. "Whatever we find, it only reinforces what you knew to begin with: Quendius has to be stopped, and Trevilara with him. We can't let the two of them bring whole-sale death to Kerith. To our friends. To our *family*."

She gifted him a tremulous smile at that. "You're right. I may need reminding again someday . . ."

"And I'll be here to do it."

"See that you are."

He grabbed the blanket she tossed him, and began to snub out their campfire. The rains had not yet begun in these highlands on a steady basis, and he wanted no spark or heat left behind them. It made for difficulties if they had to return to a previous campsite, but he would cope with that if necessary. Better than trying to outrun a wildfire. They were packed in short order, Grace waiting for him with her hand stroking her horse's soft muzzle and the animal affectionately nuzzling her back.

He led them out of the highlands by a gentle, circuitous route, unwilling to meet any of the trappers before he was ready. It took them three days of searching before they found the headwaters which went underground in the forested area. Grace knelt by the burbling river, wide and still, not at its height by any means because the rainy season hadn't swelled it yet, and even that season would give way to the spring melt-off. It was odd to see it, though . . . this flat, lazy river flowing and polishing rocks in its bed before ducking under a ledge and disappearing. He stayed back a few paces, mindful that the ground must be far more porous than it looked, to have swallowed up a river.

Grace dabbled her fingers in the water. She nodded to him. "It's been corrupted, or a tainted source flows into it somewhere along the way, but this river has gathered from many others, so the fouling is diluted."

"We need to head farther upstream, then?"

"If I am truly to cleanse it, yes. I can possibly put a . . ." She stood and considered the spot, head bent to one side. "I might be able to put a filter on it, but that doesn't remove the problem."

"You can locate the taint, though."

"Of course," she said faintly. "Eventually. I'm not sure we have that much time." She stretched her neck, looking overhead at the dismal sky with gray clouds lowering over them. They crouched over them, slow-moving and settling in. Eventually it would rain, then rain harder, and perhaps even sleet. They could both feel it in the gathering chill.

"One more night upstream, then, if it's all right with you."

She nodded. "I think that's reasonable." She put one hand, fingers still dripping from the river, to her shroud of threads and souls. "I should know how close we are by then." She swung up and guided her horse upstream, Sevryn riding at her heels. Before nightfall, he found proof that their fur-trapping clan roamed over more distance than he'd thought: dinner struggled in a simple snare before he put an end to it and field-dressed it.

"That was someone else's meal."

"The snare is old. Weathered. I gather that, although the clan comes this far, it's not often, or it would have been gathered up long ago. I won't reset it, it's not fair for whatever game it catches. This fellow was only in it for a day or so. Any longer would be cruel. I've seen animals chew their paw off to escape."

Grace shivered. She could sympathize with the creature's desperate need for freedom. The cuff marks from her childhood had faded into barely discernible scars, but she knew the feeling. She dreamed of it sometimes still, when night was at its deepest. She was lucky that such dreams often included her Bolger friend Rufus: big and burly, forge-scarred and more animal than mortal, except when you looked in his eyes. She did not remember Quendius from her enslaved days at the forge, but Rufus remained vivid in her memories. By Kerith measuring, he was old now, extremely old for a Bolger, and she wondered if time had taken him away from her. He, too, had ligature scars on his wrists and ankles and would have had the courage to gnaw himself free if that had been all it took.

Sevryn tapped her on the chin. "All right?"

"Just thinking."

"Aye, I can tell. Not much farther tonight, is what I'm thinking. What do your souls tell you?"

She considered them. She had worn that cage for long enough that she could forget it for long stretches of time. Now that she focused on it, a deliberate pull alerted her into the wilderness. "That way."

"Then that way it is." Sevryn settled on his horse. "I should make a lean-to tonight. It's going to rain, or worse. Lead the way."

She turned her horse in the direction her anchor tugged her but did not find the source before Sevryn demanded a stop so that he could start a fire, and she put the kill up to roast while he lashed branches together for a shelter. They put the horses under a heavily branched tree and hobbled them there after letting them graze till dark. The branches bent to their shelter lent a clean, sharp odor as well as some protection against the elements and they had barely finished their meal when the rain began pattering down. It grew heavier until, in the middle of the night, she awoke to find Sevryn hunched over her, protecting her as the rain turned to hail, its knuckle-sized pellets finding their way to pummel them. It stopped almost as soon as it started, and Sevryn let her go with a short sigh.

"Are you hurt?"

"Bruised a bit. Nicked my ear, I think," and he put a hand up to the side of his head and brought a finger away slicked with a bit of blood. "Nothing much, for all that." He went to check the horses.

"They're all right but a bit disgusted with the weather."

She laughed at that. "Did they complain?"

"Oh, very much so. I gave them each a big handful of grain to help them get over it." He pushed in under their blanket again. "Oh, good, you kept it warm for me."

"Warm as I could."

She put her cheek against his shoulder. He smelled of horse and wood smoke and the pungency of the evergreen. "We turn back tomorrow."

"Unless you hit on it, seems best."

She mumbled something under a yawn and settled back down. The rain began again, but this time a soft, gentle patter that comforted her as she slipped back into dreams.

"This way."

He did not ask if she were certain. He turned his horse down the small freshet, a gurgle of water down the hillside that branched into the headwaters they were surveying. Its contribution to the overall river seemed negligible, but he could see along its banks how sterile it had become, how the growth was yellowed and blackened as if poisoned by the very touch of the water. If she couldn't cleanse it, it should be dammed off, but he hadn't time or tools to dig an earth-dam, and no desire to spread the contamination into another area. It ate at the forest, bit at it like a sharp and hungry animal. All the rain in the world would not wash this bitterness away.

Rivergrace brushed past him, giving her horse its head, and he let her go, all the while listening for under sounds in the area. Trevilara had thought it necessary to corrupt the water this deep in the wilderness. Why? What might they ride into, while in pursuit of its beginning? What strategy had the queen had behind poisoning this desolate land? The only answer could be that it was not as desolate as they believed, and danger lay in that presumption.

He watched her back, as he had for so many days since following her across the bridge to Trevalka, and she led the way as quietly and deliberately as she had always done. As though knowing the worry and vigilance he maintained. As though respecting his discipline to follow and protect. They rode a long way in silence, the sun slanting through sullen clouds overhead, the forest floor steaming as rain from the night before evaporated before their eyes.

Then Rivergrace put her hand up, halting her mount. "I'm going on foot."

"You found it."

"I think I might have."

He slipped down and ground-tied their two horses together, before joining her. She moved across the ground as quietly as she could, nowhere near the stealth of a Kobrir assassin, but doing a fair job of it otherwise. A natural mulch lay over the forest bed, and old needles and twigs ground under her steps. She cut away from the brook they'd been following, following an elbow he could not see but she felt and eventually came to a pond, ringed by stones that, if not hand-cut by men, had at least been laid out in a circle round it.

"It's an old shrine."

Rivergrace looked to him. "You get that feeling, too?"

"I do." He went to one knee. "A very long time ago. The moss, the sediment at the edge, hasn't been disturbed in a century or two."

"And the pollution is weak but definite." She began to strip, her flesh immediately going pale and pimpled from the cold. "I should not be long." She fastened their climbing rope about her. "Two tugs, bring me up, no matter what."

"Always."

She tried to smile, but she was shivering too hard and her teeth chattered. Grace ducked her head and jumped in, disappearing below the murky waters almost immediately. Sevryn squatted down, trying to see her figure and losing it, as if the pond had swallowed her whole.

It would do to spit her out as suddenly, he thought. It would gain no victory by trying to keep her captive.

The stone under his knee looked flatter than the others. The moss growing over it slid away from his questing fingertip. Indentations sank into the stone. He rubbed the growth away, to expose the lettering.

Weather-worn, he could barely read it. *Exalted Trevilara day 3278 Spirit of Water.*

Sevryn ran his fingertip over it again. Yes, that was it, best as he could read it. He had no idea what the day would be today, but he thought he could safely say that the stone had been exposed to the elements for at least two centuries.

Exalted. Lifted to godliness? Riding to her powers on the backs of her people, as Rivergrace had told him? As a Spirit of Water, no less, although he knew her for her Fire. He leaned close to see if he had missed any engraving, but the rope came to life under his knee and he quickly began to reel Rivergrace up and out of the pond.

She surfaced, spitting and coughing, a sickly yellow-green light clenched in her fist. As he brought her to shore and out, she began to cocoon it in the threads she spun from her own essence and anchored it.

She coughed raggedly a few more times before managing, "That should do it."

"It's been here a while."

Grace nodded. Shaking vehemently, she reached for her clothes and dressed as fast as she could. "I think this one was, for lack of a better term, wearing out."

He waited till she dressed and hunched over under their blanket before showing her the stonework.

"So there is where she became a River Goddess."

"So it seems."

As he had done, Grace traced her fingertips over the stone. "She poisoned it so that no one could usurp her power, at least not from here."

"She could have been deposed?" Sevryn turned his head to examine the dark water pond.

"Once. Not anymore, her strength has gone beyond that of a simple fount. Once, if we'd gotten here soon enough, we could have toppled her."

"But surely you weakened her today."

Grace shrugged. "I don't know. And I think we'd be fools to hope so."

He took her arm to help her over the ground, as she shivered and quaked so violently she could hardly walk. "You need a fire."

"N-not he-here."

"Inland a bit. Out of sight. If this is a shrine, there might be eyes on it, even if no actual visitors." He hugged her close, feeling her chilled form even through her clothes.

And candlemarks later, the fire did not seem to have helped her much. He finally built the fire up much higher than he would have normally, in hopes of bringing the color back to her cheeks and the shakes out of her limbs.

What the immense fire did bring were hunters out of the shadows, eyes narrowed, and hands on weapons as they ringed the two of them. By blade and bow, they surrendered.

Chapter
Twenty-Three

"YOU WOULD SET our woods on fire."

"You can tell better than that," Sevryn spat back. "The pit is cleared. Ringed. Far enough from the canopy that even sparks cannot spread easily. Smoke and flame yes, for she is fairly chilled. Death might come to us, but not by fire. I'm more worried about a cold deep in her lungs." He met the narrowed stare with one of his one.

The speaker lowered his bow a bit. Grudgingly, he returned, "You might have a bit of the woodsman about you, but not much."

"I'll give you that. I'm a gutter rat."

"Who knows how to build proper fires."

Sevryn shrugged. "One learns."

"What are you doing out here, so far from your gutters?"

"Staying away from our dear queen."

The bow jerked up, sharp arrowhead targeting the breadth of his chest. The speaker, a bearded and shaggy-headed man who appeared to be lean and wiry under his buckskins, did not growl, but three of those flanking him did.

"What do you say of Trevilara?"

Sevryn spread his hands out, palms out. "Only that I feel better the farther I am from Her Majesty's fiery temper."

A short stout man to the rear of the group muttered, "Do not we all."

"Sssssst. 'Tisn't wise to speak ill."

Sevryn looked down. "Even the ground has ears, aye?"

"Oh, it does. More than you know, gutter rat."

Rivergrace stirred, a little noise in her throat, a clearing, a sound of impatience. Sevryn swept a hand to her. "Gentlemen, this is my lady Rivergrace."

She stepped back as all attention swept to her.

"The cold one."

"Indeed. She has a gift of water, but nearly drowned herself earlier today."

The bearded leader looked keen. "Oh? Fell in?"

"No." Rivergrace shrugged the blanket off her shoulders, letting it drop to the ground. She tucked her hair behind her ears, each one deliberately, exposing the gentle swoop of their tips. "I could feel a taint, a curse, in the water."

That brought louder mumblings from all but the beard. His hands tightened on his bow, and string and wood creaked as he did.

"What do you know of curses?"

Rivergrace put her chin up. "I know dark water. I know how it sickens the land, how it poisons the people and animals who might drink of it. I found the curse and pulled it out, from a pond not far from here." She pointed back the way they had been. "It is sweet water now, and when it goes underground, it will stay sweet, wherever it flows."

"You can do this."

"It is done."

"Why?"

"Would you leave a thorn in a limb to fester? Would you leave a gash open to corrupt the rest of your flesh? Would you let a baby starve or find a wet nurse to suckle? We live as wisely as we can, don't we?"

The bearded man watched her, his dark eyes like coal, his face lined from decades in the elements, harsh wrinkles etched deeply. He jerked his head. "Rimble. Go down and check the pond."

"And have the runs for a week?"

"Do it. Use the proof stone if you must."

Rivergrace moved a little, barely brushing Sevryn. From the corner of her mouth, she whispered, "A stone that will turn color at poison?"

"The Kobrir had them. Once tainted, they have to be cleansed, but they can be useful." While Sevryn had no doubt their captors heard Rivergrace's slight voice, he knew they wouldn't hear his, because he pitched it for her ear and hers alone, his Talent shivering around the words.

Rivergrace nodded in comprehension. She said, louder, "Use your stone. It will show the pond is cleansed."

Rimble, who turned out to be the short and sturdy fellow, set off with a grumble which could be heard until long after he disappeared from their sight. Sevryn made a note to himself that sound carried farther in these woods than he had expected. If the fire hadn't drawn attention to them, then simply talking would have, sooner or later.

The beard indicated they should sit. They all folded their legs and came to ground, bows and short swords still at the ready. He could have taken most of them out, but at least one would have fired an arrow, and with deadly consequence. If their temperaments had not improved with word that the pond had indeed been cleansed, he would have to find a way to ingratiate themselves or extricate. Since he was fairly sure this was the clan he hoped to winter with, he would do best trying to find a common ground. The thought nagged at him to use his Talent, but these people were shrewd and he couldn't sustain a manipulation for days on end. The time would inevitably come when someone would wonder why they'd been thinking what they had and realize what he'd done. The backlash would not be worth the initial response. He'd get them thrown out on their asses, neck-deep in the snow.

Rivergrace reached over and put her hand on his knee as if she sensed his tumble of thoughts. Beard immediately went to one knee, the bow at alert. She snatched her hand back, and he nodded as if she'd obeyed a direct order.

She let out a breathy sigh. "Might I pick up my blanket and move a bit closer to the fire?"

He nodded, beard waggling, silver threads of age among the sable hair, a floppy leather hat covering his head. Calluses marked his fingers as he held the bow, a testament to his expertise with the weapon. Sevryn would not want to draw down against him, although if the man's feet were swept out from under him, he could be toppled before he could send an arrow straight.

Beard turned his head slowly to meet his eyes, as if he could hear the thoughts racing through Sevryn's mind. A tight smile curved the man's lips ever so slightly. Sevryn put his palm up again. When he dropped his hand, he rolled his shoulders forward and let his chin drop to his shoulder and his eyes close. He would not sleep, but he could keep his thoughts from showing so easily, a lesson he thought he had learned well from the Kobrir, and obviously forgotten.

They heard Rimple's return downslope as he shouted, "The stone is clear! Cort, the stone is clear!"

The beard shot to his feet and yelled back, "But not the woods, you idiot! Hold your tongue!" Birds and other small animals fled their shouts with cries and hoots and the sound of beating wings and scampering feet. Cort looked down at his booted feet and shook his head. He finally took his arrow off the string and returned it to his quiver. "It seems you tell the truth."

"Whenever I can." Rivergrace's eyes smiled although her mouth did not. "And what of you?"

"Truth is a gift that cannot be taken lightly. Now. We know the pond is cleared, but we don't know that you did it, as you claim or if you merely discovered the water is sweet and clean there."

"May I stand?"

He gave a brief incline.

Rivergrace got up. She put her hands out a little way from her body, and her face went pure and clear of expression except for one of simple tranquility. In moments, dew drops formed on her skin and about her clothes, cloaking her, sparkling, gems of water that covered her from head to foot. The droplets began to coalesce and drip gently to the ground, like the finest of drizzles. In a moment she would be drenched, and Sevryn grabbed at her wrist.

"That's enough!"

"Only if they're convinced."

"And me having to burn half the forest to dry you out and warm you again? Grace, don't harm yourself for this. We'll find another way."

Cort slung his bow over his shoulder. "Be done with your weeping, girl. You've another problem now."

Grace shook herself gracefully, like a cat which has gotten sprinkled. "And that problem would be . . ."

"You ride on the backs of souls you've gathered, to have a Talent like that." Behind the beard, Cort's lips curled in a contempt more clearly heard in his words. "You will free them or die here on the spot," as he unslung his bow from his back.

Chapter Twenty-Four

"WHAT DO YOU ACCUSE US OF?" Sevryn moved to defend Rivergrace, but she put her hand out to catch his sleeve.

"Can you see soul threads?"

Sevryn muttered something but she did not catch it, purposely, as she looked about the trappers. An isolated people, yes, but wary and with probable good reason to be wary. She would not think them afraid of anything but the mountains they lived on and the Gods themselves.

Cort shifted, his beard twitching as it muddled the expression on his face but could not muffle the scorn in his voice. "High elven with ambition made it their life's pursuit to ride on the backs of those who would carry them. I can't claim to see the vows of those who pray to such Gods, but I am not one who will bend a knee so that someone unworthy can vault over me and mine."

"Nor should you." She motioned between herself and Sevryn. "We don't either. We have Gods, yes, but we did not give our souls up so that they might exist."

"Faugh." Rimple, the stout one, juggled his weight from one foot to another. "Why are we listening here? Leave them to their own devices. The mountains and the storms will see to them if the death master does not."

"I am tempted, Rimple. I am." Cort scratched the side of his jaw, burying his fingers in the wiry hairs of his growth. "But if she did cleanse the pond, we owe her somewhat for that, eh?"

"There's no way to know what they did or not. I found sign someone had been there, and the inscription stone had been rubbed clean, but that doesn't mean they did it."

She felt the stares on her. "How could I know it was dirtied? Cursed? Am I one of you, that I know these mountains? Is he?" She glanced at Sevryn who stood with shoulders tensed, and she knew his hand rested very near one of his throwing knives.

A young man with old eyes near the back of the trappers said, "I've never heard anyone speak the way you do." She had a little trouble understanding his accent, and knew that he had the same with hers. "I am Lukarn."

She wasn't sure if he indicated a name or a geography. "Your words bring a different song to my hearing, as well. If you think we have come to your lands to hide, you're right. Does the queen search for us? No. Does she search for you? I can't say and I would not care if I knew. You all have your rights to freedom."

Boots shuffled in the dirt and dried leaves and needles. The pungent smell of the evergreens rose from the ground.

Sevryn twitched his sleeve loose from her pinch. "What does Rimple mean by the death master?"

"Nothing, he knows nothing."

Rivergrace couldn't see his face as he blocked her, but from the tone of his words, she knew his brow arched. "Nothing? But he fears the being more than the weather, the winter, in these woods."

"If you haven't seen 'em, best you stay clear of 'em. It's not a sight you want," young Lukarn offered.

"I've seen him, and lived to tell about it." Rimple planted his feet proudly, squaring his shoulders and putting his chin up.

"Only because you ran like a moss fox away."

Amidst the laughter, Rimple added, "Nothing wrong with running quick and clear like a moss fox. Saved my life." The laughs rose louder. "I saw him on the great road; none of you lot did. He strides ahead of his army like he was the God of War Himself, but he's not . . . yet. His skin is silver and he leads a ragged army that nothing can stop. Lop an arm off and they don't even bleed! Nothing stops 'em but taking their head off or a bit of fire. I saw them take on the trading caravan of Mestreth himself, with all his guards and all his goods, and there was nothing left of 'em but scraps. Scraps on the bleedin' ground, I tell you. 'Course I ran."

"The great road?"

That drew the attention back to Sevryn who grunted. "You already know we're not from hereabouts. So what is this road or crossroad and is it far from here?"

"It's one of Trevilara's trade roads. She's queen to the west, but the alliance is an uneasy one. She's garrisons along the road to make sure the allies keep their words. Damned Gortish can't be trusted," and Cort wiped the back of his hand across his mouth as if saying the word had filled him with a bad taste. "No one trusts a Gort. Anyway, bandits don't harry the great road, they wouldn't dare. But this one shows up, and it's true his followers are a bit off—"

"Off? Off!" interrupted Rimple. "They're dead men walking!"

"Told you before, can't be, but anyway, nothing stops 'em easy. This death master tells them to take a garrison or caravan, and they do. He'll be knocking heads with Trevilara soon enough. She's got spies along the great road, and there's a garrison down slope from here, which is why we're so cautious about you two. You could be spies. You could be part of his crew or come to join him."

"Or we could be refugees."

"Hmmph. Possible, but not likely. You don't look desperate enough." Cort turned on heels. "I'm minded to leave you here on your own."

"What would it take to change your mind?" Rivergrace asked gently. "I've herb knowledge, some skill as a healer. I'm certain you already have such a one, but it never hurts to have two."

"Winter's gonna be harsh this year. Two more mouths to feed? I don't think so." Cort shook his shaggy head.

A twig cracked. Sevryn moved so quickly she didn't see him, but a truncated squeal and a thump in the nearby brush stopped whatever she might have said. The trappers sprang to attention as he put his hand up, and strode through them, and cleared the brush aside to show the fallen body. Cort ran an assessing gaze over Sevryn, as if noting where more knives might be secreted on his body, his thoughts hidden. Sevryn retrieved his throwing knife and cleaned it before stowing it away.

"I hunt well enough to account for two mouths. Likely a good many more."

The trappers looked at the fallen beast, long legs akimbo and blood pooling beneath it. "Not much of a mark on the hide," noted Lukarn. "Besides the meat."

"He makes a good point for himself."

"She did clean the water."

Cort took a deep breath. His beard wagged as his chest rose and fell.

His dark eyes gleamed a bit. "All right then." He put his forearm out. "Allies for the winter."

"Done." Sevryn returned the forearm grasp.

Cort pointed about. "Dress the kill. I don't want to linger here longer than necessary." He looked downslope through evergreens thick and wind-twisted, and forest trees slowly but steadily shedding their colorful leaves. "Blood calls the death master, that I know."

"The guild master for Mestreth awaits audience, Your Majesty."

Trevilara pushed back from her desk and rose, and as she did, her wall of flames rose with her, their crowns licking about her knees. She dropped a missive as she did, a minuscule piece of paper that had reached her by wings, its contents troubling and reminding her that she wanted a change of pace. Always trouble. She felt like a gardener. Kill one weed and have another spring up in its place the moment it rained and the sun shone. She dusted off her fingers. "Good. I will see him now. No sign of Mestreth himself?"

"None, but it is possible that he was accompanying the caravan."

"He does not travel the open road often."

"No, Majesty, but gossip on the street says that he was promised a young bride in the west and thought to have a look at her, if not to finalize the arrangements."

"Really. Who'd have thought the old goat would want another troublesome female."

"Her family owns mining rights."

"Ah. Of course." Trevilara moved past her secretary. "If he died going after this nubile chit, it serves him right. All those negotiations are supposed to come through me. If he isn't dead, put out a writ of treason on him. He thought to keep me out of the deal." Her face tightened. "He made a mistake."

"Majesty, his guild is powerful."

"This means that there are at least two ambitious men below him, looking to move upward. Find out their names."

"Yes." The secretary bowed low as she passed by him, even though it brought him very near the heated flames, enough that the starch on his collar smelled of smoke when he straightened again, his skin flushed as if heavily sunburned. Her skirts swept along the marble floors, fire trailing in her wake. She would keep it in check during her interview, as she often did, but she wore the odor of burning like most women wore perfume. It kept everyone at greater than arm's length except those few she welcomed near. It had kept her alive at least two centuries longer than her enemies.

The secretary mopped his face with a handkerchief dampened with mint water, one of several he kept in a discreet, waterproof pouch hanging from his belt. It amused her to singe him, and it distressed him to run out of handkerchiefs.

The guild master dressed as befit the prosperous accountant of a successful guild. He wore deep purple pantaloons tucked into butter-soft leather boots, a wide-collared shirt under a flamboyant violet vest, and a cloak thrown almost carelessly over the outfit. He would have been dashing if he'd been a few decades younger, a few hands taller, and a good-deal less smug looking. His eyebrows were fluffed out as was the style in the inner cities, and his eyelids rimmed with liner to make him seem wide-eyed and attentive. Both were styles Trevilara despised but as she was not a man, she could hardly lead that fashion in another direction. Unless she passed a law against it. She considered that briefly, before tucking it away as a not-likely-to-ever-happen thought that would be fun to bring out and regard every now and then. Gods knew there was never enough humor in the world.

"Guild Master Nitron, how nice of you to come."

"My queen," and the man bowed as deeply as his pantaloons would allow which, to her mind, was not quite far enough, but there she was, up against men's fashions again. She came to a halt a few strides away from him, her fires quelled to a mere smolder about her hemline. This stage of her protection was as subdued as she ever let it get, even when locked in an embrace. She thought of her secretary Rohri and his handkerchiefs. She really ought to let Rohri lecture her next lover on what to expect and how to make the best of it. That she would remember.

"You have news for me?"

"Our caravan has been sacked upon the Great Road, just east of the Tantonin Mountains."

"Sacked."

"Raided. Not a parcel or crate or barrel left of the acquisitions."

"Men? Wagons? Horses?"

"Men and horses slaughtered. Most of the wagons were burned; a few were taken for the cargo."

"And who would be so bold?"

"Bandits do not run there, Your Majesty. We cleared them out long ago."

"So we did." She sat down, crossing one shapely leg over the other. "What of the garrison?"

"M-majesty?"

"The garrison. There should be one along a certain distance of the Great Road. Were any of the soldiers involved? Who discovered the wreckage? Was Mestreth there, as rumored, or did he escape? Have you had word from him?" She leaned forward intently. "Did he make his negotiations with the Gortish?"

"No Gortish." Nitron drew a sigil on his chest, one for protection. Against the Gorts or herself? "As for Mestreth, he was rumored to have been with the caravan, but I know that was an idle gossip he let run, as his path took him down the coast south."

"Did it?"

"Yes, Majesty."

"A new bride from the southern regions?"

"No bride, but a niece with some difficulties needing a guardian. Family estates. Messy business, one he did not wish to trouble you with or have bandied about the trade papers and such."

"I see." She did, more than Nitron knew. Mestreth was absconding with a share of the family business from a less able family member and taking the man's daughter hostage, to boot. The raiding of his caravan had little to do with his other affairs, and remained an unfortunate incident. With perhaps one troubling fact.

"Did you have any survivors at all? Any word brought back on the attackers and their methods? None?" That last in response to Nitron's wobbly shake of the head. She sat back in her chair. "And you said the garrison did not get involved."

"Oh, they were involved, Majesty. Just not in the defense of the caravan—there was no defense, it was taken apart rather quickly and devastatingly from the evidence. A troop from the garrison came out in response to smoke seen along the road, but by the time they reached the objective, the caravan had been gutted and no one remained alive."

"Pity."

"Quite, Your Majesty, and I will tell the families you expressed your regret."

Her hemline began to smolder hotter. "You misunderstand me, Guild Master Nitron. It is a pitiful happenstance that no one survived to bring the details to the garrison or to my staff. It is a matter of near unforgivable negligence that such a thing could have happened, no matter how strong the opposition. Every single one of the survivors of the dead is to be stripped of guild benefits, for that negligence. Am I clear?"

"W-widow and orphan benefits, gone?"

"Entirely. No caravan should be so ill-organized and planned that, under any eventuality, reports cannot be made due to any disaster or deviance in their objective. In other words, someone should have gotten out to tell the tale. Otherwise, how else are we to prepare ourselves? The negligence is unforgivable. I want examples made of anyone who stands to benefit from the deaths. Am I clear?"

"M-majesty, of course." Nitron bowed, this time so low that his nose nearly swept the floor, the heels of his shoes creaking and the seams on his pantaloons straining mightily.

"I want another caravan organized and sent out, immediately. There were items in shipment that I require—" Here, her hemline flared up entirely and she took a breath to soothe the flames down. "There are items on that shipment that are a matter of life and death, and it will be yours if delivery fails again."

"I understand." Nitron's chin muffled his response, as he still stood nearly on his forehead, his face turning brilliantine red.

"Do stand up. I'm not sure you can hear me properly with all that blood rushing to your ears. New caravan. Immediately. No excuses."

"None, Queen Trevilara. There will be none needed."

"Good. And you'll inform Mestreth he is to lead this one. Or he will find retirement to the south one of the few options he'll have left in his life."

"Yes, Majesty."

"Good. Now go on, get out."

Without another word, Nitron turned and ran, his cloak tangling inelegantly behind him as he did so. Trevilara uncrossed her legs and sat, brooding a moment at the tiny flames that might be a very inventive and vibrant embroidery upon her dress except that they were real. "I don't need survivors," she said slowly. "I know who hit the caravan and why. He chooses to vex me, this death master. He cannot march into my capital, so he waits for me to come to him."

And so she would, but on her own terms, and he would regret that. She would make certain he did.

She summoned her personal troop of enforcers and then she summoned her God.

"I destroyed this . . . when?" Trevilara looked about, feeling a tiny frown line indent between her exquisite brows. A welcome coolness blanketed her from the sea spray although the smell of the air bordered on appalling. She thought she could remember the village huddled on the bay, but then they all looked alike: gray, weathered, hunched defiantly on rocky shores.

"About sixty years ago, according to my records."

"Long enough for them to lose their fear and begin to rebuild again, it seems." She gathered her dress in her hands so that she might take a step over twisted clumps of marsh grass. Her hemline smoldered and trailed steam about as she did, the only sign of her flames suppressed into remission. "They built ships, did they not? In addition to fishing and the like."

"Boats, mainly. Smaller but quite seaworthy and agile. We had a lot of refugees on those boats, Your Majesty."

"Ah. I remember them now. They assisted traitors with their seditions."

"By building and selling them boats, yes." Her secretary trailed behind her at a discreet pace as though he expected her to flare up or explode in a split-second. Which, Trevilara reflected, she could and he knew that from experience. He'd lasted the longest of any of her secretaries, and she allowed him his little eccentricities such as his need for personal space. She wearied of training new successors frequently. She would keep this one in place, if she could, until he grew aged and trained his own successor, hopefully one with an equivalent sense of survival.

"They are rebuilding their cradles."

"So it seems. Dry docking capabilities and longhouses for doing the framing. Stocking and curing lumber. They've just begun to return to their industry."

"I wonder why." She looked over her shoulder. "How's their freshwater?"

"Their wells seemed to be stocked with sweet water, Your Majesty, plague free."

"Hmmm." That might be encouraging, that might not. Trevilara watched the tide coming in as she considered. This shoreline was beautiful in its own gray-blue way, although she much preferred the waters to the far south, which were bluer and greener in its many colors, and warmer, and the sands held a faint, pink hue. "Either the plague has run its course here, which is encouraging, or . . ." She could not think of an alternative. Her hand went to her breast bone and rubbed as if she could feel the missing pinch of her soul she'd given up to poison their waters generations ago. Had her soul faded? Would she know if it had, such a tiny, infinitesimal part of it? She did not think that either she or the God Dhuriel could be vulnerable in that way. But, if her soul had blinked out of existence here, then it could elsewhere, and there were other headwaters far more strategic where her plans could be seriously disrupted if the corruption faded. She might have to take a tour and take stock of work she'd done over the decades. That would be wearisome. Would it be necessary?

She turned about to face her secretary. "Round them up. Tell them if they want to live, they will go with my men. Don't be over-long persuading them."

"And we will do what with them?"

"Send them to the camps. They seem to be hard workers. We can always use hard workers at the camps."

He gave a half bow and strode off to deliver her orders to her captain and the troop of men waiting at the small, dirt road they'd gathered at. She had not brought a large contingent with her, transporting was difficult with numbers, but those she had brought would be able to manage the slaves capably as they returned cross-country. Dhuriel did not like transporting. He did not respond well to being at her beck and call; as a God went, he could be extremely fickle. He would be happy that the returning journey would only entail her and her secretary. He would be extremely unhappy when she told him of her plans to survey past sites. She might wait a bit on that. He worried about power and the loss of it. She needed to hook more Talent and souls into their network. More work for her, laborious and dull. She should start with this bunch.

She did one twirl, letting her skirts flare out around her, flames roaring up from seemingly nothing as she did. She pointed at the outbuildings, old and new, at the lumber stacks, at the hovels, she swept her hands over the entire port and her fire answered her. She would burn this place to ash before she let the flames withdraw. Trevilara smiled as the wood caught, despite the sea spray in the air, and began to burn with a fierce roar as though it existed only to ignite when she called it. Her heart raced. How she loved to burn!

She watched it with her head cocked to one side, her ears filled with the voice of the fire and the screams of the villagers as they ran to save what they could or fought helplessly with her men, but her thoughts gathered in one, sorry, knot.

Who exposed them? Who sent word to her throne of the renewal here? Who had watched so thoughtfully and then sent notice that the treason had begun again? Did they expect a reward for their loyalty or simply recognition? How long would it be before they stepped forward?

Trevilara paused in her rumination only to point her hand at a new target for her flames, feeling her body warm in the heat, certain only that someone else must have hated this port, these people, as much as she did. When every bit of construction had caught, she turned toward the growing knot of people being herded by her soldiers, and closed her eyes a moment, gathering her power. They held a smattering of Talents among them, nothing so powerful as could stand against her, but useful for village life. Their weakness illustrated the prime examples of the differences between high Vaelinar and the lower classes, but they would still be useful to her and Dhuriel.

She found her task easier by imagining each of her targets as a flower and she plucking away each colorful blossom as she walked in the garden. If she burned the ground hot enough, even weeds would not spring up. Not for many decades. Trevilara opened her eyes, and smiled benevolently. She loved the harvest almost as much as the burning. She stretched out her slender hands.

Chapter
Twenty-Five

THEY WERE NOT AS SILENT as the trappers in their approach to the camp but neither were they ungraceful or loud, yet a small group of women emerged from the edge of a grove to stand in anticipation of them. Obviously, they'd been heard.

"Ah," said Cort. "My wife and others. I may have brought you here, but I'm a fool if I think she will have no opinion about your staying."

His men laughed softly as they dispersed to join the waiters and disappear into the evergreen branches. Cort halted and waited till the tall, strong-jawed woman with pale green eyes came forward to greet him. She wore buckskins and homespun trousers, her colors in light green and soft blues as if she took on the hues of the sky and high forest to hide her.

"Strange prey you bring from the hunt, husband." She considered Rivergrace and Sevryn evenly. The Vaelinar multicolors of the eyes played out in hers as jade shot through with a stronger, deeper jade color and tiny sparks of bronze.

"Guests," Cort told her. "For the winter."

Her eyebrows shot up. "Husband. Is that wise?"

"Probably not, but you needn't worry about the supplies. The lady here has a gift for sweet water, and her man is well-trained for warfare and can bring home his share of meat for the table."

"There are other considerations." She looked from Grace to Sevryn and back. "Are you bonded?"

"Not by ritual." Heat surged in Grace's face.

"Lady Rivergrace and Master Sevryn, this is my wife Ifandra. She is our head councilor as well as our wisewoman."

"Elected or inherited?" Grace asked of her.

"Elected. We all must earn our way, must we not?" Ifandra deftly blocked them from following the disappearing folk.

"Is there a reason for your discourtesy?"

She gave Sevryn a steady look. "A good one. Single women in a gathering of men cause trouble. If she is yours, and you are hers, then you must be bonded."

"You'll have no problem with us," Sevryn told the tall and stern woman.

"Your concerns are not mine. It is the welfare of my people that concern me, and I will not willingly bring trouble into my home. There must be a bond between the two of you, or I will tell my husband you are barred from here."

Sevryn put his chin up as he considered the sky overhead and the growing chill. "Snow tonight in all probability."

"This is a mountain. There will be snow many nights between now and spring. If you love and would protect her, you wouldn't stand there and quibble with me." Ifandra folded her arms across her chest. "I have my people to consider."

"I protect Rivergrace."

Those light green eyes considered him closely. "And that is half the problem. A married woman needs no protection from any of us."

Grace put her hand on Sevryn's arm. "I see no harm in a ceremony." Her face still overly warm, she managed a smile for him. "It's not what we'd planned, exactly, but I can't see waiting for something that might never happen."

He shifted weight. "You don't mind?"

"We are together. How should I mind?"

"We should have a celebration, not a mandate. I can't force this on you."

"You're not."

"But we had planned for more. To share our becoming with others. Friends. Your family. Nutmeg. Lily and Tolby and brothers."

"Another ceremony when we return home, that one with hard cider and dancing and the smell of good toback in the air." She smiled at him.

"All right, then." He gave Ifandra an ironic bow. "Wisewoman, would you bond us? I hope that it is not an overlong ritual."

"Tomorrow eve." She clapped her hands sharply. "Follow me, then, and I'll assign you a home." Ifandra turned on her heel abruptly and they had to hurry to keep from losing her among the evergreens.

They had almost twice as many empty abodes as occupied, sturdy solid huts with at least one wall to the mountain which rose abruptly from its shelf here, the remaining sides woven from branches and plastered over with mud, then fired so that moisture would not disintegrate the plaster. They would be snug, relatively safe against bugs and the environment, but they were little more than two-room dens. One for sleeping and the other for cooking and work. Latrines were in steep pits outside the home lines and away from the small stream that trickled down and around the community from the other side. Grace knew as she looked at it, that it was far more primitive than the seaport they'd stayed in, and yet it seemed natural huddled against the stone side of the mountain which pushed up from the forest here in a jagged peak before giving way to more forest. The trappers had found a place which surrendered to their habitation even as it sheltered them. Rivergrace frowned slightly as she looked about. Few children could be seen. Where was the abundant life needed by any habitat?

Sevryn pitched his words quietly. "You don't have to do this."

"We need a home for the winter."

"We can go south. Or back to the sea."

"It's not that. It's . . . why are these homes empty? What has happened here? Are they asking us to live where others died inexplicably? What might we be exposed to?"

Sevryn stopped in his tracks. Ifandra and Cort ranged ahead of them. The tall woman turned. "You hesitate?"

"I wonder," Grace said to her, "why so many are empty. Where are the young?"

Ifandra's shoulders slumped. "A generation has passed since they were filled. We have a queen who wars against those who speak out. Some fled to be even safer, others left to fight, and our young leave because they are restless, as youth always has been." She looked at them sharply. "Have you a problem with that?"

"No more than you might have a problem with strangers who are no more trappers than you are bakers with sweet shops in the city."

The corner of her mouth quirked. "So we are agreed in certain matters, then. That is good to know. My husband," and she smiled faintly at Cort, "is as like to bring home orphaned critters as he is fine pelts and meat. He has a good heart, you see."

"Which you do not wish taken advantage of."

"Yes." Ifandra spread her hands. "Has one of our homes taken your eye?"

Rivergrace considered the huts. One had a small hanging near the front threshold, a wind chime whose dangles were corroded with patina from wind and weather and yet twisted stubbornly from rawhide thongs, determined to dance in the wind and sound their melody. "There," she pointed.

"A good choice. That one belonged to my sister-aunt and her husband. He was lost in an avalanche on the mountain's far side and she, it is said, died in Throne City when she went to join her parents and take care of them in their elder days. We are not certain of her." Ifandra looked away. "We never received word from her."

"It can be a hard life here," Cort added.

"Only dying is easy," his wife finished for him. She pulled aside the still supple hide from the doorway. "The furnishings were left here. We do not borrow from the empty homes, in hopes we can someday fill them. The only thing you will need is lamp oil. We will share, to a point, but it is wise that you count on making your own as soon as you can. There is a nut pod we gather and press for that. And firewood, of course. We always have a need of firewood. You are welcome to take from the central pile for a night or two, but again—"

"You expect us to be self-sufficient. We will." He moved to replace Ifandra from the door.

"Tomorrow night, we will hold your bonding feast. The moon should be bright, and our plates should be full."

Rivergrace ducked inside, and immediately a certain warmth and quietude greeted her, broken only by murmuring outside as Sevryn came in, with a skein of oil in his hand, the hide door rolled back so that a slanted beam of light fell inside. By that waning light, he filled both lamps and lit one.

"Is there wood on the hearth?"

"Yes." She moved to light it with a quick spark from her hands, but he reached out and caught her.

"Let me check the chimney pipe first. It could be filled with debris or even nests." He ducked back outside and she could hear him on the roof of the hut, creeping cautiously overhead, the framework of the small building creaking and complaining under his weight. A brief squeaking and squabbling broke out overhead, and then he called down the pipe. "Light away. I don't want the mice to think they can move back in."

She knelt down and touched her fingers to the dry kindling under a small log bundle and let the briefest of sparks go. The ancient wood caught fire quickly, smoke sucked up the chimney pipe eagerly, and she swung the iron framework for the cooking pots to the side so she could use them later. For now, the cot in the corner of the other room, which was hardly enough of a room to qualify as one, beckoned. She was lying on it, herbs from the pillow-mattress still giving off a sweet and comforting scent as Sevryn entered. He plopped down beside her.

"What about hunting?"

"I will later," he murmured, "the night doesn't bother me, but a nap sounds better than a meal."

She fell asleep with her hand laced into his wavy hair, pulling his head back against her chest.

She awoke in the night to the sound of rain, a steady drumming that grew louder and fiercer until she carefully slipped free of Sevryn and went to the doorway. A round wooden disk, reminiscent of a foot soldier's great shield, had been forced into place, and she shouldered it aside so that she could pull back the hide covering and peek out. The noise grew with every move she made, and the sight of big, white hailstones bouncing upon the ground did not surprise her. Rivergrace watched them fall, melting soon after they hit, so that the white carpet of ice did not build up but stayed in patchy cover. The wind off the mountain howled round and rattled at her wind chimes and tried to tear the hide door from her fingers. She watched until the hail stopped and the rain began again, leaving great, slushy puddles. For a moment, she thought of bringing in the chimes lest the rowdy wind tear the aging artwork apart and then decided against it. It had, after all, hung there for many a season already. As she regarded it, her sleep-hampered eyes opened enough that she saw the tiny rag woven amongst its base, and pulled it free. There seemed to be writing upon it, but she decided against lighting the lantern to read it. Morning would be soon enough. Uncertain that it could even be meant for them—had it or had it not been woven there when she first looked on the chimes? She put it from her immediate worries. When she dropped the hide and muscled the wooden door back in place, she found Sevryn half-awake and yawning.

To his soft, nonsensical inquiry, she answered, "Rain and hail," before returning to the cot. He protested at the chill of her body but pulled her close anyway, his eyes shut before she could say anything else and his breathing dropping back into deep sleep. He rarely slept that way, she knew, having learned the art of observant rest from the Kobrir, so she let him gain what slumber he could. His sounds drew her back into sleep herself and she did not even dream.

Morning rushed in, gray sunlight flooding the opened doorway as Ifandra entered. "Rise, rise, we have work to do. Beware of ice patches," and the headwoman was gone before either of them could answer. With stifled yawns and scrubbing at eyes itchy with sleep, they emerged to be handed bowls of cooked grain with a splash of milk and what looked to be honey over it and joined the others in hurriedly finishing their meal.

Sevryn finished first and went to corner a few of the men, concern creasing his face, but he looked less worried when he rejoined her. "They're pleased with the weather last night. It bodes well for one of their major crops, and we leave to help with setting up for harvest."

"Here? On the mountain?"

"So I'm told. This," and he swiped a fingertip through the topping of her cereal, "is not honey. It's a syrup made from tree sap. They tap the trees for sap in the winter, and now that you've helped with the river water, they're confident of a good harvest. So we go out today to learn how the taps are put in the trees, which trees, and to hang buckets to catch the sap."

"Trees' blood."

"Sssssh." He put two fingers over her lips. "They know we're different. How different, we can't let them suspect."

Rivergrace set her lips together tightly. He released her after a lingering moment. After a stubborn pause, she said to him, "But how can trees exist through such a process? Would it not weaken or damage them?"

"You would know better than I."

She trailed a step after him. "Perhaps," she considered. "If they're not a fruiting tree."

"You tasted the syrup yourself."

"Yes. Like honey almost but distinctive." She added reluctantly, "I liked it."

By then they'd caught up with the others. Aprons with vast numbers of pockets were passed out, each pocket filled with a small but simple faucet and handle. Poles with buckets hanging on either end, carrying loads of other buckets, were shouldered quickly. Eyes flashed with excitement although voices became muted. Rimple said to them, "Voices carry in a cold

snap. The trees we tap for our syrups are down a way, out of the evergreens. It's a journey, but worth it, and our camp stays safe for being a
distance." He patted Rivergrace's bare head. "You'll need a cap, both of
you, against the winter. I imagine there are some knitting supplies in the
hut, or maybe not. We'll find you something." He broke into a jog to catch
up with his own dumpling-shaped wife who made her way down the faint
forest trail with a good bit of speed.

By the time they reached the lower groves, she felt exposed among
barren trees whose leaves had been stripped by the heavy rain and hail.
Her boots slipped now and then on the muddy ground and fallen leaves.
They spent the day learning one from another, a painstaking process for
neither of them were familiar with many of the species of trees on the
mountain, even in its lower groves. Rivergrace had finally gotten a tap into
the tree she'd picked and stepped back to look in satisfaction on it when
Ifandra swooped in and promptly removed it.

Her jaw dropped. "Why—"

"Because the sap of that one would pucker up your lips and give you
the sours for a week." Ifandra smiled at her. "Look at the bark. That's how
we know one from the other. See? It has sun-colored patches where it peels
away. Sour! Often you can tell if we've tapped a tree from past seasons and
know that one is safe to use."

By the time their long day finished, her hands had gone numb and her
apron pockets emptied of the equipment. Sevryn came to pick her up, his
pole barren of buckets. "Ready?"

"More than." She fell in behind him on the narrow trail. "What happens now?"

"They pick up the buckets every few weeks, consolidate them and bring
the sap up to be processed. I gathered they have barrels they fill and send
down to traders in the spring. This is a winter harvest."

"Actually," she countered. "I was thinking of this evening."

"Oh. Oh! I have no idea. No one has seen fit to tell me, and I haven't
had a thought to ask." He swung about. "What do you think?"

"I think I need to make caps and gloves."

He dropped back to her side with a soft growl and tugged on a handful
of her hair. He found easier purchase on the somewhat slippery ground so
led her up the mountainside by one hand and dark had fallen before they
straggled into the camp.

Ifandra met them just outside the lantern lights' soft yellow glow. She held a steaming plate in each hand. "For tonight, your dinner is prepared."

Rivergrace took the offering slowly, baffled, before remembering that their ceremony had been promised that evening. She smiled. "Smells delicious."

Sevryn bumped shoulders gently with her as he took his dinner. Ifandra nodded. "It's a simple porridge, with nutmeats and jerky, cooked long enough that the jerky becomes moist and soft. It's a staple." She winked. "You may become quite tired of it by spring." She motioned for them to have a seat at the circle.

The lanterns threw a little heat as well as light, but the muted bonfire at the center sent out the most warmth as Grace folded her legs and sank gratefully to the ground. Someone passed her a spoon and she dug into the porridge which managed to be hot, savory, and sweet and felt wonderful going down her throat. Beside her, Sevryn ate even faster, although he stopped suddenly, nearly finished, and made an odd sound at the back of his throat. He knocked the plate from her hands, his eyes gone wide and frantic. She looked in dismay at her dinner on the ground as he began to curl over, trying to speak.

They'd been drugged. Her own thoughts began to curl up in her mind and disappear in puffs of useless smoke. She fell as if every cord in her body had been severed and nothing obeyed her.

Sevryn rolled onto his knees. "Kedant and . . . what else?" The palm of his hand went to his boot top, the current holster for his best throwing knife.

Everyone scattered except for Ifandra and, behind her, Cort.

"Tell me now. I have a tolerance for kedant but none for betrayal."

"I don't know what this kedant is, but what you've been given is traditional. We call it desert rose, named for the small coral-hued snake that lies curled on barren rocks, looking as though the barren lands itself bloomed a small rose."

"That would be what we call kedant. Its effect on those of our bloodline is considerable, Ifandra, and I doubt you aren't aware."

"Too much can kill, yes. A little frees the senses, allows truth and passion to arise. We consider it an aphrodisiac." She spread her hands.

He swayed a bit. Rivergrace could not will her body to do more than turn her head to watch and listen to the battle of words over her. Her stomach roiled in protest and her mouth dried to sand. A dozen heartbeats and more drummed in her ears.

"That isn't all you fed to us." The blade made a noise as he drew it halfway from his boot.

"No, it's not." Ifandra moved a step closer, presenting herself as the target in front of her husband as if she thought Sevryn might hesitate to strike a woman. "I added some powder of a flower we call Truthbringer."

"Because it loosens the tongue." Sevryn spat to one side, bitterly. "If you wanted to know more of us, why not ask us?"

"Because you seem to be two people who have much to hide." She looked down at Rivergrace who fought to keep her eyes open and alert. "Who has not heard of honey sap trees? Their syrup and candies are legendary. Our industry here is small, but there are vast groves to the north famous for their sweetness. Children line up for boiled bits of their chewy candy, yet the two of you knew nothing of it. We asked ourselves then, where you could possibly have come from that you could be so ignorant? We barely survive here. What have we decided to harbor?"

Rivergrace found her voice. "You can't begin to imagine."

"Which makes whoever you are and whatever your purposes sound that much worse."

"You're better off not knowing."

She swung from Grace to Sevryn. "Never tell me that not knowing is better. I can't make sound judgments on my ignorance."

"I think it's enough to tell you that Trevilara is our sworn enemy, but she does not know our names or that she should be hunting us." Sevryn stood then, his blade freed and in his hand.

"When she learns them, will she come hunting?"

"If she does, perhaps. Our trail won't lead here, when she does."

"You can promise that."

Fingers curled tighter about the handle of his weapon. "Promises like that can be foolish. We would do our best to leave our friends in the shadows."

Cort murmured, "All that we can ask." His wife glanced back at him, her lips tightened.

"Having been here at all, the damage is done. How much damage remains to be seen." She put the toe of her boot out to nudge Rivergrace who, slowly, managed to leverage herself off the ground and onto her knees. "I've taken the Truthbringer as well, for it opens eyes. Tell me why I see a cage of fine wires about you. We know what it can mean and it is despicable."

"You ask me if I enslave others to me?" Rivergrace pushed a cascade of auburn hair from the side of her face as she tilted it to look up at Ifandra.

"And if I asked that, what would my answer be?"

"That I am the anchor to tens upon tens of souls, in hopes of keeping darkness from devouring them. I am no parasite, living on the souls of others." Rivergrace looked aside and added softly, "if anything, they live on me."

Their audience had crept back, close enough to hear, and now their murmurs of disbelief broke louder. Ifandra raised an eyebrow across the fire at them as if that alone could silence them, and it did.

"We all face darkness. Sometimes you cannot help but let another pass into it if they will not save themselves."

"I can't. It's not in me to let someone drift away, if they can be helped or protected. Not to the darkness and not to Trevilara. As to the why—you're a healer. Would you let an insidious disease you could cure lay waste to your patient? Your village?"

Ifandra shifted her weight, not answering, but Grace knew she'd made a point. The woman raised her chin again. "What, if anything, has this to do with Trevilara?"

Sevryn looked down on Grace, and she up at him, as if they could trade their thoughts. Grace shook her head ever so slightly as he said, "It has all and nothing to do with the queen. I won't be like her. I can't let her try to swallow me up as well."

From out of the shadows came a tenor-voiced suggestion: "Kill them now, and be done with it."

Grace looked in the general direction of the shadow which spoke. "Kill me, and the darkness is that much closer to cloaking Trevalka." She wouldn't speak of Quendius or the demon Cerat he used. These people would turn on her, inevitably, if they knew, good people turned cold with fear.

"You speak of it as if it could be slain."

She shook her head again. "A foolish hope," and she paused to lock her gaze with Sevryn again before amending, "that darkness has a purpose now, if we can keep it banked. It hides us even as it searches for us."

"Make yourself clear. You have a use for it, or it has a use for you?"

Rivergrace flushed. "We use it, cautiously, and it is unknowing."

Sevryn gestured. "We are all better curtained, because of what is rumored to prowl the roads. We've heard of a dread army, its soldiers being neither alive nor dead. They would hunt that darkness and make it their own."

Rimple came out of the shadows to stand, trembling, by the fireside. The light and shadows made harsh outlines of his face. "They don't lie about that, Ifandra. I heard tales last time I went to meet with the traders. Most unnatural and unsettling. Men that can't be killed. We have no home left, and I won't ask Rivergrace to find quarter on that road. We don't want to fall prey to that army."

Ifandra bowed her head. "You're asking a lot of us."

"Shelter for the winter. That's all."

"And you can wait until spring before you must act against this darkness? To keep the Undead from finding and claiming it?"

"I believe so." He shrugged one shoulder. "Nothing is for certain."

"But death. Yes, we know, all too well." Ifandra turned about to her husband. "It is your choice."

"Mine?"

"I have the truth and can't offer anything more than that. You're the one who minds the trails, the sign we leave upon the mountain. If you think they will expose us, it's your decision. Until spring." She passed him by to go stand in the shadows with the rest of her community.

Cort put his shoulders back as he considered them. The weathered creases at the corners of his eyes deepened in thought and worry, as did the knife-sharp lines alongside his mouth. Sevryn kept his silence under that regard and signed at Grace she should hold her quiet as well. He would not force the issue of their staying, and if they were going to go, he wanted to be quit of the mountains before winter closed its hard hand on them.

Cort shifted his rangy frame uneasily, betraying the war inside him. He lifted one hand and then the other, looking into his open palms as he took a deep, steadying breath. Finally, he looked at Sevryn.

"You are welcome for the season. But when that time comes that you must accomplish what you came for, you leave. And you take all the care that you can not to leave a trail back to us."

"I can do that." Sevryn inclined his head graciously.

"Done. And now, I believe we have a bonding to perform." He bowed to his wife who came forward with a scarf in one hand and a small stone knife in the other.

Sevryn helped Rivergrace stand, whispering in her ear, "Are you all right?"

She answered back, "The sooner we're in bed, the better I will be. I need you." Her hold on him tightened, and he could feel the fire in her blood. Sevryn smiled crookedly.

Chapter
Twenty-Six

Kerith

"I CAN'T DECIPHER his conduct. His tutors tell me he is unmanageable." Diort paced the canvas floor of his traveling pavilion, hands clasped behind his back, his face heavily etched. "One moment he is childlike; the next, his thoughts are knotted up, secretive, and suspect."

"You don't trust him."

"He does not leave room for that, anymore." Abayan stopped pacing long enough to look Ceyla in the eyes, by putting a gentle finger under her chin and lifting her until her gaze met his. "I need you to dream for me."

"I can't—you know I can't dream on demand. It doesn't work that way, not with me, not with my . . . gift."

"Bregan's life depends on it. If I can't gain some sort of perspective on him, I will execute him."

"What?"

"He's dangerous as he is. I haven't a hold on him, can't persuade him to give me his trust—"

"No wonder if you're thinking about killing him!"

"He deals with Gods that are as undependable and unfathomable as he is."

"You're his guardian. You accepted that burden, but beyond that, your entire people were created to serve the Mageborn, to be their guides and protectors."

"And perhaps the Mageborn would exist today if one of us had had the sense to end the lives of a few of the murderous bastards. Even just one. There might have been no escalation of egos and power, no devastating war."

"You can't judge that."

"No, not now, not from where I stand. I didn't live then, it wasn't my burden centuries ago. I can only act as I perceive this Mageborn, here and now." He took a deep breath. "He is as he was when a Master Trader, ego-centric, self-indulgent, arrogant. The only difference is that he was a man then. Now he's like a child."

"Whom you promised to teach."

"A promise I made without knowing him! He's unteachable. He listens to no one. He hadn't room in that Kernan head of his; the Gods have thrown everything out, including his common sense. These Gods . . . They're not mere Gods we might perceive as images of ourselves grown lofty. No. The Gods of Kerith are primal elementals and if they react, they will tear this world apart."

"You made a promise."

"One which I cannot, in good conscience, keep. Every day, he learns to be more dangerous. The Gods offer me no hope."

"I didn't know you were a religious philosopher."

"I'm not. But I have some understanding. I held Rakka in my war hammer, Earth Shaker, a God that could move mountains. Strike rivers into the earth. Send city walls into bits of gravel. A sliver of that God, the slightest thought of Rakka, had been imprisoned in my weapon. I don't know how Quendius put it there, but I do know that the weaponmaster thought it would bond me to him. It had the opposite effect. I used it as I needed to, but I turned from the master, the demon, who would attempt such an atrocity. Unlike Quendius, I had the ability to be afraid, to imagine what it could do if truly aroused. I was relieved when the hammer struck a blow that finally spent it and released the demon spark back where it came. I can't see my ward doing that."

"So you would kill Bregan."

"I would have to. He doesn't leave me much choice. He treats with these Gods as if they were his playthings, and they are not. They are the very foundations of creation and destruction, and we are best off if they never notice us because we are, truly, no more than grains of sand to them. Still, like an oyster, they can feel irritation, and they do not like it in their sleep."

"Bregan says they're already awake."

"Then we'll tiptoe if we have to, until they sleep again." He paused. "I wanted my destiny once, yearned to be what I was created for, and now I know that I'm capable of more. Trust me, Kerith is better off without Gods."

"Without kings, too."

"Sadly, though you meant it to be sharp and hurting, you're probably right." He moved his hand from her chin. "Dream for me. I need insight because I am blind on this, Ceyla, and I don't like killing as the only option."

"Is that my king's order?"

"No. I wouldn't do that to you. It's a friend's request, but it's not being made lightly. I ask your aid."

Ceyla closed her eyes briefly. Normally she would see a flash of darkness, with the sunlight burning beyond it in the daylight, nothingness if it were night. This time, however, she caught a sense of figures moving, of color, and she could hear a murmur of sound. It waited for her, this vision, as though Diort's words had called it up, out of her. How could she deny either?

She opened her eyes and began to retreat into the tent which had become her home. She had begun to sweat. "Don't awaken me. Have Mallen sit at the flaps, listen, and write. But don't let him awaken me, no matter what." Her skin chilled suddenly as the sweat evaporated off her in the dry wind. "No matter."

"Done, and let me thank you now." He put his hand on her shoulder, bent, and his lips swept her cheekbone.

Ceyla froze at the threshold to her own tent as he left her and she felt, for a moment, as if he had taken all the light and air in the world. She stirred, feeling light-headed, and entered her sanctum. She would have sworn she wasn't sleepy, that she could never rest with the storm of thoughts tumbling through her head, and she would have been wrong, for she collapsed on her pallet and was asleep almost before her eyes even shut.

Mallen came as soon as Diort beckoned, dragging his stool and box of instruments and paper with him. The lord had told him to wait until he spoke with Ceyla, so he readied and consequently rested in place almost the moment Ceyla disappeared within her tent. He rolled his graphite stylus in his fingers, poised over the precious sheets of paper his king had purchased for him. Not as permanent as ink onto parchment or vellum, perhaps, but slightly less costly to obtain and easier to use. Mallen had, however, long ago become accustomed to the permanent ink stains on his fingers. They spoke to his position as a scribe, just as Diort's facial tattoos spoke of his bloodline and training. They were both equally proud of their indelible markings.

He heard a soft cry from within the tent and knew that Ceyla had already sunk deeply into her dreams. She would remember some of them and relate them when she woke, but they had discovered that it was even more beneficial to the oracle to have someone write what she called out— as difficult as it was for people to speak in their dreams, she had become adjusted to doing so, within the safety of Diort's care. He listened, his writing instrument at alert in his hand.

He is stooped and bent with age, hairy body gone nearly bald to expose his leathery skin. His tusks are yellowed. Children scream and cry with fear at him. He is viewed with disdain and suspicion, like all of his people, for being animal. But he is not. He is a friend of the high courts and warriors. He has fought beside the greats and he has come from his retirement among his people to fight one last time.

Mallen cocked his head as the words fell to silence. He made a small note of his own beside what he had written: Bolger? She began to speak again, cutting short his own wonderings.

Pastures once grazed now fallow. Streams fed with melted snow. Below lies the sickness of the Mageborn. Nothing good can come from here now.

Two small children play on the grass. Their guard watches. Too much time passes.

The Gods are speaking. Who are we to answer? What shall we answer?

The Great Mouth opens. Its teeth march out, sharp though dark with rot. Its breath is smoke, its tongue is flame. Yet we allow the Mouth to open and stretch wide its jaws to snap at us! Why?

Do not trust the heavens.

The trader leads down a crooked path that must be followed and then judged. All will be shattered.

*   *   *

After many lapses, broken by fitful speech, Ceyla falls into a deep quiet. Mallen stretches his hand for a moment, his fingers having gone tense and tight about his writing instrument. He scanned what he had been able to copy and fear tickles the back of his mind. Abayan Diort won't be pleased with what he has to show, and the Oracle will not bear the brunt of that displeasure. Instead, he will face the questions: did he listen closely? Was there anything said that he could not transcribe in time? Did she utter words he could not translate or understand? Whatever flaws in the dreaming, he would bear part of the responsibility. Mallen sighed. He sat very still for a long time until he heard Ceyla rise and stumble about her tent, her dreaming done.

He hated to relinquish his papers when Diort came to claim them, but Mallen did as expected, gathering up his little wooden case and instruments, bowing, and leaving. Behind him, Ceyla walked out of the tent to join the king. As the two of them bent over the papers, the last he could hear was, "I don't remember what I dreamed. How could I know what it means?"

"If you don't remember, then I have to act upon my own judgment."

"You'd still put him down."

"Like I would an animal suffering a mortal injury? Out of necessity and care? Yes, I would."

"Then go," she told him. "Go and see him now. Don't do anything until you go and see him, and report back to me. Then, if your mind is still fixed, do what you must."

He straightened, his back as tight as if he'd a spear fastened to it, unyielding length pressing his spine rigidly.

"You challenge me."

Ceyla tore her gaze from the papers she held and smiled faintly. "I've no need to do that. You challenge yourself. It's one of the many things I love about you." And she looked back down to the prophecies in her hand, frowning as she thought to decipher them.

The Gods speak, indeed. He might as well go try to understand what it was they might have said. He left her and went in search of Bregan. He found him without too much trouble on the outskirts of the camp, and the trader tilted his head, noting his arrival.

"They are sunk into the very bones of the earth."

Diort halted short of where Bregan sat on the ground, his legs spread wide as a child might sit, his fingers grubbing about aimlessly in the dirt, pulling up bits of grass and pebble. Diort paused but a moment before responding. "The Gods."

"Of course! Who else?"

"One might think you speak of the dead. Or of the gems and minerals we pull out of the ground. Or even drops of rain, sunk deep enough."

"Ah." Bregan scratched at his neck. "I didn't think of that."

"So you are deep thinking without philosophical depth."

Bregan ignored him as he squinted about, eyelids narrowed to near closing, wrinkles about them clenched, fingers curled. "I can hear them dreaming."

"Do they say anything of interest or do they merely snore?"

Bregan twisted to face him. "You are mocking, guardian."

"Yes. I could be. The question that vexes me, however, is wondering if it is you who mock."

"Me?" Bregan repeated, in outrage.

"You. I sit you with teachers and you ignore them. I could understand if you wished to share this philosophy of yours with them, or if you argued with them outright about past history as you know it, or you challenged them . . . but you ignore them as if they did not exist. How can you learn if you do not learn to ask questions and listen to answers? What use is it to try to teach you?"

Bregan's expression fell. He combed his grimy fingertips into the dirt. "The noise of the Gods fills my ears. I can't always hear."

"You must hear something."

He looked away. "Sometimes."

"And?"

"I . . . don't listen."

"And we're back to the beginning of our discussion." Diort squatted, a position he could hold for hours, a stance drummed into him as a youth when all his people were nomads and rested that way at the fireside or the tent. He would know he had indeed grown old when his body refused to lower and raise him. "You don't listen. You will not learn. Tell me if I am wrong—do you know everything you need to know about being a Mageborn?"

"I don't know anything." Bregan's lip twisted. "And neither do they."

"Then I should find you new teachers."

An upward glance. "There are no Mageborn to find."

"There are librarians and historians who have studied the old Mageborn.

Perhaps the ones I brought you aren't expert enough. All theory and no practice."

"No one knows."

"You do."

Bregan's nails dug violently into the soft dirt. "I'm not learning it right. Nor do I know it well enough."

"If you know the history, you might find a way to tap what is inside you. A caravan master needs a map and a destination, but he doesn't always have to have traveled the route to navigate it successfully."

"You're upset by what I did to Tolby Farbranch. You'd be far more upset if I brought the Gods of Wind to an entire city and laid waste for their blasphemy."

"Unless you've studied, you have no way of knowing if it is true blasphemy or not. Do you?"

A shake of the head for an answer.

"You attacked Tolby because the Gods urged you to?"

"They spoke to me. A whirlwind carried me."

Abayan drew a small symbol in the dirt with his index finger before wiping it out with the side of his hand. "Men often hear voices that speak no good to them. I can't, however, explain away the whirlwind."

"See—"

"Unless you called it up yourself."

"I don't know how!"

"But the power to do so might reside with you, untapped. We don't know. We are not likely to know until you've studied a bit. Gods exist, good and ill, and there are demons which are always ill. How can I know which you talk with, and which you believe, and whose word you will act upon? How can I trust you if you are not learned?"

"You can't."

"No. And if I cannot trust you, if you persist in turning away all the guidance I try to make available to you, that trust will never develop. You become a wildfire upon the grasslands, one which I must put out, before all is consumed. Do you understand?"

Bregan tossed his hand outward, scattering dust to the wind. "You'll kill me."

"I will execute you, yes. For the safety and well-being of my people."

"How is that different?"

"To you, it isn't. To me, it means I did it because I judged it, and weighed it, and tried to find recourse around it, and could not. It was the only viable decision."

Bregan cackled. "Death is not viable."

"No."

"Either way, I'm still dead."

"Regrettably."

"You wouldn't regret it as much as I."

"The dead are merely dead. I doubt they feel much beyond the grave. The living feel for quite a while longer." Diort stood. "I'm not threatening you, Bregan. I'm trying to understand what makes you unwilling to try. To let you understand how I view your actions, both petty and otherwise."

"What did Ceyla say?"

"Nothing that would save you."

"Oh." Bregan looked up at him. "Nothing?"

He shook his head. "Nothing."

Bregan let his breath out in a long, drawn-out sigh.

"Did you expect her to?"

"I thought she might hear the Gods, too."

"She is Vaelinar," he reminded the other.

"True. How unfortunately true. Could you find a Kernan oracle?"

"Not a reliable one. The best oracle is you telling me you will listen and learn, as best you can."

Bregan stood, dusting his hands off. His breeches hung with dirt and grass clumps and he dusted uselessly at them as well. Finally, he muttered, "I will try."

"And I will get you some new tutors."

"Do that!" Bregan shouted at his turned back. "And I'll do this!" He pushed his hands into the sky and spoke a word Abayan didn't recognize but felt in the depths of his skeleton.

A whirlwind rose up and grabbed them both in its turbulent spirals. Diort felt the sickening moment when his feet left the ground and he began to spin so fast he couldn't center himself, his stomach revolting and his breath torn from his lungs. He put a hand up, and the wind's pressure immediately grabbed it, flinging his arm wide. He pulled it back to his side before his shoulder could give out and hugged himself, completely helpless in the whirlwind's grip. Somewhere in the swirling dust and chaos, he could hear Bregan's delighted howl. Diort closed his eyes tightly. Only a madman would enjoy this ride. They plunged, and Diort's eyes flew open.

He could only see clearly straight up and straight down. Downward, the ground sped under his feet in a blur, dirt undistinguishable from rock and grass and shrub. He forced his chin up and looked upward through the spout toward bits of blue sky and white-streaked clouds, a view that dizzied him even more.

As suddenly as it began, the twister stopped, dumping him unceremoniously to the ground. Bregan landed next to him, giggling maniacally. The funnel retreated from them but stayed near, clay-colored dust rising in its depths, feuding with the storm-colored cloud that seemed to comprise most of the phenomena.

"I told you! But you didn't believe me!"

"I did believe you. There was no other way you could have covered the distance you did, but—" And Diort looked at the whirlwind. "I didn't understand you."

He cautiously got to his knees. He did not recognize the wilderness where they'd been brought. A strange fragrance hung in the air. Birdsong started up, as if it had been quelled by the twister and then released. Bent thistles underfoot crunched as he stood and took a step away.

An eerie voice, more whine than words, spoke up. "Do not stray. The land here is unforgiving."

An insect with an uncommonly long stinger paused by his eyebrow. Diort refrained from smacking it out of the air only because experience had taught him that such creatures normally only stung when threatened and that if he missed, he would invariably be stung. When he swung about slowly, he saw that he stood at the edge of a place where dirt did not rule as the ground, a miasma of color did.

A curtain of mist rose up from the rainbow and broke off into unnerving shapes before dissipating with a faint howl. Trees at the far boundary grew from raw edges of ground in twisted, knotted shapes that bespoke a wind which blew here, and often, that he could not yet feel. A . . . thing . . . flowed through the colors, triangular head up, blazing green eyes reflecting the sunlight, a brush of a tail following after, a thing which ignored them entirely as it trotted past, looking for prey. It might have been a sand fox, once. Or perhaps not. It was the gait and the tail that hinted at its origin but not convincingly so, for its hide was an oily black and there had been a red cast hidden deep in its green eyes.

Diort wanted to step farther away from it, but he seemed to be on one of the few pieces of actual ground. Bregan looked as if he might launch himself into the midst of the coloring pot, but Diort caught him by the collar.

"Don't."

Bregan froze, reluctantly, with a doglike murmur of disappointment as he sank back down. He fiddled with a clasp on his brace.

The fine and familiar piece of craftsmanship no longer adorned his leg. In its place, a contraption of mottled black wood and thorn wrapped about Bregan, looking as painful as it did useful. The briars ranged from thumb-long to as long as his hand and looked to be locked into Bregan's flesh and muscle. Blood did not spring up from the various places where the brace hooked in, but bright, crimson flowers bloomed there, small and tightly curled buds of incredibly brilliant color. Bregan picked at one, his own expression crumpled and hurt.

The whirlwind spoke again. "It does not belong here; therefore its aspect is alien and hostile."

"I need it off."

"It won't leave you. It's not supposed to." Diort only guessed but he felt correct.

Bregan ran his hand over it, palm down. It seemed to have no effect, but the etchings of pain left his face as he did. When finished, he leaned back with a sigh.

"We're at a badlands."

"War is coming."

Diort laughed, a short burst of scorn. "War is always coming. If Gods stayed awake and paid attention, they would know there is scarcely a moment of true peace for the world to treasure. It takes no prophet to utter that."

"The coming war will be as this one was." And as the whirlwind's voice grew sterner, so did the chaos in front of them increase, boiling like a pot set over a blazing fire. "This is what happens when Gods go to war. There is no surrender. There is no victory. There is only destruction."

"The Mageborn were men. Foolish, arrogant ones at that."

"Men who thought they were Gods. Men who believed they could harness such as Myself." The whirlwind churned faster, turning dark. "They turned their backs on their fellows and perverted their gifts. They sought to climb into the heavens on the backs of their victories and destruction. We did not allow that. Not then, not now."

"I'm not aware of such actions now, not even from the Vaelinar."

"War comes," proclaimed the high, thready tones of the whirlwind. "You are warned that we will not allow it."

"Frankly." Bregan cleared his throat. "From what I know of the Vaelinar, you may not have much choice or power against them."

A spray of gravel flung into their faces and both flinched aside, covering their faces as the whirlwind swept in angrily. Abayan had a thought in which to breathe deep and then he knew nothing until the Wind God spat him out, Bregan tumbling after. They grabbed each other by the forearms to steady themselves and found, Diort on his feet and Bregan on his knees, that the primal force had left them on an island, surrounded by the boiling sands of chaos. If either swayed or stumbled, they would pitch into the uneasy power churning about them. He had no idea what the magic might do to him, but Diort held a distinct image of the flesh melting off his bones until nothing was left of him but a skeleton bobbing in the magical discharge.

"I am one of the bones of the world," the God told them. "We are sunk deep into Kerith and we do not parade about as mortals to gain affection or attention. We are what we are. Take heed of our anger and our warning."

Then, as quickly as they'd been set down, they were plucked up again, air sucking from his lungs and drying his eyes with an incredible itch. The whirlwind bore Diort off and the only way he even knew Bregan had been brought along was through the grip holding to his forearm. He curled his fingers tighter, taking care not to be ripped away. Just when all the air had been dredged from his lungs, and his mind went light and dizzy, the whirlwind dropped him, gasping, upon the ground. Diort saw Bregan's brace flash in the sunlight as it returned to the metal from which it had been forged.

Bregan rolled to one side and let go of Diort's arm. His eyes lifted. "Are you still going to kill me?"

Diort had no answer he wished to give.

Chapter Twenty-Seven

"HANDS UP! Now down. Center your body and be ready to face me again. No cheating by looking ahead. Those moments when you look ahead, you're not in your body, you're in mine. I can take you out in that pause. All I or any opponent needs is a moment's hesitation from you. Live in the now, Lara, and come at me! Now!" Bistane wove in front of her, his voice cracking out orders like a whip, snapping her attention to him. Her stamina fell far short of where it had been and that worried him. He drove her because he had to.

Sweat dotted her forehead and exertion colored her cheeks and she fought for breath she shouldn't have needed as she dropped back into her ready stance to face him. She carried a throwing dagger in her left hand and her sword in her right, using the one to parry with and the other to lead and strike; he faced her with the same blades. Her left arm trembled a little with strain. Lara shook it off impatiently. Instead of waiting for him to make the next move, she came at him. Over, under, and with a swing about, her booted foot aiming for the solar plexus, she nearly caught him.

Nearly. "Good move if you'd succeeded. But you didn't, and that put you out of balance and open."

"Cold hell, I know that."

"So why did you do it?" He closed on her and the blades *whinged* as they met, and he held her on the last cross, face close to face, so close he could see her nostrils flare as she sucked in a deep breath.

"Because if it had worked, you'd be doubled over and at my mercy."

"But only if it worked." He leaped back a step and into a new position, his flank to her, offering very little in the way of target. Before she could totally register the change, he swung about with a foot box of his own, clipping the side of her face. Lara dropped to one knee with an *oof*, but she covered her body with both her blades in shield position.

"Good."

"You dropped me."

"And, if you were at peak physical condition, you'd have rolled with the kick, hit the ground, rolled again, and taken out the back of my knee."

"All that?"

"Hopefully."

Licking dry and cracked lips, she stood up and gathered both her blades into her right hand, putting her other palm up. "Break. I am beyond thirst."

He retreated to the end of the training arena and stowed his weapons. Leaning back on his elbows, Bistane watched her down a goblet of water. She slammed the cup down when finished.

"If I had been in peak physical condition, we'd be done. We would have fought each other to a standstill already." She wiped her mouth and then her forehead with the back of her hand.

"Indeed." He noticed how sweat dampened her shirt and made it cling to her slender form, the fabric cupping her breasts and hugging the curve of her legs. He also could not help but notice that curves now graced her figure, much needed muscle and some reserve that she'd lost during her illness. He wanted to cross the room and bring her up against his chest, to feel the still racing beat of her heart against his own, and to cup his hands around her butt. Bistane turned his face away to grab up his own water but not to drink. He poured it over the top of his head, dousing away thoughts of her. "Take a break. There's something I need to show you."

Her attention sharpened. "What's wrong?"

"Must there be something wrong?"

"I've been in my bed for two years. There are bound to be many things wrong that you haven't wanted to share with me yet."

"That's a possibility, but no. This came to light recently." He caught up the water jug and made his way to a trainer's table. "It's this."

Lariel looked at the clothing stretched across the table in front of her. "Definitely Kobrir, though faded." She fingered a ragged edge. "Singed. Bloodstained. It has to have belonged to Sevryn."

"We might be able to gain proof of that."

"How?"

"Your healer should know, if they ever worked on Sevryn for training injuries and the like. I am told they can differentiate blood from one patient to the next."

"I've never heard of such a thing, but if it can be done, do it." She pushed her chair back away from the table, her blue-upon-blue gaze held to the bloody garments in morbid fascination. "It would be proof that they reached beyond the portal, if nothing else, although this . . ." and she stirred the rags with a nail. "Does not portend favorably."

"Blood never does." Bistane stepped back to the halls and gave a shout. When one of the maids came, he told her who was wanted although not why. On his way back into the conference room, he stopped at the table to pour a drink and crossed to offer it to Lara.

She wrinkled her nose. "You pamper me."

"Don't cross your eyes at me. You lost a lot of fluid in training this morning."

"And have the bruises to prove it." She sighed as she accepted the cup and downed half the juice in three gulps.

"Less bruises than you gathered last week."

"Is that your way of telling me I'm making progress?"

He inclined his head. Whatever he might have added was interrupted as Healer Sarota hurried into the room, Farlen Drebukar on her heels. For a brief moment, Lara looked at Farlen and thought she saw his uncle Osteen, and her pulse jumped. It was not that she didn't remember Osteen had died but it was the way Farlen moved, a huge, self-assured block of a man. Farlen had had his tentative years with her, and she realized that while she slept, Osteen's nephew had come into his own. That realization filled her with relief. Another solid friend to count on.

Sarota's face lost color as she looked down where Lara had the garments spread. Without saying a word, she emphasized what the rest of them knew instinctively as warriors and fighters: no one lost that much blood and thrived. Perhaps not even survived.

"Who," the healer asked as she came to a stop.

"We are hoping you can tell us."

Her jade-and-gray eyes looked up. "Only if I treated them before, and perhaps not even then. It's a portion of our Talent and not many of us have it in depth. If I may . . ." and she reached for the rags.

Lara took her hands away as Sarota lifted them and put them to her mouth. She opened her lips and took an edge of the old, bloodstained fabric in, sucking on it briefly, before lowering it and standing with her eyes half-closed, her expression one of intense concentration.

"More than one blood here. The second is female, I can't tell more than that, but I would hazard the opinion that the major . . . donor . . . is male and should be Sevryn Dardanon." Her eyes flew open, her expression aghast. "Sevryn!"

Lara shivered as she took the shirt from Sarota's trembling hands. "It was feared."

Farlen rumbled, "Where did that come from?"

"The portal," Bistane told him.

"From that slit? I wouldn't have thought even a blade of grass could make it through."

"It was given to me by one loyal to Lariel who is in the Returnist camp, watching events for us."

Farlen's face curled in a snarl. "Bastards. I thought you cleaned the river of them."

"All but a handful. They wanted representation, I gave it to them." Lariel folded the rags into a semblance of order. "We can surmise that the other blood may come from Rivergrace—or it may not. We've no way of ascertaining that."

"The woman's was only a trace. The vast amount is from Sevryn."

Lara nodded at her Healer. "I understand." She looked at Bistane. "How long has our spy had this? Was it dry or wet when it came through?"

"Less than two weeks, I hazard, as I visit the camp regularly to keep pressure on them to vacate. As for the condition of the shirt." He stopped with a shrug. He did not add that Lara would not look at the shirt for a week while she regained her strength and began her training with him, as if she could not quite bear to take on its burden then.

"I don't know what to make of it."

"I do," said Farlen. "It's a warning of more blood to come, and on this side of the portal."

"Do you think?"

"I think it's probable. Sevryn himself, or someone for him, put it through. A bloody flag. What other sense can we make of it?"

"We can think," Sarota said slowly, "that he himself tried to make it through and died in the attempt, leaving nothing of himself but shards of what he wore." She met the others' looks. "What? Could I not be right?"

Farlen shook his heavy head. "No. He never would have tried to get back without his Rivergrace, mortally wounded or not. He's fearless about death, that one. Even his own wouldn't stop him, I think, especially when it came to his ladylove. If he couldn't make it through whole, he'd make damn sure she would. I would count this as a warning, Lara, and a damned good one."

"And your recommended response?"

"A troop, guarding. Birds for messaging."

"Round the clock."

"That goes without saying. And we need to bivouac more troops here, Lara. Our forces have been lean for several years now."

Bistane said, "I'll bring men in."

"What do you think might come through that portal?"

"Quendius went through it, with a small army of Undead behind him. Who knows what may wish to return? Whatever it is, we have to be ready. It'll be bloody." Farlen finished with his gaze fixed on the pile of rags between Lara's hands. He nodded to Sarota. "We're done here and I've my orders."

Bistane watched her. "What are you thinking?"

She glanced up. "I'm thinking that I have to train harder." She crossed to the weapons' racks, knowing he would follow. The others left, and the arena grew quiet except for the faint clicks and clacks as she examined the blunt practice weapons in her hands. Her skin held its own paleness that came not from her heritage but from her weakness.

"That's not the way to do it."

Bistane pivoted. His father stood in his corner of the arena, leaning on a shield stand, face half-shadowed with a bit of a smile showing for all that. He looked the same, his ghost, and Bistane supposed that was because time, along with life, had ceased to exist for Bistel. Perhaps that was why his father's ghost took so much interest in Bistane's time. He visited often enough. "And what would you do?"

"Stop looking at her like a woman. She is an opponent who must be stopped, at all costs."

"Lara or Tressandre?"

"Whoever it is you are truly facing. Lara's gift, as you noted, does her no good in a short-term fight. She can't afford to indulge in possession if it takes her out of here and now. Tressandre will eat her up and spit out the bones and gristle."

"Lovely image."

"But true. Isn't it?" Bistel moved a bit, out of the shadows, and as if having caught Bistane's attention and belief, his apparition strengthened.

"She has to go for the kill."

"Yes."

"What?" Lara pushed off from her equipment table and started across the arena floor.

He put his back to his father's ghost. She had his attention, again, fully. "You don't go for the kill."

Her mouth twisted. "We Vaelinar kill in the dark, not the open. We can't afford any more enemies than we already have, or any less population. That is one of the lies we tell."

"That's your excuse, not hers. She's come at you several times already; I wager that this time she won't stop. There's nothing to stop her. You have a paltry excuse for an heir and you're weak. She doesn't respect you and won't, no matter what you do."

She gathered up her weapons, face tilted down as she examined her hands, the left with four fingers, and the right with all five. "You're telling me I can't win if I just drive her into the ground and then walk away."

"Yes."

"Death or nothing."

"Yes, again."

She swished her long sword through the air, back and forth, back and forth, in time to her thoughts perhaps. "I'm not sure Sinok would agree."

"The old king did play by his own rules. I take it he stopped your hand a time or two."

"He did. He had a timetable sunk in that crafty old mind of his, but didn't get a chance to impart it. He died before he thought he would."

"Which in itself should tell you his strategies are far from perfect." He tried not to watch a droplet of water that hung from her chin, as it dropped to the deep V of her shirt and began to slide down into the delicate valley between her breasts.

A smile came to her reluctantly. "True." The sword swung. "I'm not convinced there's another way."

"To the death or just beating her into the ground—" He grabbed his weapons and jumped at her. "Either way, you still need training!" Their blades rang loudly against one another.

The arena chimed with their strikes and parries and Bistane got little chance to think as Lara met him with a renewed confidence and fury. He tested her as she met him, finessed him, and returned with challenges of her own until both panted like a bellows, his clothes soaked through, and he could smell the heady aroma of her heated body. Her hair came undone from its tight knot at the back of her neck, flowing about her body in platinum-and-honey–colored streams, like a fine wine made from silver and sunlight. It masked her face and intentions, and she caught him off guard, sweeping his legs from under him.

Bistane rolled as he went down, catching her on a backswing, bringing her to one knee beside him. He crossed his wrists over hers, pinning her weapons, and she let out a low growl of frustration.

The sound moved him, not unlike a noise made while in the depths of lovemaking, a primal note from deep within, and he responded to it. He rolled to his right and brought his left leg up, securing her on the floor with him, locked between his leg and his arms. Her expression narrowed in frustration and she bared her teeth as if she thought she might bite her way free. She strained against him, unable to free herself.

"Yield."

"I thought this was to the death."

"Then you would be the one who'd died."

"What?" Her voice rose higher.

He jabbed his dagger hand into her rib cage just below the swell of her breast, a sensation she had evidently not felt moments earlier. She inhaled sharply.

"Oh."

"Even on her back, Tressandre ild Fallyn can be devastating, or so I've been told."

"You never slept with her."

"No."

They stayed entangled, her breath as she spoke gentle on his face.

"Why not?"

"I never wanted her."

"From what I hear, that made little difference if she wanted you."

Bistane shook his head slightly. "She wanted many people. She even called Sevryn to her side briefly. I believe he only went because you ordered him to."

"And men will talk."

"He didn't, but then, he didn't have to share details with me. Others did, from time to time, over the years. She is a voracious mistress. I believe the only man she ever really loved was Alton—which is why she will kill you."

"Because I killed him."

"Actually, it was Sevryn who dealt the killing blow, but that came out of mercy. Your jewel-studded armor blasted him into a living death, half man-half corpse burned beyond recognition. So, yes, Tressandre wants you for what happened to Alton as well as to clear the way to your title and your lands and whatever else she can grab."

Her hair pillowed her head on the arena floor, setting off the magnificent blues of her eyes. Her gaze rested on him, and her mouth curved softly. "You're watching me."

"Always."

"Waiting for me."

He inclined his head briefly.

"Why?"

"Because I couldn't not watch you or wait for you."

"And I never looked at you."

"Now that is blatantly untrue. You've danced with me, plotted war with me . . ."

"Yes, but, not like I'm seeing you now." And she moved a bit under him, reminding him how close their bodies were and how much she tempted him.

"I'm hoping that's a good thing."

"Oh, it is." She wrenched a hand free and put it up to trace the corner of his brow and brush back a stray bit of hair there. "It's too bad Sinok and Bistel are gone."

He frowned a bit. "Why?"

"Because they would have pushed for this alliance."

"I was a boy when your grandfather ruled."

"True. He held a certain distrust for your father as well. He couldn't understand why Bistel would have the inherited title of Warlord and yet be happiest tending the fields and groves of his lands. Or why the aryns flourished so greatly for your blood."

"My father used to say the guilty had just cause to be wary of the innocent because the innocent had never found their limit yet, so they didn't know how far they could be tested."

Lara laughed softly at that. "A man must be broken."

"A man must know what could break him, so he can be prepared to handle it rather than be shocked or used by it."

She wiggled under him again, getting comfortable, despite his ever increasing awareness of her. "And that was why Bistel was a Warlord. He looked at life like a strategy for . . . well, living. Victory."

"No. Not victory. Survival. And, once having survived, being able to reach for fulfillment. Joy."

"Joy," she repeated. "I hadn't thought of it that way."

"Why bother to live if there is no joy in it? No love?" His nose nearly met hers with her soft mouth just a touch away. He thought of hesitating, of pulling back and releasing Lara, and then he thought of what he'd just said. For once, he thought he knew exactly what Bistel had meant. He claimed a kiss from her—soft, slow, and gentle at first—with a heat behind it rising that she answered eagerly. After that kiss came another, and then the desire to taste her skin and her response to nibble him back and that progressed wonderfully until it didn't matter who was the victor and who the surrendered, and he had taught her what he meant and needed by love and joy.

The morning passed into late afternoon before they were truly done with one another, and Lara lay so quietly beside him, he thought she'd gone to sleep. He tensed his muscles so that he could ease from under her outflung arm, letting her rest, but she lifted her head.

"I hope you have an explanation for this, when my dresser asks me how I got the imprint of a dagger's haft on my ass." And with her other arm, she wrenched the blade from under her and held it up, only to let it clatter back to the arena floor.

"My apologies! I'm only sorry you didn't discover it sooner."

"I was . . . occupied." And she kissed the side of his jaw.

"I was going to use that for my excuse."

She laughed.

"That's a rare sound."

She nodded. "I'm much too solemn, I admit. It seemed the rulerly thing to do. I didn't dare laugh before Sinok passed, and I had little to laugh about after."

"Tranta used to coax one out of you now and then."

She tucked a wave of molten gold behind her ear. "He had that easy way, didn't he? Of course we all knew his true love was the sea."

"No woman could stand that competition."

"Indeed."

Silence curled up about them again. Lara slid a hand into his. "I'm going to say something, and I want you to consider it seriously."

The corner of his mouth went up in curiosity. "All right," he said cautiously.

"Not that it wouldn't be helpful to me, to Larandaril, but mostly because it's something I want—marry me."

His mouth worked, but not a word came out.

Lara considered him. "Is it that bad?"

"N-no! But unexpected."

"Perhaps I should have approached it strategically."

"There'd be no argument there, if I were to consider a diplomatic viewpoint on the proposal."

"But you have an argument?"

Bistane cleared his throat. He said, carefully, "No argument as long as you think you could love me, someday, as much as I love you."

"There's an argument in there?"

"An important one."

She traced his lips with a finger. "I plan on it. I hope for it. Only time will tell us if I'm successful. But I already do love, and that's a beginning, isn't it?"

"One of the best." He sat up, and drew her close to him, his lips at her delicately pointed ear. "Marry me, as I will marry you."

"Done." She laughed again and threw her arms about his shoulders.

"When do you wish to make the announcement?"

"My scribes will want to do fancy engravings and printings, but I think I will have them send birds out tomorrow morning. I don't want to wait any longer. I hear," and she brushed her lips over his cheek, "that Abayan Diort camps on the border, to be helpful if he might and to be a suitor, if called for. I think it's time we thanked him for his attentions."

"He has been a help."

"I know. But he's not for me."

"Understood. And what about . . . everything else."

Her eyes sparkled. "Everything else? The ritual, the celebration? I don't want to wait. I want to take the Moonlit Walk with you as soon as the skies allow."

"Now you're in a hurry."

"Yes. I've wasted too much time already. I want to be selfish."

"Done, then. I remind you it was your decision to wait this long."

"I'm glad I waited, but I do miss one thing about the young man you used to be."

"Oh?"

"You used to sing. Quite a lot."

"Ah. Well, it doesn't feel seemly for me now, what with minding the troops and two kingdoms and all."

"Right now, you're not minding anything but me. Sing me something."

He looked at her eyes, those same brilliant eyes before they'd made love, but now her lids curved into a sulky, pleasured expression. And so he sang for her one of his favorite songs of years past, about a boy wondering on the love he'd just discovered, a long leisurely song which put both of them to sleep before he could finish.

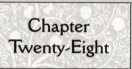

Chapter
Twenty-Eight

BISTANE SAW IT COMING. He saw it, he felt it, his muscles all bunched to move but not fast enough, and red pain lashed up the side of his head, taking him down. He threw out a hand to catch himself and felt his wrist tweak as it bent under his awkward weight, adding another lance of sharp pain through him. He hit then, in a cloud of agony and darkness that descended on him so quickly, he only caught a bit of Lara's dismay and scream.

He rolled onto his back. The lack of pain or even feeling anywhere except in his skull told him that something untoward surrounded him. That and the fact he could not see through the shrouds of ebony around him. He tried his voice.

"Where?"

"Where all good soldiers go at some time in their life."

Bistane put a hand to the side of his head where he'd been hit. It came away sticky as he thought it would. It smelled of blood, that metallic tang, that subtle other scent that people couldn't quite identify but any of the war dogs he owned would. Gradually his vision returned until he could see his hands, his fingers smeared with crimson, but not the surface he had fallen upon. He realized he couldn't hear Lara at all.

"Father."

"Son." Bistel moved within view, folded his long legs, and sat. On what, Bistane couldn't quite tell, but it was something. Tree stump, ottoman, saddle, cushion—who knew.

"Am I dead?"

"Of course not. Why would you think so?"

"Because of what you said."

Bistel's even voice rose a bit. "What I said? What blame do you put on me for foolish thoughts—ah. Yes, you could have misinterpreted me. Forgive me, then. I meant only that you'd had all the sense knocked out of you. Occupational hazard, I would think."

"Not if one can help it." Bistane sat up, head aching, but not his wrist which gave him pause because he knew he'd done damage to that as well. He flexed his right hand cautiously. Nothing. He shrugged and looked to his father. "Nice to have the company, I suppose."

"There's nothing nice about this visit. It is necessary." Bistel cut his hand through the air, his signal to prepare for a charge, and all the darkness about them fled before an onslaught of light. "This is a court of Gods, and they are about to convene on Kerith. You must know what you're facing."

He raised an eyebrow at the table revealed, with various high elven sitting about it, arguing amongst themselves, their aspect handsome yet brittle as though the comfortable, honest, qualities of aging had been carved away from them. "Are they aware?"

"Of you in this moment? Not yet. Of Kerith, very much so."

"Are they our Gods?"

"If you speak of Kerith, no. If you speak of Trevalka, our home, yes."

Trevalka. The spoken word jolted home internally. Brought a sting to his eyes and a momentary halt to his heart, as if he'd been struck with an ineffable power that touched him, seized him far harder than he'd have thought possible. He leaned forward. "Our lost world."

"Not so lost and, more probably, no longer ours." Bistel scratched the underside of his chin thoughtfully. "I barely remembered it, and you never had cause to think of it as home."

"Is it what you remember?"

"No." Bistel stood. As he did, he became more solid and clearer, his boots, his hands, the clarity of his sharp blue eyes deepened. "Our writings, what few remained, and what few we could decipher, for the magic that brought us here was meant to devastate us in totality, and nearly did . . . what few we could count as memories . . . told us of a fertile land. A land made prosperous by our ability to invent and build well, and to hold our farmers and tradesmen in kind regard for the work they did. What I see now is poisoned. Troubled. A land that is dying. And it was done to keep one woman in power, to increase her power, to put us in exile who would have opposed her."

"And what of these Gods? They wouldn't stop it?"

"They ride on the backs of the people who believe in them. They draw their godly powers from those same souls, having none of their own without that support. I'm not sure I would even call them Gods, except that now they do have power and a capricious ability to use it."

"And you said they had their eyes on Kerith."

"Yes." Bistel nodded to him. "Kerith is young. Promising. New. Fresh. For all the damage the Mageborn did to it, it's still relatively unspoiled. The pooled magics of the badlands are, unfortunately, an additional enticement to those who can siphon them off. Having been given a glimpse of our world, over the bridge Trevilara had built, the Gods want nothing more than to rule Kerith." Bistel turned his face away, assessing the court.

"We have our own Gods."

"We do, indeed, and they are beginning to rouse, but they are not such as these. Kerith's Gods are sunk deep into the basic elements of the world, and are dispersed throughout, no one with any great power in one place except for those anomalies such as earth-breaking events or terrible storms which can arise. They cannot defend themselves against such as these, unless it would be to band together and destroy the world as a whole, to destroy these Gods." Bistel faced him again.

"What can I do?"

"What any of us can hope to do. Live. Rise to meet the challenge. Prepare. Take whatever life offers you while you can." He paused. "Oh, by the way, congratulations on finally having taken steps with Lara."

Bistane would have answered that, but pain began to throb in the side of his head, and he became aware of warmth sliding down his face, at war with a cold, rough cloth in the same area, and a massive throbbing ache that ruled his wrist. The court of Gods grew blurry though not before all of them turned, en masse, and focused on him.

"We have another one of them," a beautiful but hollow sounding woman said.

"He knows how to break the chains. Crush him now."

Caught between one heartbeat and the next, Bistane could only curl his lip in defiance at them as Kerith reached up to snatch him out of harm's way. His last awareness was not of the Gods of Trevalka hurling epithets at him, but of his father's calm voice saying, "It is war, Bistane, but we are warriors."

He wanted to tell his father something important that occurred to him just as he was yanked away, his thoughts reeling and then impaled on sharp blades as he began to gain consciousness. He grunted and threw a hand out to protect himself as a cold, rough cloth scraped over the wound, bringing his eyes open.

"Gods above and below," Lara said. "I thought I'd killed you!"

He caught her and then yelped as it sent shocks through his wrist.

Lara scrunched down even lower. "Sarota is on her way. Your wrist, too?" She probed at it gently.

"Tried to break my fall."

"Of course." Lara damped her rag and put it to his head again, and he gently took it from her fingers and held it in place himself. She rocked back a little. Her hair hung in gold-and-silver wisps about her face, and there was a tear trail down one perfect cheekbone, through the dirt on her face. "I thought I'd killed you," she said again.

"Not for lack of trying."

"You should have rolled with it!"

"If I had seen it coming a little sooner, yes. As it was, I managed to keep my head on my shoulders."

She put her fist to her mouth, muffling her words. "I know. I didn't realize you'd gone to rest and we'd disengaged. I have no way of catching you that much off guard otherwise."

"Actually, you do. You've trained well. And I—" He thought to stand, but the world went sideways and slid out from under him. "I think I'll just wait here on the ground for Sarota."

"That might be wise." She started to add something, but then the shadows of approaching figures touched them and she fell silent as Sarota hurried into the area, a basket of simples under her arm.

"Now," Sarota commented as she dropped down beside Bistane. "I was expecting to see my lady on her ass, not you."

"Her technique has improved."

"So I see." Sarota frowned as she pulled his hand and cloth away. "You'll need stitches. Honey should be a good enough poultice. I have a few herbs for a drink you'll need to take. You'll have a dashing scar just behind your left eyebrow and over your temple."

"It'll give me that sardonic look I've been lacking."

Sarota traded looks with Lara. "Seems you haven't jogged his brain too badly."

"Hard to tell."

"I know, it often is with men." Deftly she cleaned his wound, not caring if he yelped or gasped, and even more deftly pulled the skin flaps together and stitched it. Something she'd put on numbed the skin a bit, but he was used to stitching and put it out of his mind, except for the pulling. That always unnerved him a bit. He could tell when she knotted the thread off and broke it, albeit sharply, between her fingers because the last tug pulled smartly and he hissed through his lips.

Sarota laughed softly. "Such a brave one. Now let's have a look at the wrist." He put his forearm across her thigh while she expertly probed the wrist, then popped it back into place with a gentle manipulation. "Wear wraps on it for a few days. Soak it as you would one of the horses. You'll be lame for a bit, but nothing is broken. No more sparring till it heals sound, or else you'll tear a ligament permanently, understand?"

"Perfectly." He rotated his wrist a bit gingerly, but it felt better than it had. It would be sore for the better part of a week, though, unless he missed his guess.

"I'll have that potion sent . . . where?"

"My offices," Lara said. She stood smoothly and brought him up by the elbow.

"Done."

"Our thanks."

Sarota waved it off. "It's what you hired me for." She closed her basket as she walked off, telling the young apprentice who'd said not a word but stood nearby watching with keen eyes everything that had transpired, and now took notes, hurrying to keep up with the long stride of her teacher.

"Your office?"

"We have logistics to plan, haven't we?"

"I thought we were just going to Calcort."

"I think a visit to Hawthorne as well would be advisable."

"You'd leave Larandaril alone that long?"

"Farlen knows what must be done."

"The ranks are thin."

"Don't you think I know that? I saw most of them die; to me, it's as if it happened yesterday." She took a moment. "I have to recruit."

"Yes."

"Calcort isn't big enough to fulfill the needs. Hence, Hawthorne."

"It's your ass," he told her. "You've not done that much riding in a long while."

"And what's wrong with my ass?" She feigned a look over her shoulder as they crossed the arena.

"Nothing, but it's going to be too sore for me to so much as think of touching it before that trip is over."

"Then make sure my saddle is padded with a skin."

"Majesty! Are you that green a horsewoman?"

"Evidently. And as I do love it when you caress my ass, it should be protected. Make a note of that as soon as we get upstairs."

And so he did.

Tolby unrolled the message scroll, small and precise as it must be. He read carefully.

Lara, Warrior Queen of Larandaril, sends greetings and hopes of good health. I have planned a visit to Calcort to celebrate the engagement of myself and Bistane Vantane and begin a long overdue acquaintance with the children Merri and Evarton. Expect arrival soonest.

He let the slip of paper snap back in his fingers.

"Engaged? She is engaged?" Nutmeg bounced to his side, eager hands reaching for and capturing the message from him. "I imagine you'll be at the shop, too." Tolby raised an eyebrow at her.

"With Lara?"

"Who else? The queen has announced her engagement, has she not? I expect there's a need for a fancy gown or two, aye?"

Nutmeg's hand flew to her mouth. "Bright apples! That almost completely flew over my head. She finally took a look at Bistane!"

"And liked what she saw, sounds as if. She's made a power match, for certain, and one hopes love is worked in there, too. I know Bistane has had eyes on her since he was a boy who could see."

"Think he'll be good for her?"

Tolby nodded. "It spans beyond my years, but from all the tales I've heard, his father Bistel loved only two women in his long life, Bistane's Vaelinar mother and then the Dweller woman who birthed Verdayne. I'm not saying there might not have been a dalliance or two through the centuries, but Bistel had a strong heart, he did."

"I thought that of him."

"And rightfully so. I think Bistane is an apple that will not fall far from that tree, and Verdayne as well."

Nutmeg shook her head as if to dodge a truth in his words she wasn't ready to hear. Instead she read the message again. "I can't believe she's coming here."

"And why not? She's eager to see the babes and she has recruitment to begin. Her losses were considerable and although Bistane has been able to hold his domain and hers, that cannot continue indefinitely. She has to rebuild her troops and I imagine she'll be looking to Kernans and Dwellers to do so, the ranks of the Vaelinars being thin." Tolby took his pipe from his mouth and examined it for a moment before continuing. "She's right if she thinks I won't be 'allowing' my family to move back to her manor."

Nutmeg's jaw set. "It's my family."

"What? Oh. Well, that it is, that it is. Yours and . . . hmmmpf, well. Your decision."

"Not that your advice isn't well noted and often taken."

A small cloud of blue smoke drifted up.

"Where will she stay?"

"Oh, at the mayor's inn, I imagine. For sleeping and eating, but doubt she'll be there for much else."

"Then I expect I had better start cleaning." Nutmeg inhaled deeply.

"Your mother would appreciate that."

"I had planned to start working there half-days, now that the children are grown a bit."

"Yes, you need a life beyond the needs of small children. Not that your days aren't busy, but your mother and I see a young woman who can handle more."

Nutmeg shifted uneasily as her father's words hit a little too close to home. She picked up her shawl against a raw spring wind that had picked up outside. "I think I should have a word with Mom about the letter. Clean house or a ready workshop."

"If I know your mother," and his eye gleamed a bit, "and I daresay I do, she'll manage to have both."

Nutmeg pulled her shawl tight. "I'll be back before luncheon," she called out, as much to her auntie as to her father.

"If not, I expect Corrie can handle it." Tolby clamped his pipe and added, "I'll be in the cider barn." Tolby watched his daughter go out the farmhouse door and begin her short walk down the lane. "Pot calling the kettle black," he muttered to himself. "Good thing I've got a pipe to stick in my mouth and not say what I can't bring back." He put his shoulders back with a mild grunt as his spine creaked a bit before making his way out to the cider barn. Dayne should hear the news as well, and who better to give it to him? The lad was made of the same stout stuff as his father and brother. Still, curiosity prickled at Tolby as he wondered how his audience would take the news.

Corrie slid away from the doorway as heavy treads moved outside. She looked into the playroom where Evarton listened to Merri's babbled instructions on whatever it was they were building with their busy little hands clasped around their blocks. They would be occupied for a few moments at least, until Evar tired of his sister's bossiness. She slipped into the small, adjunct bedroom that served as her quarters.

It was, truth be told, as big as the small room that had served as her bedroom with her husband, but it seemed much smaller than any other room in the vast farmhouse, in comparison. She ought not to be comparing. She ought to be grateful for what she had, a good job as an auntie for a year or two, enabling her husband to work his farm free and clear of debt after the drought. Ought to be, but this position now strangled her, closing in about her heart and throat until she could scarcely think. All that she loved she no longer saved but put in deepest jeopardy.

She sat at her desk, a shelf that hung down from the wall, over the sink basin, and took out a tiny scrap of paper, her pen, and ink. Laboriously, for her work-worn hand could barely cramp small enough to make the letter as dainty as it needed to be and when she'd finished and blotted, her knuckles stung. Corrie reread the paper to make certain she'd said what she ought, before tidying away her supplies in a lower drawer of the wash basin and folding the shelf up against the wall.

She had no writing desk at home. Nothing but a table, worn and sanded now and then against the outrages of everyday living, the nicks and stains. But it had been her table, and her grandmother's before that. Corrie sighed. She slipped the paper into her pocket as she stood.

"Merri! Evarton! It's a beautiful day. Shall we go for a walk? If you behave, there might be a candy twist waiting for you."

She could hear the blocks falling as two little bodies scrambled to get to their feet. By the time they reached their doorway, she had their little duster coats ready to hand to them.

"Where we going?"

"Where? Hmmm." She seemed to consider. "We could go out to the vineyard."

Merri wrinkled her nose. "Smelly."

Indeed, it was. Tolby and Verdayne had just sprayed it a day or two before, to protect against voracious insects getting to the fruit just beginning to emerge from the blossoms. "Right on that. Where else?"

"I want to see the birds." Evar smiled winningly up at her.

"The messengers?"

Merri bounced. "Dose ones!"

Corrie returned their cheer. "All right, then." She opened the door to shoo them out. "It's a long walk. Don't dawdle!"

As she went through the threshold, she checked her pocket to make sure she had the letter and a coin for payment secreted deep within.

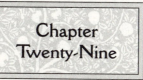

Chapter
Twenty-Nine

TRESSANDRE STRIPPED HER GLOVES off her hands, back half-turned to her seneschal, who stood tentatively in the threshold of her audience room.

"I take it this is something that cannot wait until I've cleaned and dined?"

"Best not to, my lady." His voice faltered on the last word and Tressandre frowned in response. She came around.

"What is it, then?"

"It concerns our high pastures."

She glowered at him, a line like a dagger deepening between her honey-colored brows. "What of them?" They'd been seized at great risk two centuries ago, but neither Bistel nor Lariel had gone to war over it, though they could have. Instead, what passed for a Vaelinar tribunal ordered fines which went to those of Kerith who had owned the lands, and the matter had been forgotten. "They comprise some of our best meadowlands. How could I forget them? We are horse-breeders, Waryn, not farmers." And lumberjacks and mercenaries and slavers. And damned goat herders, for only the goats could live as they did, leaping from sheer rock to sheer rock. She waited for the tall, spare man, with his one shoulder twisted out of sync with the rest of his body, an injury that had never healed straight, incurred in a fight with Alton when she and her brother had been very young. They had been deadly even then, she thought with a little pride, and tilted her head to encourage the man to finish his message.

"We had to bring the herd there down and pasture them elsewhere. The pass should be blocked off so that they won't return if they get loose."

"And why must we do that?"

"It's gone bad, my lady."

She didn't need to hear this now, not now or at all. She rubbed the ball of her thumb over the strong bridge of her nose. "How can that be? Weeds? We can bring in sprayers and have that sorted out in a season or two. Damming the pass seems a bit overreactive for that, don't you think?"

He shifted weight uneasily. "The wranglers have seen a leakage from the badlands nearby."

"A leak?"

"Chaos."

"Waste from the Mageborn Wars. The twisted magic."

"Yes, and a substantial flow. It's perverting much of the area."

"How bad?"

"We'd had one three-legged colt and one two-headed colt born this spring. And . . . other things are infiltrating the meadows. Vermin. Predators, mutated, that shouldn't be there. They put any animals we have on the range at great risk."

She should not be surprised as she'd seen this befouling before. "Plant aryns." The only good ever to come out of House Vantane, as far as she and hers were concerned. The trees thrived on a bit of chaos.

"We did twenty years back. They can no longer cleanse what is leaking in; it's too massive a breach. Nor do I think we will be able to obtain more, under the present circumstances."

Betrayed by the Vantanes again. Even their precious, dear-held trees could not keep her meadowlands clear. What use either of them, then? Her frown deepened, to the bone it felt like. "You've cleared the area?"

"Yes."

"Then we must obtain additional pastures. First, is the incursion of the badlands known? Do the Kernans bandy about gossip and talk behind their hands about the misshapen foals?"

"The village is not what it used to be. Winters have grown too harsh for them, and much of the population has moved on. But those left behind, yes, they know what's happened."

"Good. Remind them that the land is tainted when you take new but clean pastures from them."

"My lady . . ."

"What did you fail to understand?" She stared at a spot on his brow.

"Nothing. Will we pay for these new fields?"

"As little coin as you can. We are, after all, doing them a favor as we move the last of them out of their homes or they might be subjected to the Mageborn waste as well. Ensure they understand how benevolent we're being. Then get the trees, I don't care how, raid the damn orchard if you must—Bistane is still playing at guardian for Lariel and Gods only know where the half-breed has gone to these days, so the estate is far from fully-manned. Plant the aryns as soon as you can, before the summer heat makes it disadvantageous, and we'll plant a second grove in the fall. We won't save that pasture, but we can't afford a spread." She slapped her gloves against the thigh of her riding pants. "Bad luck, then. All right, let the wranglers know they've done the right thing, but don't . . ." She paused for a long moment, thinking. "Don't block the pass."

"My lady?"

Tressandre smiled slightly. "Having a bit of perverted magic handy might be a distinct advantage, don't you think? There was a time when we had the Talent to use that Chaos. Who knows? Our program might bring that ability back. It would be a shame to have made the ashes of the Mage-born unavailable."

"My lady, yours are the strategic skills. I merely do my best to implement them." Waryn bowed, a slight crease of pain etching across his face that faded when he straightened. His bones popped faintly as he did.

"Neither of us is bound to forget that." Tressandre dropped her gloves on a nearby table. "I will be dining alone in my rooms."

"I shall notify the staff." He bowed again and left, a little stiffness in his gait. He was not pure-blooded, by ild Fallyn standards, although a good bit of his bloodline had been recovered through their programs. He showed it, however, in the aging of his body. She ought to be making plans for the seneschal who would replace him, when the time came. It would be sooner than expected; it always was with these races of Kerith who had nothing like the life span the Vaelinar held.

"Oh." He came to a stop, having remembered something.

"Yes?"

"The harvest you ordered commandeered has been taken successfully, and traded. The Guild reports that monies have already been deposited in estate accounts."

"Paperwork?"

"All done by handshake. Untraceable."

"Excellent. Plan the next one."

Smiling, he left again.

"Waryn."

He stopped three paces beyond the threshold and moved about to face her. "Yes, my lady?"

"Find that young man . . . Borvan?"

"The tall one? All meat and muscle?"

"Yes." Her mouth curved in memory. "That would be him. Have him cleaned and sent up to my rooms. Oh, and a draught of kedant, as well."

He bowed in response and left again, Tressandre smiling faintly in his wake. He had tried but could not quite suppress the dislike in his expression when she'd mentioned the viper poison, but he had never found it as useful as she had. In proper quantities, that should be noted. Tressandre trailed her fingers over her jacket, to her buttons, and began to undo them one by one as she took the bank of stairs to the rooms of her apartment.

She did not, however, hear the steps of an eager lover moving down the hallway to her open door. Instead, a bump and scuffle and shuffle gave her pause. Danger? No. It sounded like two of her staff fought each other at the top of the stairs.

"You bring her the news. You downed the bird and rode here with the scroll."

"She'll kill the messenger. You know that as well as I. Give it to one of the servants and let them grovel for their life. I won't. I've trained for my position, and I won't lose my life because I've done it and done it well."

"You have only accomplished half the task."

"And dying at her hand is the other half?"

"Your duty is the other half."

"My duty was upheld when I delivered the message here. Now you're the one who refuses to complete the task."

"Me? I'm only an apprentice scribe."

Tressandre overheard as much as she cared to before rebuttoning her jacket, sitting at her desk, and shouting to the hallway, "Quit scuffling and someone discover their balls. If there is a message, it needs to be delivered."

A sudden quiet fell outside her apartment. Not for the first or last time, she wished that Alton were lounging in the chair nearby, for it would have been he who got to his feet and went to fetch the errant messenger and message. She waited and not patiently. After a long moment, the huntsman entered.

She looked him up and down. Pale under his tan, he looked as if he'd ridden a decent way, covered with dust and dried sweat upon his face. He would not look her in the eye but held out a message tube, still sealed with the wax and appropriate signet of Larandaril.

"I am well aware that the Warrior Queen has been revived. What other ill news could come out of her kingdom?" She snatched the tube from his palm and peeled it open. Before unrolling it, she grabbed the huntsman by the tip of his ear. "Perhaps you heard gossip on the road?"

"N-no, milady. Nothing. I took no time to stop once I shot the bird down."

She put her hand under his chin to force his gaze up. "Am I that fearsome?"

He froze for a long moment before saying reluctantly, "Yes."

"Good. I am someone you should fear." Tressandre turned her attention back to the message tube, opening it and sliding the scroll free into her hand. "When did you bring the bird down?"

"Yester eve, milady. They sent flights out near sunset."

"Really?" That meant they were of some importance, to send the birds out so close to night and their nesting time. She crumbled the wax seal off between her fingertips, sharp nails shredding the wax. Her eyebrows knotted toward each other as she narrowed her gaze to read the paper and fine, small writing upon it. She would have to find a healer skilled with eyes, Tress thought fleetingly, for she was getting a bit long-sighted. She focused on reading.

The words burned into her and her hand fisted about the paper, going white-knuckled. The huntsman stood his ground, but the blood drained out of his face so that he looked as white as the parchment she'd just crushed in her hand.

"You may go."

The huntsman inclined his head and fled with long strides. Tressandre had dropped her head in thought, but she watched him leave through bangs the color of dark and wild honey. In another lifetime, she might have steered him to her bed. Sometimes fear made sex all the sweeter. But not today.

She yelled for Waryn. She could hear the hallways fill with skittering boot steps as the search began for her seneschal.

Tressandre uncurled her hand. She picked the wad of paper out and put it on the desk, smoothing it out just enough so that Waryn would be able to read it for himself. A bitter laugh escaped her.

"Sooner or later, this alliance between north and south would come about. I knew it, we all knew it—Bistane has haunted your shadow for years, unwilling or perhaps even unable to look elsewhere. But this is a match you should never have considered making, for it leaves Abayan Diort to me." She spread the missive out a bit more. "He will want to listen to me."

Auntie Corrie took a chair quietly in the parlor, her mending work in her lap, and her eyes on the polished kettle which reflected to her, round and brassy looking, a view of the children's room where Merri and Evar sat playing. They knew only that she had withdrawn within earshot and that they were free to play a bit before naptime, the room already gathering a heat to its edges and corners which would add to their sleepiness in time. Smart as they were, and both of them smart as whips, they had not yet cottoned onto the tea kettle mirror that reflected them to their caretaker. Corrie doubted she had more than another moon's length to observe them unknown. Evarton would spot it, or Merri sense it, and her advantage would be flown. In the meantime, both sides enjoyed these little times of freedom, illusionary though they might be. Corrie picked up her needle and wooden egg so that she could darn the socks waiting in her lap.

She could hear them, too, and the children always seemed well aware of that, careful to keep their voices pitched down, but children's voices carried far easier than an adult's muted tones. Eerie children they were, like wise and educated old souls stuffed into new and young flesh, and she did not like it when they watched her as if they would know all her secrets. Her needle clicked about the wooden egg as she drew yarn through and wove it. For all that the one was heir to the throne and the other her fast companion, there were few women about willing to play the auntie to these two. Uncanny, they whispered. Sweet children, but strange. Passing strange, and Corrie did not think their doting mother had the slightest idea.

Merri said, "No making."

"Not a puppy," her brother told her.

"No."

"I make. Mama's ears like ours. Eyes like ours."

"No."

Evar huffed. "Already did it."

Someone pushed a jumble of wooden blocks about. Corrie guessed it to be Evar, sulking. He could have a temper, that one.

A much softer "No." Merri, the peacemaker. Always smiling, even when she cried over something, as if she knew something better was just around the corner. "Here. Make this." And it sounded as if she pushed something toward Evar.

A moment of silence followed, but it wasn't a serene silence. Corrie put her sock and egg in her lap, an intangible something in the air that made the fine hairs along her arm crawl and a chill go up the back of her neck. She had no words for the feeling that crawled through the air but fixed her gaze on her tea kettle mirror to see what the two were about. Evarton held one hand in the air as if he were about to reach over and tap Merri on the head. She sat, wide-legged with her attention close on him as a . . . Corrie could hardly find words for it . . . a bridge of wooden blocks assembled itself in thin air, arching ever higher until it ran out of blocks to use.

Evar let out a soft grunt. He made a fist and waved it in the air and the blocks, which had been vacillating and wavering, hung in the air as though stuck there.

The feeling that had slithered over Auntie Corrie's skin fell away, leaving her breathless. She knotted her fingers into the socks she had been repairing, scarcely aware of the needle jabbing into her fingertip. What had the boy just done?

"There," he said, with victory spiking his voice.

Merri climbed to her feet, chubby hands in the air, reaching to touch the blocks which hung between them. She cooed in approval. She ran her fingers over the blocks she could reach, tugging on them, and they stayed fixed in the air, hanging on . . . nothing. With a delighted chortle, she bent over, grabbed a rag horse from nearby and proceeded to gallop it over the bridge, at least as high as she could stretch. Then she pulled a stool over and clambered to the top and continued her toy's progress up and over the bridge until she could land her rag doll happily on top of Evar's head.

"Yay!"

Evar snorted. He helped her down from the stool and proceeded to march two of his clothespin soldiers over the same bridge, into her territory. They proceeded to have a bit of a battle on the bridge, as children will do, bringing another stool into play, but since they were child-sized stools and not built for longer legged adults, neither child stood very high in the air at all and Corrie saw no reason to step in.

She returned to her darning, keeping only an occasional glance out for the two and after four pairs, carefully mended, lay across her knee, she heard Evar mumble, "I'm tired." And with that, the bridge collapsed noisily and unceremoniously all over the nursery floor, blocks scattering. He staggered off to his little cot and climbed into it, his eyelids fluttering to sleep almost immediately while Merri, hands on her hips, stood and watched in doubt until her companion let out a soft, toddler snore.

"Hmmph." She kicked a path through the blocks to her own cot and climbed into it, tucking her rag horse under one elbow and soon fell into a nap herself.

Only then did Corrie feel free to move to her writing desk and jot down a little of what she'd seen, to be sent away later. Her mistress seemed hungry for observations of whatever power either of the children had. This ought to serve for a while.

"You will be tempted," Ceyla said, smothering a yawn. She fluttered her eyes a moment, trying to get the dust of sleep out of them. The day was nearly opened, still gray and dew-sparkled, but it would be hot later. She could feel the dryness in the sun's rays already. A moment's worth of homesickness struck her, surprising her with a yearning for the seacoast where the ild Fallyn Fortress perched. No hot, sticky days there. If anything too much damp and chill, but today that sounded almost inviting. Almost. She might be drawn into a midday nap, but the oracle poked at her relentlessly and she had to say what she knew. Had to deliver the vision she'd been given. Luckily, her audience did not mind, nor did he give her greater credence than she deserved. He valued her but he was not enslaved to her words. That kept tension and misgivings away from her as little else ever had.

As if knowing she thought of him, he leaned forward. "And what might tempt me?"

"Few things in life, I deem, from my time spent with you." She grinned at him suddenly. "Maybe you'll have a chance to push Bregan off a cliff."

He grunted at that. "That might indeed interest me unduly. But is that all you truly have to tell me?"

She nodded. "Little came to me but that, an envoy, a shapely one, bearing news and an offer."

"No wisdom on whether to accept it or not?"

"Not revealed to me." Ceyla looked down at the scrub grasses and dirt under her sandaled feet. She felt reticent, all of a sudden, unwilling to share her innermost feelings with Diort.

"Nothing?" He curved his strong hand and raised her chin.

"I remember being jealous. That's all."

"Ummm. I shall tell this envoy to watch her back when I tell her to leave, then."

Her face went hot and burned under her chin where his fingers stayed, lingering. She said nothing else until he dropped his hand and moved away.

"And when will this envoy approach?"

"Soon." Ceyla scurried away then, to the women's long tent, where she could hide among the workers. She could feel his stare on her back, somewhere between her shoulder blades, and her face refused to cool. She should have stuck to the vision and nothing more. She'd said too much. It could be the death of her.

Chapter Thirty

Trevalka

DHURIEL SET HER DOWN with a growl. The road turned this way and that through a nondescript valley, but it led to many a city of riches beyond, after a considerable journey. A thin layer of dust hung over the hillocks, betraying an approach from the other direction and a reluctant yield of the pass to end of winter weather. The ground about her stayed frozen, the grasses and shrubbery brown, but beyond thawed enough that dirt could be churned up. The air shivered about her, warning of more snow and winter's grip tightening soon.

"Don't be crass," Trevilara told him. "It's as much to your benefit as mine."

"I am not a pack animal."

"Nor am I a pack." She shook the skirts of her dress out as if he had rumpled it while carrying her in his arms. The simple muslin showed stains, old and new, and smelled of grease and wood smoke. Her blouse was frayed on the placket where buttons strained against the button holes. Trevilara tapped one thoughtfully. It was not that she was so big-busted, she had never been, though the dress certainly seemed to fit her in that way. Her hair hung down in oily twists and she felt thoroughly disgusting. She straightened her sleeves. "Now slap me."

"You tempt me."

"Fool God. I want to look as though I was beaten and left on the road. Do hurry, I can hear them approach."

Dhuriel shimmered close enough that she could see the manlike form at the core of all the flames, his eyes tight with disgust and anger, his hand within his soot-dark sleeve rising, but she did not see the actual swing. The blow, ice-cold and red-hot in equal measures, stung across her face and rocked her back onto her heels before she curved her body protectively, for Dhuriel seemed to enjoy it far too much and she thought he would hit her again. And he did, faster than she could dodge, with a short burst of a laugh before he curled away, edges bright blue among the orange-and-yellow flickers. When she straightened, she tasted blood on her lip and the air hitting her rib cage where the dress's bodice tore open. She ached, but she would not make a sound other than to say, "Well done." She'd give Dhuriel no satisfaction for abusing her.

Trevilara shook her head to clear her thoughts. "Wait nearby."

Within the fire, she saw Dhuriel's lip curl. "If I wish."

She licked some of the blood off her lip. "I implore you."

"You needn't. You've already sealed the bargain to be brought here and brought back. You forgot to stipulate when."

"I don't know when." The sound of hoofbeats filled her throbbing head. "Please do not abandon me when the moment arises that I need you." She hoped she sounded subservient enough; she held little patience for this fool of a God. She fed him his strength. What would he be on that day when she decided to rescind her support? Nothing. Not even a hot ash smoldering out in the night. She would see to that.

The manlike form within the fire watched her with soulless eyes. His nostrils flared. "Very well."

"Thank you," and she swept a deep curtsy.

He turned his back on her in answer.

Trevilara swallowed tightly. She would not have to resort to these measures if she had the Ferryman and Daravan by her side. But the Ferryman, alas, had succumbed to plague, of all things, and Daravan had not yet returned from his tasks on Kerith. He worked to prepare it for the two of them. The world would be a little small for her, after all, but clean and bursting with possibilities, not sunk into its festering decline. She allowed herself to feel sorrow for the dying of Trevalka, and crumpled to her side on the dirt road. She waved a hand at Dhuriel. "Leave me," she said, "until I call for you."

White-hot heat flared out, not touching her but very, very close, and then the God disappeared. Trevilara fanned the heat from her face, feeling the tiny drops of sweat that covered her profusely. Fool God. She closed her eyes. Cold thrilled through her in Dhuriel's absence as the wind came up in a thin, chill wail about her, and she wrapped her arms about her knees as proof against the cold. The next time she came out wearing another's skin, she'd make certain a cloak would be involved. She could, of course, put up her fire, but that would ruin the image of abject poverty and helplessness she wished to project. She sank into meditation, awaiting discovery.

Winter's chill bit at her, from the inside out. Her bones ached as if they could split open, burst from within her very marrow by the expanding ice. She had heard old people complain about the various aches and pains in their elder years, but she did not feel this was her lot. No, the cracking pain came from deeper within, seeded by disappointment, fostered by fear of losing. She was the only God who had the will, the courage, to live as she did, and the others cowered before her rather than look her in the eyes. She ate from them just as she feasted on the subjects around her. It was her right! Only the strong could take and hold, only the steadfast and Talented. Only she who had chosen the road she walked. The loss she feared could be nothing more than a misstep, a teetering on the edge of her path.

So she sat in the moment, wrapped in another's skin, someone who had not had the will or strength. Trevilara shook herself slightly. The other's skin itched, the area unreachable because it was on the underside of the disguise where it rested over her own, and no way to scratch it could be managed. She clamped her teeth shut against the irritation. Nothing more than a gnat, she told herself, compared to what she'd gone through and was prepared to endure in the future. Her world was poisoned. Her purging efforts failed. Her cleansing efforts had not yet shown success and were likely as not to fail as well. Survival would be won only by the strong. She judged herself able and no longer cared how any other might judge her. She had moved beyond that.

She felt the vibration in the ground before she heard the approach. The hoofbeats, the boot stamps, of an approaching army reverberated throughout her body. Trevilara lifted her chin, bringing her fully out of her thoughts. Her right knee, cloaked in cloth and silk, itched abominably. She slapped at the irritation and felt her borrowed skin sting before all sensation faded. In answer to her plight, before the question could be asked by those who approached, she leaned over and began to rock, wailing, and found tears she could shed. She pulled moisture out of the air around her and condensed it about her eyes, feeling the drops form and roll down her borrowed cheeks.

The road crested slightly and then curved behind her. She could hear the jangle of bits and the creak of leather as well as the slow drum of hooves. Not all were mounted. In fact, most were not. As she huddled over and rocked back and forth, her wailing dismay growing louder, she peeked at them from under one arm curved about her head as if to protect herself from any more blows of fate. The army was a much smaller size than she anticipated, without uniforms, most of their clothing little more than rags. Did her lieutenants and spies think her a fool for reporting this . . . this crew of stragglers as a formidable foe? Or had they even carried out their duties and approached this band as ordered?

She studied the leader riding to the fore. He alone wore clothes in one piece, his silvery skin showing through the open vest he wore rather than a shirt, a garment of curly white wool. Black leather pants stretched over muscular thighs. And a gossamer-like sheen wove its way about him. She wondered what magic he carried about him like a veil.

She would know in mere moments. She thrust herself to her feet crying out in warning, and at her reveal, a troop of men sprang out from behind the trees and scrub bushes, attacking from ambush. War cries shrilled in the air. Horses reared. The ragged crew dropped back in formation and, with only their hand-carried weapons and a few archers to the rear, answered the attack.

Feigning fear, Trevilara fell back, off the road, huddled against a tree and watched what should have been a rout by her hand-picked troop. They had the weapons and the discipline, dismounting and moving confidently into the fray. She knew after the first confrontation that this man's soldiers were no ordinary mongrels despite their looks. They fought without fear and total disregard for their bodies. She'd never seen anything like it or the total slaughter which she witnessed in a handful of moments.

The soldiers did not bleed. They did not bend from steel and their bodies, appearing ragged and frail, turned blades aside as if they were wood and stone. The only two she saw fall came from beheadings, while her own men collapsed under the sheer repeated weight of the attack. When silence fell, far too soon, she found herself trembling and wondering if Dhuriel could reach her in time to bear her away.

Trevilara straightened. If she had to, she could shed this borrowed skin and flame up protectively although that would not solve the problem of getting all the answers she needed. This . . . man . . . if he was a man, and his troop, had been marching and raiding along the perimeters of her kingdom for two very harsh seasons now, yet they had not marched into Throne City. From what she could see of their tactics, few could have stopped them until they reached her. Spring would bring them like a flood when winter thawed.

So why did they hesitate? What did the leader intend? Only words with him could tell her what she wanted to know, if he would talk.

As if sensing her observation of him, the man turned his horse about and paced it forward. He stopped close enough to talk but far enough away that it would be difficult to truly engage him. He had magnificent Vaelinar eyes, gray with obsidian arrows and the darkest of sable flecks. She sensed no power about him other than the stink of death and blood. He did not look to her like a full-blooded Vaelinar, but if another race, from a little-traveled continent, ran in his blood, she did not recognize it.

"You warned us."

"I am an envoy. Queen Trevilara sent me to treat with you. My escort"—and she flung her hand out to indicate the fallen bodies—"disobeyed orders. They beat me for disputing their intentions and set me aside. They would have killed me when they were done with you and your men. I think they thought me dead already." And she let part of her borrowed skin sag away from her torso in a bloody, flayed strip.

She did not see a reaction, familiar or otherwise, light in his eyes. Did the man feel no sympathy or understanding? Did he, like the warriors he'd directed, not fear maiming or death? She fumbled back her silk clothing, holding the skin back to her ribs, debating her actions.

"What did your queen send you to say?"

She looked up. "Your presence has been noted. Your actions have been reported. She wishes to know your intentions. Are you carving out an empire of your own or do you wish to enter into hers?"

"Queen Trevilara is known to me, as well. I am, for the moment, called Quendius."

She bit the inside of her lip. No true answers. Would he give them up only in the presence of a ruler?

"She asks why she should not send her army to dispatch your threat. Will it be peace or war between the two of you?"

"Do I threaten her?"

"Do you not?"

"It seems to me that I was the one intended to be intimidated and threatened. Either she attacked me, or troops of her so-called army are ill-disciplined. I would hazard a guess that a good ruler doesn't allow bad discipline." His horse pawed the road restively, but he sat at ease on the creature. She recognized the breed, one of the prized war horses of the south. Had he come from the south, from dens of rebellion there, or had he merely acquired the animal along the way? The other few and spare horses of his troop looked as though they were strays, picked up wherever convenient upon the road. Whatever the manner of his equipping, he sat still and watched her shrewdly, obeying the first rule of engagement which is to listen, and keep listening until your opponent blurts out that which he is afraid for you to learn.

Trevilara decided she did not deal with a fool and let her head drop in shame. "I did not warn you. That was a signal for the men to attack. I was ordered by my mistress to set up an ambush to see if you and your men were as capable as her spies had told her. You may kill me, if you wish, and send my body back as your answer. I live to serve her." She looked up to meet his gaze. "That will not, however, answer her fully as to your intentions."

The dark shards in his gray eyes seemed to glitter. He crossed his wrists on the front of the saddle, leaning forward, bringing his chiseled face closer to view her better. "She is willing to sacrifice whatever she might choose for information, including yourself. How close are you to your queen's magic and counsel?"

She could not think of a ready answer for him and stammered a bit. He stopped her. "Enough. You smell of blood and lies, and the blood is not fresh nor the lies believable. If your queen wishes to treat with me, she must come herself. Tell her I can help her cross the bridge."

They locked gazes.

She only had one bridge that she could not cross on her own and wished to, and that one closed since the apparent death of Daravan beyond. She tried to think how he might know of it, or how he might be baiting her. She did not immediately ask which bridge, and he smiled slowly. "See what I can do for her." He turned away in his saddle to face the carnage behind him and raised one hand.

As he did so, one of her dead soldiers got to his feet, tottering, before steadying himself. He turned blind eyes to her, swung about on one heel and fell in with the ranks behind Quendius. Then another. And another.

Until all stood but the one or two who were so utterly destroyed they had not enough limbs to stand or swing a weapon. Yet that was not the worst of what she watched. When her dead men stood and fell into ranks behind their new leader, his men fell in with them. Embraced them. And when they stood, flank to flank, heel to heel, hip to hip . . . their very flesh began to waver. To grow transparent. To melt. With a shouted command, the pairs of soldiers, his and hers, stepped into each other, becoming one. Taller. Thicker. Indubitably stronger. No longer recognizable as the men they had been, their features swallowed by the soldiers who absorbed them. When Quendius was done watching them, he squared around to her. He drew his sword and flayed her disguise away from her in three quick slashes, and she stood naked and bare, her stolen skin in bloody strips about her feet.

"War feeds us. Defeat only strengthens us," he said to her. "Tell your queen that."

He reined his horse about and ordered his men, his Undead, back down the road.

Trevilara stayed quiet, afraid to move, until they passed from sight and hearing.

RIVERGRACE WOKE SHIVERING. She sat up, rubbing her arms and then the exposed flesh of her legs, but nothing helped. The shivers intensified until she was quaking. Violent tremors ran from her toes to her chin, and she hugged herself tightly in hope of quieting the storm.

Then she realized that the hut itself wasn't cold. Coals still glowed red-edged in the banked fire pit, sending out coils of muted heat. Trails of smoke hung lazily in the corners where air did not circulate well. Not only were the outer flaps closed, but Sevryn had pulled the wooden shutter down tight sometime during the night. She put her hand out and felt the edge of the blanket. Still warm. She could even feel a faint heat emanating from her love's sleeping form.

Rivergrace spread her hands in front of her. No discoloration from chill. No goose bumps. And yet she could hardly hold them still in front of her, fingers dancing as though she wove at an invisible hand loom. She knotted her hands to make it stop; nothing helped.

It wasn't her shaking. At least, not from the inside out with an icy chill. No. Her soul strings pulled and tugged at her, and her body answered like a puppet obeying its summons. Her limbs flopped about uncontrollably.

She could not contain herself. The violent shivers and quakes became contortions that knocked her off the bedding and onto the floor where she lay, caught in seizures not from her mind but from her soul. Her jaw and mouth worked, yet she couldn't call out. Finally, finally, she managed a moan, a guttural wail. Sevryn, in as deep a sleep as she'd ever known him to have, for he rarely slipped soundly into a rest, didn't move. He did not seem to realize she'd left their bed, stolen away from his side.

Rivergrace writhed about and hammered her foot, jerking in an oddly timed rhythm, against the cot. The third time she hit the bed, he jerked awake, sitting straight up, hand filled with a throwing knife as he did.

He blinked. "Grace?"

Her body ground itself into the flooring of their hut. She would have sworn it clean, for she brushed it out daily, but she could feel the grit of dirt and gravel under her. She shook in yet another massive fit. He reached down and pulled her to him, wrapping her in his arms, murmuring words of alarm she couldn't quite make sense of.

Abruptly, the fit stopped. She took a deep, gasping breath and shoved her forehead into his chest, embracing him back for dear life.

"What is it?"

A minor quake returned, rattling her, but it calmed as he tightened his arms about her. He hissed with a bit of pain at first but didn't pull back, for that meant he would suffer the same shocks again. His warm breath grazed her ear. "Shall I get the wisewoman?"

She shook her head sharply and, amazingly, he knew it for a refusal, a movement separate from the involuntary gyrations of her body. Soothingly, he stroked her hair back from her face and put his lips to her forehead. She knew it was as much to check her for fever as to comfort her, and she closed her eyes.

"What is it?"

"The soul anchors." She got in another deep breath. "I think."

"Suddenly?"

"Jerked me right out of bed, as though I were one of those stringed puppets." Now air flowed evenly, as it should, and the buzz in her ears calmed. She pulled back to eye him. "Quendius has to be near. Very, very near."

"You're certain?"

"No, but I can't think what else could cause my bonds to act like this. I couldn't move on my own, aderro, but my body convulsed until I thought my bones would break." She lifted a hand to push her unruly hair back from her forehead.

"Are you afraid?"

Afraid? No, how could he think—and she realized he felt her heart as much as she did, fighting against her ribs like a wild bird would fight a snare, wings thrashing wildly. "No. I'm angry."

He kissed the side of her mouth. "I can imagine."

"I have to learn how to control this."

He nodded slowly before resting the side of his face against her temple.

She pulled back suddenly. "Gods, Sevryn. If I feel this—they must feel something as well."

"You can't know that."

"I know they have to feel *something*. My reaction is too strong for them not to. I could . . . I could be pulling them here. We have to do something. We can't allow that. These people will be slaughtered. They took us in, and we can't . . . Quendius can't come here."

"All right." He took her hands in his. Now she was cold, and he warmed her. "We'll dress and go down the mountain. To the road?"

She thought a moment, feeling cautiously along her slender chains before nodding. "Yes. It has to be."

He let go and turned to finish dressing, kitting himself as if he were going to war. Rivergrace shook off a last quake and joined him.

Dawn seemed far away as they stepped out of their hut. They passed only one sentry on the village's borders, and he sat with his chin dropped to his chest, his snore a thin, reedy noise upon the night. Sevryn hesitated as though he might awake the man . . . was that Cort, under his oddly flapped headgear? Instead, he shook his head. No questions asked, no lies need be told. Cold lay heavy about them, but the snowfalls of the last few weeks had melted away for the moment, hinting only that winter had not laid a firm grip upon the mountain lands . . . yet. Their breath fogged before them as they made their way down the mountain, Rivergrace maintaining her silence except to let Sevryn know when her anchors tried to pull her strongly in one direction or another. Each time that happened, her heartbeat doubled before it, too, steadied. If she had ever doubted that she could track Quendius by this connection to him, that concern was gone now.

They made their way through near dark with a low-hanging full moon at their backs that glowed through the forest with its own eerie light. Small patches of snow, behind a sturdy tree trunk or in the shadow of a boulder, gleamed like silver puddles before them. Sevryn moved quickly, and she followed him closely enough to have grabbed the hem of his long coat, to keep him within her reach. The moonlight, thin and patchy as it was, still kept her from stumbling, and they were able to make their way down the peak at a good pace, reaching the meadows at its foot with the dawn. He settled her in one spot before doing a quick recon of the area, returning to ask, "What are you feeling?"

"The pull is strong, but I'm in control."

"Good. I'm going to build a quick fire to warm some stones for the mugs. You look like you could use a hot drink."

She nodded, and he went to work. He was more right than he knew; the mug and drink felt glorious—both in her hands and going down her throat when ready. When he'd finished and she neared the bottom of her mug, he looked at her.

"Which way?"

"That way. The connection is stronger than it was when I woke."

"But you have it under control now."

She made a face. "I'm pulling back. It seems to even out the tug-of-war effect."

"All right. Signal me when you lose control?"

She drained her mug, thinking. "I'll . . . I'll . . ." When she lost control of the anchors, she'd lose control of herself as well, or she had before. Ruefully, she told him, "I'll probably hit the ground behind you."

He chuckled softly. "Hopefully not, but I understand." He took the empty mug from her. "Ready?"

"For now."

He packed his small knapsack and stood to kick the fire down to its last burning ember, shoveling damp dirt over it with the side of his boot. She summoned a handful of water to drown the earth. No wildfire here, if she could help it.

With the sun on their backs bringing light if not warmth, they jogged across the meadow until the sight of a road cutting across its wilderness brought them both to a halt. A winding ribbon, they could see little detail upon it, but she knew that somewhere close by, Quendius rode that road. A frisson of anticipation went down the back of her neck. Sevryn patted himself down, reassuring himself that none of his weapons had shifted or been lost, and she did the same although she had possessed far fewer than he did. He waited until she finished and pointed.

"Half a day that way."

"What? How?" The urgency of the pull on her had abated, yes, but it had been so strong.

"We came down the mountain the quickest way. That wound us about it. Our camp is actually there," and he pointed up the peak, to the far side facing the dawn.

"So I feel the pull less because, although we traveled down, we also moved farther and farther away."

He nodded.

"Good. And bad."

His eyebrow went up, the one that had the tiniest notch in it from an old, barely perceptible scar. "Bad?"

"I hate to walk."

"I learn something new about you every day." He danced a step to the side as she swatted at him.

"Narskap and Quendius marched me over half a continent, I swear, on foot and on horseback. I much prefer using a horse's feet to my own, and I'm not ashamed to admit it."

He laughed. "No chance of that today. I want to sneak up on our targets."

"Of course. Maybe we can procure a mount for the trip back."

"It would be butchered for the meat when we get home."

She shuddered. "Truly?"

"Probably. I can't see them supporting a grazing animal through the winter, and meat is always welcome."

"I'll walk."

"I thought you might."

In companionable silence, they made their way across the meadowland, following a border of scrub trees and bushes that stubbornly edged the road. By the time the sun topped the sky, she could feel a wind had risen as well, a stubborn wintery wind that more than offset any warmth the pale sun might try to provide. She was dressed for the heights of the mountain, though, and warm enough. The terrain had grown broken, studded with hillocks as well as groves of twisted trees, their leaves gone but their branches thick for all their bareness. Come the spring, these groves must be nearly impenetrable, providing good coverage for the mountain looming behind them.

She felt a twinge on her soul strings, a jerk, and responded by reaching out for Sevryn ahead of her and jerking at the corner of his coat flapping in front of her. He spun about, yet she could say little, losing control of herself again, standing there and shivering as if she'd just climbed out of an icy river.

He took her hand, which helped more than it should have, and went to his knees and then stomach, crawling up brown-and-blackened grass on the hillock in front of them. She crept at his side, not wanting to let go of his fingers. As he crested the view, he ducked down slowly, sucking in a long breath.

"That's Trevilara on the road."

"What do you want to do?"

He scratched the side of his jaw with a contemplative thumbnail. Then Sevryn shook his head. "I don't want to meet her, and neither do you."

"I can hold my own."

His other hand tightened on hers. "No, Grace, you can't. I don't even want you trying."

"You have no faith in me . . ."

"No. That's not it. I've faced her. I know the power she can call up. When the time comes, we'll have to take her down together. It's going to take both of us."

She wasn't sure how much truth she could hear in his words. "You followed me here. From our home, across the bridge, to here."

"Yes, and I would follow you anywhere." He looked over at her, lying on the ground next to him. "I've tangled with her. You haven't."

"I know what she must command."

"I don't think you do. She's a God. Nothing less."

"She rides on the backs of her followers. I know. She has sucked them dry of whatever Talents her people might have had, once, and consolidated them within herself." She freed her hand from his. "I can take her. She is vulnerable now, down there all alone."

"Not alone, if Quendius is within earshot, I think. She has to be waiting for him. She might very well have troops of her own around the bend, hiding and ready to defend her if the meeting doesn't go as she anticipates. We can't let them ally. Quendius must be cut down first."

"Because your hate for him is greater?"

He looked at her again, silver-gray eyes steady but with a gleam deep inside them. "No," he said evenly. "Because if we try to kill her and manage it, and he still lives, he will raise her as an Undead. And that we cannot afford. He has to go first."

His words: quiet, still, and cold. But true. Terribly, awfully, true. She found the breath to say, "You're right."

He touched her shoulder. "I fear that I am. Can you track them?" He cleared his throat before reaching inside him to bring up his Voice and asked for them to be unseen as he made a way where Rivergrace guided him, where her chained souls pulled her. He did not need to see them to know when they neared. Her efforts to quell the convulsions that ran through her told him. Against old fallen trees that the wind had claimed winters ago, he pulled them into a niche and rested his arm over her shoulders until she got command of herself.

Rivergrace flung her hand out to grip Sevryn's shoulder. "It follows him."

"What does?"

"The portal. Like an eye overseeing all of them." She pointed with her other hand, unable to keep a tremor from it as she did.

"Does he know it's there?"

"How could he not?" she answered slowly. But even as she spoke, she leaned close over Sevryn to see the troop all the better. "I don't think he does. I don't think any of them do."

"Quendius has to know. It's—it's like pulling Kerith behind him. He has to feel its weight, its presence."

She shook her head. "He cares nothing for life, never has. I think the only thing he can truly sense is death and dying. So Kerith doesn't exist for him in the way that the here and now does."

"That is a blessing in its way, then." Sevryn laid his hand over hers. "We can end him here and find our way across."

"We're not ready."

"We'll never be ready, because the answers we need to some of our questions can't be found until we confront him. Until I confront him." Her hand grew chilled under his. "You can't cross Trevilara, Grace."

"I know you don't want me to, but it may be inevitable."

"But not yet."

She slipped her hand away from his. "That remains to be seen." She bolstered herself on both elbows, aware that the ground under them had frozen and despite the blanket they'd thrown down, it remained uncomfortable. Below her, Quendius and his troop remained on course toward Trevilara's Throne City. She could feel faint tugs on her soul strings, urging her to follow after. Her mouth tightened. Her father's enigmatic remarks to her remained no clearer than they were on the day that he died and left her alone with the burden of stopping Quendius. She backed onto her knees. She felt weary. She slept at night but it never seemed enough anymore. Did the winter weigh on her, with its dark and dreary days and bone-cracking cold? Or was it from within rather than without? Did she pine for home and family, or did something inside her chip away at the self she'd always known? *Was it the soul strings?* Made with her own will and a pinch of Cerat . . . was it enough for the demon to eat her, inside out?

She lifted her chin. "How wearing is it on you to Compel?"

"It's part of my Talent, it's natural."

"I know that, that's not what I mean."

He rolled over on his back to eye her. "Then what do you mean?"

"Does it sap you? Can you do it on the run while you're attacking?"

"Not usually, and yes . . . usually." His eyebrow went up. "What are you thinking?"

"We should go after him. Now."

"We're not prepared."

"You, perhaps. I'm as prepared as I will ever be. We know we can't let the two of them ally, but that is what he is marching to, Throne City. By the time he reaches it, he will have passed every test she could have set for him. He will be worthy. We can't let that happen! They cannot partner. Once they do, our task will be nearly insurmountable."

"It will be that much more difficult, I agree, but what do you find so daunting?"

"It's what you already said, that should we bring down Trevilara but not Quendius—he will simply raise her up as one of his Undead."

"Gods and cold hells." He looked down at the road as the marchers began to come into clear view. "So we are in accord that he has to be dealt with first. But that does not mean that I agree with you that now is the moment."

"We don't have our own army. We won't ever get one."

"But we do have friends."

"People who have no idea of who we really are, or what we have planned. We can't drag them into this, Sevryn. Every day is an exercise in survival, nothing more noble or long-termed than that. If we drag them into our struggle, we take even survival away from them."

He sucked air through his teeth. "With Trevilara gone, their lives will be better."

"There will be a power struggle in her absence. I think there's a good chance the greater population will still be striving."

"Yes, but their goals will be their own, the reward not shared, the punishment for failure lessened. Is that not better?"

He shrank back a little so he could kiss her forehead, just above her eyebrow. "One can hope."

"Exactly. We can give them hope, and that's no small thing, is it?"

"Never."

Thick brambles edged the trade road, but they bent before him, giving him a way to ease through. Vaelinar magic. She wondered if this world had ever seen magic like the two of them held. He put his mouth to the curve of her ear.

"Can we do this?"

She gave a jerky nod.

Sevryn claimed the shadows as he advanced on Quendius. He could catch the slight noise of slow moving water, a brook or river trying to resist the edges of ice that had formed on its banks overnight and now melted slowly. Rivergrace followed in his wake, not quite as adept as he, but quiet enough that she did not ruin his efforts. When her touch grazed him, her cage of souls bit, like a sharp snap of energy, buzzing in his ears. The slightest touch transferred the pull to him. He put his hand back to slow her.

"Don't follow me any closer."

"You'll need me."

He might. He knew that he might, and so did she. "When I do, then," he conceded. He pulled aside a bit of bracken and saw Quendius on the riverbank, watching his troop, some mounted but most on foot, ford the river. The river would give him something of a boundary but not enough once he attacked. He said over his shoulder, "Can you make a wall out of that river?"

"Possibly. It wouldn't hold long. The best I could do would be to bring it up, floodtide. Without a good downstream flood, it would subside to its normal level soon."

"All I need are a few moments." He pressed her hand tightly. "If anything goes wrong, get out of here. Any way you can."

"I won't leave you behind."

"It won't be me anymore if he gets a hold on me. You know that."

Silence answered him. She did know it, all too well.

He got on one knee, waiting until the last trooper crossed the ford and Quendius stirred in his saddle, shifting his weight to lean forward and rein his horse after. There was a moment when he knew he'd seen something he hadn't quite identified, something important that escaped him, and it nagged at him even as he pulled a throwing star. He heard Rivergrace murmur a soft word or two, and then the river rose, surging about its banks in a flurry of white water and foam.

Quendius' horse backed up nervously, fighting the bridle, eyes going white with fear. He let out a shout, of anger and command, and it rang out over the roar of the river. Sevryn launched to his feet, stars flying. The first thunked deep into the shoulder and the second grazed the neck. Quendius bailed from his saddle, landing on his feet, and tore the star loose. The horse wheeled away where it ran into a tree stump and halted, jerking its head up and whinnying in dismay.

The shadows bled away from Sevryn. Quendius stopped casting about for his attacker and straightened to face him.

"So. I called for one to follow me from Kerith, but you're not that one." He tossed the crimson-stained weapon from one hand to another, avoiding the many sharp edges. "I don't place the clothing, but I do know the weapon." He turned it in his fingers and then set his eyes on Sevryn again, frowning a bit. "My forge boy," he finished, in recognition.

"Never yours."

"I remember differently." Quendius examined the star again. "I didn't create this, but it's good work." He tossed it into the dirt behind him. "Just not good enough to put me down." And he began to close the ground between them.

The frothing water border that Rivergrace called up continued to hold, but Sevryn could see the troops milling on the other side. It was then that he realized what had been nagging at him. It drove a cold lance through him.

The colors of Trevalkan troops blended in and amongst the dirty rags of the older Undead.

They were too late. Quendius had already met up with Trevilara, and although he could have taken the men in a skirmish, the possibility of an alliance existed.

He pulled his sword and dagger. "Run, Grace. Now."

Without a look back, he closed with Quendius, confident she would do as they'd discussed, and the sound of blades clashing sang through the air. It should be quick and dirty.

She gathered herself, preparing to bolt back through the shadows Sevryn had draped over their passage and which lingered still, as though the winter sun weren't strong enough to dissipate them. She could hear the grunts and gasps and sounds of those bodies circling, attacking, falling back, circling again, testing one another's strength and speed and agility. Sooner or later, one of those blows would cleave flesh.

She could feel her control on the river begin to slide away from her, water running through her fingers. Grace clenched her hands and plunged back the way they'd come, brambles pricking and tearing at her as if angry she'd left Sevryn behind. She shrugged and pushed her way through, punching if she had to, knowing the roar of the river would cover her for a few more moments and then she would have to drop to her stomach and find whatever concealment she could use to get back to the hillocks beyond.

Without Sevryn. Her mouth dried, and her pulse beat tightly in her throat. She could live through much without him. Torturous days behind Narskap and the Undead had taught her that. Those days had also taught her that she did not wish to. He completed her. He was the person to whom she would turn when she was troubled or when she was happy.

A recalcitrant bramble blocked her way and she fought with it for a moment, finally bending it out of the way, twisting its branch back upon itself, with much tearing of fingertips. She cast a look back and saw no pursuit, the small river still in flood but its surge wall gone. Overhead, a singular silver thread arched through the air, as tenuous as a spider's single silk, catching a bit of sunlight and shining brightly. She could not reach it even if she tried, and as she looked upon it, she realized that she looked at another soul anchor, not black or gold as those she wore, but a living string, arcing across a spiritual plane, where she could not touch it. Not by reaching up with her hands.

She did reach out, spinning out a bit of her own soul, as if she might tap into it herself and as her exploration crossed it, energy sizzled at her, a bolt of stinging bite. Yet she knew it, and knew it well: Sevryn's anger and spirit zapped at her. She recoiled, curling her hand back against her chest. But it wasn't Sevryn's soul spinning across this line. She tasted Quendius, with the blood-and-sulfur accent of Cerat underneath. Foulness filled her throat, and she spat to one side. She fought not to retch again. No time for weakness.

He had indeed met with Trevilara and, with or without her knowing, he'd spun a link between them. He pulled on strength and power sunk deep on the other end of that strand, and she knew there was no way Sevryn could defeat him, not with this well of power feeding him. She had to sever that conduit, no matter what she'd promised, no matter what it took. She tasted the line again, foul and corrupt as it was, with sparks of Sevryn dancing along it and she feared that Quendius had spun a hook into him as well. She should have stayed.

Rivergrace caught her breath a moment. Then she pinched off a bit of herself, to forge her own chain, her own line, and tossed it across the silvery cord above her, one bit of ethereal power across another. It caught. She felt it surge deep inside her, throttling her ability to breathe as it set her heart to drumming loudly in her ears. It tried to set its hooks into her, to take her up into its network, and her whole body seemed to waver about her. Her vision grew dim. She could feel her blood cool in her body. The brambles that had been setting her skin on fire faded away to nothing. She felt herself start to drift away, her life braided into the very line she needed to destroy.

Grace raised her hand, skin so translucent she thought she could see the vessels carrying her blood clearly, the sinews and bones of her fingers and down into her wrist. The emptiness of not being tore her remains away, layer by layer. She gritted her teeth and reached down deep inside, where Quendius did not have his hooks set yet, and then poured the energy she found coiled there out of her. Out and into that bright strand, brilliant sparks hitting where one met the other and then—SNAP! The chain shattered. Energy rained back into her, all around her, bouncing like tiny bits of hail. Bits here and there felt tainted, and she rolled away from the corruption as her sight cleared.

She could smell fire then and knew she hid not far from the fiery being of Queen Trevilara. She hitched up on her elbows and crawled closer, the thicket fighting back now that Sevryn's influence dissipated. The heat told her when she'd drawn near. Rivergrace lifted her head and saw the woman standing by the side of the road, all but naked except for a few shreds of clothing and the orange-and-blue flames that licked as high as her creamy white shoulders. A skin, not unlike that which might have been shed by some great snake, lay about her ankles and feet. For a long heartbeat, that's exactly what she thought it was until she saw it had a face, crumpled and boneless, in its ruins.

The woman stood with her hands out and took a great, leaping breath of air as though she, too, felt the instant relief of the bond being cut off. She cast about, eyes wide and luminous, Vaelinar eyes of gold and brown and green, her nostrils flared slightly as if she might scent something as well, every portion of her body on alert. She knew somebody was nearby, even if she did not quite know who or where.

Rivergrace had gotten close, very close, to the edge of the road where Trevilara waited or had been abandoned or ruled, so close that she could see the colors in those eyes very clearly. So close that the circle of flames ringing Trevilara sent its heat over Grace. She thought of roasting and narrowed her eyes against the searing air being cast off and then saw that the queen shed water like tears, a faint but dewy cloak of them, to keep herself from being annihilated.

They shared Talents, the two of them, dominion over fire and water. Rivergrace got to her knees, thinking on what she knew of herself, her strengths and her weaknesses, and understood why Sevryn feared her meeting this woman. She was as nothing compared to Trevilara. She did not have the power it took to keep the elements balanced against each other and yet at work near constantly.

She also realized why no one had ever been able to take down the tyrant. Like fine hairs that dapple the skin naturally, a thousand thousand bits of soul waved about her. Infinitesimal Talents and lives woven into Trevilara's essence maintained her. Grace doubted that anyone had ever been able to approach her without the queen's express permission.

However, she had that one, singular chink in her armor. Trevilara knew that someone had just been leeching off her. Did she know who?

Rivergrace shoved herself to her feet.

Trevilara came fully about to meet her, flames rolling and cresting over each other before settling like ocean waves breaking upon a shore. "Who are you and where have you come from?"

"I'm no one, but I crossed the bridge you made." Grace leaned forward, putting steel into her voice, wishing that she had a smidgen of Sevryn's Talent.

"Did you?" Trevilara tried not to show interest, but she looked Grace over, carefully. "You're Vaelinar, so if you're telling the truth, you're a traitorous exile like the rest of them. You're the reason this world is poisoned."

"I'm not ignorant like those you keep your heel upon. Your gatekeeper isn't coming back to you. Daravan is dead. And we are different on my world. We have *power*." And she gave a flick of her hand, bringing a wash of rain out of the air, to douse Trevilara's flames. Smoke and ash hissed into the air. Before the queen could react, she pulled her blade and stepped inward. "I weakened you. I cut you off from your souls—" She ran the palm of her hand down Trevilara's arm. "And I will end you here in your tracks."

"The best assassins are silent," Trevilara responded. She turned on one bare foot, bringing up a blade of flame, swinging in one quick motion that Rivergrace could not quite block. The weapon jolted against hers, spilling heated air and fire over her, while Trevilara kicked out with her foot, hooked her behind the leg, and brought her down, all in one smooth movement that made Rivergrace realize that the queen did not rely solely on her Talents to keep herself alive.

She twisted as she fell, to keep from landing on her own long dagger. Trevilara knocked it aside as Grace tried to turn it and thrust it upward, with half a thought because the other half was bringing up her own shroud of dew so that the fire could not burn. She curled a lip as she looked up, defiant, wondering at the back of her mind what she could try next to kill the queen. Because if she did not—here and now—Trevilara would trace her steps back to the river and find Quendius and whatever might be left of Sevryn, and their mission here would be lost. Kerith would be lost.

"I'm not afraid to die to bring you down." And she wasn't. She could expend everything she had, and it might be enough. Might.

"And you think that's a strength, do you?" Trevilara looked down at her. "Anyone can die, and while it's true that fearlessness can make one bolder, it's not enough. You need the will to live, at all costs, the need to survive to beat me. And you haven't got it. Because you've tasted death once, you're not afraid of it—and you should be. You should be afraid to lose every chance you have to eat and drink of what life has to offer down to the very last crumb and drop. You need to honor the life that you hold." She pushed her booted toe into Rivergrace's rib cage. More than a nudge, less than a kick.

It should have been a kick. One that would have knocked the breath and sense out of her, but because it wasn't, Grace lashed out, slammed her arm into the back of Trevilara's knee. As they touched, she summoned the last of her strength, shaped it into an icy lance from the waters raining down her skin and knifed it deep into flesh, sinew, and bone. Trevilara screamed. The sound itself became a weapon, slashing at Rivergrace's eardrums and skull so that she rolled free, grasping at her face to muffle it, even as Trevilara fell to one knee on the ground. She fisted one hand and brought up her wall of flames, fire that hissed and spat against Grace's skin but did little to harm her, unable to even turn her tears to steam. She rolled away and rose to her feet, as the ring of fire licked upward and danced a closed circle about the queen. The heat seared off her face and Grace retreated five quick skip steps backward, before throwing her hand up, palm out, and bringing up her own cooling mist thicker and icier.

Fire and water, the two of them. She controlled the water portion of her Talents better than fire, in opposition to the queen, making Grace careful. Very careful, lest her water become scalding hot in answer to the flames.

Her body ached as though Trevilara had tried to peel her skin and flesh from her bones, and perhaps she had. But she hadn't succeeded. Grace lived, and in that realization, she understood what Trevilara had said. And she also knew that the queen uttered words she did not wholly understand or believe in herself.

She had no faith in death. Or rebirth and redemption. Or of a future beyond this time and this flesh. Or a knowledge of memory and love and where they anchored you in the place of things known and unknown in this or any world. Nothing that Rivergrace knew deep within herself and that wisdom that would transcend her body.

Grace drew herself up. She could feel the wall grower hotter with every licking flame reaching upward. She would burn if she stayed. She felt that inevitability. So she turned and ran, her cry of dismay ringing in her ears.

Trevilara hadn't meant her to run and survive. The queen had meant her to give life up, prove her words, and die at her feet.

Grace ran faster and then dove into the air, letting her body dissolve into the mist that called her—cool and fleeting and diaphanous—beyond the queen's reach. As she moved away from Trevilara, she could hear the sounds of the battle Sevryn waged, and her heart . . . more an image in her mind than a reality in her flesh . . . leaped.

She could feel the mists of her form tearing apart as a sharp wind arose, a wind that smelled of burning cloth and flesh, heat that whirled as it ripped through her being. The River Goddess rose in her without asking, wet and angry and gasping at the searing hand that grasped at them. They rained through that hand of fire, cold and quick but not quick enough to get through intact. She could feel herself sizzle away, burned off into a vapor she could not control or contain. Bits of her gone forever, ripped off and lost to an inferno of flame and hate. She could turn on her attacker, on Trevilara, but she could feel Sevryn's distress through every fiber of the being she had left, and that tore at her, too. His was the call she must answer, if she would survive on any plane. She gathered the River Goddess and her heritage of fire tightly and rode the thermal, gliding just above the fury until she could thrust herself beyond it and soar across the distance to her goal.

Rivergrace felt her soul splitting, her life shedding into rain and mist, her other self begging to have full and total hold of her, the River Goddess trying to return the two of them to their most elemental form, to survive, to have done with thinking. Her thoughts, her intent to find Sevryn, tried to dissolve into the mists and shade of cool water, into primal nothingness. Firmly, she grasped her inner awareness, clenching herself—her image and knowledge of herself—as tightly as she could, knowing that if she let go, she would slip away. Fall to the ungentle earth of Trevalka as rain and fog and disappear forever into its corrupted soils. It wouldn't have her, not now, not yet, not until she reached Sevryn and freed him.

She tasted the coppery sense of blood first, seeping into her misty being, and then she felt the flesh, torn and jagged in pain, gaping, bleeding, and then she saw him. She reached for his broken body, splayed across the boots of Quendius as he reached down for one last slice, aiming for the throat.

Rivergrace felt his life, weak but determined, his will to protect her at all costs, throbbing in him as she wrapped herself about him and took him up, twisting and calling on the last of her strength to spin about on the river they straddled, a water spout twirling out of the death master's reach. The water in her and about her cried in joy at the release of energy, and she fled downriver with all the power of will she had left in her, going blind as the deepest of blues rose to consume her.

RIVERGRACE WOKE on the muddy banks of a river, a fading warmth against her, the taste of blood and sweet water on her lips. As she put her hands underneath her to rise, her flesh grew out of the puddles, forming her body bit by bit as she reclaimed it. Excess water ran off her in cascades as she did. Rivergrace looked down and saw Sevryn's wet form huddled next to her, soaked in blood, but alive. Still alive. For how long, she could not tell. Crimson soaked into the puddles and mud, dribbling away in vivid streaks.

She had to stop the bleeding and get the two of them away before they drew predators and Quendius to the scent of blood. Her body ached in every fiber and her gut knotted up in ravenous hunger, her flesh drawn beyond its limits to sustain her. She knelt at the river's edge and drank, gulping down its cool sweetness until she could no longer drink, and sat back, panting a little. Then, and only then, did she look at and seriously assess Sevryn. She brushed his hair back from his forehead, darkened by the wetness and by blood. His flesh held life's warmth but felt cool to her touch. She tore her outer skirt to ribbons, wondering a moment that her transition to water and back had transmuted her clothing as well. She bandaged his gaping wounds quickly, sealing the edges of flesh together as well as she could. Stitching would not help him, only a Vaelinar healing, and she could not manage one here. Nor could she heal as a true Vaelinar, but she was the only hope he had.

There were other wounds that troubled her more. Slits in and about his vitals, bleeding on the surface and hinting at great damage unseen. He could easily be bleeding out internally, giving her little time to get him somewhere safer. Rivergrace pushed her hair from her face, knotting its heavy tendrils at the nape of her neck and scanning the countryside. They had lost the road, or passed over it as rivers and bridges have a way of doing, and their mountain stood tall and indomitable in front of her. She might build a stretcher she could drag from the driftwood that littered the muddy bank around her. Even as she shaded her eyes, she could see movement down the mountain, a rippling on the horizon. Not movement on foot or even horseback but on wing. As she straightened to get a better look at the phenomenon, she realized she saw river birds coming down out of the evergreens where they nested in the early evening, gliding on the afternoon air, quiet except for a low call now and then, a sight like she'd never seen before. They came as if summoned, and they came silently as if knowing her life might depend on it, and they glided to a halt all about her at the river, wings of blue and gray and brindled brown folding, and their sharp bright eyes upon her.

And behind them, they brought the trappers.

Ifandra helped her settle Sevryn on the cot in the corner and sent for bandaging. She watched as Rivergrace sliced one wrist free of the bloody scrap and put her hand over the gaping cut. Her arm shook as a like wound began to open in her own arm, blood springing free. A sudden blow knocked her across the tiny hut, where she rolled onto her side, gasping and clutching her freely bleeding arm tightly.

"Bloody cold hell," Ifandra cried at her. "What do you think you're doing? Is that the only healing you know? You can't handle his wounds that way, or we'll have two dying people on our hands instead of one."

"It's what I know," Rivergrace said painfully, as she sat up slowly. "Healing is not one of my main Talents."

"It'll do for a bruise or strain or a single cut but not now. Look at you. Wrap that up and concentrate on closing it yourself. I'll be back with the healing woman."

Rivergrace could not think of anyone who carried that ranking in the small clan of trappers. Surely she did not mean Greyla, the simples woman, whose skill with herbs was well-enough earned though no greater than her own. Someone thrust a bundle of bandages through the door but came no closer. She grabbed a clean strip and began to wrap her own slicing cut tightly as she crouched near Sevryn, listening to his heartbeat, slow and steady but too low. The bleeding outwardly slowed, but she did not count that as a victory. Internal bleeding might be threatening his very life and she could not help him because Ifandra was right, damn her words. She would die trying to save him and no good would be done. He'd die anyway.

She leaned close, putting her cheek to his. "We can't die again, we've too much living to do. Do you hear me? Hold on. Dying is too easy in this world, so don't you surrender. Don't give in. We've a fate to honor, and then we have love still to be shared. Hold on to that. Hold on to the love."

Soft, small footsteps alerted her to someone's approach, and Rivergrace lifted her head. A child not yet a woman joined her. She smiled tentatively. "I am Rimple's daughter, called Leyle. I have some skill in healing by the mind's eye." She went to her knees next to Grace.

"He is sorely wounded. I'm not certain . . ." her voice staggered to a halt.

"I can give you power."

"Thank you. But even that—"

"I know," answered Rivergrace softly.

Lines deepened at the corner of Leyle's eyes. She put her hand on Sevryn's bloodstained shoulder, her face bent downward, her breathing steady but light. She had hair the color of nut-brown bark, and skin tanned from hunting, a soft golden hue that might carry a hint of the gold coloring some Vaelinar had. Her eyes, before she'd shut them, had been gray with flecks of green and brown, and she had scarcely a wrinkle upon her skin. Her knuckles, however, were crossed with tiny scars, which came from bramble bushes harvested frequently. Slowly, she raised a trembling hand and placed it on Rivergrace's shoulder. In a faint, whispery voice, Leyle told her, "He is bleeding inside out. I am tracing it as best I can. This man has been butchered."

"Don't tell me. I know. Just concentrate." And Rivergrace put her hand over Leyle's small, slender, scarred fingers. She could feel the tension in her young form, the focus, the determination. If Leyle could not heal Sevryn, it would not be because she hadn't tried. She poured what she could into the other; not just her strength, but her very knowledge of his body, flesh and soul. How he moved, how he thought, what he could endure. Every intimate detail that she cherished and hated, she gave to the girl so that she might have the best chance of healing him. Leyle flushed faintly as if acknowledging the depth of their contact, but said nothing, her face bent over Sevryn in deep concentration now, her energy almost a palpable aura Rivergrace could see and even touch.

Sevryn took a gasping breath, interrupted by a deep moan. His hands opened and closed, grasping at the blankets knotting under him, his back arching in agony, his pale face nearly disappearing under a sheen of sweat. She wanted to turn away but could not. She opened her Vaelinar sight and saw the threads of energy pulsing about them, and the slow, erratic pulse of his body. She was losing him, albeit ever so slowly. Which meant they could pull him back, bit by bit . . . possibly, but only because they had not lost him yet.

A stifled groan escaped Leyle's mouth, and she bit her lips to hold back the sound. Rivergrace squeezed her fingers in encouragement and got a sharp nod in return. Before them, bleeding began to slow.

"I have located the internals," Leyle managed, forcing each word out with a gust of air. "One. At. A. Time." Her fingers knotted into Sevryn's shoulder; Rivergrace reached across, tearing away the shreds of his shirt so that she could touch bare skin, making the contact even more efficient. "Oh. Better."

Her face reflected the struggle she fought, and Rivergrace followed each tiny frown, every grimacing twist of her mouth, the drops of blood that fell as her teeth gripped her lip to keep her from crying out in pain, and that moment of quiet when Sevryn finally fell into dark unconsciousness. His body collapsed, his frame slack in that nerveless way the unconscious and the newly fallen dead hold.

She closed her hand more tightly about Leyle's, willing herself into the healing itself, following the girl's energy and concentration. The girl's power took her with it, into the intricacies of what she attempted to do: find the lacerated organs and veins, close them, and start healing which would progress on its own. The healing would not be finished when Leyle was done; it would have just begun, but that she could manipulate the process where Rivergrace could never have touched revealed a truer Talent than she had ever met before. When Leyle finished, long hours must have passed. Her shoulders were cramped, sweat plastered Grace's hair to her forehead, her shirt clung to her uncomfortably, and her knees felt as if they'd turned to jelly and could no longer bear her weight. They unlaced their hands, and Leyle fell kneeling to the floor where she took quavering breaths. When she spoke, however, her gaze, still sharp, held Grace's.

"Can you hunt?"

"Can I—" Grace stopped herself. Of course. This was a self-sustaining community and they could ill-afford dead weight through the winter. "Yes.

Yes, of course. And skin and dress and smoke, although I am not good at tanning."

"Good. I will tell them our efforts are not wasted, then." Leyle put up her hand and Grace took it, pulling her gently to her feet. "He'll be a long time healing. I won't ask what happened, but it was a monstrous attack. And . . ." The girl paused, and her steady gaze fell away, to the floor. "He's not alive, lady, not as you and I know it. He's not dead either. I can't explain what I don't understand."

"His mind is not there?"

"Perhaps. More of a feeling that his soul is not."

A chill went through Grace, but she shook her head in denial. "It's his way of dealing with extreme pain. His thoughts have just gone elsewhere. He'll be back, as his body heals."

"You've seen this before?"

No. "Yes, although it's not common. He, however, is an unusual man and has his own ways of dealing with things."

"I've seen his scars."

"Not all of them."

"A hard life, then. But you feel he'll recover."

"Yes." An even harder life, if one was thought to be useless. Rivergrace held herself very still.

"I pray so." Leyle paused at their water bucket and drew herself up two quick ladles, one to dash over her head and the other to gulp down. "I'll check on him tomorrow?"

"If you must. I can handle it from here."

"Give him water. Broth later. But you probably know that."

"Yes, and to turn him and such." They both were talking days, perhaps weeks, of recovery. Leyle glanced at Grace's arm and put her hand about it. Though a faint tremor of weariness ran through her, Rivergrace could feel the warmth of healing speed through the bandages about her gaping wound and the flesh knit tight. "Now you both heal." She smiled faintly, bent her head, and left their abode.

Grace could hear murmurs outside and knew that Leyle reported to Cort and Ifandra. She expected Ifandra to enter moments later, but it was Cort who pushed his head and shoulders inside the door flap.

"Well enough?"

"Yes. Give my thanks to Ifandra and let her know I will talk to her about payment to Leyle."

"You women handle those details." He passed his hand through the air. "May I ask what happened?"

"Come in and sit." Grace folded her shaky legs and let herself collapse, more or less, to the floor. Cort entered and took up one of the chairs. He shut the door before he turned to face her, so that their words would not carry. She wasn't certain if she appreciated that courtesy or not. She would have no witness if she had to dispute what he reported later. But did she want one?

Cort wrapped one of his big hands about the other. "Leyle says he will heal, but it will take a while."

"If he had had only two or three wounds, her abilities would have restored him completely, I think. But he was . . ."

"Butchered," Cort supplied.

"Yes."

"And so the question I would ask is who and why? The two of you left us early in the day, and none of us noted your going. We found you to the west, not far from the trade road, as it runs, twisting about the base of the mountains."

"And there is another question you must ask."

His wiry eyebrow quirked.

"If we will bring that same danger to the clan."

He inclined his head. And waited.

Rivergrace sorted through the various answers she could give him. He would not accept the total truth, she'd be thought mad, and they would be turned out. She clawed her fingers through her tangled hair.

"We are not from here. You know that from the Truthbringer when Ifandra drugged us. You know that from our dress and manner of speech. Trevilara has never been our queen."

His face remained neutral, but his pupils widened. "You did battle with her?"

She shook her head. "No. We tried to stop her from meeting with the leader of the Undead that march the road. The master of death wants to ally with your queen, and the darkness we pursue would be unleashed, shadowing—crushing—the lives of everyone it touches. We tried to stop it. He tried to stop Quendius."

Cort looked to Sevryn's body on the cot, still lying in various pools of blood that now congealed and dried under his form. "And this Quendius did that."

"Yes."

"Can he trace you?"

"No. He is as new to these regions as we are, and he hasn't the resources or friends that we have, as near as we can tell. He's the one who drove us to hiding and to these mountains."

"He is still formidable."

"Very."

"What do you ask of us?"

She studied his impassive face. He was a rebel, they all were in this clan, but only in the sense that they stayed as far from the city and Trevilara's rule as they could. They made huge sacrifices to accomplish this. "The winter you promised us. I can hunt well enough so that we're not a burden to the community. We ask nothing more. No more rescues. No soldiers. No arms."

"A winter. And what will this enemy of yours do in the winter?"

"He'll go to ground. Take over a village near the trade road, loot its stores, bivouac his men. He won't be looking for us. He'll be biding his time until spring, if the winter hereabouts is as strong as I have been led to believe it is."

"Portents and signs of the region have told us this will be a harsh winter. The road will be closed—most of it. There is a pass to the west that snow and ice will block. Your enemy will survive only if he hunkers down to the east." An unspoken hope threaded through his words, that the winter would kill their enemy for them.

Rivergrace studied Cort's face. "Our enemy cannot be killed easily. Not by weather or by weapon."

That wiry eyebrow arched again. "Is that what he tried?" He looked at Sevryn.

"Yes."

"And failed."

"Because I wasn't with him. I have Talents that would have helped."

"Such as?"

Weariness had crept over Rivergrace, a fatigue that went all the way to her bones and sat there, like ice, through her body. But she put her hand out, palm up, and summoned flame. Cort rocked back in his chair.

"Not like her. Never like her. I share no blood with her, and I certainly don't share her twisted ambition. But fire is a good weapon."

Cort got to his feet, putting his chair between them as she closed her hand, snuffing the flame out. "You have water. And . . . fire."

"You've seen it." She got to her feet and began to attend to Sevryn's limp form, turning him so that she could change the linens. "I've told you our truths, and add this. We need you to get us through the winter, but if you must turn us out, at least wait a week or two, until he's on his feet. If you can."

He let out a sigh. "I will let you know."

"Thank you." She turned her back on him as she worked and heard him go out the door, dropping the flap into place and then shutting the door behind him.

All she could do now was wait.

Wait for Quendius to make his next move. Wait for winter to drive Trevilara back to her palace. And wait for Sevryn to mend. She smiled softly to herself, thinking it was a blessing she didn't have Nutmeg's impatience.

Even so, she had worn herself to a nub waiting for him to awaken. Three days dragged by, even with her leaving long enough to go out with some of the women to set traplines and retrieve what small game they caught. She sat, tired, her legs stretched out in front of her, warmth returning to her chilled feet in now dry stockings when she caught a change in the rhythm of his breathing.

Grace did not believe it when Sevryn's eyes opened, and he stared at her face for a long while as though he could not recognize her before wetting his lips to speak. She'd felt him awaken. It was the misrecognition that startled her. Then he caught his sense of her, and his eyes narrowed, soft gray eyes suddenly going hard.

"You are still here."

She brought a ladle of cold water to his mouth and let him drink before answering, "I wouldn't be anywhere else."

"You must go. I'm not the one you expect."

"Sevryn. A fever has you. Just drink for me."

He flung a hand up as if to protect himself from a blow. "That one is gone."

"Gone? What are you talking about? You're here. You're healing. I came and brought you back from Quendius. I have you."

"You can't." His voice turned into a cold hiss. "There is no coming back. Sevryn is gone. There is no returning."

"You're spewing nonsense." She hugged herself briefly. "I won't listen to it."

"You must. For your safety, for the safety of the others. Sevryn is beyond your reach."

She put the ladle down and reached for a damp cloth instead, bathing his face and neck even as he turned from her.

"You waste your time."

"Love cannot be wasted. I have it to give away. What you do with it is your decision. But I'm not leaving you, not like this."

"I'll heal, one way or the other."

"You're not driving me away."

"I have to!" He lashed out at the cold cloth and batted it out of her hands. "Sevryn is gone, and all that's left is what was forged from him, the king of assassins. I will live, but only so that I can kill."

"You're delirious."

"No. I can see the clear light of what I'm meant to see, for the first time, as a Vaelinar. I was cast in this, but too foolish to recognize it until now. You've come as far as you can with me, and I'm telling you that now you must go. What filled Sevryn is now empty, and the only thing waiting to rush in . . . is anger. Anger and rage."

She bent over, grabbed his chin, and forced him to look at her face. "I'm not giving up. I'm not afraid to live and you had better be cold-damned afraid of dying on me!"

"I'm not dying. Nor am I living. Do you understand?"

"Sevryn, he didn't make an Undead of you. I know that."

He shook his head slowly, a clench of pain stopping him. "He has me, and I'm caught between, in a cold hell where there is no living or dying or even undead. Do you understand? I'm a . . . a shade of what I should be. You can't be around me. No one should. Put me out on the mountain for the winter to take. That would be the only kindness that will do me any good."

"You think Quendius has you."

"As chained to me as I can—" He stopped. Tugged his arm in the air as though physically pulling on the chain he meant. He tilted his head in consideration. "He has me and yet he doesn't." Sevryn's gray eyes caught hers. "You've one hope. Chain me as well, and while my soul hangs in the balance, you might find a way to bring me back."

"You're here, now."

"No. I talk to you, but my mind, my thoughts . . . do you know where Quendius is now, with the troops?"

"No. How could I?"

"I know. They've gone to ground, all but him. They have dug into old farm land where the dirt is relatively easy to dig, being fallow at the end of the season. They bury themselves against the cold and frost and rain. They're going dormant."

She thought about what he said. "Except for him."

"Yes. He's deciding whether to go find Trevilara or stay near the troops. He doesn't fear villagers from nearby. They'll either accept him or die. I damaged him and he needs healing, but he'll survive." Sevryn paused before adding coldly, "I can hear his thoughts even as he thinks them." He closed his eyes tightly.

She grabbed his wrist. "Don't listen."

Sevryn's eyelids flickered, like a man caught in a nightmare. "He will kill all the Vaelinars he can. End this world. He can feel its throes beginning under Trevilara. He enjoys it." His eyes opened again. "Then he'll bring all the death he can muster back across the bridge to Kerith."

"We knew that." Or they had guessed it, at the least. Rivergrace rocked back on the stool and turned away from Sevryn's face. The expression in his eyes, the tone of his voice—as though he was a stranger to her. She didn't think she could fear death having died once, but this terrified her. To be alone. To be disconnected from memories of life and love. Did Sevryn drift as alone as he sounded? She raised her hand to his face. He flinched but did not push her hand away.

She had marked him. Put a small anchor on him so that he might find her if she became lost again, when they crossed. That briefest of touches, slightest of holds, still lay on him. It must be all that kept him from being swept over into nothingness and belonging to Quendius.

She wove it stronger, that spider silk of a thread. Wove it with all the heart she could, and hope, and brightness. After all they had been through, she could not, would not, lose him now. Not like this. There would be a day when they both would leave the material world again, perhaps together, more likely apart, but they would not be sheared away from their souls and the lightness of their memories when they went. Gods willing.

When she finished, she dropped her hands into her lap, as spent as if she'd run down and back up the mountain, her chest tightening for air.

"Are you finished?"

"For now."

"When I am healed. When winter thaw hits, you must let me go."

She had stood up and begun to turn away. Rivergrace stopped in her tracks. "Go where?"

"To him. He'll accept me. He'll think he has me. And when the moment is right, I'll turn on him. I'll kill him and then myself, and we'll be done. You'll be able to go home."

"Not without you."

"There is no me. This . . . is a shell. What is left is a thing not to be desired or loved. It has no capacity for that." He turned his face from her. "You'll have to turn me out. I'm deadly if you don't. Everyone here is endangered."

"I'll bring you back."

"And if you can't?"

"That is a bridge we'll cross when we have to." She began to move away, but he caught her by the wrists.

His gray eyes looked like a storm coming, darkening. "And if you can't, know this. When I recover, Quendius will find it very hard to kill me. That is good news. The bad news is—so will you, if you have to. Rage is all I have left. Think on it. The better decision might have to be made now." He dropped her hands. His eyes closed, shuttering away the storm that approached. She could feel an energy leave the small hut as he dropped into sleep.

Grace stood, rubbing her wrist where the cold reached all the way to her bones, setting in an ache she did not know if she could chafe away. He'd warned her. She moved to tuck a stray lock of his hair from a bloodied bandage over one eye. He slapped her fingers away.

She couldn't abandon him. She had woven him a lifeline and she didn't intend to let go.

"Aderro," she murmured softly. He muttered a soundless answer as he turned on his side, already nearly asleep.

But he'd answered her endearment. Not snarled or slapped away. Answered.

She would take whatever hope was being offered.

Chapter Thirty-Three

TREVILARA ENTERED HER ROOMS and shed her gown, dropping its silken folds to the floor as soon as the flames went out, and kicked it aside. The blanket of warmth and protection snuffed out, leaving her in her underclothes. Her bare skin immediately felt the chill of the room and the cold draft flowing through it. She thought of summoning her fire again, but fatigue pulled at her, yanked at every fiber of her body. Power. She needed more power. Each day it became more difficult for her to summon what she needed. Her people weakened. She needed a new people: tougher, more resilient, with more magic in their core to offer her. She ran her fingertips over her torso and down the inside of her arms. As always, her skin quivered slightly under her touch, so very sensitive because of the constant flames despite the moisture barrier she kept up, but she prided herself on her mastery of two elements. She was, without a doubt, the most exemplary manipulator her world had ever seen, and she would only increase. She leaned down and stroked her legs, from the inside of her ankles up to the top of her thighs, where her silken drawers stopped her touch. The sensations buzzing over her heightened sense was much like that of having had the sun reddening the skin too much, reminding her of how dangerous fire could be. As she herself could be.

She straightened and realized the cold draft into her rooms came from more than not having a fire set at the hearth yet. Trevilara took a few steps forward to her weapons stand, wrapping her hand about the hilt of the crossbow leaning up against it. Her favorite sword rattled a bit within the stand as she did so. The crossbow came up, already wound and ready, two lethal bolts in place.

A deep voice, speaking her native language but with an accent it took her a moment to unravel, came to her. "Surely there is a consort within this vast palace who could stroke your skin and bring much more satisfaction." A drape rustled and moved aside. Silvery against the corner's shadow, the trespasser stood with one shoulder to the frame of the window he'd left open to the wintry night, the corner of his mouth tilted in an amused smile.

"I would ask how you got into my rooms, but an answer would beg the obvious. Instead of how, I ask why."

"But we haven't explored all of the how yet. How is it I do not sleep with my men, as your spies reported to you? How is it I know it was you who accosted me on the road? How is it you have come to be allied with my enemies from my past?"

Her mouth stretched into a tight line before she answered slowly. "As for the hibernation of your troops, it is not unreasonable to think I have spies posted who would observe and report to me. As to your enemies, I've not met with anyone save yourself since my Tide Caller disappeared. And to the third point, I've no idea."

"You wore the skin of a dead woman, and betrayed yourself. You know little of me, but you should know in your very bones that I recognize and welcome Death. You might call me the Death Bringer. Your attempt at a disguise demeaned you and belittled me. I can forgive the spying—it's something I myself have been doing, and expect of a ruler. Presenting yourself as the spy tells me only that you cannot always rely on those you think you can. As to the last . . . either you lie or you do not. We all have enemies, do we not?" He looked upon her, his dark eyes as harsh as coal, and spread his open hands. "That crossbow won't kill me. I don't believe I can be killed, at least not in the conventional way."

Trevilara looked him up and down. "You've recently healed scars. That tells me you can be injured. Some of them look . . . grievous."

"I do. But the man who came at me had the skills of an assassin and could not bring me down." He rubbed a forearm ruefully. "Not for lack of trying, however. I learned a lesson from that encounter."

"So it was not in vain."

"Not for me. For him, perhaps. He's now tied to me, his soul is on my chain, and I will be winding it in soon." He pantomimed jerking a line to his chest and stood for a moment, fist curled to his rib cage.

Her eyebrow rose. "What do you mean?"

"His lifeline is anchored to me. He cannot live or die without my pulling him to it. If you can, look at me . . . I am weighed with many such lines."

Her other eyebrow arched, matching the height of the first. Did this arrogant being not truly understand who she was and what she could command? Did he think he could stand and insult her, and live? Why did he not fall to his knees at the mention of the Tide Caller, the man who strode across two worlds and more? Because despite his confidence, he reeked of ignorance. Ignorance and the peat fires of the village where he'd been holed up against the winter.

Trevilara licked lips gone suddenly dry. He tilted his head slightly, waiting for her action. She should fire her bolts despite his argument against their ineffectiveness, and take him down for his insolence. To whom did he think he spoke? Yet she hesitated, for the color of his skin.

The color of his skin spoke of a long line of sorcerer-kings, that rare charcoal hue that indicated great strength of mind and will. Did he know what blood he had in his veins, or had the exiles become such mongrels they had no clue?

"Perhaps," he said, "I am mistaken. Perhaps these are not the rooms of the incomparable Queen Trevilara, and I've accosted the wrong woman. A well-favored servant, perhaps. My time is valuable. I should spend its coin elsewhere," and he began to turn away.

She spat. "You speak of much and understand little."

He paused. "Am I worth educating, then, to you? You look but don't see me." He turned slowly about, like a slave on display, his mocking smile growing broader, his muscles rippling, a primitive, hulking, fine figure of a man. Her lips grew even drier and she licked them again.

With a slight inhalation, she brought her Sight up to see what he claimed, many dark but fine threads bound to him. They seemed almost insubstantial and not of this realm or plane, but she could sense they were very real. Chains, if she looked closer, anchored from deep within his chest and stretching out to finally disappear in the air, extended until they could no longer be seen with any vision. They were not unlike the bindings she had upon her own people, tapping the power they gave her to rule. Her bonds were not chains, however. Trevilara preferred to think of them as stepping stones, stones that would pave the way to Godhood. She anchored to magic, not souls, although there were those philosophers and dissidents who claimed they were one and the same. If she could get near enough to touch those the trespasser wore, she might be able to discern how he'd spun them. His seemed more efficient and less of a burden.

Trevilara pursed her mouth in thought. She carefully lowered the crossbow to the floor, near the corner of her bed. His smile opened wider as he watched her.

"You have a definite Talent for imprisoning the dead," she told him.

"Oh, they're not dead. Not quite. And they don't want to be, so they hold far tighter to these chains than I do. They know a cold hell awaits them when they let go."

"So they follow you." She closed another few steps between them, seemingly unaware of drawing closer.

"They're fighting men. They have little else to do in this or any world except follow the wars."

"And you."

"And me." He inclined his head.

She edged another step and then paused, her nostrils flaring. "You stink."

"My men carry a certain stench with them, and I am close to that. It doesn't stink to me, however. To me it smells like loyalty and power." He countered with a move forward of his own. "They will do anything I ask of them and they are extremely difficult to be taken down."

"They heal?"

"They do. Slowly but very solidly."

"Do you intend to threaten me with your army?"

"Do you wish to be threatened? Do you like the feeling of being helpless and at the mercy of one stronger than you?"

"I think there are moments when all of us enjoy that."

He advanced again. "And is this one of them?"

She put her chin up, as if considering his impertinence. She baited him, knowing that the open throat could be considered submission and this one looked as if he thrived on baser instincts.

"There is a song about you where I come from. It was thought to be a song about a longing for a former realm, a home, but now I know the song is about you. Many of us used to sing it."

"Used to?"

"Now we know that we are your exiles, those you cast away in fear or hatred. The song now has a . . . a different flavor."

"I haven't changed. Perhaps you have." So he was one of them, the traitors, the rebellious, one of those who would have destroyed her if they could have. Her gaze slid over him slowly. Time seemed to pass on Trevalka much slower than it did on that world the Tide Caller had opened for her. How many generations lay between this man and herself? She could not trace a lineage in his face, rugged as it was, handsome as it might be considered, and yet not familiar at all to her. She thought of those generals who rode for her and then ultimately against her, joining with the rebels who would defeat her. None of their visages matched with the man she assessed now. If Daravan had not died beyond the bridge, he would have advised her, but he was gone, caught in a trap he thought he'd woven too well for it to turn on him. This one, though. He did not have the Talents of the Tide Caller, but he had other strengths she could use. He caught her examination and flashed his smile.

"We may have things to discuss."

He inclined his head slightly. "An opinion I share."

"You crossed many roads closed by winter to reach me."

"Perhaps the sun warmed a path only I could follow."

She scoffed softly at that. "Speak plainly or leave. I'm tired of sparring."

He passed by her then and sat heavily on the bed. "Good, because I grow impatient. You opened a path to another world."

"I did not; my sorcerer did. We were fighting a war. There was a knot of traitors that I needed to be gone, and he found a way to dispose of them without their deaths being blamed on me."

"Why not simply defeat them? It's a message that no one would forget."

"There were complications."

"There are always complications. It's part of life. You were unprepared."

Trevilara shrugged. "I was not aware of the depth of the resistance I would face. Now I am, and they are banished, and my kingdom thrives."

"My ears bleed again."

"From what?" Her voice chilled, but she could feel heat in her cheeks. "You've been to war. You know that there are variables that cannot be controlled. We'd fought to a standstill. My people . . ." she faltered there. Her people had turned on her, but she had no desire to tell this stranger that. She had other desires, but not one for confession. "It matters only that a solution was offered, and I took it."

He eyed her, a tiny spark in his dark eyes. Not Vaelinar eyes, she noted; no sign of the magic he should be carrying in his blood and bones. Yet the chains she'd seen told her that most definitely he possessed a Talent although she might not necessarily classify it as such. There were common sorcerers about Trevalka but none with power that could match a high-tiered Vaelinar. She doubted that he carried that blood within him. Her father had tried to wipe out the corruption a generation ago and, generally it was thought, succeeded.

"You have no trust in me."

"No, I don't. Have you given me a reason to trust you? You break into my palace. You've been harrying my outlying posts for seasons. I have no idea what you want here or why."

"I want your army. I want you at the fore of it. I want to return across that bridge with such a sweep of power that all bow in Death before us."

That nearly stopped all words, indeed her very breath, in her throat before she managed, "And what then?"

"Then we rule this new world together. Clean water. Untainted fields. Unquestionable loyalty from the few we allow to live. A new start."

He knew about the water, then. About the plague. About her misguided attempts to bring an unruly populace that she had lost control of into line, leaving corruption that could not sustain a kingdom. He knew why Dara-van had brought the Raymy to his world and what he'd hoped to accomplish and how he had failed.

He reached for her roughly. "Let me show you a way to build trust." He pulled her down beside him, but she met him eagerly and they made love that was as much a war as it was a surrender the first time.

Then, after the candles had guttered out and the open window showed the darkest of nightfall outside, they made love again, long and slow and sweet, both of them crying out softly and falling to quiet satisfaction in each other's arms.

That was when Trevilara got out of bed, picked up her crossbow, and shot him.

Quendius grunted as the bolts hit home, throwing him deeper into the bedding. He raised himself on his elbow, looking down at his flank with eyes narrowed both in pain and disbelief. He levered himself up and swung his legs out of the bed, his silvery skin darkening a bit. "Cold hells, woman, if I didn't please you, just kick me out."

Trevilara dropped two more bolts in place, lowered the crossbow to use her foot to cock and wind it, and brought it back up to aim. She watched as he reached down and gingerly plucked both bolts out of the muscles of

his flank. Blood began to fountain from him. He looked at the tips before
he dropped them on the floor.

"I have no reaction to kedant."

She set her jaw. She had been counting on a reaction, one way or another. Slight paralysis at the least, mortal illness at the most.

He stood. "I thought we had established a certain bond between us."

"Trust? We have, to a point. I thought I'd test your veracity."

He ran a thumb along his wounds and murmured a word she could not
quite catch. The flow of blood stemmed and then halted altogether. "If I
had been standing, they would not have dropped me. Now that I am standing, the earth pulls at my blood yet my body denies it. My Undead take my
injury and heal it, and my blood strengthens them instead of being spilled
uselessly. Is that what you wished to know?"

"You said you would be quite hard to kill. I dislike idle boasts."

He covered the area between them in two gigantic strides before she
could tense to move and knocked the crossbow out of her hands. "I don't
boast. These bolts hardly cost me a moment's pause, except in my evalua-
tion of you." He pulled her close to him, so close that the sticky blood
staining his body glued them together. His fingers tightened into hard
bands about her arms.

Trevilara burst into flames. Quendius leaped back, out of range, with a
smothered curse. He eyed the ring of fire at her feet, with flames growing
so high they nearly licked the underside of her breasts. He stretched his
arms out, checking for damage again.

"A woman of definite Talent," he managed. "I thought it was your gown
that burned, but it appears you govern Fire." He took a step to one side and
then to the other, judging the barrier. He smiled slightly before leaning
back and crossing his arms about his chest, his wounds thinned to small
lines upon his skin. "It must weary you, though, to maintain that. A formidable defense but one so very exhausting . . . draining . . . to your resources."

"It serves its purpose. You'll not touch me again, unless I invite it."

"Perhaps. I was a weaponmaker in my old role on Kerith. I've worked
the forges nearly all my life. You'll find I have quite a tolerance for flame,
but I will withdraw for now. Have we an alliance come spring?"

The dew upon her face ran down like teardrops. "To take Kerith." Not
a question from her lips.

"To take Kerith. To leave this world to the dying rabble and to conquer
a viable kingdom."

She considered her options. Daravan had promised to open the bridge for her and had failed, but now here stood another. Not a sorcerer, with Vaelinar Talent she knew, but still a man with abilities she could use. He did not seem properly awed by her, but she would take care of that. Lessons to be taught and learned.

"Why spring? Why not take them unawares now, when everyone is drowsy and hiding from the weather?"

"Because then my men will be rejuvenated and very hungry."

"Ah. Very well, then. Come the turning of the storms."

"Good." He dressed and left the way he'd come in, through winter's icy window frame.

Trevilara allowed herself a faint smile. She'd almost agreed to what he'd asked. Almost. Winter would give her a decent amount of time to plan.

Chapter Thirty-Four

Kerith

A BONE-COLD WIND whistled off the high ocean cliffs at Fortress ild Fallyn, drilling its way through stone and mortar and fog-misted sky before skirling into the parade grounds where Tressandre had ordered the assembly. It carried the unforgiving odor of the sea: salty and brisk and unrelenting. Here, the surf pounded on treacherous rock, blue-gray waves that never warmed, never carried a fishing fleet because there were no coves or bays to cradle them, and because the wind incessantly whipped up white caps that rose as high as mountains. Any bounty from these northern seas came seldom and was hard won. It was the last place in the First Home to welcome her people, and they would not have stayed, but they had been given little choice.

Harried relentlessly after the House wars, the ild Fallyn had been forced into a retreat here. At first, the geography had seemed propitious: a hard-driven sea to the west to protect the flank, forests and meadowlands to the east and south to feed the mouth and purse. They had no way of knowing that the Mageborn native to Kerith had warred here first, and spilled their toxins into the ground, and that little harvest could be gotten. Relegated to eking out whatever living they could, as if they were no more than the mud-covered commoners of these lands, they struggled to regain what should have been theirs. The struggle neared its end. It would not be long before the sacred River Andredia and its verdant valleys would belong to her, as they always should have. It would not be long before the cold stone towers that stretched over her now would be used as little more than a lighthouse upon the coast. It would not be long till all she and Alton had worked for came to fruition. She mourned that he could not be here to see it realized. These people standing before her now would feel the vengeance that fueled her, for him and for her House. These people would help her gain the final victories. She could crack open Larandaril like an egg and plunder its hidden riches.

Praised for breeding generations of fine tashya horses, she could not understand why they were then reviled for breeding back the purity of their powers and Talents into their own people. Where did the difference lie? In small minds, unable to comprehend what the foreign blood of Kerith's mud dwellers had done to the purity of the ild Fallyn. Other Houses had not suffered such deviants, or they kept their mistakes close. Close or dead. Death served best, and the ild Fallyn returned that service.

As for the Returnists, she would send those dissident miscreants back to the hell through which they had spilled. If the ancient history of the ild Fallyns here on Kerith had taught her anything, it was that a bird in the hand was worth two in the bush. Returning to their lost home was as chancy as any bush hunt she'd ever seen.

Tressandre paced the lines, tapping a riding crop against the outside of her knee as she walked, her seneschal Waryn following at a respectful distance. Their breathing could scarcely be heard as the fear pulsing through their blood sounded much louder. She kept her thoughts to herself, enjoying the atmosphere. Her audience put their shoulders back straighter and held their chins up higher as she inspected them, their gaze trying not to meet hers but few finding it impossible to stare straight ahead. It was instinct to watch a dangerous thing when it approached one.

These were the best of their breeding program, the mission she and Alton had laid upon their shoulders almost before they could walk, and the efforts had been arduous.

Tressandre spoke, raising her voice little, enjoying the silence that reigned so her audience could listen. Their attention snapped to her, and stayed.

Her tone ominous, she said, "I have gathered you here this morning because of the hard work you've done. It is time I find a reward for you."

She heard muffled gasps and one smothered cough.

Pivoting on one heel, she strode to the far right of the line. She chose a young man, handsome enough by any standard, even hers. His eyes did not flicker to hers but his chest expanded slightly as he drew himself upward. She tickled the end of the crop about his rib cage. "What reward would you like from me?"

"Permission to subdue the enemies of your House, my lady."

The corner of her mouth quirked. She stepped onward, returning toward the center. This time she paused in front of a woman, a woman with a drawn face and a slightly rounded stomach proclaiming that she was with child. She had carried three fine sons previously for the ild Fallyn. One had died trying to carry out the recent assassination of Lariel Anderieon. One fell fighting the Raymy years ago and the third while hijacking a rich caravan. All in the name of the House. This woman did not know the fate of her sons and held no great Talent on her own, but she bred back marvelously. "This woman," Tressandre proclaimed, "is proven. She has given fine children to our cause and stands ready to do so yet again." She gave the woman a nod before passing on.

Her pace brought her to a stripling, a child not yet young adult whose features did not tell Tressandre if they were male or female, the only distinguishable marking a bracelet about one forearm marking the wearer as a jumper of distinction. Levitation, by far the most dominant Talent of the ild Fallyn, useful in warfare and building. This one would be worth a great deal in the not too distant future. "And you? What would you seek?"

"A . . . a home," the stripling whispered hoarsely. "To your honor."

"Indeed?" Tressandre drew the tip of the crop under the youngster's chin, lifting it so she could meet the eyes. Startling, near gold eyes, with the merest trace of brown within. Strange eyes, even for the Vaelinar. Not so many years ago, a baby with eyes this color would have been left in the wilderness for predators to dispatch. "We shall see."

Tressandre withdrew to the center of the parade ground, raising her voice only a trifle, enjoying the silence as all strained to hear her, even faithful Waryn still trailing behind her. "I am the sole heir to Fortress ild Fallyn. My brother Alton should be here, standing shoulder to shoulder with me, as I gaze upon the results of decades of effort. He should be here to consult with me upon the reward due you and here with me to confer that reward. He is not. Because he is not, the tasks ahead require my presence, taking me away from the stewardship of my bloodline. Waryn is my seneschal, but he is not enough. I need to ensure that my House will live on, despite the efforts of others to deny us. Today, I offer each and every one of you a destiny. I am asking you to shed your surname. To drop whatever divided loyalties you may have. To reach out and grab a fate I am putting before you. Today, I lift you up and put you in my House. You will leave your cots and find rooms in the fortress. You will say good-bye to the mud that spawned you. You are now ild Fallyn!"

A stunned silence fell, and then a choked cheer or two broke it, and then wild noises, as well as a quiet protest from Waryn.

"My lady . . ."

"Hush, Waryn. These twenty have earned it, bled for it, and will bleed again, even more if I ask them to. Without Alton, I cannot accomplish what must be done. With them, I can." She watched them as they hugged one another and shook fists at their brethren who ranged in curiosity behind the gates to the parade grounds. "Find them new clothes and rooms as soon as you can, and write their names in our books. I will need to learn them, I suppose."

Waryn gave a half bow. "If it must be, my lady."

"It must. The machines of vengeance run on flesh and blood, and the ild Fallyn heritage has run low. Now we have been renewed." She tapped her crop on the heel of her boot, a satisfied smile growing over her face. When she turned on Waryn, triumph flushed her face. "I have matters to accomplish and will be gone a while."

"I have your back, my lady, as always."

"I expect no less. When I return, be ready for great things."

He bowed his head. "From your lips to the ears of the Gods, my lady."

She laughed softly. "I don't need Gods. I have ild Fallyns."

"The Gods tell me I must cleanse their lands." Bregan tugged at a forelock of hair, ragged and shaggy because he would not let a barber or servant within arm's length of him with scissors, and scuffed his worn boot in the soil.

"Here? This does not look like badlands to me." Diort gazed about them and spread his hands in the air. "I am in the First Home at your behest, Bregan. But I have a city. I have lands. I have a kingdom to the east where we both lived well and you trained until you convinced me to come west. I am here at your behest. To tell you that you are erratic and your desires unmanageable is like telling a slime dog that it stinks. What would you have of me? I cannot let you wander about freely anymore."

Bregan looked up at him slyly. "As if you could fence me in."

"I could. Have no doubts. The Gods work as strongly through me as they do through you." He held the other's gaze until Bregan looked away. "Give me a direction, and I will move the camp that way if you indeed have a destination in mind."

Another scuffle in the bent grasses and trampled ground. Bregan's lips moved as though he held a conversation with himself. After a moment in which he fidgeted and fussed with his own body as if at odds with it, he lifted his head and straightened.

"To the west, half a day's ride."

"What accompaniment do you need?"

"You. Water. Food."

Diort raised his voice so that his first officer who worked at grooming his horse nearby would hear. "A brace of guards and supplies for a day's ride out, ready tomorrow morning."

"Tomorrow?"

"Yes." Diort nodded to Bregan and watched his eyes glitter. "Pleased?"

"We are very pleased!" He did a little jump in the air and spun about.

Diort's officer merely shook his head, returning his attention to the hoof he held in his hand, and his trimming knife. "We'll be ready, Your Highness."

"Good." Diort put his hand on Bregan's shoulder and felt energy running through him as wildfire runs through a dried grass gorge. "Rest for the day. Eat and sleep well. You'll need your strength for this task set upon you."

Bregan nodded his head up and down several times. "I will. I will, indeed." And he walked away, mumbling to himself, his hands gesturing as he explained something to a companion no one else could see.

His officer's horse relaxed as the man set his hoof down. He eyed the trimming knife in his hand. "How can you be certain whether he is God-touched or merely simple? We have both seen the afflicted who talk and dance in contortions to beings we cannot see."

"This one sees what we can't although I grant it's driven him nearly off the edge. But that is my concern. As his guardian, I am meant to help him define what is real and honest against what is merely his madness. I wonder if I am capable of the position."

The officer patted his restive mount on the shoulder as the horse rolled an eye at the knife he had not yet put away. He did so, folding it in two and tucking it back into his kit. "If anyone is, sir, you are." He gathered up the lead shank. "I'll have your detail ready at first light."

"Good." As he walked back to his canopied tent, the hairs at the back of his neck prickled. He glanced over his shoulder but saw no one watching. He thought of Ceyla and her words. For whom did he watch and wait?

The visitor did not come until after the dinner hour, when all had been consumed and cleaned away, and he lay back on his chaise full of food and drink but hollow with a vague discontent as the sun lowered in the sky. He felt uncertain that Bregan had been truthful with him about the task given him, and certainly not about how he hoped to accomplish it. He wanted to do with the man what he had been doing most of the last two years: give him a regimen of meditation and exercise, with very little flexing of his Mageborn muscles. Abayan Diort would not even be in the lands of the First Home except for Ceyla's visions that had brought him here, and then Bregan had bolted, necessitating a chase. Not that he would not have come sometime this spring anyway, to pay his respects to the sleeping queen. Did she still slumber? He'd had no word, although Ceyla had murmured to him that the Kobrir were effecting a cure and her time would be near.

His mood lightened immediately when his guards came to him and said that a woman, a Vaelinar woman who wished her name held secret, asked for entrance to the camp and his tent. He stood and watched as she crossed the grounds, swathed in shadows and a dark cloak, yet with her grace and sensuous curves clearly suggested. His heart leaped for a moment, thinking that the Warrior Queen came to him, foolish heart knowing that Bistane had kept her close these many months, and as she neared, he could see that his heart was more than reckless, it was wrong. As she paused at the edge of the light flung soft into the night by the lantern poles outside his tent, he could plainly see Tressandre ild Fallyn as she stopped and pushed back the hood of her cloak. Her hair, a smoky dark and streaked blonde, tumbled about her shoulders as she did.

His heart wanted to refuse her immediately and send her away, upset by the pretense it might have been Lariel. His inner voice, that one that ruled him as a Guardian King, told him to be circumspect. He pushed aside the tent flap.

She smiled. "Fair eve to you, Guardian King Diort. Shall we wager who is more surprised—myself at your return to these lands or you at seeing me?"

"I doubt that would be a good wager for either of us. I've made no secret of my traveling here and imagine your scouts informed you days and days ago."

"Come as an ally once again?"

"No, actually. I've come at the request of my Mageborn, here to tend to some arcane matter. But since your people are lately come to Kerith, after the Mageborn, perhaps you are not fully aware of their history."

"I know as much as you do, I think." Her smile widened, lips glistened a bit. "I have ridden a long way to meet with you, given that the Ferryman no longer exists on the shores of the Nylara with his Way of shortening distances, and my journey was not what it should have been."

"Forgive me. Come in and be seated. Wine? Chilled or warmed?"

"Wine, chilled, would be fine." She inclined her head as she stepped inside, and a cloud of fragrance hit him, the smell of horse and leather, but also of her skin's own natural perfume, and an infusion of florals and fruits that she had applied. She paused by the weapons rack to the side which held his war hammer. Even without its reputation, it stood on end, a massive, deadly tool. She ran her fingers over it.

"I remember when Rakka dropped, the very stone spoke back to it as the earth shook."

"As do I. But its voice is dead now, the demon which imbued it gone. Mountains no longer fall when I strike it."

"But its wielder stands as mighty as ever." She looked up at him through her lashes, dark honeyed blonde like her hair. "I wager it is still nearly as potent, if you intend it to be."

"It's effective." He watched her closely, weighing her movements against her words.

She dropped her cloak beside her chair as she sat. "When my people squabbled about who would reign over your people and raise them up from the backward slump forced upon them by the Mageborn Wars, my House lost advantages it might have held." She paused as he summoned a guard and ordered their wine. She continued only when the two of them were alone again. "Our fortress has a few advantages but also many disadvantages, being bordered on the east by badlands, for one. The old, toxic magics which washed up have rendered much of our land unusable."

He raised an eyebrow. "I wasn't aware."

She raised and dropped a comely shoulder, not clothed in the usual sturdy travel garb but in fine, translucent fabrics that seemed to breathe along with her, a gown that clung in many intriguing ways. "We don't make it widely known. Long before your father, or even your grandfather, was a twinkle in anyone's eyes, one of my bloodline was perfecting a method of cleaning up the magical sludges, of gathering them as one would mud in a bucket, and transferring them elsewhere."

His mind hurried to keep up with his racing thoughts. "You developed them as weapons, those 'buckets.' To be used in catapults, perhaps, or dumped in strategic water sources. The Vaelinar stopped the Bolgers with catapults."

"I cannot confirm or deny that. After all, it was your toxic waste. Who knows where it might have come from originally?" She paused again as his man brought in a tray, bowed, and left, and Diort handed her a glass of golden-white wine. "As for its effectiveness, my ancestor blew himself to bits quite early in his trials, and we abandoned his techniques shortly after. One war won, and all the others . . . lost." She swirled and then took an appreciative sniff before sipping.

He sat down across from her, his familiar old leather campaign chair creaking a bit with his weight. "I can't say I'm sorry to hear that."

"The way of progress, is it not? Ideas. Failure, success. Now and then a person comes along who makes a difference despite the trials faced." She took another sip. "Such as your oracle Ceyla."

The slight cold from his goblet of wine grew icier and spread from his fingers to his chest, even as he realized that fear chilled him. Tressandre smiled over the rim of her cup.

"If she is the person I suspect her to be, she is a runaway, one of my many wards. We lost her not long before the great return of the Raymy and the attack upon Larandaril." Tressandre gave him a close, detailed verbal depiction of Ceyla before concluding. "Would you say that description matched your oracle?"

He wouldn't give Ceyla up to the ild Fallyn. He forced himself to take a drink of wine and appear to savor it. "I cannot say one way or another. There are certainly many about with a mix of Kerith blood and Vaelinar lines. Your forefathers were a lusty sort. It would be difficult to single out such a person, although I can try if you insist. However, if any live under my protection, then that is where they would stay."

Tressandre waved a hand negligently through the air. "And that has nothing to do with the business that brings me here."

Diort's heartbeat steadied a touch. Mentioning Ceyla had just been a preliminary to the détente, informing Abayan that she was more familiar with the inner workings of his rule than he might have thought. Of course he knew she had spies; what Vaelinar would not have a spy?

She held her glass up to the lantern light as if appraising its color. "I came to bring you news, and an offer." She lowered her glass.

"And you have my full attention, Lady Tressandre."

"Warrior Queen Lariel has awakened and is regaining her strength and vigor." She paused. "And she has announced her engagement to Warlord Bistane Vantane."

The first he heard rumors about on the wind, though he'd not been formally informed; the second bit of news hit him like a hard blow to the gut. Aware that she watched him closely, he kept his expression smoothed but inside, he seethed. To dismiss him, Abayan Diort, out of hand, despite what Bistane had done for her over the years, she ought to have been more of a diplomat than that. His army had come to her aid at crucial moments more than once. Their alliance would have extended the influence of the western lands eastward to the inner part of the old lands, which had lain fallow for centuries, even though his Galdarkan nomads crossed them back and forth. He had much to offer her had he been allowed to court her. Instead, she had given her hand to the first man available, regardless of the consequences. His stomach twisted a bit, his wine going sour.

"Of course, she would make him her selection, being unaware of the many contributions of the rest of us to maintain Larandaril while she recovered. Bistane marshaled her information closely, unfortunately." She put her glass aside. "I don't think we will receive the gratitude deserved."

He fought for his thoughts and frowned, slightly, in memory as he collected them. "I arrived at the battle a little late, but I thought I heard that it was you and your brother who brought her down. For that treason, I don't think you want to collect what she owes you."

"Those rumors! They will plague me the rest of my life, and no way to put them to rest. Her own man attacked her, parrying off our attempts to block him, and her magical armor backfired on all of us, destroying Alton. When Lara collapsed, Sevryn then followed his master Quendius across the bridge to safety, leaving the rest of us behind in ruins." Tressandre's face crumpled in distress for the briefest of moments. "I lost everything to that maggot's actions. My brother. My child with Jeredon. The trust and respect of Lariel's allies. But in spite of that, I helped regain and keep the peace of her lands. My people reside there still, making what repairs they can to the Andredia and its corruption."

"Your people are called squatters."

Her lip curled. "Bistane controls many perceptions. I have been healing and in mourning."

"You seem to be recovered and lovely as ever."

She looked up, meeting his eyes. "Thank you. You are a self-made man, made without the conniving and corruption of the likes of Bistane, and are well aware of the sacrifices one must make to rule."

He felt the corner of his mouth twitch and tried to hide it behind his goblet by pretending to take a sip, though—his stomach still soured by her words—he would not partake.

"We both have debts and considerations we are owed, and ambitions which should be followed to the benefit of our people. I propose, Abayan Diort, that we ally against our injustices."

"You wish a wedding."

She tilted one shoulder down provocatively and twisted a curl between her slender fingers. "That is exactly what I propose."

Ceyla came to him late in the evening long after the guest had left, after even the restless horses had fallen to sleep, and the third-shift guards had only just gone on duty. Someone sang softly at the camp's edge, his voice true, and others joined him in a quiet song meant to gentle unsettled horses and live-stock. She paused at the door flap for a very long moment, likely telling herself what she would say to him, as was her habit. He heard her slipping through the tent, canvas whispering about her body. She knelt by his cot.

"You sent her away."

"I did."

"She will add you to her enemies."

"Yes, but I have added her first to mine." He put his hand out to entangle it in her hair at the back of her head, drawing her closer to him. "She knows who you are."

Ceyla stilled.

"I told her I won't let you go. You have my full protection."

She trembled next to him, the tiniest of tremors, relief and . . . did he dare hope, another emotion? She turned her head, whispering against his palm, "Thank you, my lord."

Her reflected breath smelled sweet to him. "My thanks are to you."

"What else did she want?"

"She wanted me to marry her."

"What?" Ceyla sat bolt upright, almost knocking him under the jaw with the top of her skull as she swung about. Her shock amused him.

"Did you not foretell that?"

"Well . . . no. Not in so many words. She must be furious."

"She was. She brought news of Lariel's pending marriage to Lord Bis-tane, and thought we would commiserate by allying with each other."

"And you refused her?"

"Naturally."

Ceyla took his hand in both of hers. "May I ask why? It might have been a good move, politically. I know that you had considered, perhaps, that Lara would give you her hand. Tressandre might have been a decent second choice."

"Firstly, I don't like her. Secondly, Galdarkan and Vaelinar cannot have children together, so such a match cannot extend my legacy. Thirdly, if I were to join with any Vaelinar despite that . . ." He paused for a long moment.

"Yes, my lord?"

"It would be you, my oracle."

He could feel the brilliance of her smile even in the twilight of the tent.

"And did you foresee that?"

"No, Diort," she whispered. "I just hoped for it."

WHEN TOLBY REACHED THE CIDER BARN, Dayne was already about, shuffling through the new batch of books sent down by Azel from the library of Ferstanthe. Although the tincture they'd been sending up worked, it seemed to work far better at the hands of Dayne and Tolby than when administered by Azel or any of his staff. It made the work longer and more frustrating, for the black mange that attacked the pages made them incredibly fragile during treatment and somewhat brittle after, the mange being neither fungus nor animal but magical. Tolby thought perhaps that even his efforts were not the turning point but the skill of Verdayne who had, after all, aryn sap running in his veins in addition to blood. Not that he actually thought the lad had real sap in him, although where it concerned the Vaelinar, he'd heard odder things. But it was indisputable that it was his father, the late Warlord Bistel, who had brought and planted the aryn wood staff which sprouted miraculously into a tree, which could then be propagated both by graft and seed. The properties of the aryn trees were nothing less than magical.

Tolby gripped his teeth a bit harder about his pipe stem. He would love to experiment with the wood, given the opportunity, but he hadn't approached this idea yet with the lad, things being as they were. Verdayne was practically a member of his family—but had not yet become one officially. He had only himself to blame; he was as stubborn as the summer day was long, and his darling Lily had plenty of backbone herself. Dwellers, they were, through and through, and Nutmeg herself an apple which had not fallen far from the tree. He puffed out a fragrant cloud of smoke as he reached Verdayne.

"How goes it?"

"Well enough. I wish they didn't have to cart the books down. The infestation increases even on the journey, try as we can to stunt it. I was thinking—and call me on this, Tolby, if I'm too far-fetched on it—I was thinking of trying a bit of aryn powder. I know it's dear, but since I'm a supplier, I can get us a discount."

"I'd say you were a mind reader, lad. Think it might work?"

"I would say it can't hurt."

"Then let's do it. Have we any spare aryn wood?"

"Not about. Just your staff, and I wouldn't be asking you to use that."

"What I propose would take nothing more from it than a light sanding and wouldn't be missed. It won't weaken my staff. I'll send for more aryn wood, of course, but that will take a handful of weeks. And we can start today, if . . ."

Tolby thought on it. "Three tinctures or sprays we'll need. Three different potencies with aryn wood, I should think."

"Then I'll do the sanding and gather the sawdust we need."

Tolby thought to warn him. "Be circumspect about the mess. Meg and Lily are like to be in a dither about cleaning up. Lariel is coming for a visit."

Dayne halted in the doorway. "With my brother?"

"Aye. They've announced their engagement and are coming to meet the two little ones."

"Engagement? And you didn't think to tell me that first?"

Tolby took his pipe from his mouth and considered it. "I would have thought it his place to tell you."

Dayne's face flushed. "Well, there's that, but he didn't. Is he coming here?"

"I believe so. The message was not so clear."

"When?"

"Ah, now that I have some idea about. Lara said soonest." He shrugged.

Dayne threw his hands up and went out the door, turned abruptly and came back in to search the tool boxes for a file, went out, came back in and rummaged about till he had a bit of canvas to catch the sawdust, and finally departed totally. Tolby let out a soft chortle before he put the pipe out and in a pocket while he went to check his batches of spray. He scratched his chin as he leaned into the storage cabinet and the faint whiff of chemicals reached him, pondering the matters of high elven with long lives.

For all that Lara sent that they would be arriving soonest, they did not. Word came of a stop at Hawthorn, capital of the First Home and in the opposite direction from Calcort because Larandaril lay roughly in between and north of the two cities, but finally birds came heralding their nearness with no actual sight of them. The guards ducked out of the day's heat, and Corrie fussed from the depths of the house as she prepared the children. Nutmeg watched the street closely. Dayne came by, a jug of cool cider in his hand.

"Rest a bit?"

Her curls bounced as she shook her head. "I can't."

"I'll pour you a cup of cider. You'll have plenty of time once their approach is seen." He picked out a shady spot in the porch overhang. "Sit. I have something to discuss with you before they get here."

Dayne pulled a chair out for her. Nutmeg looked from his hand to the seat of the chair, but she didn't ask the question that seemed obvious from her expression. Wiping her fingers dry on her apron, she sat perched on the seat's edge, her legs tucked under so that she could bolt away if need be. "I can't tarry. Corrie's waiting for me, to help tidy up the children."

"She'll wait. I vouch this is a bit more important."

"Why?"

"It's about the children."

Her spine stiffened.

"Listen, just a moment or two. Give me that."

"They're babies."

"No, they're not."

"They are! Barely two years of age and you know that as well as I do."

"I probably remember a wee bit better than you." His eye caught a sparkle. "You were busy at the time."

"Undoubtedly." One hand twisted at the apron's hem. "I won't be letting you take their innocence away. They are babies, for all that."

"Meg, you were farm raised, like I was. You've seen a horse or pony birthed. How long before they're on their hooves, ready to nurse and then run after their mother? They're born long-legged and ready to move. How many Vaelinar children have you seen?"

Nutmeg twitched and Dayne held up his hand. "Full-blooded."

Her mouth quirked. "None."

"Like horses, they're born with long legs and are ready to run, a defensive evolution, I suspect because of our devious natures. Once ten years or so grown, they are on the edge of developing the final traits of adulthood, but that's when they begin to slow. Immensely. It's not much different from those of us with half-blood. We just don't grow as tall. And then the maturity begins, and that will take centuries."

"Vaelinars mature slower because we live longer. That is the usual way of it, and Dwellers also take their time, but I am not talking about their frames." Dayne paused. "It's the look in their eyes, Meg. They have thoughts and souls far beyond their years, bursting to get out. They're not mature, but they are far more grown than they appear, and you've got to be prepared for that, because you don't have babies. You've got Vaelinar blood. They can't express the words they need, and in Evar, that drawback drives him to fury. We've got to show him the way to live with his true nature. To take hold. We need to be teaching them now."

"You mean their Talents."

"That will come, too, but I'm talking about the core of what they are. It's already there. It's not going to take a hundred years to form."

The corners of her eyes glistened. "Merri can barely walk."

"Yes, but she listens and learns. She watches you, me, Lily, Tolby—your brothers. She watches and learns by leaps and bounds. And she's smart, like Evar, far more than the average person. You know that. You're her mother and you will always be, but you can't expect to spend your days mothering a helpless child. She's not helpless. She's just . . . trapped. We need to educate them."

"And draw more of Tressandre's attention than we already have?" Nutmeg shook her head vigorously. "No! And that would expose Evar as well as Merri. Who could we trust to teach them if we did? I cannot think of a soul I would trust."

"I would do it, if you would let me."

Her mouth softened a moment before she put her hand up. "No."

"And why not?"

"They're not ready."

"I disagree. I think you're the one who's not ready."

"And why would I be? Why would I want anyone to lead them into a pack of scheming Vaelinars, ready to take their place in the ranks of those seeking power beyond anyone's notion of what is right and just?" She bounced to her feet. "If Lariel had any other heir, I would never even consider what obligations they might hold. But she doesn't, and so I do. But they're still mine, and I won't give them up."

"She's awake now . . . and she will want them."

Nutmeg's lip curled. "Train them in her footsteps and mistakes."

"Would you have them be ignorant of what their fellows are like? What they must accept and avoid?"

"Lariel needs them far worse than they need her." Nutmeg looked at him, her eyes shining with hurt and worry. "I don't want to have this talk with you."

"I can almost guarantee you'll have it with her. They should be prepared. They are no less than crippled, for all your love. It rankles at them, most especially Evar." Verdayne paused, thinking of young Evar with his little hands knotted into fists. "The longer you leave him go, the harder it is for him. He struggles to find the words that he needs to fit the action he wants to seize. It isn't good or wise to try to muffle him. He's bursting out of his skin, and I don't want him to feel he must explode. It's not good for him to ignore his frustration and needs."

"Take your brother aside. Tell him no, and tell him to lead her to comply."

"You overestimate my brother's influence with the Warrior Queen."

"He's a Warlord!"

"And do you know what the Warlord does, amongst the Vaelinars? He's a general among generals, nothing more. She wears the title Queen."

"Then tell him to—tell him to challenge her for it. He's been holding the Houses and Forts together all these seasons while she slept."

"It's not done like that."

"I don't see why in the cold hell not." Nutmeg looked down at the ground, furious, her hands shaking on the back railing of the chair. "They'll all be fine. The Vaelinars abide. They're doing quite well with only Bistane to guide them, despite Tressandre nipping at his heels. Their Houses won't fall." Her breathing fell into a sudden quaver. "My house won't survive without my children. It won't."

Her tremors upset the patio table so much that her glass of cider slid over the edge and shattered abruptly on the ground. Dayne moved. "I'll sweep it up."

She ran a hand through her hair, dragging it away from her face, and looked up, the color bleeding from her cheeks. A cloud of smoke appeared from the southernmost end of the road into their quarter. A pounding of hooves preceded the appearance of a rider, racing toward their farmhouse.

"She's coming!" Hosmer, resplendent in his uniform for the City Guard, pulled his horse to a plunging stop in the road. "She's passed the main gate," he told his sister as he swung down and began to lead his mount away to the back courtyard.

"Oh, it's about time," Nutmeg said. "I'll be back." She turned, ducking into the house, and Dayne pointed Hosmer away from the shards of the fallen cup. He had it all cleaned up and put away when the group of them reappeared, Evar and Merri trailing behind their nurse, busy with some mischief they didn't wish seen. The guards took up watchful posts as Nutmeg dried her fingers on her apron again. She reached back for her children's hands, to draw them out from behind Auntie Corrie's voluminous skirts and found little fingers damp and sticky. "By the cold hells. Who keeps giving them toffee apples? Corrie, get them cleaned up, again, and I swear—" She cast a narrow-eyed look about the assembled group of Farbranches and guards. "If I catch you sneaking them treats, I will run you out of town wearing nothing but toffee and feathers!"

"Not me, I swear!" Dayne raised his hands in defense and stepped out of everyone's way as they made a mad dash back into the farmhouse for repairs.

By the time the children made it back outside, their little faces and hands scrubbed within an inch of their lives and a shiny, near apple red from the efforts, Lariel and Bistane had drawn their horses to a stop in the middle of the street, their accompanying guards, who numbered a modest four, and the pair assigned to Calcort exchanging loud and vivid salutes and shouts of loyalty. The mayor, a retired trader of stout Kernan blood, waved to them all. "The inn awaits your pleasure. Simply send a runner ahead to notify them when you wish your meals and your beds turned down, my lady, my lord." He gave a toothy grin for which he'd become famous, Tentith the Toothsome, reining back and bidding farewell with a grand flourish from his saddle.

Bistane helped Lariel down from her dappled gold tashya, but it wasn't a Lara Nutmeg could easily recognize. Her time of illness had reforged her. This Lara appeared dangerously thin under her clothes, although her muscles stood out like cords along her arms. Her beauty had always been great, even among the slender and beauteous Vaelinar, but now her cheekbones stood in such stark relief that they looked almost sharp enough to cut. The silver in her golden hair burned brightly in the sun, almost difficult to view. Her eyes looked wider and brighter, her gaze harsher. Her riding leathers were tailored to fit her closely, yet seemed too loose even at that, and she carried a riding whip curled in her hand like a defensive weapon. She wore light mail over her leathers and a long sword at her back, crisscrossed with a bow. A quiver of arrows hung from the front of the saddle she had just left. Nutmeg stared at her and wondered if she would now make friends with such a woman, all harsh edges, if she had not already.

Lara smiled tightly as if aware of Nutmeg's sudden inability to talk and advanced, her arms outstretched. "Nutmeg, you look wonderful. Mother-hood obviously agrees with you."

Nutmeg found her face wet with tears and hugged her back, tightly, whispering in her ear, "I did not think to see you so alive again! Bright apples, and here you are!"

Lara let go slowly. She looked downward at two suddenly shy figures. "And the children." She frowned slightly. "Are they . . . well? They look fevered, their faces so pink."

That broke Nutmeg's lock on her words. "Fevered? What? Oh, no, Lara. Just scrubbed. Very, very, well scrubbed." She drew Lara to her again and hugged her tightly, feeling for herself the thin but rock-hard form within her embrace. "And Bistane!"

She turned to the Warlord who had locked arms with his brother and was finishing up, "Send you to Calcort with a job to do and you never come home?"

"Things kept me busy," Verdayne threw back at him and drew Nutmeg up so that Bistane could grasp her hands and kiss them fondly.

Bistane looked upon one and the other. "I don't doubt that you have been occupied."

Dayne's cheeks heated a bit. "I've been home at least as much as you have."

"Ah, good. That means we still have crops and aryns and obligations answered!" Bistane stepped back.

Nutmeg moved back and introduced Corrie, but Lara's gaze was fastened on the children, both of them, and she slowly dropped to her knees at the edge of the roadway, her leathers creaking and her mail clinking softly as she did. She reached for their hands. Merri slipped into Lara's hold eagerly, but Evar stayed back, aloof, head tilted, eyes on her face.

"We tho't you'd never get here," he said solemnly.

"Nor did I." Lara placed both of Merri's small hands in her left one and reached for him again. He stepped forward slowly then and took hold of her. She studied him for a very long time before looking up at Nutmeg. "I think we have much to discuss. And best not out here on the street."

In the shaded house, the words fell like pebbles into a pond, spreading ripples. "You knew I had twins."

"Yes, but I'd been told of the ruse and how successful it had been." Lara sat back in her chair, her hand shaking a bit as she reached toward Bistane. "It might have worked in the past, but anyone who sees him now, who knew Jeredon at all . . . will know immediately. He might be a bit small in stature, but he is most assuredly Jeredon's son."

Nutmeg looked across the table to where the two sat on the floor, engrossed in putting together a wooden puzzle that Bistane had emptied out of one of the many saddlebags they'd brought with them. Her mouth closed and lips curved slightly. "I see it in him, but I wasn't sure who else might. Sometimes I think I might imagine it."

Lara shook her head. "So the question is, what shall we do with them?"

"That is a question I've already answered." Tolby crossed his arms over his chest.

"They can't stay here."

"You were not all that safe at Larandaril."

Bistane said tightly, "We have taken measures."

"I'm certain you have, but the fact remains that if we had been in residence when the ild Fallyn struck, you might have lost your heirs as well as Lariel."

"I didn't lose Lara."

"Nearly."

Lara reached over and took Bistane's hand in hers. "He is right, you know."

Bistane looked down angrily, but his countenance softened at the sight of her fingers lacing gently into his. "I fault myself for it."

"No, you blame Tressandre."

"True. Her first and myself second. I should have remembered the depth of her ambition."

"And who else would try to kill a dying woman?" Lily arched an eyebrow as faces turned toward her. To Lara, she added, "Bistane did not report great optimism on your recovery. He walked a fine balance between the news of your living and your languishing, to keep your enemies off-balance. It is plain Tressandre tired of waiting for the inevitable."

"And equally plain she will soon know that Evarton is an heir of mine as well as Merri."

"She might even put Merri aside in her mind and focus entirely upon him. He has the looks and the bearing even for one so young."

A silence fell over the table as if aware that the clamor and babble of the children at play had stopped long ago and they looked to find the two staring back at them.

"They've never been that quiet," Nutmeg remarked.

"Yes, and no one can say they aren't observant." A smile quirked the corner of Lara's otherwise stern face. "What do you know of their abilities? Both have the eyes, although Merri's are quite subtle. I know they have much more to grow, but they must be showing some tendencies already."

Nutmeg tilted her head in thought. "Merri is a conciliator, a soother. I would say she is the more diplomatic of the two, and very likely a Healer. They get their bruises and scrapes, but they rarely show them more than a day, and Evar heals first. I think she takes care of her brother."

"A Healer? Hmmm. A good Talent."

"And she talks with animals."

"Really?" Lara fastened her attention on the speaker, Dayne.

"Like a lot of small ones, she spends a great deal of time talking to them. After a while she convinced me that they must communicate back."

Keldan sat forward eagerly, pushing his forelock from his head. "Oh, they do. She's told me a number of times about this one complaining that the saddle rubbed because the blanket was too thin, or a stone was caught in the frog, or the grain was going bad. She was right every time, although she's got a bit of trouble finding the words for what she wants to say. She knows far more than any child should."

"But no one told me." Nutmeg sounded a bit affronted. "About the animal talk."

"We thought you knew," Dayne and Keldan said almost as one.

That definitely brightened Lara's face as she laughed softly, sitting back more comfortably in her chair. "Jeredon had a great affinity for animals and their ways although he was more a ranger and a hunter. He understood about them, although not directly. I think it would have bothered him to hunt otherwise."

Merri made a sniffling noise of sympathy. Evar reached out a comforting arm and drew his sister close. That immediately cut off her sniffling as she pushed him off.

"And what about Evarton?"

They traded looks about the table. Tolby spoke, each word deliberately. "We're not sure. He is a bright and strong lad, but he keeps his true nature hidden, except when he's about his sister. That he has Talents, we're fairly certain, just not what."

"Does he anticipate things when he shouldn't be able to?"

Bistane put his hand on Lara's wrist as she spoke, as if to delay her statements. She looked down, and then covered his hand with her own.

"He's a leader and convincer. He knows how to persuade everyone in this room. But I don't think that's a Talent."

"And perhaps he has an odd ability not easily revealed or recognized. Many think to this day that I have no Talents."

"Persuasion could definitely be indicative of a Voice Talent."

"He's more of a charmer." Lily demurred and then smiled indulgently at her grandchildren who had returned to playing, although their voices to one another had dropped quite low as if they didn't wish to be overheard or wished to be able to listen to the adults while they skirmished.

"Despite his eyes, perhaps he has no Vaelinar magics. Jeredon and his father weren't greatly accomplished, which is why Sinok had Jeredon's father put aside and forced your mother to marry again." Bistane paused. "Jeredon's abilities came forth later in his years, disproving Sinok, but disinheriting had already been done."

"And I don't suggest it now, either," Lara told him. "I'm only curious about them. This is my first visit of many."

Tolby shifted in his chair. "Every time you visit, you put my family in danger."

She looked to Tolby. "This is my way of getting to know them."

"Perhaps letters and reports would have sufficed."

"Would you have been happy with letters?" Her gaze locked with Tolby's and did not shift. Nor did his.

"Of course not, and I respect you as a queen, Lariel—but my grandchildren were not brought to life so that you could have a successor. They belong at their mother's side and whatever heritage or legacy belongs to them, I would have them earn. Nor will I have you treat them slightly, just so that you can know which one to train and which to forget."

"I couldn't forget either of them! They are my brother's children, my only legacy of him whom I loved greatly, and those whom I hope to love as much one day."

"If they live."

"Then bring them to Larandaril where I can keep them safe."

"They are already home and already safe. Or they were before you traveled here and reminded people of their place in your life."

Bistane shifted uneasily in his chair as if he might join the argument, but his mouth thinned and stayed shut.

"I don't do this for whimsy! I thought long and hard about what my actions might cause. The gap between us didn't happen because I chose to lay abed for two years and more! And do you think I slept, soft and easy? There were times when I could, but most days my body held me prisoner, my eyes and ears aware and yet beyond my control, with no way to signal anyone that I was a prisoner locked inside. No one came to give me news or comfort except for Bistane. He told me of the babies. Of the funeral pyres burning in Larandaril. Of the devastation of the tashya herds and my troops and what he was doing to rebuild them for me. Of the bold Returnists who squat upon the banks of the Andredia, befouling her as they do. He gave me hope when I had none, resolve when I needed it, and love when I would have refused it. You visited me twice in my rooms and neither time was I aware, but even if I had been—" Lara caught her breath. "I could not have held them. I could not have loved them as my brother's children, as I wish to do. So my move to come here is calculated, weighed, and I came anyway, a decision I made with as much great thought as I did when I agreed to marry Bistane."

Tolby's expression did not soften. "Of course a Vaelinar would greatly weigh the military and political advantages of a marriage, against the wishes of the heart."

Her face blotched. "At least I did not bring two bastards into this world first."

Lily gasped, but it was Dayne who reeled back in his chair. Nutmeg sat up the straighter. "Now we get to it. At last a bit of truth from the high elven. You hated what passed between Jeredon and me."

"Yes, the truth. Oh, Meg, I love you and the children, but it would have been so much easier for all of us if my cold-damned brother had just married you before he died. Or not chosen you at all." Worry and fatigue thinned Lariel's words.

"He did not marry me because I never got a chance to tell him I was with child, although . . ." And Nutmeg paused for a moment, caught in a terrible memory. "I think he guessed. Even then, knowing, he wouldn't have married me. He thought he protected you by becoming a decoy to Tressandre ild Fallyn, and I doubt he would have done anything differently. Nor did he want to bring the scandal to your throne. He never quite came to terms with the fact we loved one another."

Lara inhaled for a moment before responding. "We weave a lot of unnecessary knots into our fates, don't we?"

Nutmeg let out a gathered sigh. "We do, indeed."

Lara leaned a bit toward her. "Let's not stop with the truth telling here, then. Tell me what happened to your eyes." Her fingers swept a few of Nutmeg's curls aside from her temple. "And your ears. Why would you have them cut so? What would possess you to don the costume of one of us? Why do you feign at having Vaelinar blood?"

Nutmeg shook her head away angrily. "Why should I play at that? I've been changed, and it was the doing of your two heirs, before they were even born."

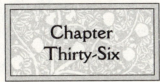

Chapter
Thirty-Six

L ARA JOLTED UPRIGHT, one cheek ablaze as if slapped. Bistane
reached one hand to her lower back, steadying her. She made a try at
saying something, failed, before trying again. "It happened while you were
carrying? You think the babies changed you."

"Yes."

"This is serious."

"I know." Nutmeg tapped her cheekbone. "I can also now read
Vaelinaran."

"Impossible."

"But helpful."

"I cannot think of an instance where something like this has been
chronicled." Lara put her own hand, her mutilated left, on the table in
front of her, spreading her fingers out . . . three fingers and one thumb, the
missing finger's joint marked by a ragged scar. "We know," she said slowly,
"Of the rumors, the folk tales, that women who have loved the Vaelinar
and carried their children often live longer. There was no real reason why
that would be so, but it was, unquestionably." She looked at Verdayne.
"Your own mother's life would verify that."

He nodded.

"We have always attributed that to the care and lifestyle we offered:
better housing, food, healing. We know that Kerith affects us, in many
ways unnoticeable and in some ways, very apparent." She held her left
hand in the air. "My family's pact to the Andredia is one of flesh and blood,
a magic of this world and not our heritage, and one which binds me to the
river." She dropped her hand. "Now, perhaps, we must consider that the

unborn have a way of matching their mother's growth more closely to their own. We have our own longevity; we take our time in maturing. Perhaps the young have a way of changing that pace. But as to the rest." Lara took a breath and studied Nutmeg closely, who returned her frank gaze with an even one of her own. "I have never heard of such a thing, of the physical being remade."

Bistane took a breath. "Nor have I, but I'll be the first to admit that young mothers would hardly confide in me. Transforming what already exists might be a survival trait, an unconscious act that doesn't last beyond infancy."

"We have two-headed calves born now and then, but there's nothing t' suggest they wanted to be that way."

"Dad! I won't have my children compared to a two-headed calf!"

"Nobody is doing that. It needs pointing out that strange things can happen to the unborn and many of them unfortunate. It has little to do with Making or Unmaking."

"You're a level-headed, forward-thinking man, Tolby, but the old superstitions have a way of roaring back." Lily gave a grim smile. "Don't be forgetting that we were attacked by that madman proclaiming he is a Mageborn, returned to us."

"What madman? What attack?"

"Bregan Oxfort." Lily gave a slight nod.

"Bregan has been odd since he was attacked by the Dark Ferryman and suffered a severe stroke of mind and capabilities, but Mageborn? When did this occur? Why wasn't I informed?"

"So much has happened," Bistane said mildly. "I thought I had caught you up on Bregan. His transformation came about at the battle of Larandaril. Abayan Diort is now known as the Guardian King, having taken Bregan under his protection. If the man is indeed Mageborn, it's driving him insane. He has some primal powers, but they're very erratic and his mental state is even worse."

"He attacked us here when Tolby was giving one of his talks to bring the news and the story behind it to Calcort, particularly of the latest attempt on your life. He's against the Vaelinars because the old Gods of Kerith are awake."

"So. If Evarton does have a Talent to transform, we face opposition from renewed religious beliefs among the Kernan."

"That would be a simple response. We really can't gauge how much of a following Bregan has, or if he could incite anyone to join him, and Diort has kept a pretty tight lid on him while trying to teach him what little he can about the Mageborn."

"Yet he attacked you?"

"Indeed. A whirlwind brought him in and deposited him on the doorstep of th' Bucking Bird. That was an interesting afternoon."

"Interesting? He came to attack our children, and you call it interesting?" Nutmeg folded her arms across her chest.

"Aye, that I do. You see, my lady, he had no idea who he was attacking—no interest at all in Merri and Evar—he was after me for blaspheming, and that tied his mind in a knot."

Lily muttered something, and her lips thinned and paled.

"Diort came riding in just behind him, with his little Oracle, and all was put in order soon enough."

"If Bregan has become a menace, he should be dealt with, and not lightly."

"He didn't expose the children. His rantings and ravings went against his reputation if anything, and I'll wager Diort has him well in hand now."

"Still . . ."

"Not still. The matter seems done. What should concern us is that revealing either of the children's Talents can potentially have a backlash not only within our own community, but also with the new-sprung religious leanings of the Kernan."

"That might be overstating th' facts, but it seems wise to keep our Gods in consideration. They are awake, and they may not like what they're finding."

"Which does not help us with our question of what Evarton may be able to do."

"If anyone had these Talents, our Houses have kept the knowledge close. Transformation would be close to Illusion, but Illusionaries are scarce. Our eyes see too well to be fooled."

"Perhaps we have the first inkling of an even rarer Talent. He could be a Maker."

"A Maker?"

"Permanent change or creation. That would take a lot of power."

"A Talent we only assume could exist as an extension of building. No one has actually been found to be one. The closest would have been Bistel, who took a greenstick staff and made a tree of it."

"A Talent for growing, only. He didn't create something out of thin air." Bistel's eldest son sat back in his chair.

"And Evar belongs in that vein. He might have made a dog out of a statue."

"What do you mean, Dayne?"

Lily folded her arms across her chest. "We decided that dog got in from outside somehow."

Lariel leaned forward intently. "A Vaelinaran war dog? In Calcort? Had it been set upon the children? Why did we not get a report on that?"

Dayne shook his head and did not stop until he held their attention. "I had a statue. Life-sized. Poor work, just a mud-fired effort that my brother sent me as a jibe. The statue disappeared. I noticed that Evarton had gotten it and towed it away to their playroom and hidden it in the corner. It was a bit heavy. I said nothing but I admired how he must have wrestled it about, even with Merri's help. When a live dog got into the rooms, it was in a murderous state. It killed Gryton and nearly myself and Brista. After we dispatched it, she went to make sure they had gotten out and were all right while I secured the scene. Imagine how I felt when I saw the thing turning back into stone. Evar, Merri, and I made a solemn pact—"

A little voice shouted out, "Cake!" and Dayne could not help smiling as he amended. "We made a solemn promise over cake not to talk about the dog. I've been doing a bit of studying, armed by some of the books the Library has been sending for repair, but a Talent such as Making is not really discussed head-on. It seems to be one of those things which, if held, would be greatly feared. Perhaps even the owner of that Talent would be killed to keep others safe."

"You didn't even tell me."

He turned toward Nutmeg. "No. I meant to, but the time never seemed right. We had so many other things to worry about." He cleared his throat. "Annnnd it does explain the proliferation of toffee apples."

"Those scamps."

"The Talents of a Maker are considerable. There's danger there, real danger. Our history is littered with the deaths of those who thought they could make a Way, who could twist the fabric of what is into what they willed—and died when that fabric snapped. A Maker violates far more laws of the world than that."

"I thought that Bistel was the last of the living creators of a Way."

All eyes turned to Nutmeg. She shrugged. "Wasn't he? He talked about it to me once." She dared not mention that discussion had come through the pages of his journal.

"He was, and he wasn't. Others came after but few survived their attempts to found a House based on the ability to successfully create a Way. And, today, most of those Ways have snapped back to what they were before they were tampered with. It's as if the yarn can only be stretched and twisted so far before it fails." Lara studied her hand a moment. "It appears that the portal Daravan created is a Way in itself, only it tampers with two worlds instead of one."

"Making it even more dangerous."

"I believe so. When it snaps—and I think it has to sooner or later—the energy released could be catastrophic if it's unexpected."

"And if it's anticipated?"

"We might be able to shield Kerith from the effects or dissipate them altogether. Remember the stories of old of when the Vaelinars were first cast here? The explosion and devastation was as great as a volcanic blast. I should imagine it would be the same."

"Someone should explain that to Tressandre! She's been pressing the Returnists to do all they can to widen the Eye."

Bistane shook his head at Nutmeg. "She'd never believe us. She'd be certain we were hiding something wonderful and critical from her. We intend to deal with the Returnists and then Tress."

Lara looked to Dayne and cleared her throat. "You've been reading the *Books of All Truth* from the Library?"

"No, just some of the lesser volumes sent with them. I wouldn't violate the trust of the Library or its keeper." Dayne leaned on his elbows over the table. "We have to know what we're dealing with, how to train them and how much to let the world know about them. They can't be kept ignorant as well as hidden."

"Bring them to Larandaril. I'll see them taught. The border wards will go back up at Larandaril, and no one will be able to get in. We have secrets to be kept veiled."

"Don't make promises you can't keep, Lara. We've already got squatters there we cannot evict."

Her attention snapped to Bistane who tilted his head slightly. "You've never been forthcoming about the extent of your own abilities."

She shut her mouth tightly a moment before saying, "There are reasons for that."

"And to you, they are excellent reasons, but to the rest of us, you're cloaked in secrecy which may or may not be valid. It's one of the main causes the ild Fallyn have, and why they continue to deny your right to your title. They believe you have no significant ability and are too weak to be Warrior Queen. They are wrong, but they remain convinced that the title was stolen from them despite your win in the trial."

"So you suggest we leave the children here and hope to educate them and continue to hide them?"

Tolby pulled his pipe out of his pocket and examined it as if preparing to light it. "The ild Fallyn will not stop until you are gone or they are."

"I will not stoop to her level."

"You don't have to. She can trip you up just fine from where she is." Tolby tapped the pipe bowl on the table, shaking out some ashes and brushing them off with the side of his hand. "She's never wanted a fair fight, Lady Lariel, she's only wanted a victory."

Lara rubbed her temple as Bistane said quietly, "It's been a long and tiring ride. The mayor has a table and a bed waiting for us, so we'll take advantage of the hospitality and talk things over."

Lara stood, with one of his hands on her, and gave a faint smile. "I can find a teacher for Merri, but I'll have to think long and hard about who would do for Evarton. That someone would have to be skilled, discreet, and ethical. There are things that can be Made which should not exist under the sun."

"I would offer," Verdayne murmured.

"Commendable, but you wouldn't be able to keep up with him, soon."

"But I am here now. It would give you a chance to research quietly and recruit. Even more quietly."

Lara nodded after a long moment's thought. "I'll take that under consideration. Being a teacher, however, might undermine the position you already hold in the family. It's settled, then. We bring in teachers as soon as possible."

"Understandable." Nutmeg scratched at her temple, thinking, and added, "But don't replace Auntie Corrie. She's been wonderful with them."

"No. Of course not." She let Bistane guide her to the door, fatigue of thought slowing her more than anything else. Nutmeg watched her go, realizing that she knew days like that, when it hurt more to think and plan than it did to actually live. Days when the first light of sun hurt like a slap across the face, when the first audible noise screamed in the ears, when the thought of just existing felt too painful to consider. The chasm of not being stretched in front of her, seemingly too formidable to cross.

It had been far worse when she'd first lost Jeredon. Now she hardly considered it, except for when she had to make these decisions about their children. Odd, that. A pain she'd never realized had been healing. After the door shut behind them, she swung on Dayne. "When did you figure out the toffee apples?"

"Oh, not long ago," he said, backing up. "Just a day or so ago, really." He ducked his head. "Taking a pipe, Tolby? I'll join you outside for a smoke, myself." And he was gone before she could say anything else.

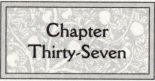

Chapter
Thirty-Seven

LATE SUMMER EVENING HAD FALLEN, and the Farbranch homestead had given up to peace and quiet as the children were finally put to sleep, and the last of the kitchen was cleaned up and prepared for the next day. Lanterns in the cider barn had been shuttered, as well as the great doors, and even the stables seemed quiet with only an occasional shuffle in straw as a horse lay down or a pony got up to rattle at his feed bucket. Dayne's pipe barely warmed the palms of his hands as he held it and contemplated the ash growing cold.

Nutmeg slipped out of the back door and came to sit with him. He scooted over to give her ample room, but she sat close enough that their shoulders and thighs almost touched. The aura she gave off was warmer and far more fragrant, smelling of herbs and spices from whatever tomorrow's baking might warrant and her own scent which had always intrigued him.

She gave a short sigh, pushing her heavy hair off her shoulders and twisting it into a knot at the nape of her neck. "I am thinking of going back to work."

"Truly?"

"Reluctantly, but yes. Mother reminded me while we were making packets for tomorrow's lunch of the one thing Tolby will not admit."

"And that is?"

"That he is growing old. There will come a day, sooner rather than later, when his body will fail him when he needs it most." She paused. "Do you know why Garner stays away from the family?"

He'd only met the eldest wandering Farbranch son once, and that briefly, for the naming celebration for the twins. Garner had come home on a whim, it seemed, mildly amused that he could be there to celebrate as well, and had left as quietly as he'd arrived. "No."

"Because Garner told me that Dad won't let him go. He raised us all to be good, fierce adults, but he doesn't want to let us go."

"Do you miss your brother?"

"I'm used to it now, so days can go by before I lift my head and think: I wonder where Garner is. What's he up to? Is he planning a family, or will he be a rover, and how will I know?"

She shrugged. "He has his own ideas to follow. Now Hosmer . . . he is as steady as a rock wall, so I don't have to worry that Dad won't have anyone t' lean upon. Keldan stays now because of the horse trade, but he might be tempted to leave someday, to ride the wind."

"Not meaning to offend or argue with you, but I don't think Tolby is going to go feeble on you any time soon."

"It's not that. But when you and I were taken, he faced Vaelinars with abilities he couldn't counter. Any man is bound to fail against the likes of an attacker who can leap higher than the house."

"He gave a cold-damned good try. If not for the fire, we might have routed them."

"Might. Might. And his heart could go out while he tried to fend them off the next time." She sighed again. "You know they will try again. All the harder if anything we suspect about Evar and Merri proves true. They'll either be taken to use as a weapon against Lara, or they'll be slaughtered outright." She put the heels of her hands to her eyes as her voice broke. "I couldn't live through that, Dayne. I can't lose them! I have to keep them safe and happy, close, somehow, some way!"

"You won't lose them. We'll stand in the way."

"It would be better with a troop of Lara's and Bistane's best to stand with you, and she can't afford to station a troop here. Not now, with her ranks so thinned."

He dropped his head a bit. "I'd have to stay with Tolby. The books and all."

"Oh. I hadn't thought. And your estates, too, of course." The knot at the back of her head unraveled on its own, almost as if connected to her plans.

"We might be able to move our operations to Larandaril, but then Tolby would not be part of it because I doubt he'll go, and he is the master."

"I understand."

"If I were you, and I'm not, but if I were, I'd keep them here at home as long as you can. Your hand and Tolby's, Lily's and Keldan and Hosmer . . . those are the hands and voices you need raising them, at least for a few years longer, as long as you let them grow. Any teachers they have will be neutral. Cold, even. That's the way of Vaelinaran teachers. Trust me."

"You know."

"I do. The Vaelinars have few children and adore the ones they do, but they are turned over to teachers, not like your teachers but tutors who feel they must not favor. Must not encourage. Must not love." His tone roughened a bit, with his memories.

"You can't plant a seed or sapling without giving it water. Compost. Sunshine."

"But these seedlings are already growing and they, those tutors, fear to be a wind that might twist the growth in one way or another. All they offer are words. And, from what I know of young Evarton, they might have to be stern ones now and then."

That made her laugh slightly. "I'll keep them close for a while longer, then and see who she sends. And I'll do as you want, look on them with closer eyes, and see if I can help them unlock themselves. You were right to tell me they weren't babies any longer." She patted him on the knee. "It's agreed, then. They'll go to Larandaril when we're prepared."

Neither of them heard the door open faintly behind them, a small crack, through which Corrie watched and heard, as she had partially during their earlier conference. Things she was being paid to tell, paid with the lives of her family: Larandaril's borders soon to be closed and now, the children to be taken back. She would have to send word. Fearfully, she eased the door shut and left, her heart thumping unevenly in worry.

"Decided. But not until you and Tolby are ready," Dayne added.

"Not until we are good and ready." Nutmeg smiled, at ease.

When Lara and Bistane returned in the morning, little more was said between them. The Warrior Queen got down on her stomach in the playroom and learned how to play with her heirs, Bistane offering strategy now and again. In the afternoon, they worked the vineyards with Tolby and taught the twins how to drive the small pony cart up and down the rows. Evar, thanks to his taller stature and leaner muscle, had a knack for it. Smaller and chubbier Merri's response to the pony pulling on the reins was to fall over giggling as if the beast had said something outrageous to her, and perhaps it had. When she clambered down out of the cart and went to walk by the pony's head, it rested its muzzle on her shoulder and followed her sedately down the row of grapevines. Lara raised an eyebrow at that, looking to Keldan who nodded at her.

They shared a family dinner at which Lara announced she would be leaving in the morning after a talk at the mayor's inn, aimed at recruiting new troops for Larandaril, but she'd come back soon.

"An' Bis'ane?" Merri asked.

"Most especially Bistane."

The little girl's face lit up. Bistane put his hand over his heart.

"What is it?"

"I've seen the future. That smile will have a hundred men and more on their knees."

Merri looked at her nose, eyes crossing, as if to see whatever Bistane saw, and frowned when they all laughed. She shrank back at the chorus. Evarton put his hand out to pat her in comfort. Auntie Corrie came in from her room and gathered the children up for a bath and so that the rest of them could talk amongst themselves, but no one had much to say except for Hosmer who warned them about certain Calcort families who might or might not volunteer and what their agenda might be.

"Although," he finished, "I doubt you'll be wanting to turn anyone away."

"We may have to. As you would say, one bad apple turns the barrel rotten. I need troops, but I can afford to be discerning about who I accept into our ranks. Still, I'm pleased to hear your thoughts on the matter, particularly with the squatters I already am confronting. I thank you for your insight."

At that, Lily got up and brought in two pies and sent Meg for a fresh pitcher of cream and crockery to serve the pies on, and conversation fell quiet again. When Lara left for the evening, she did not ask Nutmeg if or when she was coming, and Meg did not tell her. They hugged briefly, and then the Warrior Queen was gone. It would be a day-to-day decision, one that she would keep as close to her as her apron. She thought upon Garner again, and Sevryn and Rivergrace who felt as though they must have gone beyond death, but she would not count it as such. After all, had she not stood on the road and watched them both return full of life once already? So many had truly gone; she didn't want to think on others that weren't certainties. And she had friends who she might never meet again beyond her knowing.

So much in all of this was beyond her knowing. Her thoughts spun a bit hopelessly before she caught fast on the fact that she had family, and for now that would keep her busy enough. The others would have to bide their time.

In the cliff dwellings where Rufus lived as the eldest chief any of the Bolgers ever chanted about or remembered in their many centuries among the lands of the First Home, a summer night fell. Rufus fell into sleep early, as befit his tired bones and leathery frame, but he roused midway through the night, wide awake and staring at the stars through a deliberate rent in his dwelling, awakened by a dream of his death. He rumbled to himself, remembering it fitfully, a vision of dying amidst the other folk of Kerith, so different and disdainful of his own people. He was more a beast than a man by their standards, he knew, he'd always known. Yet he counted some of them amongst his closest friends, the Vaelinaran beauty he called Little Flower who others named Rivergrace among them. This nightmare had been a dream of her.

He knew it was a death dream because he'd felt himself dying, his heart lunging in his chest beating wildly and the blood pouring out of an immense gouge in his right flank, and his eyes going dim even as he beheld a bridge of rainbow beauty. The air held the metallic tang of blood and more death. The air thundered with screams and warfare. It felt to him as the end of all days not just his own. He held a clear, singular memory of sight and sensation as Nutmeg, the Dweller sister of his Little Flower, clutched his hand tightly and tried to staunch his bleeding. Nutmeg's face was the last sight his fading eyes caught.

Rufus did not fall back asleep. He had had such dreams before and heeded them, and although his time had come very close then, he found himself still very much alive—if bone-aching and muscle weary and greatly aged among his people. He did not know why he'd outlived all of his peers though he thought perhaps the Vaelinars had cursed him with a touch of their own longevity so that he could remain embroiled in their plots. He thought long and hard on what he remembered of his vision. Ordinarily, he would have discussed it with his shaman who had been a Bolger with great wisdom and insight, but that friend, too, had passed a handful of seasons ago. He did not trust the new shaman who was too young and relied too much on gossip from the other clans and villagers to be well-versed and confident in his own shamanism. What did a shaman so green know of experience? He also thought that a nightmare of death would not be considered odd or unexpected by the young Bolger, for the end of life must surely be near one carrying the years that Rufus did, and a view of rainbows would seem most auspicious.

Rufus didn't think so.

He levered himself up from his bed which was little more than a woven blanket stuffed with fragrant rushes and leaves. Pallets had been adopted in most of their clan sites, but he thought of them as annoyingly soft. His bones had grown into adulthood bedded down on the forge hearths of Quendius' weapon mills. A good blanket held enough comfort for him. As he moved, the aroma of crushed herbs surrounded him, intended to soothe aches and a clouded mind, and promote sleep. Rufus grunted as he squatted by his fire pit. He'd left it banked, for hot as the days were now, he oft times felt damp and cold at night. His age, again, he knew it well. He stretched his neck one way and then the other, hearing sharp crackles and snaps, and then did the same to his back. He put his arms out, flexing them against old wounds and bone spurs and the other ailments that plagued him, but he could not discount the knowledge that, despite his years, he had all four limbs, and yes, even the fingers attached to his hands, although one crooked one would no longer bend. He used to be able to remember when he'd injured that finger so, but it escaped him now. He pulled his packs out and began to stow items, sorting through carefully, placing things to stay behind in significant piles as was tradition for the women to come in and tidy a dead Bolger's residence. This for the heirs. This for the Gods. These for the clan's good. When done, Rufus laced his packs and hefted them over his shoulder, letting out a low grunt of effort as he did so, then clamping his thin lips shut tightly against any future sound.

He paused his preparations long enough to seek out his clan's ruling chieftain: his grandson, a Bolger much wiser in the ways of the First Home and even Vaelinars than Rufus thought one could ever be, their world being what it was. They were a defeated people, kept down and often in financial slavery, but now their stature had grown and chieftains had to treat with them, even with those who drove them away from towns. Rufus was not fond of the tusks that had been ground down so much that they barely protruded from Bylar's jaws, but it made for effective speech. The other folk were fond of much talk. He himself was not, even from Little

Flower and her Dweller sister who talked even more so, but he could listen. He learned much that way.

He hunkered down in the long tent, the clan communal building, across from Bylar who worked at making a leather sheath, his strong fingers propelling the needle through quickly and finely. It would be a very nice piece of work when finished, a handicraft Rufus knew his old eyes were no longer up to.

"I leave."

Bylar glanced at him and paused long enough to scratch an even fingernail under his jaw. "Now, I see. Where to?"

"I go see Spice." Rufus's name for Nutmeg, better than Big Talker, although not as apt, he thought. Nutmeg had not liked being called Big Talker.

Bylar nodded. "No word on Rivergrace or Sevryn yet?"

Rufus shook his head.

"Do you need trade goods to take into Calcort?"

He shook his head again. He thought a long moment before tapping the small leather bag he'd tied about his neck and put under his leather apron, bringing it to Bylar's attention. "Not be back."

Bylar put aside the leather sheath and needle. "Grandfather," he said, and took up Rufus' free hand. "Are you certain?"

Rufus grunted. He shifted away at the emotion he saw brimming in his grandson's eyes. It was both painful and good to know he would be missed, as he would miss his family. "Dreams."

Bylar nodded. "But the Dweller needs you?"

He shrugged a shoulder. "Maybe. Maybe not."

"Then you may return to us yet." Bylar squeezed his hand. "We will chant for you."

"I have much pride in you." Rufus made himself say the words carefully, this Kernan talk, so much more complicated and expressive than their speech had been. Few spoke it now. His mastery over it faded with every year, the Bolgers having no need for the language of a long-lost past. He held his grandson's hand tightly a moment longer before letting it go. "I have made friends for you, for my tribe. They should stand by you." His own tusked mouth ill-spoke what he had to say, but he could see in Bylar's eyes that he understood. He stood up, drawing himself tall. "Scatter my things at the last chant. My house is sorted."

"We will do you honor." Bylar stood as well. When he straightened,

Rufus found himself surprised and impressed. His grandson surpassed him now in height. With a slap to the other's shoulder, he took what he felt certain would be his final leave of his blood and his tribe.

The herdsman asked no questions when he cut out his mule from the stock and saddled him up. He picked out a second mule and loaded it with the packs and goods he thought he would need.

Only the two of them—Chief Bylar and the herdsman—watched him ride out into the thinning rays of the morning sun. It did not matter that no one else saw. They would tell of it in the chanting, when his time came.

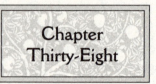

Chapter
Thirty-Eight

THE DAY GLOWED BRIGHT HOT along the packed dirt streets of the quarter. Even the vineyards shimmered in the light, waves of heat rising off the vines and tendrils and clusters of tiny, immature grapes. Few people were out and about at this point in the summer day, attending to their business indoors until the sun's merciless rays began to slant and shadows could fall easier over Calcort. The sullen river flowing across the city's edges did little to ease the heat, but added to the humidity hanging over its territory. The wise, who'd lived many summers in Calcort, did as they did every summer and left the heat and the humidity to the young and foolish.

Two small figures crouched in the shadow cast by the Farbranch cider barn, about the only coolness at that far end of the quarter. One figure was shorter and rounder than the other, and kept tugging at the curls bouncing about her face and neck, trying to pull the kerchief meant to bind them up into place. The second, taller and slender, and most emphatically the leader of this nap-time escape, drew in the dirt with a stick and then dropped his pottery figures into areas of importance. Merri gave up on her crouch, dropped her rump onto the ground, and smoothed her skirt about her dimpled knees.

"Where's the princess?"

Evar grunted and tugged a small doll of rags out of his tunic. "Here." And he dropped it behind enemy lines.

"Ohhh." She pursed her lips in dismay at her princess having already been captured and behind the enemy camp before the game had even started and opened her mouth to protest when a door swung up and slammed shut behind them, on the farmhouse side of the barn. Evar grabbed his twin, and the two of them shrank back against the cider barn as pelting footsteps came near, and their Uncle Keldan could be seen at the street's edge.

He did not, however, look at them when he plunged to a halt at a sharp whistle. Like a wild pony, he dashed his long dark hair from his face with a whip of his neck and torso, and looked back at the house.

"And where might you be going?" Lily's voice, Grandmother, sounding stern.

"The ild Fallyn's tashya horses just came into the stockyard. I've got to go pick out my bids for the auction. It's the *horses*, Mom." And his business, too, which he did not remind his mother of as he straightened his vest and tried to look professional.

"Tressandre did not come with the herd."

"No. And even if she did, I'd not give her a look." He shifted his weight uneasily. "I cannot help it if her horses are some of the best."

"I know you can't. All right, on with you, then, but you'd best not be slamming any more doors, hurry or not. Those two scamps are down for a nap and Auntie's resting as well, and we could use the peace and quiet."

He tipped his hand to his forehead. "I will." He gave a broad grin. "Sure is quiet with them asleep."

"And I want to keep it that way. Now go on with you." The farmhouse door closed with a soft click. Keldan pivoted and took off at a run.

He did not see either of them pinioned to the shadows and holding their breaths as he ran past. Merri tugged her kerchief off completely with a "pfhuff" and spread it on the ground, then moved her doll onto it. Evar gazed off after his uncle as he disappeared down the winding street, clouds of dust in his wake.

"Uncle Kel loves horsies," Merri declared.

"But Mama doesn't like the Sandra."

"No," she answered agreeably and began to set a few of the clay men on her side.

The two heads bent over the battleground, voices soft and muted, even Merri's objection when her princess promptly got captured all over again. They did not notice when the shadow covering them grew quite long, and cooler, or the stooped figure that halted at the edge of it to watch them.

"Look at you, sweeties. Playing so nicely."

The two of them looked up at the withered woman, shawl spread over

her head so that her face could scarcely be seen, wrinkled and covered with
sunspots, like the backs of her hands, a crack of age in her voice. Dust
covered her, everywhere, muting the faded black garments she wore into
a kind of dun nothingness. She held her shawl tightly under her chin with
one palsied hand. Evar stared with a kind of fascination, but Merri tilted
her head and promptly said, "I'm older."

Evar shot her a look. "Not supposed to tell!"

Merri shrugged. "She's not anyone."

The woman gave a crackling laugh. "Such pretties. Are you fighting?"

Merri pointed at the figures which had changed position yet again. "My
princess."

The woman came closer, with a hobbling, broken step. "Keeping her
safe, are you?"

Evar's nose wrinkled. "Big war," he said. "Over the princess." He bent
over his figurines, marching them about in the dirt and clashing them together, bits of dirt flying as he did.

The woman's bright eyes watched them avidly.

Merri glanced at her once. "Auntie," she commented.

"Not ours."

"No, indeed, dearies, not your auntie. And where is she?"

"Nap." Evar drew some more lines in the ground at his feet.

"We mustn't wake her, then. She must be tired."

"The guards are napping, too," Merri told her helpfully as she lifted her
doll and tidied her up a bit.

"Are they, now?"

Merri nodded. She looked up at the old woman who'd hobbled so close
that she now stood right next to them. Her eyes looked sharp with interest.
"I sang to them," she confided.

"You did."

Her loosened curls bobbed about her little round face as she nodded
confidently.

"I can make people sleep, too," the old woman said. She struck, a dagger in each hand. As she pulled back, each little body curled over and fell
silently into the dirt.

BRIGHTLY COLORED BOLTS OF FABRIC lined the wall of the tailoring shop, each in its wooden slip carefully crafted by Tolby and Keldan Farbranch from the finest of lumber, sanded and polished to a gleam so that nary a splinter could snag or harm the yardage they contained. Their textures varied as much as their rainbow of colors, from the soft cottony gauzes favored by the Galdarkans and Vaelinars of the Far East, to work with their bells and veils, to the heavy quilted fabrics of the northern lands and their own woolens such as the pattern she prepared to weave now. As she scanned the fabrics, her gaze lingering on one and then another, she found she could see the handiwork that went into each creation more closely. This one was done in a huge factory building by a young weaver tired and thin, worn and worried her work might not pass inspection. A sadness hung about it, cast by her travails. That one was made in a large room just off a warm kitchen, where the sisters, mothers, and cousins gathered to work. And that one—strangest of all, black silken material with silvery stars and streaks in it—made in the stone cellar of a faraway hold, the rock of the room old and steeped in religious ceremony, in a city far, far to the east by Kernans she knew little about. These were things the old Nutmeg could never have seen before.

Lariel had surprised her by noticing family secrets almost immediately. Why would she not? A Warrior Queen certainly held more abilities than that of leading a troop into a battle. She knew how to govern. How to ask for and receive commitment. And she knew how to observe, and even though she'd been asleep for quite a long while, nothing had escaped her attention when she'd come to see the children. Nutmeg knew that, but just now found herself accepting it. She felt as though she had passed inspection.

Not that Lariel had had much choice in the mother of her heirs, not like she might have wanted at one time, but Jeredon and war had taken many options from them. Nutmeg rubbed the end of her nose on the back of her hand as tiny fluffs of wool made her want to sneeze as she set up her work for the day. Too much thinking, as her mother would say, and not enough doing. She would do! And let the thinking fall where it may, often in the quiet of the evening when she needed to sleep.

She found it a relief, though hard work, to be back in the shop. The twins (the children, she amended in her mind, she had to stop thinking of them as twins because to the outside world they couldn't be) hung on her every moment, full of questions she could not always answer, and filled with energy she couldn't match. Having Corrie for an auntie gave her half days now that she could spend working with her mother again, and she appreciated the relative silence. Not that her family did not spell her when they could, but the children were still too young for Tolby to take into the vineyards and orchards themselves with him for the day, although they often played in the quiet, huge barns which held the storage vats and barrels, or the cider barn when the presses were not at work. And Dayne, well, he had unlimited patience for their bounce and play and questions and had even been known to help create small stages of games for them, lying on his stomach on the floor with them, marching about toy soldiers or critters carved from wood to their dictates. He did take them into the groves, though for only short periods of time. She could not see Jeredon indulging in play had he lived to be their father, although he would have taken both tracking and hunting when they got older. But he had never shown the well of patience or interest with the young. Dayne, though, never seemed to tire of the attention whenever the two scamps chose to shower him with it. He would even—

Nutmeg felt the blow to her chest, the thud as the hilt hit home against her flesh, the numbing yet fiery pain of it, and it drove her to her knees. The loom shuddered as her weight hit the frame and she hung there, fingers twisted in the threads, the machine bracing her slack body. She looked down in surprise for the killing blow and saw nothing. Nothing. Threw her gaze up to the door, the windows, and saw them empty. A cold twist went through her body, as cold as hell itself. What had she felt?

Nutmeg flailed about, patting a hand down and finding nothing, not a single thing which could have stabbed her so deeply and as she did, a second stab hit home, this in her thigh. Her leg began to cramp and convulse and she cried out in pain, her voice strangled and thin. Lily rushed to her. "What is it?" Fear ran through her tangled body, cold, hard fear.

Nutmeg caught at her mother. "Home. Find my babies! Hurry!" as her throes toppled her to the floor, her vision of her mother bending over shrank and shrank until everything went dark.

Lily turned and threw open the shop door, bell jangling in protest. "I'm leaving!" she called back. "Help Nutmeg!" and she raced into the dirt street, pinching her skirts high in her hands, feet flying. A tear streamed down her face even as she caught her breath, running as she had not run since her children were little and, more often than not, in danger of falling from an orchard tree. Her breath rasped in her throat. Had she left Nutmeg behind, dying for some reason? Or had her daughter sensed that something struck from without? They had guards—where were the Vaelinars? Her breath hot and gravelly in her chest, she could see the farmhouse and cider house, with the green slopes of the ripening vineyards beyond covering the horizon.

Lily skidded to a halt in the cider barn's wide open doors, startling Verdayne who stood poring over the latest progress on the recovery process of the books pinned here and there about the great, wooden, lunch table. He looked up. "What is it?"

"The children! Where are they?"

"Napping. Or they should be. Lily—" But she did not stay to hear another word, throwing herself out the cider barn and toward the house. Little puffs of dust sprayed from her boot toes and she could hear Verdayne behind her as she slammed open the door to the farmhouse. Silence greeted her in a house where silence never reigned.

The two Vaelinar guards lay slumped against the kitchen wall, fallen over, their mouths slack in mild snoring. "Oh Gods," Lily muttered. Verdayne passed her, kicking each in the bottom of their boot soles until they grunted awake, but she did not pause to see anything else. She went to the back room, the children's room, with its adjoining bedroom that had been fashioned for the auntie. Toys scattered from her frantic steps as she dashed through the small room, throwing open the cupboards and closets and looking under the beds. Not a mischievous face met her. Verdayne joined her.

"Found them?"

"No! They're nowhere!"

Verdayne shouldered open the door to Corrie's room. It lay silent and sterile as if never occupied, and all trace of the woman gone. Lily joined him and they both stood in shock a moment. "It's like she'd never been here at all."

"She took them!"

"Or turned them over. Not a drop of blood spilled." He pushed Lily gently out of his way. "Let me check the grounds."

Lily put a hand to her throat where she could feel the wild pulse of her racing heart throb. There had to be more, didn't there? For Nutmeg to have been stricken as she was? But no blood found yet. That ought to be good, even if Evar and Merri were missing. Her head swam for a moment, thoughts chasing each other in frenzy. Where could they be? What should she do? Outside, she could hear Verdayne calling their names, but she couldn't hear an answer. Not that they'd answer if they were hiding, the scamps, but it couldn't be that easy, could it? Not with the heirs to Larandaril and with the ild Fallyn in play. Lily's fist crumpled her skirt. Nutmeg had felt it and been struck down by it.

So where were their small, fallen bodies? What had the auntie done with them—and why? Did it suit Tressandre ild Fallyn's purposes to have the fate of Lara's heirs go unknown? She heard a soft, keening cry and turned about in the children's room. A wooden soldier went skidding out from under her shoe as she realized that it was she who made the cry. Verdayne returned to her and put a bracing shoulder under her arm.

"Come to the kitchen and sit down." His voice, low and firm, pierced her whirling thoughts.

"Nutmeg?"

"Waiting in the kitchen. Pale and scared, so you need to gather yourself. She needs you. And . . . I have a question or two."

She hadn't realized how much taller than even Tolby he was until he guided her across the farmhouse to a waiting chair. Nutmeg sat, so pale even her freckles seemed to have disappeared, one hand wrapped about a cold cider.

"Auntie Corrie?"

"If she was taken by force, it appears she anticipated and packed for it." A grim expression roughened Verdayne's statement.

"She's in on it," Nutmeg said. "How could she? We trusted her. They were like her own babies."

Verdayne poured another cider and pushed it into Lily's hands. "I found a trace of them outside. First, Merri had that dolly made of yarn, didn't she? That one with the incredible mop of hair."

"She has one. I don't know where it is, but—"

He put his palm up. "Thought I remembered it, but couldn't be sure. They have a fair number of toys."

That brought a bit of color back into Nutmeg's face. "A child needs toys."

"I did not mean criticism." He held up a bit of twisted yarn between his fingers. "I found it by the side of the farmhouse, along with a bit of a mess in the dirt, some marks and tracks." Nutmeg reached for it as the two Vaelinar guards stumbled in.

Amett rubbed his face. "They're gone?"

"It appears that they were taken, yes."

"Bloody trees. Bistane will have my hide for this. When I was sent to replace Gryton, I had the book read at me. Protect the children, at all costs." Amett slumped into a chair.

"You're lucky you were both asleep. If not, you'd be dead."

Brista met his gaze. "You're certain."

"Fairly. The children had sneaked outside. I found a bit of a dirt fort and a few soldiers and marks as if they'd decided to roll about in the dust. Those body prints had one or two drops of blood each, but—" And he held up his head to forestall gasps from both Nutmeg and Lily. "Not enough to show great harm."

"I'd say we were charmed to sleep. It's happened before." Two high spots of chagrin colored Brista's face. "I never mentioned it because I didn't think the little squirts could manage it, being on our guards against it and all. But for them to be dropped, sudden and deadly like means it has to be kedant. Likely on a dagger blade, as a Kobrir would do."

Nutmeg sucked in a shaky breath. "That venom kills."

"If enough is used. We Vaelinars are particularly vulnerable to it."

"Who knows what a child's body can tolerate?"

"None but the Vaelinars are so affected. And the children are only half-Vaelinar, are they not? So the taker took a risk that their dose would be effective at all. Still, administered by a stabbing—not a merciful way to dose someone. Takes a cold calculation, that does."

"Tressandre ild Fallyn would not think twice."

"And her tashya herd is in town for sales."

"We were told she didn't come with the herd."

"We were not told what disguise she might be wearing."

"Disguised?" Nutmeg turned the bit of yarn about in her fingers. "You think she took them alive?"

"Yes. Which means they will stay that way until she either has what she wants, or decides that the children are no longer worth anything to her."

Nutmeg stared at the kitchen table and her mug, which she had not yet touched, for a long moment. "Her plans will have wheels within wheels. That works to our advantage. She will keep them longer."

"And I intend to find them." Verdayne smiled briefly. "Just beyond the farmhouse grounds, I found that, as if dropped. And by the vineyard border, another twist. And yet a third headed toward the back alley toward the town gates. So pray, Nutmeg, that Merri's dolly has a prodigious amount of yarn on it, because someone is leaving us a trail."

The farmhouse which had seemed so very deadly quiet in the early afternoon now filled with noise. Bins being opened and closed. Packs being filled. Voices quarreling over details small and large. Bodies moved to and fro, like gears in a great mechanism bypassing and mingling with one another without a single clash until a firm and loud voice rang out.

"I'm going and that's it."

"No, Tolby, you are not. You're needed here to guard your home and Nutmeg, especially if either of the children finds a way to send word or come home themselves." Verdayne put his hand on Tolby's pack, gently lowering it to the floor. "I will not tell you, sir, that you're too old to ride this trail because you alone know that, but I will tell you that no one is in a better position to protect your daughter than yourself. Hosmer has his duty owed to the city guard, and Keldan has his duties with the horses. Garner is . . . roaming. That leaves you to do as you've done so well, be the head of this household and hold them together."

Tolby glared up at him before shaking himself like a water-soaked dog. "You make a certain sense."

"I do. And, besides, our work on the books is nearly done and could be vital if the ild Fallyn and their alliances declare war on the rest of us. There's tincture to make for the Library, and we can't fall behind on that."

Nutmeg stood, her arms crossed over her bosom, her hair tied back and her eyes flashing more cinnamon than golden-brown. "Lara's visit set her off. I knew that was ill-omened."

"Lariel had never seen her heirs and you declined to bring them to her. The queen needed to see the children. They're the only family she has left."

"And in trouble because of that. We took them away before because of the danger."

"And it followed you here." Verdayne held his hand out to her. "I promise you I'll find them."

She looked at him, and her teeth grazed her lower lip as if to stop it from trembling. "But you can't promise me you'll bring them back."

"I can only vow that I'll die trying. So will all of us here."

They held gazes for a long moment before Nutmeg looked away with a sigh, a movement of her hand indicating the search party. "You're not taking any Farbranches with you."

"Am I not as much a Farbranch as any of you?"

She turned back slowly to him. As busy as the room had been, the great room now seemed cleared of all persons but the two of them. "You should be," she answered, her words slow and faint.

"Then send me away, telling me that I am, that I am as much a Farbranch as you are—and you will be as much a Vantane as I am." His half-smile stayed frozen on his face. His hand stayed held out to her. "Your answer won't keep me from going and searching, nor will it bring me back any faster, but will be something I carry with me, a hope to make my heart lighter."

Keldan paused by the front door, looking much like a wild pony or tashya caught for a moment in mid-gallop, his hair falling about his face like an unruly mane and his eyes askance. "I don't under—"

"Shush," his mother told him. He clamped his lips shut.

"Verdayne."

His hand never wavered nor did his gaze into her eyes.

"Are you asking me what I think you're asking?"

"You're the only one here who wonders." His half-smile grew a little wider. "Except for Keldan."

"I just . . . I just wanted to be sure." Her eyelids fluttered a moment. "Yes. I . . . yes. I will be waiting for all of you to come home to me."

Tolby dropped his pack and grabbed Verdayne about the ribs. "About time you found the courage!"

But he only had hold of Verdayne for a moment before Nutmeg tore him away to fill Dayne's arms, her head on his shoulder, her tears wetting the collar of his shirt thoroughly before he tilted her face up to his and they kissed.

A cheer went through the house as they did, and Keldan's voice could be heard saying, "Now *that* I understand."

Before letting her go, he said fiercely to the curve of her ear, "I will do all that I can to bring them back safely. You know that."

"Yes. And take care of yourself, too."

"For you, I will." He let her go reluctantly, and smoothed away the tears on her cheek with the ball of his thumb. "And you must promise the same."

Nutmeg made an inarticulate sound that he took for an answer. It filled his heart for all of that, and he took that joy with him when he went out the door. Brista fell in step behind him.

Chapter
Forty

RUFUS WATCHED as his mule flicked his long, glossy ears forward and back, his swinging pace easy and yet unhurried, even as it covered ground. Bolgers seldom rode horses. Horses objected to their beastly scent and their somewhat awkward carriage when mounted. The scent he could do little about; it was part and parcel of being a Bolger. Rufus had developed a saddle that was more suited to the Bolger frame than other skeletons, it was deeper and more canted in certain areas and proved vastly more comfortable. The stirrups hung differently as well, and were shorter. The headstall and reining system remained the same, but with a mule it hardly mattered. They knew a road when they saw one, even a path, and were hard to convince to take a more difficult route. They had sense where the well-being of their legs and hooves were concerned. This one fellow Rufus called Butter because his stride was so smooth, one of the finest mules he'd ever cut out of a herd. He had tashya blood in him as well as the dunka that made him the mule he was. The pack mule following was Kernan draft and dunka, a blockier mule with hooves like frying pans, giving her a tough gait to ride but a lot of stamina on the trail. He didn't know if they'd survive the trip any better than he would. He'd been days already and no nearer knowing what his dreams had sent him to do.

Summer heat beat down on all of them, and the mules snorted at him when he drove them through a small brook after they'd gotten their fill drinking and decided to stand a while in the cool, sluggish water. It made more sense to them than continuing down the dusty trail, headed for the wider caravan roads. He growled at them and clapped his boot heels to sleek flanks. With a shake of their heads, they followed orders. When he had started on his ride, he'd had only a vague idea of where he wished to go, but with every swinging stride of his mule, he headed toward Calcort. Rivergrace would not be there; no one had had a sign of her since she'd followed Quendius. Others told him he would know if she were dead, their bond being so close, but he knew that to be false. How many times at Harvest Meetings had he joined with other tribes and found to his surprise that this chief or that tribesman or shaman had passed and he'd had no inkling? No, the world of death did not bow to him and let him know when friends and loved ones had gone to it. He had no idea if Little Flower and her man still lived anywhere because there was no sense he carried which would give him that truth. But he knew that Spice did, and if anyone might understand his dreams, she might. If she stopped talking long enough to listen to him.

A growl of laughter welled up in him, momentarily stilling his thoughts. It was then he noticed what he might have noticed earlier had he not been trapped in memories. Butter's stride had shortened. He snuffled with suspicion every few steps, his head slightly tilted, ears back and nostrils flared. Something lay ahead that he did not like, and he showed it by his reluctance to approach. Mules had good sense, and Rufus pulled them to a stop, stretching his legs in the shortened stirrups a bit, and standing in them.

He could hear scavenger birds, muted and faraway, but clacking and cawing to one another from somewhere on the road ahead. He knew if he rode closer, he'd smell the metallic tang of blood and torn flesh on the air. The only question left to him was not whether someone or something had died—but how many. He dismounted and looped the reins about the front slope of the saddle, snugging them under a leather hook made for that purpose, and tied the pack mule's reins in as well. He smacked Butter on the neck. "Stay."

The chestnut mule rolled an eye at him as if to agree emphatically. No way was he going where he could smell blood and carnage. Not even if hit with a stick. Rufus patted him again as he slipped past, off the trail and into the high brush which had been lushly green with spring and new growth and now had begun to turn a golden brown. The chaff rose as he did, and he rubbed his nose roughly to keep from sneezing. The noise of scavengers grew louder as he drew nearer, and the smell of death on the air grew unmistakable. He touched the pouch hanging about his neck once or twice as he stalked closer. This seemed nothing like his dream, so he did not worry overmuch, but taking care seemed prudent as always. He had not gotten to this old, inconvenient age by being careless. Dust and dried foliage rose about him, spiraling about like snowflakes, and he slowed to little more than a crawl, unwilling to set off the birds when they spotted him. It was not the dead and dying he feared. It was the combatants who could lie among them, waiting for a fresh attack.

He raised himself to one knee and the palms of his hands, peering through the tops of the waving grasses. The scattered remains of a vast caravan littered the road beyond. Broken wheels and shattered cart beds. Carcasses of the massive forkhorns bloated, torn open, and being savaged by the birds, so many skraws their black feathers blanketed the naturally dun hides. Blood had been spilled, much blood, but the cargo seemed to have vanished. Rufus ran his tongue along one of his corner tusks. From the size of the caravan, he decided it must have been carrying grain. Grain precious enough to kill in wholesale slaughter. Not a trader remained alive, drawn and quartered, their body parts thrown about, making the bodies near unrecognizable. He listened for long moments, trying to hear if someone yet moaned, yet lived. Nothing came to him.

Rufus stood then, rising slowly out of the grass and weeds, setting off a few of the nearest scavengers, but most were too busy eating to be deterred by one mobile body amongst them. A few of the birds swooped at him, talons out and beaks open, screeing and cawing, but they flopped away when he swung at them with a growl. They perched not far away, eyes blinking in surprise that he was yet among the living.

He stopped at the side of the nearest wrecked caravan, its buckboard bottom belly-up to the sun and sky. He rubbed a finger along the wood, catching bits of grain, confirming his guess as to the cargo.

Rufus raised his gaze, eyeing the long row of devastation. Someone had decided to murder and steal what they could have bought in the marketplace. Grain was not yet so dear that a mortal life should be traded for it. He wondered at the piracy. It was not until he had traversed nearly the entire length of the twenty caravans making up the trading train that he found a scrap of a clue which stood out among the traders' bodies and artifacts. The sleeve of black with silver workings on the cover glittered dully in the sunlight.

Rufus' lips curled back from his teeth and tusks. Ild Fallyn. He'd heard that their hard-won farmlands had not produced well this season or last. He wondered how they could be short of coin with the hot-blooded tashyas they were famed for breeding or their fur and mineral trade. Such things could be chancy. His own people lived on the fortunes which rose and fell without warning, but then, his own people lived far less ambitiously than did the ild Fallyn. He tucked the sleeve inside his leather apron. There were some who would believe his story, even without the sleeve, but there were more who would not believe a word he said. Such was the worth of a Bolger among the other races of this land. He could not change it although he had spent his whole life trying. If Little Flower were here, she would take his evidence and understand. They held much respect for each other.

He didn't hold much hope that Spice would do the same, but he would try.

Rufus eyed the road ahead. It did not lead to Calcort but cut across the road which did. This was a main trading route, from out of the warehouses of the capital Hawthorne, and into the East, traveled for moving vast volume without stopping on the way until it reached its journey's end, with less chance of spoilage by doing so. A bold move had been struck here, one of desperation and planning. If the ild Fallyn had struck once, and killed all who might have witnessed, they would strike again and do the same. He would take backroads—hunting and migratory paths—not easy riding but out of the way of whatever traps the Vaelinars might have laid. It would be safer to do so.

He touched the pouch at his neck again, a habit he had begun to develop. These were his death herbs, to be spread upon his funeral pyre; if he died alone, they would be smothered in their essence but still guide his soul to where it should go. He told the pouch he had things to handle first, and that his destiny must wait.

Dropping his hand, he strode back into the bush to retrieve his mules, leaving as little evidence of his passing that way as he could. His animals flicked their ears back and forth uneasily and breathed hard, disturbed by the smell of blood spilled upon the earth and the noise of the feeding scavengers, but they went willingly, eager to get away from the massacre. Even as their hooves quickened, his reluctance grew. Something nagged at him, something he'd seen but not recognized or had not looked for. He twisted in the saddle's frame, looking back to what he could not see, remembering what he had seen.

He reined Butter to a halt. "I am a crooked and foolish old Bolger." Glossy chestnut ears flipped forward and back. He swung his leg over and got down, this time tying both animals to strong bushes where they could crop the grasses but not pull themselves loose easily.

This time he did not sneak up, and the birds fled in a great cloud of dark and cawing annoyance at his appearance. He waved his arms and growled as the greedy ones who did not wish to fly took off sullenly, one or two diving at his face and darting away as he swung. Feathers scattered.

He stood at the head of the caravan now, rather than the end where he'd approached before. He looked among the debris and savaged bodies, uncertain what it was that had bothered him. Not one attacker had been left behind, if indeed any had been taken down by the defense. He toed a drawn sword here and there.

Then Rufus squatted low to take a closer look at the caravan guards to the fore. He put a finger to an exposed blade to be certain. He stood, walked down a few strides to the next downed guard and noticed the same thing. Crisscrossing the massacre for nearly half the length of the caravan train brought the same observance.

They'd gone down fighting, but none of them had a single bit of blood on their swords and knives, except for one near the very front. They had, to a man, done a poor job of defending the caravan and themselves. As he strode back to the front of the line, he noticed something else and again, squatted low to inspect it. He straightened and began to walk back and forth, avoiding the drying pools of blood and bits of flesh the scavengers had thrown about. Then he went to the wagons, which were stripped and battered apart but not burned as they might have been. Wheels lay apart from the axles, but no one had stripped the metal from them, valuable he thought, or at least to his tribe: cogs and nuts, screws and bolts. Great water bags were empty as well, hanging loose off their hooks or tossed upon the ground, and that told him more than he could have guessed. The only reason to have emptied every waterskin, bag, and barrel would have been to dispose of their contents. He pulled one of them up and hoisted it to his nose. Nothing to smell, even though Bolger noses were, in his opinion, superior to any of the Kernan, Dweller, or Galdarkans. He put his tongue to the wet interior.

The tiniest of buzzes along with moisture tickled the end of it.

Drugged. Not a strong drug. No one would have fallen from their saddle or cart in a stupor, but strong enough to have impaired anyone who drank from it. Other tongues and noses would not have detected it until too late. He dropped the water bag. So now he understood why the guards could not mount a decent defense.

This caravan had been sabotaged before even leaving the Guild warehouses. As his gaze scanned over the dead once more, he noticed one last remarkable, damning thing: there was not a Guild trader in the lot. All—every single man and woman on this caravan—had been hired help. He knew that because of the flesh and muscle left on the corpses: tanned, muscled, wiry. No soft bodies such as belonged to traders, not even those who traveled with the caravans frequently. Not a one of them walked or sat a horse when they could ride in a wagon. Not a one of them held harness to callus their hands or cared for forkhorns or draft horses. Not a trader could be found with the scars and hardened hands to wield a sword. They hired others for all those hardships. He'd known one who cooked, once, but the busty Kernan did it because she liked good food, even over campfires.

No trader had been lost in this savage attack and he knew theft had not likely lightened any trader purse: that was what insurance was for. No questions would be asked when the remains of the dead were found. Banditry happened. The sabotage would go unnoticed, even as he'd first overlooked it. He stopped at the one body who'd managed to draw any blood at all from the ambushers and looked down. A familiar line to the jaw caught his attention. He stooped down, trying to make sense of the beak-savaged face. Then he saw the necklace laced tight about the neck.

He knew this one. This one was Spice's brother, the one called Garner, the one who wandered so far from home, sometimes a guard, more often a gambler. He pulled the necklace loose, sad that he would have to bring her this news. Of all the dead here, he'd done well, but he should not have been here at all.

Rufus searched Garner's pockets, clothing drenched with drying blood, stiffened and awkward. He found the letter of hire, and another letter, waiting to be mailed to Tolby Farbranch of Calcort, and knew that he had not mistaken the identity. He shoved all these into his apron. If another Bolger had found them, they would have been of little value, for he was one of the few who knew his letters and writing well. This knowledge told him that it had been foreordained he be the one who found these ruined lives. This one he said the chant of farewell over, a respect from his tribe, a lament and salute for the family. But he could not burn the body as required. It had to be left as it was.

Rufus walked back to his mules. They stamped back a step, at the smell of fresh blood on him and he spoke roughly to them about their nonsense before gathering the reins and lead, and mounting. He tapped the pocket on his leather apron a last time to ensure he still had the items, and then turned the mules southwest, toward Spice's home.

He knew he would not be welcome. But then, Bolgers usually were not in the towns of men.

Chapter
Forty-One

"I CAN'T SEE." Tiny, muffled voice but not so muffled she couldn't sound peevish, even to herself.

"I can."

Silence followed as Merri digested that and did not protest, for she had long ago accepted her lot in life that Evar could do things she couldn't, like pee standing up. Her mother assured her that there were many things in life she would do that he couldn't. She just couldn't remember them under the circumstances. After a long moment, Merri asked, "What do you see?"

He shushed her before she heard him squirming about in the cart bed—it must be a cart, because it felt like wood planks to her bottom and she could hear the thud of pony hooves and the jangle of harness, and a splinter had worked its way into her ankle where her sock always sagged. She felt the pressure of his body against her side. "It doesn't look like home anywhere." He rubbed the side of his head against hers, burlaps sacks scratching. He amended, "Dere's a hole in my sack."

"Ohhhh." That explained a good many things if not the old woman who'd stabbed them.

"My head feels better."

Merri grinned to herself. That was one of the things Mama always told her that she could do and he could not.

"We are alone," he added and that took her smile away instantly.

"No fambly?"

"No fambly." Evar's voice stumbled a bit as he choked or perhaps the cart just bumped them both about.

No family. The thing that always worried Grampa Tolby most, being alone. She wondered what would happen to them. They had already been stabbed. Would they be killed?

She began to cry, but softly, making as little noise as she could because Evarton had shushed her earlier and it seemed important to be quiet. The cart began to bump about at a terrible rate and she fell over, Evar settling half-atop her legs with a soft plop. She could hear him sniffle as well and did not feel so bad that she was crying. Both of them sniffled and gave off muffled sobs until they fell into sleep, and by that time the cart had settled to a less rugged road whose bumps felt more like Auntie Corrie's rocking. In her dreams, Merri could see her mother shrinking farther and farther away until she became no more than a dot. She wondered what was happening.

The moment she heard the twins begin to hum, she put soft beeswax into her ears, threw a change of clothes and shoes in her carpet bag, and grabbed a burlap bag from the cold bin in the kitchen. She had little time, Corrie knew, and she had to flee while she could. The children would be out of their cots in moments and sneaking out to play, toddling out to meet their destiny. A tear leaked out of the corner of her eye. She wiped it away hastily and shut the door behind her quietly. Her own cot had a blanket rolled into it. No one would know that she had not fallen asleep like the guards. As she pressed her back to the corner of the farmhouse, she listened for the patrol. Not a footfall reached her ears. Her heart thumped in her throat. For family, she told herself, she did this for her family. Out of her carpetbag, she pulled up a small, colorful bird and unhooded it. It cooed and blinked at her. She hesitated a long moment before raising her hand into the air, releasing the bird. It gained the sky quickly and confidently, far quicker to seize its freedom than she was.

She found the tashya mount promised to her tethered across the street behind the herbalist, and she was all but certain no one saw her lash her carpetbag to the saddle and mount. Pinned to the front of the saddle was a small map painted on silk. She grabbed it up, balling it into a knot in the palm of her hand. She would follow it when she got far enough out of town, the one detail in her orders she would not follow. Her instincts and role as an auntie, as well as a wife and mother, could not be thrown in a ditch quite as easily as the ild Fallyn hoped. She rode to a crossroads she knew well and waited.

The pony cart already stood in the shadows, the pony with its head down snoozing, and one leg relaxed with its hoof balanced on the edge. She stayed in the shadows, feeling the hot sun's rays trying to bake her despite the shade, but she did not move from cover until she was certain she was alone except for the cart. She threw her leg over and jumped down, grabbed the pony by its headstall, and pulled it into the shade as well. They lived, their breaths short with sniffling and an occasional gulp of fear, but there was little she could do for them.

Corrie could hardly bear to see their small forms dumped into the pony cart, sacks tied about their heads and their hands and feet tied. She searched the area again to be certain that she was alone, that no one could be near enough to spot her. The rider who had brought the children here had taken the more traveled fork away, leaving a false trail while the cart waited for its driver to catch up with it. She leaned into the cart quickly, stuffing what she could into their pockets. Their faceless little bodies turned to her, mewling in distress.

"Shush. Don't cry now. I've put trail biscuits in your pockets."

A muffled "ugh" from Evarton.

"No, don't be that way. You'll want them later, I know. You'll be hungry later."

"Hungry now."

She patted Merri on the head and tried to fluff the bag up so she could breathe easier. "You'll be hungrier later. Now listen, and listen good. It's the ild Fallyn who's took you."

"Auntie," they both acknowledged her.

"Don't tell them any of your secrets. Not one, no matter what. Not even if they say they're going to hurt either of you. They mustn't know your secrets. Understand?"

Two sniffling "yes"es answered her.

"If you do tell, they will break you and throw you away." They wouldn't understand killing or death, not quite yet, in spite of Merri's abilities and even the war dog. They couldn't possibly. But being thrown away, that they'd understand. "And it will hurt, fearsomely, for a very long time."

Someone took a long, quavering breath. The other said, thinly, "Throw us away?"

"Yes, but so broken no one will want you, ever, not even Mama. So broken, Merri, and no one could ever fix you. Keep your secrets, both of you. Don't show them. Don't tell them." At her back, Corrie's horse threw up its head and she knew she had to leave. "Remember!" She hurried to her beast and mounted quickly, pulled the reins, kicked her heels, and took off at a dead run.

"Auntie? Auntie!" But no one answered Evar's call.

After very long moments, so long they fell asleep, someone got into the cart and clucked to the pony and it began to jolt off. That brought them to drowsy awareness.

Merri leaned against her brother. "My head hurts," she whispered.

"Mine, too."

"Are we broken?"

He nudged her chubby little form. "Not yet! And we're not gonna be." He wasn't sure what it took to be hurt enough that she couldn't help the two of them, but it struck a deep, dark fear in him, and he meant never to find out. He found her hand again, damp and sticky from the heat and laced his fingers with hers. In moments, as he knew she would, she had taken his headache from him and he could breathe clearly again, too. Whatever that lady had stuck them with, it had hurt and then pounded, even in his sleep.

Merri squeezed lightly. "Better?"

"Yes." He squeezed back. They rolled up together, each trying to take the hard bumps and jolts of the cart bed for the other, and she hummed them both softly back to sleep again, the only way to make the journey go faster.

It took days. They only knew that because they were taken out of the cart sometimes to squat by the side of the road, which became less and less roadlike as the journey went on. Nights, they were taken out and the hoods lifted, so they could eat bread soaked in milk with a touch of honey and slivers of meat that tasted smoky. They drank ladles and ladles of water and lay back quietly on their blankets, afraid to talk to the quiet, frowning man who drove them. Sometimes another would join and ride alongside the cart for a while—that they could not see, but heard. At no time did they see the old woman who had stabbed them, but another one, the Lady, was talked about in deep whispers they weren't supposed to hear. Evarton gathered his strength until he was certain he could Make something that would free them, perhaps a gigantic animal from the smaller animals he could hear rustling in the bushes out of the campfire's light, but he considered the possibility that the Animal might then attack them. That could not happen. And even if he freed them, how would they get home, such a long way to travel without help?

He decided to wait. Grampa and Dayne would come after them, he was sure of that. But would they be found?

Merri had been leaving signs at every squat. She would bring a flower bush to bloom, one that never bloomed in the summer and told him that it would bloom all winter long, until the longest night killed it. This pretty yellow-flowered bush littered their trail all the way back to the first day. But would anyone pass it? He wondered how she'd done it, because he was the Maker between the two of them, but she said only that it came from seed crumbs in the trail biscuits Auntie Corrie had left. That made him feel a bit ashamed, for he'd gobbled his biscuits right away, every speck of them, so hungry he'd been, but she had saved one back for its seeds. He didn't feel his shame long, however, for the frowning man saw to it they were both fed well. A request for apples, however, had turned the frown into a growl.

They jolted to a halt that seemed final because the cart pony gave off a whicker which was answered in return, and the frowning man made a grunt of satisfaction as he swung down from the seat. He grabbed them by the seat of their pants and hoisted them into the air where Evar had an odd sense of being flown about as he would fly one of his wooden birds before setting them on a patch of grass that still smelled sweet in the summer heat.

"I smell horses." Merri sounded emphatic. He did, too, but he knew she meant a lot of horses. Her nose had always been better than his.

The frowning man sawed away at the bonds on their wrists and ankles, setting them free. Evar clawed off his sack immediately and then helped Merri whose curls had somehow gotten caught in the sack strings. The sight that met their freed gaze struck them silent. They had seen the vast vineyards on the low rolling hills at the end of their street and farmhouse and had been up and down the rows with their grandfather as he talked to them about sun and rain and grapes. Never had they seen a vast valley such as this, with lush grass that still waved blue-green in the summer sun. Nor had they seen hills looming all around, high and jagged, and some with white tops and a chill wind coming down off them. Of horses, they saw only three, but the valley which was a little bit in their very young memories like Larandaril, but much more raw, was lined with fences. Empty pastures and training rings and great barns on the far outskirts, farther than they could really see, their eyes a little blurry after days under their burlap sacks. It seemed wild and more than a little dangerous, far from Larandaril and even farther from their home at the end of the street in Calcort. The immensity weighed down on them and little Merri began to cry silently, great tears streaming down her cheeks at the loss of her mother and family.

Frowning man went on one knee next to her. "That's enough, hear? We've got work to do." He pointed at the low ramshackle house behind them and the weathered paddocks beyond. "There's been horses here, a lot of them, and we have to gather their patties, dry ones."

Evar put his arm about Merri's shoulders. "Why?"

"We burn them, see. Against the cold at night, and it will get cold. Very cold." The frowning man straightened. "There's already snow up there." He pointed at the jagged mountains about the valley. "There will be snow down here, soon enough. You'll work, you little beggars or you won't get fed. I'm no cold-damned nursemaid. Now get moving."

That made Evar cold inside. The frowning man intended to keep them there. Perhaps for a long time. Or perhaps just long enough to figure out if they were broken or not. He drew Merri close to protect her as well as he could. They started out across the old pastures where the droppings littered the grasses. They picked as many as they could, Merri retching from the smell now and then, her little face streaked with tears and fear.

At night, tired and grubby, with only enough well water drawn up to wash their hands and faces, Evar waited until the frowning man fell asleep before he rolled off his cot and went to the tiny window. He latched his sore fingertips on the bottom sill and pulled himself up a bit, so he could look out. He knew that it was a low window, but not quite low enough for him. Behind him, Merri stifled a yawn and joined him, her whispery mouth next to his ear.

"Whatcha doing?"

"Feeling it."

She smooshed another yawn into her mouth. A long pause was followed by her own attempt to stand on tiptoe and look out, but she couldn't manage it and let out a huff of disappointment. Then she clapped her hands over her lips. "Sorry."

"He won't wake."

"Whyn't?"

"We hummed him to sleep."

"Oooh. Right." Merri turned a bit to lean on him. She smelled of sunshine and grass but not the nasty bits, 'cause they'd washed up really well.

Mama and Grandmamma would be proud of that. He patted his elbow on the top of her mussed-up curls.

"Whatcha seeing?"

"I told you, I'm feeling."

"What, then?"

He tried to find the words for what he felt inside and outside the bunk house, and along the pastures, spilling down from the sharp hillsides surrounding them. It was like a washtub, or maybe the drinking trough when they played in it, filling with water and surrounding them, gliding all around them and sinking into even his bones. He wasn't sure what it was. It wasn't sunshine. Or bathwater. He didn't have the words for it. He turned slightly to look down on his sister, but she had slid slowly down his body until her rump hit the floor and she'd tumbled forward a bit, and snored faintly in her own little way. Just as well. He didn't know how to explain what he felt to her, only that it was important somehow.

He didn't know what the frowning man or the old woman who'd stabbed them wanted from them, but he believed Auntie Corrie. The ild Fallyn had hidden them here. They thought they had won the battle by doing that. They thought they would learn the secrets.

Evarton's fingernails curved into the window pane, bringing up bits of old paint. The ild Fallyn had no real idea. The two of them were there because the world wanted them there, at that moment, for something important. He could feel it. All around them, and sinking in.

HE TOOK THE EARLY NIGHT WATCH on the tenth night, bone weary but aching more for the fact he had no news to send back to Nutmeg. They'd doubled back twice on the trail and found the merest of traces, but nothing they could track. The yarn twists had stopped, for reasons of their own, or been blown away or plucked up by birds looking to fatten their nests. He refused to think of any other reason.

Dayne supposed he should thank the Gods and fates that he hadn't found their bodies, laid out in a display of spite for all to see. That realization gave him little comfort. The absence of bodies did not mean that Evar and Merri had survived. They could be nowhere near where Tressandre had decided to take her vengeance. There was, he knew, an entire world of harm out there which he could not see from where he waited.

He'd already ridden one horse into the ground, his fine tashya gelding foundering and nearly dead on him when Dayne had traded him for a Kernan horse and tashya cross at a small camp now far behind him. The Dweller lad had rubbed the gelding's soft muzzle, not saying a word about the horse's condition but with condemnation simmering unsaid in his eyes. He wore a farmer's well-worn coverall and shirt, but his boots were sturdy with new laces fresh bought from a local trader, and he had kind eyes and callused hands.

"He'll recover," Dayne told the Dweller. "You'll have a fine saddle horse on your hands when he does."

"And if he doesna?"

"Send to Calcort. Ask Keldan and Tolby Farbranch for your due. Coin or another mount, they'll be good for it."

"Farbranch?" The lad's face lit up. "I'm a Barrel, I am. You tell 'im we crossed paths, a'right? Old master Barrel has passed but I'm Joniah, his grandson, and we're back with orchards and fields on the Silverwing."

"I'll remember." Dayne scanned him, realizing he had found an insight into Nutmeg's past. Tolby had brought his family from their orchards in the early days of the Raymy infestation and eventually come all the way to Calcort. "You're a far piece from the Silverwing."

"Oh, aye, don't I know it. Came down t' meet a trading caravan, I cut across their roads now and then, do a bit of tradin' on my own without having t' go to the towns."

Dayne smiled to himself at the thought of the enterprise. "Any luck?"

Joniah frowned and wiped his nose on his sleeve. "Nawt. Th' caravan didn't show."

"Bad luck, that. Better luck next time."

"Donnae I know it." The lad smiled. The gelding whickered softly. Joniah put his hand back on the beast's neck. He hesitated before asking, but then he did. "What happened here?"

"I'm tracking."

"I kin see that. In a cold-damned hurry, too, t' founder a fine horse."

"I'm chasing someone."

"But na caught them yet, aye?"

"No." He shook his head. "But there's no time to waste. The ild Fallyn have taken Nutmeg Farbranch's child. Children. Two children, Merri and her playmate."

"No! It canna be." Joniah frowned heavily.

"Yes, and if you see them, they have to be stopped. I don't want to be putting this on you and you alone, but we can use any help. Send word to Calcort if you spot their tracks. Or double back and find me, I'll be ranging northwest, bit by bit."

"I will. I can track you by Bessie's shoes. Handmade, y'see, by my brother."

Dayne found a smile at that. He'd taken up her reins and left them, the Dweller warming a pot over a spit to boil up some grain for the horse and nurse him a bit.

He rode Bessie in a swinging circle, much slower than his former pace, and caught up with the rest of the trackers the next midday, with no one having found anything of use. Despair screwed its way inside his chest. He could not even think of returning to Nutmeg without some sign, some token of hope, if he could not find the children themselves. The despair crawled deep within and carved out a space for itself there, and he felt it with every breath. When they made camp and he took the watch, his thoughts chased each other around like a pack of street dogs after a butcher's bone.

He heard a click in the night. Stone against stone or maybe a shod hoof against stone, and it brought him awake and alert, taking him out of drowsy memory. Any other night, he might have called out a warning hail, but not this night. This night he left the shelter of his tree and moved quietly, lethally, into the foliage in search of the noise. He moved as quietly as he could until he thought he reached the noise and put a hand up carefully to pull a branch down, and felt something hard in his shoulder blade as he did.

"Don't be moving."

Dark as it was, tired as he was, he could not mistake the voice.

"Tolby. You're getting slow, I thought you'd catch up with us by last night."

The sheathed knife moved away and Tolby grunted. "And I never thought I'd catch you snoring on watch."

"I wasn't snoring, just thinking deeply. Was I?"

"I won't be telling Nutmeg, never fear. Let her find out for herself." Tolby Farbranch moved past him, leading his mountain horse, its head lowered in weariness, toward the small river. He tossed the reins to Dayne. "Hobble him up for me."

With Tolby's tired mount joining the others, the two of them sat by the dimming fire drinking a last bit of soup, talking quietly so as not to wake the others: Brista and a Galdarkan who had also found them on the road, sent by Bregan and Abayan Diort, he claimed.

"No sign."

"Not yet. They could have gone in any direction." Dayne sat back with a weary sigh. "Though I think she'll probably have sent them to the fortress. It can be impassable, if she brings the bridge down."

"She won't be doing that."

"And why not?"

"Because she can't march her forces out without a bridge, and have no doubt, she wants t' bring war to Larandaril."

Dayne rubbed the back of his hand over his forehead. "I confess, I don't understand the hatred between the two families."

Tolby refilled his tin cup with soup and blew across it. "I'm no Vaelinar, but this I know. Old Sinok Anderieon caught the ild Fallyn slave trafficking, after it had been settled amongst the high elven that the natives of Kerith were to be respected. Sinok rained his wrath down upon them, and when he was done beating them to a pulp with Bistel's help, he confiscated their Holds. Drove them to the ocean, where the ild Fallyn clung like th' stubborn barnacles they are. The ild Fallyn have never forgotten and vowed they would one day take Larandaril as their due." He sipped for a moment. "I'm a bit surprised that wasn't among your history lessons."

Dayne could feel his face growing warm. "I was never good in history. It seemed so long ago, all of it."

"To one like myself, aye, but you . . . you're going to have life spans on me."

"I know, I know. The only history that caught my attention was the aryns. I grow them. Sometimes even dream them. They're real to me."

"And now the ild Fallyn are real to you, as well."

"Tree's blood, too real." He stood. "I've a bit more on my watch, so I'll be making rounds."

Tolby rinsed his cup out. "And I'll be sleeping', lad. Never doubt it."

He turned on boot heel. "I met a lad a bit back, traded my horse for his. Says to tell you his name is Joniah Barrel and his family is back farming on the Silverwing."

That brought a spark to Tolby's eyes. "Are they, now? That was a good family. Don't know of any Joniah, though."

"He says his grandfather has passed, but he knows of you."

"Ah. See, lad. His grandfather knew my father. History again." Tolby gave a sad smile. He unrolled his blankets and was good to his word in minutes. Dayne looked in on him after his third circle and watched him a moment, trying to decide which of her father's features Nutmeg had, and what of her beauty came from Lily instead. He hadn't made a decision when it came time for him to pass the watch and go to sleep himself. He did not think even a moment's peace could find him, but he was wrong.

He awoke to the sharp smell of a revitalized campfire, smoking and snapping, and the aroma of a breakfast spitted over it. Others had been awake far sooner and gotten busy, he thought, as he leaned over to pull his boots on. The Galdarkan, Egarth by name, knelt by the spit, testing the carcass for doneness as he stood to join him.

"The others have ridden out already. This is the second hopper we've spitted this morning. They split theirs and this awaits us."

"They will catch us on the road later, then, as we've been doing."

Egarth nodded. He took a stick from the fire, blew out its leaping flame on the tip, and sketched in the dirt. "They are headed thusly."

Dayne nodded. "And we in the opposite direction." And by the time they both weave their way back to the main road, they will have covered a great deal of territory, in a grid fashion. He scrubbed his hands. "Smells like breakfast is about ready. I'll go wash up."

When he returned, the Galdarkan had removed the spit, scattered the coals so they would cool before he doused and buried them, and had cut the carcass in two, laid out on plates. Dayne grinned and sat down for a hearty meal with his stomach growling a welcome.

With four of them, they worked a faster spiral, one on the faint road and the other three riding to the fore and then circling, back, spiraling inward, until they met upon the road again. The off-road searchers had a tougher ride, through bracken and last-summer tangles, gazes sharpened to spot whatever they could, so the three of them traded off. They covered a lot of ground with no results. When a late-summer light drizzle began one darkening afternoon, he rode up to see Tolby had a canopy put up amongst the trees and a good smelling soup simmering over the fire. Tolby's attention snapped to him, and he shook his head as he dismounted and drew the reins over.

"Nothing and more nothing."

"I've had thoughts on th' direction, but even though Tressandre would be a fool to send the children to the fort, I think she'd have them hid somewhere nearby, at hand. She's taken them as hostage against Lara, so it would do her no good to have them so far out of sight she couldn't get to them fairly quickly."

"I agree." He patted Tolby's shoulder as he passed to the patch of grass and hobbled Bessie so she could graze there next to Tolby's horse.

"So why are we failing, lad, if we should be so close to their trail?"

Dayne hunkered down and filled his cup with fresh-steeped klah. It would taste better with a touch of cream and honey, but it was fine without as he sipped it gingerly. "I can't go back to Nutmeg with empty hands, but it's not just that. Those are my children as much as they're not. I helped birth them with you. Steadied their first steps. Wiped the jam off their hands and cheeks. Sang them asleep. They're a part of my heart, and I can't leave them out here." He cast a gaze to the sky, the sun now gone but the last of its rays still a faint glimmer among the shifting gray clouds.

"It's possible that Tressandre has sent demands to Lara. We've no way of knowing."

"And equally possible she hasn't, that she will withhold her taunts to hurt us that much more."

"Aye, lad, that woman has no heart. Just fury knotted inside her." Tolby stirred his soup vigorously. "She'll peel the skin off them if it would help her cause."

"If she finds out Evarton could be a Maker . . ."

"She'd have no way of knowing that! And they may be little more than babes, but both are sharp. They have old souls in them, I've seen them looking out at me. They know more than a child does, even though our Meg would have them stay babes forever. Tressandre will turn them inside out to look them over. No, she has 'em stowed somewhere while she is out and about tending to her schemes and her Returnists. They're not under her nose yet, and that's a worry off our minds." Tolby lifted his head. "Here comes Egarth. And he's got a bag wi' him." Tolby stood quickly, dusting his hands on the seat of his pants.

The rain had slackened, and the last rays of the setting sun set the Galdarkan's skin to even more of a golden glow; he looked molten as he tossed his bundle down to them before dismounting. "I found a dead woman to the south. Gave her the honors, and gathered what I could for her relatives. Might you know her?"

A hand-dyed scarf had been stuffed with items and knotted. Both men knew it the moment they held it between them. The woman known to them as Auntie Corrie had worn it often, a present from her family before she'd come to work for Nutmeg.

"We know her."

"How was she killed?"

"Attacked from ambush. Archers from trees, it looked like. I took three of these out of her," and Egarth handed Dayne three arrowheads. They looked lethal but gave no hint as to their making. Dayne rolled them over a few times on the palm of his hands to see if there was anything he missed.

"South?" Tolby repeated.

"Yes."

"And traveling alone?"

"Except for her killers, yes." Egarth turned his horse out with the others, dropping his gear to the side under the canopy.

"Her family farm was to the south, near the coast and the great salt bay, the haunted one. Hardscrabble farming there, which is why she left it to become an auntie."

"And I'd say she was heading back, quick as she could." Dayne watched as Tolby sat to untie the bundle and reveal its contents. What the Galdar-kan had thought important enough to retrieve might not be worth anything at all or it might have been quite telling. Tolby sorted through quickly. He stopped at the three brilliant gold coins shining up from the center of the goods.

The finding shocked Dayne. There was no way Corrie had earned that working for them, which meant she'd earned it elsewhere.

"Blood money."

"But not a lot of it." Tolby sorted the coins back and forth with the tip of his finger. "Hawthorne coined, so no ild Fallyn marking here. Easy enough to obtain from the exchange. Bandits killed her on the road but ne'er thought to take her coin from her?" He snorted.

"Wait—what's that?" Dayne leaned over and found something buried in a rolled handkerchief. He tapped it on his palm. "Message tube." Its contents, rolled tightly, had to be pried out. He picked at it carefully with nails that had grown ragged during the ride. Unrolled, he read the message aloud:

Abandon your post when you see the horses. Your family is free.

"The horses. Tressandre's tashyas being brought to market, though we didn't spot her, and that makes her hand clear in this. They had to have taken Corrie's family for leverage. They excel, it seems, in taking small children. The coin must be for spying on them." Tolby watched him restore the missive to its leather tube, his dark eyes bright.

"That gives our auntie some rationale for her treason, although it would have been better if she'd come to us at the first with her trouble. We might have saved her grief as well as her life." Dayne tossed the tube back into the scarf at Tolby's feet.

"I know the southern farmers. They trust little. The weather is against them, the traders drive hard bargains for their goods, and they dislike outsiders." Tolby knotted Corrie's goods back together. "I'll stow this for a bit, but if it takes up precious room, I'll be leaving most of it by the wayside, just like she left my grandchildren." He set his jaw.

The drizzle continued through Dayne's watch and even lulled him into a deep sleep when he finally fell into his blanket, but the day dawned with crisp, sharp rays promising to dry the trail out soon. Tolby had all the horses saddled and ready, and the campfire already kicked out, his portion put to the side on a warm rock.

"I'm going to have Egarth take me to where he found Corrie."

"What do you expect to find?"

"Nothing but I want to backtrack, if we can. This rain was light, it might have straggled through, hitting only here and there." He swung up. "If it was ild Fallyn who hit her, and I'm sure it was, it will be worth knowing where they came from. You go on with Brista, and we'll meet in a day or two."

"Unless you find the ild Fallyn first."

"If we do, I'll still be meeting you. I'll not let the bastards go without an accounting."

"Watch your back."

"Aye, that's why there are two of us going." Tolby tipped his hat and rode past. Dayne threw Egarth a look that said all he could without putting words to it. Bring Tolby back.

Abayan Diort's man gave him a solemn nod as he pushed his mount past them, and Brista merely shrugged into her all-weather coat, tightening the hood about her face.

When they met again days later, they had no further answers, but their horses were all thinner and trail worn, as all four of their riders looked. No luck and no sign. He wondered what he could possibly tell Nutmeg when they returned.

He dismounted as Bessie seemed a bit off and waved the others ahead. "I'll catch up for dinner."

They left him running his hand down her legs, looking for heat, and finding none. Then he lifted each hoof and carefully inspected her feet. A tiny pebble was just about to work its way into her frog, and he plucked it out. That might account for a bit of the soreness, or not. Like it or not, the hard riding could be just as troublesome. He didn't want to have to go looking for another mount replacement. He surveyed the area. They were far from any settlement he knew about, though he did not know this area well, but any quest for additional mounts could take him far from the search.

Dayne patted the mare on her shoulder. "How about I just walk you a bit? We'll catch up soon enough." Her answer came by a flip of her ears. She fell in beside him as he went after the faint trail, and her walking seemed steadier. The late afternoon murmured quietly about him, punctuated only by the creak of the leather tack, the sound of Bessie stealing an occasional hunk of grass, and the thud of his footsteps. Insects circled them lazily, drawn by the scent of the sweat drying on their bodies and both her tail and his hands swatted at them now and again.

Dayne composed in his head the letter he knew he should write to Nutmeg yet could not find the words for. How could he encapsulate his disappointment in finding no trace and repeat his promise not to come home without them in the few words a bird messenger could carry? She already knew, he believed, had to know, because if Merri and Evarton had been found, she'd have word, no matter how many horses he broke getting them back to her or how many Vaelinar magics he'd called upon to let her know the news. There would be no aching emptiness.

Dayne rubbed the side of his head where a dull throb pulsed as if his thoughts wanted to pound their way out. He scrubbed an ear where one of the insects, somehow or other, had delivered a sharp bite and it now itched like crazy. His ear rang as he rubbed it harshly and when he stopped, he realized he couldn't hear anything.

No, not exactly true. He could hear Bessie plodding along. But the small noises of the countryside around him had fallen into a hush. Earth sense, one of his Talents, rose up. Riding alone, it hadn't been dampened by the presence of others, which often tended to drown it out. Now he knew he wasn't as alone as he thought himself. He quickly took in her reins, his fist under her chin, and turned her off the broken track and brought her into the shade in the shelter of a tree. And he waited.

He waited after Bessie's head dropped and she fell into a light slumber, while his quickened heartbeat steadied and the headache that had been threatening tailed off, and only his ear still stung. He waited until he thought he might have been mistaken save that the everyday clicks and clucks and rustles and wing beats and bird call and insect buzz did not return. The wildlife, like himself, had hunkered down in caution.

Then he caught the faraway sound of an approach. Two sets of hoofbeats, hitting leisurely upon the ground, two riders not at all in a hurry. Dayne tied Bessie to a stout-looking branch and made his way through cover for a closer look. To his astonishment, two mules tied together walked sedately toward him, the lead with an empty saddle and the second with packs lashed securely across its back. He blinked at the sight, trying to decide what to do, when the smell of wildflowers rose about him, strong and clean. He looked down at his boots, wondering what late summer patch he'd wandered into, and felt the knife edge at the side of his throat.

"Stand slow."

A strong yet guttural voice, one which had trouble with the sibilant sounds. Dayne did as he was told. A bold, musky aroma came to his senses. A Bolger hulked behind him.

"I never caught wind of you," Dayne said, thinking that he'd be dead already if he was meant for it, and if the knife wielder was thinking, too, maybe conversation would change his mind. His captor grunted.

Dayne took a chance. "Chief Rufus?"

"No chief for a long time. Warlord's son?"

"Aye, Verdayne. They call me Dayne."

The Bolger gave another grunt and took the knife away. "Get animals before they leave. Hungry, they go."

Dayne backtracked to his horse and when he came out of the bush, the old chieftain had both his mules in hand. A great, shoulder-bowed beast he was, his skin now more of a burnished brown than the russet it had been, his hair gone to only a few bristles of silver on his head and a tuft or two on his chin, although the chest covered by an old blacksmith's leather apron showed a thick hedge of russet-and-gray hair. He put his hand out for Dayne to shake, hand to wrist.

When Rufus dropped his hold, he surveyed Dayne up and down. "You are Nutmeg's man?"

"Yes. Well, that is, we're spoken for each other but not married. Yet. Soon, I hope."

"Then why out here?" Rufus, brow wrinkling, looked up.

"It's a long story, but Nutmeg's children have been taken."

Rufus hmphfed deep in his chest. "Long story can wait for dinner. Mules need grass. I need food." He pointed down the way where the others had disappeared into the forest. "We not catch up till dark."

"Graze the animals. We'll have dinner with the others. Just how long have you been tracking me?" Dayne asked as they walked toward the sunset.

"Since mare picked up stone. I have story, too. Wanted to have right listeners."

"You have to show me how to move that quietly with two mules."

A smile creased the old Bolger's face. "Deal."

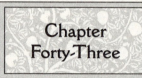

Chapter
Forty-Three

RUFUS TURNED THE TRAIL BISCUIT about in his hands several times, peering down at it, leathery forehead wrinkled in observation. He sniffed at it suspiciously. Dinner fare steeped in the pot, and Dayne counted himself lucky that it was a big pot and would feed them all. He'd surprised them when they'd caught up to the camp, but Tolby had thumped Rufus on his shoulder before going out to stake the mules on the horse line. He grinned at the Bolger's hesitation.

"Just grain and seeds and dried berries."

Rufus dug a nail at it. He picked out a seed. "What?"

"Oh. That's a—" Dayne peered at it from across the campfire. "Sunface seed. A cheery little yellow flower with this nutty center. Tastes good. Really."

Rufus rolled back on his rump, still examining the seed. "From where?"

"They grow around Calcort. And south. They take a lot of sun. Warmth. Seeds are a little hard to digest but healthy for you. We press an oil from them as well, but they're popular in baked goods. Muffins and cookies and the like."

Rufus put the seed to his mouth and took an extremely long time to taste, chew, and swallow one relatively small seed. Dayne didn't know whether it was because of his age, or teeth, or suspicion. The Bolger nodded. "Sunface."

"That's it."

"Understand." He tucked the rest of the trail biscuit into his apron and patted it as if to assure himself which pocket contained it, then frowned and withdrew something from another pocket. "I am old." His bald, leathery forehead wrinkled deeply.

"You are long-lived among your people," Dayne assured him.

Rufus rolled an eye at him. "Pocket reminded me. I need Pipe Smoke. Something to give him. It is why I trailed you."

"I can give it to him."

Rufus shook his head wearily. "No. I carry it." He patted Dayne on the knee. "Is not a good thing. My sorrow."

Dayne looked at him, but could not see what the Bolger's long fingers gripped in his other hand, eyes squinted a little in distress, and he decided not to press him. "All right, then." The campfire lent little illumination against the deep of the night, but he could see Tolby's silhouette across the way at the horse line. Dayne straightened to go fetch Tolby.

Tolby joined them, smelling of the horses and mules he'd been grooming. He folded his legs and sat down cheerfully next to Rufus. "Looking good, Rufus. Still wearing your apron."

Rufus curled a lip back. "Good armor."

"That it be." Tolby pulled his pipe out and examined it. "Want a pinch of weed?"

Rufus shook his head slowly. He put his hand out on Tolby's. "Stop. I have . . ." The Bolger's deep voice broke a little. He did not finish his sentence but turned one of Tolby's hands over and dropped a small bundle into it. "Found it on body."

Tolby tucked his pipe back into a vest pocket before opening the cloth, the bloodstain dried and stiff. He looked at the amulet necklace for a long moment, saying nothing, although his breathing grew harsh. Dayne felt ice grow in the pit of his stomach. He'd last seen that amulet hanging about Garner Farbranch's neck.

Rufus rumbled, "Died fighting."

"Did he?" Tolby's hands began to shake, and he pressed his palms tightly together, cupping the amulet. "Where? When?"

"Not far. Not long. Died in trade caravan. Guard. Only one fought."

Tolby rubbed his thumb over the items. "You're sure?"

Rufus nodded.

Tolby closed a fist about the object. "I always thought someday he'd bring a wife home. Maybe a babe, too, just to meet with family before he was off again. My good lad. Always restless, he was always so footloose." His breath gargled a bit in his throat and he cleared it roughly. "You said it was close?"

Rufus nodded.

Tolby's eyes narrowed. "Near here? Who in the cold hells would attack a caravan train this close?"

Rufus shifted, dug into his apron pockets, and produced another bit of cloth which he handed to Tolby. "Destroyed all to hide, but I found."

Tolby unrolled the sleeve. "Black and silver. Bloody ild Fallyn."

"Bandits. Caravans smashed. Waterskins, jugs, all drained. Bad smell. Drugs," Rufus told him, speaking laboriously through his tusked teeth. "No one fight back but him." He poked a finger at the amulet. "He fought hard. Too many." Rufus growled lowly. "You take to Spice. You take to Lara guard. You tell."

"Ild Fallyn drugged their water supply and then hit them on the trail?" Dayne shifted as he sifted through Rufus' words. "Looks like."

"Any survivors? Maybe someone crawled off the road and hid?"

Rufus shook his head.

"Cargo?"

"Gone. Was grain, much of it. Everyt'ing else smashed." He leaned forward, adding, "No traders in caravan."

"No traders? They always carry a trader or two. Apprentice, if no one else. Are you certain? How can you tell?"

Rufus sat back, giving Tolby a little resentful look. "No soft men or women. No rich rags. Only hired. Tough people. I saw. Skraws at work, eating, ripping. You not see."

Tolby waved the sleeve. "But I have this. Did you bring a waterskin?"

Rufus thought a moment before nodding. "One. Red stripes."

"I'll take that, too. Maybe someone can identify the drugs." Tolby took a hard breath, and his eyes brimmed a little as he looked at Dayne. "I can't stay with you, then. I have to go back. I won't be letting the ild Fallyn get away with this, either. They killed my son as well as took my grandchildren." It took him two tries to get to his feet. Rufus grunted and handed a third object up.

"Caravan flag."

Tolby nodded. "That will identify the cargo and crew." He wrapped it about the sleeve and amulet and tucked it into his pipe pocket, switching the pipe to a less secure spot. "My thanks to you, Rufus, even though it is bad news you carry."

Rufus peered up at Tolby. "I stay. Find kits for Spice and Little Flower."

"You do that. I'll tell her."

Dayne stopped Tolby from brushing past him. "Stay the night," he counseled. "We all need the rest."

Tolby's mouth thinned. Then he gave an abrupt nod. "A'right, lad. There's some sense in it. But I'll be off with the first light." He pushed away then and went to the far edge of the firelight in the fading day, and sat down near the hobbled horses, his shoulders bowed, his chin dropped to his chest. Dayne decided it would be best to leave him alone, at least for a while.

Chapter
Forty-Four

THEY CAMPED UPWIND of the massacred trade caravan and little met their eyes now. White bones lay bleaching in the air amongst shreds of clothes, beasts of burden with little left to their carcasses but their heads and hooves, and the skeletons of the carts and wagons they'd been pulling. Lara folded up, the strain on her face emphasized by the pale bruises under each eye, their search for the children fruitless but word sent from Calcort directing them to this tragedy.

"No evidence to find."

"We were not meant to, certainly. Rufus told us true. I trust his word and Tolby's on what happened here." Bistane threw one leg over the top of the saddle and sat, off-balance, surveying the area behind her.

"If they'd stayed by the river, they might have survived."

"Nonsense. If not ambushed here, they would have been taken somewhere before they crossed the border into Galdarkan lands. Just because they eschewed the river here, and had to rely on their own water sources, did not lead to their downfall. They were sent into a trap and meant to do exactly what happened: ride into it and get cut down."

"For grain that could be bought at a fair market price."

"If a domain is penniless, with credit tight, no price is fair enough. If there's any blame to fall on this, it falls on my shoulders." Bistane shook his head. "I failed to realize how desperate the ild Fallyn had gotten. If I had . . ."

"You'd have gone to war against them."

"Yes." His teeth flashed white at that. "I'd have brought our old enemy low if I'd caught but a whiff of their desperate scent."

"You were busy at the time."

"Never should have been so busy I did not see them weaken! I had thought the First Home was facing an ordinary uptick in bandits, common after any warfare, and never thought to investigate deeper. No, this is my fault, and I will enjoy picking apart the ild Fallyn who did this." His gaze swept the killing ground again. "Although without old Rufus coming across this fresh, we would have had no inkling of what happened here." He dismounted and tied the reins loosely, setting his horse free to graze.

"There is that." Lara unhooked her own canteen and took a hearty gulp. She wiped her mouth with the back of her hand and looked at it as she lowered it, the scarred stub of that missing finger. "Old Sinok used to say that all rivers flowed into the Andredia. I believed him when I was small, riding at his knee, and even more, he believed it himself. He thought by our sacred pact with the Andredia, he could influence this part of the continent, any part of it which might be touched by the merest drop of the river water. If he'd been right, I should be able to go to any river and ask for word of the children, and receive an answer. Get a testimony as to the ambush here."

Bistane's horse moved restively nearby, cropping with anger as if unhappy with the browning grass dried by the summer heat, and stamped as he moved across the small meadow. Both turned to look at him, checking their surroundings and other mounts, before looking back at each other. Lara scrubbed a wetted scarf over her face, feeling the sun and grit in her skin. Her legs felt knotted and chapped from the hard riding, and a kink had settled in the right side of her neck, stubbornly refusing to ease. She spread the scarf over the ground to let it dry, grubby though it was.

"But your faith and his was wrong?"

"Yes. It's close, the Andredia is a great river that runs mostly underground throughout these western lands before emerging from the mountains and into the valley of Larandaril, but it's not the only great vein of water. If it were . . ." Her voice trailed off as she looked outward, seeing without seeing.

"What would you do?"

"I would call on the blood and flesh we gave her to seek out my heirs and return them."

He looked at her hand, the four-fingered one as she rubbed the scar unconsciously, unknowing that she even worried at it as she talked. "What is this pact, exactly?"

The corner of her mouth drew tight. "We don't talk of it."

"Not even with the consorts and heirs who inherit the consequences of it? I want to know what awaits me and mine."

"You have a point."

"I do."

"Sinok was the second generation of our family, but you know that."

He bowed his head even though she still did not look directly at him, seeing him only from the corner of her eye.

"He was born when the Anderieons had conquered a large portion of these lands for themselves. As he used to tell me, he was born early and a sickly babe and it looked as if Kethan would not have an heir, despite his prowess as a Warrior King and his subjugation of Kernans, Dwellers, Galdarkans, and Vaelinars alike. But he forgot one important aspect of this world, of Kerith." She stopped rubbing the scar for her missing digit. "He forgot that the peoples of Kerith had Gods, just as the Vaelinars had had them."

"Sleeping Gods."

"Not all of them."

"Oh?" Bistane leaned close. "This was a tale I've never heard from any of the first, not even my own preternaturally long-lived father. The Gods of Kerith seldom manifested themselves."

She inhaled deeply on the threshold of imparting truth which her family had kept silent for centuries. He could sense her hesitation.

He fell quiet then as if afraid of interrupting her confession. "I don't think Sinok even wrote this in the *Book of All Truth* he submitted to the library. He was like that his entire life, keeping the foundation of our line and our secrets to himself. But, then, they were all like that. I have a feeling that the powers and Talents we are born into were changed by Kerith. Made stronger. Made different. We did not share our knowledge with one another." She paused for quite a while. The meadow had its own serenity, broken only by the occasional birdsong or whirring of wings or the cropping of the horses.

"He had his own secrets to keep close, the truth of the rape of his daughter and my birth out of incest, of his disinheritance of Jeredon as a grandson because he found my mother and her husband at the time too weak for the dynasty he intended to establish. He kept my Talents secret. His alliances secret." She laughed without humor. "A Vaelinar to the core."

She lifted her hand, palm upward as if she might hold something. "As a sickly babe, Sinok had little value to Kethan, but that Warrior King knew that he was unlikely to find a different heir. We have never been prolific in our families. The explosive entry of our people into this world had awakened a singular God, a God of diverse and yet devastating power, the Goddess who held the River Andredia." Lara shifted her weight on the hard ground. "Kerith Gods are elementals, the bones of the world, as it were. He decided to make a pact with this God for a guarantee of succession, with a sacrifice of blood and flesh which he thought would appeal to this primal force. Kethan offered the life of his son Sinok for the promise of Larandaril and a ruling heir."

That startled Bistane. "Sinok was not the firstborn?"

"Oh, but he was. The God of Kerith returned the child to health, with the further pledge that Larandaril be kept sacred, that the peoples of Kerith would benefit just as much from its bounty as the Vaelinars who held it, and that the waters of Andredia would hold the throne of this Kerith God, and be worshipped as such." She gave Bistane a sidelong look as he raised an eyebrow, absorbing this.

"You protect a Kerith God?"

"I do. We did, for centuries, until Quendius seriously jeopardized that God with his weapons forges, poisoning the mountains with his corruptions and the font had to be cleansed and the pact reaffirmed. Again, flesh and blood." She lifted her maimed hand into the air and dropped it. "My grandfather was never a particularly religious man, even sworn to a God, but I feel the burden differently." Her mouth twisted again. "Rivergrace has her own pact with a minor Goddess of the Kerith waters, it seems, the spirit of the Silverwing, but the presence which imbues the Andredia is the primary force in all her glory. I would call on her if I could, but what Daravan and Tressandre have done—and I haven't rectified—may have cost me my honor and my word."

"You don't know."

"No." Lara looked to her hand again. "The Andredia might just feel that the sacrifice of Evarton and Merri is . . . apt. I'm afraid to ask. I don't think I can bear the answer."

"You've been to the river."

"Yes. To make sure it is cleansed of the war I waged on its banks. I haven't tried to communicate with Her."

"Then every day compounds your guilt, Lara."

"I know." Her hand curled on her trouser knee.

"From word sent me by Tolby, the Gods of Kerith are getting to their feet, shaking themselves, and are angry. I wouldn't wait long before you reconcile with Andredia."

Her voice thinned. "I know." She stood, gathering up her horse's reins. "We've found nothing out here. No trace of them. Not found by us or any of the bounty trackers eager for a purse of gems or even by Dayne who was closest on the trail behind them."

"Then we should return home."

"And give up?" Her attention snapped to Bistane.

"No. We return and force Tressandre's hand."

"And how might we do that?"

"Send every last one of those Returnists still squatting on the Andredia back to her doorstep, send them running. You're not finished cleansing the banks of your river."

She tilted her head a little. "No. I'm not."

"Whatever blood you draw, you can dedicate to your Goddess."

Lara drew her reins through her fingers slowly. "She is a God of peace."

"Even more so, then. The war that Daravan and the ild Fallyn directed to her shores was an affront to all her sensibilities. And yours." He mounted and leaned forward in his saddle toward her. "I have it on good authority that the ild Fallyn have no sensibilities."

Her cheek twitched slightly as the corner of her mouth drew up. "You push me. I've held back because my sleep left me weak, as you know well, and because . . . because I don't want to start a civil war among the Houses. We bicker enough as it is."

He shook his head. "I am only encouraging you to do what you've known you had to do, yet hesitated. I could never push you." Bistane paused. "Let me correct myself. I would never push you. I stand at your side, to help how I can, even if you demand flesh and blood of me."

"What did I do to deserve you?"

"I don't know. But long ago I asked our Gods to let you look upon me and really see me for what I was and what I could offer. Don't make me sorry for my plea."

She reined about so that their horses stood near enough that her leg rubbed against his. "Never." She took a deep breath. "Then it's home, and forcing Tressandre's hand. I can't prove what she's done to Evarton and Merri, but by all the Gods, I can get her for this."

Chapter
Forty-Five

"WHAT ARE YOU DOING?"

"Looking."

Merri tugged at his shirt hem. "But what do you see?"

"A lot of things." He pulled her up beside him. "You're tall enough to look now. On tippy-toes."

Merri shook her head in disbelief and then did as instructed, her eyes growing wide as she found she could indeed look out the small framed window. She cast a sideways glance at him. He no longer had to stretch to his tallest to look out. With a small hmmm of interest to herself, she looked back through the window as night in the valley spread out before them. It was, as always, empty. As empty as their hope for something good to come after them. No one would come. They weren't wanted. They had been given away, to keep raiders away. They'd been told that, every day since they'd been taken. No one wanted them. No one looked for them. No one cared, except the grumpy man who looked after them, and he cared as little as he could. His heart seemed as empty as the fallow pastures stretching all about them. There was nothing to see.

But now.

A silvery glow danced over the bending grasses, and the trees at the far side seemed to dip and sway in time with it. A star hung low enough to be one of the moons, but she wasn't sure about that. Her eyes didn't see as far or as well as Evar's; she was always missing things he tried to point out to her, and the sky was no different. She stretched her little legs a bit more. Her chin could almost reach the bottom sill. Evar's face occupied the middle of the glass pane. She wet a finger and marked where his chin hit.

"What's that for?"

"I think you're growing."

He knew he was. His pants had shrunk so much almost half his lower leg stuck out, and Merri's little coverall was getting very short and tight on her rump. He could talk better, his mouth almost able to keep up with his thoughts, for once. He no longer felt like a sausage that might burst its casing, or tinder that might burst into flame with his anger at what he could not do. His body could almost keep up with his mind, and Merri's, too. They were changing, even in the weeks they'd been here. It proved him right. Something in the valley filled him up, and Merri as well. But what?

He stared back at the empty pastures, wondering what his sister saw. He saw lines of power that he could tug on and knot and stir around but knew he shouldn't. What lay out in the open, coating the pasture during the day, felt wrong. Nighttime brought a different power, sprinkled in dewdrops over the bent grasses and weeds. Silvery dots came out of the ground and bounced along until they formed a small river, more than one, ribbons of silver wavering along the fence lines and pathways and groves. They looked so real, he thought he could poke one with his finger if they went out to see. The frowning man slept, but he had a lock on the door, and even though Evar could get his fingers on it, he hadn't quite puzzled out how it worked. Yet. The floating ribbons had to wait. Perhaps another week. Two at the most. And after he poked them, what then? What if they struck him down, like a sword slicing through him? He hadn't ever seen a sword do that, but he'd seen the curved scythe the frowning man used to keep grasses and brush clear of the cabin. Swish and gone. A man would be much harder, but metal could cut deep if swung hard enough. He thought of all his clay soldiers left behind, left at home. Now when he played, he'd understand what happened to them when they fell over. They could be cut in two. Or lose an arm or a leg. He shivered.

Merri tugged on him again. "Can you see it?" Her whispery voice tickled the side of his neck.

"See what?"

"The man." And she pointed a finger which had once been that of a chubby toddler but now was more like his, slimmer and definitive.

He squeezed his vision tighter, unable to believe she could see something he didn't. "Where?"

"There, sitting on the fence. He's got all white hair and sharp blue eyes. He looks like one of your soldiers."

Evar blinked rapidly two or three times, and then he saw the figure, head turned as if he could see them watching through the window as he balanced on the top railing of the fence. The man's head turned back and Evar could see he watched something else, something Evar couldn't see. "What's he watching?"

"He's watching Dayne. And a hole in the sky."

"What?"

She waved one small fist. "A hole. In the sky. And Dayne is standing there, and he's got his sword out and . . . oh, Mama! Mama's there!" Her voice rose in excitement. He had to whirl around and clasp his hand to her mouth to muffle any further words. Her mouth worked against the palm of his hand. "She's covered in blood, Evar!"

He pressed hard. "Don't wake up the frowning man!"

She grew still in his hold. When he pulled his hand away, he had to wipe it on his pants, and she wiped slobber from her mouth on the back of her fingers. "Ick."

"Quiet."

"I saw Mama! She looked all fierce and she had a sword and she was all covered in blood. She was hopping mad. I saw it!"

"Then you saw something awful, Merri, and you can't talk about it."

"Awful? Was it bad?"

"Yes, if Mama has blood on her, it's bad. Very bad."

"She didn't look broken. She looked . . . she looked angry. Like the time she caught the blacksmith whipping our pony when he wouldn't stand still for new shoes."

Evar remembered that. It had happened when the days first started getting really long and really hot. The smithy had come by to do some shoeing and their cart pony wouldn't let him pick up his hooves or stand still. The man had gotten redder and redder in the face, with sweat soaking his shirt and pouring off his face until finally he'd let out a string of very loud words and began to whip their pony. Nutmeg had charged out of the house kitchen and grabbed the whip out of the smithy's hand with a few loud words of her own. She held a pail of cold water in her other hand and promptly dumped it over the top of the man's head before leading their pony off and yelling at the smithy to go away. She had been very very angry then. As angry as he could remember, even at them. Merri had told Evar then that the pony would have stood still if she could have talked a bit to him. The big, sweaty man scared him.

At dinner when Nutmeg told them, Dayne had clamped his mouth shut, unable to say a word, but Grampa Tolby had rocked back in his chair and laughed and laughed until Grandma Lily had to go and get him a clean handkerchief. Then he'd leaned forward and kissed their mother on the cheek, saying she should always look out for those who couldn't defend themselves. Evar and Merri had stayed quiet, unable to express what they wanted.

Evarton took a step back from the window. He couldn't remember understanding at the time, but he understood now. She'd stopped that man from beating their pony which hadn't known any better and couldn't help himself. He ran his fingers through his tangled hair. What he didn't understand was why Dayne hadn't said much.

"He's gone," Merri told him. "It's all gone."

He didn't know what any of it meant or why Merri had seen it and he couldn't until she told him about it, and he didn't know what he could do about it. He scrubbed his nose.

"Can I look again tomorrow night?" She peered up at him, her small face trusting.

"Yes. Every night till we figure it out."

She threw him a happy smile before lowering herself from the window and walking very quietly back to their cots where she climbed in, rolled onto her stomach, turned her face to the window, and fell asleep. Evar watched her. She did not ever seem to worry about anything for long. He already knew, even as a child, that his world was far different from hers, and he had to protect her from it. He wondered if his world would change or if hers would?

The frowning man liked them to work. When they'd found all the dried patties they could and stacked them up, he sent them to look for kindling wood. Merri enjoyed that, because it sent them into the shady fringes of the pastured valley, along the tree line which edged the grass. There were many small branches and twigs to be picked up and even the tiny bugs that crawled among them didn't dismay her. They invariably bit Evar and left him with a variety of welts and itchy spots which his sister would soothe away with a touch and a grin, telling him, "They don't eat me! You must taste good."

He did not find that as funny as she did. To compensate, he would occasionally dump a handful of crumpled fall leaves down the back of her coveralls. The frowning man thought that unacceptable and would yell at both of them for their antics. He sent away for clothes and shoes, grumbling that he'd been lied to, they weren't toddlers at all but clearly children, and children who'd reached a growth spurt at that. The shoes that came by special horseman were too long, but he packed the toes with a soft sock and showed them how to wear them. Merri's fit quite a bit better, but Evar had to take his socks out after a week or two because his foot was growing into the shoe. Even with new clothes, his pants never seemed to cover his ankles and calves.

What the two of them noticed more and more was that Evar grew almost too tall to look out the small window comfortably, while Merri shot up so that her nose would touch the exact center of the window glass when she did, and he had to crouch down a bit. Growing up made things easier, but it scared Merri. She got out of bed one night and crept over to Evar. She did not dare get in bed with him, because he struck out in his sleep and she might get hit. She sat quietly on the edge and looked at him, fixed her eyes on his face, and tried to not even blink. It always worked. Eventually.

"Gah! You're staring at me again." He wrestled his blanket aside.

"I can't sleep."

"And why not?"

She scratched at her knee. "I'm afraid Mama won't know us when we see her again. We're growing."

"She'll know us."

"Do you think?"

"A-course. Mamas always know their children!"

Now she scratched at her head. "But you're taller! And me, too. And thinner." Her mouth arched downward.

"When we see Mama again, she will yell our names and run forward and grab us in a hug."

"Both of us?"

"Both of us. At once."

"Are her arms big enough?"

"Yes," he said firmly. At least, as he remembered her, they were. If they weren't, she'd try at least. She wouldn't give up. He didn't think about Auntie Corrie often, she had never been one for hugs, and Dayne . . . well, Dayne was the one who would toss them in the air and then give them a big, swooping swing-about till their heads grew dizzy. Grandma Lily would put one or the other on her knee while she worked at the loom, and

Grandpa Tolby would walk the vineyards with them, slowly, so they could investigate the growing fruit, and then he would walk home with first one, then the other on his shoulders. They all gave them hugs but none so tight or wonderful as their Mama. What he didn't understand, and what he couldn't convince either himself and his sister of, was why no one had come for them. His nose prickled with heat and, afraid he might cry in front of Merri, he scrubbed at it, hard.

Merri touched her fingertips to his cheek. "It'll be all right."

He grabbed her hand in his. "You know, the lady is coming to see us soon."

"I know."

"She wants our secrets."

"Probably."

"No probably about it—that's why she stole us! And we can't let her know. She's not a good person."

Merri turned her face up to him. "I won't tell. Not even if she hurts me."

"And I won't even if she hurts me," Evarton vowed back to her. But he stopped then, and it felt as though his tongue had fastened itself to the roof of his mouth. He wasn't at all certain he could be quiet if the lady or anyone decided to hurt Merri to make him tell. He took a deep breath. He might have to do something then, something big and terrible and deadly.

Evar swung off his cot, took his sister by the arm, and walked her to her blankets to tuck her in. She curled on her side, and he rubbed the back of her neck until he heard her slight, fuzzy snore before he left her, but he walked to the window instead of to his bed. He did have to slump down a bit to see out, but the sight that met his eyes made the effort worthwhile. Silvery ribbons of light and dew danced over the grasslands, overflowing from the brook which edged the valley. He longed to touch them, to see what he could make of them, and he pressed one hand flat against the barrier of the window. He drew in the misty exhalations of his breath with his other hand, his fingertip making spiral dances that matched the movement of what he watched. As he did, a woman arose out of the dew and sparkle, her body ghostlike but clearly a woman of beauty and grace, as different from his mother who he knew to be beautiful as he was different to Merri in looks. The river woman wore a cloak of running dew drops that caught the dark blue of the night as well as the silvery fog from the grass. She watched him, but when he reached for her with his thoughts and his intent to make her real, a gust slapped him back from the window, nearly slamming him into a wall.

Evar straightened, shakily. He came back to the pane but did not dare touch his hands to it. The river woman wagged a finger at him in denial. Not yet, she told him silently. She floated across the grasses, through the fencing and came near the small cabin. He could feel a sudden chill in the air as she dipped down so she could look him in the eye.

Words spilled over into his head. *Call me Andredia.* And she bent near enough to the window to look him straight in the eye, and he recognized the stern yet handsome face of Warrior Queen Lariel masking the face of the river woman. *Remember.*

Evar took a hasty step backward as he could feel the power build up yet again, but she did not slap at him. Instead, she grew tall and he had to press his nose to the pane to see all of her though his heart beat loudly in his chest as he did, cold fear rising. She seemed to be waiting.

"I-I-I'll remember."

The woman nodded at him and then strode away from the cabin, each step taking in all the dew and fog on the ground, inhaling it, until all silvery magic dancing over the pasture disappeared into her figure as she stepped into the small river and disappeared. He thought about Merri's vision which she had not seen again, although she sometimes talked about a great bridge with terrible things marching on it, things she wouldn't tell him about. He thought about the valley filling him and his sister with . . . well, he still was not quite sure what it was. He thought it felt like magic, even if it was not the magic he'd been born with, or if he could do good with it. It had grown their bodies to fit their deeds, and he feared it wasn't done with them yet.

His hands shook as he tumbled into his cot. He lay on his back looking at the night-cloaked ceiling for a very long time before sleep finally came for him.

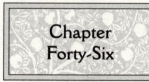

Chapter
Forty-Six

"COME ON, COME ON, wake up, ya little bastiges." He yanked the covers off of them and slapped their bare feet with his hand. "Rise and shine, ya whiny bags of snot."

Merri rose with a gulping snuffle, but Evar shot out of bed, his lips curled back from his teeth like a disgruntled hound. However, the frowning man paid him no attention, already beyond reach of his bite, if he had intended one. In the darkness, his defiance went unseen. Daylight had yet to flood the dusty old bunkhouse, and it looked as muddy and dark as the bottom of a well. Merri tried to swallow down her dismay, but her snuffles turned to hiccups as she did until even her brother shoved her in the shoulder.

"Stop that!"

"I—I can't." She plopped down miserably on the bed's edge and waved a shoe at him. "My shoes hurt."

"Whatcha mean?" He thought he might guess, because his own shoes pinched his toes horribly and he wasn't even sure if he could get them back on his feet. So soon after he'd thought he had her fixed for shoes, but that was before her nose reached the middle of the small window's pane. He sat down next to her, the wobbly cot creaking under both their weight. She shifted and the cot made a low groan as if it would collapse completely. He took the shoe from her hand. "It hurts where?"

She pinched the toe. "I'm all squinched up."

He nodded, looking at her shoe. The weather still held warm days, but the nights had started going cold. She needed shoes on her feet. Evar got off the cot and padded into the kitchen, looking for a sharp knife. It took a lot of tries before he found part of a broken-off scissor, a single blade with handle. He sawed the end of her shoe off, his face knotted in concentration, his breathing harsh until he muscled the leather off. Then he did the same with her other shoe and when he was done, Evar secreted the blade away under his straw mattress, in case he needed it later. His own shoes would be ready to be cut open in a day or two, he reckoned. It was the meadow filling them up and now, spilling over.

The side of a fist thundered against the little wooden door, shaking the entire bunkhouse. "Git your scrawny little butts out here, NOW."

Evar shoved himself into his clothes and took Merri by the elbow, hauling her along with him while she hopped on one foot, getting her shoe on the other. Her little pink toes stuck out, but she'd stopped crying and turned her face on him, aglow with a smile. She bustled out the wooden door and grabbed her bucket by its rusty bail and stood at attention, waiting for the frowning face to give her chores until breakfast.

Evar took his place beside her, and he could hear the tiny rumble of her stomach, soon to be echoed by his own. They'd be lucky if they had breakfast. Frowning face didn't always like to make porridge, and there were days when he went off hunting for himself, coming back empty-handed but smelling of wood smoke and grilled meat. He'd been told to keep them alive, but he'd once hauled Evar up by the shirt collar and lifting him up off the ground till their noses nearly met, told Evar he didn't have to keep them plump.

"Scour the groves. I want tinder and kindling, the small, dry stuff from you two. I'll haul the bigger branches. Rain is in the wind, and it'll be a wet night. Wet season is nearly here. Best to get wood ready for the next few days, or we'll all be freezing our asses off. Got it?"

Merri nodded rapidly, hair bouncing.

Evar lifted a shoulder, looking up. "We need a breakfast, later."

"Mebbe. Mebbe not." Frowning face ran his fingernails through his stubbly beard. "If you git your jobs done quick. Bring back your buckets a coupla times and we'll see."

Merri took off running. Evar let her go and stared at frowning face. "We get breakfast."

The man shrugged. "A'right, a'right. Now on with you, shit for blood."

Evar went after Merri, not wanting to let her get too far ahead. The woods hereabouts seemed devoid of large prey, but that could change as autumn weather bore down on them, and the big predators got hungrier as the cold dropped its curtain. These things he'd heard from Tolby and

Dayne and Hosmer when he was still small, but he remembered. She could protect herself, he thought, if she could gather her scattered thoughts. He could feel the frowning man staring at his back as he ran.

The bails dug into their hands as the buckets gained weight, so Merri stopped gathering long enough to braid soft rushes to wrap about them. He wandered off as he heard a buzzing, and when he found the hive in a fallen tree trunk, he plundered as big a piece of honeycomb as he could manage without too many stings, and wrapped it in his handkerchief, and stuffed it in his trousers. Merri had to heal him of his stings before they started filling their buckets again. All the preparations slowed them down and by the time dawn had stretched to midmorning, her stomach growling had grown louder and louder. They had gathered three buckets each to the frowning man's one wheelbarrow load of wood as he sat on the front stoop, drinking from a tin cup and enjoying the sun's rays while he could, as the promised clouds curled at the sky's edge. Merri sat down as Evar filled the sheltered trough with the last of their kindling and dropped the buckets.

"Breakfast."

"Think you earned it, do ya?"

Evar grabbed his sister's hand and showed him the blisters and streaks of blood, despite the reed covers she'd made. "We did what you said."

"Aye and took her fair time, dincha? Go on, there's a pot on the fire." He jabbed a thumb in the air, pointing behind him.

Merri bolted to her feet and led the way, but she stood over the pot with a disgusted look on her face. "It's all dried up. Burned on the bottom." She pulled a wooden spoon out, holding up a clump of what was meant to be porridge and now clung, solid and chunky, to the spoon.

"Don't worry." He patted his pocket. "We got that honeycomb we found earlier. We'll just paint the honey over the bad parts and dream of Mama's cookies."

And they did, eating the chunky, dried-out yet still warm cereal with honey drizzled all over its nooks and crannies and it was almost good. He wrapped his honeycomb back in his handkerchief and stowed it away with the scissor blade, thinking that he was growing a treasure. He did not like to think what else he might have to use the blade on, but he felt a little better for having it. They washed up and set the pot to soaking after they had scraped it as clean as they could. Then he had to help Merri wash her face (how did she get honey stuck in her eyebrows??) before going out to see what other chores the frowning man had for them.

He'd fallen asleep in the sun, hands clasped over a belly that showed under his thin shirt. The frown had almost slipped away, leaving heavily tanned skin that showed few lines. He had an underlying copper tone to his Vaelinar complexion as a few did, but Evar was fascinated by the change in the frowning man. He looked almost . . . nice. If he looked nice in his sleep, in his dreams, then it was something dreadful that turned him nasty when awake. Evar couldn't think of anything he and Merri had done to earn such hatred. It just simply seemed to be.

He turned away before the man could wake and before he said anything, but as they slipped past, Merri stubbed her bare toes on the rough-hewn steps and cried out. He came awake abruptly, eyes clear and forehead immediately sinking into deep lines, hand going to his belt where he kept his weapon sheathed, a wicked and curved short sword. It wouldn't be much good for stabbing, but it would be a devastating slicer, Evar figured. That much he knew from the many toy soldiers he'd once had and the times he and Dayne had spent skirmishing with them. He rubbed his forehead. So many more thoughts got in now than used to. The valley kept filling them up every day, and he wondered if his head would begin spilling over like a too full pot set to boiling.

The frowning man waved over to the pastures. "We got fences to fix."

Merri stood on one foot with her hand about her other one, in midair. "I don't know how." She worried at getting the other shoe on and finally achieved it.

"Oh, don't ya worry, little shit-blooded bastige. I'll be teaching ya. Follow me." He glanced at Merri's feet. "What th' cold hell did ya do that for?"

"My shoes won't go on my feet." Her face wrinkled up, eyes brimming. "So my toes have to stick out."

"Doncha be crying over that." He cast his knotted-up gaze on Evarton. "What about ya feet?"

"Shoes are tight. Sir."

"Weeds. Filthy choking weeds ye are." He spat off into the dirt. The frowning man made a noise deep in his throat. "We'll see about thet. Now, on with ya. Plenty of daylight left for work."

By the time the sun hung directly over the horse pastures, Evar had learned what he could of fence building and most of that was that neither he nor Merri were big or strong enough to do it successfully. The frowning man didn't seem to care if they did it right, only if they struggled hard while doing it. Merri's hair grew damp with sweat, and her face which already carried their mother Nutmeg's natural apple-blushed cheeks grew vibrantly pink. Post splinters filled their hands, and dirt buried itself deep under their nails. The bales of braided wire sprung on them more than once, flinging one or the other halfway across the fallow meadows, much to the amusement of the frowning man.

Evar heard his sister's cry behind him as the wire snapped into its coil once more, this time imprisoning her inside and he rushed to free her, the sound of harsh laughter at his heels. He burned at the sound of it, punctuating Merri's plea for help. He grasped her trembling hand. "I'll get you out."

Sweat or maybe it was tears slicked her face. "It hurts. All over."

He could see the purple bruising on her arms and ankles and where her shirt had pulled away from her stomach. She chewed on her lower lip. He knew what she prepared to do, and she couldn't, not here, not now, not with the frowning man watching. He leaned close.

"Don't make it better."

"But it *hurts*, Evar."

"No! We can't show him what we do. Remember what Auntie said." He took his mouth away from her ear and concentrated on pulling the wire rounder open so he could tug her free. He could feel the silver energy from the valley coiling up inside him. If he wanted, he could make wire fences all along the pastures, so many they would never need a fence again. He could do it. It swelled inside of him, up his throat, until the words and power shoved to break free.

But he did not dare. Merri couldn't, and he couldn't. This was terrible, but something worse waited for them if they did. He didn't know what, but it had scared Grampa Tolby and Grandma Lily and Mama and Dayne and Auntie Corrie. They were broken somehow, inside, and if they showed it, the frowning man might hurt them dreadfully. This beautiful valley, lonely and stretching in front of them, held a deadly trap waiting to chomp them up. He knew it.

"Pull," he told her, swallowing his power and his fear. "I'll get you out."

They grasped their hands tightly, small hands compared to those of the frowning man, but Evar could feel the strength and magic running through them. He knotted his fingers about it tightly and slowly, determinedly, pulled his sister free. She lay on the grass at his feet for a moment, curled up in pain and gasping a bit, and he said nothing but stared at the frowning man. Stared hard enough to burn holes. The man turned his face away from them.

When Merri uncurled, he set her on her feet. The two of them brushed her off and about, making sure she hadn't broken a bone or was bleeding anywhere. She hissed between her teeth at nearly every touch but made no attempt to heal herself although she trembled with the effort not to. He pressed her shoulder gently. "I know it hurts."

Her eyes looked up at him hopefully. "Tonight?"

He nodded.

Balling her hands into fists, she wailed, "I can't wait."

"You have to."

"It hurts me all over."

"Merri, you can't."

She put the knuckles of her right hand to his cheekbone where the wire had whipped up against him. It'd hurt sharply then, but he'd nearly forgotten it. He winced now as she touched him. "It'll make a mark." She opened her hand and laid her palm to his face; he felt a brief, warm glow. "There. Better."

And when she dropped her hand, she balled it up again, her knuckles white. "I won't do anymore," she told him. "Till tonight."

Over the top of her head, he could see the frowning man watching them intently again. Evar hugged Merri carefully as the man called out gruffly, "Back to work or there'll be no dinner."

Evar stooped to the braided wire and loosed just enough of his power to make it more supple and easier to handle. The metal warmed under his fingers in answer, telling him it was ready and eager to do whatever he asked of it, but he bit the inside of his cheek instead, a warning to himself that they were being watched most carefully.

He pulled the wire bale open, instructed Merri to stand on it while he unrolled the rest of the length, and then the two of them struggled to cut the length and hold it while the frowning man nailed it firmly into place. They set new posts the rest of the day until Merri fell to her knees with a little whimper. Then the frowning man glanced at the sun low in the sky.

"That'll do," he told him. "Get back and clean up. I'll check the traps for dinner."

And while it wasn't cooked long enough to be truly tender, the long-ear stew they had tasted really good. Long after the sun had set and a sliver of the moon appeared, the frowning man finally fell asleep, and Merri could tend to their wounds. She did so, shaking with tiredness. Evar could feel the power flickering in her like the fretful flame of a candle with wind flowing over it, but they were mostly better before they fell into their cots.

Evar didn't know why the frowning man hated them, but he knew that he hated the man back. He also felt sure that he would grow to hate him even more over the coming days and nights.

THE APPROACHING NIGHT shivered over him. Bregan sat hunched with his arms folded over his head, enjoying the silence of the evening, the silence that had settled about him like a mantle for weeks now. Blessed quiet. He couldn't train in the quiet and knew that, but he didn't mind it for his ears still felt raw from listening. The Gods did not speak in patient or gentle tones. No, they railed at him. Shrieked and hammered. Whined until they hit a high note that sliced through him. There was one voice, soft and low, but what it said was so appalling, so disgusting and gruesome, that he would rather the voice disappear in a cacophony of noise like the others than to be audible. Sibilant, it cut through the other voices easily, but it was the voice he wished to hear the least of all of them. It made his head throb and his stomach knot, and it dripped like rancid grease down the back of his throat. When that voice had left him a day or so ago, he rejoiced although he knew it was only a matter of time until it returned. He had eaten and slept better than he had in too many seasons to recall, and he wished he could count better than that, but memory eluded him now more often than not.

No, he embraced the silence he found now, not knowing how he'd achieved it but infinitely grateful it had come to him. Bregan put his arms down at his sides and rolled his shoulders to ease the tense muscles there a bit. Today, he felt almost like himself again: Bregan Oxfort, a Master Trader, son of Willard Oxfort, head of the Hawthorne Guild of Traders.

He dipped a hand in his pocket, finding nothing more than a loose thread or two and some lint. Should he not have a few gems and some gold pieces in various denominations, and perhaps even a crinkled paper bill or two? It seemed he eschewed wealth as well as his former status.

He peeled his shirt away from his rib cage, scarcely more than a rag, and wondered at his wearing of it. The tattered trousers that covered his lower limbs accomplished the job only a bit better, and his elvish brace gleamed from ankle to mid-thigh over the one pants leg, giving it a chance at fewer tears and holes than the left. He peered at his feet, hardened and brown, shoved into old sandals though it was obvious he often went barefoot. Had he fallen, or had he simply degraded into this state? Bregan tilted his head to one side, remembering rich clothes and jewelry as befit a Kernan of Master Trader status.

That was, of course, before he'd lost his mind as well as his purse. He knotted his fingers in his trouser leg and, not surprisingly, the fabric gave way to a gaping hole. He'd have to beg for more clothes. A chilly tug in the wind told him of the changing seasons with winter near. He'd have to do his begging soon, or the cold would accomplish what the voices had not. He rubbed his hand over his arm. The skin, brown and freckled and weathered, reminded him of the arms of caravan drivers, free-striding and living men that Bregan had never thought he would, or wanted to, resemble although he had escorted his father and his own caravans many a time. He had, however, worn shirts with billowing sleeves to protect his arms, as well as long, soft pants to cover his legs, boots as soft as a baby's skin, and a wide-brimmed hat to keep the sun from his eyes and face. He must have shed all those long ago.

The wind came about again, a tiny puff against the side of his face, a tease. He flicked it off, like an annoying insect. The wave of his hand left an arc of color in its wake about his head, and he stared at it for long moments until the colors faded away completely. The ground underneath him trembled slightly, as if a very heavy footfall nearby sounded, although he knew of no one large enough to make the very earth shake. The earth shook when volcanoes stirred to life—only one or two on this vast continent—but it was said the island continent to the south held a number of active volcanoes which could rumble to life. And there were those times when whatever God who wore the world on its back simply tired of the burden and shifted, often carelessly and without heed for whatever destruction might be caused. The world was full of structures laid low, all with little or no warning.

Bregan lifted his chin a bit. In past days, the old war hammer Rakka had shaken city walls and even mountains from their foundations when struck by its wielder. Diort built his empire from those struck down by the hammer when they would not yield to him, but he had given warning, in all fairness. In those past days, a God of Kerith had been laid inside the war hammer while it was being made, and a bargain had been struck between the maker—Quendius and his hound Narskap—and Abayan Diort. His guardian had not kept that bargain, ultimately, and the demon fled when the hammer fell at Ashenbrook, helping to save the day for Bistel and Lariel's forces, fell for good rather than the total domination Quendius had intended. But those were the last times Bregan could remember anything making the earth rattle beneath him, quite as it did now. Memories moved him now.

He spread his hands out, palms up, as if he could reflect the dusk from them, reluctant to give up the day to night, savoring his quietude. He so rarely knew who and when and where he was these days. The power of the Mageborn burned through him like a hot knife through sweet churned butter and left him behind in a puddle, more often than not. He had no more control of his powers than a newborn did of its body, and despite Diort's patient guardianship, the situation did not seem to be improving. Unless one could count these days of silence as an improvement, which gave him hope that there might be more facing him.

When the first purple shades of true night began to creep over his form, devouring him bit by bit, the whispering began.

Bregan dropped his face into his hands, hunched over in despair. Yet these were not the voices which normally excoriated him, reviling him for being unable to follow their needs and desires. No. These voices spoke more kindly to him, offering hope and even praise, as a moment which might change all drew near, and gave him a role to play in it. Redemption hung within his grasp, redemption and mastery of his powers, along with retribution for those who had affronted the Gods. All that had bedeviled him these past years, now boiled in a stew. Yet around all the pleased, encouraging voices surrounding him, the other voice slid in, stealthy and beslimed, hissing its disagreeable suggestions that made it all the more unpalatable.

Bregan whipped a hand out in a snap of power and caught it by the neck, this thing that reviled him. He could not see it, but it writhed and snarled at him, the air about it disrupted as if something yet unseen existed there and flailed about in a great but useless struggle.

Bregan blinked. He stared at his left hand, grasping something un-known but definitely filling his hold, as his hand and even his own arm bounced up and down in the struggle to keep it bound. His ears filled with the vile cursing of the thing, the voice no longer promising rewards but vowing a thousand terrible deaths to both him and his soul. Bregan swallowed tightly.

Then his other voices rose in quiet and confident praise for his capture, strong words that overrode the blight of the other's intonations, that drove it down even as his grip did, until it hung, quiescent, in his hand. It had not surrendered to him, but to the overbearing strains of the Gods and for the briefest of moments, Bregan shared a sympathy with whatever it was he'd caught, just as cowed and browbeaten as he was although he sensed the condition would not last.

He found himself spiraling inward into the crazed reality he could not avoid, but he retained enough of his former presence of mind to keep that thing in a firm hold. He staggered to his feet, with a single goal in mind, in this mind that the Gods controlled and pestered and corrupted to within a pinch of his life. He crossed the broken ground, heading toward the faint light of campfires and tent lanterns, in a single-minded journey.

Ceyla closed the tent canopy, before turning and looking at Diort who half-sat, half-lay in his familiar chair, his leather throne as it were, for he seldom returned to the city he had named his capital and where his true throne stood. She wondered if the nomad in him kept him camping in lands far from the center of his rule, shying away from city walls and paved streets. She sat on the tent floor next to him, crossing her legs and tucking her feet a bit under her, enjoying the smile she awakened. "Dinner and a reading?"

"Dinner, of a certainty, and no, not a reading. Just company tonight, unless you mind."

A flush of happiness stained her cheeks. How could he think she would mind being asked to stay with him? He forced her into nothing, not conversation, not prophesying, and never love. But it remained wondrous to her that if she were to offer any of those, he eagerly accepted, and returned it equally. She had grown to love him, and he'd revealed that he, in turn, loved her. What more could she ask? There were few things she could even call to mind.

He put his hand on her shoulder. "I take your silence as interest?"

"Interest and wonder."

"Wonder?"

"Yes. Always. That one such as I—" Her thought caught in her throat, and words failed her.

"If I could take anything from you, it would be that."

"What?"

"Your need to count yourself as less. You're not less to me, you are more. You bring intelligence, soul, and beauty to my life." He put his hand out to her, to catch her up and draw her close.

Ceyla thought to feint away, to play, but something in the air pierced her, driving away her humor and leaving only the darkest of fears. The hairs on the back of her neck stood up, prickling and stiff in warning. Trouble, running at them, like a wild animal in a charge, and her voice stuck, unable to utter a warning. She scrambled ungracefully to her feet, mouth working to say what she could not, hands waving about. Alarmed, Diort came to his feet, too. The bent and shambling figure of Bregan burst into the tent, and Abayan straightened to meet him but not in time. Bregan grabbed up the war hammer, pivoted and swung before his target realized he was attacking. It slammed into the side of Diort's face. Flesh and bone were assaulted as Diort staggered back, too stunned to cry out. He put an arm out, across Ceyla, trying in vain to protect her.

The war hammer drew back for another blow. "You'll not stop me!" shouted Bregan.

Ceyla fell as Abayan did, throwing her body over his, before Bregan could strike him again, and trembled, waiting for the bone-crashing blow. But it did not strike. She turned her head and saw him thrust his left hand onto the hammer, doing a stiff-legged dance of force that she could not comprehend, but then he lifted the war hammer and pointed at the tent ceiling in triumph.

"Rakka!" he shouted, and she swore she saw the hammer twist and thrust upward as if in answer.

Diort groaned, shifting under her. Bregan spun about as Ceyla watched him, crooning soft words to her wounded lord, trying to keep him still as the agitated Mageborn eyed them both with wild eyes. She put her left hand out toward Bregan.

"What are you doing?"

His hair fairly crackled about his head with the energy sparking about him and pulling his limbs this way and that into a palsied effigy of dance.

"Rakka is reborn!" He pumped it up and down, the sinews standing out on his wiry frame as he did. "Earth-shaker will shout again, in my hands."

Diort moaned again, half-sitting up despite her efforts to keep him down and quiet lest Bregan attack him again. Blood flowed freely down his face.

Bregan leaped toward them, landing within a hand's width, and bending over, laughing in his broken voice, the gaze in his eyes piercing. He held the war hammer high as it rumbled with a voice of its own, one of a terrible thunder that threatened to shred their ears. "The Gods call me! I am going to break the world!" With that, he bounded away, out of the tent and into the night where a terrible wind arose and the canvas about them rippled as if asail on a high and troubled sea before all fell into a deep quiet.

"Gods help us." Diort tried to stand and failed as she caught him up again and held him tightly, the wound from his temple and scalp bleeding what seemed to her to be buckets, cascading over both of them.

"We have to stop him."

Diort pressed his hand wide-fingered over his head, blood leaking through abundantly, streaming down the back of his wrist. "And how might we do that?"

"Rakka is yours. Surely it will still answer to you."

"Did you not see him shove another demon into its being?"

"Saw and felt."

Diort rocked back on one heel, almost leaning back more than he could balance, and his other hand closed tightly on her shoulder as he fought to save himself. "If you're counting on my being able to stop Bregan, don't. The Gods have set him loose. These are my Gods, not yours, and they are awake and angry."

"Someone has to be able to stop him."

Leaning heavily on her, Diort threw back the tent flap as men came scurrying to her call for aid. "If the Gods have called for him to break the world, it's likely none of us can stop him. I fear all we can do is hope to survive."

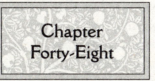

Chapter
Forty-Eight

DAYS PASSED WITHOUT WORD, except a tiny patch of letter that Nutmeg got from the Barrels, dispatched by the local tinker-trader who wound her way down to Calcort eventually. They reminisced about their acquaintances and rued that the legendary Robin Greathouse no longer traveled the roads, and finally the tinker passed over the missive, sent by one Joniah Barrel whom she remembered as being shorter than knee-high last time she'd seen the Barrel family. He wrote word that he'd come across Dayne and traded a horse to him. That had been, by the time the crumpled and wax-sealed page reached her, an age past. She carried the letter in her apron, for all the comfort it gave her, and watched the vineyards, knowing that she would have to hire whoever she could for the harvest which should be handled any day now. Wait too long and the rains could blight the grapes. Wait too long and anything horrible could happen. Had already happened, and more might befall her. Tolby had sent Lily a briefer letter saying only that Corrie had been found dead, killed by those she'd been in league with. Not a letter anyone would cherish.

She stood outside the cider barn and stretched her back, achy and tight from having leaned over the curing table since early morning, checking the progress of the restoration. The fine dust of the aryn added to the current batch of tincture seemed to be the final ingredient necessary for success. Dayne and Tolby had been remarking on it, just the day before—was it?— the twins had been taken. She kicked the barn doors closed behind her.

She did not expect word but thought that somehow, some way, they would find her children and get a message sent home. Summer edged to autumn, denying her that hope. Nutmeg folded her arms. Lara had not sent any further word other than that she had troops searching as well, having given up the search herself because of other responsibilities. No hint of ransom for them. No message of self-satisfied arrogance from Tressandre. Nothing but silence.

Nutmeg snatched off the lenses which not only protected her face from the curative spray but also magnified the pages on each book so that she could see definitively the work needed. Each inked letter could be delineated so clear and crisp that she could see if the black mold had indeed retreated—no—been wiped entirely from the volume.

If only Tressandre ild Fallyn were a black mold. She would wilt and collapse into a slimy heap as Nutmeg sprayed her from head to toe and watched her disintegrate—

Nutmeg pursed her lips and blew out a disgusted sigh. She took off her bonnet to fan her face, attacked by her anger as much as by the heat. She did not like standing by and waiting for word on the fate of her children.

Hers. Not Jeredon's, for he'd never lived long enough to put his hand on her burgeoning stomach. Not Lara, for all her care of Nutmeg was that she held the two heirs to her kingdom. Not her father, bless his heart, or her mother, or her brothers. No. They were hers, and here she stood in the dirt road and whined because she knew nothing of their whereabouts.

A silverwing arced by overhead, its wings catching the light with its metallic glow, and she traced its flight. Where did it go and why? It seemingly paid no attention to the cityscape stretched beneath it, and why would it? It had no training or reason to bind it to Calcort. That jogged a notion in her mind abruptly.

Nutmeg whirled around and tied her bonnet to the cider barn handle. No more. She would stand and wait no more. She'd be patient waiting for the harvest of grapes, but not this harvest. Not this one. She took to her heels and her guards, who had been lazing in the heavy sun, hurried to follow after.

Across town, where the edges of Calcort became ragged and seedy and lesser establishments filled the quarter, she found the man she wanted. As soon as she entered, he looked up, his face as sharp-edged as some of the birds he trained. "What word?"

He shook his head. "None, Mistress Farbranch. I'd have sent it if there'd been anyway."

"Unless Vaelinar coin is worth more than my own."

"No, no. I work for the mayor and people of Calcort. How can you say that?"

"You sent birds out for the auntie of my children, did you not?"

"Well, I—I—suppose I might have. A customer. She wrote to family, I thought."

"She wrote to the ild Fallyn, and you knew that as well, for the birds only go where they're trained to fly! A traitor camped in my home, and you never said a word! So how am I to know what coin rules you now?"

The bird master shrank back against the corner post of his open-air shed as she took a deep breath.

Nutmeg yelled at the bird master. She called him for his treachery and his love of monetary gain, his lack of loyalty, and threatened to set her brother Hosmer on him and his humble rookery. No one had come winging back with a message in the last few weeks. Not a single bird. Not a single letter. So he said, but how was she to believe him? How could anyone trust him again?

The guards outside the building hunched their shoulders against her shrill voice; she saw them straighten up as she darted outside the bird master's quarters, her face hot and her throat aching. She paused long enough to toss over her shoulder, "Inform the city guard that this man was sending birds to ild Fallyn fortress in secret. He should be watched."

Her breathing didn't slow down until she reached her mother's shop, with home full of empty rooms waiting for her just down the street. As she stood at the doorway, two women brushed past her, both Vaelinars but from the East coast where the wearing of veils and gauzy tunics trimmed with small tinkling bells were all the fashion. She saw the flash of their jewel-colored eyes as they looked, assessed, and moved past, veils hiding the shapes of their mouths. Approval or disapproval? No way to tell, but she could guess. The news of her diatribe had become the topic of gossip as soon as her words hit the air, racing like wildfire over dried-out summer hills. She took a steadying breath as she entered, and her mother looked up from the big cutting and measuring table that took up much of the room in the entryway.

"Meg," she said softly.

"I know, I know." She lifted her hands, still knotted in fists, and uncurled reluctant fingers before dropping her hands back to her sides. She plopped down on a nearby stool. "I know."

"What can we do?"

She shook her head. "Short of trapping Tressandre and wrapping my fingers tightly about her neck, I can't think of anything."

"You know your father and Verdayne haven't given up searching."

"There's nothing to find! She has to have them bundled away at her fort."

"We—Lariel—has spies there, we know that, and there's been no word. If she took them—"

"Who else would have?"

Lily stopped speaking a moment, lines at the corners of her mouth deepening. "It seems likely, but little evidence has been found. With Corrie dead, there's no direct connection, even if the bird master corroborates your accusation."

Nutmeg had been looking at the cutting table, littered with tiny scraps of fabric and loose threads, as scattered and difficult to read as the taking of her children. She lifted her gaze. "We know it has to be Tressandre."

"I agree, but again, we don't know that Corrie gave them over. It looks so, but we haven't proof. So, I ask, what more can we do but wait for the searchers to return, and wait for Lariel to take more direct action."

"But will she?"

"I think she loves them almost as much as you and I do."

Nutmeg let out a scoffing sound.

"Truly," Lily told her. "She sees Jeredon in Evar, I know she does."

"And Merri?"

"On the outside, Merri is a mirror to you, but inside, she carries her own Vaelinar traits. She may be the more formidable of the two. Evar can be read. Merri is cheer and laughter, but her eyes hold a much older wisdom." Lily crossed to her and took her hands up. Neither mother nor daughter had soft, unmarked hands. They were farmers and weavers, with the calluses and small scars—marks of years of hard work—to show for it. It struck Nutmeg for the first time how alike their hands were. She held her mother tightly for a moment before letting go and standing.

"I can't wait any longer."

Lily stepped back, with a tilt of her head, to watch her. "You need to be here when they're found."

Meg shook her head. "No. There has to be something else to be done. They're Vaelinars, and I've learned how to deal with them. I just have to think how to deal with this one." She brushed past her mother then, each stride quicker than the last one, until she burst into a run, heading for the farmhouse.

Inside, she sat at the old table. If she took the time, she could find the various initials of her brothers etched into the wood edge. She'd been dared to do the same but hadn't, determined then to be better mannered, a resolve that lasted until the day that she found an elven child dying on a battered and tiny raft as it carried her on the Silverwing River past their orchards. Finding Rivergrace had brought out two things in her: determination to be a leader, and a rebellion against things she felt were wrong. Perhaps it had been the wrist shackles that slipped easily off Grace's emaciated arms, leaving terrible scars behind from when they had fit too closely. Perhaps it had been the notion that she had to banish Grace's timidness and thrust her back into hearty living. Perhaps it had only been the realization that, with the addition of a sister, she was finally no longer grossly outnumbered in the family.

Nutmeg drummed her fingertips on the table. Over the years, she and Grace had learned much about the serpentine thinking of the Vaelinars, the elaborate back and forth and around. Tressandre had Lariel's heirs. What did she now plan to do with them, and how could Nutmeg circumvent that? The children had no other value than their bloodline, and without that, they possibly still would not live in ild Fallyn hands. Tressandre would dare much, but she wouldn't dare kill them now or they'd have been left for dead in their rooms by Auntie Corrie.

To kill those children now, outright, would set off a civil war among the Vaelinars, just as much as clearing out the Returnists squatting on the Andredia. Lariel had her hands tied.

But she did not. She, their mother.

A frisson crept across the back of her neck.

She crossed the farmhouse, most of it rebuilt since the fire two years ago, and went to her room. The hole in the deep adobe wall opened at her touch, even though the smoke still seemed to lie curled within, wrapped about the parcel she had hidden there. She drew it out, pushing the oilcloth aside, sneezing lightly at the smoky smell the volume retained. But the book remained intact, as she knew it had, though she rarely drew it out now, with Dayne living so close to her. Someday, Warlord Bistel had asked of her, someday she was to give this to his sons, when she deemed the time had come. She hadn't planned to for quite a while since she'd first begun to guess at Evar's abilities. And Merri, though she wasn't sure how much of Merri's magic came from her Vaelinar blood and how much from her Dweller stock. Still, she had thought the book had work to do for her own children before she passed it on. That thought had given her a great deal of guilt.

Nutmeg held the book to her chest. Who stood now for Evar and Merri? A handful of trackers scattered throughout the countryside? Everyone sent out at the beginning had faltered. Only Dayne and her father still combed the wilderness for a trail—even Lara had quit. She could not let them go. They were only children, pawns in a scheme of Vaelinar making that had been centuries in the spinning.

Now the fate had fallen into her hands and she intended to make the most of it.

She pulled several pieces of rag-paper from their stock and sat down with a pen. Words needed to be precise and counted, and she knew who would send it out. He would not dare to deny her wishes.

Tressandre. Meet at the Andredia soonest and I shall state in writing, I will lie, that Jeredon is not the father of my children when you safely return them to me.

She blotted the small paper carefully and read it over a number of times, her throat tight. Tressandre might decide other than Nutmeg hoped, but she knew full well what she was sending off this day. First, she revealed that both were hers, although if Tressandre had them, she would know from looking upon Evarton. Nutmeg had already given her something for nothing in this negotiation but hoped for a gain in return.

A lifeline for her two children.

She took the second piece of rag-paper and began to copy laboriously a chosen page of Bistel's journal. His careful writing blurred once or twice, and she bent low over it to ensure that she made no errors. When she had Tressandre at hand, and her children nearby, she would do what she had to do.

That page she sanded carefully before blotting, and put her book back into its precious hiding place. She knew little of Vaelinar magic, but this she knew. This Bistel had gifted to her in his last breaths.

At day's end, she returned to the bird master and he, pale of face and with a shaking hand, rolled up her message and sent it off. At the shop, her mother put her hand on her cheek and gave her a kiss to her forehead, without a word, not even one of comfort, for neither of them could think of anything to say to each other anymore. She arranged for hires to begin picking, as the nights had begun to hold the barest of chills which meant rain not far away, and the grapes needed to be in. Apples, brought in by wagon and cart, crate and barrel, would come later and could wait. She packed a spare pack, with only a second pair of shoes, a cloak, and a set of clothes for change, preparing for the days before she'd reach journey's end. The page she stowed next to her skin, inside her blouse and corset. She penned a quick note to her father to be read later, with as much explanation as she could bear, took one of Hosmer's city guard horses from the farmhouse stalls, and rode out.

Tolby rode into the yard of his home late, with the slanting sun throwing heavy shadows between the farmhouse and the cider barn. He'd bypassed the main gates of the city and taken lesser traveled alleyways and dirt roads to reach his quarter of Calcort, not wanting to deal with any who might accost him. His horse blew a loud sigh as he dismounted and led it off toward the stable. No one ran out to greet him, swinging doors slapping the door frame behind as they did. No one shouted a welcome to fracture the emptiness. He paused, assessing the area. Lily would be at her shop, no doubt, and he supposed Nutmeg with her. Hosmer would be on shift with his Guard and Keldan down at the stable yard where he worked and trained. He cared for his mount quickly and left it with a pat on the neck promising more attention later. The animal rolled an eye at him before shoving its muzzle deep into a rack of hay.

He should go and find Lily and tell her of the grievous news he carried, but he had no heart for it, knowing it would break hers to learn of Garner. He had another urgent task in mind which he vowed to accomplish before circumstances could sidetrack him. He threw open the great doors to the cider barn and entered, to find himself surrounded by the aroma of fresh-picked apples and of the mash left behind from the first crushes at the presses. Tolby stopped in his tracks, emotions torn. Someone had taken up his work. He found that both reassuring and disturbing that the world carried on without him, as he knew it must someday, just as they must carry on without Garner. He realized that the vineyard harvest would have been handled as well, with grapes waiting in the vats barn, perhaps even with the first barrels already filled there. He had trained his family for this over the years, the orchards, the vineyards, the harvest, the disposition of the crop, the fermenting, all of it. He had never foreseen the day when he would not be around to partake of it. That future now announced itself to him, not to be ignored. Tolby Farbranch had defied Time and knew that it would be catching up to him. He closed a hand.

"I'm still standing," he told the empty air. "And my family has done well by me." He shook himself, like an old dog upon rising from a sleep, and crossed the cider barn to find what he'd come for.

He found the small stack of aryn cuttings in a shadowed corner where Dayne had likely stored them. Most of the wood was not only dried but peeled, ready to become lumber and whatever else had been planned of it, scrap pieces for all of that, too precious to waste. He sank to his knees and dug through, piece by piece, with an ever-sinking heart. Then, his fingers seized upon that which he'd almost given up on finding: a limber branch of green wood, unpeeled, life still within it. This was not kindling. Prize in hand, Tolby rose up from his knees. He grabbed a small shovel leaning up by the door and returned outside. He paced the courtyard of his home first, and then turned to the well of sweet water that Rivergrace herself had cleansed, years and years ago, when they'd first come to this new home. He threw his head back and calculated the rooftops, the shadowing buildings encroaching upon the courtyard, and where the sun would and would not reach. And then, and only then, he paced off a small area and began to dig.

When he deemed the hole deep enough, he took up the pail from the well and drew up its waters, tying and untying the rope from the bail so he could lug it back and forth, filling the hole with water. As he stood over it, praying silently for the soul of his wayward son, drops fell into the dampness as if raindrops falling, and it took a moment for him to realize he had begun crying. He did not wipe his face, for it was no shame to cry for Garner and what the Farbranches had lost with his passing. Then he lowered the aryn cutting into the hole and, with his hands scooping the soft soil, filled it in and tamped it down. With each handful of dirt, Tolby recited a moment that they'd cherished with Garner, bits unimportant and important in his years with them, and when he finished, he crouched over the aryn, frowning a bit. He scooped up a last handful of dirt, murmuring over it, "And our wishes for the souls of those yet to depart, but who most certainly will, in these uncertain days. That those who are lost and may return to us or may not, that they may know they are loved and remembered. That those who have wronged us will know the balance that comes from living life itself, and that those who loved us will feel the joy of life in its fullest." Tolby let his handful of dirt trickle down upon the aryn to the last speck and then brushed his fingers clean.

He straightened his trousers and vest, hands patting his pocket until he found his pipe and pouch and striker. When his pipe began to fill the air with its soft, aromatic clouds, he turned to set off toward Lily's shop. He did not have far to go because he spotted her running down the lane toward him, alone, and he stopped to wait for her, his pulse quickening.

"Did you pass her? Did you see her on the road?"

"Who? What are you talking about, Lily?"

She threw her arms about his neck, holding tightly, breathless, her own heart beating wildly enough against his chest to make him afraid. When she pulled back, she answered the question hanging between them. "Nutmeg is gone."

"Gone?"

"Left. You missed her by three days."

He swallowed tightly. "After the children?"

"Of course. Weeks without word, she grew impatient. We heard nothing from you and little from Lariel and Bistane, and no one had seen the children pass by. She hatched a scheme of her own, I imagine; you know our daughter. She left word only that she headed to Larandaril. I've heard nothing since although I would think she has Lariel or Bistane woven into her scheme somewhere." Lily managed a wavering smile. She noted the tears that had tracked down the side of his face and wiped them away with the ball of her thumb. "But here you are home, and early, and without Verdayne. What's happened?"

He tightened his hand on her waist, pulled the small bundle of Garner's effects from his pocket, took her hand in his, and opened it up gently before placing the bundle into it. Lines deepening about her eyes and mouth, she let go of him and opened it, recognizing the amulet almost immediately, and noting the bloodstained cloth that wrapped it. She buckled. "Dark Gods."

He caught her, holding her up, and could feel the emotion well up from deep inside her until she began to weep: great, gasping sobs. Tears didn't come easily to Lily. She came from family like his, which knew backbreaking work was needed to succeed, sometimes just to stay even. She had not sobbed when illness took one of their babes and miscarriage the last. She had not cried when Tressandre took Evarton and Merri, holding back sorrow in favor of hope. But this, the evidence of Garner's death, brought the grief up like a fountain and spilling over as though she had reached her breaking point. He held her until her breathing steadied.

"When?"

"A few weeks ago."

She looked up. She'd been holding the scrap of fabric to her face and her tears had dampened the blood, wetting it and leaving a pink stain on one cheek. "How? How could he have been nearby and not sent word? Not come to see us?"

"He probably thought he would come to see us after this job. I cannot tell you, Lily, for his mind was never easy for me to know. All I know is that he was a guard on a caravan that was ambushed. He accounted himself well, but no one survived."

"No one?"

He shook his head.

"Who knew him, then, to bring this to you?"

"Rufus came across the wreckage."

"Ah." She took a tremulous breath and lowered her face again, and then looked past him. "An aryn. You planted an aryn, here of all places. How can it grow?"

"If there is any justice in this world, it will grow in his memory."

A smile tightened across her pale face. "If anyone could make it grow, you can." She sighed. "Is this what we've come to? People so weak that all we can do for our children is to plant a memorial for them?"

He growled low in his throat which made her bring up a short laugh.

"I should have known better than to ask. Where are you off to, then?"

"Larandaril, after Nutmeg, to find out what wild scheme she has cooked up. We should have known about the ideas that would roll about in her head—she was always so stubborn she would float upstream if she fell into the river." He pulled his wife back toward him with a solid and unrelenting hug, so that she would know how much he missed her and how much he hated the idea of leaving her again. Her arms tightened around him in a soundless answer of the same feeling. He did not find the small missive Nutmeg had left for him.

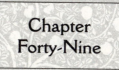

Chapter
Forty-Nine

"OUR SPIES REPORT that Tressandre ild Fallyn has left her Hold and is riding south as though her saddle is on fire." Bistane let the small scroll of paper snap back into its rolled-up shape as he handed it to Lariel.

The corner of her mouth twitched at his dry words and she took the missive. "Good. I don't know what brings her this way, but we'll waylay her original plans as best we can." She traded a long look with him. "It's time, isn't it?"

"If you're ready, then yes, it's time."

"Then I have something I must do first." Lara paused. "You can't come with me, and I'm likely to take most of the day."

"But you'll be all right."

"I might . . . return with a little less of me."

"You're going to the Andredia."

She gave a nearly imperceptible nod.

The curve of his mouth thinned into a tight and pale line before he said, "I wish you hadn't picked a God which demanded blood sacrifices."

"We don't know that there isn't a God on Kerith which does not demand a sacrifice."

"We don't need Kerith Gods."

"Because many of us think we are Gods ourselves?" She touched her hand to the back of his. "We both know that's not true. And, if there is anything good about this journey, I don't intend to travel to the font. Just to the banks of the river, nearby, to do what I have to do."

"And come home to me."

"Yes. As often as I can, I intend to come home to you." She replaced the brief caress of one hand to another with her lips brushing across his warm mouth, then turned away before he could respond and she melt into it, dissolving her resolve to leave.

She had a gelding saddled; a tall, leggy tashya with a bright chestnut coat and flaxen mane and tail who'd greeted her at the fence with an eager snuffle, telling her he wanted to go for a run that day. His swinging stride took them quickly to where she guided him. She did not go to the Andredia flowing by the horse pastures and the manor house, where she had a bench set near a small cove where the water eddied with an almost languid movement during the summer months, but headed to the west, to where the Eye rested in the sky and the fields had burned with funeral pyres she'd been told were as tall as a barn. She thought she ought to remember the beginnings of those fires as she remembered the end of the battle, but she did not. She'd shut them out of her mind: the piles of horse flesh, mortal flesh and even of the vantanes, the war dog corpses, heaped high. She did remember the blood on the water, the bodies floating, the gear and equipment of battle bobbing up and down on the current, being carried away in a rush to the ocean to the far west, save that the rocky bed of the Andredia running through the Larandaril Valley seldom gave away its treasures. She knew without being told that the riches of gear and clothing had been eagerly plucked from wherever they surfaced to be repaired and sold, or in some cases, given back to Lara's forces for a reward. The bounties of war could be many.

She put the chestnut gelding out on a long lead so he could graze a bit and drink when he was thirsty, hiking to the grove which separated this stretch of the river from the encampment farther on. Encampment. Lara scoffed at her inner voice for that title. It was a squat, full of illegal inhabitants, ones she'd chased off beyond and who'd come creeping back when they thought her back turned or those who had come to join the movement based on stirring talks given in Hawthorne or were sent directly by the ild Fallyn themselves. Discontent with a direct inheritance of her domain, they seized it bit by bit, crumb by crumb, having failed by assassination and scheming to take it more directly.

A low-hanging branch of an evergreen snagged at the knees of her riding leathers as she passed it by. She grabbed at the fragrant needles, crushing them in her hand. After a two-years'-long drought, the forest had come back, green and springy, lush and promising. Lara let the bruised needles rain to the forest floor from her hand. The sound of the river sang through her blood and drew her close. Lara lowered herself onto the grassy bank, taking off her boots and letting her feet dangle in the water that held the first chill of Fall in its coldness and in the boldness that drove its current. She spoke to it as she sat there, words barely audible, not a prayer and yet not a conversation. She told it of her apology for the discord she'd allowed into the valley, and for the lives and blood that it had carried, and of the hope she held for a better tomorrow. Of fertility and promise for all that the Andredia touched and prospered. Then, slightly hoarse, she merely sat and listened to the river as it sang back. It wove a melody that sank deep into her heart, and mingled there with songs from the past—its and hers—and filled her.

She would have to put the wards at her boundaries back up. The magic coursed through her, returned to her, as verdant promise had returned to the grove. It would keep out all enemies and allow only those she let through, unless trickery prevailed. Quendius had invaded her kingdom once, using the head of her seneschal, Tiiva, dismissed but not removed from the list of those allowed. She would have to make amends and allowances this time, but she did not want the boundary to go up until she had the Returnists dismissed from the land. If she restored her wards now, the squatters would be recognized as allowed. That she could not brook. She ran a foot through the still waters, watching a leaf as it fell and then got caught on an eddy she'd created, swirling around and around in circles.

She'd always loved the Andredia, even after her grandfather had brought her down to the grassy bank and defiled her there, pleased that her virginal blood had stained the grasses and then washed off in the warm river waters, for Lara had been just a child and he'd been incredibly rough and tearing with her. That was her first sacrifice of blood and flesh to the sacred river. She'd never told Bistane of that event, the man who was both her grandfather and father and then defiler lay beyond whatever vengeance she might take. The last forfeit had taken her finger. She had no idea what the next might ask of her, knowing that one day the river might demand her life. As long as it was her life and hers alone, she would agree. She knew an event awaited her and could only pray that she would live to meet that destiny.

She pulled her feet from the water and pulled her boots back on. The river lapped playfully after her, teasing that it might wet her from boots to chin, if it wished, as if trying to lighten the burden it had given her. She leaned down and ran her hand through the crest. It had accepted her and charged her with a duty yet to perform, but it was one that she already knew she would have to carry out. She had a judgment to make and carry out, not for her own sake, but for the lives of many, most of whom would never know what had been done. "For Kerith," she promised the Andredia, her voice barely above a whisper.

Lara stomped both feet firmly into her boots and began walking westward through the evergreens. Halfway through the grove, close enough to the squatters' camp that she could smell the charcoal fires, she heard a splashing and a muttered curse, too light in tenor to be a grown man's voice. She smiled a little, having surprised a young fisherman at his duties.

She found him westward on the river's edge, squatting by a handful of large river stones that looked as if they'd been tossed up to beach themselves, wetted enough to keep the sheen of river mosses about them. He had no pole but dangled his line by hand and from his frustrated mutters, the mop-headed boy had had no luck. He inched over and, forehead knotted up with intensity, began to lower his line again, which she could now see sported a tiny noose at the end of it. She stood and waited until he inevitably began to curse and throw his hands up in the air.

"No luck?"

His mouth twisted in surprise as he shot her a look before shaking his head vigorously. He put a hand up to stay further words from her, and crept about the end of a pair of rocks where the water came up and pooled, dropping his line again. They both held their silence until whatever prey he hunted escaped him once again. The boy sat back on the rocks with a heavy sigh.

"Not a bit. Mam sent me out to catch frogs for soup, but I swear they have eyes in the back of their warty heads. Wurse 'n fish."

Lara hid a shudder, having a dislike for frog soup that went almost as far back as her memory. "So you give up on fish?"

He shrugged and turned his surly expression to the river. "Cain't. Have t' bring home some dinner, or elst Dad will make me sleep out here till I git some. And it's gittin' cold, you know." He hugged himself at the thought. "Ruther be here than home cause they're fightin' agin."

"Your mom and dad?"

"Who elst? They fight all th' time. She wants t' go home. He says nawt, th' queen owes him a farm from the times when she chased his father off th' land hereabouts." The boy cocked his head suddenly and gave her a shrewd look. "You must be ona th' new ones."

"New ones?"

"Yup. Only sum of us stay all th' time, the rest come and go. The mayor sends 'em back and asks for new blood, to keep th' Lady Tressandre happy. So you're new."

"Yup." She took a step nearer. "The trick with frogs is, they do have eyes on the back of their head. Or rather, the side, sort of, and that gives them a wider scope of sight. Plus, you're between the sun and the rocks, so your shadow falls over them. They react to that shadow and go hide."

He pursed his lips, thinking. "Sounds 'bout right," he agreed.

"So it's best to hunt frogs or fish early, and keep the sun in your face if you can."

He sighed. "No dinner t'night and a cold sleep."

She looked at him closely, wondering who his grandfather had been, and not recognizing the features, Kernan with maybe a touch of Vaelinar a mating or two back. She'd purged the valley years ago when the Andredia showed signs of pollution and corruption, and she'd attributed it mistakenly to the sharecroppers she let work the fertile lands. She and Jeredon had placed them fairly, she thought, if outside the valley, with good lands to start over. Here was one family who'd come back, bitter and angry. Lara took a deep breath. "How about I catch a few fish for you?"

An eyebrow shot up. "You kin do that?"

"Ought to be able to."

He shoved his string at her. Lara waved it off. "I used to be able to tickle them from the water." She pulled her boots off again and waded quietly into the river where nearby trees dappled the water with shadow so that hers would not be apparent. As she bent over, she sent her thoughts out, fishlike, upstream, catching the sense of other forms, darting and swimming about lazily. Small fish, true, but enough for this family's pot, to flavor a stew or chowder. She called them downriver to her and as they swam through her hands, she pitched two of them onto the bank where the farm boy crouched, amazing him. He pounced on them, stuffing them into his burlap bag. "You did it!"

"That I did." Lara waded ashore, picking up her footgear.

He stuffed his bag into his pants, heedless of the wetness sopping through and the wriggling fish against his stomach. "I won't be tellin' m'dad or he won't et this. I won't tell him th' queen catched them."

"Ah." Lara looked down at the boy. "You know who I am."

"I'm poor, not stupid." He took a long stride away before touching his burlap sack. "I thank you for this. But you're not runnin' us off agin, unless it's over my dad's body. And mine. Got that? The true queen 'as got our backs. She's coming to take you apart." And he took to his heels as if afraid what his defiance might call down on him.

Lara watched him run, zigzagging through the thinning grove and disappearing into the tall brush and reed that fringed it. She didn't know if he would call attention to her presence or not, but she wasn't ready to meet any of the Returnists alone. She backtracked her trail to her horse, who had decided to fall asleep under the shade of a tree, and flicked his ears lazily at her appearance. Tressandre was on her way with clear intent.

When she came back, she'd have reinforcements . . . and the Andredia . . . at her side.

Chapter
Fifty

"THIS PLACE GETS INTO YOUR BONES. Makes 'em ache like broken teeth in a freeze." The frowning man glared at the far pastures and the fringe of forest holding their borders. He set his jaw, clenching his teeth as if they pained him before shaking off his thoughts. "Git along with the two of you. I'll be rid of you tomorrow."

"Rid of us?"

The frowning man would not meet Evar's stare. "They're taking you off my hands. About time, if you ask me. Don't want to be spending a winter out here when snow and ice closes th' pass. I'll die for my lady, but I'm a fighting man, not some auntie to a couple of half-breed mongrels, and I want to go with my boots on. I didn't sign on to be wiping mongrel chins and butts and coddling little snots who shouldn't ever have been born."

Evar could feel a heat growing inside of him, not a warm and cuddly heat, but one of anger. "Don't talk about my sister like that."

"She's a mewling pup, and it's glad I am to be rid of the two of you. You brawl like teething puppies and scamper about without a wit in your head—and what if you'd been hurt? Your lives are on me, hear that? Me! I was to keep you safe, all the while the two of you squabbled and rolled about on the floor, kicking and scratching each t'other. Running through th' pasture like you haven't a sense in your heads. Bolgers are more civilized than th' two of you. You'll be gone in the morning, and I will dance when the deed is done."

"Who is coming for us?"

"The Lady herself, for all I know and care. I'm well done of you. Did what was asked of me and then some. Nobody told me you'd be growing like weeds. You make sure she knows I kept you in shoes and long pants. You make sure she knows I listened to th' whining and complaints and didn't lay a finger to you, hear me?" And the frowning man shook his crooked fingers at Evarton.

Evar quailed inside a moment, wondering if he meant the old lady who'd stabbed them both so ruthlessly. The thought of Tressandre was bad enough. He fought the instinct to rub the old wound on his leg. "What happens then?"

"I don't know what she wanted from the two of you."

He knew. If not at that moment, on the street while they played, perhaps now. If not now, soon. She wanted them dead.

Evar turned his head, very slowly. The valley had stretched him. Not just his body, lengthening and strengthening him, but his mind, his thoughts. His knowledge and his reactions. And although he had not let himself think it before, he knew who'd taken them and why and what ultimately would face them. The ild Fallyn wanted them dead. That realization clawed at the back of his throat, dark and terrifying. He could feel his eyes grow hot and sting as if he might cry but did not. He forced it back. She might want him and his sister dead, but they were still alive. They still held some purpose in Tressandre ild Fallyn's plan for things, and they would be kept alive until they fulfilled it, whatever it was.

That thought steadied him. He knew already that his bloodlines, of Lariel and Jeredon, of Nutmeg, had already defeated the ild Fallyn time after time. He would do whatever he could to see they won again.

His hand curled into a fist. He turned his back on the frowning man and went to the bunkhouse, the tilting shanty which gave them shelter and saw, as he passed over the threshold what had worried his captor. The house would not make it through a harsh winter. Might not even stay standing through a heavy autumn rain. The old weathered roof and wood might just give out a groan and collapse upon itself, useless, a pile of firewood. The frowning man was a coward. Evar thumped the doorjamb as he passed through it, and the graying, aging wood gave a solid thump back at him, betraying itself as much stronger than it looked.

Just as he was.

He joined Merri at the hearth where she stirred soup that she and the frowning man had set to simmering over coals early in the day, adding herbs and root vegetables now and then, the tough old coney started from the very first and, hopefully, getting more tender with each cooking moment. It smelled good, if nothing else.

She met his shoulder nudge with one of her own. The aroma of the soup coated her like a perfume, but underneath she smelled like meadow flowers and sun. He tucked a wing of her hair behind her ear, her ear that was like his, delicately pointed and less Dweller-like than anything else about her.

"Will you be eating?"

She wrinkled her nose. "That old one was my friend." She nodded at the pot.

"I know. I would have freed him from the snare, but frowning man got up early this morning."

Merri heaved a sigh. "He was getting old. The winter worried him. Now he doesn't have to worry."

True and truer. She swung on him. "You have to eat. Too thin. Mama and Auntie would say you're too thin."

He grinned a little at her. "If they were cooking, I would eat."

She pushed her lips into a pout and turned her back on him, still stirring. Her shoes pushed out in front of her toes by a ridiculous length. His shoes almost fit, so he'd given his extra socks to her so that she could pad her shoes even more. She wore boy's overalls, rolled up and cuffed at the bottom so they wouldn't drag, but had on a girl's puffy shirt underneath, something someone had embroidered with needle and thread carefully once, but now the sun and many washings had bleached the colors out of the handcrafted thread so it was difficult to see. He thought they were tiny flowers and fruits but couldn't be sure. He realized as he looked at her that she'd lost the chubbiness she'd carried even after she'd begun to toddle and walk after him. Looking at her now, he realized why she had the nightmares she did—that they'd somehow gotten home, but even their mother had not known them. She looked the same yet terribly different, as he must look different to her, standing nearly head and shoulders taller than she did. He'd be tall, Dayne had told him. Taller someday than Tolby or Dayne himself. Evar remembered that, even as he couldn't remember the sound of Dayne's voice anymore.

Or even Mama. But he couldn't tell Merri that because it would make her cry. That would make the frowning man fiercely angry, and their caretaker already stood on the edge of harming them. He patted his sister on the shoulder and walked away to check the firewood in storage. When Mama found them again, would she spread their hands open and look at the little scars and calluses they had from working in the pasture, gathering wood and mending the fences and making snares, and would it make her cry? He didn't want that. He could barely deal with Merri and her short bursts of tears now and then.

He finished his chores and went to the window, looking out as the lowered sun disappeared and that half-light between day and night colored the meadows and forest. Though he searched for the ribbony silver lady, it was too early to see her. She appeared only when the sky was darkest over-head and the dew heaviest on the grasses. If she did appear, would she say to him what she always said: Not yet? Or would she finally tell him that his time had come?

And if it had, what would he do then? He still had no answer when he rose a long time after dinner, when even the coals on the hearth had burned away to cold, black flakes and the window called him again. Merri stirred as he slipped past her bed and he put a hand on her ankle to keep her quiet although the frowning man had begun to snore heavily.

The sight that met his eyes was not what Evar expected. Sharp shadows ringed the old bunkhouse, black and prickly, ranging here and there and yet when he moved to watch them, they disappeared, fading into the night. Yet something had fallen across the night itself, something deeper and moving quickly, almost seen, crossing from here to there and then gone. His throat ached as he tried to catch its vision and could not. Finally, be-cause he knew Merri could hear the frustrated grunt he gave out now and then, he tossed a few words back to her.

"There's something out there."

Merri yawned widely before getting to her feet. Blankets shuffled against one another as she pushed them aside and came to join him at the window. He could still feel the warmth of the bed and its blankets on her. "Is it the silver lady?"

"No. It's nothing I can see, like a shadow almost. But bushes and trees are shaking when there is no wind. Something is getting closer and closer."

She closed her hand about his elbow. "Wake the frowning man?"

"No."

"It's hunting."

"I know." He paused with one hand on the window frame. "I just don't know what it's hunting yet." And he wondered if the silver lady would show as well, and if she did, what she might make of those sharp, quick shadows.

She made a *sss*ing noise through her lips; for her, a sound of worry. He patted the hand which held him. "We're safe."

But they weren't, not really. The frowning man was giving them over in the morning, away from this valley, away from the magic that welled up from the earth and spilled over into them, away from what little safety they had. He should be used to change, but it seemed he had had too much lately. He looked down at them because the window showed him little that he really wished to see. Because the nights had been growing steadily colder, his sister was still dressed, as he was, save for shoes, such as they were. They stood barefooted on the wooden and grimy floor, and he pointed out to her where he'd almost seen something. She leaned close to the pane, watching with her bright eyes, not at all sleepy.

"What is it, then?"

"Don't know. Big as a Kernan, though." A sharp angle caught his eye. "There!"

"Ooohhh." She saw it then, too, close by, an edge of night too sharp for the shadows, closing in on them. She pressed her cheek to the window, trying to follow its movement. "I can't see it now."

"But it was there."

"Yes." She took a shaky inhalation of breath and when she let it out, it fogged the window and, for a moment, neither of them could see anything.

Something brushed the far wall of the bunkhouse. They both whirled from the window at the noise. Merri reached for her brother's hand again and grasped it tightly. Stuck in place, he did not dare move or nudge Merri to a safer corner, for he had no idea where safety lay. Silence spun down from the wood post ceiling and hung about them like spider thread, coiling closer and closer until catching them in its web, drawing tighter and tighter until Merri made a little noise at the back of her throat and the webs gusted away in shreds. Evar put his hand out, catching the edge of one, realizing that he had made the webs, spinning them off some small creature's net high in the rafters. Spinning an armor about them wasn't a bad idea, but the silk hadn't been near strong enough to protect them. He pondered on that a moment while Merri pointed a shaking finger.

The roof creaked. Dirt sifted down, a fine rain of grit and sawdust. "It's up there."

He grabbed his shoes and hissed at her to get hers on. She plopped on her rear and tugged them into place, her mouth skewed in determination. The whole building groaned faintly as if leaning in answer to the weight and movement above.

He feared going out. But he feared staying in and being trapped more. He tiptoed into the corner of the kitchen and grabbed the dull paring knife from the counter. It wouldn't be much use, unless he had to poke an eye out, but it was better than nothing. He crossed back to Merri, put his arm about her waist, and propelled her out the back door. It exploded against the frame of the building as he flung it open behind him, shattering the silence of both the hunter and the hunted. Something cursed in a low growl as it did.

Chapter
Fifty-One

FROM THE DOORWAY, Evar half-carried, half-threw Merri as far as he could across the broken dirt-and-grass yard. Something rushed him from the shadows. He ducked, shielding his sister as she let out a frightened squeak, and the bulk hurdled over him toward the bunkhouse tearing apart the opening as it did. He caught the sense of great strength and size, and a tremendous, animal smell, but he had no idea what it was as it leaped over the shattered doorway and into the building where another voice raised in a roar.

The frowning man, up and angry, shouted his loud curses as only he could do. A chair came flying through the threshold splinters and bounced to a violent stop upon the ground. The sounds of two bodies thudded against a thin wall, and the very roof shook as though it might come down. Evar stayed hunched over Merri, her little body panting in fear, as what could only be a war broke out in the bunkhouse behind them. Furniture crashed. Wood flew in pieces. Pots and pans clanged. Shouts and grunts and screams of pain and fury. Evarton knew he should get to his feet and run, run as hard and fast as they both could, but the noise froze him in place just outside. He didn't know how he could help. Who he should help.

The battle raged for more moments than he could count, and then all fell silent. Even the frowning man's shouts and swearing ceased. Something swung back and forth in a faint creaking from inside before it crashed downward in a last crescendo of destruction. The near corner of the bunkhouse sagged to the ground in a cloud of dust. Merri crept back up and shook his arm.

"Run."

He listened. He didn't know if he expected a roar of triumph or another round of cursing, but the night had stilled. He got up, pulling her after him. "I think it would catch us." But he steered her into the darkness anyway, his eyes adjusted enough that the squat bunkhouse behind them stood out even in the moonless night. They moved slowly, from fence post to fence post, edging toward the open forest that fanned about the old pastures. In there, perhaps, they could hide under a fallen tree or climb fast enough to get out of reach. He had another idea and began to lead her toward the river cutting through the near arm of the grove. They knew it well, hauling pails back and forth. Their small feet had worn a groove in the dirt and grass.

"We're going to sit in the water," he whispered to her.

"But it'll be cold!"

"Some animals hunt by heat. That'll hide us. And if by scent, the water will confuse it. And by noise, too, if you can stay quiet." These small things he'd learned from the frowning man's mutterings over the weeks when he'd gone out, bow or snare in hand. They ate, hadn't they? So the frowning man must have been right.

She made a snuffling noise, rubbed her face and headed down the muddy bank, stepping into the water so quietly Evar didn't realize she'd already gone in. He joined her, put his arms about her, and they both sat down in the shallow water which promptly rose up to her upper lip. He squeezed her tightly, feeling her rough and wild breathing against his chest.

They waited. The forest felt too quiet about them, the few birds who sang at night losing their song, and the predators that rustled about hunkered down in the brush. The thing—whatever it was that had attacked the bunkhouse—was stalking again, and the creatures about them hid from it.

Evar could feel Merri shiver in his hold. They couldn't sit here all night, or she would catch deadly cold. He would, too, as the river bit into his body. He sat, freezing and deciding what they could do when he smelled it. That thick, unmistakable animal smell that had bowled him over before it crashed into the bunkhouse. Near. Very, very near. Merri blew her breath out lightly and he hugged her even closer, unable to say anything to make her feel better. It would hear. It might even hear their hearts drumming.

Before he could think what to do, a heavy blow knocked them both out of the water, awash in a great spray, and onto the bank where they lay, gasping and flapping about like two fish. Stunned, all he could do was gasp as Merri panted next to him.

A voice rolled over them.

"Nutmeg unhappy I bring back two wet babes."

Water dripped everywhere as Evarton rolled onto his back and looked up at the great beast looming over them. Yellow tusks caught a faint glimpse of starlight as the beast man squatted next to them.

Evar's mind worked slowly, grasping, but Merri blurted out, "Bolger! He's a Bolger!"

Evar nudged her to stay quiet, as the being was scarcely mortal as they knew them. But Merri grinned brightly, catching the moonlight. "You're Mama's friend!"

"Rufus," the creature said, and took her gently into the curve of his arm. "Friend of Spice and Little Flower." He spoke in a harsh voice, hard to understand, but Merri flung her arms about his neck.

"Mama sent you!"

"And warlord's son and Tolby."

Evar got up and shook himself like a dog, trying to shed excess water as the night wind curled about him, a cold hand closing around him. "The frowning man said no one would come for us. The frowning man said we were sold for peace."

Rufus curled an arm about him, drawing him in as well, next to his sister, into a cloud of beast-scented warmth. "Lies. We looked since you were lost. Many, many days."

He began to cry. He hadn't cried, not since those first days, but now he did, the only warmth he could feel on his face.

Rufus laid his head on the tops of theirs and made a crooning, soothing growl as his arms tightened about them. "We run. Then we get fire," he told them. "Long way back. Valley no good. Old magic waits here."

"The silver lady?" Merri lifted her head from under his shelter.

"Not seen lady of silver. Might be good. Might not." Rufus ruffled her hair. He drew them up as he stood.

He walked them to a sheltered spot among the trees. "Wait. Bring mules back."

So they waited, but Evar made Merri march about with him, swinging their arms and stomping to keep warm. When the beast man returned, he brought two long-eared mules with him, lifted Evar and placed him over saddlebags and bags, and then helped Merri settle in a small patch of a saddle on the other mule. He grunted and groaned a bit as he did, and Merri wrinkled her nose. She put her hand on the top of his balding skull.

"I smell blood. You're hurt."

"Later." He patted her leg. "Hold on tight."

He turned and broke into a bow-legged but steady run, away from the pasture and the bunkhouse and their imprisonment. Evar dug his fingers under the woven ropes and straps and hung on for all he was worth, but the mule's lope was smoother than he expected. Merri's head nodded back and forth on her shoulders as she rode next to him, her little face scrunched into an expression of determination. So they moved through the night into what must have been a pass in the great mountains, not the way they'd come in, but a way that seemed lit by a silvery ribbon of moonlight, flowing up and among the rock. He leaned over to look down, for the moonlight shone so that it must be wet, brook water reflecting the heavens above, but he couldn't see it up close. Yet it stretched ever in front of them and when he looked back over his shoulder, he saw—nothing. Nothing but night.

"Andredia," he spoke quietly, not expecting to be heard over the quick thuds of the mules' hooves on the hard-packed dirt trail, slight as it was.

"Guiding river," Rufus said. He nodded forward. "Keeping holding. Long run before dawn."

The Bolger smelled stronger with the sweat of exertion and copper, but it wasn't a bad smell, just . . . strong and different. Evar looped his fingers tighter and leaned forward, and the mule picked up its pace. Merri's mount dropped in behind, as the mountain pass leaned in upon them, and they could only move through in single-file, although the Bolger did not let that slow him down. Heat from the mule's body rose up, chasing away his own slight chill, as he grew less and less damp as they rode. He could hear Merri behind him, give off a slight noise of both wonder and discomfort, alternating it seemed. He called out to her and she threw him back an "I'm all right." That would have to do.

They loped, trotted, walked, and trotted agin into bright daylight, the rocky trail behind them, and the wilderness giving way, grudgingly, to the colors of autumn. The vision surprised him.

They finally slowed when the sun began to lower again, and Rufus found a sheltered spot, not far from a small "lick of a river" that met his need.

He helped them both slide down, and leaned against one of the mules a moment to catch his breath before waving them off. "Get wood." They needed no other order, for they knew what kind of tinder and firewood to gather, leaving the Bolger kneeling at the rivulet of a brook, washing himself somewhat gingerly, great boiled leather apron on the muddy bank beside him.

Rufus praised him for it when he returned and squatted down with a load of dry wood. With the kindling Merri had gathered, he got it lit in no time, and they huddled close to the licking flames while the Bolger made them "swamp tea." They chewed on jerky, sweet and peppery, and sipped at their tin cups of the brew which was hot and nearly tasteless except for a wildflowerlike flavor. Rufus spoke little but encouraged Merri to chatter, as if knowing she had bottled-up nerves that would keep her awake until she talked them out, and Evar watched the Bolger closely. He looked far different from the Bolgers who occasionally came to Calcort. Those Bolgers stood taller and straighter, and their tusk teeth were all shaved down, so they spoke better and looked far less ferocious. But they found little business in Calcort, their main trade being across in the bigger cities. His grampa had always treated the Bolger men fairly, but Evar knew that a lot of the Calcort folks didn't like them. He decided that his grampa was right and the others wrong. He put his feet in close to the fire as it sank into the hot rocks and coals and Merri finally began to run out of words.

Rufus laid her down close to Evar and tucked a blanket about the two of them. Evar blinked slowly and realized that he missed being tucked in. The two long-eared mules slumbered just beyond the dim circle of light after having spent all the afternoon cropping up as much grass and bramble as they could reach. He closed his eyes and pulled the blanket up about his ears, giving in to warmth and hope. The last he heard was Merri's soft voice.

"How did you find us?"

"Flowers brought me."

"Sunfaces! I planted them. I thought Mama would see them and know!"

"Flowers and a silver river," his low voice rumbled. "Now close eyes."

Merri snuggled down next to him, her familiar body warm from the fire, and when she pulled her blanket up, it was not only over her but him, too. They fell asleep together.

*   *   *

She awoke in the early morning to the sound of twigs snapping as they burned in the campfire, and to the smell of something cooking that made her realize how hungry she was. Evar's longer limbs sprawled over her, and she pushed him and the blankets away carefully. As she rubbed sleep from her eyes, Rufus looked up from his squat at the fire. He looked both battered and wise, she thought, and smiled at him.

"Wash. River there." He pointed the way to her although she knew quite well where the brook gurgled along the valley's edge. She toddled off that way to take care of washing and other necessities, as the morning mist rose off the greenery just like smoke off the fire. She opened her hand, spreading her fingers, weaving her hands in and out of the mist, watching it disappear as she touched it. For the first morning in a long time, she felt like singing.

She came back to find Evar rolling up and tying their blankets into tight bundles, under the sharp, dark eyes of Rufus. He stopped Evar once and had him reroll, after showing him how to tuck the ends in better. She plopped down, but Rufus pointed a knobby finger at her. "Feed mules."

Merri looked over her shoulders. The mules had been busy cropping all the nearby grass while tethered, but they looked as if they could eat more. The chestnut one tossed his head at her, ears wobbling. She bounced to her feet and took them off with her to an ungrazed area nearby and let the lead line out to its very end so they could eat while she perched on a fallen log. The two long-legged beasts immediately put their heads down to pull and lip the grasses. Evar stayed working around the campsite and watching their breakfast sizzle.

Evar called for her then, to leave the mules and come eat. After they finished and she'd licked her fingers clean, Rufus pointed at one and then the other. At Evar: "Ride brown mule." At her: "Ride with me."

"Tired of running?"

He snorted faintly. "Am old one."

She giggled at him. Her legs stuck out a little as he tossed her on the front of the small saddle and the chestnut mule *whuffed* when Rufus mounted, adding his own weight, and the mule turned his head about to look back at them.

Rufus grunted at his mount. "Not heavy."

The mule flipped its ears, making Merri giggle. "He thinks we are!"

Rufus put his arm about her, drawing her back against his stomach and chest. She could smell the strong leather odor of his apron, old and stained. Behind it, she could smell the coppery taint of blood. She'd forgotten he'd been hurt. She could feel it now, in the stiff way he moved and breathed. She put her hand on the back of his wrist as he took up the mule's reins. With a deep breath, she gathered her golden light—just like the bright yellow Sunface flowers—to send through him. It was hard, like pushing a shovel through clay mud (something they'd had to do many days in the valley, mending fences), but she shoved and shoved until she could feel him breathe easier. She couldn't quite explain, but he felt different. His bones, his muscles. Maybe it was because he was old, or maybe it was because he was a Bolger. But she gave a little nod of her head as she took her hand away because she'd managed it anyway.

"Thank you, little Sun."

She nuzzled the back of her head against him. "Welcome."

They rode with Rufus telling them they still had a long way to go. He stopped twice a day to let them stretch their legs and teach them about the land they rode over. Berries, roots, animals, and birds he knew as well as he knew the wrinkles on his palms Evar said to her. He soaked it up like one of Mama's washing rags, and he told her at night it was because he was learning more and more about Making through what was already there. He held a handful of berries in his hand to show her. "All dried and old." He cupped his other hand over it for a short bit, frowning greatly, and then opened his hands up. The berries glistened, all plump and full of juice. The two of them gobbled them down before going to pick more for the camp-fire dinner and to share with Rufus. That sort of Making she understood. She understood the reach of it, and it wasn't that unlike her own healing. That sort of Making began with the soul inside.

If Rufus noticed Evar's ability, he never mentioned it. But then, the old Bolger never said two words when one would do, and more often than not, used a thumb jab and a frown or grimacing smile instead of talking at all. He used a lot of sign language when talking about the herbs and roots, whether to dry them or not, and to grind or stew them, and what they did in their various forms. He made Merri laugh so hard she nearly cried when he imitated a terrible stomach ache from one of the prettiest flowers she'd ever picked.

The rain hit. None of them liked riding in the rain. The pack mule stopped once and refused to take a step no matter how hard Evar drummed his heels on its sides. Rufus had to turn their mule around and go get it, and lead it by one rein until it finally decided it would have to follow no matter what. The rain made them all cold and shivery, but at night Rufus would weave branch lean-tos over them and over the mounts so they could dry and warm themselves a little. On a clear day, they rode to the top of a ridge and Rufus jabbed a thumb back the way they had ridden. She could see mountain peaks, their white tops shimmering with snow. Winter had come to the valley they'd left far behind.

"We ride," he told them. "Harder."

Winter was chasing them, too.

He often took Evar with him when he scouted the trail in front and behind them. That made Merri angry and hot inside. The two returned, with dinner which was good, but having left her behind which was not. She stood in front of them and folded her arms over her chest.

"I'm the heir. I'm older than he is! I should go."

Rufus squinted a dark eye at her, considering.

Evar said, "I'm just learning about tracking and concealing the trail, and a little about hunting."

"Stuff I want to know."

"But you're littler than me."

Her mouth tightened. "Born first."

Rufus let out a laugh, a great, booming laugh and jabbed a thumb at her. "Keep quiet, and I take."

"How long quiet?"

"All night."

Her mouth twisted back and forth a minute, holding back her questions, and then she nodded vigorously. She held her tongue all night although it was really hard, especially when Evar poked and nudged her every chance he got, and when her shoes got put too close to the fire, almost burning them up! She settled for punching him in the shoulder after she rescued them, adding a pinch to his ear when he chortled at her.

Rufus tapped her shoulder in the morning as they doused the campfire. "You tonight."

Her smile blossomed. "I'll be ready!"

By nightfall, she wasn't ready. All she wanted to do was help weave the lean-to and fall into a heap by the campfire because that day's ride through hail and rain hurt every bone in her body. But she'd asked to learn and now

Rufus stood ready, waiting for her. Evar shook out his own poncho and fastened it around her shoulders, saying, "It covers more." Then he gave her a little warm kiss on her eyebrow.

Rufus led Merri into the growing darkness. He pointed out their trail. "Rain. Less work."

That sounded good. He showed her how he circled ahead, scouting for easier trail and coverage, and he carried, not a bow this time, but a strap of leather and a pocket of hard, round stones. He showed her how to load the strap and then sling it, but she hadn't the strength to send it far or hard, most of the time losing her stone at her feet before she could even fire it.

He surprised her by bringing two fat birds down from nearby branches, after making her squat next to him in total silence for long, boring minutes while a soft drizzle trickled around them. He made her pluck the feathers after he dressed them, and showed her how to bury them and the offal, so that their hunting would not be so obvious. Other animals would dig it up, but it would be hard to tell they'd been there. Then he cut two green branches and had her drag one behind her while he dragged the other behind his prints, taking care to walk on the needle-covered ground and not the mud as they returned to camp.

Evar had stripped down and groomed the mules and had a small fire going, with lots of hot stones ready for cooking. They laid the bird carcasses flat on the stones and sprinkled herbs over, with more rocks placed on top. Soon the sizzling filled the air with good smells. She fell asleep before Evar and Rufus finished their dinners.

In the morning, Rufus woke her, his hand on her mouth, his forehead creased heavily in worry. He pointed up to the dark and boiling clouds overhead. "Winter comes," he told her. "And ild Fallyn."

The mules were already saddled and loaded and the fire quenched. He wrapped her up in her blanket, threw her poncho over her, and hauled her up after him. He turned the mule down one of the ways they'd scouted the evening before and kicked his heels hard. They bolted away into the morning. She stole looks backward, wondering how he knew.

But he did. Perhaps he'd seen smoke from a not-too-distant campfire. Maybe he'd crossed a trail a day or two ago and realized what it could have been.

Before the sun rose overhead, trying to shine through a storm-laced sky, Merri could hear riders behind them. They wove through the forest as if braiding themselves into the branches, back and forth, she and Rufus hunched forward to keep limbs from whipping in their face, and Evar brought his mule even with theirs more than once. She grabbed a look at him. Determination knotted his eyebrows over his pale face.

Rufus rode low, holding her tight in the shelter of his long arm, and urged his chestnut mount into a fierce run, cursing when the groves thinned and they rode across wide meadows, open for all to see. That was when she glimpsed the others, hard after them, not far behind.

The mules galloped, but they could not match the speed of hot-blooded tashyas.

The ild Fallyn grew close enough that they could not only hear pounding hooves, but the crack of hand-held whips and the whoops of encouragement pressing the horses. Lather from the mule's glistening shoulders flew up to splatter Merri's face. She'd bounce all over, but Rufus bent over her, flattening her to the saddle and the mule's neck. She buried her hands in the mule's stiff and stubby mane, holding to what she could. A thinning forest enveloped them, but it wasn't enough to hide them.

The mule swerved over bracken and stone, and she went one way while it went the other. She began to slip from the saddle and Rufus' arm, sliding away. Rufus grabbed for her, reining back, but the only thing holding her on was one foot and a handful of stiff mule mane.

And then her shoe, too big even with the sock stuffed in it, began to come off.

Rufus lost a rein, entangled under Merri's arm. She squeaked as the shoe popped off, and Rufus slowed the mule into a wide, loping circle. Evar shot by and then returned, his mule puffing and dancing, as Rufus caught her by the ankle and for a moment she dangled upside down but saved.

Evar went back for her shoe, but instead of galloping back, he turned in his saddle. He waved. "Run! I thought of something."

Rufus righted her in front of him and growled, "Come!"

Her brother did not move. He raised one hand in the air, and she could almost see waves of light dance about his fingers.

Rufus growled. She put her hand on his. "He's doing magic."

The Bolger grunted, saying into her ear, "No magic for arrows."

Behind them, she could see the ild Fallyn burst into the open and point through the thin forest that separated them. They were reaching for their bows.

"Evar!" she screamed with all her might, afraid he wouldn't hear, afraid he didn't know.

He shot her a look, hand poised in the air in front of him, and then smiled. He never saw the three arrows loosed at him.

Chapter
Fifty-Two

MERRI TRIED TO SCREAM, but her breath caught in her throat and froze. Her hands clenched at Rufus. She bounced in agitation.

Evar turned his head ever so slightly back to the ild Fallyn and dropped his hand suddenly. In the space between the attackers and him, trees began to explode and fall, one after another, taking out everything in their way, including arrows. The sky filled with wood splinters and bark, branches, and sticks. Evar's mule let out a squeal as it turned and bolted back to Rufus.

The debris turned the air brown and gray, as thick as fire smog. Merri's mouth hung open as her brother raced by, and Rufus kicked his mount after.

They hung side by side.

"How? What?" Merri got out, squeezed so tightly by Rufus she almost could not breathe, but she managed to talk.

"I made them old. Like the logs that fall and go to pieces. Only all at once." Evar grinned at her. "I didn't know they'd explode!"

"No talk. Ride!" And Rufus lashed his rein at the flank of the packmule, whipping both into a frenzied run.

Merri hunched down closer to the mule and wove both hands into stubbly mane, determined not to fall again. Heat rose from the beast as if it were on fire, and sweat, and lather, making everything slippery. They raced across fields and sparse groves, weaving in and out, but the mules began to slow.

Rufus chirped and growled softly at them. Their ears flipped back and went low, their legs stretched out, but they could not muster the speed he needed. Their breaths came harsh and loud and frantic, but their efforts came slower and slower.

And then Evar's mule let out a scream and went down, somersaulting as his body went flying, and Rufus reined hard to avoid both. It brought his mule to its knees in an effort to miss its work mate and Evar's now limp body. Before she could take a breath to cry out, the ild Fallyn jumped on them.

Rufus threw himself out of his saddle, bringing his cudgel around in one hand and knife in the other, surrounded by shouting riders in black and silver, horse flesh circling about him, and Merri lost sight of him. Shakily, Evar got to his feet, and stood weaving back and forth until a rider grabbed him around the waist and threw him over his shoulder like a bag of apples. Evar let out a shout of defiance and his captor shook him, and Evar went limp.

Merri kicked and screamed at the hands grasping at her, holding onto the mule for dear life, but they pulled her down, one ild Fallyn sawing mane away from her hands with a bloody knife. When she could see again, through the confused mass of flesh, horse, and mule, Rufus lay groaning on the ground, splashed with crimson as Evar's quiet form was thrown next to his.

Hard fingers pinched the back of her neck. "Got her. Do we need the others?"

"Our lady said to fetch the two children." A face leaned down to look into hers. "She said toddlers, but these two fit the description otherwise." He yanked her hair back from her ears. "Half-breed, this one."

"This one, too, or small for one of us." A booted foot shot into Evar's ribs, bringing a moan, as he flipped her brother over. "He reminds me of Jeredon, though. The Lady will be glad to see 'em both, I think. Someone might be playing loose with which is an heir and which is not."

Merri swallowed tightly. He was alive, still alive, not broken beyond helping! She made a move, the tiniest of moves, to go to him, but the hand on her neck closed even tighter and she could hardly breathe for the pain.

"We take them all. She'll want to take the Bolger apart, see what he knows. Put 'em back on the mules if they're sound enough."

"They're both winded but tough as jerky. This one's scraped up a bit, but it'll do."

The hand on her neck lifted her up and shook her. "Mount 'em up and tie 'em down. Put the old Bolger on the pack animal and the two on the

lead mule. Make sure they can't wiggle free. I want no more trouble between here and Larandaril. Our lady waits and there will be cold hell to
pay if she's unhappy."

He let Merri go only when her hands had been tied tight in front of her
and she was the last to be lifted onto the saddle. The chestnut mule turned
its face toward her and blew sharply through wide, red nostrils, his flanks
still heaving from the run.

It was the only friendly face she'd see the rest of the day.

Not far into the ride, Evar woke, his breath grazing the side of her face.
"Merri?"

She'd been healing him bit by bit, as she could reach him, but she
hadn't been able to do anything for Rufus. She could smell the sharp tang
of his blood on the air and it made her sick and shivery in her stomach.
"Are you better?"

"Yes. You?"

"I'm scared."

"Me, too. Where are we going?"

"They said . . . they said . . ." She could hardly believe what she'd heard.
"Larandaril."

He went silent for a very long time. Thinking, she hoped.

"They will use us to hurt her."

"We can't do that."

"I know. But I don't know how to stop them." He leaned against her
and she could feel him both tremble and tense.

She had no idea how to stop the ild Fallyn either.

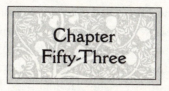

Chapter
Fifty-Three

Trevalka

THE CHESTNUT-AND-SABLE-STRIPED crown horn ripped a mouthful of grass free and pulled his head up to eat, eyes and ears alert to the sounds and shadows around him. Sevryn stayed on one knee, letting the sun and shade work for him, his hand on his throwing knife. He'd sneaked out, away from Rivergrace's constant watch and that of the others in the colony. His legs were not quite steady under him, but being inside another day clawed at his thoughts. And, a bit down the mountain, he'd found this target. Luckily downwind, he'd have but one throw at this magnificent creature that would bound away on long, slender legs if he'd missed. There would be meat there for a good week, plus throughout the restless end of winter in the form of jerky. His mouth moistened at the thought of a fresh chop. If he missed, no loss, but if he hit and only wounded the crown horn lightly, he'd have a chase through the lower forest to retrieve his dagger. Does the king of assassins miss? he asked himself. There would be no question of a miss if he'd brought a bow and arrow.

The crown horn could startle at another sound or smell. It hadn't grown this magnificently big and horned by being stupid and slow or unaware. He was lucky to have found its trail, but the first big thaw of the season had melted as much as it would, and nighttime would drop the temperatures back to freezing. The grass the big buck had uncovered with his hooves was not green, but sparse and brown. He shifted now, turning his head crowned with that formidable bit of horn, toward Sevryn as if growing suspicious. Now or never.

Sevryn straightened and threw in one sinuous movement. The knife thunked deep, the buck threw his head back with a startled bark of sound and took off running. With a muttered curse, he sprinted off after. He wanted the meat, but he needed that knife back. He should have been hunting with a bow, he thought, but he'd gotten so close without alerting the crown horn, and the dagger had practically jumped into his hand while he thought about his shot. Meat did not come easily. He would not curse his luck or lack of it, but his common sense. He should have been thinking like a hunter and not an assassin. Putting a hand down, he vaulted a fallen log and reached the spot where the stag had been hit. A bright splotch of crimson marked the ground as well as a single leaf, still trembling on its withering stem. He could smell the heat coming off the blood. He could see which way the crown horn sprang, startled, and he went after it, with no wish to leave a wounded beast behind. It struck him that he did have some feeling left in this shell of a shade. It was not born of compassion, however, but pride. He needed the meat to prove his value and to finish the job of slaughter he'd begun, nothing more.

Sevryn broke into a jog over the broken ground, the grass pushing across snow and ice, mud puddles from the melt meeting his boots unexpectedly where he could not see them lurking, and seemingly dead branches whipping across his face with the buds of tightly curled new leaves waiting to unfurl. His own blood warmed as he ran, singing in his ears, doing its best to remind him of a time when he lived fully and felt deeply. He shoved those reminders aside and concentrated on spotting the blood trail, not steady but splotched frequently enough that he could keep to it. He'd almost caught up to the crown horn when he realized that tracking it had been far too easy and that it seemed the buck was circling around to flank him. He'd never considered that the crown horn, a grazing animal, might have predatory traits.

He came to a wary halt. He could hear his own breath blowing lustily through his lungs but nothing of the buck, so much bigger, running so much harder. Sevryn cast his senses about as he stepped into the shadow and shelter of a large tree trunk and took a look at its lowest branch. A bit of a leap but nothing he couldn't manage. A loud crack sounded beyond and to his right, and he made that leap, catching the springy branch and pulling himself over it and into the fork of the tree as the buck came out of hiding, one lordly step after another. His dagger pushed its way out of the meat of the beast's shoulder and fell to the ground.

The crown horn's wound closed and healed as if it had never been.

Sevryn set his teeth for a moment, looking down at his dagger, wishing he had it still in his hands, before looking up at the buck. Its antlers reached high enough that they could entangle his ankles and pull him down. He had indeed not been hunting what he thought he had. This was no mortal flesh. He spoke bitterly.

"Where were you those months ago when we first came into Trevalka and met the others? I and my companion noted that there was no God of forests, of beasts and the hunt, and the seat on the court stood empty."

The crown horn snorted.

"I am not talking to air or an animal. Show yourself. I'm in no mood for godly games."

An all-too-mortal voice answered.

"I was tending to my flock, as it were, something the others rarely do now that they have given their divinity over. You crossed over and I felt the two of you, blood of our blood and yet now, flavored with the taste of other stars and universes. And then, when I would have made myself known, you hid among my closest children, and I decided not to disturb the innocent. But I would know what you intend to do, having brought this new Goddess to my country and what she intends to do." The buck pawed at a patch of crumbling snow and nosed it away to reveal the old grass hiding beneath. He lipped at it, as though the God's hold on his creature was not all that tight.

Sevryn pondered his words before responding. "She's not a Goddess."

The buck snorted, stems of grass still hanging from its lower lip, and one eye rolled up to view him sitting in the tree.

"She is no Goddess of here," Sevryn amended. "Nor does she intend to be."

"Where a God rules is more and more a decision made by the followers than the God."

"We have but one purpose and that is to stop Quendius and keep Trevilara from opening the portal again."

"The portal has never closed."

"So we noted once arriving here. Our purpose remains. We won't let Trevilara poison our world as she has yours."

"So you are the seed of exiles." The buck chewed its grass calmly, lifting its muzzle high to view him with its animal eye, seeing him with far more than an animal's senses.

"We are. The world we left is a good one, though fraught with its own ambition and warring."

"We are aware. From time to time we bring our exiled souls home, wrenching them from out of the hands of other Gods, just so that we might weigh the situation." The crown horn shook its head. "Trevilara did us no good by her actions, but neither were some of us convinced of wrongdoing. We become our own Gods, and the people get what they deserve and promote."

"I've seen no proof of that."

The crown horn jerked its head up higher, threatening rack at his ankles.

Given an unexpected explanation for the wrenching and unsettling disposition of bodies on Kerith, bodies and souls occasionally Taken and torn asunder, Sevryn took a breath. So the event did have otherworldly consequences. "And what about you? You seem to have a consideration for your followers that Trevilara doesn't." Moving slowly, leisurely, he pulled his legs up to sit a little steadier on the branch, still not quite out of range of the crown horn's antlers, particularly if he sprang, but there were branches still higher and in reach above Sevryn.

"It depends upon your intentions."

And who could know how a God might judge actions? Sevryn looked again at his knife, lying fallen on the ground, now behind the buck and seemingly forgotten. He did not trust Gods, not even the River Goddess braided into Rivergrace's core. "We came to stop Quendius. He's a master of death, and he gathers the newly fallen to make an army of Undead. To what purpose, I couldn't tell you, I can't see into the man's head. But . . ." He paused. "I don't think Quendius plans to stop until he's the last man living."

"Is there nothing mortal he desires? Wealth? Flesh?"

"I think Death is the only thing that touches him. That gives him pleasure. Death and dying."

"And it was your world that made him."

He had no answer for that. The crown horn dropped his head and snagged another thatch of grass, chewed and swallowed.

"You will go to him," the beast told him.

"It seems inevitable. I'm not quite an Undead myself, having failed to take him down when we met."

The stag's head dipped twice. "You will go to him. You'll have but one last chance to meet and stop this Master of Death, I think, and your Goddess will feel much grief."

"Don't say that."

"You don't wish to hear that? Then you're not as far from feeling as you hope you are." The buck reared up a little and pushed his muzzle against Sevryn's branch, rocking it vigorously. "She holds your hope and his demise. She's as chained as you are, but she wears it better. But know this—she needs to spend you, as if you were nothing but useless coin. She cannot hesitate to use you however she must.

"When the time comes, call me and I will come to help as I can."

Sevryn sprang to his feet, both hands on the branch above to steady himself, but the beast didn't bring him down yet. "Why do you tell me this now?"

"Because you're too late to prevent Quendius and Trevilara from meeting and forming an alliance. Because what your River Goddess and you came to this world to do, must still be done. And because the two of you cannot do it alone, I offer my aid."

He blinked down at the creature. "You'll come?"

"I will. Trevilara has poisoned the roots of my country. We may not survive her, but we can't even begin to heal as long as she still walks this earth. I can't promise that any of my fellows will assist. Most of them are bound to her, shades of themselves, just as you are. But then, Sevryn Dardanon, that gives you an advantage."

"What?"

"Only you will know how to truly reach them."

He did not feel as he knew he probably should have, gratitude at the offer and despair at the news. He felt only a faint tug on the strings that enslaved his soul and he knew the touch to be that of the death master. But even if it had been Rivergrace, he would feel little different because his life in the shade left him little to feel with. He wondered if he should thank the Trevalkan God, but his hesitation stretched awkwardly. The buck snorted then and rattled his antlers against the branch, forcing Sevryn into dancing for his balance as the beast lowered his head to the ground and sprang away with a clatter of hooves among the stones and ice.

Chapter Fifty-Four

Kerith

T HE LETTER MAY HAVE BEEN part of the impetus, but Tressandre knew as soon as she hit the sweet, fragrant air on the ridge above Larandaril, that she could not have stayed away long. Her being craved this valley, the hills that sloped about it, the river rushing through it, the lush grasses that grew in its pastures, the quilting of its farms downstream, the ripening of its orchards upstream. She ought to appreciate her Fort, for all the hard work her people had done to place it, to build the vast bridge that led to it, the ocean salt mist that rose in spray and fog about it. But she didn't. She hated her toehold at the edge of a vast shining sea that did not care that she occupied a niche on its shore. Her family had been herded into her tiny empire like vermin into a trap, and the longer she stayed there, the more she hated it. Those she'd just given her name to thought that living in its rooms instead of hovels meant something. She knew better.

She put her heels to her roan tashya, reining him down off the ridge, her guards trailing in a brace behind her, and hit Larandaril's wards. She recoiled in her saddle at the mental hit. For a moment, she couldn't think at all, the ability smacked away, and she almost lost her seating as her horse danced back under her. She threw up a hand to halt her guards as she recovered, with a shake of her head and a low curse. Her ears buzzed as if surrounded by a nest of stingers, and her stomach made one last flip-flop.

Tressandre rested her hands casually on her mount's shoulders. "Why it appears our little queen feels well enough to have put up wards again." She tilted her head. "They're not as robust as they have been." If they had been, she'd have been lying unconscious on the ground. The boundaries of Larandaril were never crossed lightly when the wards were up in full. They might even take one's life, if Lariel intended it. Of course, that would not happen under an extended breach, but who wanted to be the first or second to die while the rest got through? She caught the glances her guards passed now as they waited for her orders. Waryn gave her a meaningful look, as if he could lecture her on marshaling her troops. The two packhorses in the back sidled against one another with their ears back, as sensitive to the magic as any of them.

"Take a breath," she told them. "No one will die here today." A nosebleed perhaps or a persistent, ringing headache if one insisted on passing into the valley. Usually the prudent stopped their trespass and waited for one of the Warrior Queen's border guards to ride out and send them off or grant them passage. Or run them down.

She didn't think Lariel would be that forceful today. Her fingers fiddled with a tuft of silken mane, as she decided how to react. The choice was taken from her, however when a vantane came winging in from downslope, circled about them, and came to a stop on a nearby tree stump.

"Fetch the message."

The raptor folded its wings and watched her man closely as he dismounted and approached it, putting out his gloved hand to take the big bird up and unfasten the message tube. In moments he had it in her hands.

These lands are not yours to hold, nor is this border yours to cross. If you proceed, be prepared to meet me in combat.

Tressandre smiled widely. "My lads, we have been challenged. The Warrior Queen forbids me to visit my countrymen encamped on the River Andredia, even though they have sent to me in distress over her treatment of them. I think I shall take up that challenge!"

The guardsman holding the vantane asked, "Shall I send back an answer?"

"No. Shake the bird loose. I give my answer as I cross her border." Tressandre put her heels forcefully to her tashya's flank and set it into a run into the valley. With her shoulders set, she barely reeled in the saddle as the ward hit her again, and she didn't look back.

The encampment greeted her with little regard as she swung down. She signaled at Waryn to greet the pudgy little man who came running to meet them, and looked for some sign that her hand of soldiers had arrived ahead of them. The little man bowed again and again, panting as he spoke hurriedly to Waryn.

Her seneschal straightened. "There's been no sign of the children and their escort."

"No sign?"

He shook his head after trading a look at the mayoral personage whose jowls swung as he gave the negative.

"What do you mean, you don't have the children? My men were ordered to retrieve them and drop them here. I want them found, at all costs. I'll dispose of them myself after I finish the business at hand." Tressandre's attention snapped to the speaker whose face had already been pale and went gray at her look. Hurriedly, he pressed papers into Waryn's hand and fled back behind the encampment gates. She stretched her back and then her legs. The hard riding sank into her bones, and she disliked it. She straightened. "And why does this . . . village . . . smell like swill? Set me up outside, on the pasture. Even fresh manure smells better than what these squatters have built." With a snap of her fingers, she stayed her men outside the warped and unsteady gates the Returnists had built to protect themselves.

The mayoral figure bowed low again. "I only report what the messengers give me."

"Hmm." Tressandre crossed her arms over her chest as she watched her entourage scurry to set up her canopy, rug, and chairs. "I have the advantage. Although—" And she raised her voice. "It would help if I. Had. The. Children. What in the cold hells happened?"

Waryn put a hand in the air palm up, as he scanned the information passed to him. "Valek was killed at the ranch, my lady. He put up quite a battle, according to reports, but the children were taken from him."

"Is no one competent but you and I?" She rubbed at her temple. Bloody wards and bloody headache.

"You have trained quite a number of competent men. While it's true Valek lost the children, the force manned by Hywat found them, with some losses to the troop, and they're not far from here."

"Good news at last, although it felt like I needed to pull teeth to receive it." She assessed Waryn with a faintly raised eyebrow. "What other good news need I pry from your jaws?"

Waryn allowed a small smile at her words, and gave a slight bow. "Mistress Nutmeg is just across the river, waiting to ford it."

"Ah. That was almost worth waiting for." Tressandre brought her hands together as she turned to survey the work progressing. Her men tightened down the canopy poles and ties as she watched. "This might be fun. I intend that it shall certainly be satisfying, if she stands by her trade."

"You must have some idea."

"She offers a Writ of Parentage. She's willing to wager the lives of the children that it will satisfy me. I won't know until I have it in my hands if it's worth losing the leverage I have over Lariel." She scanned the encampment. "Although, there is nothing that says I can't just take her statement and keep the children. She offers me an official lie, but Lara knows better. Writ or not, she wants the two, and I think she'll keep her distance if I have them. The little Dweller is banking on her association with Lariel and Bistane to keep her untouchable. She's wrong."

"Your word . . ."

"I'm willing to sacrifice the honor of my word to gain these lands. My brother gave his life to this goal; why should I not surrender the value of my word? His is an uneasy spirit waiting for vengeance, and I'll have that for him." Tressandre put the tip of a finger to her full lips, thinking. "I want the children kept back, from both Nutmeg and Lara, until I give the word."

"Done. Once they get here. Our scouts signal me that our riders are on the ridge."

"A candlemark before Mistress Farbranch then, if that. I shall have to put up a front."

Voices hailed from behind her, alerting them the shelter was in place and ready. Waryn bowed. "I'll prepare a hot drink."

"Do that. I wouldn't want to seem inhospitable." Tressandre took a seat in her leather sling chair and crossed her boots at the ankle. "I only require that my guest arrives before the duel. It shouldn't be too much to ask." She stilled as Waryn rattled around in the field kitchen, preparing a draft to be heated. Wine with spices, she thought she smelled, as he uncorked a bottle and brought out a few tins. She would not drink much, expecting that Lariel would return with a challenge at hand, and that business she took far more seriously than bartering with a Dweller woman for her half-breed children. That supposed connection interested Lariel far more than it bothered Tressandre, save for the preservation of Jeredon's lineage. She could wait, she supposed, for the next generation to grow old enough to be dueled, because Tressandre in no way intended to let Lara Anderieon continue living. She would be cut down in atonement for the horrendous death inflicted on Alton. An exceedingly slow and painful vengeance awaited.

Tressandre mentally reviewed the gear she wore, appropriate for her expectations of combat later in the day, and decided that she was most adequately equipped and more than a match for her opponent. Lara was neither strong enough nor fit enough to duel, not after her imposed sleep of two years. She should have taken the woman down last time they met, but surprise had frankly made Tressandre hesitate, and by the time she'd recovered, she found herself being forced from the field. And Bistane had been there, more than ready to come to Lara's aid.

"Remind me to have a brace of men on Bistane if he shows, as well."

"Prudent," answered Waryn as he handled something that sizzled faintly.

"And necessary. He won't refrain from coming to Lara's aid if he thinks she needs it. That is devotion when what she needs is leadership from strength. When she's gone and I acquire the title, the world will take notice of what a Warrior Queen should be. I won't tolerate Galdarkans on our borders or tribal fiefdoms. Kerith should be prepared to fall to its knees before our superiority. That's what we've done wrong from the very start, trying to uplift these peoples who were so far behind us that they couldn't even walk in our shadows. Instead, we meddled, and look where it's gotten us? Reviled by most of Kerith instead of respected and feared." She held her hand out and took the goblet that Waryn offered. "We all thinned our blood out because our ancestors couldn't keep it in their pants. My father had the right of it, breeding back to repair the line, and threatening to excommunicate the dissenting Houses from the Council. But they chose not to listen and now the Council meets every so many years and all we do is discuss our grievances. Discuss? They should be settled in blood, like we should have drawn the line in blood, and dared the others to trespass!"

She took a cautious sip, enjoying the sweet and spicy echo of the wine down her throat. Her tone quieted. "A good vintage, if not aged quite enough. I do hope we stole it from someone who's going to miss it a great deal."

"That, I couldn't tell you, my lady. I don't keep tabs on all our contraband."

"Pity. I was beginning to be impressed with your mind. I shall take solace in that you have room for me to improve it." She took a second, shallow sip, appreciating the flavors both subtle and bold, making a note to find out who the vintner was for future reference. She had a number of things to plan.

Nutmeg reached the sloping valley floor and considered the River Andre-dia's waters. She yawned a bit to shake off the effect of the last ward which had passed her through reluctantly. Her horse shifted under her, for the river could and often did run deep, throughout Larandaril, but she knew this spot to be one generally favorable for fording. Lara had never gotten around to building a bridge, using the river itself as a protective barrier for the manor and outbuildings.

Nutmeg found herself a little surprised that no one had met her on the slopes, but now she saw a handful of riders, wearing black and silver, as they pulled up across the river from her. She searched their faces, finding arrogant expressions and the high cheek-boned beauty of the Vaelinars but nothing other than their clothing to readily separate them from the other Vaelinars she'd known and befriended all her life. What was it buried in-side of them, the ild Fallyn, that made the high elven war upon each other with such fury and cold dedication? Had it all started, centuries ago, with a situation like the one she faced now—beloved children taken hostage against another's future? She could imagine that, she thought, blood feuds that would last her lifetime, although the thought that blood pays for blood did not sit well with her. The earth abides. That was the truth she and her family held to, love nourishes the balance while the earth abides.

She could see they had no intention of putting their mounts into the river to escort her, but waited impatiently upon her action. If any of them had been full-blooded ild Fallyn, they could have crossed the river in a single bound, but Alton and Tressandre's relentless press for power had greatly diminished their ranks. In fighting for their line's heritage, they had nearly extinguished it.

The page might kindle it anew. Should she give it to Tressandre in hopes Evarton and Merri would be returned to her, if the Writ did not prove sufficient. The resolve she'd had days ago before she started on this quest began to evaporate. Nutmeg set her jaw. She would not relinquish anything without seeing her children first, without getting assurances that a trade would be made. The fact that Tressandre waited, here and now, implied the deal had been accepted. She took a deep breath, lifted the reins, and put her heels into her tired horse's flanks to cross the river. The chill spray of the water made both of them toss their heads back as they breasted the crossing and climbed the steep bank on the other side.

Her horse shook itself like a wet dog, catching the guard of ild Fallyn who had immediately closed in about them, taking the bridle under the horse's jaw to control it, but not soon enough to prevent the spray. Nutmeg pressed her lips firmly together to stifle her amusement and ducked her head down a bit.

She slid a hand inside her coat, to feel the paper secreted inside her corset. Warmed by her body, it released a heat to her fingers she could feel even through her gloves. Under her breath, like a silent prayer, she asked a favor of it. *If it comes to this, Lord Bistel, let me see through Vaelinar eyes, Gods of Kerith forgive me.* She thought she could feel a flare of assent from it, a warmth across her skin. She then patted the long knife in its thigh quiver, strapped to her leg inside her pants, divided riding skirt over that for warmth and disguise. Dwellers did not war as Vaelinar did, did not spar with dagger and sword, did not scheme for revenge. But her father had not been a renowned caravan guard before he returned to farming for nothing, nor Verdayne a son of a Warlord for ill, nor did she have trouble holding her own in a family full of boys. Tressandre ild Fallyn had no idea of her measure. Reassured, Nutmeg sat back in her saddle to let her enemy close its trap about her. They rode her across the trampled fields which just this spring, she noted, had finally begun to recover from the battle waged across it. A golden canopied tent awaited them, with a seated occupant in front.

Tressandre rose from her chair and watched her as she dismounted, a matter of kicking her feet free and then making a collected fall to the ground, her Dweller legs too short to make the maneuver a graceful one. As she straightened, she saw the expression of disdainful amusement cross the ild Fallyn features before being hidden, and tucked her chin down to hide her own thoughts in return. Of all the peoples on Kerith—Kernans, Galdarkans, even Bolgers—the Vaelinars underestimated the Dwellers the most. Did they think all the Dwellers could do well was brew ale, grow pipe weed, and tell tall tales? Nutmeg counted on that being Tressandre's undoing and set her face to show no expression. A quick sweep of the surroundings quickly undid her confidence. She saw no sign of her children anywhere.

"Where are they? Our deal depends upon the safety and return of my children!"

"Our deal? We have no deal. You made an offer. If you'd stayed holed up at your little farm in Calcort, you might have gotten my answer, refuting the charges that I know anything about this little kidnapping. But you made mention of a valuable paper, and I'm ready and willing to witness your signature, in exchange for the affront you've made against my reputation and that of my House."

"Not without my children!"

"But they don't seem to be here, do they? Not in that miserable Squatter's hovel over there, or in my tent, or anywhere near here."

"A Writ—"

"Words on a paper. Valuable, to a point, but not enough to force me to give up any collateral I might hold. You'll offer the document I need, or your children will never see their mother again." Tressandre waved a hand. "Take her off and hang her by her boots and shake her until something interesting falls out. I knew of your deception with the children before you offered that nugget to me. Did you and Lariel think you could hide the true heir forever? String her up, the sooner the better." Tressandre paused as she turned away, adding, "When you're ready, let out a scream or two."

Nutmeg lunged in the hands that fell upon her, to no avail, but she spat her words at the other anyway. "I'll sign nothing until I see them, safe and sound. Otherwise, even the Gods won't be able to help you!"

"I don't need any help, Dweller. You're the one head-high in trouble, and threatening me won't lessen that. Take her off." Tressandre lowered her head to enter her canopy and stopped for a moment, shading her eyes as she looked away. "Waryn, find me whoever passes for the head man of the squatters' encampment. I want to know what's happening with the portal. It's begun to pulse. Get me someone who professes to be an expert on that thing."

Nutmeg tried to dig her boot heels in as they dragged her away, shouting, "Where are my children? Where are Evar and Merri?"

The scent of bruised grasses filled the air, grasses and blood, the war of seasons ago not so buried as she had thought. They twisted her arms as they pulled her after them.

To the ones who held her, she said savagely, "She has no honor. She'll break whatever promises she's given to you as easily as she breaks hers to me. If you have a pinch of Talent, she'll use you and throw you away." Her voice broke in her throat, thin and high. Pain flashed up the side of her head as the one fisted her, and the other pulled her to the nearby grove. Her page burned like a small sun inside the ribs of her corset. It wouldn't fall out if she swung by her heels, but they'd uncover it when they stripped her. She counted on it, and that they would stop searching when they found it and she could get her hands on her long knife.

They tied her boots at the ankles and hoisted her up so that she swung, her hair bouncing free, and her ears singing as three of them pushed her back and forth. Nothing fell but her eating knife and they kicked it away, laughing. Then rough fingers pulled her long coat from her and her outer blouse, and someone used a knife on the back of her corset strings and a cheer went up when the page fell free. Her blouse flapped about her waist and the corset slipped free entirely, falling to the ground. She took a long breath as a rough hand on the rope stopped her swinging.

"You there. Get that to her ladyship and see if she had need of that."

"All this for a bit of paper?"

"Don't read, do you?"

Someone spat nearby. Nutmeg couldn't see who, from her vantage point and through the mane of her hair.

"It has import, or she wouldn't have been carrying it hid like that."

A copper-toned Vaelinar bent to pick it up and sprang away in a light run to carry the prize. The hand on her rope spun her about.

"What d'you suppose Jeredon saw in this little bit, huh?"

"We've got what we came for. Her ladyship will want her taken care of."

"That's what I mean. I'd like to take care of her. I bet she's tight, huh? So much smaller than us. Maybe that's what Jeredon liked."

Behind her, a deep-toned voice answered. "I like 'em small. I don't like feeling like I'm a spoon stirring a big pot of soup."

"We don't have time for this. We've holes to dig and cover over in the dueling ground."

"Won't take long."

Her ears buzzed louder, but they jostled closed as they argued around her, and her heart began to thump.

"A'right, then. Stuff her, but make it quick and leave her for the rest of us."

She could feel fingers on her trousers, tearing them open, and then a shout.

"Lady Tressandre wants us on the grounds. NOW. Lariel approaches."

She twirled about and about on the rope as someone shoved her with a curse. Lara? Did Tressandre also bait her with lies about the children? Or something else?

"But—"

"Oh, cold hell. Just hit her one and leave her. We'll be back."

Her spinning stopped with a crushing blow that brought a squeak to her lips as they left her. Her head pulsed viciously, and she thought she might be sick for a moment.

Nutmeg waited long moments, head throbbing and lip split, but she had a hard head. She'd survived much worse falling from the old apple trees. As soon as she knew she was alone, she began to bend at the waist and pull herself up on her own body until she reached the knotted rope.

Tressandre smoothed the page out with her fingertip, a smile growing on her face. "She already had it written. Not witnessed, but it makes no difference. This," and she beamed up at Waryn, "will undercut Lariel. It will shake her to her core, and that will give me the advantage. Our Warrior Queen does not have the stamina nor courage she needs to take me on."

"Then take it, my lady. Show her and leave the field. You don't need to meet Lariel Anderieon now, if that paper will undo her kingdom."

She lowered an eyebrow. "Are you suggesting to me that I quit? Run like a coward?"

"No. Take your victory home and defend it. You'll have it and the children, and Lara will be unable to move against House ild Fallyn again. She will wither and die, last of her line, and you will prevail."

"I can prevail here. I want flesh taken for Alton."

Waryn leaned close to her, his long face creased. "You know the boy looks like Jeredon. You have little advantage to press."

"They've spent the summer in the pasture we had to abandon to the old magics, the wastes of the Mageborn war. Who knows how corrupted their young flesh is? How twisted their powers have become? If my mares gave birth to two-headed colts and three-legged foals, will they be any less touched? If they are even mortal enough for their own mother to want to reclaim? If they are clean enough for the Warrior Queen to trust her throne to? Why do you think I had them put there?"

She paused and ran her fingers over the page. "It seems you fear my ability to take down Lariel."

"I don't."

"You do, or you wouldn't advocate running to a stone hole where I can defend myself. I won't kill you for your advice, Waryn, but I won't forget what you've revealed by it."

"You've great skill. You're better than Lara in every way, but she's always managed to survive, even when we've thought it impossible."

"I will avenge my brother. I will avenge every slight the Vantanes and the Anderieons have piled upon my blood. This should have been my land, my valley, but it was denied my bloodline. Our blood, lest you forget."

"Then do it tomorrow from the safety of our fortress."

She slapped him, with the full force of her arm behind it. He staggered back and started to raise a hand to his face before stopping himself with great will.

"Now leave me, and see to the preparations I wanted."

Waryn bowed stiffly, the side of his face flaming red, and left her.

Tressandre went to her weapons' rack and began to choose, with infinite care, what she would show to be wearing, and what she would have hidden on her person. She had no intention of meeting Lariel Anderieon on equal footing when she had every chance to prepare a more fortuitous end to their meeting. This meeting, this duel, should be their last.

Chapter
Fifty-Five

THE MORNING COILED ABOUT THEM with a cold and icy mist, that did not dare to part before the sun's weakening rays, and broke only after they left the kitchen and went into the arena. She shivered as she stripped down so he could equip her. The challenge she'd left for Tressandre as she'd crossed the borders would be answered.

Bistane wrapped her wrists with the thin chainmail, bare splinters of the shattered Jewel of Tomarq glittering as he did. He should salvage more from the Jewel's cliff site, but without Tranta to sanction it, the effort did not feel proper, rather like stealing a relic the man and his brother had died trying to protect. The last scion of the Istlanthir family had floated to shore, dead, with an unknown assailant also drowned gripped tightly in Tranta's hands, taken over the cliff with him. Tranta had survived one fall off that massive cliff; it seemed too much to ask that he would survive a second, but Bistane would have asked it if he could. Bistane missed Tranta's laugh, his wry humor, his friendship, and his longing for the sea. So many peers had gone, torn apart by the greed of Quendius and the ambitions of the ild Fallyn and the machinations of Daravan. Yet now he stood, preparing Lariel and asked himself if they were falling into yet another trap. His lips tightened as he clipped the links shut one by one with the needle-nose pliers he gripped. "Too tight?"

"No."

He slapped her leg lightly, and he wrapped another bracer about her lower thigh, covering her leg and her knee. Again, he slipped just enough links in to clip them shut, essentially closing her into the mail. In order, he did her right side, wrist, elbow, then thigh and knee, his expression closed in concentration.

He tugged on them gently. The mail did not move over her skin, each link digging in slightly. "Get up. Dance about. Give me some positions and action, I want to see if the braces stay in place."

More than half naked, Lariel did as bid, a look on her face that showed him she was thinking of teasing him and dragging him down to the arena floor with her where she could kiss away the frowning intensity of his concentration. But she did not. They were working too seriously at keeping her alive. He patted his palm down on the bench. "Those two need adjustment." And in moments he had her mail tight enough that she pulled back with a tiny sound of protest before giving in. He pulled her toward him and set her on her feet instead of holding her close as she craved. Lara shut her eyes tightly for a moment, as if willing herself to accept the seriousness of the moment. He wondered if she tried to avoid it as he did, knowing somewhere behind the knot in his stomach, he felt afraid.

"You look worried," she said.

"Because I am."

He touched his hand to her forehead, and his fingertips were chill but barely colder than her own face. That touch sent a current leaping toward her, cutting through the chains that surrounded her and in a moment, she understood exactly what he felt. Lara leaned back. Fear welled in a tiny, ice-cold bubble that threatened to fountain and overwhelm her, and she shoved it back down.

"Now I'm going to tell you what to do, and you're not going to like it."

Lara kept her gaze on him, watching him with a slight curve to her mouth, thinking of how much he reminded her in that moment of his father Bistel, the matchless Warlord of the north, her great friend and adviser, as well as the son with whom she'd fallen in love.

"This duel should last no longer than bare moments. Do you understand? You go in with a dagger in each hand. You go for her vulnerable spots, the same ones I just protected on you. Go for the joints and then for the arteries. Slice her to ribbons. Here, here, here, and here. She can't last if you do. You'll be boxing, kicking, shoving her off if she closes, slashing before you've driven her off. If she has armor of her own, then you will have to step back, gather, kick her legs out from under her before she takes to air, and come in under the rib cage."

"Brutal."

He nodded at her. "Yes. Don't give her warning. Don't stand there and pronounce her guilt and treasons. She knows what she's done to you, to your brother, to your grandfather, to your heirs. She knows and she doesn't care. Save your breath, you'll need it. I want you to explode at her. Both hands. All the skill and energy you have. Cut her arteries to ribbons and let her drown in a pool of blood. That is all the judgment you need. Do you understand?"

"I do, but—"

"No. You can't waver on this. If I think you are, I'll take you out of the duel and put myself in as your champion and you know what will happen?" He gripped her by the arms and drew her close to his face. "She'll kill me, Lara, because I don't have the Talent you do. I can't anticipate what she'll do by even the merest of a moment. She will find a way to kill me, as skilled as I am. She thinks this is her moment, and she'll use every last trick she has."

He took a breath. "And while you stand there, stricken, at least I think you'll be stricken if I drop dead—she'll close in and kill you as well, while you're off-balance. She's going to go for it, and she won't care this time if she wins your lands fairly and cleanly or not. She's going to get what she wants."

"I won't let her."

"Not by all the ice in Hell." He shook her, lightly. "You had better not let her." He ran a critical eye over her as he let her go. "Don't depend on the crystals to do much."

"Why embed them, then?"

"They will spark at her attack. Just a moment of distraction, of hesitation on her part because of what they did to Alton, and she *will* remember that, and that will give you an advantage you need."

She had nearly forgotten the force of that scene, the fury of the jewels flaming out and taking him down as he closed in to kill her. It wasn't a memory she could reach easily, hidden by her long sleep, but she touched it now before letting it go. "You want me to slaughter her."

"No. This is a duel and she'll be fully prepared, weapons and hatred in hand. I want you to be, too. This is her last, best chance, to become the Warrior Queen and take Larandaril. She knows it. She craves it, Lara, like we all crave air. Food. Water. And some of us, love."

"I don't know if I can—"

"You have to do this. I won't let you go out unless you're ready. Are you ready? You have to give it your all."

"And if I fail?"

"Then I will defend Larandaril as long as I can, as long as it was not a fair fight, and it won't be. The ild Fallyn blood in her ensures that. They have never entered through a door when a window beckoned. It's not in them."

"You're saying she will cheat."

"I'm saying she cannot help but cheat. Which is why you must be ruthless. If you give her one quarter, she'll take your life from you." He tapped her chin. "You cannot afford to be one bit less on the offense than she is. And I know you. You are already thinking that, if you can but pin her down once, you might be able to force a surrender. And, if you do that, you are considering what you will do with her. Where you will imprison her. Where you might exile her. Perhaps Abayan Diort has a dungeon deep enough for her. You don't know that she hasn't already gotten to Diort and made a deal with him. He wants all these lands united, like the Mageborn who gave birth to him, but he's not willing to start a war to get what he wants. He's been trying diplomacy instead."

"I can't trust anyone."

"You can trust me, and you can trust yourself. If you steel yourself." He rubbed his palm lightly over her arm and she felt the caress ripple through the mail he'd fastened in place to protect her there. Protecting her vulnerable spots. Just as he tried to use his words now to give her a layer over her worries and feelings.

Lara rubbed her hand under her nose where it suddenly itched terribly. "I will," she told him.

"All right, then. Get dressed. Word is she's on the upper hills of Larandaril already."

Lara stretched her neck uneasily. That was what she had felt, tensing her muscles and trying to knot her temples, the borders of Larandaril trying to tell her they'd been crossed by an enemy. She moved for her leathers. "I'll be ready." Her voice sounded brittle to her ears. Brittle and false. She swallowed tightly. She would be ready. She would.

"This is a duel, you realize."

"And we both know she won't follow any rules put to her." Bistane stepped back and looked her up and down, assessing his work.

"I have a different standard."

"So do I," he told her. "My standard is that you live. Not only for me, although the Gods know I can be selfish. But you need to live for the sacred Andredia, and Larandaril, and Evarton and Merri as well. We all need you."

A pleased blush tinged her face, and she looked down, fussing with her leathers and gear, as if unwilling to let him know her true feelings. Bistane smiled to himself.

"Ah," said Bistel in his ear. "The wonder of a well-placed love. You give and it returns."

He wanted to turn but did not, wondering that his father's ghostly presence would be with him, with Lariel so close. She'd never given any indication of being able to see Bistel, but he did wonder from time to time about just how tangible the phantom might be. He thought about what his father had just said and answered. "Do you think Tressandre loved Jeredon like that?"

"He loved Nutmeg although he would not admit it to himself. As for Tressandre, the only thing she's ever loved was her brother Alton, and that only because he mirrored her." Cold waters, whispered to his ear in a chilled fog of a breath.

"She hates easily enough."

"To the bone."

"You're muttering to yourself again," Lara said, as she finished fussing with her laces and pulls, flexing her arms to make sure she had the room she needed and that all else stayed secure. "Talking to the ghost?"

"Ghost?"

"You must have one. You talk to yourself a lot."

"Ah. Perhaps. Perhaps I'm just discussing what I fear to say to your face."

"And that would be . . ."

"How beautiful I think you are. How you worry me."

"Is that all? I would think your ghost would be nagging you for grandchildren."

"All in good time," Bistel whispered in his ear, before a cold wave washed over him that told him his father had left him yet again. But not, it seems, without a few words of hope that he and she might survive this entanglement with Tressandre. It did not seem enough to hold on to, but it was all he had.

"Not yet," he answered Lara. "His first thoughts are on the duel." He lifted his chin. "You look ready."

She took three deep breaths. "Let us pray so."

He did. He patted his thigh as he stepped back, a slim almost imperceptible dagger—a dart really—coated with the king's rest secreted in an outside sheath. He would not lose her, even if it meant sending her to the depths of endless sleep and cold hell again. It saved her once from death and he dared hope it might save her again, but he could only use it if he himself survived Tressandre and Lara lived long enough for him to get to her.

The sun on high revealed the Returnists' squat, buildings bleak and weathered and aromatic, crowd gathering. Tressandre waited at the fore, leaning on a sword, her wrists crossed, her expression one of open contempt. Lara dismounted, giving up the reins to Bistane who left his saddle and took both horses aside to stake them. As he took a watchful stance not far from her, two ild Fallyn in black and silver melted out of the crowd and flanked him. Lara's glance flicked away from him and back to Tressandre.

"Well met, at last, Tressandre ild Fallyn." Lara lifted her chin.

"Only now well met? We have known each other most of our lives. Fellows, I do believe the Warrior Queen has insulted me." Tressandre halfturned and a few half-hearted laughs met her look.

Lara took out her daggers. "By virtue of that title, I not only insult you, I judge and sentence you. I convict you for your attempted treasons by assassination, for sedition among our people and the people of Kerith, for theft and plundering, for enforced slavery, and for the kidnapping of my heirs. This is a blood sentence and a debt I intend to collect. You're guilty in my eyes, ild Fallyn and I don't care if the Gods judge otherwise."

Her words caused murmurs among the crowd but no shouted denials and Tressandre merely looked amused. "Kidnapping, you say? I'm sure those wayward children are floating around here somewhere."

Floating? Caught by surprise, Lara looked toward the Andredia, expecting to see wretched bodies adrift on the river. Tressandre leaped.

Lara leaned precariously backward, feeling the swoop of air over her chest as Tressandre's slash passed over her, the sword humming. She thought she could even smell the tang of kedant venom on its edge, but that might have been her imagination. Gaining her balance, she jabbed upward, not expecting to hit but forcing Tressandre to jump back a step and give ground. She twisted as she did, giving no target other than her flank, chain mail rippling across her torso. Her wrists sang out a tiny protest of pain and weakness which she ignored.

Her body worked on its own, muscles remembering drills pounded into her since she stood tall enough to hold a sword. She let it react the way it had been trained, and experience had honed it, while her mind leaped ahead and they circled each other a moment, judging each other's reach. Tressandre carried sword and knife, she carried two daggers. A confident look crept over the other's face as she calculated her reach.

They sparred, blades slicing the air to ribbons when they missed, her armor sparking when Tressandre did not, and she flinched back in alarm just as Bistane had predicted. Lara's shirt fabric began to shred as Tressandre's superior reach landed blows that Lara could not parry, and her sleeves hung about her arms, revealing the bracers and bands so carefully laced into place by Bistane. Tressandre's lip curled, but she said nothing, pressing on the attack instead. The weapons howled as they played off one another, metallic shrieks accenting their breathing.

Lara could feel herself growing tired. Dagger play was quick and fitful and nasty, not meant to be a long and drawn-out fight. Her ankles ached as she moved, back and forth, side to side, pivoting, turning, leaping, as her hands dueled almost without thought, meeting and tagging Tressandre wherever she could. She could feel her skin sting where Tressandre had sliced her, not deep but deep enough to draw blood, just as she could see where she'd drawn blood on the other. But there would be no end to this until life itself had been taken.

Lara shook her head slowly, denying Tressandre's arrogant expression. "You're not going anywhere this time."

The whites of her eyes accented her smoky jade and greens as Tress stated, "You haven't got what it takes."

"To kill in cold blood? You'd know what that takes. But I can't justify mercy anymore. You've gone too far."

"Such pretty words. Cruelty. Treason." Tressandre stepped forward and crisscrossed her sword and knife cutting across Lara who met them and shoved them off with a muffled grunt.

Tressandre gave a scoffing hiss. "Give yourself whatever reason you need for your failures." Her booted feet crossed over each other nimbly as she circled about Lara. She would leap again, Lara told herself, when she threw her balance forward onto her toes. She had Tressandre's tell, now.

"It was no failure to wait and see if you were a poison I needed to purge. You are, and I'm ready." Lara baited her.

Lara threw herself aside, feeling the rush of air implode as Tressandre leaped. With all her preparation, with all her training, with all that Bistane had sacrificed to bring her this far, it would not be enough. She reached out her soul and caught at his, him standing nearby, his sword clenched in his hand, holding back the watching crowd and aching for her. Solid as a rock he stood, as solid as he'd been all through her life, even as a young girl and he just barely older, with a deceptive song on his lips. Songs that did not hide his soul as she'd often considered them, but now knew revealed a side of himself that he could not hide and did not want to. He loved life. He praised it in all its forms and nourished himself from the nurturing of it. He had a Vaelinar heritage as close to that of the Dwellers as he could get, and he chose not to hide it but celebrate it, for there were few Vaelinars who could understand. She understood, now, and in that split-second before Tressandre would descend upon her, she saw him anchored deep into Kerith with all his love and hope of life. He was exactly what she had always needed to love back. She'd sensed it and committed to it, but now she gave her all back. She threw her soul about that anchor and held on tightly.

She knew enough about her Talents that she could possess and look ahead, sometimes fractions of moments, sometimes years. She always feared never being able to return, so Lara had never let her Talent loose, had never unfurled it to its lengths even with Jeredon helping her. Now she had Bistane. She would never live past this moment in time if she did not reach for another. So she did. She seized not flesh or soul but Time itself.

Her senses darkened a moment. She knew a painful and disorienting jerk, like being at the end of the movement playing Crack the Whip. Then her eyes flew open and she stood on her feet, bringing her right dagger across and down. Her ears thrummed with the pressure of her movement, but she spun on her left heel after the slash without waiting to see its full effect—she knew she'd connected—and reached out, grabbed a moment, and whipped herself forward again.

She caught Tressandre stumbling on a jump, blade-filled hands flailing as she struck impotently at emptiness. She kicked one foot out at the back of Tress' knee, bringing her down, and rolling, and lashed out, getting the inside of her thigh deeply. Crimson spurted in the wake of her strike.

"Tell me where the children are."

Her lip curled. "Like curs, waiting to be sacked and sunk in the bottom of the pond, where good-for-nothing mongrels should go. You'll never find them without me." Tressandre bent over her leg, one forearm up to shield and the other frantically ripping apart the bottom edge of her shirt and trying to wrap the thigh wound. Lara hung back long enough to let her make the ineffectual gesture, trying to shrug off the cold dismay Tressandre's answer stabbed through her.

If they lived, she still had a chance to find them, but she would not take that chance from Tressandre. She sucked in her resolve. "What I learned from Sinok was that it isn't enough to be right or powerful. You have to be ruthless. Today I embrace that."

Tressandre began to levitate, her arms flung out and her hair spread upon the winds of her movement, readying to flee.

Lara lashed out with the back of her hand and the butt of her dagger's hilt, smashing the side of Tressandre's temple and laying her out flat on the ground. Winded, she took a deep breath so she could raise her voice. "For every traitorous act you and your brother Alton have committed on the peoples of Kerith, I condemn you. I judge you. I execute you."

"You can't kill me."

"You think I won't? Again, you've been wrong about me, ild Fallyn."

Tressandre flung her hand out, digging her fingers into the grasses, new grass grown over old blood and ashes, her nails digging down deep. "This is mine! It should belong to me. By blood and spirit we shed here, I claim what is rightfully mi—"

She brought her dagger across Tressandre's throat even as the woman's face curled in spite, and she shouted out a single, indistinguishable word.

Warm blood splattered Lara's own face; she dropped her daggers in the grass, straightening and wiping her face on the back of her sleeve. She noticed then that her own shirt and jerkin hung in tatters about her, exposing the mail bracers Bistane had so lovingly secured in place. Tressandre had gone for every weak and vulnerable spot she could reach, and met the mail with every slash. If he had not prepared her, and if she had not reached out to Time itself, it would be Lara lying in the pool of blood on the trampled meadow. Her eyes blurred a moment and she had that sense, she had that fleeting moment of knowing that Time seized her back, and she looked on another field of death, and heard the voice of a God in her ear.

Then she returned, with a shiver, and Bistane held her up by one elbow. "Are you hurt?"

He held her away from him and checked, limb by limb.

"A few cuts," she answered. "Nothing deep. You had me covered where she intended to strike. We can't stand here. She had orders in place."

He swept his gaze over the retreating crowd, the pale of face and disbelieving, the Returnists and squatters and her men, all of whom had lost all they'd hoped to gain. "To do what, you think?"

"Kill the children at the very least. Set the world on fire if she could have managed it. Or—" Lara lifted her head and looked at the Eye, pulsing as it hung in the sky, and a chill fell over her. "Open that."

Chapter
Fifty-Six

BREGAN'S MOUTH tasted of dirt and ashes when the whirlwind deposited him at the hills above Larandaril. He staggered as it dissipated around him, his skin chapped from the dry heat of the elemental as well as the grit and debris that had been caught up with him. He had not been able to summon the God for days as he wandered across the wilderness, and when it had finally found him and taken him up, it hadn't crossed the land directly "as the silverwings fly, the Dwellers might say." It had meandered where it would, reminding him that the Gods of Kerith were both capricious and distinctly not mortal. He spat as he could, but he had little enough in his mouth that he could not clear the taste of his journey from his throat.

He wobbled down the small slope, listening for the rush of the river, heading for the water which was the only thing on his mind. His burning thoughts had quieted for the moment, leaving him only with the need to drink and perhaps find food wherever he might. But water, sweet water, stayed foremost on his mind. He could see its vibrant blue ribbon winding its way across the valley. He did not even notice the war hammer he had stuck through his belt, great thing though it was, covering two-thirds of his body and bouncing against his one good leg as he made his way downhill. Drying grasses tore at his ragged clothes, and stones pushed at his toes however they could be found, until he stumbled onto the last muddy bank and half slid into the river awaiting him and nearly drowned himself.

But the Andredia had suffered a fair amount of fools in her time and eased away from him, enough that he might turn his head to breathe while he sprawled half-conscious at her mercy. When the coolness of the water lapped at his face and neck, bathing away the grime and sunburn, and when he'd drunk all he could consume, he got to his knees. His brace creaked a bit. Bregan looked down in surprise. The smoothly geared contraption rarely made a noise or stuck or hampered him in any way since he'd been fitted with it more years ago than he would like to admit. He could see that he'd battered the elven machinery over the years; tiny scratches nearly invisible to the eye could be seen and also bits of wood and stone caught in the cogs and wheels. He stepped into the river and cleaned it as best he could, for without it, he stood and walked little better than a one-legged man, and that one without a crutch as well. His brace caught the light as he emerged, gold-bronze and brilliant, and when he stepped, it moved as smoothly as it ever had. Bregan smiled. He began to move down the Andredia toward his next goal where it hung, barely imperceptible from his vantage, the golden eye low in the sky over the forest, the portal that began to hold a crimson hue as though that eye bled.

As he gained ground, memories of the man he used to be flooded him. Wastrel, gambler, a man women flocked to, a Master Trader, a master swordsman, even after being crippled when he had to switch sword hands and relearned his skills. He wasn't sure why the Gods let his mind come back together again, although he supposed it was for some reason of theirs. He wanted to say that he would have come to them, even if they hadn't split his mind apart, but he wasn't sure of that at all. He knew he hadn't much choice when he had turned to the Gods of Kerith, because they were the only ones he could perceive in the days after his mind crumbled. Even Abayan Diort and Sevryn Dardanon, with their bold presences and sharp weapons, had barely existed to his senses in the first days of his new self. Even now Diort looked upon his charge with a somewhat beset upon, if benign, expression. The Guardian King had never seemed certain of his guardianship. He could not fault him or Ceyla his oracle; both had cared for him as they could within the range of their experience. Bregan knew he was difficult. He could not change that. The demands of the Gods were excruciatingly difficult. They were angry with their people and with their own complacency, choosing to sleep for centuries as if all had been well.

That would change. That and everything would change. Bregan caught the edge of that fleeting thought as it sliced through his awareness, that edge as sharp as razors. He had been given this task and would do it as they asked of him, but at the same time, he wouldn't absolve those Gods of their forgetfulness. Of their sleep, of the deaf ears they'd turned to their people.

They'd been called upon and chose to ignore those pleas. He, Bregan, newly discovered Mageborn, would exact a penalty on both the errant people and their Gods. Only he could do it. He would suffer whatever punishment they lowered upon him gladly, and as for the future . . . there would be other Mageborn coming along, sooner or later. He had but to blaze the trail for them.

He knew they would take far better steps than his own shuffling, struggling ones. They had to be better than he—he rested with the dregs at the bottom of the barrel. But, then, perhaps that is how he and his line escaped the purge that took the Mageborns out of Kerith for all these centuries. It was not the best and wisest who came surging back, but the least of the unwanted.

Good camouflage, he told himself as he rounded yet another lazy bend in the great river and then heard the singing in the sky of the portal which had never been closed. His neck stretched as he threw his head back to look at it, great slit in the clouds, with auras shifting behind it, hinting of untoward things happening in faraway elsewhere.

His brace glided smoothly the faster he walked and the closer he got to his goal. It more than held his weight; it seemed to be upholding the other leg as well, lending strength and speed to both. He hated the weakness that ruled the right side of his body. He'd seen old men and women cursed with it, a stroke of the brain, folding them up and spitting them out without unwrinkling them, leaving them tottering upon the face of the world. It was his own fault, though, he admitted that to himself. He had charged at the Dark Ferryman, a phantasm who was no more mortal than a . . . a . . . stump of a tree, and he'd been hit with the full force of whatever magic it was that ran it. The jolt knocked him across the river, blazing pain into every fiber and bone of his being, and he thought he'd died except for the agony that coursed through him with every laborious beat of his heart. He should have died. He'd attacked a Way, accusing it of deception and dishonor as you would a mortal, but it had never been mortal, that Vaelinar Ferryman. Well, Bregan told himself, that was not the story entire. He had been mortal, once, brother to the Vaelinar traitor Daravan before caught in a web of magics and transformed into the Dark Ferryman who could ford any river, no matter the flood or wind or ice, who could and did escort any barge or ferry brought to him. And whom it was said, could also transport a wanderer across any water if his name was invoked.

Bregan doubted that last, but he knew those Vaelinars who had traveled far more swiftly cross-country than even their hot-blooded tashyas could carry them, so perhaps there might have been an inkling of truth to that assertion. Perhaps. If so, he needed the Ferryman now. His body ached and his belly growled with hunger and his lungs wheezed with every step. Then Bregan realized he'd broken into a run, an easy run that his body resisted but answered to, anyway.

The Eye grew ever closer.

If he kept running, his rib cage heaving and rasping, he'd die before he reached it.

Bregan dug in his heels and clenched a fist. "Take me there in my own time, or I'll drop dead. Then where will you all be with your plans and prophesies?"

His run staggered down to a walk, a long-striding, quick walk, but a walk nonetheless. He muttered gratitude to the thin air, not caring if it was heard or well-received. He was Bregan. He knew what he was about, what he'd gone through to get here, but not what he'd go through to get out. The memories, painful and harsh, crowded him, and he'd bat them away if he could. Better to go on as he had been, obstinate and odd, but clouded. Whatever he must do, it seemed his reason was needed. He realized he had the great war hammer, Rakka, in his belt and laid one hand across the hammer end of it, against his chest. He remembered not only himself now, but also the crazed Mageborn he was, and that the time had come to break the world.

Dayne crouched by his small and meager fire, warming the palms of his hands because it seemed that that would be the total output of all the warmth to reach him. He'd had a cup of hot klah—the last of his store—and porridge made from some of his grain and a half handful of the horse's. He hoped the horse wouldn't miss it because he'd been hungry, terribly hungry, and the horse had grazing, after all, ample grasses just now bending to cold nights. He squatted closer, spreading his hands wide, hoping that if he warmed them before he shoved them into his gloves, the warmth might spread through his entire body.

Brista had given up and returned to Larandaril, her quest to find the children failed and her confidence eroded. He alone stayed out, searching, weaving across the countryside, hoping to eke out some clue, some sighting, some evidence that Evarton and Merri had been taken this way. He had one last journey to make, and wasn't certain in his mind if it would do any good, and what his brother and Queen Lariel would think of it, but he'd decided to storm Fort ild Fallyn itself and demand answers. And not in a diplomatic way. It would probably disgrace the Vantane name and he doubted the ild Fallyn had an honest tongue among them, but he wanted to know what they would say to his face. He would get some satisfaction, if poor, because he was the son of Bistel Vantane, and that bloodline they had to respect even if they cared little for his half-breed son. But they could not spit outright in his face, and he thought of himself as a good reader of what was not said, as well as what was.

He'd at least glean if they'd taken the children. At least that.

His throat ached with the thought there might be little else he could take back to Nutmeg.

Verdayne rocked back on his heels, letting his rump hit the cold and stony ground, putting the heels of his hands to his face and holding them there for long, quiet moments in which he might have cried or at least tried. Despair fell upon him, a deep dark cloak from which he didn't think he could emerge. To have lost Merri with her bubbling laugh and mischievous eyes, and Evar, with his curiosity and determination. To never see them again . . .

Dayne forced a long breath down his throat and shoved himself to his feet. Another day and then he could turn his trail toward the coast, toward the nest where Tressandre ild Fallyn curled. He kicked dirt over his fire and then poured the last of the klah on it. Little smoke wafted up, for he'd barely had more than a few sparks there to heat the rocks which had warmed his cooking pan. He'd have to find a homestead or village soon and buy whatever supplies he could—little enough on him to barter or trade with, but he might be able to beg some credit on Tolby Farbranch's name. His wouldn't be believed. With a sigh, Dayne stirred the ashes to make sure they'd cooled and gone damp. No sense having a wild fire on his heels as well.

He scratched his mare under her chin as she raised her head to take the bridle, and she shoved at him a bit, though whether in affection or irritation, he didn't quite know. Probably irritation from being kept from her meal. She'd lost little enough flesh, though, over this ordeal, unlike himself who'd had to punch a new belt loop just last night. He rubbed her head as he gathered his reins and prepared to give the half leap that would gain him the stirrup and then up and over.

That's when he saw the smoke, a thin trail he might have missed, but the mare had her head raised and her ears outlined the wispy white trace. Dayne froze in his tracks and shadowed his eyes against the morning sun. The squeak and rattle of small beasts in the grasses and shrub did not abate, so the fire makers weren't terribly close.

Neither were they awfully far away. Nor were they shy about revealing themselves as the smoke grew thicker and higher. A good fire for a morning's breakfast of people who undoubtedly thought they were all alone.

At first Dayne thought that he might get some supplies, if they were well stocked. And then he wondered who they could be at all. A tic in his throat grew painful and he rubbed a chilled hand over it, reminding himself that he'd forgotten to pull on his gloves. He did so, hurriedly, without urging the mare to take a step.

Whose fire?

Tolby might have ridden back out, hoping to cross paths with him, and resume the search. Brista was days gone, so unless she'd doubled back, she hadn't made a camp. She'd gone south, and this fire lay north of him. North and west, a bit.

He put a gentle heel to the mare's flank, urging her forward, at a steady walk, and reined her through the terrain over the least noisy path. He wasn't sure he wanted to sneak up on the campfire, but he wasn't certain he wanted to ride in, assuming courtesy. Not after the massacre of a trade caravan on a public road. Not after the taking of Lara's heirs. Not after the general breakdown of rules he had once assumed to be inviolable.

When he drew near enough to the fire that he could smell it, he dismounted and pulled the mare into shade between trees, its branches sparse but still covered in foliage, and let her drop her head to graze again which she did willingly. As he moved, he caught the lay of the land and realized—how could he have not known?—that he had circled south as well, with the hills that marked the boundary of Larandaril immediately to his south, a ride of only a day or two. He was likely to have come across a few of her huntsmen, then, although the bounty of the valley should have provided all of their needs. Perhaps someone riding down to Larandaril, then. Perhaps someone spying on it from the ridges, which gave him pause because the only Vaelinars he knew who would keep such a surveillance wore black and silver. If that was the case, it was fortunate he'd been cautious approaching and should remain that way.

He unlaced his bow from the saddle and took the quiver. Less than half full, it had provided fresh meat now and then and he'd regained his arrows whenever he could, but in the way of things, he hadn't found every arrow shot. He had enough to hold off a few men. More than a handful would cause him a great deal more trouble than it would be worth starting a fight.

Dayne sucked on his teeth a moment, deciding. Then he slung the quiver over his shoulder and advanced with bow in hand. Because the season had begun to close in on what would become winter, leaves had fallen and dried. The odd twig here and there. Even entire tree limbs, weakened by beetles or storm. He moved as quietly as he could, trying to make no more noise than a nut wrangler might do among the roots and grasses, a poor effort unless it was a terribly big-footed nut wrangler. When he finally went to ground and lay, listening, he could tell that those at the campfire had not detected him and seemed particularly unworried that they might not be alone. It was, after all, a big patch of wilderness they were riding in from, and they rested on the border of a kingdom with civilization and a militia. He dropped his chin and pitched his pointed ears a bit with the effort, in order to hear better.

"There's ridge runners hereabouts. Keep your yaps shut before you draw their attention."

"Ridge runners?"

"It's not only wards Queen Lariel uses to keep her borders safe. There's creatures. Never seen one, but I've heard of them. They run loose on these hills and cut down anyone who crosses their path."

"Old wives' tales. You're worse than an old Dweller blowin' smoke. No such things hunt along here, nothing other than the creatures we all know about."

"There's been deaths up here no one can explain."

"Those are from the wards, if anything, but she's weak now and so are the boundaries. Our Lady got across them slicker than snot on a slime dog and we'll get across, too."

A rude noise cut across the arguments.

Dayne lifted his head and crawled closer, cautiously, near certain what he'd stumbled over, and not liking it. He knew the banter of troops, the friendly scorn they held for each other, and the vitriol for the energy. Before he rode down to Larandaril manor, though, he wanted to be sure.

A horse whickered. Not a noise of greeting though, more like an irritated "shove over" from one grazing mate to another. He froze in place. The horse line seemed to be upwind of him, on the other side of the campfire which meant they hadn't winded him. No one suggested that the horses be checked. He elbowed himself closer another stride or two. A faint breeze rose up, whispering over the ridge and its twisted grasses and shrubs and leaning trees that attested to far stiffer winds. It brought a scent to him, a musky, sweated, and dried blood animal scent that would be far stronger if he sat at the camp site. For a moment, Dayne did not quite recognize it, and then it hit him between the eyes.

Rufus.

Dayne mulled over his options. He decided he didn't like the idea of Rufus with troopers who followed a Lady with movements "slicker than snot." He could back off and go on his way, and send a party back to investigate or he could go in now to free Rufus. He flexed his hand about his bow several times the way Bistane would drum his fingers on a tabletop, thinking. It came down to the numbers and odds.

Then he heard a high-pitched and peevish voice declaring, "That is not right. That is lying!" A chill slid down his back. Merri. It had to be, not so babyish as she had been, but then it had been months since they were taken. Months in which to get steadier in her steps and words and thoughts. Months without her mother and the family that loved her.

Another voice responded, also in higher tenor, "It's not lies if they believe."

"Then they're ignant."

"Ignorant."

"That's what I said!"

"Shut your mouths, both of you. And keep them shut or your dinner bowls stay empty."

A low, muttered, "Lying liars."

He could picture Merri folding her arms across her chest and settling back with a stubborn look on her face. He knew that look, although he usually had only encountered it assigning chores. And nap times. And yes, bath times, too. The corner of his mouth pulled back in a smile, in spite of himself.

They were *alive*.

First, to free Rufus. Then, get the children. And he needed to plan his action very carefully to ensure they stayed that way.

Chapter Fifty-Seven

Trevalka

SHE COULD HEAR the patter of rain off and on during the night. It had started sometime after the moon's zenith, and she'd kicked off her covers, finding the small hut oppressively warm. Sevryn did not rouse, for which she found herself overly glad. He was up more and more now, terribly weak but gaining strength each day, and during the nights as well, and she'd hoped for a sleep straight through. His mental restoration far outpaced his physical, although hard to discern for he was either ill-tempered or remote. Only in her dreams did he even approach the old Sevryn she remembered and loved, and Rivergrace found herself losing hope that he would come back to her this time. She woke herself up, unhappy and unsettled, and lay on her back staring up at the dark ceiling and listening to the rain. The snows would melt if it kept on all night, a false thaw, because within the week or two, winter would be back with all its cold wolfish intensity, at least on the mountain. As soon as the wind came up and the storms came in, the cold would settle in and bring back the snow and ice.

Rivergrace closed her eyes after a bit and tried to go back to sleep, listening to the rhythm of the rain dripping on familiar outside objects: the cooking stones, the communal benches, the hard-packed ground near the horse lines, and even off the roof of the vast hide tent where they wintered the horses, their own body warmth and blankets keeping them fairly comfortable down the hill. She thought she could hear the soft trill of a perimeter guard whistling to another as shifts must be changing. She'd stood her share, shaking in the cold, eyes stinging from the expanse of whiteness shining the moon back at her. She'd handled the night shifts, the hunting, the skinning and more. Everything that Sevryn would have done, if he'd been able, she'd done. Her body ached when she went to her small cot and it hurt even worse when she rose, if that was possible; the pain of waking reminded her that she was still alive. But she wouldn't have it said that their presence in this colony was a burden, that wintering them was something that should not be allowed.

Because she had awakened, she began to pull carefully on the threads of every soul she had bound to her, counting their numbers and found them, to her relief, the same. Quendius was quiet then, as quiet as his hibernating Undead, and their shade count did not differ nor had he added to them. If he added souls that she had not been able to anchor as well, their numbers could overwhelm her, inundating and drowning her. She loosened her touch on her anchors, finding their dreams bleeding into her, uneasy dreams of great hunger for blood and pain, terrible, harsh visions that she could not stand to have wash up against her. She shivered under the onslaught of their desires and wondered if the same dreams haunted Sevryn. Neither living nor Undead, he existed as a shade, an essence in between, and drifting every day farther and farther from a man she could reach.

A drop of water fell on her forehead and slid down the bridge of her nose. Grace threw her head back and stared into the ceiling at a leak she felt but could not discover. She reached out with her water sense, and turned the rivulets of rain aside from the top of her roof, at least until sunlight when she would see what needed to be patched. Another drop fell and then the wetness halted. She swung her feet out and quickly shoved them into a warm pair of boots as the winter tried to seep in through the cold floor. Pulling the door open and then the insulating flap aside, she could see a few lone figures moving about outside.

The nearest one paused. "Rivergrace? Are you coming with us, then?"

"Checking the traplines so early?"

"Yes. We need meat for the soup pots."

"Wait for me. I'll finish getting my gear." She dropped the flap down and retreated long enough to layer herself for the morning which felt as cold as it was damp. When finished, she threw a look back at Sevryn who either had not awakened or played dead on his cot across the hut.

His hand streaked out from under the blanket. "Aderro."

For a moment, she melted, and he grabbed her wrist, dragging her down to the cot. As she fell awkwardly across him, his hot mouth went to her neck and bit down, holding her in place while he wrapped his arms more tightly about her.

"What are you doing?"

"What comes naturally." He gripped the edge of her shirt in his teeth and pulled it open, then raked the edges of them down the hollow of her throat and across the mounds of her breasts. He growled as the soul chains snapped and bit at him, little zaps of energy, and gave him pause.

"They're waiting for me!"

"Let them. You're mine." His rough chin forced the front of her shirt open further and now his teeth were on her nipple, biting and sucking. Her back arched. His attention thrilled her and she wanted to respond, but she couldn't. Others waited for her. The meat larders lay nearly bare after what had been a long, harsh winter, with more bad weather on the horizon after this respite. The animals would be out hunting for their food, and they should be out to cull those ranks for their own needs.

"I can't." Her words came out muffled and then he elicited a soft moan from her. She got a hand up and in between them, pushing. "I. Can't."

"What a cold fish you've become. More water in your veins than blood." She couldn't see it, but she could hear the disdainful curl of his lip.

She pushed more firmly. "I want to be able to meet you, like the partners we are. But the hunting party is waiting to leave."

"I don't want a partner. I want a mate!" And his mouth left her breast hot and throbbing, his sharp teeth nipping at her ear, drawing blood. As he spun her away from him, she lost her footing, landing on one hip on the floor.

Rivergrace's hands went to her shirt, doing up the buttons as well as she could, feeling her face warm with anger, words stuck in her throat. She got up, ready to answer blow for blow, but Sevryn turned over on his cot with a snort, putting his face to the wall.

A sharp knock on the door called her out. She grabbed her scarf, coat, and gloves from hooks and shoved her arms into sleeves as she went.

She shut the door firmly behind her. He had only reached for her intimately once in his recovery, and that the moment had been brief and violent, signed to her that the man for whom she waited might be far beyond her reach. The man inside their hut had no real idea what aderro or love might mean.

Their boots whispered down the side of the mountain, through melting snow and puddles of bone-cold water as they walked. The others talked amongst themselves, having little heed for Rivergrace despite the days they had spent together. Grace thumbed the hilt of her hunting knife at her belt and listened to the wind snaking through the evergreens and rattling the bare branches of the other trees as they passed through them. The trappers' camaraderie toward her amounted to little more than the cooperation they needed to hunt successfully. The realization pricked at her, reminding her always that she did not belong here. Not in this world, not in this time, and even sharper because it told her she had nowhere else to go, not until that final moment when everything would end.

Her arm hurt where Sevryn's iron grip left marks and she rubbed it now and then, until she saw Leyle casting a look over her shoulder at her and frowning. She didn't want the healer's aid and took care to stop drawing attention to herself, but Leyle dropped back to keep pace with her anyway.

"Did you anchor him to yourself?" the girl asked, watching the ground carefully to see where she walked, unwilling to look Grace in the face. "After the healing, I mean. I told you how far away he'd gone. Did it help? Did he come back to you?"

Rivergrace considered her answer before she spoke. "No, he didn't return to me, not entirely, so I'm not sure if catching his soul helped."

"I'm sure it must have." And Leyle nodded her head, agreeing with her own statement. "I saw where he wandered, very dark and cold. I wouldn't want to live with anyone that close to the cold hells. He would scarcely be mortal. And I've seen him out and about in the last weeks, getting stronger. He's healed, I think, yes? He's not the same, but he's not lost to us. Not yet." She lifted her head long enough to throw Grace an encouraging smile.

"Do you think so?" Rivergrace knew that Sevryn got up and about when he thought she wasn't aware or would find out later, slogging through snow and ice, building back his strength and stamina. The strength he had, she could attest to that. As to the rest of his healing, she could not gauge.

"I do. I know you worry. I should have told you sooner!" She linked her arm through Grace's. "I've seen him watching you when he thinks no one else is looking. He struggles with his love for you. It comes and goes with him, unfamiliar to his lost side, and very much wanted and valued on his other side."

"You see that."

"In his eyes. I can feel it a bit, too, I think." Leyle had reverted to watching the ground for exposed roots and stones, but she tilted her head to one side as she thought. "I think he is trapped. So, mind you this. He may pretend there is no love so that he can do what he has to, without warring with himself. Both of you have great foes to face." Leyle stopped in her tracks altogether and tightened the arm she had slipped in with Grace's. "The others don't like to mention it, don't want to face it, fear being exposed to Trevilara. We *are* safe in these mountains, but they don't think so, and they worry and they shun." She tapped her other hand on their braided arms. "I hope you don't mind me talking."

"I don't mind at all." Rivergrace found a smile, quick and then gone, still genuine for all that. "You bring me a bit of peace."

"Good!" The group up ahead stopped and began to separate, to follow the various trapping lines. "Let's hope we find some game. I hate this time of the winter, when stores get lean and I get hungry."

Hunger pangs gnawed at Grace as well and she split away from the group, following a snare line that led deeper down the mountain, into its shaded side, where snow drifts still glistened. The wind whispered low to her, but she'd no way of understanding its words and wished that Sevryn were here, her friend and love, Sevryn, with his Talent of Voice that could often hear and know what the wind and sea and stone tried to sing to them. If she had to guess, what she heard now would be a bit of a warning, a revelation that the days were not what they seemed, not yet, for winter still lay upon them despite what it seemed. As she wove between the evergreens, snow caught on their branches fell and plopped wetly to the ground, splashing as it fell. She brushed off the knees of her pants as she followed the line and caught up with the first snare, still coiled and empty, beneath an overhanging limb. There were tracks about it, though, and it appeared some of the bait had been carried off.

Rivergrace opened the bait pouch and bent to scatter another tidbit. Though the emptiness of this snare seemed discouraging, the sight of activity was not. She hurried to the next on the line and found, as she'd hoped, an inhabitant. The little furry body lay frozen on the ground, having fought to be freed and death catching it in the icy night. She untied it and began putting it into the game bag. Its eyes flew open to sparkle at her. A voice filled her head, a sound not from a single throat but many, saying, "We are not dead and we are coming for you."

The rodent fell from her hands to the ground, eyes now shut again, whiskers and paws still and iced over. She toed it with her boot. It did not move or speak again. Grace took a deep breath before bending again to pick it up and stow it away.

It did not move in the game pouch, its brief spark of unlife spent and gone. She brushed the back of her glove against her mouth, steadying herself as she realized what she had truly heard.

She plucked at the cage she wore, soul strings quivering in agitation. They were awake again, every single one of them. Awake, their winter-imposed sleep banished by the temporary thaw. Or, perhaps, in the low-lands, spring had come awake, sluggishly, reluctantly, but enough that the ground thawed. The buds of new life struggled through the dirt to make themselves known. *And the Undead had awakened, hungry and rampant.*

Rivergrace hurried down the trapping line, finding two live and ex-hausted strugglers. She chose the fattest for the cooking pot and released the other, unsettled by the thought of slicing them open and dressing them, warm blood and the smell rising about her. She and Sevryn would have to be quick and merciless before they had caught enough to feed themselves. Stuffing the skinned carcass into her game pouch, she rebaited the snares and hurried back to the point where they'd all separated.

Sevryn met her in the glen. He was dressed too lightly for the snowy mountain but rather for the quickness and agility he needed for combat. He carried her weaponry in his free hand.

"They call me. Did you hear as well?"

She nodded. Then, to match his gear, she shed her overcoat, game and bait bags, and outer trousers, stripping down to the green-and-russet leath-ers underneath and taking what he offered her, placing sheaths and bow and quiver where they belonged. The sun, not quite overhead, slanted down at them. She patted herself down a second time, assessing what she had and what she might need, a slight tremble in her hands. She looked to him.

"Do they anticipate us?"

He shook his head. "All they feel now is the need for meat and blood. It rises like a flood tide in them, a yearning that can't be denied." A hand crept to his throat and he swallowed, and she realized he felt the hunger, too. "But he waits for a woman on the road. He waits for Trevilara to re-turn to him."

Return. That meant that they had met and allied. Rivergrace closed her eyes for a moment, warding off the fear that swept her. "If they fight to-gether . . ."

"She hasn't reached him yet."

"We have to run."

"We have some help."

She opened her eyes, steeling herself, and saw the huge russet crown horn that walked out of the forest into place at his elbow. "What—"

"A mount to carry us, faster and stronger than we are afoot." Sevryn reached for her, putting his hands about her waist and tossing her aboard the massive stag.

It held a natural warmth, breathing gustily as she settled on its withers. Whatever it was, or where it had come from, she accepted the beast for divinity. Sevryn leaped aboard behind her and she reached for the small hump of mane decorating the base of its proud curved neck.

It was both spring and not as they rode to meet that which was both dead and not.

Chapter
Fifty-Eight

THE CROWN HORN raced down the mountain in springy leaps yet Rivergrace kept her balance on its back without effort. She gave up breathing for a few moments as they sprinted downward, before accepting that the stag would get them to the road. By the time she began breathing again, Rivergrace knew that she rode upon a God. Which one she could not be sure, nor had she any idea how Sevryn had made its acquaintance, but she thought it would be the God of forests and animals, the hunter God who had not held a seat at the council she'd first met. That seat had been empty, yet it was not because the God had ceased to exist but because it did not believe and act in concert with the others. It had also, apparently, thrown its lot in with them against Trevilara.

She wanted to ask Sevryn how they had met and what, if any bargain, Sevryn had made, but it occurred to her that it might be crucial whether he'd met this God before Quendius had taken him . . . or after. The kind of bargain he'd be willing to make or accept might be markedly different. How different was something she didn't want to consider. She leaned into the wind, feeling Sevryn at her back and then, with a jerk and a jolt that nearly unseated her, the ties binding her to the Undead yanked at her, filling her with a blood rage and lust that turned the world around her crimson and tried to tear her heart from her chest. The air about her crackled and snapped in violence, stinging both her and Sevryn who breathed raggedly at her back. She thought she'd had control, but that assumption ripped away from her, leaving her defenseless and overwhelmed. She managed a sound, a whimper, at the back of her throat.

The stag leaped sideways, over a fallen log, its cloven hooves raking the decayed sides and exploding the bark like seeds from a thistle. Rivergrace squeezed her eyes tight against the onslaught of thirst from the others. She knew, she could not help that she knew, that they boiled out of their barrows, ravening like animals after hibernation and anything breathing and with blood in its veins attracted them. Fur and hide, flesh and blood, flew in chunks over the muddied landscape, and they fought amongst themselves for whatever scraps might remain. She knotted her hands until her nails bit into her palms, staving off the sensation that she ate and drank with them. Sevryn growled angrily.

"Hang on," she whispered. "Hang on!"

His arm tightened about her waist. His chin dug into the top of her shoulder, hoarsely breathing at the curve of her ear. He said something she could not hear over the thrashing of the flight downhill, the crackling of brush and limb and hooves over uneven ground. She wasn't sure if she wished to know what he said or thought, gripped as he must be. Could she trust him at ride's end?

Forest bled away before them as she opened her eyes again, the road a ribbon through the bleeding horizon that grew closer with every leap and bound. The soul strings pulled on her, dragging her down that road, and she leaned close to the crown horn's bowed neck.

"To the north," she cried, and it flicked a russet ear at her, and its direction turned slightly, as the stag leaned toward the northern road. She did not want to go—dared not—but to hunt, she had to. Her hunt would be different, Grace told herself over and over. Her hunt would stop the bloodshed and hunger, a righteous kill. Her voice coursed through her body: *kill, kill, kill.*

"Stop it, Rivergrace." Sevryn's voice, husking at her ear. "Stop thinking." He pressed his jaw against the side of her head tightly.

As the stag hit the flats, more or less, its speed doubled, the wind in her eyes bringing blinding tears; whatever thoughts she had seemed to be snatched out of her mind. Sevryn settled behind her with a muffled groan. She held no help for him. Whatever she might have given him would be lost, carried away, in the floodtide of speed. Her fingers cramped as she curled them deep into the thatch of mane as the crown horn put his head down and the ground blurred beneath them.

The crimson wash over her sight faded. The blood rage faded. Quenched? She feared and yet hoped it might be. Would the Undead be slow and sluggish now, a well-fed beast? Or, with their thirst fulfilled, did the battle rage now begin to rear up in them, the clash and slash for the sheer joy and power of it? Rivergrace's head throbbed, and she should be afraid, deathly afraid, but a kind of calm settled over her, like a cloak. She knew what she had to do.

Suddenly, the stag began to slow until he was pacing in little more than a trot and she could see it clearly ahead, the army on the road. She could scent it as well, the flesh beginning to putrefy at last, the clothes mildewed and musty, the horses flecked with manure and blood and gore. Fewer horses, and she imagined without wanting to how many of them had been torn apart alive and devoured, fresh gobbets of warm flesh. Behind the army, a great and open eye watched over them, the portal that Quendius did not seem to realize followed them. He did not seem to either see or sense it, riding to the fore of his ghastly army, a massive sword resting on the pommel of his saddle, catching the sun as if he held a lightning bolt. She knew a sword of that ilk; she had once carried its brother, imbued with Cerat. That had been her first acquaintance with the demon and she'd destroyed that sword, but the weaponmaster had forged another to carry in its stead, a formidable blade even without Cerat caged in its metal. The sword stood in place of striking the colors, meant to strike fear in the hearts of those he would encounter.

And almost as if they were expected.

But the stag had them among the tall growth and the shadows of a few sparse trees as they paced to a halt, its flanks heaving with exertion, heat rising from it as if it were on fire. She didn't think they could be seen. Sevryn took one arm away from her waist, and she sensed he patted himself down, checking his weapons.

She relaxed her own hold on the stag's mane, opening her hands and flexing them. The heat grew hotter and hotter. When she looked up, she could see a ball of fire curving from the north, a falling sun heading their way. Like a falling star across a night-dark sky it blazed until it burst over the road.

She put her arm up to shield herself; when she could bear to look out again from their meager shelter, a woman had stepped down from the fire, alighting as if from a carriage, herself on fire—not with a white-orange heat but a cooler, red blaze. Trevilara put her foot down on the road and patted her gown into place, its hem a corona of fire.

The fireball re-formed into a torch behind her, as she turned her head.

"My thanks, Dhuriel. I'll be calling on you again as we move down the road. We have kingdoms to conquer."

"Your wishes are always heard," the torch answered without words which Rivergrace heard as a wash of heat and emotion across her mind. She ducked away from the exchange, not wanting to be singed or have her presence felt. Still the God's answer sizzled and danced in her thoughts.

The torch grew smaller and smaller until little more than the size of a candle's light which Trevilara reached up and pinched out. In a swirl of hem and fabric, she started toward Quendius.

She called joyfully to him, and he put a heel to his horse to hurry and meet her. As they touched, the Eye behind them opened wider, pulsing. It responded to her, and a secret of it opened suddenly to Rivergrace's awareness.

"No," whispered Rivergrace. "No, no."

"What is it?" Sevryn asked, sounding somewhat recovered.

"We thought it keyed to him, because it followed him, since Daravan is gone and can't command it. But Daravan had anchored it to her, because he had created it that way. He was more trusting of Trevilara than I bargained."

"We knew they intended to cross over."

"But I had hoped that they couldn't. That we could corner them here and bring a stop to it. Now . . ."

"Now we do what we must. Have you a plan?" and he ran his fingers across the cage of soul strings that surrounded her. She felt the fiery tingle of his touch on every one: a plink, plink, plink of sensation that sparked. He hissed with the pain as if enjoying it somewhat.

A plan. Her father's Undead whisper in her memory, one of the last times they spoke before Quendius destroyed him: *Remember this," he said. "Cerat is never diminished no matter how many times he is divided."*

The demon who ruled the Undead, whose God sparks anchored them to both her and Quendius, the demon she'd faced before and could quell but never destroy, the great corruptor who licked at her soul. She hadn't understood Narskap's statement. He'd shaken her as if he could sift his words into her very soul.

"What are you telling me?"

"What I must. He lives to corrupt. Innocence is the most perfect bait to catch him. He is most powerful whole." Narskap shook her lightly. "Will you remember?"

And she did, although she still did not quite understand what he meant. She kicked her foot over the stag's shoulders and jumped to the ground, putting a hand on the warm flank. The beast had slowed its panting as it recovered from the run. "What would make the Gods of Trevalka fight?"

The stag lowered its great antlered head and shifted to look at her. Its wise eyes widened a bit. It spoke within her. *Jealousy. Territory. Power.*

"Would they fight against that from another world?"

Gods from another world could not transit here. Although you . . .

"My life is braided with the essence of another, yes, but she is not in possession of me; she is not even a second skin, yet she exists within me." This forest God knew that, as well as she did, but she thought she might find another truth within it as she said it. Rivergrace watched the road thoughtfully as Quendius dismounted, dropped rein, and held a free hand out to Trevilara. The crossing had nearly ripped her apart. What had Narskap been telling her? Now she hoped she understood why.

The stag pawed a foot as if growing restless while Sevryn jumped lightly to the ground beside her. Sevryn cleared his throat, caught by the hunger the Undead felt, even though he was a shade, a being caught in between with all the haunts and none of the advantages of either the living or the Undead. He'd been eating meals daily, so he was not starved by hibernation as they'd been, yet that hunger had burrowed through him, and his skin paled with it. He looked fit. He looked like both the man she loved and the beleaguered being she hobbled with her love. He hadn't recovered, although she'd given him a lifeline to seize and follow, so why hadn't he? He stood, King of the Assassins, and she realized now that he was coin to be spent, a weapon to be thrown at a target, and she no longer had the choices she thought she might. She would probably lose him. Rivergrace turned her gaze away as her eyes began to fill with tears she didn't have time to shed.

She grasped at threads of action. "I'm going to incapacitate Quendius. Whether it will be enough to stop him, I can't tell you. I don't think we'll have another chance to go after him without bringing down his anger on innocents." The thought of what his retaliation on others would be gave her a shiver. They already had a taste of what the Undead had done upon awakening.

He limbered his hands. "And the army?"

"Fire should do it, confuse and perhaps even drive them off. They're like dry tinder, and so they should run, leaving him vulnerable."

"Any advantage you can give me." He quirked an eyebrow. "And you?"

"I," she stated firmly, "have Trevilara."

"She nearly killed you before."

"And he nearly destroyed you. But we are wiser and stronger now, I think, and we have come to this, as we knew we would. I'm not afraid to die." To live? To live as herself with or without Sevryn? Possibly. She wanted her home, the Farbranches, Lariel and Bistane, the sweet Andredia and the Silverwing Rivers, the taste of a Tolby-grown apple, all of it. She loved Kerith. She wanted it safe. The thought of Trevilara invading it, pouring her corruption over the borders into the lands of her home, steeled her. No. By all the ice in cold hell, no. Not her family and friends and people. She leaned down, dusting off the green-and-russet leathers that fit her well, and held weapons within pockets and sheaths, just as his own clothing did, setting herself just as he had. She knew what weapons she had: flame and water, bow, blades, and will, and her tie to the nether-world between living and death. She mastered storm and shadow. Far behind, beyond the curving of the road, she could see a dust cloud forming. Trevilara's troops were not far behind their queen and whatever she and Sevryn could do, they had to do it now. She reached inside herself and pulled up dark cloud and fire within it, and all the rain she could muster up. Storm and lightning wrenched their power from what she had locked away deep inside, and it hurt as they tore loose, bringing her to her knees until she put her hands to the ground and filled the well inside of her, dew dappling her from head to toe. The horizon danced with the fury she unleashed, yet so distant was it she could not hear the roll of thunder nor taste the sizzle of the lightning. Grace forced her thoughts to center again. She looked up to find him watching her. He put his hand down to haul her to her feet.

"What happens to me?"

"When I cut you loose?"

"Yes."

"You find your way back or not. I can't help you more than that except to tell you." She leaned down again, fussing with a boot lace. "I love you."

"You've power. Bring me back if you have a care for me. Before I go after Quendius."

She shook her head slightly, not thinking it possible, that it would empty her of all she had and still not be enough. She had enough love for both of them, but he needed to open up that part of him, to search for himself in the void where he drifted because even though she could keep him from being lost forever, she could not bring him home. He had to want that. He had to find his way back. All she could do was show him the light awaiting him.

She tugged on the essence of herself, water and flame, and considered its threads in the air and whether she could weave him a lifeline and realized, to her sorrow, she could not. She'd already woven one for him, and he'd ignored it. It still floated in the netherworld somewhere, if only he were not so blind that he could not sense it.

Rivergrace touched his cheek. He flinched as if she'd struck him. She tried to tell him. "Think of all night, the night that covers all those who are lost and all those who are gone. There is a window onto that night, with the glow of an everlasting and burning lantern hung in it. Search for that light, Sevryn. If there are shadows, there is a light. There is an anchor and a rope to grasp."

"I'm blinded to it!" He spat.

"I'll keep that lantern lit, but you must find it, however you will. By sight or feeling the heat of it or even by the smell of what fuels it or the sound of it in the dark. There exists a way to find it. If I could, I would put it in your palms." She half-turned away. She wanted, with all her heart, to reach out and take hold of him, until the old light came back in his eyes and the word aderro, beloved, truly meant something in his soul. She couldn't feel it for him, and they both knew it.

"I'm afraid I'll drag you down with me."

"Don't fear. Hope. I have my own anchors. A silver river glows through my night, and a sister's smile, and the memory of you, burning brightly. I know what awaits me."

Sevryn shrugged uneasily. "I shrink from what awaits me."

"Then we've already lost everything, you and I, but they haven't. Not Nutmeg or Lara or Tolby and Lily and all the others. Not yet. Not until we fail here, and I don't intend to fail. You do what you've been trained to do and put what heart you've left to that. Can you do that for me?" He put his fingers under her chin and brought her gaze back to meet his.

"Free me, and we'll deal with whatever may come." He looked steadily into her eyes.

Grace nodded. It wasn't enough, but it was all he could offer.

A shout upon the road brought their attention about sharply, and she looked to see Quendius had reached Trevilara and swept her up in his arms. The portal hanging in the sky shook as though a great wind struck it. She felt it, the burning queen, and twisted in his embrace to point at the gate. Quendius roared as though he'd been blind himself and she now let him see. It had followed him, but he'd had no mastery of it. It gave her heart to know that but, at the same time, Trevilara showed the power she held over it. Daravan's cursed legacy, this bridge, this culmination of all elven Ways.

"Forgive me," she called to Sevryn and burst into a run, carrying her to the road. Sevryn shouted hoarsely behind her, to stop her, and his cry turned Quendius and Trevilara about.

Her heart and breath thundered through her and her soul caught on fire as she touched the demon she'd used to bind hapless souls to herself as well as to Quendius. She pulled on Cerat through her strings, buried deeper within her; the demon splinter of darkness and unquiet and unending ambition and hatred rose up in answer as she promised him freedom and a hero to conquer, his triumph of power dropping her to her knees yet again.

She did not fight to get up this time. Quendius shouted at her, but her ears filled with Cerat's growling triumph, deafening her to all else. She surrounded him with the shining silver of her inner self, that river of life biting at him, keeping him at bay, sending him out of her skin and into the chains writhing about her. Gold and silver and ebony, sparking with snaps of wildfire and magic, the cage surrounded her. She raised her arms up in supplication, in hope, and snapped the cage that bound her even as she unbound them, and the God sparks leaped free. Power arced through the air. Cerat surged within them, his visage with jaws open to devour what was rightfully his, that which had been pledged from the very beginning: the half-lives of the Undead. She could see them swarm Quendius, enveloping him.

Quendius staggered back, his charcoal gray skin paling as the force hit him, all his army, all their pieces of Cerat, never diminished no matter how many times the demon had been divided to make new Undead. Cerat filled him, rushing in with a victorious shout. The other's body twisted about in raw agony and the sounds of his sinews and bones stretching, cracking and popping, could be heard across the span. Then he straightened with effort— and grew. And grew.

Chapter Fifty-Nine

THE VISION OF QUENDIUS, grown to colossal, burned itself into his eyes just before the blow hit him. Sevryn felt himself snap in two when she released her hold on him. The moment of whirling away into nothing took all his senses away and then back into him, hitting as hard as a bolt, knocking the breath out of him. He fought to breathe. Then he fought to see and feel as his eyes bolted open and he saw Quendius gain the flank of his horse where he retrieved that great sword. The weapon-master towered over the horse as he hefted the sword in the air, both diminished next to his bulk. The being turned about and grinned in his direction, and crooked his finger, beckoning. "Come to me!"

His heart leaped into his throat at that, hot blood coursing through him to replace the moment of cold fear. His bowels twisted and he wanted to run—needed to run—but could not. The compulsion to obey jumped in him as well and he shoved it down, pushing aside the will to join Quendius, either as part of the army or to meet him in combat. The urge to battle shoved aside his fear. He desired to launch across the road after Quendius, to tackle and bring him down to size. He *had* to, but his training compelled equally. Sevryn ducked into the bracken and thickets, loosed his Voice and asked to be taken in and hidden, to have the darkness. The world butted against him and he took a moment to answer its challenge, seconds moving in desperation, and then it opened to him. Sevryn laced his way through the dark, his target in sight. Quendius bellowed in frustration as he lost sight of Sevryn.

"Come out, you bit of shit on my boot heel! Come and face me like the man I know you are not!" The sword cut the air about him in a great arc, singing its need for violence. His army, roused, began to shuffle into position near him.

Even as he went to one knee, Sevryn realized he'd left Rivergrace behind. He looked back over his shoulder to see if she'd gone to ground as well, but there was no sign of her. He would send up a prayer if he knew one he could trust, but not with these Gods and not with his own lack of heart. What prayer could he make that would be heard? He shoved that worry aside along with the others and gave himself up to the hunt and the prey and the fight awaiting him.

The sword swung again, and he swore it sang just overhead, so close and loud and sinister its sound. He answered with a call of his own as if he were also made of sharp and tempered metal.

Quendius turned, peering into the underbrush. "So you are near. Come out then and meet me, or are you afraid of the shackles of your slavery once again? My blade tells me it wishes to taste sweet meat."

Eagerness made him shudder, reminding him of a war dog waiting to be unleashed, but Sevryn held still another moment. Just another moment longer. He edged closer into position.

Fire shot up with a crackle and roar of heat, and the Undead fell back with cries and moans in their throats, arms flung up to shield their faces. Embers shot outward, falling about them, bits of uniforms going up with a fizz before smoldering out as they smacked themselves and each other, and every one of them fell back from their leader with a shuffling wariness. Flames reflected orange and blue on their gray faces, dancing with an eerie light over their dead, impassive surfaces. Their panic showed in their movement, quickening and furtive, leaving Sevryn a shot at getting close to Quendius but giving him no clue how he could avoid the man's now gigantic reach.

Two hand daggers against that reach and that sword meant any close combat would be suicidal. Even with a sword . . . Sevryn crouched on one knee, weighing his options. He might muscle a weapon off one of the Undead, that he could manage, and get through the flames with little or no injury, but staying outside the striking ability of Quendius would also put him outside doing his foe any damage. And he wanted to bring Quendius down. Needed to, if only to protect Rivergrace and Kerith. Rivergrace who had taken his heart from the first moment he'd sighted her, that dark auburn hair that tumbled down her shoulders and back, those eyes of riverwater blue and storm-cloud gray and deep blue as at the sun's first and last appearance in the sky. The mouth that quirked when he made a joke, the lips that touched his with both passion and tenderness, the hands that gave him strength and took away his pain. How could he have forgotten her and all that she meant to him? He'd lost his life before and not abandoned her. Quendius must have ripped it away from him. Never again. He would never lose her like that again!

That wish, that need, dove deep inside him, burning its way into depths that had gone cold and numb, torching his soul. Sevryn gasped at the pain of it, of feeling again, of reaching for life again. He ducked as he heard the sword hiss by, and felt the slice glance off his upper arm, a flesh wound if that, little more than a scratch, but it brought him back, whole and wary. Even as he watched the weaponmaster, he saw flesh melt from the other's face, and a skeletal vision force its way through, a demonic visage with little mortality left in its structure. Blazing eyes searched him out, and with Cerat doing the looking, he knew he would be found. The demon had senses beyond those of this earth and plane. The shrubbery rattled next to him. He looked under his elbow and saw the muzzle of the crown horn, nostrils flared as the beast snorted at him.

In a blur the creature disappeared and in its place fell a spear and a small wrist shield, the spear of seasoned wood and its three-pronged point of antler, its accompanying shield looking to be carved and shaped from hoof. Sevryn put his hand on the spear, not much different from the weapon he'd mastered until the tutelage of the Kobrir assassins. If it were tough enough, and being God-made, he hoped it would be, it should serve his needs well. "My thanks," Sevryn said gratefully. The God had promised help, and delivered. As to the rest of the God's brethren, they'd seen no sign. He curled his hand about the spear's shaft and reached his free hand to the shield, strong leather straps at its back. The moment he hefted the items, Quendius swung about, attention snapped to the shadows that wrapped about Sevryn.

Quendius purred. "Therrrrre you are." He turned away from his army and the barricade of fire that held them back, his steps crossing the road in two massive strides.

Sevryn leaped aside, pulse roaring in his ears, ready to meet him.

It was Trevilara who screamed, "No!"

Rivergrace felt Sevryn fade away from her side and her senses, hearing the faint *thrum* of his Voice as he asked for concealment from the surroundings. A tremor passed through her, a loss of faith and confidence. Had she done the right thing? Had she abandoned him? And yet, in the sense that bothered her, hadn't she already lost him? She shouldn't have freed him the way she did, sent him spiraling adrift. Grace clenched a fist. She had to. She would not be like the woman she was stepping out to face. She wouldn't ride on the back of his soul and power as Trevilara did to the people she enslaved. If anything, all those she'd just released had leeched from her until she felt as transparent and insubstantial, her soul unlike that of the demon Cerat greatly weakened with each division and now that she had herself back, she felt leaden.

The portal hanging over the army of Undead flexed in the sky, opening from a mere slit to a doorway. Not yet big enough to admit the army through, but big enough that a person could slip by, and threatening to grow ever larger. She'd miscalculated, greatly. The wall of flames she'd set served now to herd the Undead toward that portal. If they sensed it. Trevilara saw it, her face carved in a triumphant smile, her hands beginning to sketch a sigil of magic and power toward it. Rivergrace could feel its strength as it began to build. This was the magic of the Vaelinar who built Ways.

Behind it, though . . . behind on the road stretching back to her capital, Grace saw the power that fed her.

Hundreds of Undead, making their way slowly from the coastline of Trevalka, in answer to the summons of their Queen. A hundred hundred. A force that must have been on the move days before this thaw, days before anyone could know that Quendius and his men would be on the road to meet her. Trevilara had not only hidden the slaughter of this massive force, but she'd moved it in secret, not a sound or smell giving it away, but as she channeled her powers now toward the portal, the revelation hit.

Quendius had taught her his Way of death. While she and Sevryn had been in hiding, buried in winter, these two had met and begun the undoing of Kerith. She had not anchored these, so she couldn't free the sparks of Cerat buried in them. Trevilara held those leashes but no longer contained the need to hunt and feed.

Her heart froze in her throat at the sight and knowledge.

She moved with only one thought, to stop them at any cost.

Rivergrace flung her right hand out, throwing more heat into the wall of flames licking at the things which followed Quendius. She could hear their hoarse bellows in response. She caught a glimpse of them scattering, arms waving to beat off embers flying in the air, and diving off the road into a ditch on the far side, with sprays of water pluming up as they hit. That caught her a bit off guard, realizing that her targets could react well enough to avoid the fire and possibly come up on Sevryn's flank, but she had no time to do more as Trevilara stepped out to face her. Grace took a deep breath to steady herself and reached down into the land, to touch its hidden waters, to strengthen herself. The flow she tapped was the very font she'd sweetened last autumn, and it rose to greet her eagerly as if its elemental self could express gratitude. She gathered in its welcoming and held it close, turned her flank to the burning queen, and raised her own hand to meet whatever Trevilara might cast.

As her fire touched Grace's ice, Grace could feel the chains binding Trevilara to the massive army looming down the road, a thousand more sparks of Cerat, eager and able to do whatever their queen asked of them, more dead than alive, but this army still lived. Mortally wounded from the soul outward, each man retained his flesh and agility, his intelligence and ability, his soul burning with Cerat's terrible needs. If she'd feared to set the Undead loose on Kerith, the thought of these men being targeted on her home nearly drove all reason from Rivergrace. Living, they would fight not only because the woman commanded them, but because of the rewards they intended to reap: their freedom, treasure, rape, pillage, victory. Twice as driven as any that Quendius held in thrall and twice as dangerous because they could think and plan on their own. Fire would not blindly goad them any more than blood lust alone. They would seek their own dark desires and fulfill them.

Yet as their Talents touched for a brief, blinding moment, Rivergrace felt a fear in Trevilara, a fear of her, as the queen rocked back on one heel and cried, "Nooooo!"

In that split-second, she knew that she held something that terrified Trevilara, that showed her defeat could be near, that shook her to the bottom of her being. But what?

Rivergrace broke away.

She turned and ran back a few steps, retreating to the side of the road where the grass rose up to tangle about her booted ankles, life rising to meet her. She raised her hand again, shivers of ice before her, preparing to meet Trevilara's onslaught. She could hear Trevilara's army now, boots marching in quick step, a muted thundering on the road, dust rising behind them, the colors of their uniforms a blur upon the horizon, marked by silvery flashes of the sun upon their unsheathed weapons. They would have swords. Pole arms. Perhaps even bows and arrows for the archers.

She would stand out, a bold and unmistakable target unless she could finish Trevilara and shatter the chains held upon their hearts. She had stepped onto the road knowing that she would have to meet whatever Trevilara threw at her with equal or greater force, this match one that would be, if the other wished it, to the death. She gripped that resolve tightly inside her. It was not enough for Grace to be willing to die; she had to be willing to do whatever she must *to live*, and if that meant Trevilara must die in her stead, so be it. It lay inside her uneasily, but she grasped it, hard. She would do whatever she must to keep Trevilara from sending her army through that Way, that gate from here to home. She would not let that army fall on the throats of her people, her friends, and her family. *Never.*

They locked gazes. Rivergrace could see the silver flash in Trevilara's gem-green eyes, the infamous Vaelinar multicolors signaling the magic they held within. Her flawless skin of porcelain with the faintest of copper glows stood revealed by the dipping neckline and off-the-shoulder gown draped about her figure. She looked as if she had just stepped off a dance floor to duel Rivergrace, save for the fire that hemmed the ivory-and-gold gown. The flames licked higher as Trevilara took her measure and then deliberately looked away. She flung a hand out to the portal trembling in the sky above Quendius and sketched a sigil, leaving a brand of cobalt blue burning in the air before her. Trevilara called out three words in a language that tolled harsh and clanging upon her hearing, and the doorway began to open.

Rivergrace abandoned her assault, put her head down, and ran as a bridge arched over the road.

Sevryn held tight to the spear, keeping his back to the barrier as he moved into position with Quendius. He did not have the advantage on reach, but he no longer had a disadvantage. In fact, the overgrown Quendius had to bend to strike at him, and jump aside faster, something his new bulk hampered. As long as he could keep his shield up, he might be able to worry at Quendius/Cerat long enough to blood him, and let that blood loss weaken his opponent. The Kobrir had taught him to move in quickly, deal as mortal a blow as he could, and move out. That tactic would not work here, not entirely, as it would put him too far within reach of that sword. He wished he had his ithrel with him, that cunning blade that acted as a pole arm and then could be doubled upon itself as a blade, sharp and lethal. The spear warmed a bit in his hands, the wood solid and familiar, centering him. The moments he'd felt wildly adrift, like a feather seed aloft in a high wind, blew to shreds around him. This, he knew. This fight, this war, this mortality. And he knew down to the marrow in his bones, he did it for her. Would do anything that she asked of him, and would keep any harm from her, that it was within his power to do. He'd thought himself alone. He was not. His mind and his heart filled with thoughts and memories and moments of her, crowding in, filling him. Others followed: Tolby, Rufus, Nutmeg, Jeredon, Gilgarran who'd fostered him, Lariel of the capricious nature, and more. His people. Her people. Like wicks in candles, they lit and burned brightly, illuminating his soul. It wasn't innocent. It wasn't pure. But it was loyal and fairly honest and it was *hers*.

He narrowed his eyes as Quendius struck at him, Cerat chortling as the sword swung so close he could feel its icy breeze alongside his jaw. He ducked but not to the side or down as anyone else would have done, he ducked forward, carrying him inside the arc of the swing, stabbed into the calf with a vicious twist and leaped onward then, out of range. Quendius let out a mad howl of pain, Cerat's skull sizzling through his face again, like bubbles under the surface that kept bobbing up as he boiled.

Sevryn bounded back on guard. Hot blood trickled down from the wound he'd earlier deemed a scratch. It seemed more than that now, pulsing with the beat of his heart, dampening his shirt and pattering to the ground. That slice would be more dangerous to him now than he could afford, blooding and weakening him. He needed to tie it off and put pressure on it, an impossible task. He wove with Quendius, back and forth, always presenting him with his flank, as small a target as possible and felt his heartbeat count off the moments he could keep up the fight. A muffled growl behind him caught his attention, and he turned slightly only to find himself facing one of the Undead who'd braved the curtain of fire and charged him, ragged clothes blazing, hands brandishing a two-handed sword.

Sevryn threw himself to the ground, letting the impetus of the other's movement carry him over and then lifted up, throwing the Undead at Quendius/Cerat. He picked up the sword long enough to bury it in Quendius's side as the Undead muddled all efforts of Quendius to leap aside.

Sevryn had no time to give the sword a good twist as Quendius/Cerat bellowed and tore the blade out with his own hand. Sevryn got his shield arm up in time to block a tremendous blow that drove him back to the ground, on his knees, and quickly rolled away. He groped to regain the spear he'd dropped and felt it slide back into his grip, caught on his back and looking up at Quendius as Cerat's madness gleamed back at him.

It was Rivergrace who saved him then.

She sprinted past, her dark green-and-russet leathers a blur in his vision, as the landscape rippled up and up, bridging the distance between the road and the Way dancing in the sky.

He rolled to his feet and bolted after her, if for no other reason than to put his body between hers and Quendius, to take whatever might be aimed at her. The archway shivered and shook under their pelting steps, lifting them over the Undead and their strangling cries below, punctuated by Quendius in full voice shouting: "Stop them!"

Nothing reached them on the bridge. Sevryn gained her side, saying, "I'm here. I'm here."

She looked into his face and smiled widely in understanding. "Aderro."

Her next words came more matter of fact.

Chapter
Sixty

"CAN YOU HOLD THEM?"

"It all depends on what is happening behind us."

Grace spared a quick look. "I think they are either trying to close the Way or destroy it."

"Either works to our advantage unless we wish to go home."

She shook her head. "There's no going back for us, not alone. We have to hold here."

"Then we will."

Grace shot a bolt of flame that took out an arc of arrows, turning them to cinder whose ashes fell harmlessly short of them, but the hand she aimed shook before she dropped it down and tucked it in her vest. If she thought he would not notice, she found herself greatly mistaken.

One-handedly, he managed to rip off a piece of his shirt and tie it about his arm, and she laid three fingers over the bandage. A flush of warmth went through him as she sent what healing she could, but the damage had been done. His heart pumped wildly and he could feel the weakness in his limbs from the fight and the blood loss. "We can't hold it much longer."

She pushed at her temple with the back of her free hand. "I can't kill Trevilara. It will unleash that army into Cerat, fueling him anew. We'd have but a heartbeat or two before he destroys us, if he gains that much power."

Enough time for him to shove Grace through the Way they guarded. Enough time for him to get her through and gone, hopefully to safety. He did not know if his Voice and his blood could bond to the Way and make it do his bidding, but he was willing to make a try of it once she was free and clear. Living things responded to his Voice. The Way appeared alive enough to him. She stated the obvious.

"We have to take Quendius/Cerat down."

"I've been trying."

"I know that." A shiver shook her, far more than a simple shiver should, nearly knocking her off her feet, and Sevryn threw an arm about her shoulder to steady her. "I'm going to take Trevilara as far down as I can, and then throw everything I have to you. We'll go for Cerat then."

She leaned against him, her voice softer. "You came back."

"I could not help but come back to you. I doubted that and shouldn't have."

"But that wasn't you."

"Not much of me, but enough. I won't let myself get so far away from you again." His lips brushed her forehead lightly and then he shoved her away abruptly. "Heads up!"

Quendius/Cerat had gathered Trevilara up in one arm, like an auntie carrying a child, and came back at them, sword in hand, their moment of respite finished. Heedless of the flames that licked up her dress and body, he growled at the two of them. He gained the bottom of the bridge which shuddered under his weight.

Rivergrace stepped away from Sevryn, giving him space to fight and then stood her ground, one hand in the air in front of her, cupped. Water began to trickle through her slender fingers. She could feel Trevilara's essence, faint but compelling, in every drop, and through her, sense the many souls linked to her. She could feel the soldiers as they quick-marched to join her, their drumming on the road, the pulse of eagerness running through their limbs, the breath gusting in their lungs, the excitement thrumming in their nerves, the hope to do worthy battle on her behalf and gain the rewards she'd dangled before them, before she'd taken most of their souls. They'd come through storm and shadow to answer Trevilara's call and even as she died, they did not falter.

"What are you doing?"

"Taking water from Trevilara. She uses it as a shield against her fire. I can only take so much, can only afford to weaken her a little, unless . . ." She turned and considered Sevryn who kept his attention on Quendius/Cerat who mounted the bridge cautiously, it trembling under his great weight. The flames about him licked higher, but Cerat Soul-eater showed no care. If the blaze consumed the flesh of Quendius, he still lived and moved. Sevryn kept him fixed in his sight, his jaw tight as she watched them both.

Rivergrace bit her lip as the thought came to her. She dismissed it, but then it came stubbornly right back.

She could affect the chains Trevilara had woven. That realization had brought the scream from the burning queen's throat, the denial, the fear of losing the army Trevilara had brought into her spirit slavery. Grace could touch them. She didn't dare free them . . . they would run amok, heedless, bringing blood and battle, and utter chaos. But perhaps she could transfer them, channel their power into one who could use it.

She blinked, realizing she looked at Sevryn, weighing him, assessing her options.

He threw her a sideways glance. "Unless what?"

She tightened a fist about the water in her hands. "I can't kill her. But I think I can strip her of the chains she's woven, just as I broke the ones I created."

"But you just said the power would leap to Cerat."

"If the chains are broken, yes. But if they are transferred—"

"Not to you. You can't take it. Grace, you're thinning, becoming transparent, moment by moment. That's out of the question."

Quendius/Cerat took two more steps up the bridge, shifting Trevilara in his hold, and the smell of burning flesh hit them.

Rivergrace did not answer his objections, saying, "We have to hold them here. However long we can. We've few choices." And, with a deep moan of effort, she reached out for the souls bound to Trevilara and ripped them away, replacing Sevryn as their anchor.

He staggered back against her, fighting to see and hear and keep his spear arm up and shield ready, as his ears roared with a hundred hundred thoughts and bodies and knew he had to stop them on the road. He shook his head to clear it. Grace could feel the emanations off him, a thousandfold, even as he grabbed them and bound them to himself. He screamed a war cry that shrilled at her ears and made her turn away.

Trevilara cried out; Quendius/Cerat dropped her at the foot of the bridge, and bounded toward them.

Sevryn reached his shield arm over to grab Grace and push her through the doorway behind them when the Way exploded with shattering noise and blinding light.

Chapter
Sixty-One

Kerith

NUTMEG REMEMBERED CURSING every sit-up and touch-toes she did after the babies' birth, but now she found gratitude for the flat, hard stomach she'd created with all those rigorous exercises. It flooded her with a rush, even as her pounding blood heated her ears and face, dangling upside down. The herbalist had taught her, lecturing, that carrying twins could do harsh things to a body, but muscle tone could be brought back if one *worked* at it. She had to get down. Had to. She'd kill Tressandre, so help her, but she had to get down first. No, she wouldn't kill her, she'd torture the cold-damned woman. And when she'd given up the children, then Meg would kill her. She grasped at her plan as she flexed those stomach muscles and bent herself in half so she could grasp her ankles with her hands. She slid her hunting knife out of her boot's shaft and began to saw at the ropes binding her.

Just before the rope began to part, she twisted so that she would not fall on her neck or the knife. The neck she remembered from her youth at the orchards on the Silverwing River . . . trader Robin Greathouse coming by the farmhouse and telling of the young boy (and Meg scrambled to remember the name, the Dweller family who suffered the tragedy but she couldn't) who'd fallen from a tree and paralyzed himself from head to toe. Garner had exclaimed incredulously, "How can anyone fall from a tree?" regardless of the fact they all could, and did. But they'd learned to control their falls, going soft and limp so that if anything, the slap on the back of the head and butt was about all the damage they took. Hosmer had broken his wrist one year, but that had come from a kick from a neighbor's vicious cart pony. Falling on the knife took no great lesson other than itself. One didn't fall on pointed objects.

So as the rope gave way, she spread her arms wide and twisted in mid-air, before landing on one hip and shoulder. The thump took her harder than she expected and she lay gasping a moment, the wind knocked out of her. She curled up and then got to her knees and stood. Anger curled through her and singed the very air she took back into her lungs. She would take the ild Fallyn fortress apart stone by stone. She would not rest until Merri and Evar were hers and home again!

She hoisted up her trousers and knotted them together and slid her blouse back into place, but the corset she toed with her boot before leaning over and ripping it open. Inside, between stays and lacings, she plucked out another piece of rag paper, with a different kind of writ. A Writ of magic. A writ that made her head throb to attempt to read, and her eyes stab with pain as she looked from words to the world around her, attempting to see it with Vaelinaran eyes. Eyes that could see the threads of the world as if she were a God at a loom, ready to weave or unknot its patterns. She could barely discern the makings. Nutmeg blinked fiercely, her eyes welling with hot, stinging tears of pain. She was not made for this! Evar perhaps, as Lord Bistel had been, but she was only of Kerith, not of the elven who made Ways across the lands as if reality existed to be rewoven by their hands.

Her nose began to run as freely as her eyes. She couldn't do this!

She crumpled the paper in her hands and shoved it deep in her pockets, its scant two sentences of words burned into her mind. The power which had begun to well up from the ground about her, like a misty fog in the early morning, sank back down. Perhaps the threat of what she might do would be enough.

Perhaps. She wiped her face on her sleeve. Took a lace from the discarded corset and tied her hair back. Broke into a run, for she'd tarried too long and who knew what might be happening outside the copse.

The ground seemed a little unsteady as she crossed the grove, her steps stumbling or catching now and then until she finally put a shoulder against a crooked tree and paused. Mayhap she'd rattled her brain more than she thought, although she'd taken enough tumbles in her life to know that she had a much thicker skull than most (bless the Farbranch blood). Perhaps the Vaelinaran working had curdled her from the inside out. A thundering roar, muted, but still powerful, filled her ears. She listened a moment to identify whether it came from inside or outside, and then lifted her gaze to the sky peering between tree branches where the rip between worlds pulsed and bulged as if it might burst. Its voice filled the air with the roar of a whirlwind. It shone with the brilliance of a second sun, a bloody sun, colors rippling across its surface in an insane pattern that pounded the head to watch. And below its glare, on the lush and green Larandaril meadow, she could see two combatants engaged in a deadly dance: Lara and the ild Fallyn Tressandre.

Speech froze in her mouth. The wind she'd had knocked out of her and gotten back fled again. She could see Bistane held back on the sidelines by men wearing their black and silver and knew that the moment Tressandre had engineered for centuries came to a close.

Except that she was losing. Tressandre struck and instead of a spray of blood, sparks would fly, and Lara spin away and close back, to slash home herself. Tressandre staggered back and spun about, and Lara closed again, a hornet stinging her opponent to death with a thousand quick strikes. Perhaps not a thousand, Nutmeg found her thoughts, and wiped her dry mouth on the back of her hand and nearly sliced herself with her own knife.

"Rotten apples!" That would be a fine fix, wouldn't it, to have survived ild Fallyn henchmen only to cut her own throat carelessly. She braced her left hand on the tree, digging her fingers into its crackled roughness, her eyes fixed on the sight of her Warrior Queen finally, finally, taking the fight to Tressandre and *winning*. Warmth crept through her body until she realized that every time sparks flew, Tressandre landed a blow that should have driven the life from Lara.

Lariel wore armor peeking out under her loose, white silken blouse that blood now streaked, and with each hit, a new slash revealed her protection. Armor studded with Tranta's jewels, just as she'd worn the day she'd been struck down and sent into a deathlike sleep. Tolby had told the tale of those gems many a time, bits and pieces of Tranta's Jewel of Tomarq. And though those bits of gem protected her again, they wouldn't, couldn't, last, running out of power even as the two female bodies kicking, lunging, stabbing, and whirling away would run out of stamina. Lara might be winning now, but the tide could turn and viciously. Even so, Nutmeg thought she'd never seen anything so deadly and beautiful as the duel before her. She clenched her hand tightly about the hilt of her knife, her every muscle tightening with the need to help, but knowing she could do nothing.

Then Tressandre hit and scored hard, blood flying.

Bistane threw his head back and pulled against the hold of his captors with the same futile urge. He pulled one arm free as Tressandre took to the air with a follow-up roundhouse kick, but Lara ducked under, cramped and hunched, breathing hard against the pain.

And then, then three more passes and Lara had her on the ground. Hope surged through Nutmeg, the battle over, Tressandre spitting but finished—and Lara slashed her throat apart. Blood sprayed up, and Nutmeg would have screamed but could not, the words, the wrongness stuck in her throat. Dead, finally, at last, but oh, Gods!

A wordless scream tore from her throat. Her children! What of her children? The truth to their taking died with Tressandre and Lara walked away from the deed, uncaring. No, no, no.

Hot tears spilled down her face again and she sank to one knee, shaking in every limb. Lara had her down and defeated! How could she strike fatally at the one person who knew where Evarton and Merri had been taken? How?

Sun glanced off the knife blade in her quavering hand. Nutmeg stared at it, unthinking.

No queen like Tressandre does her dirty work alone. There must be someone, somewhere, who knew what she had done and was planning. *Someone.*

Small hope, but she would hold on to it tightly until it grew into something bigger. Nutmeg rubbed her nose on her other sleeve and got back up. Betrayed by a Vaelinar, how could she ever have thought that Lariel would act in anyone's interest but her own? Bistane would give her heirs of her own; she did not need two bastard half-breed children to rise to her throne. If Nutmeg wanted her children back, she would have to gain them herself.

And they would not be the first things she would take back.

Nutmeg wove her way through the last of the grove, not watching Bistane and Lara as they approached the Eye which lowered and threatened in the sky above them. She watched instead, as Tressandre's men picked up her body, taking care and placing it within the shaded canopy that bore the ild Fallyn banner and insignia. They would have formed a watchful square about the body, but a tall, spare man came out of the depths of the tent and shooed them away, as he might children or pests. He moved into a position with head bowed and hands clasped over her, and Nutmeg might have thought he prayed. She recognized the cut of his clothes and his manner, titling him as high in Tressandre's royal household, perhaps even her seneschal. No one saw Nutmeg as she took a place outside the tent flap, just out of view of the watcher.

Shouts rose as Bistane and Lara ordered her troops to dismantle the encampment. The watchful servant observed these actions for a moment before ducking back and bending low over Tressandre's limp body, beginning to arrange her clothing. He spoke to the body, a running of hurried words that Meg could hardly differentiate.

"You can't be dead, my lady, you're too strong for this. Too stubborn. I've stopped the bleeding, you'll see, I have a bit of healing in me, not much, my father tried to beat it out of me for a soldier's ways, but I still have it, and I give it to you, to our Fort, our House. You'll rise again, you'll see."

Outside, a wind began to rustle the canopy, even as Lariel's troops started to topple the encampment, the voices of the squatters crying loudly in anger and despair. In the furor of dismantling the squatters' homes, no one saw Nutmeg as she slipped inside.

"She took my children. Where are they?"

The seneschal raised his face to look at her.

"Do you see them by my side? A bargain made with lies is no trade. I'll take you apart until you tell me what I need to know. She put them somewhere, and you must know what she did with them. Do they live? Did she have them killed?" And the point of Nutmeg's long knife circled in emphasis.

The man drew himself straight. He clenched a worn piece of paper that she recognized and waved it about. "I'm Waryn ild Fallyn and the House lives. Tressandre will have her legacy yet! Your mongrels will die at our hands." Pulling his own long knife, he lunged at Nutmeg.

She did more than duck. She threw herself on the ground, knife point down, and drove it into Waryn's foot, twisted it, and rolled away. He screamed in pain as she leaped back to her feet, and backhanded a slash at him, across the top of his knees. He stumbled back, but her knife caught flesh and crimson cascaded. She would slice him to bits, if she had to, from the feet up until he met her Dweller height!

"You gutter rat." Waryn limped back, breathing hard, gathering himself.

"Not gutters. My kind lives in trees." Nutmeg felt her mouth pull into a smile as he moved again, and she parried him easily. The knives sang as they ran against each other. She let the momentum turn her about while he fought it, the torn leather of his boot hampering his movement as much as the wound. He dropped his left hand to his thigh wound, squeezing it tight, blood seeping through his fingers. Taking a great breath, he leaped at her, and caught her, his blade digging deep into her shoulder muscle. She screamed then, as much in anger as pain.

"I should let you live, to see me kill them when they arrive." Waryn flexed in triumph, baring his torso.

She had her answer, of sorts. They still lived. They were expected. Nutmeg stood fast and plunged her blade into his stomach. With a grunt of effort, she sliced the knife up and out, stepping back as his hand went limp and he doubled over. He gave a last sputter before crumpling to the ground in a bloody pool. She calmly reached up and pulled his blade from the meat of her shoulder where it hurt, but had hit nothing more vital than a little muscle. She bent to retrieve the Writ before leaving the tent, stepping over first Tressandre ild Fallyn's body and then that of Waryn.

She wiped the back of her hand across her face, shaking from the pain. What if he'd lied? Or she'd misunderstood him? She had to believe they were still out there. She had to.

She staggered into the sunlight as a ragged figure burst from the trees across the river and forded it with great, bounding splashes. He stopped, waving a massive war hammer over his head and crying, "I am come to break the world!"

Bregan Oxfort stood on the banks of the Andredia, swung the hammer about his head three times, and let it fly at the portal in the sky.

Hammer and Way collided with a massive boom and a scream that sounded from a hundred hundred throats. Blazing light poured out like molten gold from a bucket, blinding in its brilliance and shocking all who saw it.

Magic spilled out from the Way as if a dam had broken.

The demon she'd come to know as Cerat stumbled through with a roar that deafened Nutmeg. He drove two people in front of him, dwarfed by his immense figure as he emerged, and he combed the land of Kerith in front of him, looking for new blood.

H E SEARCHED. Glowing bits of sparks and embers bounced off a crude pathway arching from the Way to the banks of the Andredia, dancing and drifting through the air with fervor as though each and every one sought a target to strike. Nutmeg felt his burning touch as the demon sifted through her soul, scorched her hopes and fears, turned her inside out as if she were nothing more than a rag on the wind, made her an offer which she, jaw clamped shut against the pain and horror of Cerat, refused. He prodded at her again, opening new wounds, offering a sudden, striking hope which she almost grabbed before pushing the demon away. Her children! He offered them to her, dangling them in front of her aching soul like an auntie might offer a treat, and Nutmeg shoved him off, her sobs stuck in her throat. Torn, she almost grabbed after him, afraid to refuse but she clenched her fingers instead to stave him off. His God sparks showered about her, spitting and biting, a thousand white-hot hornets piercing her. He struck at her a third time. She screamed at the onslaught, the demon's patience gone, his encouraging entreaties dropped, and only cold-hell promised for her and hers if she refused him again. Nutmeg wrapped herself in Dweller stubbornness, passed down in barrels by both her father and mother, and spat back the demon's threats.

Nutmeg ducked her head and threw one arm over herself, knife still in one hand and Writ in the other as she ran to the river's side, because she saw figures outlined in the doorway, two figures struggling. Cerat left her then. She felt raw and bared to the world, but she could see two others who fought to keep him from crossing the bridge to Kerith, and she knew them. "Grace!" she called hoarsely. "Sevryn!"

Her voice shredded on the wind which rose, circling about them, a whirlwind being called up, tearing away her calls even as Bregan sprawled on the ground, his life spilling all about him in prismatic color.

She did not see, behind her as those God sparks blanketed Tressandre ild Fallyn where Waryn had laid her out as befit his sovereign. Did not hear the gasp of unlife which issued in the midst of Cerat's presence.

She did not see the shadows grow to envelop it. Nor did she see what rose in its place.

Bistane took Lara's hand, noting, "Your vision was wrong," as he stepped to her flank and they both took a stance to consider the portal and its increasingly agitated state. He noted the slashes in her clothing, the metal and crimson that showed through, and fought his desire to take her off the dueling field to home, where he would mend her yet again. But she didn't feel the sting of the wounds yet, or suffer from blood loss, her heart's pulse he could feel even in her hand—strong and quick, filled yet with the fury and excitement of the fight. The dart he carried in his thigh quiver remained a precaution he thanked the Gods he had not had to use. Not that she would have thanked him if he had sent her back to the imprisoning sleep of the king's rest. He took a deep thankful breath for that respite. She had won the right to be here, so he abided and teased her instead.

Lara's eyes narrowed. "What do you mean, wrong?"

"You're not alone. I'm in this with you. I have your back, and you have mine."

She felt her expression lighten. "Indeed, you do." She put out her left hand to cover his, and he squeezed it lightly in answer. "I can't guarantee you—"

He raised their joined hands to his lips. "You're the Warrior Queen, and I your Warlord. We have this moment to live. And, if there are others to be savored, I'll still be at your side." Bistane grinned, suddenly. "Even if I have to haunt you as my father does me."

She laughed softly at that. "Fair warning. I intend to take you at your word."

"May I be held accountable by you for all the words I've ever said, or will say. Or sing!" He leaned his head forward and lightly kissed the end of her nose. Before she could react, he swung her about by their clasped hands and she came about facing sky.

She saw the War Hammer Rakka slung through the air, the spindly

figure dressed in little more than tattered clothes except for the bright
bronze metal structure that encased his leg, the elven brace. Bregan
screamed in defiance and danced a mad dance as his Hammer hit the portal and it burst open, spilling a massive demon and more onto a bridge
which now arched to her beloved Andredia.

"Dear Gods."

Bistane had no response, as caught off stride as she. Shaking him off,
she ran her hands over her bracers to prepare for more fighting.

"Send for troops. We don't know what will come through. Raymy or
fighters, plague or swords. Go now!"

Bistane let out a sharp, piercing whistle that caught the ears of those
dismantling the squatters camp and the few who held ild Fallyn fighters at
bay in surrender. He had no intention of leaving her alone to face whatever
might come. Her soldiers turned and saw the unbelievable, even as they
raised their swords to rally. Bistane called for a messenger, and one of them
angled off, heading for his tethered mount.

She did not sense the figure behind her, at her flank. She did not see a
shadow darting in from behind. No glint of warning came off the sword in
hand, even as it drove between the two of them. Buffeted aside, Bistane
staggered back. Lara let out a small cry of pain and astonishment as the
sword slammed into her three more times. Bistane wrenched them apart,
and then Tressandre whirled about on Bistane, knocking him to the ground
with a blow from the hilt. The guardsmen and guarded scattered in disar-
ray, the ild Fallyn recovering quickly.

Tressandre reached down and grabbed a handful of Lara's hair, silvery
blonde unlike her own which fell as a dark, smoked gold, and she let out a
bark of a laugh. Her complexion so pale as to be more gray than porcelain,
her lips white lines in a face no longer beautiful, she looked like the Cold
Lady herself as Lara's blood spurted onto her booted feet.

As quickly as she'd hit, her men fell on Bistane and dragged him up on
one knee as he called out.

"Told you. I can't be killed. Unlike you." And she shook Lara's body.
"No mourning for you. No lying in state. No weeping." She began to walk
to the river, dragging Lara with her.

Without a sound, Bistane lowered his head and lunged at Lariel, his
hand brushing her as Tressandre dragged the body past. Tackled at his
ankles, he got his hands on her for but a moment before her men hauled
him back, their hands and feet battering him until he curled into a

defensive position and felt warm blood coursing down the side of his skull. He did not make a sound other than grunts as they pummeled him, but he did not take his eyes off the procession.

Filled with—what was it? Not life, no, because she knew her heart did not drum in her chest, but brimming with a sinister energy as she savored the triumph of her kill. It had been offered her and she'd taken it, without a second thought. Whatever swept her up and brought her back, she intended to worship. She'd been damned and died. She'd been there long enough to know that hell indeed lay cold and deeply dark ahead of her some day.

Now she was returned, returned in triumph. Tressandre did not miss a beat on her determined march, though the smell of their blood, Lariel's and Bistane's, filled her head with a throbbing need that she burned to quench. She wanted to fall on her knees and lap the warm, coppery syrup. It increased with every imprint of her boot upon the ground, a drummer that sought to marshal her into its force. She heard a faint moan from her captive as her form bumped over rock and stone, toward the Andredia. The noise gave her pause. She hated to make the same mistake her enemy had made. Was there enough left of Lara to destroy further? Perhaps put her to a pyre and light it well and thoroughly?

Tressandre shook off the thought. She had a kingdom to claim, and the Eye of the Portal yawned over her, filled with far more potential than the unlamented Warrior Queen of Larandaril. She could hear a battle at the Way's threshold and knew she could steer its fate. She stopped at the Andredia and took a breath, quelling her blood lust as best she could. This afterlife she'd brought on herself had some interesting demands, but she would conquer it as well. She eyed her latest conquest in satisfaction, noting the blood pooling slowly on trampled grass, the skin growing ever paler, the look of faint surprise etched on Lariel's face, the look of defeat that had escaped Tressandre so many times and that she had obtained at last. Now she had a demon to attend.

Tressandre looked down at the muddy bank where bluer than blue water lapped, in waiting. "Blessed river. There have been many rumors about you. Let's see if this one is true. Here's my blood sacrifice to seal our vows." And she kicked Lara's crimson body into the waters.

Bistane raised his head, blinking as blood ran down into one eye, searching through the figures circling him, all his hope centered on the

Andredia as he watched Lara sink below the surface. Did he see a glint of metal buried in her shoulder? Had he struck home, clear and clean? Such a small bit of metal, scarcely more than a hand's length, his dart. Had he hit home, or had he finally lost her? Or would the River Andredia claim her as its right?

Her body floated limply as it was borne away by the river, drifted out of sight, turning over and over, her face above the surface and then under. Above. Under. Above . . . Surely she had stopped bleeding, although red ribbons laced the water behind her. He craned his neck to watch her still form.

A last boot toe to the side of his head smashed in torment, and blackness flashed through him, bearing him into the dark.

Bregan Oxfort lay, spent, as the bridge arched over him and he sobbed into his forearm at his failure to destroy the Way. When he raised his eyes, his blurred gaze fell on Rakka which had fallen back to earth not far from him. He began crawling to it, determined to raise it one last time, if his failing body allowed him, one last blow at the blasphemous doorway from other Gods to his Gods and nearly reached it when a boot planted itself in his back and held him flat. The sole and heel ground into his spine.

"Sorry," Tressandre told him, as she bent past and picked up the war hammer. "No one denies me what I want anymore."

Her smell, her Undead musty odor, filled his nostrils as he turned his head about, trying to catch her in his vision where he would pin her, Bregan hoped, like an unwary insect. But she would have none of it. He had no hold on her, the Gods skittering away from both of them. She hefted the hammer high. Her eyes of jade that were rimmed in black glinted. "When you see them, tell your Gods they have no heirs to this world. It is now *mine*."

The Hammer fell and Bregan felt his elven brace jerk out as though it might save him yet, and that was the last he knew but for one last, agonizing spear of pain that tore him away.

Tressandre looked up to the bridge, uncertain if she wished to open the Way further or destroy it—if either was in her power. She gripped Rakka in her hands before shaking off a bit of the gore that had once been part of the mad Mageborn Bregan and strode to the base of the pathway. The slope was not considerable and yet enough that she could not see clearly through the portal, at what loomed behind Cerat. Two shady silhouettes struggled at the demon's feet, two figures locked in combat, not with each other but with her new lord. What would happen if she attacked the bridge with Rakka? Would she open the gateway further or slam it shut? And which would give her the most advantage? She was no Returnist wanting to return to the unknown, but she might willingly welcome a powerful ally, someone else to worship at her feet.

Cold hells, indeed, Tressandre thought. She was no virgin to stand about bewailing her fate and whatever might await her. She drew the hammer up and dropped it as hard as she could, fueled with her Undead fury and power, upon the Way.

It sounded.

A note of the deepest, purest timbre came from the depths of the stone and bones of Kerith, rising and striking, with one clear and pure echo after it. Now that, she had time to think, was how Gods should call. As the bridge widened and firmed its approach upon Larandaril, Tressandre recognized the two who fought to hold Cerat back.

Lariel had only been the first and greatest of her enemies to fall. These two would be next. Tressandre threw her shoulders back, drew up the hammer, and began to climb the bridge after them.

She hurt. The Andredia lapped about Lara, over her body and occasionally over her face, cleansing her gently, but it did not take the pain from her. She hurt until death, and even that did not seem as if it could soothe her. The Cold Lady rejected her, pushing her back into agony, pain that she could not push away. The current of the river, slow and easy, barely moving, turned her over and her eyes came open, looking through the water to the stones at the river's bottom. How polished and perfect they looked, even with small minnows swimming among them and waving bits of grass and reed. *Daughter.* A soft, even voice washed through her, one she thought she might have heard many decades ago but could not be sure. It eased her fears, took away the hurt, rocked her in its sincerity and serenity. If the Andredia had a voice, it must surely be this one until Lara remembered the river in its full flood and fury after heavy rains and snow melt, when nothing wise should stand in its way. Few things could exist in the face of that much power. The voice must be different in those times even as it spoke to her now. *Daughter*, the waters murmured again, this time with a faint shaming tone. She remembered she both loved and feared her great river.

But the pain thrummed back into her and Lara flipped face up again, unable to move, or even breathe, though it seemed as though she did because her ribs sent a lance of agony with every movement as she gasped for air. One prick hurt her more than all the others, deeper than the other wounds, blade still buried within her. She did not wish to move, only sleep, and let the Andredia carry her wherever it wished, even out of Larandaril and all the way to the sea. She would sleep wherever Tranta slept, dear lost friend, and even as she thought that, she thought of those she would leave behind.

If she slept that final sleep, she would lose Bistane. Evar and Merri. Nutmeg and all the other Farbranches. Dayne, Farlen, and her troopers. The names stretched on in her mind, all those she'd cared for, even if only as a commander of a great and demanding House. Too many to lose. She was not ready.

Lara wrenched an arm and hand out of complacency, reaching for that thorn buried deep in her shoulder, the thorn that kept her from dying and yet kept her from coming back to the life that the Andredia poured into her. With a tug that tore at her, she pulled the small dagger free and let it drop to the river's bottom. Even as she did, she could feel the soothing touch of liquid cleansing her, restoring her, healing her. The river rushed in to embrace her fully.

Lara came wide awake, dreaming no more. Alive still. And fighting. She rolled over and began to swim, one slow stroke after another, her boots dragging at her ankles, her chain mail and leathers fighting to weigh her down, but she toed the shallows soon enough and stood at the river's edge, soaking wet. Behind her the doorway and bridge to other lands gleamed and roared with the sound and smell of battle and fire, and the very rocks of the valley echoed with the great noise. She wished she had not dropped the dagger now, small as it was. She would have to pick up something useful on the way back.

As she walked, the trees lining the river bent close to shadow her figure, arching their branches over her, a roof of protection from all who might see her on the edge of the Andredia.

Evarton burst into the clearing ahead of them, Merri on his heels and Dayne had to rein back the mule hard before it jolted Rufus following them. He put a hand out and grasped Rufus by the shoulder firmly.

Rufus said nothing, but his eyes flew open and he pulled himself up in the saddle. "The river."

"And more." Dayne did not like the scene on the far side of the river, black and silver fighting with blue and gold. The eye in the sky stood wide open, unblinking save for the figures that barreled through on the arch it birthed, fighting men, with gaunt faces and little more than rags for clothes, guttural shouts uttered from their throats. "What manner of men are those?"

Rufus rolled a Bolger eye. "No manner," he answered. "Fight or be killed." He took the mule's reins up in his gnarled hands, tearing the lead away from Verdayne, clamped his boot heel to his mount and charged across the river, spray flying. In dismay, Verdayne started after and halted in front of the two young riders. Merri stood in her stirrups, pointing.

"Mama! Just like I seen her!"

"Saw," muttered Evar who also stood in his saddle. Both their high-pitched voices raised in shouts. "Mama! Here! Over here!" Their hands waved wildly to catch her eye. Dayne kicked his horse in between them, saying, "Not now, not now!" his heart in his throat as he wheeled around, watching Tressandre ild Fallyn, a massive war hammer in her hand, close in on where Nutmeg stood, blocking the bottom of the portal's bridge, a small, fluttering bit of white clutched firmly in her Dweller hand.

"Stay here."

Both of them answered as one. "No."

"You have to stay here!"

Merri closed her lips tightly and got that light in her eyes, the one he knew so well, an echo of her mother's stubborn gleam. She shook her head. "No."

"I've no time to argue!" He could see Rufus skidding the mule to a halt and his bailing out of the saddle, more a fall than a jump, his wounds hampering him.

"It's just like I saw," Merri added. "Except the general with the white hair and really blue eyes."

Another chill went through Verdayne. "Who?"

"You know," Evar told him. "You *know*."

"You saw this. Merri did, I didn't. I saw the River Lady, though. Several times."

Dayne couldn't think.

They'd been nonstop chattering at him since he rescued them. He'd freed Rufus stealthily, and the two of them had laid low the five ild Fallyn at the camp. Hard work, but Evar had used a bit of his Talent and Merri had turned her healing on Rufus though without much result. The old

Bolger had taken mortal wounds, and she'd only put off the inevitable. The night and half day's ride had filled Dayne's ears—and his heart. He had been hard put to match the two children to the two toddlers who'd been taken, but it was them, aged beyond reason over a mere summer, and he knew them. They told him stories of labor and mistreatment and loneliness and fear and hope. And now Evar looked at him with the expression of a wise, old soul despite his seeming six years, and Dayne believed him. He knew who the man with the shock of snow-white hair had to be.

The ghost of his father who haunted Bistane's footsteps was somewhere on the field, amid the chaos, amid the death, himself undeniably still a force among the living.

"Where?"

Merri and Evar scanned the havoc across the river. Then Evar pointed a grubby finger. "There! He's sitting on something. He's like . . . he's like a boulder in the river. The fighting just parts around him as if no one can see or touch him."

Dayne sighted along the gesture, and then caught the division in the pitched battle outside the squatters' camp, a blur he could not distinguish above a fallen figure. He knew the leathers, though, or thought he did, on the body.

Bistane, lying face down in the trampled grass, as still as death itself.

Dayne's thoughts went skittering as he saw Tressandre close on Nutmeg, and his love swing about, a small blade in one hand, white fluttering bit of something in her other, skip back even as Rakka swung through the air, just barely missing her. She slashed out, low even for a Dweller, catching Tressandre across the top of her knees, before falling back as the ild Fallyn struggled to regain her balance and pull the hammer back into position again.

A yodeling challenge split the air, a Bolger cry as primitive as the old chief could manage, as he charged Tressandre and Nutmeg.

Dayne could hold back no longer.

"Stay here!" he demanded as he put heels to his mount.

"No," they answered again. "Rufus and the old Vaelinar will keep us safe." And they set their horses at his heels, splashing through the Andredia after him.

Nutmeg saw Rivergrace and Sevryn as Cerat drove them backward along the arch.

Within the demon, she could see Quendius, dissolved and merged to Cerat's flesh. He roared as Cerat did. As he lowered his head and bowed his shoulders, making ready to charge, his face changed, melting and re-forming, then melting again, as the maddened eyes of the demon Cerat looked down at her. The God sparks he shed were like a blacksmith's when he hammered hot metal, rivers of malevolence flowing about him.

"Home!" he bellowed, and her ears rang with it, and her courage fled.

But not entirely. She looked up and heard her sister cry with resolve. "Hold him!" and the two, side by side, presented their flanks and raised their blades, and set their feet in determination. The Undead boiled at Cerat's back, tumbling through the portal and falling from the arch, heedless, to the land below. Most got up, growling and ready to fight. A few lay too broken to move.

Nutmeg's hands trembled so wildly she nearly dropped Bistel's words. She looked down and curled her fingers tighter about the sentence that promised the Unmaking of a Way. She didn't know if she could power them, but she could read and speak those words. Still grasping her knife, she scanned the Vaelinaran cursive, praying for justice. Justice that would undo all that Trevilara and Daravan had done. Justice that would protect Kerith and those she loved. A wind rose around her. She felt Tressandre and jumped in fear and reaction as Rakka swept past her. Those maddened ild Fallyn eyes, not so different from the demon raging above them, caught her. She slashed back in defense, low, where the wound would not be mortal unless she hit a major artery but where she could hurt and slow her opponent down. She stumbled backward again as Tressandre hissed wildly and regained her balance.

She heard the shout—Dayne, crying in alarm, "Nutmeg!"

But it was Rufus who tackled her and bounded up with a growl, throwing his body between hers and Tressandre ild Fallyn as the war hammer Rakka swung wildly through the air. It connected with a solid thud, cracking bone and splitting skin.

His body bowed at the hit and he staggered back with a low moan, but he stayed up and reached out, wrapping his leathery hands, hands strengthened and toughened by decades of work at a forge, and he held on.

Tressandre screamed as she tried to wrestle the hammer back, setting her heels and pulling. Nutmeg, still raw from the demon trying to turn her inside out, could feel Tressandre's strength, mined from the dark magic that ran in her veins in the place of blood. Cerat leaned out of the portal to give a laugh of approval, and they locked eyes a moment. He bowled a handful of soldiers through the doorway, even as his bulk shuffled forward, pushing Rivergrace and Sevryn back. Their blows sliced him, his flesh healing before they even pulled back, and he howled in joy. Flames followed him.

Nutmeg felt herself pulled away from the fight, the hands on her firm but small and slender like her own and she looked up into Dayne's face. Her smile that blossomed lasted but a second before she said, "Cover me."

He did not ask why. He made certain she stood firm on her feet before he turned his back to her and prepared to take on all comers, even the Undead who had been thrown past Rivergrace and Sevryn and now came running down the bridge, brown and jagged teeth bared, rusted swords in their hands.

Rufus groaned from deep in his throat as the sinews stood out on his wiry arms and blood began to flow from wounds that had barely stopped bleeding, his leather apron going red and slippery as he hung on to the hammer. His foot slipped on the grass as he went down into a crouch and could not straighten again, and Tressandre's face blazed in victory.

"It is mine." And she clenched her jaw before giving one last, all-powerful tug to the hammer, all her attention and all her rage focused on the Bolger.

Rufus let go.

He did not want to, but two Undead lunged at him headfirst and he found himself impaled on a pair of blades that nailed him to the ground, his throat bared to their grinning faces. His body failed him as he struggled to free himself. He could smell that they were not men. He could smell the corrupted flesh and blood that surrounded them. He let out a last bellow of Bolger courage and tried to get up, fighting to the last, because he could not give up. A vision of light blond hair, adrift on the wind, and blue upon blue eyes, filled him as he fell back one last time. He wanted it to be his Little Flower, his Rivergrace, but it was not.

"Die again, Tressandre ild Fallyn," a soft, determined voice said behind her as Tress waved the hammer high.

Tressandre pivoted, bringing Rakka about, but Lara stood inside her swing, face-to-face, sword in hand. They grappled before Tressandre shoved her away and bent back to aim the hammer. She feinted with the effort, kicking up and out, catching Lara in the throat and driving her to her knees. Choking, Lara took the fall all the way to the ground, rolling and coming up to her feet even as Rakka thundered down where she had just been. Lara reached out, her hand skimming the hammer head as Tressandre began to pull it back. With a grimace and a smothered cry, she pulled something from the weapon, something not quite visible, something wily and spitting and oily smelling, swung it about and threw it into the Andredia where it hit with a smoking hiss. Ripples thrashed wildly in the river until something uncoiled and sank unseen. The hammer itself twisted in Tressandre's hand as she nearly dropped it, the weight and balance upset. Tressandre's eyes flashed coal-dark. She shook her head, dark-honey hair bouncing off her shoulders, and set her feet. She swung, much faster and quicker, catching Lara off guard. Lara plunged to her left, but not in time. The war hammer hit home, hard enough to stagger her back on her heels.

She tightened her grip on her sword. As Rakka raked across her, she made a noise through her teeth and swung about, turning even as the shaft bounced off her shoulder. Lara wrapped her other hand about her first, lunged forward, and buried her sword to the hilt in Tressandre's throat. She made a great thrust and then a slice, taking off her head.

Tressandre's head bounced to the ground, mouth opened in a soundless cry. Lara kicked it away from the body and picked up the war hammer. She pointed at Dayne as he caught up with her, Nutmeg across his horse's flank.

"Deal with them." She nodded at the two Undead who had begun to feast on Rufus's still warm body. He let Nutmeg off and the two of them waded through, blades flashing, to give the old Bolger peace and honor.

Then Lara looked to the doorway and the bridge, and weighed the hammer in her hand as if uncertain what course to take.

Nutmeg began to read, to recite, her gentle voice gaining strength, stumbling now and then over a word in Vaelinaran that she seemed uncertain of pronouncing but continuing stubbornly despite the troops being thrown off the top of the bridge like boulders in a catapult, Rivergrace and Sevryn unable to stop the flow even as they advanced on the being that was both Quendius and Cerat. She felt a presence join her, bolstering her, augmenting the working she'd begun and looked up for a moment, and then behind her. A boy and girl sat near a fallen figure on the ground, Bistane perhaps in stained leathers, the fighting between ild Fallyn and Returnists and Larandaril troops all about them, as if they sat on an island in the middle of a raging river. The boy raised his hand and her eyes brimmed, she could feel the hot tears stirring, as she thought, but dared not think: Evar? And the curly-headed girl next to him. Merri? Not her babes, her toddlers, but children, long-limbed and straight and fearless as they stood to wave to her. A blur near them moved, and she saw, she thought she saw, for a flicker of a moment, Lord Bistel with his brilliant blue eyes and shocking white hair, plain as anything could be seen on that horrific day. Dayne fought his way to them all, lopping off heads as quickly as he could, building a wall of fallen bodies in front of them.

Nutmeg put her shaking hand to her mouth and tasted the tang of blood as she did, before returning to the sentences she'd read and waited to feel something, anything, stirring in her blood. But she was not, after all, Vaelinar.

Only then did Lara look to her. She smiled faintly as if having made a decision and raised the hammer high above her head with two steady hands.

A fiery figure ducked under Cerat/Quendius, emerging onto the bridge. She burst into the air of Kerith, Trevilara, her ink-black hair, singed and in patches upon her head, her ivory gown so besmirched with soot it could hardly be called pale anymore, her flames licking along her body so eagerly they appeared to be devouring her. She raised her hands and flung herself at Rivergrace.

Grace saw the wreck of the woman hurtling at her and dodged, one foot slipping over the edge, nearly taking her off the bridge as she danced backward. She pulled for water. Hesitation slowed her resolve. She could smell the burning, the crisping of flesh, the stink of scorched hair and clothing, the desperation as Trevilara flew through the air at her. She could feel the purity of Kerith coming down on her shoulders like a cloak, and pulled it to her with a deep breath. This, then, was hers. Hers to save from the corruption that dripped from Trevilara's every pore. Grace would not surrender her world. Her land, her loves, her people. Hers to give her life and her soul to.

Rivergrace opened up and claimed what she had feared more and more, not understanding it, not wanting it, but oh, by the Gods, needing it. Now, more than ever. She thrust her hands into the air, and called on the Storm fury buried deep within her. Reached down and down and down, past her thought, past her flesh, past her soul and that of her River Goddess, past her intense love for Sevryn and Nutmeg, Tolby, Lily and her brothers, and all else. She delved deep into Kerith itself, felt it welcome and answer her—stone, fire, water, and air—answer her as if she'd drilled for it and the well fountained up to fill her. It surged within her until she couldn't contain it and shouted, letting the Storm out. Lightning flashed. Clouds roiled up overhead, heavy and ominous and thunder clashed. The lightning leaped from billow to billow and the air stank of ozone. She reveled in it, owning it, giving it liberty to fill the skies.

Then she closed her fist and pulled all the moisture she could grasp, taking all of it back into her. Trevilara screamed as the conflagration exploded about her. Nothing answered her as she fought to put out her own flames. She raged at Grace, toppling to the bridge in absolute, unapproachable flame that took her in a flash as if she were nothing more than dried bone and rags, tinder for the Storm's fury. Then and only then did Rivergrace take control of the Storm and brought it back to her, bit by bit, swallowing its power within her own till the skies calmed into a gray mist. Just as she had claimed the Storm's power, now she claimed regret for the damage wrought, for the sorrow rained down.

The portal shook as it sucked back in the debris, still on fire, the Gods of Trevalka reclaiming their own. Cerat howled and came after them.

Sevryn thrust his arm out and pushed Rivergrace off the side of the bridge, and set himself against the demon. As Cerat towered over him, Sevryn moved, suddenly, swiftly, and instead of aiming upward, went for the ankles in an attempt to sweep the demon's legs from under him. He was her coin to spend, and he took it upon himself to answer that responsibility. The demon snarled at him, the face of Quendius within his jowls, and that took Sevryn aback for a moment.

All the hesitation the demon needed.

Cerat moved, his great sword swooping down, to nail Sevryn, stuck all the way through him and into the bridge. He gave a satisfied purr as he leaned over.

The pain hit him so hard, Sevryn thought he would vomit before he realized he could not move, not without tearing his body wide open, not without Cerat pulling the sword free. He could not make a sound though the cords of his throat strained for expression. He tried to raise his head, to see if he could find Rivergrace below, if she'd fallen safely, if she'd gained her feet, if he sent her to friends. He could not. Tears of agony filled his eyes so that he could hardly see, even as Cerat leered over him.

The demon put out a finger and dabbed it on the blood swelling up slowly from the base of the sword.

"I could pull it free," it said in Quendius' voice. "But you would bleed to death all the quicker."

Sevryn fought to breathe, to talk, but his throat stayed rigid and unresponsive. He glared upward, unafraid even as the torture curled into paroxysm. He managed a hand gesture that even a demon would know and take offense at.

Cerat responded by reaching down and wiggling the sword the tiniest bit. Sevryn's body spasmed and his heels drummed under him, sound finally escaping his convulsed throat in a high-pitched whine.

The demon laughed. "I would linger, but I have a hundred hundred men at my heels, waiting to be loosed upon their promised land."

It pulled the sword free with such force that Sevryn felt himself rise off the ground with it before falling limp off the blade as the last of it left him. Cerat kicked him out of the way as he began to lumber down toward Kerith.

Sevryn never saw Lara step forward and raise the hammer.

Lara looked to Nutmeg. She saw Rivergrace fall from the arch ahead, landing in a rather undignified but not dead pile. She heard Sevryn's keening moan as the demon drove his sword deep, and she winced at the mortal blow. She caught a glimpse of a boy child weaving through the fight, to reach Nutmeg's side and slide his hand into hers as Nutmeg's voice rose and fell in cadence. The air shivered about Lara, pressing upon her senses as the others wove power and magic unfamiliar to them both. It cloaked her and fed her strength and spoke to her in voices she did not recognize save that they were Vaelinar and ancient. The force wove itself about Lara and Rakka, needing a tool to wield it. She wanted to fight it off, this alien strength, this summoning that tried to take possession of her even as Cerat had obviously taken Quendius. Above it all, the boy's voice rose soprano, strong and determined, light with his age.

The hammer spoke to her in a low, growling voice of authority, stern as she resisted, and then within it, she heard another note, a note of promise and clarity. It almost—but how could it—sounded as Warlord Bistel had whenever ordering a charge.

An undertone came to Lara, a woman's voice, with grace and gentleness. It sounded to her like her mother's tones, a voice she had not heard in centuries. It spoke to her of love. She had not courted love, not counted it among her blessings or desires, had never hoped to hold it out or be given it in return, without obligation or obedience attached. She had love now, unexpected but most wanted, and Lara realized that Bistane had not only given her himself, but a raft of friends and peoples that she valued and held dear, not merely as a ruler but within her heart.

And this thing that encircled her, that Nutmeg and the boy had called up, wanted to be used, but only in the best of ways, in defending those she loved.

She raised the hammer high and dug into the strength and magic being offered. She twirled Rakka for momentum and pounded it onto the bridge just in front of Cerat as he charged her. Her soul ripped out of her and struck with it.

There are those who say Kerith ended that day, in the blink of an eye, and was remade in the following blink. The shrieks of a hundred hundred men struck down beyond the portal, never to see the light of any day again, peeled through the air. The Way to Trevalka collapsed on itself with a great sucking in of air and light, became an ebony blight in the sky that shrank and shrank until it winked out of sight.

Lara, bent in two, straightened and saw the demon Cerat also shrink and shrink until it was little more than a mote on the air, before it zipped away, born off by one of the Gods of wind. It was, after all, one of the elementals of Kerith, all but unmade but still entitled to be part of the world.

She took in a great breath and backed away from the falling debris of rock and rainbow, stone and blood, fire and rain. She saw Rivergrace take up Sevryn's form, her hands pressing over his in futile attempt to stop the free flow of blood, and they traded looks before Grace lowered her gaze to her love again.

Lara turned slowly, looking for Bistane. She thought she saw him, but it was not him—it was the lean, white-haired form of his father who stood and backed away from a figure lying face down in the trampled grass. Bistel grew more and more transparent as she neared. A girl walked slowly away from the ghost, a girl with an unruly mop of hair and blue-button intense eyes as Lara went to the figure. She stood on watch as if she thought she might be needed. Bistel inclined his head to her and faded away to nothingness as Bistane groaned and rolled to his side.

She cupped his face.

His eyelids twitched open. His mouth twisted a little to one side, swollen and cut, and he managed, "You live."

"I do. But if you ever use the king's rest on me again, there will be cold hell to pay."

He laughed, coughed in pain, and reached up to pull her down on the grass with him.

Nutmeg knelt by Rivergrace, bracing her as she tried to tend Sevryn. The boy stayed with her and called to be joined, and it wasn't until they both accosted her, that she realized who the two were. Heedless of Grace, she began to sob, unbelieving, as she pulled them tighter into her embrace. "Merri! Evar! Oh Gods." And she lost her ability to talk coherently as she hugged them and cried happily, looking up long enough to see Dayne, and put her hand up to draw him to her as well.

Merri pulled back long enough to say, "I can help."

Nutmeg blinked. Merri struggled past her to put her hand on Rivergrace. "I can help," she repeated firmly.

Grace shook her head, but Merri leaned closer in determination. She closed her eyes, and her brother Evarton took her other hand and closed his eyes.

At first nothing happened but that the flesh of her hand grew warm under the other's touch. Sevryn fought to breathe, his chest gurgling and wheezing with every spent attempt. Grace shook her head again.

"Kinder to let him go."

"No."

Rivergrace looked and saw only a child looking back, a child with a dirty face streaked with spent tears, a child with dark gold curling hair and eyes that reminded her of someone, and then looked to the boy, and saw an echo of Jeredon. "You don't understand," she said to them, to Nutmeg's children. "We've been here before, both of us. We know what death is. We're not afraid."

"But do you know what life is?" the girl countered. And she squeezed her hand over Rivergrace's.

Grace realized suddenly that the blood had stopped welling up, that her hold on Sevryn which had been slippery wet began to dry. He took an easier breath. His body relaxed in her hold. She knew that Merri was bringing him back.

She caught Nutmeg's gaze. "I hope you know you've raised some very cheeky children."

And so it was that Tolby Farbranch came late to the fight for the first time in his life, to be greeted by his daughters and grandchildren, covered in blood but very much alive.

Chapter
Sixty-Three

THE ARYN TREE planted as a memorial for the fallen by Tolby Farbranch in the courtyard of his home grew beyond his wildest dreams. It gained even more fame than his wondrous cider and spirited wines. There were those who were astonished, as aryns did not flourish this far south of their first plantings by the infamous Vaelinars, but this tree did. It grew so tall that it dwarfed the old farmhouse and even the cider barn, and could be seen from the farthest corner of the vast vineyards on one side and the great city on the other. When the wind blew through it, it sounded as if it held the Great Sea in its branches. There were those who vowed it could even be seen leagues away by riders approaching the Calcort city gates. Although more were planted here and there in hopes of the same success, most did not grow so tall or beautifully. They said it was because Tolby's tears had not watered them as his own tree had been. Or perhaps it had been the addition of Rufus' ashes among its early roots. No one knew for certain. Dwellers could grow near anything, if they put their mind to it. Heal most anything. Survive most anything, even the Gods.

Tolby lived to see the tree in its youth, reaching outward with green and leafy eagerness, to be a canopy over the wedding vows of Dayne and Nutmeg, followed by his son Keldan and his horse-trading bride who were only the first of many to be married under its arching branches, and not the only of Kerith's many races to enjoy its blessing.

Glossary

aderro: (Vaelinar corruption of the Dweller greeting, Derro). An endearment, meaning little one

alna: (dweller) a fishing bird

alphistol: a garden flower

astiri: (Vaelinar) true path

avandara: (Vaelinar) verifier, truth-finder

Aymar: (Vaelinar) elemental God of the wind and air

Banh: (Vaelinar) elemental God of earth

Cerat: (Vaelinar) souldrinker

Calcort: a major trading city

Daran: (Vaelinar) the God of Dark, God of the Three

defer: (Kernan) a hot drink with spices and milk

Dhuriel: (Vaelinar) elemental God of Fire

emeraldbark: (Dweller) a long-lived, tall, insect and fire resistant evergreen

forkhorn: (Kernan) a beast of burden, with wide, heavy horns

Hawthorne: capital of the free provinces

kedant: (Kernan) a potent poison from the kedant viper

klah: (Kernan) a strong, caffeine-laced drink from ground and stewed beans

Lina: (Vaelinar) elemental Goddess of water

Nar: (Vaelinar) God of the Three, the God of War

neriarad: a flowering, drought-resistant shrub that is highly toxic in stem, seed, and flower

Nylara: (Kernan) a treacherous, vital river

Nevinaya aliora: (Vaelinar) You must remember the soul

quinberry: a tart yet sweet berry fruit

qynch oil: a pressed oil used as a base for many purposes, including cooking

Rakka: (Kernan) elemental Demon, he who follows in the wake of the earth mover, doing damage

rockeater: a venomous, dry country serpent

skraw: (Kernan) a carrion eating bird

staghorns: elklike creatures

stinkdog: a beslimed, unpleasant porcine critter

Stonesend: a Dweller trading village

tashya: (Vaelinar) a hot-blooded breed of horse

teah: (Kernan) a hot drink brewed from leaves

ukalla: (Bolgish) a large hunting dog

Vae: (Vaelinar) Goddess of Light, God of the Three

vantane: (Vaelinar) war falcon

velvethorn: a lithe deerlike creature

winterberry: a cherrylike fruit